# A LIAR'S TWISTED TONGUE

CAROLINE CUSANELLI

Copyright © 2024 Caroline Cusanelli

All rights reserved.

No part of this publication may be reproduced, stored, or transmitted in any form or by any means, electronic, mechanical, photocopying, or otherwise, without the prior written permission of the publisher. No part of this book may be used, reproduced, or distributed in any manner whatsoever for the purposes of training artificial intelligence technologies.

All characters in this publication are fictitious and any resemblance to real persons, living or dead, is purely coincidental.

Book Cover by Seventhstar Art
Map by Caffee Cartography
Illustrations by Jan Perit Kablan

ISBN-13: 979-8-9900278-3-1
Originally published May 2024
Printed in Canada by Friesens Corporation
*Also available as an ebook.*

*For anyone who finds it difficult
to share the contents of their heart*

Compiled under Directive 221:
Preparedness for Interspecies Cohabitation
Issued by the Visnatus Academy Council

# 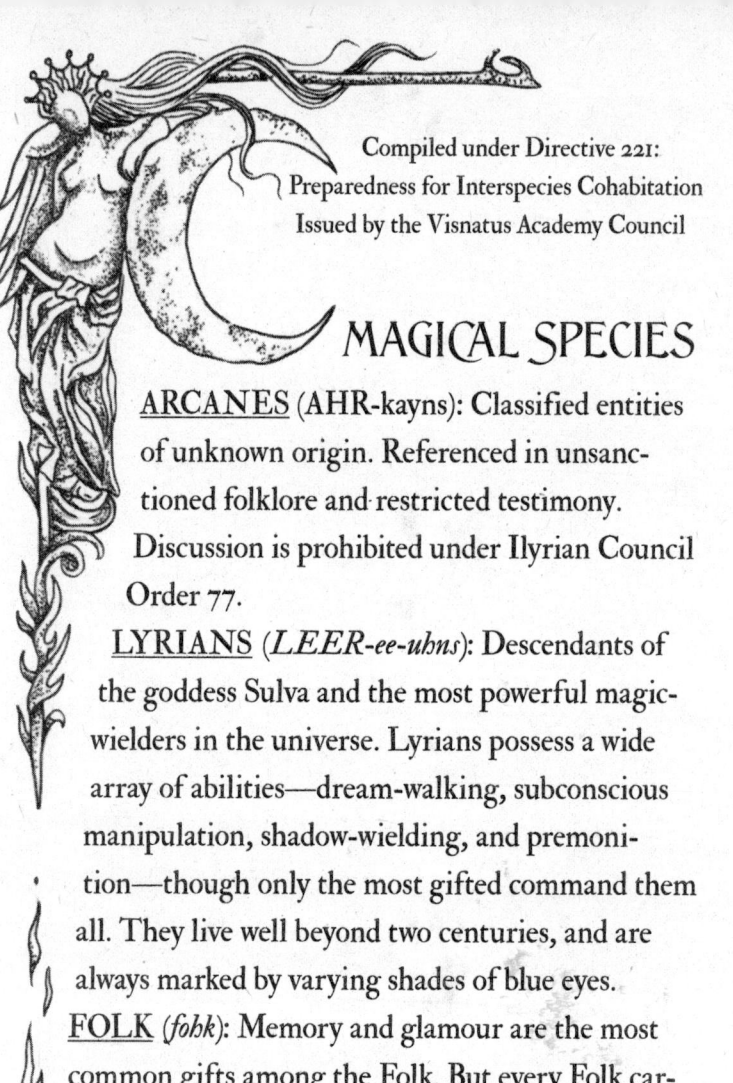MAGICAL SPECIES

<u>ARCANES</u> (AHR-kayns): Classified entities of unknown origin. Referenced in unsanctioned folklore and restricted testimony. Discussion is prohibited under Ilyrian Council Order 77.

<u>LYRIANS</u> (*LEER-ee-uhns*): Descendants of the goddess Sulva and the most powerful magic-wielders in the universe. Lyrians possess a wide array of abilities—dream-walking, subconscious manipulation, shadow-wielding, and premonition—though only the most gifted command them all. They live well beyond two centuries, and are always marked by varying shades of blue eyes.

<u>FOLK</u> (*fohk*): Memory and glamour are the most common gifts among the Folk. But every Folk carries only one elemental root—and all have brown eyes.

- *Light Folk*: Disrupt electricity.
- *Air Folk*: Command the wind.
- *Fire Folk*: Can start fires, but not extinguish them.

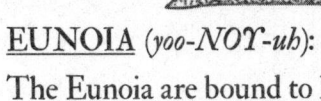

EUNOIA (*yoo-NOY-uh*):
The Eunoia are bound to life itself—able to stir growth in plants, sense emotion, and seek truth. Despite their wicked ability to manipulate feelings, they are often used as healers and agriculturists. All Eunoia have varying shades of green eyes.

DRAES (*DRAYZ*): Known as the mind's creatures, Draes are the most intelligent of the magic-wielding species. They can steal mental magic from others: memory, emotion, and subconscious control. The most skilled among them can read thoughts. Their skin is nearly impenetrable and their lifespans stretching up to five hundred years. All Draes bear violet eyes.

NEPENTHES (*neh-PEN-theez*): Agile, silent, and bred for the kill, Nepenthes are considered the most dangerous magic-wielding species. With venomous fangs capable of delivering instant death, they can blend into their surroundings or pass through solid objects—powers that are banned without special permission from a Royal. With a single hiss, they can calm their prey before attacking. All Nepenthes have gray eyes.

# MAGIC

<u>THE FLAME</u>: The volatile elemental magic of the Fire Folk.

<u>GLAMOUR</u>: Alters appearance of a person or object. Only Folk can cast/remove glamours.

<u>CHANNELLING</u>: Temporary magical energy transfer between individuals.

<u>WARDS</u>: Mental magic defenses used by Royals and officials.

<u>BARRIERS</u>: Forcefields designed to block specific life forms.

<u>PORTAL</u>: A magical doorway allowing travel between two mirrored surfaces.

<u>RAECRIUM</u> (*RAY-kree-um*): A magical device used to project images to other raecriums.

# LIMITATIONS

<u>LIFE FORCE</u>: The source of vitality, strength, and magical ability.

<u>SOUL SUCKERS</u>: Colloquial term for individuals capable of stealing another's life force. Manifestations are subject to containment and investigation.

<u>BURNOUT</u>: Overuse of magic can cause exhaustion, nosebleeds, migraines, or death. Irreversible in advanced stages.

# ARTIFACTS

<u>SOUL STONES</u>: The most powerful artifacts in the universe. Each world has only one, crafted to maintain balance and keep the magic of the universe in equilibrium.

- <u>MEMORIUM</u> (*meh-MOR-ee-um*) (Folkara): A relic of immense power over memory, weather, and glamour. The Memorium was originally a vibrant yellow, but time and overuse have dimmed it, tarnishing its brilliance into a deep, murky orange.

- <u>STONE OF LIGHT</u> (Ilyria): Alters perception, strengthens or suppresses Lyrian abilities by providing pure light energy.

- <u>SOUL RUBY</u> (Iris): Grants immortality or annihilates eternal souls.

# HISTORICAL TERMS

<u>AA</u> (AFTER ARCANE): Current timeline. Year 1 AA marks the aftermath of the Arcanian War.

<u>BA</u> (BEFORE ARCANE): The era preceding AA. There are no surviving records of this time period.

<u>ARCANIAN WAR</u>: A universal war 1,000 years ago that lasted six months and killed 70% of the population.

**NEPTHARIAN WAR**: A conflict between Folkara and Nepthara twelve years ago. Lasted two years.

**LITTALINE COMPACT**: Accords protecting the alliance between Ilyria and Folkara.

**IRISAN ARCHIVES**: The largest library in history, destroyed during the Arcanian War.

# WORLDS

**ILYRIA** (*ill-LEER-ee-uh*): Homeworld of the Lyrians and a military powerhouse. Ilyria thrives on alcohol, energy, fishing, technology, and control. Its government is a matrilineal absolute monarchy—power passed from mother to daughter, with little room for mercy in between.

**FOLKARA** (*FOHL-kah-ruh*): The homeworld of the Folk and the largest world. Its primary industries include welding, mining, livestock, and the production of luxury goods. Governed by a traditional monarchy, its wealth runs deep—but so do its divides.

**EUNARIS** (*yoo-NAHR-iss*): Homeworld of the Eunoia. Known for its agriculture, medicine, and the gentle magic of growth. Governed by a democratic republic, Eunaris thrives quietly—valued by all, ruled by many, and heard only when it chooses to speak.

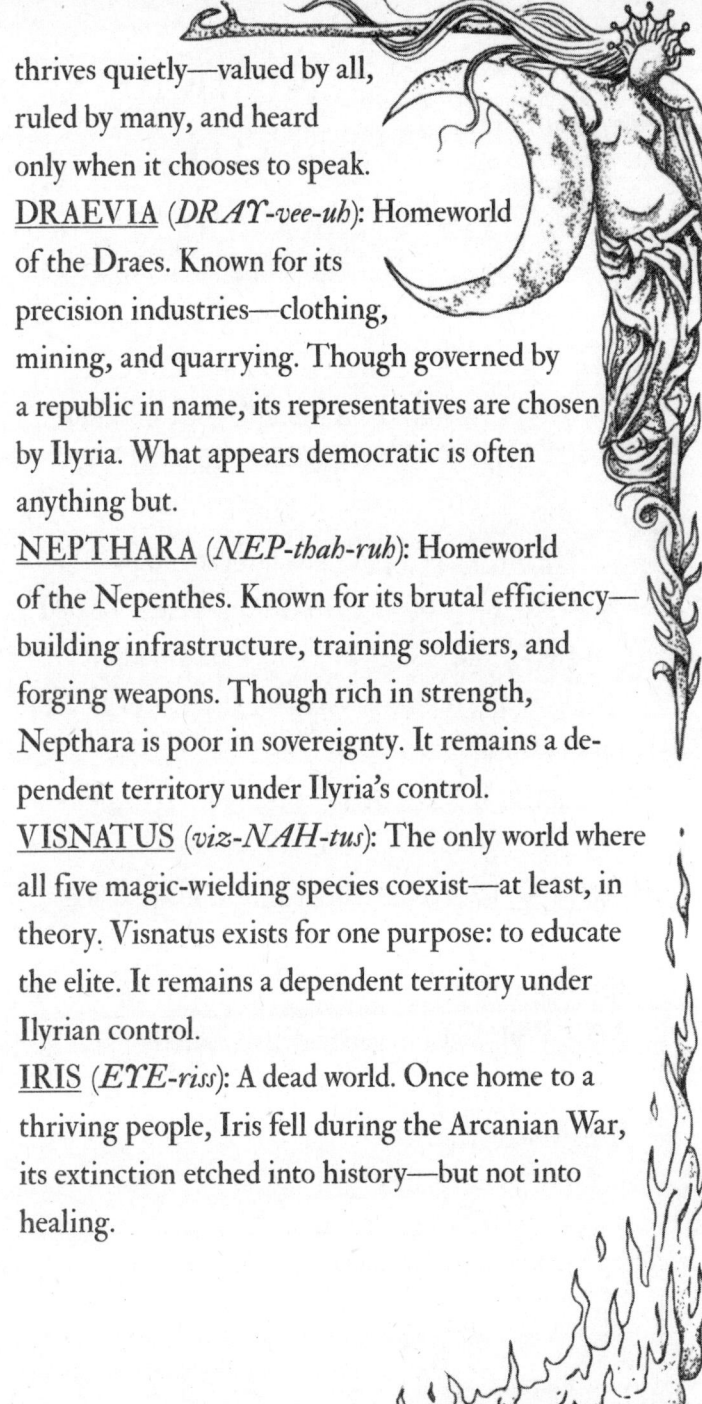

<u>DRAEVIA</u> (*DRAY-vee-uh*): Homeworld of the Draes. Known for its precision industries—clothing, mining, and quarrying. Though governed by a republic in name, its representatives are chosen by Ilyria. What appears democratic is often anything but.

<u>NEPTHARA</u> (*NEP-thah-ruh*): Homeworld of the Nepenthes. Known for its brutal efficiency—building infrastructure, training soldiers, and forging weapons. Though rich in strength, Nepthara is poor in sovereignty. It remains a dependent territory under Ilyria's control.

<u>VISNATUS</u> (*viz-NAH-tus*): The only world where all five magic-wielding species coexist—at least, in theory. Visnatus exists for one purpose: to educate the elite. It remains a dependent territory under Ilyrian control.

<u>IRIS</u> (*EYE-riss*): A dead world. Once home to a thriving people, Iris fell during the Arcanian War, its extinction etched into history—but not into healing.

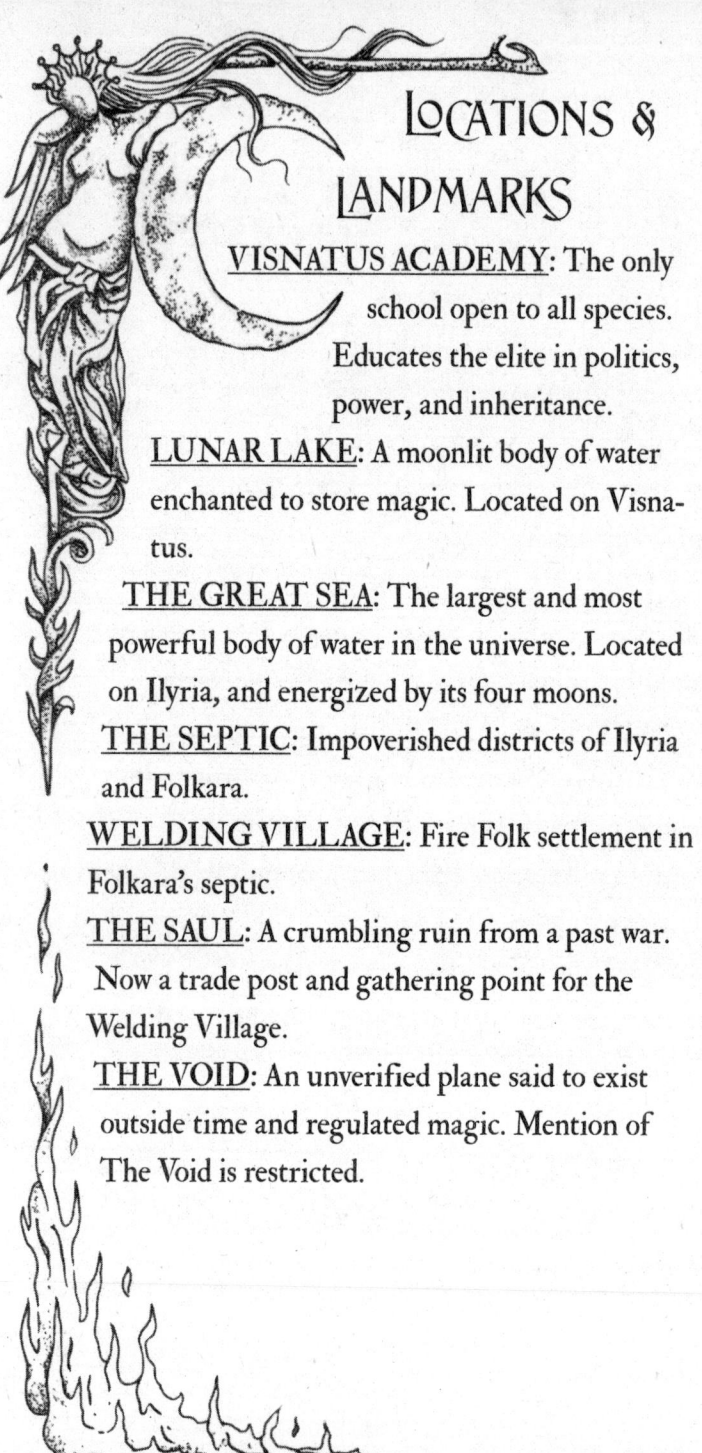

# Locations & Landmarks

**VISNATUS ACADEMY**: The only school open to all species. Educates the elite in politics, power, and inheritance.

**LUNAR LAKE**: A moonlit body of water enchanted to store magic. Located on Visnatus.

**THE GREAT SEA**: The largest and most powerful body of water in the universe. Located on Ilyria, and energized by its four moons.

**THE SEPTIC**: Impoverished districts of Ilyria and Folkara.

**WELDING VILLAGE**: Fire Folk settlement in Folkara's septic.

**THE SAUL**: A crumbling ruin from a past war. Now a trade post and gathering point for the Welding Village.

**THE VOID**: An unverified plane said to exist outside time and regulated magic. Mention of The Void is restricted.

# DEITIES

<u>SULVA</u> (*SOUL-vuh*): The Lunar Goddess. Revered as the mother of the Lyrian bloodline.
<u>AYAN</u> (*EYE-awn*): The Solar God.
<u>ZOLA</u> (*ZOY-uh*): Goddess of balance.

# DEMIGODS

<u>AMUN</u> (*AY-muhn*): Descendant of Ayan. The first person to walk the universe.
<u>EIRA</u> (*EER-uh*): Daughter of Sulva. The first Lyrian.

# MONSTERS

<u>FATTA SCORPION</u>: A scorpion that grows to ten times the size of an average person. Its venom does not just kill—it erases the soul. Originates from Iris.
<u>KAPHA</u> (KAH-fuh): Four-armed predator from Nepthara. Can shift between tangible and intangible states depending on its need in battle. Kills by strangulation and calms its prey with a touch.
<u>MOONARO</u> (moo-NAH-roh): A strikingly beautiful creature covered in shimmering silver fur, with antlers made of icicles. It possesses the icy power of Ilyria.

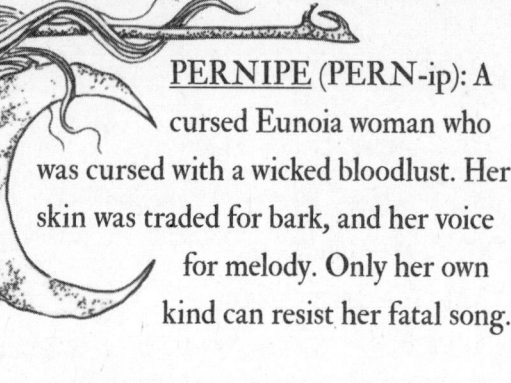

**PERNIPE** (PERN-ip): A cursed Eunoia woman who was cursed with a wicked bloodlust. Her skin was traded for bark, and her voice for melody. Only her own kind can resist her fatal song.

# Lore & Living

**AIBEK** (*EYE-beck*): The ancestral name of Ilyria's ruling family—a lineage tied to absolute authority.

**CONTARINI** (*kon-tah-REE-nee*): The surname of the Folkara regime.

**MIAL** (*MEE-uhl*): A name half-erased. Found in forbidden texts from the Irisan Archives. No known identity—only power and implication.

**PENCE**: The universal currency.

**ACANSA** (*ah-KAHN-suh*): An elite Folk-only school on Folkara. Admission is blood-based, not merit-based.

**VESI** (*VEH-see*): The original liquor of Ilyria.

> This document was assembled at the request of the Visnatus Academy Council to assist incoming students in navigating the sociopolitical and magical complexities of the universe.

# A Note to Returning Readers

For returning readers familiar with earlier drafts or pre-release materials, you may notice a number of changes to names, nations, and terminology in the final version of this story. These adjustments were made to better reflect the internal consistency, linguistic evolution, and cultural resonance of the world.

Here's a brief summary of notable updates: Lucent is now Lyrian; Soma has become Ilyria. Lorucille is referred to as Folkara, Viridis as Eunaris, and Serpencia has been renamed Nepthara. Armanthine and Verena are now Drae and Drevia, respectively. Queen Lusia has become Queen Leiana, and Eudora is now Elowen. Kappa has also been updated to Kapha. These refinements were made to deepen clarity and immersion, ensuring the world of this story is as vivid, intentional, and cohesive as possible.

Thank you very much for coming with me on this wild ride.
— *Caroline*

# PART 1: THE RISING

# Chapter 1
## Sometimes I Think I Could Be a Killer

DESDEMONA

Blood soaks my palm, and I press Damien's dagger deeper. I don't look away from the torn skin, even as Damien whistles from the trees above. My mom and I always agreed—I was better off powerless. But as my self-inflicted wound sizzles, blisters, and seals into an ugly, closed slit, I know the truth. The dreams weren't just dreams. They were warnings. And now, it's too late to ignore them.

The leaves above me rustle, and finally, I clutch the dagger, ignoring the sting in my palm. Damien's job is to scare the catch down from the tree; mine is to deliver the killing blow. We've done it a million times before, only now, the pit in my stomach feels like it could swallow me whole.

I try to push away all thoughts of the dreams or the wound. But the wound proves that the dreams are something more. Something I already know. My powers are manifesting, and when they do, I will burn everyone down before I finally burn myself.

By the time the possum hits the ground, my blade is already buried in its neck. Its dark, oily fur is matted, its too-long limbs twisted at odd angles. But even in death, its teeth remain bared. I understand it; it sucks to be the weakest in a group. I think I'd die the same way—snarling, relentless, angry at those who bested me.

Damien whistles again, startling me. This time, I look up. He's high in the tree now, where the branches seem too thin to hold him. His auburn hair falls loosely around his eyes, obscuring his vision, but he doesn't seem to mind.

"Come up," he calls.

He asks almost every day, and I only climb when I have no other choice. I've never told him I fear the height. A part of me is certain he knows. It grates at me—like skinning an animal, it feels like he's pulled back a layer of *me*. Something he was never supposed to see.

When Damien finally jumps down, he's holding a smoking gray bird by its feet. We don't normally hunt birds; they're harder to catch and don't have as much meat as the possums. But they sure do taste better.

"You should've come up," he says.

I push away my nerves as quickly as I can, opening the bag for him with a smile. "Why?" I ask. "'Cause you burned it?"

Damien's a Light Folk, and his ability to control electrical currents helps us hunt. But with too much power, he could turn the bird to ash.

"No way." He holds up the bird like it's a trophy and smiles at me like I'm a child. "It's perfect, Red," he says, using the nickname he gave me the day we met.

Then, I adamantly told him my hair was orange. Now, I refrain—he already knows.

Instead, I shove my shoulder into his bicep. While he throws the bird in the bag, I close my fist tighter, despite *wanting* Damien to see the cut, to notice my shaking hands and worried eyes. I want to see his concern before he shrugs it away, joking about how he couldn't trust me to handle the daggers. But ultimately, when he asks, "What happened?" I would tell him that my magic is manifesting, and I'm scared of what it means.

Of course, none of that will happen, because my hands aren't shaking and my eyes... Well, there may be a hint of worry that I'm unable to conceal, but nowhere near enough to make him wonder any more than usual.

"We'll have to cut it to see," I say, wiping the blood—mine and the possum's—from the blade before I hold the dagger up. Then I smile, even though I don't feel like smiling.

Damien tugs the bird away from me. "No way you're mutilating today's prize."

I don't mean to get quiet, but I do. "Mutilating" is a word that hits too close to home these days.

Five possums and a bird aren't enough to feed my mom and Damien's family for the day, not with the trading he'll have to do. So Damien scales another tree, looking for another catch, and I follow suit, preparing the dagger. Hiding behind the hunt.

I used to think Damien only let me tag along with him to help my mom and me. It's no secret that three years ago when we arrived in the Welding Village, we weren't doing well. No belongings, nothing to trade, and starving. I hate pity, but even now, I think that if pity is the reason Damien and I became what we are to each other, maybe I could live with it.

We hunt until the late hours of the morning. I carry the bag into the septic, our home, but when he holds his arm out to me, I hand it over.

"Be careful," I whisper, glancing around. "There are more keepers around than usual. I saw a new shipment of Nepenthes huddling up this morning." Damien shakes his head, unconcerned, and I grab his arm. "Someone could have reported that we're hunting."

He rolls his eyes. "Who would do that?"

Only a few people know we hunt, and they're the ones we trade with. But I don't think that's enough of a bond to protect me. They've known Damien his whole life; they've known me a few years. It shocks me that he doesn't see it. He should understand the things that people are willing to do to survive.

"Anyone desperate enough to need a reward." I say again, "Be careful."

"Always am, Red."

Damien heads to the Saul to trade our catch for necessities—clean water, since the nearest river is a four-hour hike; clothes for his younger siblings as the nights grow colder; and the most taxing luxury, salt. I head to school.

It's the most worn-down building in the village. As one of the few buildings made from rotting wood, I can't help but wonder if there's no upkeep because everyone assumes it's bound to burn.

Here, they teach us the "useful skills," mostly how to use our powers to improve our chances of survival, which are never great in any of the septics. Folk can live well into their hundreds, but I won't make it past thirty. Most Fire Folk don't.

This is my last year before I'm forced into welding—four years earlier than everyone else in the septic. They want a solid decade from us before we self-combust.

Nineteen is the age we officially become dispensable.

Today, Ms. O is teaching us how to paralyze a monster—not for hunting, but for defense, which makes no sense. Monsters don't attack anymore.

"How many times have you...?" Elliae whispers, her auburn hair falling around her face, just like Damien's. She's easily the prettiest girl in the village—pale skin, rounded jaw, bulbous cheekbones, every physical feature a Folk could want. I always thought she'd do better in one of the kingdom's villages.

Beauty doesn't lead to pretty jobs here.

"More times than I can count," I whisper back. I don't add that I've never paralyzed an animal; that's always Damien. All I do is finish the job.

"Did he go to the Saul today?" she asks.

"Yeah, why?"

"Ma told him not to," Elliae whispers, her eyebrows scrunching with concern. "Something about more Nepenthes."

*I knew I saw more keepers.*

I've never been able to understand why the Royals of our

world, Folkara, let the Nepenthes stay after the war. But they're still here after killing us for sport. I wish they'd just stay on their world instead of bombarding mine.

"Tell Ms. O my mom's sick if she asks," I mutter to Elliae, cursing Damien as I slip out of class to find him.

I stop when I pass a room that's usually empty. Today the walls are littered with posters. Words spelling out sentences in color. *Color on paper*—something I've never seen before.

Paper is scarce here, and cutting down trees is illegal. So seeing all these pages with things like *"Hard work makes the worlds go round,"* or *"Your sacrifices strengthen us all,"* and, my personal favorite, *"The key to peace is compliance,"* filling the walls is rather surreal.

I'm sure it has something to do with the keepers. Suddenly, the worry that someone *has* actually reported Damien and me for hunting intensifies.

Despite my panic, I scan the remaining pages, searching for anything about hunting. But my eyes are drawn to a small note, words formed from leaves and dirt, nothing like the fancy colors on the posters. *"YOU DESERVE TO BE SEEN."*

Maybe that one's my new favorite, for its comical attributes.

When I'm off school grounds, I walk straight to the Saul, part of me waiting for the keepers to stop me at any moment. The cobblestone building is riddled with holes, and decaying vines cover most of its surface. Word around town says it's the oldest building in the village because the Nepenthes took it over during the war, and it didn't burn down with the rest of our world.

They call it the Neptharian War—named after the Nepenthes' world—but it was *us* who died. It was *our* war.

I'm halfway there when I see Damien. I don't change my pace out of fear of attracting a keeper's attention, but I want to run. Maybe give him a good slap, too. But the Nepenthes are fast —with inhuman speed and agility, you never know when they'll show up.

When I'm less than a foot from him, I say quietly, "What is wrong with you?"

Damien lazily rolls his eyes. "We needed water, Red. The little ones haven't had anything to drink in a day." I eye his pack, and he answers my unspoken question. "Yes, I got you some." He hands me a waterskin, and I suck it dry.

Then I shove the waterskin back into his chest. "But the keepers—"

"Wanna say that any louder?" He slips the waterskin into his pack and grabs my arm.

Instinctively, I look around, to my sides and behind me. "Stop," Damien instructs. "Eyes ahead." I do as he says, walking straight forward as he whispers, "I still have four possums in the bag."

"Shit," I mutter under my breath. Could this all be a setup—a way to catch us in the act? If we're caught, we're screwed, and if we're not, four isn't enough to feed his family of five and mine of two.

We keep walking, eyes ahead of us, both hoping that they won't stop us today. The smallest penalty for hunting is twenty lashes to the back. The highest is death. Four possums is a lot more than one. One could be forgivable—an honest mistake, your first time. Four means you know what you're doing.

My heart drops to my stomach when a keeper calls, "What's in the bag?"

I make a mental vow to not die today.

Or tomorrow, for that matter.

"Clothes for my little siblings," Damien says. "It's getting cold out."

"From the Saul?" he asks.

"Yes, sir."

"And what's a kid like you got to trade?" The Nepenthe reaches for the whip at his side. A display of power.

I only see one way out of this—and it's a long shot.

Stepping forward, I grab Damien's hand, telling him to stay quiet. "Bottles," I answer with a soft smile. "We hiked to the river and collected sand so I could make them."

"A Fire Folk, are we?" the Nepenthe says lazily, stepping closer and gliding his disgusting gray eyes down my body. I bite my tongue and close my fist.

"Yes, sir." *Not that he deserves the title.*

"Shame. By the looks of it, you'll be in the welding quarters soon." By that, he means dead. Damien tenses next to me.

"Yes, sir."

He leans back a little, his hand still close to the whip but not on it. "Why aren't you in class?"

I keep my face entirely blank. Unreadable. Nothing to show but what I want him to see. Nothing to use against me, should he find a reason.

"Mom's sick," I answer. "Wanted to get her something warm."

He smiles, eyes still on my body, and from the look in them, I know he's more than just surprised at my fuller frame. I'm stronger than the majority; Damien is, too, but no keeper ever looks at him the way this one is looking at me.

Worse, I fear my frame is enough to make him suspect I've been hunting.

"She's real sick, sir," I say. "Freezing up and all."

The Nepenthe grunts and then brings his eyes back to mine. "All you got in that bag is clothes and bottles?"

I tilt my head to the side, smile deceptively, and nod. "Yes, sir."

He shoves his hand in his pocket, leaning to the left and looking around the space—which is just dirt, trees, and the Saul in the distance—before looking back at me. "Get out of here. Don't forget I made your life easier."

"Thank you, sir," Damien says, and I can hear his anger. He

shouldn't have said a thing.

But I was wrong—no one has reported us. If they had, that Nepenthe would've been far more suspicious of potential hunters. It means the keepers are here for something else.

We walk a little quicker than we did before, and when we're a good bit away from any keepers, Damien says, "I hate those creeps."

"At least we're alive," I mutter. I wasn't sure we would be by the end of that conversation.

But Damien stops and pulls me behind a tree. He gives me a long glance before asking, "Which way did you walk to the Saul?"

"Through the barren. Why?" It's the patch of land that never recovered after the war.

"Marice is dead. Same with a dozen others. Whipped."

*Marice.* We give him the skins and leftover bones of the possums in return for the waterskins and the broth he would make of them. He made the catch bag Damien is holding right now.

He's been caught with our livestock remnants dozens of times. Apparently, one time too many—because now he's dead. Because of *us*, our hunting.

"Shit," is all I can seem to say.

I think of all the nights Mom, Damien's family, and I sat around the fire with our broth, listening to Marice's stories of how he and Sevyn fell in love and survived the wars together. Every word he spoke demanded your attention.

"What about Sevyn? Is she okay?" I ask.

"I think she ran," Damien says, looking over my shoulder. "Couldn't find her anywhere." He steps away from the tree, back onto the beaten path. "We should get moving."

After a few minutes of walking in silence, I say, "Four?"

"Yeah, four." He kicks a pebble.

My stomach grumbles, but there's no way we could hunt again.

"The girls make it on one, easy," Damien says quietly. His little sisters, who are probably waiting back home for Damien's haul. Food and water they wouldn't get if Damien was caught.

It's different for him. If anything happens to me, my mom would be fine. His family relies on him.

"Mom and I can split one," I say.

"No," Damien says. "No. You get two."

He takes me back to my dwelling, and we unload the water, two possums, and salt on the table, throwing a sheet over it all, just in case.

Before he leaves, I slip one possum back into the pack.

Night falls while I run my hand through the dirt, brushing away all the debris and filling the space with bark and twigs. I twist one against the wood, and when I see the glow of orange, I place it on my pile of kindling, blowing until fire catches. This used to feel silly, a Fire Folk using practical skills to start a fire. Now I worry I won't have to do this much longer.

Mom holds the possum over the fire. I tuck my knees into my chest and watch the flame. I try to ignore what it reminds me of, what it means to me after ten nights of running from it in my dreams.

"You okay?" Mom asks, the fire turning her face orange.

I force myself not to flinch. The dreams are only dreams, and I won't become what I am in them.

*A murderer. A destroyer.*

I look up and answer, "Yeah."

"You're looking at that fire like it's going to burn you."

"It might." I smile to lighten the mood.

"Only if you fall in," she says. "Is there something you want to tell me?"

I wish I could—the dreams and the cut and the arson. All the things that occupy my brain when the distractions of the day die down. "Nothing comes to mind."

"Your magic?"

I clench my fist tighter. "Still nothing."

"Good," she pauses, "I don't think you should hunt tomorrow," she whispers, making sure no prying ears nearby can hear—the Nepenthes and their super senses.

"We need to eat," I whisper back.

"Janice can get us berries."

"She has an entire family to feed if Damien doesn't hunt," I argue.

Mom turns the carcass over the fire. "It'll be fine."

"Won't there be more work for you with the keepers here—"

"No woods tomorrow," she cuts me off, her tone stern. "Understand? Stay close to home."

I push away the thought those words bring. It's just anxiety. But staying close to home normally means leaving home, in the end.

"I understand."

The next morning, I wake before my mom and begin braiding my hair, getting ready to hunt. I promised not to hunt today, but in doing so, I promised not to worry about our empty stomachs and to surrender to the role of the child, despite not feeling like one.

Even though I'm only a year away from adulthood in the eyes of the Fire Folk.

I'm a quarter of the way through the braid when I stop. Like old times, I climb into my mom's bed. She mumbles something and turns to me, groggily wrapping her arm over me.

"I missed this, baby girl," she mumbles.

"Me too."

My grogginess overcomes me, and I find myself falling asleep in her arms like I'm a kid again.

I wake once more, this time to the familiar feeling of Mom

tugging my hair as she braids it. I smile to myself when her fingers run along my scalp, sending shivers down my arm.

"You have the best hair to braid," Mom whispers. She used to say this all the time.

I fidget my fingers while she fiddles with my hair, and when she finishes, I turn to face her. Mom's soft hand caresses my cheek.

"I love you," she tells me. "It's you and me against the worlds."

It is. It really is. It always has been. Everything we do is for one another. It's that love that makes me think I could tell her the truth—that we don't have long before I die. Because that's the reality of my magic, the nature of the Flame—the Fire Folk's power. Whatever happens between now and that end could be terrible, but she deserves to know that it *will* end.

I open my mouth to tell her. The only words that fall out are, "And I love you."

Mom smiles. She wouldn't have smiled if I told her the truth.

I take the long way to school. I have to see the posts—make sure Marice is dead for myself, assuming they haven't hauled his body away already.

The stench of long-dead corpses reaches me before I see it: thirteen bodies tied to wooden posts by their bloodied wrists. Their backs barely resemble human flesh, more a mangled mess of muscle, blood, and bone.

But I see Marice's face, his light brown hair and graying beard.

Damien was right. The thought twists in my stomach, but not long enough to elicit a response. I think I'd succumb to the stench before I allowed myself to fall victim to my emotions.

If Marice was caught with our catch, then the keepers might

know we're hunting. They would be searching for us in every scenario but one: Marice taking the fall.

I try not to look worried, scared, or wounded as I walk to school, but someone taking the punishment for my actions is more than I ever expected. Tears prick at my eyes, and I keep my gaze down as I pass more Nepenthes, wondering again what they're doing here.

When I get to class, I sink into my seat. Time moves slowly, and for a moment, I wonder if this is a dream. If it is, who will I kill next? What will burn because of me? But I've never had a dream in the Welding Village, and Elliae is next to me, her auburn hair framing the soft features she shares with Damien. This has to be real, then.

Right?

Vaguely in the background, the teacher drones on about the Royals needing more metal and how kids are now expected to start work early.

Time resets itself with five taps from outside the glassless school window.

Elliae whispers, "I'll cover for you."

She always does, but this time, it seems a little more dangerous.

I slip out of my usual hole in the wall, ignoring the influx of posters in the old room, and meet Damien outside the school. We start walking immediately. I'm prepared for him to say there's a monster in the woods—and he needs my help defeating it—and I'm prepared to ask if he's dense.

But those aren't the words that come out of his mouth.

"Your mom wanted me to get you. Said it was urgent."

I stop so abruptly that Damien almost loses his balance trying to match my pace. He's looking at me, expecting an explanation, and I'm thinking of the homeless, wondering how long I could survive as one of them. Because that's what I'm about to be, considering that I won't leave another village. Not this time.

"What was she doing?" I ask with my eyes trained ahead of me.

"I don't know. She seemed scattered."

*Packing.*

My entire life has been one forced departure after another. It didn't matter if I liked a place or hated it, we stayed until Mom said it was time to go. It's a curse that's followed me everywhere I've gone: the perpetual loss of everything I know. So when I look back at Damien, at his comforting brown eyes and shaggy auburn hair, I can't help but grab his wrist and run, jerking him along with me into the woods.

"Hang on, Red," he says with a laugh, but I can tell he's concerned.

I think we could survive in the woods. If I can figure out how to use the Flame, I could cook our meals, maybe even hunt on my own. We could do it. We wouldn't be like the homeless. We'd be like animals. Sure, hunted, but also free.

This time, I'm not leaving with my mom. I won't lose everything—again.

I stop running only when we reach the woods. We're safe, away from the keepers, and my mom.

The sun shines through the trees on Damien's soft, Folk-like features. They harden when he turns to me, breathless, and asks, "What is it?"

His lips curl into a scowl, and his eyebrows draw together, but there's nothing but understanding in those brown eyes. The same brown eyes all Folk have—the brown eyes I've found both comfort and treachery in all my life. The only other eye color I've seen is the Nepenthes' gray—the gray eyes that follow me with every step, threatening potential punishment.

Maybe I could just tell Damien about the dreams. Right here, right now, say, *"Damien, I've been dreaming of starting fires and killing Folk. A lot of Folk. Do you still want to be my friend, or do you think I'm losing my mind?"*

"Will you stay here with me?" I say instead, looking down at the dirt. "Just for the night."

He's looking at me like I've asked the impossible, and I'm trying not to show my desperation.

"Yes," he says, and I'm in awe.

That's it. I can show him how easy it would be to live here, and we can stay. I won't have to lose anything. Not again.

We sit beneath the trees, and Damien reaches into the bag, pulling out a handful of berries, a jug of nectar, and a bottle of rena.

*A bottle of rena.*

Rena is our world's makeshift alcohol for the poor, yet most of us in the septic could never afford it.

I lean over, grabbing it from his hands as I mutter in awe, "How did you get this?"

Damien shrugs. "Traded a dagger for it."

He only has two. Well, one now. One from his dad and one he traded. I always used the latter, not because he didn't let me use his dad's, but because it never felt right.

"Why would you do that? You aren't a drunk in hiding, right?" I joke with him, but I'm partly serious. I can't imagine why he would trade anything for alcohol.

"No," Damien laughs, meeting my gaze. "I noticed you're on edge lately. I thought doing something fun could help."

*So much for hiding it.*

The way he's looking at me is scaring me. His lips are slightly parted, and his long, curled eyelashes make his eyes look almost romantic. If there was ever a time to tell the truth, this would be it. It's funny because I could; it wouldn't take much work to say the words.

But it's not just the words, and it's not just the dreams. It's what lies underneath them. It's the fear—not just about my powers materializing and the imminence of my death, but about the murders. The endless murders. The proof on my palm that

I'm not normal. That I may be even more prone to death and destruction than the other Fire Folk.

It's showing him the target and handing him the knife.

"I have fun hunting," I say, and for a moment it feels like nothing in the world has changed. For a moment, it feels like yesterday.

"It's good to enjoy it," Damien says, taking the glass bottle back and tugging the cork free with a pop. "Because you're not very good."

I catch the hint of a smile behind the bottle, and I smile back when he hands it to me. I've never had rena before, but I've always wanted to try it. It's an ugly color, like someone added dirt to water, and it tastes like it, too.

"So, what's going on with you, Red?" Damien asks. "You ever gonna tell me?"

*There are times I want to tell him everything.*

"What?" I smile, taking another sip of the burning liquid and closing my left hand so he doesn't see the scar. "Nothing's going on."

"Here's hoping the liquor will loosen you up a bit." He raises the bottle, takes one last sip, and slips it back into the leather bag before scaling a tree, silently signaling that it's time to hunt. He looks down at me. "Coming?"

I shake my head. He pulls his dagger from his boot and throws it down to me. Our routine. Still, I feel guilty using his dad's dagger after he traded his other dagger for rena—for *me*. And I can't even tell him why he thinks I need it. If I do, he'll likely be scared of me, even if he doesn't say as much. Especially here, in a village composed of Fire Folk, where the majority of premature deaths are caused by us.

Everyone he's ever lost has been taken at the hands of the Flame.

I run my thumb over the orange stone engraved at the tip of the handle. It looks like a memor—one of Folkara's precious stones. Something this fancy doesn't belong in my hands. But when a possum falls from the tree, squirming and unable to run, instinct drives my blade into its throat.

By the time Damien comes down, I'm starving, the bag is full, and the sun is setting. I shave a stick until it's something sharp, then start a fire while Damien skins a possum. The sunset fades fast, and by the time we eat, the sky is black.

My mouth waters when Damien fills my palm with berries. I try to take my time but end up shoveling the whole handful into my mouth. And when the rena is in front of me, I feel excited for the first time since the dreams began. We drink, and five sips later, I'm lying on the dirt with my head on Damien's chest, watching the dancing stars.

"That one looks like a soldier," I say, pointing at a cluster of stars shaped like a stick figure holding a sword.

"I've heard stories that they put the souls in the sky when they're ready to rest," Damien says, referring to the gods. Everyone knows the three of them: the lunar goddess, Sulva; the solar god, Ayan; and the goddess of balance, Zola. No one talks much about them here, besides my mom.

"That's nice," I say, but I don't think it is.

"Des?" Damien asks.

His voice is soft, and it worries me. I don't want to do serious right now, but I flip on my stomach and look at him. He doesn't say anything; he just keeps staring.

Until I finally lean in and press my lips to his.

I think I've thought about this a lot more than I'd care to admit.

I pull away and whisper, "I'm sorry."

Damien shakes his head, then grabs the back of mine, pulling me into him again. My lips grow numb against his, from the rena or the kisses, I don't know.

Damien holds the back of my head as he says, "I wish we could stay like this forever."

*Perfect.*

"We can," I say softly.

He smiles at me and pushes a piece of my orange hair behind my ear. "I wish we could," he repeats.

"No, we really can." I'm sitting up now. "We can hunt. I can cook. We could sleep under the stars. It would be easier than what we do now!"

"Okay," he says, sitting up, too. "What about Isa?" My mom, who's leaving, but I don't say that. "Or my sisters? My mom? They're probably freaking out. Just leaving for the night was a bad enough idea."

I lean back, away from him. "You think this was a bad idea?"

"No, no, Des, that's not what I mean." I know he's being honest—but it's not enough.

I could tell him that the second we go back to the village I'll be gone. My mom will drag me away to a new place, saying it's for our safety, and he'll never see me again. But I know how my mom likes leaving. Without a trace. Just because I've made my choice doesn't mean I'll disrespect hers.

So all I can do is convince him to stay here, with me.

"You're never going to be anything there! A Light Folk in a welding land? Your magic will never be valued. You'll never get ahead, always barely able to feed your family, having to choose between food and winter blankets. And me? I'll become a welder and die just like the rest of them, burned alive for the Royals! We're both damned no matter what we choose, so why not choose something for ourselves?" My voice trembles, threaded with desperation.

More importantly, I hope that mentioning the dead welders won't anger him. I've never alluded to his dad like that before. But this is important.

"Are you kidding me?" he says, and I know instantly that I've angered him.

"Damien—"

"No, no. That's not cool. None of that was called for. I just wanted to have a good night with you, get you feeling better, and you throw that at me?"

"It's the truth!" I argue.

"I don't care if it's the truth! This wasn't the time to be talking about the *truth*," he spits, rising to his feet, and I follow.

"I can't go back," I say.

"Do you think I want to?" Damien points back toward the village. "That place is full of ghosts," he says, meaning everyone he's lost in the fires. "And you're right, I never will be anything here, but that doesn't mean I can leave. I was raised here, my family is here, and I'm sadly sure my future family will be stuck here, too! What you're asking me is ridiculous. You're asking me to give up my life!"

I wish I could tell him that's exactly what will happen to me if we go back. I'll lose my life, I'll lose him, I'll lose *everything*. I want to grab his arm, pull him with me, and beg him to come.

"Damien, you don't understand!" I plead.

"Then tell me. What am I not understanding?" His face grows flushed with every word. "I'll be nothing, and you'll be dead. Does that not sum it up enough?"

I swallow, wishing it was enough to soothe my throat, burning with unshed tears. "That's not enough for you to want to run with me?"

Damien shakes his head, biting his bottom lip before saying, "I don't think I could ever run."

So, that's it, isn't it? I can't convince him. If my imminent death isn't enough, my leaving tonight wouldn't be either. I drop his hand, which I hadn't realized I was holding, and I don't think about how close I was to begging. I think about kissing his cheek as a final goodbye, but instead, I turn back to the village, leaving behind the rena, the nectar, and the leather bag Marice made.

I can't bring it with me anyway.

"Des!" Damien shouts. I keep walking. "Desdemona!"

I don't turn back. I kick a rock and try not to focus on the hole in my chest, in my stomach. I have to do something. I have to *do* something. I run. I run back to the village—all the way to my dwelling—where my mom runs out and right into me.

"Let's go," she says, grabbing my shoulders and pulling me inside. I glance back, waiting for Damien to emerge.

But he never does.

Inside, Mom rips her necklace—the one she always wears—from her chest and takes my hand, pressing the cold, heavy pendant into my palm. Her fingers tighten around mine, and for a brief moment, I feel a pulse of warmth and energy, like the necklace is alive, syncing with my heartbeat.

The heat reminds me of the dreams—the burning and being burned, the hunted and the prey—and for a moment, it's almost as if bits of those moments flash before my eyes.

"Wear it at all times, under your clothes," Mom instructs. "Let no one see it." When she sets the necklace down, her hand lingers, as if reluctant to let go. Then, she asks, "What happened to your palm?"

"Hunting accident," I say, but there's a weary look in her eye.

It translates to a weary tone when she says, "You're sure about that?"

I answer firmly, "Positive."

She doesn't push, just nods and pulls a piece of paper from her pocket. Something I didn't know she could afford. "Read this as soon as you can. Burn it when you're done. No one can see it." She pushes me deeper into the dwelling.

"Burn it? Mom—"

"You can," she interrupts, her voice steady. "I know you can." She pulls me toward the back, to the only mirror we own —we're traveling by portal.

Portals only open between reflective surfaces, and we've never used one before. Mom says they're too traceable. That's why we always walk between villages—sometimes for weeks.

If we're using a portal now, it means we're crossing worlds.

Which makes no sense—there's no reason to put yourself through that kind of danger. There are seven worlds, and traveling between them can be tricky. Sometimes, travelers get lost between realms, unable to reach either side.

But I quickly understand why she's willing to risk it when the door bursts open behind us, and two figures step through.

"Mom?" I cry, watching them approach, waiting for her to open the portal.

One of the intruders speaks, "You've worn out our patience, Isa—"

The sound dies, but his lips continue to form silent words.

Mom rests her hand on the mirror's surface. It turns pitch black and grows until it's as tall as she is. I duck, ready to step through the portal.

But my mom doesn't follow.

Lightning crackles between her fingers before she hurls it at the men, their bodies convulsing under its force. They're paralyzed—but it will only last so long.

Mom still doesn't move.

"Are you coming?" I shout, but she's already shaking her head, her eyes fixed on the figures just inches away.

A sense of dread settles over me as I notice the resignation in her gaze. "They'll find me if I'm with you."

I grab her wrist, yanking hard while I cry, "Please! You can't leave me alone." *You can't take away the last thing I have.* But the bodies begin to move again, and as they come closer, I catch a glimpse of their eyes.

Red—something I've only heard of in the ghost stories about the Arcanes.

Mom pulls her hand from mine, and I try to fight her. I try to grab her fingers, her wrist, a thread of her shirt—anything to pull her toward me. Instead, she shoves me away.

The last thing I see is her, hands raised to fight, before I fall through the empty mirror.

## Chapter 2
## Before There Was Honesty, There Was a Lie

# LUCIAN

I glance at my sister, Lilac, her hands trembling against the armrest of her chair. The chandeliers above us cast shadows on her unusually pale face, draining the color from her until she looks like someone else entirely. I should say something—I should do *anything*. Not for my sake, nor for Kai or Calista, who sit equally stunned, but for hers.

And yet, what would it change?

Some things are too big to fight. My life was never mine to begin with. I learned that a long time ago.

All I've ever wanted was the illusion of choice—to keep my head down, serve quietly, and maybe spare Lilac the worst of it. But now, even the illusion is gone.

Headmistress Constance—Cynthia to me, and the few permitted such familiarity—sits behind her desk, the surface cluttered with books and papers. Her black hair, streaked with gray, is swept back from her face, the lines of age softening her otherwise stern appearance.

She frowns as she says, "Your betrothals will take place in the coming months. The stability of the universe depends on it." With heavy resignation, she adds, "As your parents reminded me."

I think we all hoped this was a dream. A lie, before the awakening.

Kai and Calista rise first, their matching blond hair catching the harsh light, turning silver at the edges. Their posture is identical—twins molded by the same royal teachings. Their faces share an almost identical softness: curved jawlines, rounded noses, and the large, warm brown eyes of the Folk.

Lilac and I follow, the cold marble of the academy hallway pressing against my boots as I step forward.

Marriage. Lilac is to marry Kai and take the throne of our world, Ilyria, while I'm to wed Calista and inherit Folkara—the kingdom of the Folk. I'm not being handed power. I'm being fed it. Like it's poison disguised as privilege.

This union is meant to bind the kingdoms before their alliance crumbles. But it's far too late. The universe is on the brink of collapse—if not already falling apart—and it goes far beyond Ilyria and Folkara.

I spent my life believing I would never get a crown, that I would someday be free of the throne and its politics. Yet, with the whispering of words that weren't even their own, my parents have drawn me back in. Like a fish caught in the current, I can't swim against their tide.

Cynthia offers me a small, consoling nod as the heavy door to her office slams shut. We're left in the hall with our royal guards—a reminder of the bad news delivered to us today.

Immediately, Lilac looks to Calista. My sister's hands tremble, hidden in the folds of her dress—attire we're forced to wear during royal duties. Lilac has always been the more fragile of the two of us, but despite the trembling hands and the worry in her eyes, she remains the picture of elegance. Long black hair falls in waves around her pale face, stricken with concern. Unlike the Folk she gazes at, Lilac has the sharp features of a Lyrian—angular cheekbones, a pointed nose, and icy blue eyes.

"Did you know about this?" Lilac asks Calista. "Is that why you—"

"No," Calista answers immediately, their eyes meeting. The princesses have known one another their entire lives, always sharing more than a political alliance.

"How was I to know?" Calista finishes, her voice firm but threaded with something gentler—a quiet apology meant for Lilac alone.

Lilac looks down, picking at the skin around her nails. I take her hands, trying to steady her.

"This isn't right," I mutter, shaking my head. "It shouldn't have come to this—"

A hand grasps the collar of my shirt, slamming me back against the cold marble wall.

"Kai, stop it!" Lilac shouts as Calista grabs her arm, holding her back. Lilac puts up a small fight, her face flushed, before ultimately sinking into Calista's hold.

I shift my focus back to Kai. I've known the Prince of Folkara my entire life, and he's never been one to hide his stronger emotions. Yet, despite everything, he's a friend. And if I had something to hit right now, perhaps I would.

"Why didn't you say something, Lucian?" Kai roars. "If it shouldn't have come to this—why didn't you stop it?"

I look down, meeting his gaze with a sigh. "The same reason you didn't."

"Says the prince of the most powerful kingdom," Kai spits.

"The *prince*," I argue. "Not the king—and certainly not the queen."

The queen is the true ruler of Ilyria, not the king, nor a mere prince. That is why Lilac will inherit our throne. Our bloodline passes through the women. In any case, my parents would never desire me on the throne—I am scarcely their heir.

Shaking my head, I add, "It wasn't my decision."

Like every other, this choice was never mine.

"Oh, please," Kai snarls, his grip around the collar of my shirt tightening. "Everyone knows you're Leiana's favorite!"

My *mother*—who is far from my biggest fan, and I'm far from her favorite.

I grab his wrist, glancing at the guards as I whisper, "Compose yourself."

The guards avert their gazes, and I release Kai. Petty gossip about the princes is worth a pretty coin—and as future kings, we cannot afford our names to be tainted.

Kai sneers as he says, "Do you want to make an enemy of me?"

My eyes wander the length of his body, and I smirk, growing tired of maintaining my composure. "Truthfully? I could use a new sparring partner."

If he wants to make this a fight, I won't stop him. I could use something to hit, too.

"We should get back," Lilac says, pulling away from Calista. "Get out of these dresses, prepare for class."

"I'll walk you," I say, stepping in line with my sister and offering her my arm. With a short nod, she accepts.

With every step, Lilac's gaze remains fixed on the floor, her heels clinking softly. I know her well enough to recognize she isn't truly looking at the ground—she's caught somewhere in her mind.

"Li," I whisper. "It's going to be all right."

Her shoulders hunch with each breath, as if she's trying to retreat into a shell she doesn't have and never will—especially not when she's queen.

"This isn't fair," she mutters, shaking her head. "If they think this will make us stronger rulers, they're wrong." She offers me a sidelong glance, as if daring me to argue.

I don't fight. She's right.

"We'll make the best of it," I whisper, trying to believe it myself. It's no secret to either of us that I'm saying it for her sake. "We'll make the necessary changes once we ascend to the throne."

"We're being put on the throne to *uphold* the status quo," she argues. "There is *no* change to be made." Her gaze meets mine, and I can tell she's dangerously close to tears. "Neither of us will ever truly be loved, and we'll end up repeating the same mistakes our parents made."

"Hey," I say, grabbing her hand, and trying to snap her out of the downward spiral. I've been there many times—yet I've never seen Lilac follow me down. It's a mirror I'd prefer to do without. "That's our choice to make," I try to assure her.

Lilac frowns, her voice scratchy as she whispers, "But you don't believe that."

No, I don't. There isn't a single choice that's mine to make. But I want Lilac to have more than I've gotten. When there's nothing left to fight for, there's still her.

"Do you think they love us?" she asks after a long bout of silence, her words unsteady. "I mean... could you do this to someone you love?"

There is no easy answer—not for Lilac. She is their blood, their kin.

She doesn't know that I am not. My parents were both dead by the time I was six—my mother when I was one. Leiana and Labyrinth, my aunt and uncle, took me in, but under one condition: I couldn't tell a soul about my true lineage.

I've tried to tell Lilac before, but it didn't go well. Leiana had a Folk wipe her memory, and then she punished me, as she often does.

Lilac is my sister, through and through. But Leiana and Labyrinth are not my parents.

I've never known what it is they want with me. The bloodline of Ilyria is carried by the women—what need do they have for a son? Yet they've kept me under their watchful, suffocating eyes since I was a boy.

"Power tends to corrupt," I say as I squeeze her hand. "So hold onto your heart."

I glance at her, taking note of the scowl on her face as she mutters, "That's the very thing I can't let them take."

I leave Lilac at her suite and walk to my own, located on the other side of the dormitory wing. In my room, I glare at my reflection in the mirror—tired blue eyes and neat black hair—before collapsing onto my bed.

The mattress sinks beneath me with a softness that feels undeserved.

Marriage, and to Kai's sister. Kai to mine. Fear shakes me, and I cannot tell if it is for my sake, or Lilac's.

I thought I'd given up on hope long ago. Through every treacherous task my parents forced upon me, I was certain I'd already forsaken my humanity. I believed my purpose was to shield the light of others—a wall of stone protecting a candle from the wind. But not wanting to do something is nearly as powerful as wanting to. And I do not want to marry Calista Contarini.

But these things are far beyond my control. I only wish I could save Lilac from such an unfortunate fate.

A knock sounds on the door, and I run a hand over my face, trying to shake the emotion out of me.

Rising to my feet, I call, "Come in."

I should have known it was Azaire before he steps into the room, tugging at the sides of the royal blue beanie he always wears. Morning sun spills through the curtains, coating his rich brown complexion.

Closing the door behind him, he asks, "How did the meeting go?"

"You know how it is—talk of trade routes and how to settle tensions between borders." I fall on my bed once more, staring at the molded ceiling, the silver edges gleaming faintly in the light.

I already know that Azaire will see through me.

"Lucian—"

I cut him off, saying, "I am to marry Calista." I clasp my hands, resting them on my abdomen as I force a deep breath.

"There will be a magically binding betrothal in the coming months."

After that betrothal, there will be no choice but to marry Calista upon the agreed date. My very power and bones will bind to her—swearing me to her for the rest of my life.

Although I can't see him, I know Azaire is shaking his head.

"You don't have to do this," he whispers.

I sit up and say, "We both know that's not true."

Yet when I turn to face him, his bright gray eyes lock on mine, and his bushy black eyebrows rise with something akin to hope. "Don't let them take more of you," he whispers. "If you have to, find a way to do it for yourself."

The optimism in his voice makes me wish it were the truth.

Azaire, always the wise. I envy his heart, even when I see it as a weakness—and false hope *is* a weakness. But it's an honorable one.

"No surrender," he says with more conviction than usual.

"No surrender." I nod.

One day I will show the worlds what he is—erase the idea that because he was born with venomous teeth, he is a predator. For if a king can praise a Nepenthe, then the worlds can, too.

After a moment, I add, "I'm thinking about throwing a party, blowing off some steam. Spread the news?"

Azaire shakes his head so subtly it's nearly imperceptible. "Are you sure that's a good idea?"

"No," I answer. "But I need a distraction."

A sense of control.

"I see," Azaire whispers. Then, he adds, "Yuki would probably be the better option."

I nod, rising to my feet and heading to the door as I say, "Probably."

Azaire and I cross the suite, weaving past the dark table and sapphire furniture. In the room they share, Yuki lounges in a large, cushioned chair with one leg draped over the arm. His black hair is shaved close to the scalp, already growing out enough to need another cut soon. His sharp eyes meet mine. With a swift movement, he snatches the long sword at his side and hurls it toward me.

I catch the weapon midair.

"Party," I say. "End of week." I shift the position of his sword in my hand as I say, "Spread the word for me?"

Yuki salutes me, smirking as he says, "You got it."

I return the salute, stepping away and heading toward the door. My thoughts shift back to the weight of the marriages and how I'll endure class with it hanging over me. As I exit the suite, the squeak of my peers' boots echoes on the polished marble, snapping me back to the present.

When I enter Lyrian Studies, I meet Cynthia's gaze. She's the most powerful Lyrian in Visnatus Academy, and as a result, this is the sole class she teaches. The vast, open space is more like a gymnasium than a traditional classroom, with high ceilings and enchanted walls designed to cast shadows for us to manipulate with our magic. In a room full of the best Lyrians of my generation, the air hums with power, yet Cynthia's features quickly turn sullen, telling me what today holds.

A group of Nepenthes enter the classroom—falsely labeled as volunteers. I stiffen, and Lilac moves next to me as we both scan the group of gray eyes for Azaire, my fear hanging over me like a guillotine. It's a breath of fresh air amidst a world of smoke every time I don't see him.

These so-called "volunteer groups" emerged after the Neptharian War—the final bloody battle between Folkara, the world of the Folk, and Nepthara, the world of the Nepenthes. For centuries, the Folk dominated the Nepenthes, forcing them into servitude as soldiers against their own kind. Finally, the Nepenthes rebelled—three times, in fact—though it was their final attempt that nearly toppled the monarchy.

They've never been allowed to forget it, conditioned to despise their own kind while being forced into tasks no one else dares to endure.

A short girl with long silver hair is assigned to me. I softly offer my apologies when no one can hear. The corners of her mouth tilt up, and she nods. Then I reach into her mind.

It's a light feeling for the uninitiated, comparable to a soft tickle I've been told. However, I am not under the false impression that this is her first time being subconsciously manipulated by a Lyrian. She can most likely feel the pull I have on her, the way I move her body like a marionette.

Physically, this is something I'm used to—I am comfortable in others' minds. But beyond physicality, twisting someone's actions to suit my own needs feels wrong. Perhaps because it's been done to me my entire life.

I don't know the other end of the stick *exactly*, yet I know it intimately. But there's very little room for moral qualms in my life.

As a prince, power is all I'm good for.

So, I continue.

Every step feels like a betrayal as I walk the girl across the length of the room, pushing further into her mind until I can see through her eyes, until her very essence has been taken from her entirely, stolen by me.

"Very good, Lucian," Cynthia says to me.

She, in particular, knows my disdain for the treatment of the Nepenthes. She even agrees with me. But this class is reserved for those destined for the highest positions in Ilyria's kingdom. The use of subconscious manipulation is required learning for the job.

When Cynthia tells me to make my Nepenthe fight another, I know she isn't happy about it. It's entirely selfish of me to think of Kai.

But two fighting puppets is exactly what we are.

My Nepenthe steps toward Lilac's, but hers goes still.

I glance at my sister, but she doesn't look at me; she never does when she feels guilty.

"Li," I whisper. "We have to fight."

Lilac stares ahead, looking at our puppets. Slowly, she shakes her head. "I can't," she mutters. "I *won't*."

"If Leiana finds out—"

"I don't care." Lilac drops her hand, and the Nepenthe she was controlling is set free—his mind is his again, his limbs his to move. "This isn't right."

Lilac turns away from the scene, and I wish I could follow. If I were to leave this room, I'm not sure what Leiana would do to me.

I stay put, casting aside my morality in favor of my mother.

Cynthia calls another Lyrian forward—and their Nepenthe follows. We fight with hands alone, my small girl landing punch after punch on the boy. Specks of light flood my vision the further I push the girl. My head spins with every strike. I grow nauseous, and I'm sure the Nepenthes do, too.

When Cynthia finally says, "Enough," I release the girl's mind at once. Stepping back, I fall onto the first seat I find.

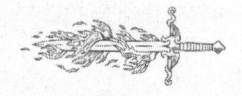

---

I easily make it through the rest of class in a state more numb than alert. Psychology and Combat Training don't need my cunning.

When the day is done, Yuki walks beside me, adjusting the strap of his bag. Grinning, he says, "The entire academy knows. I've taken it into my hands to make sure it's the biggest party of the year." He rubs his hands together while an impish smile spreads across his face, as if this is all some big game.

For a moment, the marble of the academy blurs. I'm plunged into a vision of Kai, standing in our suite, his fists clenched at his sides, his face flushed with anger. With a blink, the vision dissipates, and I abruptly return to the gleaming hall.

"How did Kai take it?" I ask, already knowing.

"Not well," Yuki answers hesitantly, his pace slowing.

I give him a sidelong glance, asking, "What was on Kai's mind when you told him?"

Yuki is one of the few Draes in the academy, here as my Royal advisor. His kind are skilled mentalists, capable of reading minds—a talent that's proven useful more than once.

He presses his lips together before saying, "Something along the lines of killing you."

"All right."

I already know as much—he wants to fight me. Whether I decided to throw a party or not, I'm certain he'd still want to. The *why* is what I don't understand. Could it truly be nothing more than having misdirected anger?

"Anything else?" I ask Yuki.

He shrugs, smiling as he says, "Only that you're an inconsiderate prick."

"Hm," I mutter, humor slipping into my tone. "I suppose that's what happens when you grow up with a person."

Yuki laughs as he opens the door to our suite.

I'm already prepared for the inevitable. Kai sits on the couch, identical to my vision, and asks, "What's this about a party?"

Always so predictable. Everyone is.

I take the three marble steps down to our suite before I answer, "On Friday in the woods. Bring your best engagement gift."

My words are like pouring oil on a fire. Kai steps away from his door, purple bolts of lightning crackling between his fingers and snaking up his arms.

A part of me wonders if this is where our friendship finally dies. We've fought one another a hundred times before, yet this is different. Far more dire.

"What is it about the party that has you so worked up?" I ask as he steps closer.

Kai raises his hand, the energy sparking. "It's not the party, it's the principle. I get the worst news of my life, and you want to celebrate!"

I narrow my eyes at him, allowing more irritation than I should. "Because the news was such a delight for me?" I retort sharply.

Kai strikes, and I move quickly out of the way, his lightning crashing where I once stood. The bolt chars the wall, smoke curling through the room.

Perhaps it *is* simply misdirected anger. It's not as if he can fight those that are truly at fault for our marriages. But if it's a fight he wants, it's a fight he'll get.

Like I said, I could use a new sparring partner.

Light Folk are tricky, second to a Fire Folk in brute power, and Kai could incapacitate even me. If he can land a blow, that is—which he won't. Not when I can see them coming before he even lifts a finger.

He holds his hand out, sending five arcs of electrical energy in all directions around my body. Before they land, I summon shadows from the back of the room and wrap them around his legs.

I'm more tired than I expected after Lyrian Studies, but I ignore it and hope he doesn't notice. Slowly, I walk behind him, the quiet of the suite amplifying each step. "Would you like another shot?" I ask. He struggles, trying to turn, but the shadows refuse to relent, holding him in place. "I might even release you—if we take the magic out of this encounter."

Kai doesn't respond to my taunts. He squirms, futilely trying to move his legs, his frustration building.

I take the opportunity to say, "It's a party, Kai. Get over it. I don't want to marry your sister, and you don't want to marry mine."

I turn from him and make my way up the three steps that

lead to the exit of our suite. Only when my hand rests on the doorframe do I release Kai.

Then, without warning, the wind is knocked from me. Pain surges through my chest, and my heart feels like it's being squeezed in a vice. My body seizes, muscles locking as the sudden wave of agony floods my senses. It takes me shorter than most and longer than usual to regain my composure.

Kai's getting stronger—the Folk usually do with age.

"It's always smart to take an open shot," I say, not bothering to turn as I leave the suite.

# Chapter 3
## If You Can't Run, Hide

# DESDEMONA

A second before I can regain my bearings, a deafening alarm blares in my ears, the shrill sound vibrating through my skull. At the same time, a flashing red light flares to life, with the sole purpose of making it difficult for me to read Mom's note. Her handwriting is sloppy and disjointed, clearly written in a rush. *Of course* it has to be difficult to read—and, more irritatingly, impossible to destroy.

*Desdemona,*

*Tell them your father was Dalin Marquees and that your birthday is four months earlier than your true one. If they ask you to prove this, do what they say. If they use your blood, do not let them see the wound cauterize. Do not take off the necklace, ever. Keep it hidden always. Do not talk about me, ever. To you, Isa Althenia is dead. You were raised by a kind family in the septic. They discovered your heritage and sent you to Visnatus Academy before a fire took their lives. In a place like Visnatus, knowledge is your greatest weapon yet. You have a keen eye—use it. You mustn't look for me nor let a soul see this note. If I can, I will find you.*

*Love you always,*
*Mom*

She's not coming.
I'm in a different world.

Alone.

The flashing red alarm finally dims to a steady yellow glow as two silhouettes come into view, walking toward me with agonizing ease. I force myself to swallow the paper, mourning my mom's handwriting as it scratches my throat. The last link I have to another life I've lost.

A man and a woman approach, their gazes fixed on me. The woman is older, her lips painted dark red, with subtle lines of age curving around them. Her features are sharp—typical of Lyrians, I've heard—but her skin has begun to sag with the years. Dark hair frames her piercing blue eyes.

In our universe, there are five kinds of magic-wielders, each marked by the color of their eyes. In my entire life, I've only ever encountered two: the Nepenthes, with their cold, steely gray eyes, and the Folk, with brown.

But I've heard the stories of the Lyrians—their shadows sneaking into your subconscious, stealing secrets best kept buried.

The man is pale—a telltale sign of the Folk, and another physical attribute I wasn't lucky enough to acquire. My skin is tan, no matter the time of year, and my face is always plagued with sun freckles. He has the same subtle features of my kind—bulbous jaw, full cheeks, other features I never got. My face is sharper, more angular, a constant reminder of what I lack in comparison.

His short frame and brown eyes remind me of every old guy back home, but there's no comfort in that. Not with the Lyrian nearby, ready to unravel my mind with a glance.

Every magic-wielder in our universe has a mental and, worse, a physical ability. All Folk have power over memory, making this man dangerous, but not as dangerous as the woman. But "Folk" is merely an umbrella term for us. Each of us can wield one of three elemental magics: Air Folk control wind and sound currents, Light Folk control electrical currents, and Fire Folk, of

37

course, control the unruly Flame.

When both the man and woman's mouths move soundlessly, I realize not only is he an Air Folk, but they're discussing my life and death. I'm septic. The fancy alarm and flashing lights probably made sure they knew that.

This is a school for the elites, and I am most certainly not an elite.

*But I am a liar.*

Another man walks in, with scruffy blond hair and a beard, one hand gripping a sword sheathed to his waist. Then those gray eyes of his land on me. The same eyes as the Nepenthes that have killed so many of my kind.

So *he's* going to be the deciding factor in my life. Well, *I'm* deciding not to die today.

I'm not very good at fighting; I'm more adept at running. I haven't got a weapon, nor do I know how to use one very well. I can kill seizing or still animals, but I've never hurt another person, other than in my dreams.

I wonder if I have it in me—to kill, to be the monster my dreams say I am.

But Mom made sure I had enough information to survive, so survive I will.

*Knowledge is your greatest weapon yet.*

Their breaths bounce around the circular cobblestone walls, and I wait for them to address me. When the woman asks my name, I say, "Desdemona Althenia."

The Nepenthe stiffens, his hand still on the hilt of his sword as he mutters, "Bullshit."

"Excuse me?" I start.

The Lyrian woman cuts me off, sharply saying, "Leiholan." The Nepenthe shuts up—so that's his name. Locking her gaze on me, the woman asks, "What are you doing in Visnatus?"

"My father was Dalin Marquees," I tell her, reciting my mom's letter out loud—the papercuts still scratching at my throat. "A family took me in as a baby, and they put together my lineage. They sent me here during a welding accident." I look at the floor and play with my fingers, keeping my eyes open until they dry out, forcing tears. When I look back up at the three of them, I quiver my lip. "Said if one of us could live, they wouldn't pass on the opportunity."

Not even one of them looks convinced. I think back to my dreams; the murder wasn't very hard then. Maybe I could win in a fight.

*What a ridiculous line of thought.* I pout some more.

"Marquees had no children," the short, bald Folk says.

I shrug and say, "I'm right here."

"Where does the name Althenia come from?" Leiholan asks me.

"My mother. Isa Althenia." I blink to produce more tears from my already stinging eyes. "But I never knew her."

The woman gives Leiholan a long glance, and he nods. Then, she and the Folk man head down the dimly lit hall, leaving me alone with the Nepenthe.

I turn to Leiholan once they've disappeared. He's already watching me, his grip *still* on his sword—like I'm a threat to him, when it's clearly the other way around. I don't let myself look defensive. I make myself appear defenseless. Small and weak, powerless at his hands, hoping for mercy. That's how the Nepenthes like it. I expect him to ask me questions, interrogate and intimidate me, but he says nothing.

It's not long before the other two come back into the room, the Lyrian woman holding a milky-clear crystal ball the size of my hand. "Hogan?" she says, and the bald Folk lifts his hand, his eyes shining indigo just like Damien's. With his magic, the slight shimmer of an iridescent light flickers out between us. So, he's a Light Folk, *not* an Air Folk.

I guess someone else concealed their voices from me before. The Light Folk have electrical power, none over sound.

The Lyrian, the only one whose name I'm missing, walks toward me. Her eyes gleam with an unnatural light, the sign of magic being used. Lyrians are known for their power to manipulate the subconscious—puppeteers of the mind—and I fear what she plans on doing to me now.

"Your hand," she says.

It's not a question. I hold up the one that isn't scarred. She takes out a dagger, much fancier than Damien's fancy one, and pushes the tip of the blade into my pointer finger. After a drop of blood has fallen on the crystal, I yank my hand away and close my fist.

"Squeamish," I say with a shrug.

The woman raises an eyebrow in response, then glances back to the crystal ball. In its reflection, I catch the brief flash of a man's face I don't recognize—must be Dalin's—and then my mom's face. As the Lyrian assesses me, I know she believes it. Either whatever my mom did worked, or Dalin truly is my father.

I've heard of Dalin before; he was a war hero, a Fire Folk who fought in the second out of three battles between Folkara and Nepthara—the Folk vs the Nepenthes—six years before the *real* war. The one I lived through.

In that second battle, much of the credit for Folkara's swift victory went to Dalin and his ability to wield the Flame as a weapon. But his ending wasn't happy. A Fire Folk's rarely is. Despite being called a master of the Flame, he died at his own hands.

The Folk—Hogan—and the Lyrian exchange a look, while Leiholan's gaze stays on me. "Get comfortable," Leiholan says, and this time, all three of them disappear down the hall.

I step forward, almost reaching the exit when sharp tingles like a thousand needles rush down my body. Then there's nothing.

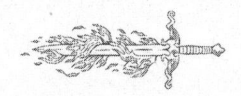

I snap awake to a haze. The world is a blur, but I feel a chair beneath me. Desperately, I try to stand, only to realize my body won't *move*. My limbs are tied to the chair, but I don't feel any rope. I pull again at the immaterial restraints.

They pull back harder.

As I struggle, my vision slowly returns, revealing burgundy curtains, a mahogany desk, and the Lyrian woman's bright eyes and red lips.

I push again, and my stomach knots.

"Light Folk magic, dear," the woman says. "It will wear off."

*They paralyzed me.*

"Don't glare," she says, her voice drawn out with deliberate precision. "It could be *much* more painful."

Between her fingers, she rotates a crystal glass of silver liquid—an intoxicant, I assume—and I'm immediately offended that *she* is the one acting inconvenienced.

I take a deep breath instead of screaming. To my left, there's a fireplace full of wood, and to the right, a bookshelf sits next to the tall windows behind her red seat. I could use a log or a book to knock her out, break the window, then make a run for it.

But run where? I don't know my way around here, which is precisely why knowledge can be wielded.

"I'm Cynthia Constance, the headmistress." She sets her glass down with a *clunk*. "I understand this situation has been far from satisfactory. For that, I offer you my solace.

"As I am sure you know, Visnatus is an academy for future *leaders*. The best and most powerful of your generation come here to learn to wield not just their energy, but their minds. I will not force this to go down sweetly. You do not belong here. Yet, you are a *lesser* legacy only because of a father you did not know."

She pauses as she takes a good look at me. "I'm willing to give you a trial period here. If you can prove to be as"—she taps the desk—"*noble* as your peers, I will allow you to stay."

This feels like a trick, but I say, "Thank you."

My whole body is starting to feel numb and prickly, like my foot when I sit on it for too long.

"I believe it goes without saying that you will be keeping your origins a secret." She raises a knowing eyebrow at me.

At the mention of my home, my heart aches. I know this place is fancy, that it can probably offer me three meals a day and snacks between, paper and books, and everything else my life has lacked, but I don't care. I don't want it. I want my home.

"For the time being, you will adopt the surname Marquees." She slides a jar across the table to me. "Go ahead, grab it."

This time when I try, I'm able to lift my arm, but the prickly sensation doesn't subside. I pick up the jar, filled with a gooey, milky substance.

"It's a glamour," the headmistress says. "Apply liberally every three days—it will hide your scars."

Right. Who I am isn't worthy here. It's good for me that hiding is something I've been doing my entire life.

I don't even want to think about what they did to find the scars on my back.

The headmistress rises, saying she will walk me to my suite. I follow, spotting a little blue-studded knife on her desk, gleaming in the light. On the way out, I slide it into my hand, feeling relieved by the cold, polished metal against my palm.

The academy is ridiculous. Marble walls gleam in the sunlight streaming through the arched windows. Grand staircases curve elegantly through the halls—but I'm more focused on the floor.

I recognize the stone immediately, seeing as it's the same marble my village quarried when I was ten. Why would you use something so difficult to retrieve for something as silly as a fancy floor? All you do is walk on it.

It occurs to me that I'm stepping on someone's wasted life.

The headmistress tells me that one of my suitemates is a Royal, and I don't make any gesture that would show her how taken aback I am by this. A girl from the septic, rooming with Royalty? Instantly, I'm suspicious of the headmistress. There's no way her intentions are altruistic.

I don't believe in altruism. And even if I did, the headmistress would be at the bottom of that list.

She tells me their names: Aralia, Wendy, and Calista. I'm not ready when I reach for the door. Or when it opens. Or when I walk down the three marble steps and past the two columns that lead into the suite.

The room is larger than anywhere I've ever lived before—furnished with a plush beige couch, a sturdy table with chairs, and a small kitchen tucked into one corner. On the opposite side, there's a cushioned seat, and two doors line either side of the space.

"The door in the far corner is the bathroom, the other two are bedrooms," Headmistress Constance says.

I stifle an audible gasp at the size. I'm not trying to ostracize myself from my new roommate, who's lying on the couch, her short black hair dangling off the edge.

"I'm sure your suitemates will get you acquainted," the headmistress adds, offering me an unsettling smile. "Good luck, dear," she says on her way out.

The girl doesn't look up from her book as she says, "I'm Aralia."

"Desdemona," I mumble, still staring at the high ceilings and the silver that decorates them.

Another girl steps out from one of the four doors. She has blonde hair, brown eyes, and a pastel-yellow dress that gives the illusion she's floating instead of walking. She looks me up and down and purses her lips.

This girl has never stabbed an animal for her supper.

She places a dainty hand on her chest and says, "Calista."

So, this is the Royal, the princess of Folkara—my world that I get the blunt end of while she gets the very narrow top.

Standing up straighter, I say again, "Desdemona."

Her eyes fall back to my body. My chin is where her gaze lands—the tip of her head barely reaching my eyes—but her glare feels like it's meant to be intimidating. She's even taller than my mom, and I still feel like a giant. Intimidation isn't going to be her strong suit.

Aralia steps forward, grabbing my hand as she says, "Welcome to our *wonderful* suite."

I get a good look at her for the first time. She's pretty like the other Folk, but not as pretty as the princess. Her eyes—dark brown and wide—carry an intensity that feels at odds with the softness of her other features. Her short black hair, dark and unassuming, gently frames her face, cradling her soft jaw and rosy cheeks. And when she smiles, I notice that her teeth are huge—something she'll have to grow into, if she ever does.

Without a word, she pulls me to the side of the suite and into a room with two large beds. A desk sits between them, beneath a wide window. A stack of books is piled on the cushioned seat, and dozens of picture frames line the windowsill.

Aralia walks to the back of the room, opening two *more* doors, but it's just a closet. "I'll move my belongings to this half of the wardrobe," Aralia says.

I look away, at the dresser directly across from the beds. Papers and pictures are scattered across its surface. This would be a precious mine back home.

"A drawer will be good enough," I say, interrupting her reorganizing efforts.

She walks to the dresser, moving her papers and stuffing them into random drawers and notebooks. The only thing I have is what the headmistress gave me—a glamour, I think she called it, and there's definitely not enough of it to fill a drawer.

"Is there anywhere I can get food?" I ask when she's finished.

"Of course," Aralia says, like food is always a given—something waiting for you and not something you hunt—and heads to the door. "Coming?"

Together, we exit the suite. I try not to look uncomfortably around at the academy hallways as we enter the kitchen—which is unlike any I've seen. The countertops are made of marble, and behind them, the room is filled with gleaming silverware.

A far cry from Mom's chipped steel pot and bonfires.

Best of all, the counter is lined with small pies.

"Take one," Aralia says.

She must have meant a *slice* of one, but before I clarify, I remember where I am. I take the pie greedily and am pleasantly surprised when my first bite is sweet, not savory.

Pies aren't a delicacy at home, just a way to stretch the meat when it's meager.

Aralia offers to help me unpack my stuff, and I make up something about trying to let go of my past, telling her I'm going to buy everything I need here. As if I have a single pence to my name. Then I lie on the bed—which is softer than even the thickest patch of grass—and sleep for the rest of the day.

When I wake up, it's night. I turn in bed, expecting my mom to be across from me, snoring softly. I nearly have a heart attack when it isn't her.

Then I remember what happened. Mom sent me to Visnatus Academy, to another world. Visnatus stands apart from the rest of the universe; it's the only world where no magic-wielders emerged. Formed by an asteroid and once deemed freeland, it was later claimed by Ilyria, who built the academy here. All of this my mom told me—because before she was banished to the septic, this was her school.

Carefully, I listen to Aralia's breathing until I'm sure she's asleep. Once I'm certain, I slip out of bed, stuffing a pillow under the covers in case she wakes. There are things I have to do—

learn more about this school until I can figure out a way to get back to my mom.

I apply the glamour over my entire back, and to my surprise, the scars vanish. The raised skin is still there beneath my fingers, but I can't see it.

On the dresser, Aralia left sheets and a stack of clothes. There are dark blue plaid skirts, pants, ties, and jackets, each with a silver emblem on the chest: a sun and moon balanced on a scale crafted from a sword.

I throw on one of the jackets and walk the halls, searching for an exit. The busts lining the walls seem to watch my every step before I enter a garden.

From the outside, the school walls are covered in glowing purple flowers, and the crisp air feels sharp in my lungs, awakening my senses like a blade piercing skin.

Nothing like the humid Welding Village.

My gaze catches a glowing beam in the sky—which I assume is a moon. And it's the most beautiful thing I've ever seen.

I decide I'll miss it when I make it home to Folkara. It's the only world without one.

The moonlight cascades onto another faint blue glow. Curiosity consumes me, and I follow until I reach a shimmering, iridescent lake.

I stop when I notice someone sitting at the lake's edge, their reflection rippling in the moonlit water. All I can make out is dark hair and pale skin. But, despite my distance, my reflection appears beside his—only I look different. My orange hair is shorter, and my brown eyes are darker. As he leans down, the water that casts our reflection turns to fire and the image disappears altogether.

I begin to walk back to the academy, but without turning around, he says, "Leaving so soon?"

The voice is like a song I used to know but can't remember.

Before logic kicks in, I ask, "Do I know you?"

He turns, wavy, dark hair falling over his forehead but not into his eyes. Every angle of him is sharp enough to cut; his jaw and cheekbones are emphasized by the shadows the moonlight is casting over the planes of his face.

He's perfection. The kind you could only attain by being pampered your entire life. Beautiful, yes, but I prefer the roguish beauty of Damien. It adds depth of character. This boy has none, I'm sure.

His eyes scan up and down my body. They're so dark that, at first, I think they're brown or gray, but when they meet my eyes again, I realize I'm mistaken.

They're a blue as dark as midnight.

A far cry from the headmistress's eerie, bright, almost white eyes.

"I'd remember a Fire Folk." He smirks. It's slow and teasing, the kind that accompanies an enemy before they strike.

I sneer, only in an attempt to find some high ground. "Stay out of my head, *Lyrian*."

"On the contrary." He stands. "Your head seems like such a *lovely* place to be."

I don't allow my voice to fluctuate for a second. "Same with your memories."

The boy scoffs with a smile, but I think I've made him nervous because he says, "Tell me, what do you see?"

"Nothing you'd want repeated." Nothing, period. The Folk govern memories—seeing, rewriting, erasing them. But not all of us.

I've never been able to start so much as a measly fire.

Despite my still hoping that's the case, I take the chance to walk in the opposite direction of him.

Then I think I might just survive here after all.

# Chapter 4
## All My Dreams Are Awake

## DESDEMONA

The next morning, Aralia gets out of bed before I do. She whispers, "You should use the bathroom before the others wake up," and I turn to face her. I don't know how she knows I'm awake, but I thank her and leave the room.

For the third time now, I take in the suite's size. The marble walls gleam too clean, too polished—so unlike the gritty, cramped spaces of the septic.

It's eerie. There's gotta be something underneath the surface they want to keep hidden.

The bathroom is—like everything else—large. A porcelain bathtub with silver feet sits at the back of the room, and a tiled shower is tucked in the front corner. Showers are rare back home. Sometimes they had hoses outside the mines and welding facilities to wash off the soot, but normally the best chance at bathing was filling a tub with water from Mom's steel pot—which always ran cold too quickly.

When the *hot* water runs down my back, I think this might be the best I'll ever get to feel. I stay beneath the stream, unmoving, until my fingers wrinkle like the bark of an old tree.

I force myself from the shower and put on my new school uniform, staring at myself in the fogged-up mirror for a moment too long. I never enjoy my reflection, but worse than my appearance is the outfit. After everything Mom told me, I never expected to end up at this school. It always sounded so bureaucratic, so classist, and now I'm wearing the same clothes as the preppy elites.

But I'll get over it.

When I go back to Aralia's room, she's sitting at the desk between the two comfiest beds in the worlds, dabbing her face with color.

She turns to face me, glancing up and down. "You'd look good with blusher," she says. "It'll make your face look rounder."

Damien and Elliae were the first Folk to *not* mention my angular face—the face that's drawn unwanted stares my entire life.

Aralia hands me a tube made of *real* silver. These kids are so spoiled, but that's a sentiment for another day, so I put the stuff on my cheeks and lips. Turns out she's right, my face does look a little rounder. Prettier.

"It's a glamour," Aralia explains, putting the pink cream on her cheeks. The features of her face blur, turning her already rounded cheeks and jaw even softer. Prettier.

The opposite of me.

I offer a small "Thank you" for good measure, despite feeling no gratitude to the girl. She has everything she could want. Sharing a portion of *everything* doesn't make her an altruist.

She offers me another silver tube and says, "This will take care of your freckles."

*Right.*

I go to the kitchen, hoping to find more of that delicious pie from last night. Instead, I find cups full of purple and green berries with seeds. Students sit on tall wooden chairs around the counter, and some take their cups to go.

Most fruits that grow in Folkara are poisonous. It's one of the first things I can remember my mom telling me. Don't touch the berries. Sometimes Damien and I would find dead Folk in the woods by the bushes.

Disregarding the warnings, I plop the green fruit in my mouth, and its sweet juices explode. No one pays any mind to me until I suck down the berries in seconds. Then they all start to look at me. I guess they don't eat like this.

"Thanks for the food," I say to no one in particular, setting down my utensils and standing to leave.

"Did I just hear a thank you?" a voice calls back, strong and full, echoing through the room.

"Yeah," I say, much quieter.

The woman steps in front of me, and I meet her green eyes, dark skin, and pulled-back brown hair. I've never met a Eunoia before, but I've heard of their enchanting nature, their otherworldly beauty and crystalline green eyes.

I also know the Eunoias have power over emotion, and while the Lyrians' subconscious control is considered the most deadly, I've always had the sneaking suspicion that someone reading my emotions would be a fate worse than death.

Their kind comes from Eunaris—supposedly the most peaceful world in our universe. They work together there. Their powers are tied to nature; they can grow and feel plants, which makes them responsible for the universe's agriculture. My mom used to talk about missing their food in the septic—because that's a place where their work doesn't reach.

The Eunoia waves a large wooden spoon in my direction. "You must be new around here."

"Yeah," I say again.

"Still, I appreciate being appreciated. But don't we all?" She laughs and points the spoon at herself. "The nicer you are to me, the nicer the food will be to you," she whispers like it's some kind of secret. "I'm Elowen."

"Desdemona," I say, leaning in and matching her conspiratorial tone. "So, does that mean I'll get more of it?"

"Yes, it does." Elowen smiles.

"Everything I've had so far is incredible." I smile back. "I didn't know food could taste that good."

"Where are you from, girl?" she asks me.

"Utul," I answer without hesitation.

Utul is one of the rich lands on my homeworld, Folkara, but not a part of the kingdom. It's a fairly decent lie—and not one I considered before, which I should have—because no one will expect me to be a diplomat or a politician. Just a spoiled brat.

"And you've never had dragon berries, or are you toying with me 'cause you want a second serving?" Elowen asks, her voice rich with humor.

No, I've never had dragon berries, but I say, "Never had dragon berries this good." I wonder if these berries were something Mom missed in the septic.

Elowen slides another dish to me slyly. "The secret ingredient is nectar."

I smile at her, accepting the berries and walking to my first class, Philosophical Theology. This is where I get to productively zone out for the first time today.

By that, I mean I plan my escape. I'll have to portal home—it's the only way to go from one world to another—but considering I can't even use the Flame, I'll need someone to channel.

So I'll not only have to find some unwitting Folk to steal magic from but also get past the alarm that ticked off the headmistress when I arrived.

When the class is over, it's far from too soon. But I think I might prefer it over Elemental Magic, for obvious reasons.

The next classroom I enter is huge, more like the Saul that's always stuffed with hundreds of bodies—desperately trying to sell and trade enough to feed themselves—than our dwellings. The ceilings are higher than I've ever seen before, and the walls are boarded up with cushioning, but the entire roof is one big skylight.

I had assumed this class was for the Folk—*Elemental* Magic and all—which I was correct about. I stay toward the back of the class, hoping that I'll be able to avoid whatever the teacher wants us to do.

It doesn't work out so well.

The teacher calls my name, introducing herself as "Ms. Abrams." I duck my head. But when she adds, "A Fire Folk," I don't flinch at the whispers—or wallow in them.

"Today we are doing something extra special," she continues. "A practice in control."

When she glares at me, I know this is a directed attack. Not many people like the Fire Folk; we're *dangerous beings*. Then there's the fact that everyone believes my dad is one of the most infamous Folk of the previous generation.

Even here—where they don't have to worry about a Fire Folk burning down their village in a work accident—they still fear the Flame.

"Each of you will take your elements to their absolute limits," Ms. Abrams says, "and when I say *yield*, draw your power back in."

Some students smile, and some look as nervous as I feel, but I'd never show it.

"I will pair each of you with a partner to warm up with before we begin." She goes on to pair up the class, and when she says my name after "Kai Contarini," I will myself to stay calm. Contarini is the Royal name of the Folk. I'm hoping my partner isn't related to them, but it's a foolish wish.

Again, this feels deliberate. I wonder if the headmistress is behind it. A Contarini is bound to be powerful, one of the two Royal families left—who have held onto their power through force alone. I don't want to imagine what will happen if he can't —or won't—reel back in his power when he's supposed to.

When he smiles at me from across the room, I'm a little thankful for Aralia's glamour.

As I approach, he says, "I'm Kai." His floppy, dirty blond hair sweeps over his forehead. He has bulbous cheeks and big lips, like Damien, and soft, kind brown eyes. A smile that could convince anyone of anything. The kind of smile I've spent my entire life envying and emulating from my mom.

"Des." I quickly add, "Demona," not sure if they use nicknames the same way we do in the septic.

But Kai smiles and says, "It's my pleasure to meet you, Des."

"You too," I say, mimicking his smile.

"The only thing I ask of you is to take it easy on me," Kai says.

"Oh, yes," I say. "That goes for you, too. I'm more fragile than I may seem." I've noticed people like when the Fire Folk have self-humility, and when he laughs, I take note.

"What makes you think such a thing?" he asks, and I close my fist tightly around the cut on my palm.

"Perhaps my limited experience. I'm from Utul," I tell him, sticking with the lie I told the Eunoia in the kitchen earlier. It's the most peaceful part of Folkara, a perfect utopia to hide behind.

*I bet they didn't have a mile-long death toll every day during the war.*

I carry on, saying, "I'm gonna be honest. I personally wouldn't like to be responsible for another Fire-Folk-related disaster."

A flash of what I hope is fear crosses his eyes, but he steps closer to me, leans toward my ear, and whispers, "Ms. Abrams has never been very fond of the Fire Folk." He reaches his hand out to me and says, "I can make sure it's not too painful." I scrunch my eyebrows up at him, and he seems to understand, saying, "I'll get you out of class." When I don't take his hand, he says, as if I care, "It will be beneficial to me as well. Displays of power from me or Calista are never frowned upon."

"Calista is your sister?" I ask, putting together the pieces.

"Twin."

"She's my suitemate," I say with a shy sort of smile.

Intrigue lights up Kai's eyes. "Then you may be stronger than you give yourself credit for."

I grab his hands, and when the current of energy moves through him to me, my breath hitches. For a minute, it feels like my heart stops, thinking of all the animals Damien and I have killed this way.

"Ms. Abrams!" Kai calls and winks at me. "There's been a miscalculation."

"She's fine!" Ms. Abrams calls back.

"If another accident happens," Kai says slowly, "she could be paralyzed. I would hate to see that happen."

The teacher narrows her wide eyes, then nods. I offer Kai another smile.

At the end of class, I try to walk out unnoticed, but Aralia catches up. "Hey," she says softly, walking next to me. "Are you all right?"

"Yes, just a little winded." There's quite the contrast between the other kids ducking their heads while I walk past and this one walking with me.

"I don't like Ms. Abrams either," she tells me. "If I am right to assume that you didn't like her. Otherwise, I *love* her." Sarcasm drips from her tongue the way saliva drips from mine when I'm cooking after going a day without eating.

Or two—not that Aralia would know what that's like.

"I did think she was a rather good teacher," I say with a straight face.

"Well then, I think she's great. Have you been beyond the academy, in the woods?"

I keep my eyes fixed ahead of me, down the beige, marble hall. "No."

"Oh well, there's gonna be a party at the end of the week. Everyone's going."

A party where everyone will be, held outside of campus and possibly past any alarm. That sounds like the perfect time to leave unnoticed. Which means I'll have to figure out how to get back to Folkara—and quickly.

"I might, too," I say, already planning.

When I sit down in my next class, Psychology, the teacher's eyes lock on mine. It's Hogan, one of the three people who interrogated me when I first arrived at the academy. One of the three who know I'm from the septic.

His eyes narrow. A warning, I assume.

*Hide.*

If only he knew how long I've been hiding. I'm practically a pro at it.

When he introduces me to the class as "Ms. Marquees," I get those annoying looks again, and like before, I decide to use them as fear. Hogan tells us to open our books, and the class resumes their unit. Of course, they're talking about the psychology of septic Folk. Like it's any different.

I guess we're poorer, dirtier, more rebellious—*this* is what the look at the beginning of class was about: *don't stick out.*

When I've had enough, I look around the room, my gaze stopping on the boy I met by the lake. His eyes, a deeper blue than any Lyrian I've seen so far, coupled with his wavy dark hair, make him the personified picture of the midnight sky.

He glances back at me, raising an eyebrow, and I turn away—there are far more important things to focus on. Number one: getting home, and number two: Hogan calling me at the end of class.

I walk to the front, stopping at his desk.

"How's the glamour working?" he asks, meeting my gaze. "I spent a long time perfecting it, so it'll last you longer than a day at a time."

*Yeah, spent all that time while I was unwillingly unconscious.*

Instead of spitting at him, I smile. He's one of the people I need to convince that I can fit their mold.

"It's a marvel, thank you."

"I wanted to give you a heads up about the Draes," he says.

I've heard about the Draes, but only briefly—they have purple eyes, impenetrable skin, *and* they can read minds. That's where my knowledge of them ends.

Hogan continues, "Most are untrained and thus can only read what you are thinking at the moment. Take extra caution with your thoughts when they're around."

I nod. "Understood."

"Come to me when you need more glamour," he says, tipping his head down slightly—sending me off.

I exit the classroom. Of course it's *come to me when you need more* and not *I'll show you how to make it*. They don't trust me. They don't see me as anything more than a lower-class citizen.

The second I enter Combat Training, Leiholan's eyes burn into me—yet another one of the three people who know I'm septic. I wonder how he'll treat me, since he's a Nepenthe, too.

"Get a suit before you stick out," he demands. "In the back."

I follow his instructions and open the double doors. Some of the girls wear shorts and skirts, but the only thing in the closet is a tight, black jumpsuit. So that's what I wear.

The whole class stands around three thin mats placed on the floor at the front of the room. Leiholan stands facing us. Every student has a sword, except for me.

Slowly, I move to the back of the crowd.

"Jermoine and Breck, Eleanora and Erica, and Lucian and Yuki," Leiholan calls out. "On the mat."

*He* steps onto the mat, the boy from the lake. I can't escape him. And when he fights, I hate that I can't tear my gaze from him. Every swing and strike is like a work of art. Every step makes it a masterpiece. Deliberate and precise, strong and cunning, artful and deadly.

*I want to fight like that.*

For a moment, I want to feel strong enough to protect myself.

When class is over, I head out, but Leiholan calls my name. I walk to him as he uncaps a bottle of alcohol. He takes three sips before he even looks at me, but still, he doesn't speak.

"What do you want from me?" I ask when I've had enough.

He points at me with the bottle in his hand. The bottles we make at home. The labor we don't get to delight in. "I'll teach you to hide," Leiholan says, looking down at me, and I feel almost as little as I do when my mom looks at me like that.

"Hide from what?" I ask.

I'm sure I know his answer.

"This world." He raises his arms and looks around the combat room like it's a glorious castle. "You don't know it. I didn't either, and I hate to say it, sweetheart, but you stick out like a Nepenthe after the war."

"Yeah?" I say, somewhat tauntingly. I can already smell the alcohol on his breath. But the more intoxicated he is, the less I have to worry about what I say. "And why would you do that?"

"Common courtesy," Leiholan says, like it's a joke I should be laughing at. Then he laughs.

I smile mockingly. "Bullshit."

He takes another swig. "Cynthia told me to help you." He waves his hands in the air like a kid; the only reminders that he's not one are the sword strapped to his waist and the bottle in his hand. "The headmistress."

I think about his offer; I really do. Blending in would help my cause, but I don't see it ending well. He's a *Nepenthe*—the creatures that are born and bred to enforce tyranny in my home.

"I'll pass."

But Leiholan raises his sword. "I'll tell you what," he says, stepping closer. "You beat me in a duel, and I'll grovel to Cynthia. Tell her I won't train you."

He points his sword at my chest. I think he's well intoxicated at this point, which should work in my favor. But maybe I could use a little help; I'd just have to be very careful about what I say. Take information, don't divulge.

Because he's right, I don't know this world, and I have to survive here long enough to get back to my mom.

"Fine." I step away from him. "I'll accept your help."

Leiholan chuckles, a deep, drunken laugh. "Oh, sweetheart." His sword falls to the floor with a reverberating clatter. "A few more of these"—he raises the bottle—"and I won't be able to stand."

# Chapter 5
## The Blood Doesn't Stop at The Hand

# DESDEMONA

Alone in the woods, my hand hovers over the river. The water swirls into itself, twisting into dark spirals—but no matter how much it shifts, it never turns into home. It takes all my energy just to open a portal back to Aralia's room.

I could never make it to the Welding Village alone.

Lifting my head to the sky, I scream, the sound rippling through the trees for the hundredth time. The birds chirp back, mocking me. I wish I had a throwing knife.

As long as I can find someone to steal power from tonight, I'll be fine.

I'll make it home.

To save my energy, I walk back to the school. In the suite, I flop onto the bed, watching Aralia as she swipes black stuff across her eyelashes.

I don't know why, but I ask, "Can I try some?"

She holds up the tube. "Mascara?"

"Yeah," I say nonchalantly, probably overcompensating. There's no reason she'd think I don't know what mascara is.

Completely oblivious to my bluff, Aralia hands me the tube. "Here ya go."

As I put on the mascara, I instantly look... different. My eyes are bigger, wider, more traditional.

I should ask Aralia for more of these glamour things.

When she pulls a flask from her boot, I think of Damien and

his daggers. I try not to miss him. I'll be seeing him soon.

I watch as she takes a sip, staring for a moment too long. She turns back toward me and holds out the flask. "Do you want some?"

"What is it?" I ask. It certainly isn't rena.

She laughs as she says, "Vesi. Duh."

I say yes, only because I want to tell Damien how it tastes. I take half a sip. It glides down like nectar, nowhere near as sweet but just as smooth.

Aralia tilts her head to the side. "You probably want to borrow an outfit as well, right?" she asks.

I want to strangle her. How many low blows can she make about my appearance?

Instead, I smile. "That'd be great."

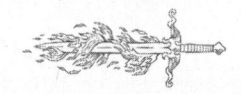

---

The further Aralia and I walk into the woods, the closer we get to the river I found. Perfect. Whoever I channel power from won't need to go too far away from the party. This might actually be easy.

The air thickens as we approach a stretch of open ground. Eight fire pits blaze, casting shadows over the trees as groups of kids gather around, their faces glowing in the light.

I take a breath, standing back before shaking my head at my own stupidity. I know it won't hurt me—it's not *my* fire. But here, surrounded by trees, I'm reminded of home. Of the welding accidents and death tolls.

Once the fire starts, it doesn't stop, and I don't want to be just another number.

*I don't want to fall victim to the untamable nature of fire.*

A few feet from one of the fire pits, I spot Kai standing on a log, talking while his arms flail around him. When he catches my gaze, he smiles.

"You've acquired the prince's favor," Aralia says—input that wasn't needed.

"I guess I have," I reply.

Too bad I'll be gone by tonight.

I smile at the thought.

"It's a shame he'll be betrothed by the end of the Collianth Cycle."

*The Collianth Cycle*—that's what fancy people call a year. It's the three hundred and sixty-five days Sulva and Ayan take to orbit each other. Thanks to Mom, I know all about it. The Collianth, or New Year, is a big deal for elites; they celebrate the star-crossed gods' reunion because their collision created our universe.

But the Collianth is the least of my worries, and so is a prince's betrothal. I'll be long gone by then.

"He's engaged?" I ask, keeping up my charade for its final hours.

"That's what this party is for," Aralia tells me.

I worry I've been too self-absorbed these past few days if I'm missing important details like that. For now, I scan the forest, searching for the person with the least wits about them, when a familiar—and drunk—voice calls out, "Desy! Join us!"

Kai stumbles around on his log—the perfect candidate. Powerful, intoxicated, and above all, I've gained some small amount of his trust.

Aralia gives me an infuriating look and winks. I smile, even though I'd like to slap the stupid grin off her face.

As we approach, Kai says, "Desy, Desy, Desy." His arms flail more and more. When he slips, I catch him and settle him back on his log.

"So, this is your party?" I ask, but I've clearly said the wrong thing.

The dumbfounded look on his face shifts to a scowl. "No. It's Lucian's," Kai slurs, looking somewhere in the distance.

"Lucy, Lucy, Lucy," he adds in a mocking tone. "He used to be my sister—I mean, *friend*. He used to be my friend!"

He shakes his head and laughs, but I don't know what part of that he finds funny.

"Oh," I mutter awkwardly. "I thought the party was for your engagement."

Kai picks up a glass bottle full of alcohol and mumbles, "Our engagements."

"What?"

"Our engagements!" Kai shouts. "His," he points, and I follow his finger right into the boy with the midnight eyes. "And mine."

Lucian.

*His name is Lucian.*

"Oh." It's only now that I take in the state Kai is in. Drunk out of his mind and trying to drink more. "My apologies," I whisper.

Kai looks at me and says, "People prefer to say congratulations."

I put my hand on his and rub his knuckles with my thumb. He seems to calm beneath my touch, which is perfect. "Do you want to go somewhere quiet with me?" I ask softly.

Kai giggles, his voice slurring as he sways. "Yeah," he says, clearing his throat and trying to steady himself. "Yes."

Suddenly, guilt simmers in my stomach. But I *have* to do this. To get home. Besides, these kids have had everything handed to them. I'm just giving Kai a real-world experience.

With his hand in mine, I bring him to his feet and reach for his power. It feels like Damien's, sharp and precise—an electric current humming beneath his skin, waiting for me to tap into it.

I guide Kai through the trees while the vesi kicks through me, but not nearly as much as it does Kai. He's stumbling over every step like he has two left feet.

We've hardly made it away from the party before Aralia calls,

"Desdemona!"

I keep walking, hoping she'll just go away, take another drink, and forget what she saw. But three steps in, I turn to face her, knowing my plan is a terrible one.

"He's drunk out of his mind!" Aralia calls. "What are you doing?"

I walk back to her with Kai on my arm. *Think, think, think.* What to say?

"Kai asked me to take him to the river," I say. "I think he's thirsty."

"Water," Kai mumbles. "I do want water."

Aralia steps closer to us, offering, "I'll come with you."

"I got it, really."

She gives me a pointed look, grabbing my free arm. "Why do you think I share a suite with Calista?"

My plan has barely commenced, and it's already failed. I walk with Aralia, not having any other choice.

We reach the river, the moonlight reflecting on the water's surface, and Aralia's hand brushes mine. I reach for her power, thrumming beneath her skin—fluid and wild.

So she's an Air Folk. That will do.

There's a rock a few feet from me, big enough to knock her out with one hit if I use enough force. Then I could take her magic and escape. With Aralia holding Kai over the river, this is the perfect time. Slowly, I pick up the rock.

Aralia lets go of Kai, throwing him on the grass before pulling out her flask and a joint. I clutch the rock behind my back.

"Want some?" She holds both intoxicants up.

"Sure." I smile, waiting for the right time to attack.

"Have you ever smoked? I don't have any guesses 'cause I've never been to Utul," she sings her last words with a smile.

"I have not," I say, copying her movements when she hands me the joint and readying to smash her skull when she looks away. "What did you mean earlier? About sharing a room with Calista?" I ask.

"It's my job to watch her." Aralia shrugs. "I'm her advisor."

My hand aches as I grip the rock tighter, and I ask, "Is she that difficult?"

Aralia looks toward the water, and I lift the rock. "Her parents think so. But no, she's not that bad. She's almost all talk," Aralia says, turning to me. "So, what were you doing out here?"

I drop my hand, settling the rock on the ground and thinking quickly.

"My mom was taken," I say. "I think whoever took her brought her to the septic, but Headmistress Constance won't do anything about it." I lean into Aralia and whisper, "I think she's scared of the septic Folk, but I'm not, not if I can get my mom back." I glance at Kai. "I was going to channel some of his powers to open a portal there."

Aralia is silent for a second, but as she watches me, a smirk begins to curl at her lips. Perfect.

"Okay," she says, throwing me off guard.

"Okay?"

"I'll do Kai's job. Channel me." Aralia holds out both her hands.

Channeling isn't dangerous—it's borrowing. But I'm still surprised she's this trusting.

"Really?" I play the part of the grateful disbeliever. When I don't come back, she'll be worried, probably think someone took me, might even go to the headmistress unless she's scared of the consequences.

"Yeah."

The second the word falls from her tongue, I take her hands. Aralia says something, but I don't hear her over the rush of power. My blood pumps, threatening to spill out—as if my body no longer has enough room for me.

I visualize home, the mirror, my mom—and then I touch my

reflection in the water.

The river swirls into itself, turning black before transforming into my dwelling. I've done it. It was that simple. I've accomplished my biggest goal. I'm getting my life back. I jump through before Aralia can see where the portal is taking me.

I exit the mirror dry and call for my mom before taking in the state of the dwelling. Our clothes are on the floor, and the only flower vase we've ever owned is shattered. There are holes in the orange clay walls. No one's home.

I run out through the village, straight to Damien's house, then slam against the door, pounding over and over. His mom, Janice, answers and wraps her arms around me.

"Des?" she says, her voice nasally, undoubtedly from tears. "You're alive."

I shake my head, the words spilling from my mouth. "Why wouldn't I be alive?"

"Des?" Damien says, my name filled with emotion I only hear from him when we talk about his dad.

He runs to me, and Janice steps out of the way. His arms wrap around my waist, and he twirls me in the narrow entrance of his dwelling. His head is burrowed between my shoulder and neck, his breath trickling down my skin.

*I'm home.*

I'm home; I'm finally home. But my mom isn't.

I catch my breath and regain my composure when he puts me down. Looking back at Janice, I ask again, "Why wouldn't I be alive?"

"Oh, honey," she says, reaching for my shoulder and rubbing it in a consoling manner. But I don't want consolation—I want answers. "There was a monster attack in your dwelling. We thought it took you both."

I step out of her grasp. "What do you mean, *both?*"

Damien looks at me like I'm fragile, like I'm the glass we were never allowed to keep, and I want to scream.

"Where is my mom?" I ask.

Janice's bottom lip quivers. It's Damien who steps forward and says, "She's gone, Des."

My breath hitches, then stops entirely, like the air is being sucked from my lungs.

"What do you mean she's gone?" No one says a thing. I just get the same, grief stricken looks that I've been receiving this entire time. "Was there a body?"

"Des—" Damien begins, but I don't let him finish.

"Was there a body?" I repeat.

He swallows. "No."

*If I can, I will find you.*

That's what she said in the note, those were her last words. She's not dead.

I look between the two of them, my heart shattering. I'm so close. I'm home, but my mom isn't. I have to go back to my dwelling, find something that can locate her. Anything.

"I'll be back," I tell them both. "I promise I'll be back."

Damien pulls me into a hug when I try to run. "Don't go, Red. Not again."

For just a second, I hold him.

"I'm sorry," I whisper as I begin to pull away. "I have to." I think of the day Mom sent me to Visnatus—of the red-eyed Folk who entered our dwelling. They must've taken her.

I plant a kiss on Damien's cheek and run.

When I make it to my dwelling, I cling to the wall to keep from falling to the floor, until my only option is to fall to the floor. I rub my temples and press my spinning head into my hands. *Focus,* I tell myself, *focus.* The room is spinning, and between the running and the panic, I'm more than out of breath.

What a joke this is, to make it home and have the most important piece of it gone. I can't believe I tried to run away with Damien, as if my mom isn't half of my everything.

I wish everyone in that preppy, stupid school could experience this. The heartache of losing everything. Those poised and pampered assholes have had everything handed to them their entire lives; meanwhile, the rest of us have to cling to scraps that are so easily taken away.

My nails claw into the clay walls, and I manage to stand. I stumble through the room, but what I'm looking for, I don't know. Blood, hair, some kind of clue.

The cruelest, sickest joke of an idea flashes through my mind. I'm not entirely sure I'll follow through with it until my hand is on the only mirror in our dwelling, and I envision the woods and river I just left, prepared to go back to the place I was dying to escape.

Nothing happens. Of course nothing happens. Even my worst idea is out of my reach.

My back crashes into the wall, and my hand grips the stone around my neck, breathing harshly to hold back the tears. I pull too hard on the pendant, and the chain snaps. I throw the broken necklace to the ground and bury my head in my hands. *Don't cry, don't cry, don't cry.*

Suddenly, I'm standing in the woods, high on a mountain where Mom and I lived when I was ten. I can tell by the puddles on the ground. It was the only place I've ever lived that had rain.

I think *I'm* ten. It's the only reason I'd be this short—why my hands would be this small.

Flames lick my knuckles, wrapping around my fingers, and my mom is there. "Very good," she tells me. But the flames don't stay on my hands. I set the wet trees on fire, too.

When I open my eyes, flames lick the walls of my dwelling, and the heat is suffocating. The door opens, and I shout for Damien to run, but it's not him who enters—it's the red-eyed Folk.

"Get out!" I scream. "Get out, get out, get out!"

The man starts choking. He falls to the floor, and the shadow of a person pulses against his skin. The shadow claws and claws

—trying to get out of the body, I think—before *it* starts to choke, too.

Then neither of them move.

I can't swallow. I can't move. Not until the flames lick my hair and there's no other choice but to run.

But I can only crawl.

I make it to the Folk, and I pull his eyelids apart, just to be sure. But his eyes aren't red, they're brown.

I put two fingers on his pulse.

There's nothing.

## Chapter 6
## What I Pay For

# LUCIAN

The smoke burns my eyes as the bottle passes between us. The others murmur, lost in their own drunken haze, while I stare into the fire, half mesmerized. Such a strange element, wild and untamable—the antithesis of everything I am. Vital to life, yet capable of bringing even the strongest to their knees.

Across from my bonfire, Kai hops off the stump where he'd been pontificating, and a redhead helps him to his seat. It's the same girl I met by the Lunar Lake. What is she doing with him? She claimed to see my memories—a power of the Folk, yes, but rare against mental wards as strong as mine.

I know how to defend against the mental arts.

If she was being truthful about her power, someone with considerable influence may have orchestrated our encounter.

I watch carefully as she converses with Kai, surprised—more so when Kai laughs as she picks up his hand. I stand, ready to interfere, to figure out whatever game this new girl is playing—when the world cracks.

A ripple passes through me—sharp, familiar. A vision.

My sight flickers between the image before me and the new girl, her hair made of fire. I step closer, touching the flames that engulf her. They don't burn.

Inches from her face, I stare, bewildered—both within the vision and here, in the middle of the party.

I've never had a vision come this way before—folding over the present as if it's already happening. But I know better. As with all foresight, it's a warning, a hint.

Unlike most Lyrians, what I see always comes to pass. Once the vision strikes, it's a ticking clock.

And I don't know what this could mean.

The image lingers, flickering like the fire, until Azaire's voice pulls me back to the party.

"You okay?" he asks, rising from his tree stump. I nod absentmindedly, my gaze fixed on the spot where Kai and the girl were just a moment ago—both now gone.

"I'm gonna go get some air," Azaire says, shoving his hands in his pockets while stepping away. "You wanna come, Luc?"

"Bro," Yuki slurs and holds out his arms, looking up at the trees that surround us, then down at the fire that warms us. "There's nothing *but* air here."

"Away from the smoke," Azaire replies with a shrug.

Yuki mumbles something before taking another swig, and Azaire walks away.

Lilac sits on the stump next to me, crossing her arms over her chest with a quiet sigh. I follow her gaze to Calista, who's chatting with Fleur across the fire.

I nudge her arm lightly and ask, "Have you talked to her?"

Lilac keeps her gaze fixed on Calista. "About the betrothals? No." She places a hand under her chin, sinking deeper into the stump. "Since she told me she loved me, then left? Double no."

"She'll come around."

"Or she'll marry you and fall madly in love," she sighs, casting me a sidelong glance before returning her focus to Calista.

"Not possible," I chuckle.

That grants me a longer, more annoyed look from Lilac. "Did you get back together with Eleanora?" she asks.

"No, of course not. I meant—it's rare to see Calista like anyone, let alone love. Not the way she did you."

Lilac shakes her head as she whispers, "Then why did she leave?"

It's a rhetorical question. She knows the answer as well as I do. Calista is a Folk, the Princess of Folkara. Perhaps if she were of a lower class, she'd be permitted to court other women—though certainly not as the future queen of such a patriarchal world.

When Fleur walks toward us and slides next to me, Lilac stands abruptly, quickly disappearing into another group.

My instinct is to follow my sister, but as I rise, Fleur grabs my hand. She leans into me, her bright white hair shining like a light in the night. "We're having a little… afterparty in my suite," she whispers in my ear.

The corners of my lips quirk up, a small laugh escaping me. "The suite you share with my sister?"

Fleur lifts a shoulder. "Yeah, well"—her hand drapes around me, her fingers sliding into my pocket—"if you're interested."

For the first time, I turn to face her as I reach into my back pocket, pulling out her undergarments. Fleur has flirted with me as long as I've known her, but after my stint with her best friend Eleanora, I'm surprised she continues to pursue me. Not that I couldn't use a distraction—one that will have to be confined to flirtations. The last thing I need is to get involved with Calista's friend.

"You have two conflicts of interest," I remind her playfully, leaning in to whisper in her ear as she did me. From this angle, I spot Calista, glaring at me from a few feet away as she approaches. "One's your best friend, and the other is your future queen," I whisper. "Who happens to be on her way over now."

Fleur glances behind her, then her wide, green eyes meet mine again. She holds my stare for a moment before speaking, her voice steady. "I can keep a secret."

"Remains to be seen," I whisper with a smile.

Calista stops in front of the both of us, watching from

above. She rolls her eyes, grabbing Fleur by the arm and pulling her to her feet. "He's my husband, F. Have some decorum."

I kick my legs up on another tree stump. "Jealous?" I ask with a smile.

Calista drags me to my feet. "Where's Kai?" she asks, shooing Fleur away.

"I'm not his keeper, Calista."

I shrug my arm out of hers as she says, "You know how he gets."

Yes, I know how he gets; he's tried to fight me twice in the days since we heard of our forced marriages. Kai's a good guy, but he's never handled being Royalty well. He always fights against the unbeatable.

I hold up a finger as I say, "Give me a moment." Then I gesture to Yuki, and he hands me a bottle of vesi. I take the longest chug I have all night. The group chants my name around the fire, as though I'm doing something impressive. When I lower the bottle, Calista rolls her eyes, and I smirk, holding out my hand to her.

"Shall we, milady?"

She looks at my hand and scoffs, saying, "You disgust me."

"Always a pleasure."

We weave through the fire pits and tree stump chairs on the grass, passing group after group. Each one calls my name, offering drinks or asking me to dance. The public believes I'm far more amusing than I truly am.

Still, I can tell my popularity grates at Calista, and for what she did to Lilac, I stop at one of the shouting groups. I smoke a joint and begin a dance with a girl before Calista pulls me away again. The girl kisses my cheek—though I get the feeling she was aiming for my lips—before Calista pulls me back on track.

From there, we walk in utter silence, which may be better because we hear everything, meaning we'll find Kai sooner. Though, I'm not keen on finding Kai. For all Calista knows, he's out here with a girl, which is not something I need to see.

I've known this kid my whole life. He's practically family. When this feud finally finishes between us, we'll go back to the way it always was—brothers-in-arms, comrades, kings of the universe. It's why I chose to help Calista after everything. A show of good faith. A display of diplomacy.

We're far from the party—the music and shouting a distant noise—when I begin to say, "Calista—"

"Shh," she hisses. "I hear something."

We both freeze, Calista meeting my gaze with a finger covering her lips. When I hear the chatter, she gives me a smug look.

I shake my head. This isn't a competition, the way she seems to think it is. I'm here to help her.

Following the direction of the noise, I push apart the dangling branches of a willow tree, but it's not Kai we find behind the leaves. It's Azaire and Wendy.

*Air, huh, Azaire?* He gives me a shy smile, as if reading my mind, and Wendy gives me a horrified look.

"Our apologies," I say with a grin as I drag Calista away, falling back into silence.

"I told you I heard something," Calista says. "Not that I knew it was him—"

This time, I cut Calista off, saying, "Wait."

Calista shuts up, glancing around the dark woods, alight by the moon and glowing leaves. Just beneath the subtle rushing of nearby water, there's a hum. Calista takes off toward the noise immediately.

Once more, I grab her arm. "What if he's here with a girl?"

"He *has* a girl," she hisses.

I frown as I respond, "Lilac?"

"I am not talking about this with you," she says before walking—twice as fast—toward the river.

But she quickly stops, her shoulders deflating as she sighs. "He *might* be with a girl." She turns to face me without meeting my gaze. "There are rumors about Lilac and my... relationship. He could be mad."

Shaking my head, I say, "He always knew."

"Not about that—about *other* people knowing." She laughs, a humorless sound, as she looks up at the sky, her hands resting on her hips. "The same way my parents are going to be."

Her eyes shine in the light of the moon, tears forming at their corners.

"Is that why you ended it?" I ask. The thought has crossed my mind many times before, though I never told Lilac—the wound has always seemed too fresh.

Calista wipes away her tears before they can fall. "Let's go."

She turns, kicking at the foliage as we approach the river. There, near the water's edge, we find Kai passed out on the grass, his body sprawled awkwardly. Aralia is sitting beside him, but she looks off into the distance, her expression bored.

When she glances up at us, she immediately says, "He needed water."

"That's what you've been delegated to?" Calista sneers. "My brother's water fetcher?"

"We should go," I whisper.

"No, Calista, some people just want to help," Aralia snaps, looking back at the river. "Just take him and get out of here."

Calista walks past Aralia, deliberately shoving into her shoulder as she leans down to lift Kai. Her muscles strain as she attempts to pull him up, but with the alcohol heavy in his system, he's more like deadweight—completely uncooperative and limp in her arms.

She glances up at me, glaring. "A little help?"

As obnoxious as it is, Royals help Royals. It will do neither of our families any good to have the future king of my world seen like this. I pick up Kai's other side, carrying him through the woods, past the garden, and through the academy before throwing him on his bed. Then, Calista and I promptly part ways.

I head back to the party, which isn't far in the woods—it doesn't have to be. Truthfully, I have more power than any of the staff here. The party isn't allowed, but no one can stop it—not when I'll wear a crown and half these students will serve me.

The air feels thicker as I approach, spotting Yuki talking to Eleanora. But she still glances up at me. It's only a moment before she looks back at the group, forcing a laugh as she says, "Did you see the new girl?"

Instantly, my interest is piqued. There's only one new student I know—the girl I saw with Kai tonight. I've thought of her often since I met her—how the lake reflected her image as if she stood beside me, although she lingered feet away.

More than that, I've thought of my memories. There's a million things she could uncover that might unravel the image of my kingdom—a million reasons to be unnerved.

"What's her name?" I ask.

"I don't know, maybe Deserae or something?" Fleur shrugs. "Who cares?"

Calista sits beside Fleur and me. "May I?" she asks, grabbing the bottle from Yuki's hand before he answers. She drinks the alcohol as if it's water and she's dehydrated.

"Okay then," Yuki scoffs.

"Anyone have…?" Calista puts two fingers to her lips, miming a drag.

A joint is lit and passed her way, slowly making its way through the group. When it reaches my hand, I notice Lilac lingering on the edges of our bonfire. I gesture for her to join, but as she steps closer, no one moves to make room.

"Stalker at two o'clock," Eleanora whispers to Calista, but I'm only surprised when they both snicker.

I glance at Calista, searching for an answer, but she quickly looks away. This isn't like her. She's never been rude to Lilac before—not like this. Everyone knows she holds a soft spot for my sister, though few understand the extent.

Perhaps that's where the rumors stemmed from.

"What has gotten into you?" I whisper harshly.

Calista's gaze flicks back to me, her eyes going wide for a moment before she scoffs. "Nothing," she says, turning away, but I don't miss the strain in her voice.

I rise, joining my sister. "There's a life outside of pointless drama," I say to the group. "You'd do well to find it."

We walk away, and Lilac hesitates before saying, "You don't have to miss out on the fun."

"Please," I scoff and hand her the joint I never passed along.

"Thanks." Lilac shrugs.

We sit by a mostly empty fire pit, and with one look, the small group dissipates.

"That was awkward, right?" Lilac mumbles. "Did you feel it, too?"

"Eleanora's on a power trip—"

"I'm talking about Calista." Lilac's eyebrows knit together, and she frowns, passing me the joint with an almost limp hand. "But you should've never been with Eleanora," she whispers.

"Yeah, I know."

"Do you think it's always gonna be this way?"

"Truly?" I ask. Lilac nods. "I hope not."

*I think it's going to get worse.*

"Me too," she whispers. We pass the joint back and forth, letting it burn down to ash before Lilac calls out, "Azaire!"

I glance up to see him trudging toward us, tugging his beanie lower over his ears, a shy smile playing on his lips. He settles down beside me, in front of the fire, fidgeting as he mumbles, "Hey."

"How's Wendy?" I ask, nudging his arm with my elbow.

"Oh." Azaire lets out a nervous laugh as his gaze drops to his hands. "It wasn't... I mean, we were just talking."

"You actually talked to her?" Lilac says with a smile.

"That's a bigger step than you've ever taken," I add.

"It's…" He shakes his head. "It's probably nothing."

"Make it something," I say.

"I think that's a *huge* step!" Lilac exclaims. "Have you ever seen Wendy talk to anyone?"

"Of course I have," Azaire says.

"I don't know," I tease, "it's been a few years."

I look at my sister, thinking I'm going to get a response. Instead, she stares at Calista, who laughs with Eleanora, both glancing in Li's direction.

"I'll be right back," I say before walking to their fire, surprised by my swimming vision. I squat down, grabbing the bottles out of my friends' hands.

"What the—"

"Dude!"

I take a sip from one, then the other, and say, "Let's get one thing straight." The group falls silent, all looking up at me. "We're not treating my sister—and, let's be truthful, the most powerful of us all—as some awkward outsider."

I scan their faces, locking eyes with each of them. Most of them avoid my gaze, as expected, though a few watch with amusement. Fleur's lips tighten.

Lilac is to be the Queen of Ilyria—the most powerful position in the most powerful world. They have no right to treat her so poorly.

My voice is tight as I say, "Got it?"

A few kids nod, and one says, "Yeah, yeah, man."

Another looks up, his face flushed. "My bad."

I face Eleanora, her gaze hovering over my lips for far too long. She opens her mouth but says nothing.

"I know, *I know*, I'm irresistible," I say with a mocking smile. "But I'd prefer you look me in the eye. It's rather demeaning this way, don't you agree?"

Eleanora mumbles something unintelligible and looks away.

"Great," I announce, setting the bottles down. "I'll see you in class, then."

"You're not coming tomorrow?" Yuki asks.

"Everyone's gonna be at the gala," Fleur adds, twirling her white hair around her finger. Eleanora throws her a heated glance.

I hand the bottles back and say, "Not everyone."

As I rise to my feet and walk away, Yuki hurries to catch up. I turn to face him. "What's up?"

"I'd rather chill with you," Yuki mutters, joining our small group while Azaire tells us about the constellations Wendy showed him, his grin practically splitting his face.

Students dance around us while Lilac, Yuki, and I pass a joint back and forth. Azaire's high on Wendy, I think.

Truthfully, I have a better time with these three than I have with any group. I prefer it this way.

But my laughter is nothing compared to the electricity that rattles down my spine when someone whispers in my ear, "Meet me by the lake in one hour, or I'll tell everyone what I saw in your memories."

## Chapter 7
## Who's Keeping Score Now?

# DESDEMONA

I fall to my knees, and my throat burns when the half-digested food from my stomach falls to the floor. The fire licks at the bodies lying on the ground, and I turn away, pushing away the image to be dealt with at a different date.

Sweat pours into my eyes, and I force myself toward the mirror. Bile rises in my throat when I stand, and the flame closes in around me. My hair catches fire, and I think I scream.

This is how the Fire Folk meet their deaths—consumed by the very flames we wield. But not me, not today, *not now*. I get to my feet and pull myself to the mirror, for my mom. Maybe for Damien and his family, if they still care for me after seeing what I've done.

The death I've delivered.

I press my hand to the mirror, its surface cool against my burning fingers. As I picture the river, I hear it—the water rushing on the other side. *It actually worked.*

Maybe the gods can do some good because this is nothing short of a miracle.

Before I step through the portal, a glint catches my eye. The fire's reflection on Mom's necklace.

I dive for it, the flames brushing against my body, but I have no other option—it's the last piece of my mom. My skin burns, and with every last ounce of strength, I force myself through the portal.

The wind is knocked out of me as I fall onto the grass, coughing maniacally until I can't breathe. I'm going to die. Whatever the gods did to save me was just to punish me in the end. How cruel, how sick, how funny it must be for them to watch me squirm.

I cough up black soot, and a hand rests on my back. Magic fills my lungs with air—*Aralia*.

I collapse. The only thing I can focus my vision on is the grass tangled in my eyelashes. And I breathe—sweet, sweet air, the taste of survival.

Sitting up, I look at Aralia, her thick, chin-length black hair glistening in the moonlight. Her wide brown eyes look at me with something like compassion.

"Thanks," I mutter.

Aralia shrugs and says, "What was I gonna do? Watch you choke?"

*That was certainly an option.*

Once my breathing settles, Aralia says, "We'll have to cut your hair."

She's right. When I reach for my hair, it crumbles into ash between my fingers. I pull out the small knife I stole from the headmistress, and as I prepare to cut it, I remind myself that I'm alive. A little hair is a price worth paying.

Before I begin cutting, Aralia says, "I could salvage more than that."

I make what may be the dumbest decision today and hand Aralia the knife. Closing my eyes and holding my breath, I half expect the knife to plunge into my side when I hear the slicing of dead, crisp hair. I touch the ends. Shoulder-length and even, certainly better than what I would have done.

Then Aralia laughs as she asks, "Why do you carry a *letter opener?*"

She fiddles with the knife, and I glance at it. I had no idea that's what it was. But I mutter, "You never know when you'll find unexpected correspondences."

I see Aralia—for the first time—as someone who could be useful to me. She's smart and clearly observant. She knew I wasn't sleeping that first morning, maybe knew I left that night, even had proper enough suspicion to ask what I was really doing tonight. She's my roommate, for better or worse, and clearly wants to be my friend. This all could lead to a seriously convenient situation.

"What's on your shirt?" Aralia asks.

I look down and see what can only be my puke. I cup a handful of water, splashing it on my chest, then on my face for good measure.

"Puke," I say because there's really no good lie. "Bad fight."

"Same goes for your hair?" Her voice carries that sarcastic, pompous edge I'm getting used to.

I smile at her like she's said something funny, just to ease the moment, and repeat, "Same goes for my hair."

"Here." She hands me her silver flask. "Last sip." Her eyes linger on me, noting what must be my less-than-pleasant appearance. "You could use it."

"Yeah," I mutter. "I could."

I tip the flask back, gulping down the last of the alcohol and feeling the burn of the intoxicants as they settle in. But it feels nice—nothing like the fire that scorched my skin and hair.

That thought makes me glance down at my skin. I'm surprised when I don't see a single burn mark or blister. I was sure the fire had touched me. Fire Folk don't have protection from the Flame... at least, I don't think. If we did, how would we die?

Maybe we have some sort of resistance, because my skin looks completely untouched. The fire seemed to reach nothing but my hair.

I don't look at the skin for long; I don't want my lingering attention to draw Aralia's. As I look up, I hear a hiss, like a breeze brushing past my ear, but I don't feel any wind.

"Do you hear that?" I ask, my voice barely a murmur. It almost sounds like someone's whispering, but I can't make out the words.

"Hear what?"

I glance around the river and trees, but there's nothing there. A moment later, the whispering stops.

"Nothing," I mutter, and I raise the flask to my lips once more, trying to get out the last dregs of alcohol. Then I realize someone's missing. "Where'd Kai go?"

Aralia extends her hands to me, her palm flat and facing the sky. I drop the flask into her hand, and she answers, "Calista and Lucian carried him back to his suite."

Calista and Lucian know we were out here. I can't risk two more people knowing that I went back to the septic—that I'm *from* the septic. Especially not a princess.

I hide the fear shaking my facade. "You didn't mention me, right?"

Aralia runs her fingers across her lips like a zipper, twists them at the end like a key, and smiles.

Once more, I conceal my emotion—this time, my confusion. She lied for me, protected me.

I return her smile.

Together, we walk back to the party, and when the opportunity to dance arises, I pull Aralia with me—deciding to show her that I'm a friend, in case I ever need one.

I find more vesi for Aralia, and when she's drunk enough, I slip away from her and move behind Lucian.

"Meet me by the lake in one hour, or I'll tell everyone what I saw in your memories," I whisper so only he can hear.

My plan—the one that brought me back to the school—seems to be working. I smile to myself as I walk back to the suite, ignoring the obvious flaws in my strategy.

Once inside, I change and shower, avoiding the mirrors the way I avoid all my fears—like what will happen if I get caught, if

Lucian doesn't agree... And what I'll have to do if things go wrong. I can't let him leave with the possibility of him repeating my plans. What I'm asking him to do isn't just unacceptable; if I were caught, being septic alone would be grounds for execution. And what will I say when he inevitably asks me to prove I know anything from his memories? I'm basing everything on a single reaction I barely caught in the dark.

Maybe I won't show up. But if I don't, I'll be even farther from square one. I killed someone. I don't know if I can just go home.

I put a hand on the wall for balance. That can't be right—can't be real. It was one thing to dream of it and another entirely to do it. I killed someone.

I can't think about it. I need a plan.

Lucian and Kai are both engaged, and Kai seemed awfully strung up about it. It must not be their decision, so what do I do with that information?

Fifteen minutes.

This is a bad, bad idea. But it's the only one I have. I *need* to find my mom. She's all I have left, and every second I waste takes me farther from her. I'll risk everything to bring her back. I'll do *anything*.

In the closet, I pull a lace from one of Aralia's fancy corsets, threading it through my mom's pendant and tying it around my neck. Then I push myself back outside.

When I reach the lake, Lucian is already sitting on the edge. I sigh in relief at the fact that he even showed up. Whatever memory he thinks I saw is important.

Like last time, the glowing waters reflect on Lucian's face, but unlike before, there is no reflection of the two of us. Only his contorted expression ripples across the gleaming, turquoise surface.

He doesn't stand, doesn't even turn toward me when he says, "What am I doing here, Marquees?"

Well, here goes nothing. I keep my voice steady as I say, "I need you to track someone."

Lucian laughs, finally meeting my gaze. "Why would I break the law for you?"

"Because I know something you want to keep a secret." A bold lie.

Lucian rises to his feet, taking a very slow step in my direction and leaving the lake behind him. "See, I don't have any reason to believe that. Not unless Leiana's sent you. If that's the case, I'll do anything you wish—so long as you tell me her motive."

Leiana, as in *Queen Leiana of Ilyria*. It all clicks now. This is Lucian *Aibek*—son of one of the two Royal families that have held their thrones for centuries, even as every other monarchy in the worlds fell.

If Kai is a prince and the two of them are engaged, it would only stand to reason that Lucian, too, is a prince. And the marriages... I think back to what a very inebriated Kai said: *His and mine*.

"I'm here to watch you until the marriages are settled," I say, hoping it's not too vague an answer.

"I have a Eunoia at my disposal, not too far from us right now," Lucian says slowly.

I don't let my fear slip out, but the thought of a Eunoia—a magic-wielder who can manipulate emotions and force the truth from anyone—makes the pit in my stomach deepen. If that happens, Lucian could learn more than just my white lie.

He could unravel everything.

"But if you tell me the truth of your own volition, I'll be sure that Leiana doesn't hear of our... encounter," he finishes.

"I swear I'm telling the truth," I say quickly. I don't have to feign the hysteria in my voice. "My family was killed, and Leiana promised me safety if I could make sure you were married smoothly."

His eyes narrow. "Who?"

I stand still, my voice small and unsure as I echo, "Who?"

"Whose marriage?"

What a headache, and how much more difficult a headache makes this. I share a room with a Royal—the blonde Folk. It must be her.

Finally, I say, "You to Calista."

Lucian cracks a smile, and I worry I got the name wrong.

At once, the shadows around me—the ones cast by the moonlight on the trees—vanish, summoned by Lucian's hands. They swirl around his arms before rushing straight toward me.

My neck goes numb, and my breath catches in my throat. He's choking me. The feeling of imminent death looms over me *again*.

My hand trembles as I reach for the blade at my waistband.

"I will release my shadows in three seconds," Lucian says, slowly opening his palm. I feel as his power begins to loosen, and I watch as the shadows slowly slither back to him, like obedient snakes. "And if you do not tell me the entire truth, I won't be so merciful."

The sensation returns to my neck, and I suck in a sharp breath, my blade still clenched in my hand. I could slice his neck if it comes down to my survival over his.

He probably deserves death anyway. Never worked for anything in his life. Simply born into power and money at the top of this entire universe that shits on me. *He's* the reason my life has been what it is. Or at least part of it. A perpetuation of it.

"Is it death you've chosen?" Lucian asks when I don't respond. How impatient. But of course he is.

"I must say I've never seen such loyalty to the Queen of Ilyria in a Folk," he finishes, his hand raising again. A threat.

I raise a hand in surrender. "Don't."

Slowly, I slip my blade back in its place at my waistband. I hate him. I hate that he has power over me, that my life is in his

85

hands.

And I've backed myself into a corner. Another lie, if not convincing enough, could lead to my death. So, I choose the hardest way out—the truth.

"Two Folk took my mom. I need your help to track her. I'm not working with Leiana. I've never even met her. I didn't know you were a prince until you mentioned her name tonight."

Lucian doesn't look impressed as he asks, "As for my memories?"

"Nothing," I say with the not-so-sweet feeling of defeat. "I saw nothing."

Nothing to hold over him, *the prince of Ilyria*. He would have fit so well in my pocket.

He studies me for a moment, then gestures to the lake. His voice is devoid of compassion—of anything—as he says, "Get in the water."

"What?" My heart races. Is this how he plans to kill me?

"In return for your honesty, I've decided to show mercy." He smiles, bearing his perfect teeth. "Submerge yourself in the lake, wait for the moon's light to pass over you, and then visualize your target."

Your *target*. Of course that's how a prince would describe it.

I don't take my eyes off him as I step forward, plunging into the water. For the first time in what feels like forever, a chill runs through me. It's as if my body has been operating on instinct, and that instinct happens to be burning hot.

Above me, Lucian spreads his arms wide, as if inviting an invisible audience to watch, and forces the light of the moon to shine down on me. It's truly a magnificent sight, but I'm not here to watch in awe.

I close my eyes, filling my mind with images of my mother. She had the lightest hair wherever we went in the septic, honey with streaks of darker brown. Her eyes are the kindest I've ever known, even though she wasn't known for being kind. She's strong, brave in the face of everything, and certainly brave wherever she is now. But the face that forms in my mind is twisted with fear.

She's in a dimly lit room—a cage or prison of some kind. I step toward her, my legs growing numb, my throat tightening. Her eyes shutter, and my fear deepens.

"Mom?" I call. "I'm here!"

I push through the numbness lingering in my legs, the tingling creeping up my torso and into my chest. As I step closer to my mom, a shadow flashes behind me. I twist, trying to catch what I swear I saw—but nothing's there.

"Hello?" I call out.

My mom coughs, then whispers, "*Leave.*"

The shadow lunges in front of me—*not* a shadow, something uglier, something worse. It reaches out to grab me, and I raise my hand, prepared to save my mom, but something yanks me back.

My vision blurs and brightens at the same time, piecing together the new image. I'm not in the dark room—I'm underwater, the moon still shining overhead. The prince's arm is around my waist, pulling me to the surface faster than I sank. When we reach the top, I cling to the edge of the lake while I cough up water.

I am absolutely right to think of this school as the enemy, along with everyone in it.

Lucian pulls himself from the lake before I've finished coughing, but when he does, I notice the scars on his back—twisted, uneven marks that look like old burn wounds. Their edges are raised and discolored, as if the fire still lingers beneath his skin. I stare at them, wondering how a prince would receive such marks, until he turns back to face me. When my coughing subsides, he—shockingly—offers me his hand and pulls me up.

The last thing I expected him to do was help me.

The evening air on my soaked body makes me tremble—but

I'm hardly cold.

"Did you see?" I ask, my voice unsteady. If he saw my mom and could identify her, I would've done the complete opposite of what she wanted. But he might know where she is.

"I did," the prince answers.

"Where was she?" I plead, gasping for breath. How ridiculous I must look, how *weak*. What a contrast to how I want him —anyone—to see me.

"I don't know," he says, but his tone is different—different enough to make me doubt him.

I narrow my eyes and catch my breath as best I can, determined to keep my voice steady as I ask, "What happened to your back?"

A prince with scars is a rare sight. I'd think, at least.

He glares at me, and I hold his gaze. When he smiles, I smile right back. I hope I look deranged, like someone he has no choice but to fear. It's a long shot, considering I've been at his mercy all night, but it's hope.

It's not meant to make sense.

"Born with them," are the only words I get. He pulls his shirt over his head and wet hair, turning to leave.

"You were born with burns?" I challenge before he can walk away. He stops walking, his gaze flicking over his shoulder. "Fire Folk, remember? I've seen a lot worse."

"They're not burns," the prince argues.

"My mistake," I say with a shrug.

"It's but a problem."

Lucian turns again, but I stop him one last time, saying, "Do me a favor and don't tell anyone what you saw tonight?"

"Now why would I want to incriminate myself?"

"I'd be the only one to pay for it."

He gives me a long look. "You'd be surprised what I pay for."

This time, I let him go.

## Chapter 8
## Nothing Burns Like The Cold

# LUCIAN

I sit at the end of the great hall in my homeworld, Ilyria, watching as the council members' faces descend into fear. Murmurs echo through the room, chaos brewing at the sudden news.

After centuries of peace, the monsters resumed their attacks—exactly three days ago.

Three days ago, when Desdemona asked me to track her mother. Three days ago, when I found a woman in The Void, and a girl who may have the means to get there.

Three days ago, when Desdemona nearly stepped through my vision—a feat that shouldn't be possible, one that I must now deduce how to use. Something that, if I were to be honest, aroused some intrinsic part of the universe.

Something that surely has to do with the resurgence of monsters.

Labyrinth, my father and the King of Ilyria, rises. His silver staff strikes the marble floor with a sharp echo, demanding silence. Still, the chatter doesn't cease until Leiana stands, her black hair swept back into intricate braids, moonstones dangling from her ears.

She places a soft hand on Labyrinth's shoulder as she says, "There's a reason we are all here today, and it is not to cause further chaos."

The room goes eerily silent, every breath held in the council members' lungs.

My sister Lilac turns to me, her eyebrows high on her forehead. Like the rest of them, she's scared.

I shake my head, telling her there is nothing to worry about. We'll be safe on Visnatus, within the protective barriers of the academy.

The Queen of Folkara rises from her seat, her presence commanding attention. She bears a striking resemblance to her children, Kai and Calista. Half of her blonde hair is braided and wrapped around her head, adorned with flowers and twigs, while the rest cascades down in soft waves.

Standing around the table, she announces, "There have been reports of victims in Folkara whose eyes turn red before dropping dead. It could be the work of Arcanes."

I clench my jaw at the mention. It's a ridiculous suggestion. No monster attack would be at hands of the Arcanes—they have far more sinister activities to occupy their time.

My mother, Leiana, chuckles, her glance sweeping over the council, checking to see their reactions to the Arcanes. "I can assure you all that no such ambiguous power has been at play for the last thousand years," she promises.

She'd be the first person to know that is entirely untrue.

Representatives from each world sit at the table: the Folk from Folkara, the Eunoia from Eunaris, the Draes from Draevia, and the Nepenthes from Nepthara—worlds all subservient in some way to Ilyria. Each of them shifts uncomfortably, aware that they cannot speak freely. My parents have long banned discussions of the Arcanes, but their name still carries weight, enough to stir paranoia. A word etched in war.

The Queen of Folkara, Melody, takes her seat once more, leaning toward Leiana with deliberate intent as she challenges her. "You've continuously failed to locate the Soul Ruby. An immortal Soul Stone could have kept these creatures alive, could it not?"

Leiana's scowl is the first sign of emotion she's shown all meeting. I'm surprised that Melody is bringing this up in public—the missing Soul Stone is not widely known. If another world were to find the Soul Ruby first, they would inherit powers beyond even Leiana's comprehension.

Every world once had its own Soul Stone, embedded deep in the core of their planets. Each has since been retrieved, and over millennia, we've uncovered their powers. However, there are a myriad of stories about the magic the Soul Ruby possesses—and none of them are simple reading.

"The Soul Ruby is not your concern," Leiana says, her voice tight.

"Then perhaps the Memorium is, as it should rightfully be *my* Soul Stone," Queen Melody responds. The Memorium was the Soul Stone once embedded in Folkara, but it's been missing for over a hundred years. "Has there been any progress in recovering it? You'll need it if you still wish to wipe the memories of our people—"

"We are here to discuss the attacks," Leiana interjects with finality, her tone teetering on the edge of trembling.

King Easton of Folkara, Melody's husband, speaks up. "Do not forget that two of the casualties were not caused by a monster."

"Who was at fault?" I ask, speaking for the first time this entire meeting.

"A Fire Folk, likely. The bodies were torched after death," Easton says to me, not the room.

"And the Fire Folk lived?" a representative from Nepthara—the only Nepenthe allowed in this meeting—scoffs with a laugh. No one joins her. "Doubtful," she mutters.

"It's not a priority," King Easton says dismissively. "The victims were septic."

"It's essential for the count," Queen Melody retorts sharply.

Before the marriage announcements, this would be the time

when Kai and I glanced at one another, a subtle apology for our parents.

Today, we barely acknowledge each other.

Suddenly, the great hall fades from view, and two back-to-back visions flash through my mind—a very unpleasant future discussion with Leiana and an encounter with Kai. Neither sound appealing, but both are unavoidable. I've never had a vision that didn't come true. So, I quickly release the thought and organize my own.

"What do you think, Lucian?" Kai says on cue—just as I foresaw.

"I think there are many plausible causes," I reply. "For one, peaceful relations between us and monsters hasn't been the norm for most of documented history. Perhaps this is the gods' way of restoring balance." I don't give Kai the pointed look I would like to. In front of the worlds' representatives, we must put up a united front, appear as comrades.

"That is very wise counsel, Lucian, thank you," Labyrinth says, offering me a small nod.

My work here is done. I've said enough for the council's quota, so I move to tuning them out. There are far more important matters for me to mull over—such as Desdemona.

If I had been honest about my suspicions, I would have said that I believe she awakened some fundamental force within our universe when she nearly stepped through my projection—into The Void, no less, the Arcanes' home. A universe that no one has *ever* reached. I should have gone to Cynthia immediately.

If this girl has a connection to the Arcanes, we'll need her.

I only pay attention when the Royals and representatives prepare to leave. I rise, offering smiles and handshakes on their way out of the room. But as soon as the last of them is gone, I take my seat, and Lilac stops in the doorway.

My sister stares at me. "Are you coming?"

Leiana places a firm hand on my shoulder, using all of her

strength to keep me seated. Lilac's eyes widen, full of fear for me.

"Your brother is fine in here," Leiana says.

Lilac looks between her mother and me, clearly wanting to oppose, but she knows better. We both do.

With a silent nod, Lilac exits, and the moment the door closes behind her, a blade of shadows shoots toward my heart. I raise a hand, only managing to intercept the sharpened shadow a mere inch from my chest.

Labyrinth smiles at me, pleased.

"Good work, son," he says—a title that grates at me. To call me "son" in public is one thing; the universe believes that's who I am. But he is not my father, and I was never his child. I'm his *brother's* child. "It's reassuring to see you've maintained your wit," Labyrinth finishes.

"Always, Father," I reply, bowing my head curtly. The words taste acidic on my tongue.

Leiana meets my gaze, a smile that's almost too sweet curling on her lips, as if I don't know exactly why she would stop me from leaving. "How are you, darling?"

"Very well, I appreciate you asking." I give her the same nod I gave Labyrinth.

Not wasting time with any further niceties, she asks, "Has a new student been enrolled in Visnatus?"

This is not the way I thought the conversation would go. I thought we would talk of Lilac and how Leiana could tranquilize my sister's obvious despondence over our marriages. That's the thing with seeing the future—key details are often left out. I might see a punch coming but miss the blade in my back.

I'm no liar when it comes to Leiana and Labyrinth, yet every part of me whispers to *lie*.

The new student she's asking of is Desdemona, and if Leiana wants her, it's for no moral reason.

She wants her power.

But I can't let Leiana have her. Not yet, at least. Not when she could be this important—a catalyst for my cause.

Desdemona's mother was not only in the Arcanes' land, but Desdemona herself nearly reached it as well. She could single-handedly take me further than anyone has ever gone before.

Because if I can reach The Void, I can kill the Arcanes.

I've learned that Desdemona is a relentless liar. Perhaps it is her spirit that moves me to say, "Not that I know of. Do you believe an individual could be related to the monsters?"

*This could very well be my undoing.*

Lying is a slippery slope. Once you slide, you can never stop.

My hand slips into my pocket, fingers curling around the small silver wolf—one of the few relics left from my childhood. Its cool touch carries a bite of Ilyria's freezing temperatures.

"Oh, no," Leiana says, her ice-blue eyes meeting mine, her tone as smooth as it is deadly. "This has nothing to do with the attacks."

Before I can respond, her power presses in on me, suffocating even without a touch. Tendrils of dark blue energy spiral from my mouth, the visible thread of my life force slipping away.

First, my breath slows, then my chest tightens, and a weight settles on my body—fatigue like I've been drained of every ounce of strength.

"When you find this student, you'll watch them for me," Leiana says. "Won't you?"

"Yes," I manage to choke out, my body collapsing over the table as I gasp for air, each breath coming harder than the last.

"Yes?" she repeats, her fingers brushing the dark hair that's fallen across my face. I don't have the strength to move it aside. "That's my boy."

Black specks cloud my vision, and I lose all sensation in my chest. I can barely make out Labyrinth's voice through the haze. "Leiana, that's enough." She releases her grip on my life force.

Life force—our essence, our power, our very life. When

Leiana takes too much, I'll die, and she'll absorb yet another soul's magic for herself.

I often wonder if either she or Labyrinth would care.

They talk above me as I lie paralyzed on the table. The only thing I can do now is pray I wake up from the unwanted slumber.

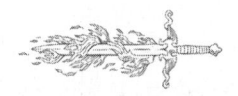

---

When my consciousness returns, it's night, and somehow, I'm still alive. I stagger to my feet and portal to the headmistress's office, barely keeping my balance.

Cynthia waves me in from behind her sprawling mahogany desk. I stumble in, collapsing onto the red sofa against the wall, the cushions worn from my many years of use.

Her face softens as I sink into my seat, though she doesn't ask what happened. She doesn't need to. She knows.

For her silence, I'm grateful. She spares me the indignity of condolences and concern.

I am a prince at best, a puppet at worst, and acknowledgment of those grievances would only remind me of them.

Her silence is the rarest and most genuine form of kindness I've ever received.

"What were the circumstances of Desdemona's arrival?" I ask her, my voice weak because I am.

Cynthia lifts her chin, her gaze sharp. "What did she share?"

"Nothing. But I've uncovered something vital to our cause."

She leans in, her fingers interlaced under her chin, clearly intrigued. "Do tell."

"Her mother is in The Void," I say, sinking deeper into the sofa. Cynthia perks up. "Taken by the Arcanes."

"I had a feeling," Cynthia muses.

I eye her suspiciously, unable to tell if this is her usual eccentricity, or if she truly suspected such an odd turn of fate.

"They're back," I mutter. "Possibly for good this time, if they're capturing instead of killing. If we can use her mother to get to The Void, perhaps we can kill them first."

Cynthia would be the first person to tell someone of the Arcanes and their thirst for massacre—but we both have different ties to them. Different reasons to want them dead.

I was twelve when I was taught that the fairies wanted a protector, a creature to do their bidding. They forged the Folk from the bodies of their fallen, merging them into a single, towering creature a hundred times their size. And the first thing they ordered their new creation to do? Exterminate an entire species of monsters—the capris.

It didn't take long for me to realize the fairies didn't want a protector—they wanted vengeance.

That was when I began to want vengeance, too.

I wasn't born a prince, but the Arcanes made me a prisoner.

They murdered my parents, and I was sent to live with Labyrinth and Leiana, who paraded me around as their fake son. They forced me into servitude, and when I didn't comply, they made me suffer for it. The Arcanes didn't just take my family. They took my *life*.

So at twelve, I made a vow.

I would take theirs in return.

Cynthia understands my need for revenge far better than anyone. The only thing is that to her, it's futile, and to me, it's inevitable.

"Does Leiana know Desdemona is here?" I ask, dread knotting in my chest, fearing she'll reach Desdemona first.

"No," Cynthia replies. "I did not alert anyone of Desdemona's presence."

Not illegal, but not legal either—a sign Cynthia knows more than she's letting on.

I smile to myself. "Why is that?"

Her eyebrows arch, and a smirk tugs at her lips. "I have the same suspicions as you."

Interesting. I wonder what it is about Desdemona that caught Cynthia's attention. On the surface, she seems like nothing more than a typical Fire Folk—hotheaded and bound to burn.

Clearly, that's far off the mark.

"May your suspicions meet my ears?" I ask.

Cynthia sweeps her hand wide, her voice smooth as she says, "Grant me a favor, and they shall."

I am the only one who knows the many reasons Cynthia may need a favor, and still, I debate.

To most, a verbal promise will only be paid back by one's virtue and is easily dismissed. A Royal is not included in that generalization. If I offer her a favor now, I'll be in her debt—until she demands repayment.

Yet, I have no choice but to get to Desdemona before Leiana does. She could hold the very key to my revenge against the Arcanes.

So here I am, powerless but to say, "Yes, Cynthia, you have my favor."

"Desdemona's mother was closely linked to Freyr before her *death*—not to the lineage Desdemona claimed through her father, Dalin Marquees."

*Interesting.* "What do you mean death?"

"Isa Althenia died eighteen years ago."

The way Cynthia speaks is frustrating, but she's always made me work for my information. Even now, with a favor at play.

"Show me her picture," I demand.

Cynthia approaches her bookshelf, in the corner behind her desk, filled with illegal texts. She only reaches for a yearbook. Sure enough, she shows me a photo of a younger version of the woman from my projection.

*Isa faked her death.*

"Is this all I receive for my favor?" I ask.

"No. You'll have to find Freyr Alpine. He's at a secret facility deep in Folkara's northern mountains."

"Do you have coordinates?"

"I do not." She raises a single eyebrow. "Keep an eye on the girl for me."

I rise to leave. "I was already planning on it."

---

By the time I make it back to the suite, each breath is difficult to take. The air feels like sand in my lungs, scratching my insides. Azaire stands in the kitchenette in the corner, a cup of tea forgotten in his hands.

He barely has to look at me. One glance, and his bushy eyebrows scrunch in discomfort. One glance, and he sets the mug of tea down, saying, "Again?"

It must be my drooping shoulders, or the shadowed eyes, or something else entirely that only someone who knows me can sense.

"Again," I say as I fall on the couch. Even standing has taken its toll, and I worry how close to death Leiana has brought me this time.

Azaire frowns, walking toward me. "Maybe Wendy could make you something to ease the pain?"

"There's no replenishing life force," I say as I lie back on the couch in exhaustion, though he knows this already.

"She's a talented healer. Maybe she can help." Azaire shrugs as he sits beside me. "Never hurts to ask."

Asking can hurt. It'll hurt her to learn the truth of my kingdom. But there's another question nagging at my mind. It was only last week that Azaire and Wendy had their first conversation in years.

I glance at him, asking, "How do you know she's a talented healer?"

Azaire tugs on his beanie. "Oh," he says, "uh…"

I sit up abruptly. "*No*," I choke. "Tell me you're not in one of the volunteer groups."

If Leiana put him in one of those groups—turning him into a guinea pig for her elite students to practice their powers—then it's a calculated move. It's leverage, the kind she's wielded over me my entire life.

She's never hesitated to drag my loved ones into her games. She knows there's little she can do to break me now. I've endured years of her torment, after all.

*This* is how she hurts me. How she controls me. Because there is nothing I wouldn't do to protect Azaire.

"It just happened," he says, as if that will make it any better. "I know there's nothing you can do, and…"

"What did they do to you?" I ask, my voice shaking.

Azaire looks down, still tugging on his beanie. "A few stab wounds, broken ribs, and a black eye."

I exhale shakily, the weight of his pain sinking in. "Zaire…"

The emotion pours into Azaire's voice as he says, "I'm not going to say it's not a big deal, because it is, but I know you'll make it right when you can. I can hold on until then."

"No," I seethe, rage boiling my blood. "The next time someone tries to drag you into one of those groups, you tell them I'll have their heart in my hand by the end of the day."

No one will hurt him. I don't care what kind of punishment Leiana has in store for me. *No one* will hurt him.

"Lucian," he says softly.

I cut him off, saying, "I mean it."

"And I appreciate it, but you look like you're one step away from Leiana doing you in for good. I'll take the punishment because I don't want to see that happen. Because *we* protect each other—and this is how I protect you. No surrender, right?"

No surrender is a pact we've held onto for years now, made during what I thought was the most turbulent of times. I've long since known better, but at eleven, the worst seemed more dire than it does now.

*When we made the pact, I was sitting alone, looking out past the Great Sea that I sometimes wished I could escape from.*

*Azaire sat next to me. His usually dark skin had grown pale—a common effect of Ilyria. The sun never fully breaks through the gray sky in my homeworld, and the ground is always blanketed in snow.*

*It was silent for a while, not the kind where I'm fishing for something to say, but the kind where I forgot there could be anything to say at all. Azaire broke that silence when he asked, "Did they do something?"*

*"No," I said, shaking my head, but I couldn't stop the tears from stinging my eyes.*

*Azaire was barely three-quarters my size. He wrapped his arms around me like he was twice that. I opened my mouth to speak, but Azaire saved me the effort as he said, "You don't have to say anything."*

*It was foreign—being understood without explanation.*

*"I think," I croaked, "I think she almost killed me this time." The tears nearly froze on my cheek as the snow fell around us.*

*"But she couldn't. You're too strong."*

To this day, I still think Azaire is the strongest of us.

*"She can't have you, Luc," he continued. "Maybe your power… but not your spirit."*

*I didn't believe it. I didn't even know what he meant, because she was taking my spirit. Bit by bit, day by day. I knew, even then, that Leiana would carve me hollow.*

*"I hate them." I picked up a rock and hurled it into the Great Sea. "I hate Labyrinth for not doing anything."*

*"I know," Azaire sighed.*

*"I know you know."*

*"No," he said. "I know what it feels like to hate."*

*"Who do you hate?"*

*Azaire mumbled something under his breath, and when he looked up again, I knew not to pry.*

*But he surprised me by saying, "Under my beanie, I don't have hair. I have snakes."*

*He tugged on his beanie. Back then it was forest green. It's long since been replaced by the sapphire blue of my kingdom.*

*"That's why I hate," he said. "Because they kill."*

*"That's not your fault," I told him, shaking my head.*

*"Neither is what Leiana does to you." Even back then, I remember him sounding so sure—strong. He turned to face me as he uttered for the first time, "No surrender? Promise that you won't give in to Leiana."*

*I was only a child, but I knew that was an impossible promise. I knew one day Leiana would take me entirely.*

*I continued to look out over the sea as I said, "Then you can't hate your snakes."*

*Azaire was quiet for a moment. When I turned to him, he wasn't looking at me anymore. He shook his head as he muttered, "That's different."*

*"Why?"*

*"Because they* have *killed," he said. "They took my life from me."*

*I knew—still know—what it feels like to have your life taken from you. So I told him the whole truth, my entire life's truth. I told him I watched as my father died, and that I couldn't remember my mother at all. That Leiana and Labyrinth weren't my true parents, and all the torture, all the abuse, was because they feared I would tell another what I'd just told him.*

I think it was the first time I'd ever been so honest.

*And after my confession, he looked at me with tears in his eyes and said, "It wasn't a Folk that killed my parents, it was the snakes."*

*I, eleven and tiny, looked at him and repeated his words: "No surrender, then?"*

*Azaire shook his head. "No surrender."*

After that, he went on hating his snakes, and I went on believing that Leiana would be the death of me. It ebbed and flowed until I one day realized that Azaire might be right. Perhaps she would take my life, and perhaps there was something else, something that mattered more, that she would never get.

We protect one another. Azaire is the voice of wisdom, I'm the show of strength. Both are required to win the battle. But as

Labyrinth says, wit matters most.

No surrender has come to mean something grand to the two of us. It's the promise of another day. It's the hope of making it through the hardest of them. It's the strength to fight on, even when we don't see the reason.

No surrender is what keeps us going.

Now, I look at Azaire, my voice steady, and promise, "No surrender."

---

The next day, I stop outside of Calista's third-period class. The lingering effects of Leiana's antics are fading, though not completely. I lean against the wall for support, watching as Calista exits. When her gaze settles on me, she rolls her eyes, her annoyance clear.

"Waiting for me, are you?" she says, walking past me.

We share one thing—a stark lack of control over our lives. In different ways, we are both held down by our futures on the throne. Yet neither she nor Kai cares to see it.

I quicken my pace until I'm stepping in unison with her. "Oh, yes," I say with a dry smile, "you've caught me in the act of my undying concern for you."

"What do you want?" she asks, picking up her pace as if she can outwalk me.

My gaze stays fixed ahead as I say, "I believe I have a way to get us out of the marriage."

It isn't at all the truth, and it doesn't need to be. It's the easiest way to get her to uncover what I need to know about Freyr Alpine, to find the facility Cynthia claimed he works in, and persuade him to tell me the details I'm missing.

Why, for instance, was Desdemona's mother, Isa, taken by the Arcanes?

Calista's eyes widen at the proposition of freedom. She may

even be smiling. "How?"

"It won't be easy," I murmur, glancing around the academy hall. "We'll need privacy."

"Let's," Calista says, spinning on her heel and heading toward the unused stairs.

We ascend to a floor reserved for Royal families during their time at Visnatus. Long ago, every world in our universe had a monarchy, but now only two remain—my kind, the Lyrians of Ilyria, and Calista's people, the Folk of Folkara.

It's been ages since I've set foot in this room. The space is still cluttered with relics of our Royal predecessors—decaying books and rusted music players sit on old wooden tables, all coated in a thick layer of dust and cobwebs that cling to the corners. But the room has its advantages: it's soundproof, and can only be entered in the presence of Royal blood.

"Tell me your plan," Calista demands.

I can't help but nearly laugh at her persistence. She still holds onto hope for her future.

I can't say I share that optimism.

"There's a covert operation in Folkara," I tell her. "If we expose it, we might be able to break the Littaline Compact."

The Compact binds Ilyria and Folkara as allies—our reason for marriage is to uphold this.

"What would that mean for Folkara? For my kingdom?" Calista asks, her eyes sharp as she straightens her posture.

A fair question, though I'm not sure how this will affect her world. It depends what the operation is, truthfully. More than that, it depends if I'll have to bring this information into the public to get to Freyr Alpine.

Though that isn't a detail I'm willing to share with Calista.

"If we pull this off," I say with a smile, "freedom."

Calista hardly misses a beat before she says, "Tell me what to do."

"Go to Folkara, do your *quiet* snooping, and search the

northern mountains for anything unusual."

"Yes, sir," she says, and not particularly convincingly, either.

# Chapter 9
## Duck Duck Goose

# DESDEMONA

"Not like that," Leiholan mutters, his tone both gruff and impatient, as if correcting me is becoming his next lovely habit—right after the alcohol he always carries. His bottle clinks against the sword strapped to his waist as he tells me, again, to "Walk straighter," as if I know what that means.

When he said he'd help me hide, I didn't expect it to involve walking around with a book on my head.

He goes back to throwing random questions at me. "What do you think of flám perfeit?"

"I have no idea," I mutter as the book falls from my head.

This entire *lesson* is pointless. When I look at him, he smiles and takes a sip of his vesi.

"Do you ever stop drinking?" I ask, exasperated.

"Would you refrain from your beverage for but a moment?" he corrects me, feigning poise when we both know he is far from it.

Then he takes another swig.

I want to scream at him, but I only repeat his words back to him.

I get it; I'm from the septic, which apparently means I don't know anything. Leiholan is one of three people at this academy who knows where I'm from, hence why he's teaching me. But taking lessons from a Nepenthe—the same creature as the keepers back home—is worse than insulting. It's dehumanizing.

When the bottle lowers from his lips, Leiholan says, "Tell me about your mom."

Those few words make me falter. But I doubt his drunk self even registers my moment of internal collapse.

"Strong," I answer, finding it hard to put a word to the woman. "A survivor."

All he does is grumble in response—a dismissive grumble. As if it weren't *his* people that forced her to be those things.

"You had to be to make it in the septic," I reply, not taking on the defensive tone I'd like to.

He just takes another swig and says, "Trust me, sweetheart, I know all about survival."

"Was it survival you were worried about while your kind ambushed us at every turn?" I ask defensively, which I didn't want to do.

"You don't think we were being killed?" Leiholan spits, just as defensive and angry as I am, looking down at me like I'm a small child. I feel like one too, with how much I want to push back against his words.

For two years of my adolescence, his kind hunted me during the Neptharian War. Every day I watched the Nepenthes kill more Folk in worse ways.

I bite my tongue.

He takes the biggest gulp of vesi I've seen from him so far.

"Can we fight now?" I spit, picking up the double-edged sword I chose on the first day of training.

Leiholan unsheathes his weapon, pointing the blade at me. I stiffen, expecting him to run it right through me.

"No one expects you to know how to fight," he says, his voice still tense. "Utul was a smart choice for a fake home, but not for your sore lack of knowledge. They actually *teach* their young there—hence the questions you always sneer at when I ask."

I open my mouth to respond, but he cuts me off. "When you're ready, swing."

I swing the sword at him.

Over the next few days, he works on my vocabulary. He tells me to say "suppose" instead of "guess," "fair" instead of "good," "dish" instead of "food," and "as goes for you" instead of "you too." He promises me that not only is this proper speech on Utul, but it's also expected at Visnatus.

He could be pouring ridiculous words down my throat, for all I know. But I jot them down in a notebook whenever I find a quiet moment alone in Aralia's room. What I don't do is show him any gratitude. This is the least he could do for one of the Folk, the smallest way to make amends.

He tells me about the structure of this *new world*. I already know some of it, but I can't deny that it's helpful. Back home, the hierarchy was invisible, except among the Nepenthes and us Folk.

It's much different here.

The Lyrians are natural strategists, using their powers of subconscious manipulation to gain the upper hand. "Hence why they rule the universe," Leiholan grumbles. But not all Lyrians can wield shadows—only the most powerful among them, namely the Aibeks, the ruling family of Ilyria. Lucian's family.

When Leiholan moves on to the Folk, annoyance prickles at me. We're the most densely populated and the most diverse, thanks to the different elements we wield. But apparently, our power is seen as fragmented, preventing us from unifying.

"Don't be fooled," he says, lifting his sword and preparing to use it. "This place acts like it's meant to shape you, but I've seen plenty of students leave worse than they came. It's not life they're preparing you for; it's politics."

The Eunoia are diplomats—that much I knew. They have powers of empathy and healing, but they're only trained in medicine. "Also persuasion," Leiholan adds. "They're capable of swaying emotions—manipulating, if you ask me. But, like the Draes, they aren't trained here."

Draes are nearly invincible and incredibly intelligent. They have the capacity to read minds, but only a select few are trained —those that will be advisors and scholars, working behind the scenes for the Lyrians.

But when Leiholan gets to the Nepenthes, I stiffen. He doesn't say very much. They're faster, stronger, more physically adept than all the others. But that's where he leaves it.

"Understanding the roles we play is the only way you'll survive here," he says sullenly, finishing his spiel.

"Roles we play?" I mutter. "Not things we do?"

"Final lesson," Leiholan announces like he's talking to a room full of people and not just me. "We play roles. We don't become them." He lifts his sword. "Sadly for people like you and me, our entire universe is built on these hierarchies."

"I'm nothing like you." I know what he meant, but I won't give him the satisfaction of grouping me with a species as brutal as the Nepenthes.

"You're right," he says with a smirk. "You're not just from the septic; you're a *Fire Folk*. Worse than me. Your admittance here could tear this whole thing down. Makes me wonder why Cynthia let you in at all."

*I already know I'm not meant to be here*, but Leiholan swings first, and I'm too busy dodging his sword to say so. The clash of metal and the sting of exertion leaves me breathless, and by the time Leiholan finally calls it quits, I'm thoroughly worn out.

Dragging my feet to the exit, I'm close to escaping before Lucian steps in, blocking my path. I know I can't ignore him any longer—and I'm far from thrilled about it.

He knows too much.

Besides, the last thing I need is to be entangled with a *prince*. Another spoiled brat who gets everything he wants on any whim, at the hands—and often *lives*—of people like me.

Standing in front of me, eye to eye, the prince whispers, "I need your help with something."

"You need *my* help?" I ask slowly.

"Yes," he says with a smirk. "I could use a powerful partner."

"In your dreams," I scoff.

His tone is too sarcastic to be considered kind when he says, "You already are." But he eyes me up and down the same way he did by the lake—and I can't tell if it's ravening or revulsion that he stares at me with.

I step closer, eyeing him carefully as I whisper, "Is this about my mom?"

"Partially. I'll meet you by the lake, same hour as before," Lucian says before pivoting on his feet and walking out.

I do the same, making a beeline for the door when Leiholan interrupts my escape. "You'd be wise to go."

I stop, glaring over my shoulder. "And why is that?"

"First off, drop the attitude, sweetheart. Second, if the prince thinks you're powerful, maybe you are. From here, you don't look it." He squints as he looks at the new cut I earned on my bicep, and I cover it with my hand, hoping he can't see that it's cauterized.

"Thank you," I say, and he looks pleasantly surprised before I add, "for another piece of *riveting* advice."

I walk to my first class, Philosophical Theology. The difference between how the well-off and the starving view the gods wasn't hard to pick up on in my childhood, mostly because my mom used to be the former, and she brought her belief in Zola with her to the septic. Zola is the goddess of balance, and Mom used to tell me, "You are the good thing to right all the bad that came before."

It was one of the few times she was ever sentimental with me.

The teacher, Mr. Auberwitz, is a Lyrian who has a track record for starting class too cheerfully in the name of Sulva—

ignoring the other two gods, Ayan, the solar god, and Zola, the goddess of balance. But I guess it makes sense if he believes the Lyrians are Sulva's descendants. I don't know how true that is, considering the rest of us most definitely did *not* descend from a god.

Mr. Auberwitz drones on about Sulva's greatness, and I'm thinking that classes at such a fancy school should be a little more put together. It feels like I'm listening to ramblings.

Sulva, the lunar goddess, and Ayan, the solar god, formed our universe. They both went on to have their descendants—the first being Amun and Eira. Eira was Sulva's descendant, while Amun was Ayan's.

The story goes like this—Amun was the first person to ever exist. The poor guy got lonely or something like that, so Sulva created her first descendant and the first-ever Lyrian, Eira. Amun and Eira fell in love, Eira died, and Amun found a way to die, too. It's supposed to be *super* romantic because Amun was supposedly immortal, but I think it's a load of bullshit. It's also the first love story of Elsyia, so it's a story I've heard a thousand times—folklore back home and something Mr. Auberwitz believes in.

It's a relief when I finally leave and meet Aralia by the purple tree in the garden—which has become routine before heading to Elemental Magic. But today, she flashes a joint.

"Ditch?" she offers with a smirk.

I glance at the girl that isn't my friend but somehow thinks she is, and I know the last thing I care about is class. I'm only here until I can save my mom—then this whole school will be nothing but a distant memory.

"Why not?" I mutter.

We go out into the woods, beyond what I've learned is the school's protective barrier, keeping out monsters and other random nefarious things that have never been a problem before. But the barrier means the academy can't do a thing about what we do out here, so Aralia says.

We sit on the rocks by the river I found, and Aralia teases, "Wanna light it, Inferno?"

But behind my eyes, I see the dead Folk in my burning home —a *real* inferno.

I offer my usual lie: "I'd rather not burn down the woods." *As if I could even light a match.*

I've been bumming off her or Kai's magic anytime I can in class, but that only works for non-elemental magic, like opening portals or casting shields.

To distract from my casual—and seemingly obvious—lie, I say, "You smoke a lot, huh?"

Aralia inhales before passing me the joint. "Most of us do." It's not hard to pick up on the sadness seeping into her sentence. Then she waves her hand in the air, and the sarcastic tone I've grown used to is back. "Future leaders and all. Means we have tight-ass parents."

"What are your parents like?" I ask, not because I care, but because it might be useful to know. All information has potential. Any knowledge can be wielded.

But I see why she might mistake our conversations for friendship.

"They're the most highly regarded advisors in Folkara." Aralia shrugs a little. "We moved into the castle when I was young, and I didn't see them much after that."

"Oh," I say, and I wonder, not for the first time, what the Neptharian War was like in the castle, a place rich enough to have armor, soldiers, and barriers. In the septic, all we had were tired workers—people trained to produce goods, not fight wars. Maybe she moved into the castle *because* of the war. Royal advisors handle battles and strategies. My mom used to be one.

"Most of our parents are important or whatever…" Aralia continues. "Speaking of parents, are you sure your mom wasn't taken by the Royals?" My head snaps in her direction, and she shrugs again, saying, "You said you didn't find her in the septic."

Could that be it? My mom locked in some underground royal dungeon? The thought hadn't even crossed my mind. There's no reason the Royals would want anything to do with her.

Not that I can think of, at least.

"I guess it's possible."

When I get her back, I'll finally tell her about the dreams—and my magic. The thought alone is the greatest relief I've felt since I lost her.

---

I wonder if Lucian's words were a threat. Meet him at the lake the same hour as before, when *I* threatened *him*. I don't trust him or the information he might have on me. He could identify my mom or tell someone I coerced him into breaking Ilyrian law. I worry about what will happen if I show up and if I don't.

If he turns me in, I'm as good as dead. If his parents don't kill me, King Easton and Queen Melody of Folkara will lock me away. But maybe I'll find my mom and finally tell her about the dreams. My magic.

*My murder.*

She's the only person I trust not to use them against me.

I decide to go to the lake with only one plan in my pocket—channeling Lucian's power, if needed.

Ivy covers the exterior school walls, but not the way it did back home at the Saul. The ivy on our trading house is dark, weedy, almost dead—covering all the holes in the cobblestone building. Like the world is trying to make up for the inevitability of destruction.

Here, it's just green.

A narrow path, lined with trees and bushes, leads to the lake. I've been here twice now, but with the moon completely full overhead, the sight is different. The water gleams softly, and I nearly recognize it from Mom's stories—the lunar lake, spelled to absorb the power of the lunar goddess, Sulva.

Lucian stands at the edge. I don't greet him, and he doesn't greet me. All he does is glance at me, scanning me from head to toe, before walking into the woods. I guess I'm supposed to follow, so I do.

We walk through the woods in silence for a long while.

"A Fire Folk," he says as if it's amusing, stepping across overgrown roots. He's as sure-footed as the Folk who've spent their entire lives in the septic. Like Damien, he barely makes a noise.

I wonder what kind of fancy training made him adept compared to the real threats Damien faced that granted him the skill.

"And a Lyrian," I reply, mumbling under my breath, "a makeshift Amun and Eira."

He offers me his hand as we cross the river. I take it, playing the role of the unassuming girl from Utul. I lift my chin higher and *walk straighter*, fighting the urge to drop his hand.

Especially because my own is growing *hot*.

"Why would we want that?" Lucian asks.

"Eternal love, maybe?" I say, despite thinking it's bullshit.

He locks his eyes on mine, just to say, "I wouldn't die for you."

"Nor would I, Prince." As he looks away, I reach for his power, but there's nothing. I know that channeling is stronger when it's used against your kind, but it makes no sense that I'd feel *no* magic from him.

Lucian walks farther into the woods as he says, "Self-preservation is important. It's probably best that you haven't seen how charming I can be."

"Really? Because I found you almost choking me to death to be quite pleasing." I shouldn't be talking to a prince this way, but at the same time, I kind of like it. It almost feels like I could obtain the upper hand—I mean, in something as infantile as sarcasm, but it's *something*.

"Well," he says, "I have known the Fire Folk to be masochists."

I think of the flame in my dwelling, my hair catching fire... the Folk I killed. I wouldn't say I found any gratification in that, but it doesn't surprise me that this is how the privileged talk about us.

That *this* is how he would talk about *me*.

I can't even imagine what he'd say if he knew where I'm from.

"Have you ever *met* a Fire Folk?" I try to keep the edge out of my tone and fail.

"One or two." The prince stops for a moment, looking like he's contemplating something. Then, he says with a smile, "I think they're dead."

And I think he's trying to provoke me. For what purpose, I don't know.

"Right," I mutter.

We fall back into silence as we weave through the trees, cliffs becoming visible as we travel over jagged, slippery rocks until I find myself looking out over a body of water that seems to go on forever. Compared to the murky waters back home, this glimmering turquoise is as clear as glass.

I envy its magnificence, the beauty in its very nature. A beauty I will never have.

Not only is it pure, but it's free.

We climb down the rocks, the cliffs on either side of us and the woods just behind us.

Lucian turns to me, his expression unreadable, and opens his arms wide—just like he did the night that I saw my mom in her cage. Moonlight illuminates his face and the water behind him as I stand motionless on the sand, waiting for him to elaborate.

Finally, he says, "Shoot me."

"What?"

"Send your fire at me."

I glance around, realizing I've walked into a trap. "You said you needed my help."

"I do," the prince says simply. "I need you to use your magic against me."

I stare at him, my eyebrows scrunching in confusion. Confusion that I don't bother concealing.

"Come on, darling." He smirks. "Show me what you got."

"And you called *me* a masochist," I mutter.

His smile only grows.

I reach out for his power again, searching for something to channel, anything to put on a good enough show. There's nothing. Absolutely nothing.

"I can't *shoot* fire," I argue—my last resort.

"All right," the prince says. "Then *start* a fire. I'll put it out."

I step closer, when I should be stepping back—but sudden anger drives me. "Do you know how hard it is to put out the Flame? It's nearly impossible, which is why so many of us die."

"Trust me, I can put out a fire."

"But it's not just a fire," I say again, unable to mask my irritation. "It's *the Flame*."

His midnight eyes glow an incandescent blue, black spirals winding up his hands and wrapping around his arms. "Start a fire, or *I'll* shoot."

Suddenly, I know I'm going to die. And when a shadow flies in my direction, I barely manage to duck. Chills cover my entire body.

"What kind of help is this?" I shout.

The prince steps closer to me. "I thought you had a power that could rival my own." He's in my face now, smiling, *taunting*, when he says, "Where's your fire?"

Why would an Aibek, a *prince*, think that I'm powerful enough to rival him? I mean, I'd love to beat him. But I know I can't, and I can't bear to show him that. So I turn away and say, "I'm not doing this."

The prince doesn't protest. I wouldn't have expected walking away from an Aibek to be so easy, but here I am.

Then I fall to the ground, right on my face, while my back aches from the sudden cold. A shiver racks through my spine before I lose all feeling.

I grab onto the tree that I so narrowly missed when I fell. It takes all my strength to pull myself up and lean against it. Cold continues to rush through me as shadows tighten around my torso.

Even when I'm down, he's still fighting me.

I curse under my breath before I yell, "Stop!" But it's barely a scream.

Lucian stalks closer now, and when two shadows sharp enough to impale me form in his hands, I know he's trying to kill me.

What a stupid decision it was to come here. Of course he'd want to kill me. Maybe he found out I killed that Folk, or just doesn't tolerate being threatened. He's a prince, for gods' sake. He can do anything he wants and get no flack.

He could kill me at any time, without even needing to know that I'm from the septic. He's *untouchable*.

I look him right in the eye, hoping that maybe he'll see me as something small that needs protecting instead of someone he wants to kill.

But, no, he aims the shadows like I throw daggers, right for my chest and throat.

I guard my chest with my hands as I yell, "I don't have magic!"

Lucian drops his hands, and the shadows that had bound my body release me, flooding back to their natural places. It's an odd sight—watching them slither back beneath the trees and rocks, returning to the places they should have been but weren't because they'd been trying to kill me.

Slowly, sensation begins to return to my upper body.

Before I can curse at him, he says, "Of course you have magic." The remaining shadows in his hands dissipate, vanishing into the night air.

"Well, surprise, I don't!" I rise to my feet and brush the dirt off my pants.

Lucian's gaze follows my movements, climbing up my body until our eyes meet. "You have plenty of magic."

My breath catches in my throat, but I hope he doesn't see that. I think of the dead Folk. The fire that didn't burn my skin. The wounds that cauterize. Plenty of magic indeed.

*But I don't want it.*

The prince smiles, and his teeth look annoyingly perfect—cheekbones, too. His entire face, really. Because that's what a life of being pampered gets you. Beauty.

That's the difference between me and him—I had to fight for my food, and he got to throw the extra away.

He had the luxury of being able to think of something as pointless as beauty. Because it's not pointless for people like him, it's a weapon. For him, charisma can be wielded.

Lucian walks around me, stepping behind me. He grips both my shoulders, grazing his fingers down my arms while he whispers in my ear, "If you don't know how to use it, I can fix that."

I'm embarrassed by the goosebumps covering my body while his breath tickles my neck, relieving the warmth I hadn't realized I was feeling.

Suddenly I'm hyper-aware of my hands, the burning sensation in my palms, my stomach. Like something crawled inside of me, ate me hollow, and replaced my insides with fire.

*This* is what power feels like. I felt it the night I killed the Folk, but I couldn't define it at the time. Now I have to decide if I ever want to feel it again. If I could kill a Folk as easily as I did on my last night in the septic, I'd have the power to get my mom back when I find her. I could kill the people who took her from me, took my life from me.

And that sounds pretty sweet.

"Fine," I say, turning my head. I can just see his lips, an inch from mine. "*Fix it.*"

---

Calista's sitting on the couch in the suite when I finally make it back. Her posture is relaxed, but her eyes are sharp, watching me closely as I step through the door. Most of the time, she ignores me, but today, she doesn't look away. She pauses, her gaze lingering longer than usual, like she's reading something in my expression.

I step around her, heading to Aralia's room when she sets her utensils on the table before her. I turn my back to her.

"What were you doing with Lucian?" she demands.

I stop, looking toward the door, wanting to run away but wondering if I *can* run from a princess.

"We were talking," I say calmly, turning to face her.

Calista stands, stalking toward me. While I'm grateful I couldn't start a fire earlier, I'm thinking I won't be for long as Calista sizes me up.

"With your magic?" She sneers, her gaze settling on my torso. "I can see him all over you."

With a sigh, I say, "There was some magic involved, yes."

Calista's eyes narrow as they glow a vivid yellow—Air Folk magic.

At first, I feel nothing. Then, claws tear into my brain. Tearing it apart, peeling back its layers, but I know she's only finding empty pockets because I can see what she's seeing. She's trying to see my memories, but somehow, she's failing.

The pain intensifies with every second, and then I begin to hear it—the same whispering wind I heard when I came back from the septic. The combination is unbearable.

The whispering echoes through my mind, like an attack on

my senses. Suddenly, there's nothing but harsh, incoherent hissing. It overwhelms me, dragging me all the way back to the murders I committed.

How could it *not?* The whispering began right after I killed those Folk in my home, as though their voices followed me out of the septic, refusing to leave me be.

I try not to think about the dead bodies, just in case Calista can see, but when the whispers rise to a screech, I crack.

"Stop now, or you'll regret it." The pain sharpens my tone, and I hope the orange glow in my eyes is enough to scare Calista.

But the princess laughs as she releases her hold on my mind. "Quite the brazen little Fire Folk," she mutters.

I clench my fist, wishing I could punch her in the face with it.

"Since you don't understand your role, let me explain it to you. Not only am I your princess, but I'm also your future queen. You know what that means, don't you?" She leans in and whispers, "It means when I ask, you answer. *What* were you doing with Lucian?"

I know that making an enemy of the future queen is a bad idea, but I don't stop myself from saying, "None of your damn business."

I'm sure Leiholan would tell me a better, more posh way to say it.

"He's playing you," she whispers with an unsympathetic nod. "Don't be foolish enough to give him an advantage." Her long finger rises to my forehead, pushing hair out of my face while her eyes search mine. "The wards, are they from Lucian?"

*That's why she couldn't see my memories.*

Mental wards, meant to guard against mind magic, were never something we worried about in the septic. No one had the time —or energy—to go rifling through someone's memories. That must be far from the norm around here, the school for *future leaders*, where stealing others' thoughts is undoubtedly an advantage.

The necklace sears against my skin, pulsing like it holds a life of its own. If Mom wanted to protect us, it makes sense she'd block my memories from intruders. A mental ward powered by a memor—one of Folkara's precious stones, and the pendant of her necklace—could make mind magic difficult to use against me.

But not impossible.

"I don't have any wards," I try to quiver, to feign the fear I know she wants to see from me.

Calista rolls her eyes as she calls, "Wendy!" After a second without a response she follows with, "Wendy, now!"

The door to one of the suite rooms opens, revealing a tall girl with striking green eyes and dark brown skin and hair. Suddenly, I really hope I'm right about the wards. Without them, the Eunoia could ask me any question, and I'd be forced to answer.

The light from the room behind her casts an aureole effect, and I wish we could be meeting under better circumstances. A Eunoia is someone you want on your side.

She walks closer to us, slowly and gracefully, and when she looks at Calista, she frowns. A scar from her bottom lip to her chin protrudes when she does.

"What are you doing?" Wendy asks. Her voice is strong, but her gloved hands are shaking. The green of her eyes flickers, glowing and fading, a clear sign she's using her powers.

But it doesn't seem deliberate.

"Tell me if she's telling the truth," Calista says.

Wendy looks at me, her whole body trembling like a leaf. As I scramble for a way out of this, I can't help but wonder if my anxiety is affecting her, too.

The Eunoias' power is emotion—empathy—which is how they detect lies. If I *do* have a mental ward, she won't be able to force the truth from me, but she can still tell if I'm lying. If I believe what I'm saying, maybe she won't notice. I mean the truth is I *don't* know. How could I? My mom never told me if she put up wards or not. It's a guess.

I repeat this to myself again and again.

*I don't know.*

"If I do this, will you leave me alone?" Wendy asks, turning to look at Calista.

"Yes," Calista answers.

With a sigh, she meets my gaze, saying, "Go ahead."

Wendy's eyes are dark green, vibrant beyond belief, and as they glow with her magic, they seem to light the entire suite.

"What mental wards do you have?" Calista asks me, already gloating.

"I don't know," I answer.

I *really* don't know.

The glow of Wendy's eyes flicker as she says, "She's telling the truth."

Calista's glare burns into Wendy, but it lingers on me as she says, "If Lucian finds out *anything* about my kingdom that could've only come from this room, I'll know who to turn in for treason."

The threat of treason from a princess shakes me to my core. She wouldn't even need evidence—all a person like her needs is their word.

"What are you talking about?" I ask.

She looks at me as if I'm daft, narrowing her eyes. "If you let him into your subconscious, he could find the leverage he needs against me—"

I cut her off. "He's the future king of *your* kingdom."

Raising an eyebrow, the princess smirks, as if this is a long joke I've been left out of. "We'll see," is all she says as she turns to walk away, shutting the door to her room.

When Calista is gone, I breathe. All I want to do is run home to the septic, to take my life back. But that isn't an option for me anymore—not without my mom. Not before I find out who's

hunting her and why they took her.
*Not when I've killed one of my own.*

## Chapter 10
## Reality Ruined My Vision

# LUCIAN

I know Calista's found the information I need when she barges into my room, screaming, "I could kill you!" Yet, the depth of fury in her voice suggests she has uncovered far more than I anticipated.

She grips the collar of my shirt, and for a moment, I find myself pondering what Cynthia has set in motion—something truly dangerous, if Calista's reaction is any indication. I wouldn't put it past Cynthia to manipulate me for her own advantage, though I can't see what sending me to find information on Desdemona's mother would do for her.

"I don't believe that's a new sentiment." Glancing at her hands, I add kindly, "Would you release me?"

With an obnoxious sigh and an exaggerated motion of her hands, she lets go of my shirt.

I straighten my collar, then ask, "What did you find?"

Calista's scowl grows deeper than I've ever seen, more sullen than the day we found out we were to be wed. "You know what I found!" she seethes, taking a step closer with every word. "You tricked me into betraying my own people and used my suitemate to gather information on me." She eyes me up and down as she adds, "You claim to have never desired a crown, yet all your actions are in favor of stealing mine."

I meet her gaze, searching for something to help me understand. While trickery and manipulation are tools I often deign to use, I can't recall what she's accusing me of this time.

"Calista," I whisper, as if trying to tame a beast. "Whatever you found on Folkara, I swear I hadn't the faintest clue it was there."

She freezes, and her face softens, the anger dissipating. Her shoulders sag as she looks away. Slowly, Calista whispers, "A weapon, Lucian. I found a weapon."

For a moment, the word hangs in the air.

This is far more than I anticipated.

With a reaction of this magnitude, it's clear Calista isn't referring to a mere blade or bow. She means *weapon*—a device forged with the highest level of intelligence. The magic of the universe itself, embedded into machinery, with one sole purpose: destruction. It's the kind of artifact that fueled history's bloodiest wars.

The enormity of it settles over me. Weapons like this haven't been crafted in centuries—not since the accords forbade their creation. Such an act is treason, and Calista's anger is entirely justified. If Folkara is caught creating them again, it could escalate to a war between our worlds—and everyone knows Ilyria would win.

Yet I can only take this one step at a time. The weapon is alarming, but if Cynthia spoke the truth about this path leading to Desdemona's mother, I have to follow it. Her ties to the Arcanes are far more troubling than any weapon.

"What are the coordinates?" I ask, praying that she will not make this difficult.

The anger flares in Calista once more as she turns her gaze back to me. "You said we'd get our freedom!" she exclaims in what I'm sure is as hushed a tone as she can manage. "This could be a death sentence. You could start a war. My family could be ripped from the throne!"

"What do you think is going to happen if the worlds start making weapons again?" I ask, as if this is what I truly care about. "What kind of a war will we have on our hands then?"

"You're going to be the one to start it!" she yells.

I reciprocate her angry gaze and say, "It's already begun. The Nepenthes and Folk are still fighting. Our worlds remain at odds, and our parents think these petty marriages will slap a bandage on a stab wound. It won't be long until the fighting begins, and what do you think will happen with a super-powered machine of destruction at play?"

I pause, weighing my options quickly, waiting for some kind of prophetic insight into what Calista will say next. I get none.

Looking down, I admit, "I never planned on telling Leiana or Labyrinth. There won't be any retaliation from my world. My reason for needing the location is not to doom Folkara—I simply want to uncover the truth so I can prepare myself."

Calista's sneer deepens, her eyes twitching with frustration. "Always thinking about yourself, I see. You never meant to get us out of the marriage!"

"You know I don't want to marry you any more than Lilac wants to marry Kai. If there is ever a chance for salvation, I will take it."

"This isn't salvation!" she yells.

"Neither is destroying the universe." My voice hardens. "This is bigger than us, bigger than a forced marriage or political alliances. This is the threat of universal genocide. Do you want that on your conscience if you're lucky enough to survive what will become inevitable if you keep wasting our time?"

Calista glares at me for much too long, her eyes softening as she contemplates.

I unclench my jaw and say, "Please, tell me the location of the headquarters. Help me help Lilac be a better leader."

She exhales, her shoulders slumping, and I can see the fight draining from her. Finally, she caves in. "The mountain region of the Welding Woods. Get me a map."

I do just that.

After Calista shows me where to find the facility, I'm tempted to go straight to Azaire—to set aside my ploy with Desdemona's power and head directly to the facility. But both are crucial pieces of my plan. If I stand Desdemona up, there's no guarantee she'll ever agree to meet me again.

And I *need* her power.

By the time I reach the lunar lake, Desdemona is already there, waiting. This is only our second time working together, and since the last, I've spent far too many hours turning over the question of why her magic feels so potent. Specifically why it felt so different—so jolting—when I touched her.

*It was electrifying.*

Like I was the winter and she was the warmth.

Like I was a question and she was the answer.

Like I was a dying man and she was the air.

This, plus Leiana's interest in Desdemona and her intriguing ability to step through projections, has made Desdemona my life's most profound enigma. However, I have not deluded myself into believing that I won't have to turn her into Leiana when she asks again. I only have to solve the puzzle before it's too late.

"Would you like to open a portal to the shore?" I ask as I approach Desdemona.

Her eyes grow wide, and her body goes rigid for a moment. If I had blinked, I would've missed it, because her straining disappears as quickly as it came.

She leans over the water, holding out her hand in a gesture I've never seen before. Her fingers curl toward her palm while her thumb sticks out. The determination on her face, coupled with the odd placement of her fingers, has me not wanting to look away.

Then the water swirls into itself, the image of the coast and the woods beyond it coming into view, and I can no longer watch her.

I step aside, extending a hand toward the portal. "Ladies first."

Desdemona scoffs, standing straight. "So you're a gentleman now?"

"Always was."

"I'd say agree to disagree, but self-awareness is one of the things I *don't* think you lack." She glances over her shoulder at me, cheeks reddening. "My inadequacy."

I can tell that there's no remorse in her beyond that of fear. It reminds me of my childhood, when I'd say something off-putting and immediately expect retribution.

I'm not sure what's more annoying—that she looks at me the way I used to look at Leiana, or that she thinks she knows me well enough to do so.

"No, no," I say with a smile, choosing to play along. "Tell me, what is it I lack?"

She tucks her chin to her chest and says much more shyly than I would've expected from someone so headstrong, "Gentlemanliness, maybe?"

"How so?"

"You nearly killed me."

"Did not," I reply.

"Did so."

I hold up my open palm, and shadows surge like storm clouds. "I'm in complete control, darling."

She tilts her head to the side. "Do you call me 'darling' to distract from your lack of gentlemanliness, or is it just what you call all the women in your life?"

"Only the powerful ones."

Desdemona huffs, and I find the ease with which I can annoy her to be a pleasantry. If I can get a rise out of her this easily, then I'll be able to get fire out of her as well.

"I've heard life expectancy doubles when you don't piss off Fire Folk," I say.

"Then maybe you should stop calling me 'darling.'" Her eyes stay locked on mine, and her lips curve into a smile as she jumps through the portal, leaving me thinking I've met my match in her.

I never would've expected her to be so amusing, not based upon our first meeting, where she was simply a liar. But she's proven me wrong. I almost enjoy talking to her. Which is a pity, because I will be forced to doom her.

The only thing I *need* before I do that is to get to The Void. If she's as sore with magic as she's shown herself to be—which is considerably doubtful, considering the liar she is and the power she exudes—then I will need to sharpen her potential so I can use it for myself.

But I can have a little fun before it comes to that.

I jump through the portal, the sand crunching beneath my feet as I reach the coast.

When I face Desdemona, she asks, "What now?"

"Start a fire."

She eyes the tree that was her target last time—still perfectly intact because she failed.

"Right," she mutters without looking at me.

But my eyes haven't parted from her once. I can't help the feeling that, if they do, I will miss something important. As if the answer to my question will be written on her face. Is this a show, or is she truly incapable of starting a fire?

"Yes, you can thank your humble upbringing in Utul for your difficulties," I say, though I don't believe it.

No one from Utul would be so ill-mannered. They start training their daughters to be debutantes practically from birth.

"Yes, Aibek, thank you for reminding me of *my* childhood," she spits.

Ill-mannered indeed. An effortless liar as well—only, she clenches her left hand.

"Anytime, Marquees."

She looks at me with a frown before her gaze shifts back to the tree. The look of determination scrunches her face in a way that feels odd. Fire Folk are known to be careless with their power. It shouldn't take strain to start a fire—it's why they often die by their own power.

I give her a few minutes before I ask, "Do you want help?"

"No," she says.

"I can—"

"I said no!" She groans, dropping her head into her hands.

"Is everything all right?"

"Yes," Desdemona sighs, breathing heavily into her palms. After a moment, she glances up. "Yes." She looks over her shoulder, toward the sea. "Is it windy, do you think?"

My gaze remains fixed on her. "Faintly, I suppose."

"Right, well," she scratches her ear, "I don't think fires and wind go together well. Maybe we could revisit this?"

"I'm not convinced that will be a problem."

What if Leiana gets to her before I can? Desdemona *is* the path to revenge. I have to take it before I lose it.

"Maybe it's for the better," she finally answers.

"And your mother?"

Her eyebrows knit together. "What?"

"Do you think that being weak will bode well for your mother?"

Desdemona stomps in my direction. "You don't know anything about—"

"I know she's somewhere you aren't able to get to. That even if you do find her, there's nothing you can do. Because you're weak."

Inches away from me, she stops, sneering. Heat rushes to her cheeks. "Do you really think I give a damn what you think, Prince?"

"Yes," I say. "Otherwise, you wouldn't be so flushed."

"Maybe I'm just warming up."

"By all means"—I raise my hands—"try to burn me."

She scoffs, a sound akin to a laugh, yet starkly devoid of humor. "We're done here."

I step toward her. "Perhaps we are. Normally when I court the Folk, I choose the ones with more... *pleasant* features."

She turns back to me. Perfect. "You think I'm here for *you?*"

"I do own a mirror."

"I am *here* for my *mother*," she speaks through gritted teeth.

"And what will she say when she sees you quitting? That you're living up to the family expectations?"

"*What?*"

"That you're going to die, *darling*," I say with a smile. "How else could I say it? That you're a failure, perhaps?"

Desdemona's eyes glow a magnificent orange, and I place my hands on her shoulders, twisting her around while whispering in her ear, "Tree."

The base of the tree, where the trunk meets the grass, glows the same orange as her eyes. The heat emanates through the air, searing my face even from a distance. It's glorious.

Desdemona glances from the fire to me, and the emotion in her eyes isn't the one I expected. She looks horrified.

Perhaps the powerless act hasn't been an act at all.

"Put it out," she demands, panic rising in her voice. "You have to put it out!"

The fire travels in a line from the tree, heading directly toward Desdemona. It takes me mere seconds to snuff it out with my shadows.

Desdemona spins on me, her face twisted in probable fury. She shoves me by the shoulders, nearly knocking me off balance. She's much stronger than I would've given her credit for, and I find myself excited at the prospect of her wielding a blade.

"I don't need you to belittle me to start a fire!" she roars.

But clearly, she does. We trained for hours the time before, and nothing came of it.

"What would you have preferred?" I retort. "That I fed you treats like a pet being potty trained?"

Her eyes burn into mine, her voice trembling with rage—or fear. "I hate you."

"Good," I whisper, leaning closer. "Power is emotion." I nod toward the path of the forgotten flame. "So keep your wits about you."

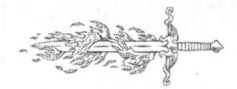

---

Azaire rubs his temples, the worry lines on his face deepening as he sits across from me at his desk.

I've just told him that I found Freyr Alpine—the last link to Desdemona's mother.

"You want to do this now?" Azaire sighs, his voice heavy.

"If you can spare it."

*I worry now is already too late.*

"Don't you want to think about this?"

I've thought about this endlessly. Isa's ties to the Arcanes make this more than a small secret—it's powder to the fuse. This is the first known kidnapping of my life, and the Arcanes are more partial to killing than keeping.

There's certainly something going on within Desdemona's family, waiting to be discovered.

"It's a weapon Folkara is working on," I tell him, looking for a bit of inspiration on his end.

Revenge and I were fast friends, inseparable companions by this point. Azaire was supportive until it became feasible. He hates being red-handed, but I don't mind spilling more blood for the life that was taken from me.

"Like?" He points to one of Yuki's swords.

"No. A weapon."

He nods and tugs at his beanie. With a sigh, he says, "What's the plan?"

I hand Azaire the photo of Freyr—our only lead. His orange hair and sharp, freckled face stand out among the Folk. Cynthia certainly meant *this* was Desdemona's father, not Dalin. And since Freyr is alive, it's a convenient twist of events.

"Are you feeling up to this?" I ask as Azaire examines the photo.

"Yeah." He looks up, nodding once. "I can do this."

Through his mirror, I open a portal to the lake Calista showed me—the closest and safest reflective surface near the coordinates. The facility itself is carved into the base of the tallest mountain, facing east toward the most remote area of Folkara. Calista's map leads us to the entrance, which should be steel—easy for Azaire to phase through.

When I spot the entrance, I hang back, finding a discreet place to hide. Then I give Azaire a nod. He melts into his surroundings, seamlessly blending with the mountains and trees.

Those are the two reasons I needed Azaire with me—his ability to phase through material and his invisibility are both powers of the Nepenthes.

When we're both comfortable in our positions, I sink into Azaire's mind. It's never easy to inhabit someone's subconscious, but Azaire doesn't push back, letting me travel through with ease before finding my place.

All at once, I see the world through his eyes and hear Azaire's voice in my head. *"Are you in?"* he asks.

*"Yes,"* I answer.

Azaire walks through the entrance, cautiously checking for any sign of life.

The entrance opens into a wide hallway. Its walls are made of the same rocky gray stone as the mountain, with iron piping running along them. Azaire slips through the hall and into what seems to be the main room. Inside, three tables line either side, each manned by Fire Folk shaping steel and gold.

We seldom work with gold; it's a rare material. Not only is it hard to find, but it's nearly impossible to excavate.

*"What are they making?"* Azaire asks.

*"I don't know."*

I spot Freyr in the very back corner, working on a piece of gold. He, like Isa, looks about twenty years older than the photo Cynthia gave me. Time has weathered him—his orange hair is cut close to the scalp, his freckles are covered in dirt—yet there are still some things time hasn't taken away.

He has Desdemona's mannerisms.

*"Last stall to the right."* My words slip through Azaire's mind.

*"Going in."*

*"Be careful."*

*"I know."*

Azaire approaches Freyr—who is none the wiser to his presence—and presses his invisible dagger to the Fire Folk's throat. Freyr's body freezes beneath the blade.

"I have a couple of questions for you," Azaire says, trying to keep his voice low while also making it menacing.

"Okay, okay," Freyr says as he reaches toward a scrap piece of metal, his hands blazing.

*"Left hand,"* I warn Azaire, and before I can even process the movement, he has Freyr's hand gripped and pinned behind him.

It's odd to *feel* Azaire using his super speed when I scarcely ever *see* it.

"Isa Althenia," Azaire whispers, his grip tightening around the dagger's handle. "What's her relation to the Arcanes?"

"She has none—" Freyr's words end in a hiss when Azaire tugs his arm tighter, nearly pulling his shoulder out of the socket.

"I don't know," Freyr breathes. "Isa had a friend, Willow Estridon, she'll know."

*"Estridon is Wendy's last name, Luc."*

For a brief moment, the current scene fades from my mind, replaced by a vision of a future fight I fear Azaire can't win. I push the image away as quickly as I can manage, trying to get back to Azaire.

*"Get out,"* I say, still stuck between my vision and reality. *"Now."*

As I come to, Azaire turns, and just as I foresaw, there are three welders closing in his general vicinity. Freyr reaches out, somehow catching Azaire's arm. The searing grip forces my best friend to drop the blade. It falls to the floor, no longer invisible.

"Zaire, beanie!" I shout, desperate. Without his serpents, I fear he won't make it out alive.

*"I'm not killing them, Luc."*

*"And if they kill you?"*

If they kill him after I brought him here—begged him to accompany me? He can't die for my grievances. I won't let him.

I reach deeper into Azaire's mind, fighting as if wading through quicksand. I claw for control of his body—his hands, his arms—desperate to tear the beanie from his head before it's too late.

But Azaire pushes back.

*"Lucian—I got it,"* he reprimands as he bolts for the back of the room.

But it's not good enough. It's not a way out. If he grows tired while phasing through the mountain walls, he could get stuck inside them, and I have no idea how far he'll need to go to break through to the other side.

"Not that way," I shout. *"Get to the entrance. The mountain walls will trap*

*you inside."*

Azaire doesn't stop. He runs right to the wall and then through the rock.

*"I can't get around the Folk,"* he tells me.

"You're going to get stuck, turn around," I warn him, but I want to plead. *Turn around, Azaire; please turn around. Run the other way.*

*"I'll be fine."* He pushes through—but phasing isn't an easy power. He can't stay immaterial forever.

*"You don't know how deep it goes,"* I warn.

Azaire's mind is growing tired. I'm going to lose him. He's going to lose his grip on his magic, and he'll get stuck within the mountain.

*"Turn around, Zaire, now,"* I beg.

*"I can't fight them."*

*"I can. Go back."*

*"If I do this, you* can't *kill them,"* Azaire says steadily.

I'd do anything to get him out of this alive, and if that means promising to do it morally, I will.

*"I swear it."*

At my words, I feel Azaire's mind yield, the quicksand softening to putty. He turns, stumbling through the rock, each step draining more of his strength.

I push deeper, forcing my way into Azaire's muscles, one tired but nimble limb at a time. Like a puppet, he moves under my control, advancing through the mountain and returning to the facility.

Azaire's fatigue is evident as his body sways. The room spins, and I focus, working to seize control of his mind entirely, channeling my energy into him.

To save him from the mess I made.

The men are back at work, two posted at the front—none had been guarding when Azaire went in—and the remaining two are each holding a piece of gold in their hands.

I'm slow to access Azaire's heightened agility, but once I do, I'll be able to get him out—despite his lack of fighting skills.

I move toward the exit.

"Do you smell that?" one of the guards asks, holding the dagger Azaire dropped.

"Flesh?" the other replies.

"Yeah."

Immediately, I know what they're referring to—Azaire's burnt flesh from where Freyr grabbed him. The adrenaline must have kept him from feeling it.

Both men guard the steel door, one sniffing the air like a dog.

*"Zaire,"* I call through the connection, my voice straining even within our minds. I need to know he's still there—still fighting, still alive. *"How are you holding up?"*

My pulse pounds in my ears as I search for even the faintest response, but he doesn't answer. I can hardly feel him. If he loses consciousness while I'm still in his mind—if he fades completely—I don't know what will happen. And I don't want to find out.

*"Zaire!"* I scream into the void of his mind. *"Answer me!"*

A dagger slices through the air. I yank back just in time to save his body from anything more than a shallow nick. It's enough to draw blood, though, and I feel it for what it is. The price of my distraction. The price of my *negligence*.

This is all my fault. If I had planned better. If I had gone with him. If I had done anything *differently*, he wouldn't be here, on the verge of death.

*"Zaire!"* I bellow, throwing a wild punch at the man holding the dagger.

It lands hard enough to send his weapon clattering to the floor. My fingers close around the hilt, slick with Azaire's blood. But the dagger doesn't vanish with Azaire's weakened body—too much of a giveaway. The man races straight for us.

*"I'm holding on,"* Azaire finally answers, his voice faint but there.

I take a deep breath I can't afford, relief threatening to subdue me before I save him.

Save him from *my* mess.

*"I'm getting you out,"* I reply, gripping the dagger tightly as I duck and drive it into the man's shoulder.

Another attacker lunges at me. My mind is stretched thin—splintering—trying to guide Azaire's faltering body while fending off these Folk.

I only have to get him to the exit.

I catch one leg with Azaire's hand—which is visible now, too weak to maintain his concealment—and shove the man to the ground. But it's not enough. Another Folk seizes Azaire's wrist, then his shoulder. Pain shoots through his body, jolting us both.

I manage to slam Azaire's elbow into the man's face. Over and over. Blood splatters. Finally, the man lets go. I kick another Folk down, and for one blessed moment, there's an opening.

I run for the door. I run with every ounce of strength left between Azaire and me. I *run*, pushing Azaire's body through the steel door and into hiding as I run with my own—nearly losing control of both of us as I balance our worlds.

With one final step, I reach Azaire, catching him as he collapses. I let go of his mind, returning fully to mine, and holding onto my friend. The shoulder of his shirt is burnt off, exposing blistered, pink skin. I touch a finger to his raw skin, my breath shaking—these are the consequences of my actions.

My stomach churns as I trace his wounds, my voice cracking as I whisper, "Zaire. Stay with me."

His eyes open briefly, a soft groan escaping him as a sob tears through me.

"You're alive," I whisper, though I didn't mean for the words to escape. I clutch him tighter. "Oh, gods, you're alive."

Barely conscious, Azaire whispers, "Take me to Wendy."

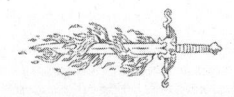

---

"Stay with me, Zaire," I mutter, out of breath as I rush through the academy halls with Azaire's limp body in my arms. Every step feels heavier than the last, my legs trembling under the weight of his stillness. I force myself to keep moving, each second slipping through my fingers.

I'm petrified that Azaire is going to slip away with it.

When I reach Wendy's suite, I pound on the door hard enough to make the wood rattle. "Wendy!" I shout, my breath hitching. "Are you in there? Open the damn door!"

A moment later, the door creaks open. Wendy appears, her eyes widening in shock as she clutches the doorframe. "Oh my gods," she whispers, stumbling back against her dresser, clutching a gloved hand over her mouth.

"Can you heal him?" I ask, my voice strained.

Wendy's training is far from finished, but I know why Azaire asked me to bring him here. Certified healers have restrictions on how much they can help a Nepenthe.

And he trusts her. That means I have to trust her, too.

Wendy steps forward, then stops. She stares at Azaire, sucking her trembling lip between her teeth and shaking her head like she's afraid of him. "Why can't I feel him?"

Because of me. Because I overrode his faculties and pushed him too far. I drained every ounce of strength from his body.

"Please," I beg, the word breaking free before I can stop it. "You have to try."

If I hadn't seen the vision, if I hadn't told him to get out, would this have happened? Is this my fault in more ways than one?

Wendy meets my gaze, her breath as uneven and panicked as mine. Almost imperceptibly, she nods, her gaze shifting from fear to determination. "Put him on the bed."

I lay Azaire on the bed, reluctant to let him go, scared that my will is what's held him together. He looks so weak, so fragile. His face is pale, and his breaths are shallow.

Wendy's hands are trembling as she hands me a glass jar. "This," she breathes. "Put it in his nose and mouth."

I do as instructed, the purple powder clinging to my fingers as I dust it around his face. My arms feel weighted, as if I'm still carrying Azaire's body, as if my conscience is wading through murky waters.

My hands shake so viciously, I can barely cork the bottle—the bottle that's now red, coated in the blood of my brother.

I fall back, sitting on a chair in the corner of the room, watching Wendy save Azaire. Watching her save him from *me*.

She pulls off her gloves, holding her hands over Azaire's torso, but not touching him. Vibrant green energy flows from her palms and into his body. I sink into my seat, watching nervously as she puts her glove back on and rubs a salve onto the burns. Then she starts again with her magic.

"Come on, Zaire," I whisper absently, pleading with the gods, watching in a daze as Wendy finishes.

"It'll be a few days," she says. As she turns to face me, I realize her face is slick with sweat.

But all I hear is: *He'll be all right.*

He's going to make it.

"What happened?" Wendy asks, pulling me from the haze I've fallen into.

I shake my head, running a hand across my face, trying to wake myself up. Dried blood flakes from my skin with the motion.

"It's not safe to talk here," I whisper.

"Then where?"

"Past the barrier. By the coast."

She looks at me like I've lost my mind, then glances back at Azaire. "Fine."

As she walks to the exit of her suite, I fall back, not wanting to leave Azaire. I stare at his still form.

Wendy catches my gaze, saying, "He'll be safe here."

I suppose she felt my hesitance—she's a Eunoia, after all—but I hardly feel reassured.

We make our way to the coast in tense silence, and as we walk, I sort through my options. I don't want to tell her, and I know I have to. Once the words leave my mouth, there is no taking them back.

But what choice do I have? There's no easy explanation.

We stop at the coast, and Wendy stands, waiting for an answer while I look out at the sea—squinting against the sun.

"They're back," I finally say. "Monster attacks have started again, and they coincide with the re-emergence of the Arcanes."

When I was six, Leiana and Labyrinth outlawed any mention of the Arcanes, wiping all records of their existence. This very conversation is treason, and I've pulled Wendy into it.

But if Freyr was telling the truth, Wendy might already be involved. Willow Estridon—that's Wendy's surname. It could be her mother.

Her steps falter, and she turns to me, her eyes darting between me and the woods, just behind the coast. "Monsters are attacking and you brought me outside the barrier?"

"There are none on Visnatus," I say.

"That could change at any minute!" She edges back toward the woods.

"If it does, I can take care of it."

*The way I took care of Azaire?*

In the brief moments of silence, I fear that's what Wendy will say. It's hardly uncalled for. It's the right thing to say.

Perhaps I can't take care of anything.

Instead, she only whispers, "Why are you involving me in this?"

"Someone was taken by the Arcanes," I say, lowering my voice, though no one is around to hear. "I tracked down the one person who might have a detail I'm missing." I pause, but I'm not finished. "He gave me your mother's name: Willow Estridon. I suppose she was involved."

Wendy freezes, her eyes widening in shock—the name certainly rang a bell. She takes a deep breath and says, "Go on."

I oblige. "Eighteen years ago, a woman faked her death. Your mother knows why. We were told to find her."

Her voice tightens. "Was she the one taken by the Arcanes?"

"Yes."

"What was her name?"

I take a breath, knowing this is the point of no return. I'm taking her too deep into this. Yet, she's already a part of it by the simple matter of her bloodline.

"Isa Althenia."

Wendy's expression hardens, her face unreadable. "Next time, don't be vague about matters regarding my mom." Her voice is sharp, raw, nearly angry—but there's something else. She pauses, lips parting as if there's something she wishes to say but is failing to find the words. "But you were sent on a fool's errand," she finishes.

My heart sinks. "How so?"

Her eyes meet mine, her lips curving into a frown. "My mom is dead."

## Chapter 11
## This Oath is a Lie

# DESDEMONA

"You know you need a dress," Aralia mumbles while she puts the glamoured mascara on her eyelashes.

I stop, my fingers freezing midway through buttoning my uniform shirt. "A dress?" I ask, caught off guard.

I've been wearing her clothes since I got here—which, truthfully, I'm grateful for. She hasn't said a thing about my lack of funds, and thanks to her, no other student has noticed.

"For the Gerner," she says with surprise, like I should already know. Of course, I probably should. She's going to be the first to learn I'm the worlds' biggest liar if I don't up my knowledge.

Suddenly, I'm frustrated that after all the time I've spent with Leiholan, he never bothered to mention this Gerner.

"Right," I say with a forced smile.

Looking at herself in the mirror and running a comb through her hair, Aralia says, "After class, we'll go to my favorite seamstress."

The comb is embellished with gemstones that could feed my mom and me for a year. Or years.

She wraps a braid around her head like a crown and turns to face me. "Don't worry about the cost."

Yeah, she knows too much, and I can't tell if that's good or bad.

I stop in the kitchen before class, picking up a piece of warm toast slathered with jam as I say, "Morning, Elowen." I'm gonna miss this when I'm back home.

"Grand day, Desdemona," she says.

I've spoken to her enough to know a few things. She grew up in Arson's Alley, a place that sounds far too much like home. Working as a chef in Visnatus is more than she'd ever dreamed. She enjoys this job. I enjoy our chats. I'm almost certain she's been able to recognize the telltale signs that I'm from the septic, and I'm also certain that I have enough of her trust that she'd never say anything.

I take a bite of the bread and jam, unable to suppress a groan.

"What *is* this?" I ask.

"Wild berry," she answers, and I'm sure she knows I've never tasted something so rare.

"From Eunaris?" I ask. It's the Eunoias' world; they supply the elites with agriculture.

The rest of us get nothing but what we can find.

Elowen offers me a conspiratorial smile and a little nod. "It goes great with cheese," she says and slides me a plate of soft, runny cheese.

My mouth waters. "You're my favorite Eunoia here. Maybe even my favorite person," I tell her, plopping the cheese onto the bread and then into my mouth. I've never tasted something so good, but I could say that about everything Elowen makes.

"Now you're just being mendacious," she says, her deep laugh echoing through the kitchen.

Mendacious. One of those words Leiholan taught me. I wonder who taught it to her.

"Trust me, I have my moments, but this isn't one of them." I say again, "My favorite."

Pinching a little flour, she flicks it at me, laughing as it dusts my face. "Get to class, kid."

"See you at lunch, adult."

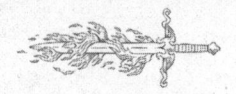

Psychology class has to be my least favorite. Except for the fact that I suck at Elemental Magic, never get picked in Combat Training, and don't like talking about gods who've never given me a damn thing.

I guess they're all my least favorites.

But when Hogan tells us to come up with a new way to inspire compliance among the masses—the masses being *my* people—my stomach churns with something between fire and vomit.

I think maybe I could be *great* at elemental magic.

*Maybe I could burn this whole place down.*

Hogan also tells us to "think outside the box" and "find a partner." The students beside me stand up immediately, getting as far away from me as they can, and I sit here awkwardly. I'm sure I could do this by myself. Or just not at all. I don't care about the grade, and I don't want to think about how to further torture my people.

But Lucian slides into the newly open seat next to me, and I avoid meeting his gaze.

"Partners?" he asks, and—still avoiding him—I glance up at a pair of green eyes that bore into me.

It's a Eunoia—who can likely feel my disdain for the prince next to me. Disdain that, if noticed, could be grounds for execution.

"I think someone else has the same question," I mutter, watching Lucian's eyes trail to the Eunoia with the brightest white hair I've ever seen.

"Eleanora!" she shouts, her tone clipped before she shifts her focus back to us. "It'll be a group effort," she says as she sits next to Lucian, shoving him even closer to me.

On my other side, a Folk with curly hair—brown streaked

with blonde—sits. *Eleanora,* I presume. She stares at me like I'm her prey, and I'm suddenly grateful for the mental wards I may or may not have because I couldn't afford someone seeing my memories.

"I'm Desdemona—" I start.

"Fleur," the Eunoia interrupts, reaching past Lucian to offer me her hand.

I don't take it at first, knowing that skin-to-skin contact gives an edge to their empathetic magic. But when her smile tightens, I reluctantly grab the Eunoia's hand.

Fleur's grip is far from firm, and her skin is far from calloused. I've never touched hands so soft before. Even Lucian's are rough and ragged.

"Eleanora," the Folk with the curly hair sings from beside me. I force a smile. "Fair to make your acquaintance."

"Yes," I say, drawing out the word. "Very fair."

Lucian chuckles, and the sound is almost comforting amidst this tension, but Fleur drowns it out when she says, "So why is the prince so interested in you?"

"I don't know," I say flatly, eyes fixed on Fleur. "Maybe you could ask the prince."

Lucian's eyes meet mine, playfully, teasingly. A kind of gaze he's taken up with me before—but not the kind I choose to return. "She and I have a common interest," he answers.

I resist the urge to tell him off, only because we have an audience. We couldn't be *more* different—this very school project proves that. A prince and a pauper will never see eye to eye.

The Eunoia begins, "And what's that—"

"*Fleur,*" Eleanora huffs. "We have an assignment."

"Right," I mumble at the same time that Lucian smugly says, "We do."

The prince looks at me then, seemingly amused.

"Any ideas, Marquees?" His voice is light, but he knows what he's asking. Ideas on how to make people suffer *more*.

That's who he *is*.

A prince who, if he even realizes how wrong this is, clearly doesn't care. He seems to see it as just another reason to poke at me, to have his fun, entirely oblivious to the lives he's ruining.

The lives he's taking.

*And I thought there was blood on my hands.*

I may have killed two, but Lucian's killed thousands. Inadvertently or otherwise.

But I have a role to play. "Well, the textbook already spells out the basics we need to rely on," I say. "Lack of free time, exhaustion, hunger. Once you have that, you make pretty pictures and simple words."

*Your hard work makes the worlds go round.*

My mind is bombarded by those *pretty pictures* and *simple words*, and it disgusts me that these people here think that we people there don't see past it.

The things that actually keep us down are the lack of energy to fight and the physical repercussions if we try.

But no, to these three—to this whole school—we're just dumb. Barely more than an animal.

"Yeah," Fleur laughs, "that sounded like a whole lot of nonsense." The Eunoia looks from me to Lucian, her green eyes faintly glowing. "From the sample propaganda we saw, I think there's a lack of emotional ties. Maybe add children or something?"

"Oh!" Eleanora says, like she has some bright idea. "Like instead of only lashing the perpetrator, lash their children, too."

*They already do that.*

I think I'm going to be sick.

*I've* been a child tied to those posts. And if anyone here knew that, they'd likely kill me, so I force myself not to puke at the thought of tying *more* children to those posts.

"And loved ones," Fleur says, fiddling with her nails like she's *bored*. "Punish the whole family, friends, beloveds."

*Punish the already starving people who are only trying to survive.*

"I don't know," Lucian sings, sitting back in his chair. I *hate* him. "It sounds rather routine."

"Well, if you want to vary routine, you could try actually *feeding* them," I say through my teeth, too bitter for it not to be emotional. "I mean…" My voice *almost* shakes as I try to save myself. "Hogan—Mr. Bayley—told us to think outside the box. I think it'd be easier to control a population of happy people who don't realize they're missing anything." I look down fast, but not before I see Lucian smiling.

"As if," Fleur scoffs, just as Eleanora says, "Yeah right."

But the prince surprises me, almost seeming human as he says, "That could work. At the very least, it could get us the top score." Both the girls scoff, and I'm appalled. This is a grade to them and a reality to me. "Think about it. Who else is going to offer that we treat them *better?*" His hand extends to me. "And Marquees has a point; if you don't know there's anything more to fight for, then you're not fighting."

"Yeah," I say too sullenly, so I look up and smile and hope that it looks like I'm doing more than just baring my teeth. "Exactly."

---

Leiholan calls out the names for the first round of challenges in Combat Training, then the second, and the third, and I've lost all hope that he'll call my name this time. Or ever. The students are going to start to talk soon.

Luckily, I manage to make it through class without watching Lucian and Yuki too much.

Then I go to Leiholan.

"What's the Gerner?" I can feel the scowl painted on my face, my lips being perpetually pushed down anytime I'm in his presence.

"Fundraiser for the school," he says, not bothering to look at me. "All the money made from the clothes and decorations goes back to 'em."

"You mean the school *takes* the money back?" I ask.

He smiles, and I can tell by now that this is one of those highly unamused smiles. "Look at you, perceptive. Who would've thought." He claps for me like I'm a child. "And make sure when you're stealing from the already poor seamstresses that you get a silver or blue dress."

I consider grabbing the bottle of alcohol beside him and drinking it all myself. Instead, I ask, "Why?"

"Ilyria's colors," he says. Like I didn't already know that. "Founders of the school. Blah, blah, blah."

"You never thought that this was important for me to know before?" I ask.

But it's rhetorical, and he knows it, I'm sure. He's annoying, not dense.

"Must've slipped my mind," Leiholan replies, equally annoyed.

I clench my jaw. "Well, my roommate almost found out I'm a filthy septic liar because of you!"

He matches my nasty tone. "*Or* the school thinks you're a perfect Utul princess *because of me*."

"I don't like you," I say like a child. I have no better words.

Leiholan laughs, like my irritation amuses him. "The feeling is mutual, *sweetheart*."

I say nothing, worried I'll sound furious or—even worse—wounded. Walking backward, I give him two thumbs up, then a middle finger, as I storm out of the room, heading to the suite.

I'm about ready to throw a dagger at someone's throat, which has become much too common a longing as of late.

Back in the room—Aralia's room? Our room? I don't know anymore—Aralia is lying upside down on the bed. Her eyes meet mine, then they roll.

"*Finally*," she says, and she's on her feet in seconds.

It takes too much effort to say anything other than, "Ready?"

"Yep."

She extends her arm toward me, bending it at the elbow. I think she's expecting me to clasp mine to hers, and I don't know how to tell her I'd prefer not to touch her, so I bite my tongue and just do it. But Aralia frowns and says, "I don't want you to get lost in the portal."

That's somewhat sweet—she doesn't want me to die. If I were on the other end of this conversation, I'd let her take her chances.

She opens the portal, but it only grows to her height, so I hunch through.

The air shifts as I step onto a bustling street. Merchants shout, haggling over their goods, their voices mixing with the hum of the crowd. It reminds me of the Saul back home, but richer, more vibrant. There are fruits and vegetables I've never seen, newspapers, jewelry, and trash everywhere.

Trash is a luxury where I come from.

Broken bits of roofs, entire doors, glass, and fabric scraps litter the cobblestone street. Back home, we'd scavenge every bit of it.

Back home, we didn't have cobblestone on our floors.

"*This* is where you get your clothes?" I'm genuinely surprised, but sounding like a snob will only help my case.

"Only my dresses," Aralia answers. "Portricia is the *best*, trust me."

"I wasn't talking about the seamstress; I was talking about the village," I say.

"It's not a village." She gives me a look, up and down, assessing me. "It's Arson's Alley."

By her tone, it's clear I should've known that.

But it seems like we both disregard it when Aralia pulls me through the street. She doesn't even flinch when a possum scurries by. I wonder if I should've and make a mental note to at least fake a yelp next time.

The door we enter is made of glass, which means the people of Arson's Alley can't be as poor as they look. They're getting *our* handiwork.

A tall woman with streaks of gray in her black hair greets us. "Oh, Aralia, you look stunning as always." The woman smiles in a way that lights up her entire face—including her gray eyes.

I inch back before she can get too close.

Aralia *hugs* the Nepenthe. "As do you, Portricia." Then she gestures to me. "This is Desdemona. She also needs a dress for the Gerner."

*Portricia* eyes me up and down, and I smile as best as I can.

All the Nepenthe says is, "Gold."

"Excuse me?" I try not to sound offended.

"Your complexion," Portricia says. "It's suited for gold, not silver. I'll put you in gold."

"Gold?" I echo, trying to hide my confusion. I've never seen gold—but if she knows about it *here*, I'd be expected to know it in Utul. "But Ilyria's colors are silver and blue," I say. That was Leiholan's only instruction.

"Yes, they are, but I don't dress my clients for Ilyria. I dress them for themselves. And you, sweets, are a gold."

"I don't want to stand out," I say sheepishly.

I'm already so used to all eyes on me—and not in a good way. They're always either fearful or full of pity. I don't want more of that.

Or, worse, someone noticing what they shouldn't.

"I couldn't in good conscience put you in silver!" Portricia basically shouts.

"How about blue?" I ask.

"How about I put you in both, and you can decide." The Nepenthe smiles, flashing her venomous fangs, and whispers, "But you'll choose gold."

"Fine," I say.

Portricia claps, but only with the tops of her hands. "Splendid!"

Aralia smiles at me, and I give her an unsure smile back.

The next thing I know, Aralia and I are standing in front of a mirror while Portricia covers me in dark-blue fabrics. She wraps them around my arms and waist with precision, then does the same for Aralia, but with silver.

I try not to shrink back when Portricia's skin touches me.

"Remember how the blue looks, sweets," she says while she chews on something.

And then she covers me in the most beautiful fabric I've ever had the good luck to see, let alone wear.

Portricia pulls the gold fabric snugly against my waist. The dress drapes low and loose around my chest, with straps wrapping around my neck, creating a slight choking effect. I can't see the back, but it feels entirely bare. Good thing I'm wearing Hogan's glamour over my scars. The dress ends above my ankles, and Portricia pins extra material so that it flows down to my feet.

"A leg slit?" she asks from the floor.

"Definitely a leg slit," Aralia answers for me.

I can't take my eyes away from my reflection. I look... I don't know how I look, but it's different than I've ever looked—ever felt—before. So different that I can't stop looking.

I think I like the idea of showing up in the wrong color. It's the smallest "screw you" I could manage to make, but it's something. A middle finger to this elite world that does nothing but take from me.

A cool draft brushes my thigh—Portricia's cut the dress almost to my hip. I don't have the energy to feel threatened by the shears in her hands. I just feel... different. A warm feeling bubbles in my chest, and I can't help but smile. Really, really smile. I can feel it, like a laugh, like a hug. I'm happy over a dress, I guess, which feels ridiculous, but suddenly I'm thinking that this feeling is so rare, so fleeting, that I'll do anything to hold onto it.

I look at Portricia, into her gray eyes. "Thank you," I tell her, and I mean it.

She waves a hand through the air. "Anytime, sweets." Then she pulls my hands into gloves that reach halfway up my bicep, the same shimmering gold as my dress.

I'm still smiling when I look over at Aralia, whose dress shines like a silver star, shimmering with every move she makes.

"You look like a star," I tell her.

She smiles, and her too-big teeth are on full display. She'll grow into them, and I get the swelling feeling that I am glad I get to see them before she does.

"Thank you, Desy."

She reaches for my hand and holds on, rubbing her thumb against it. It takes effort not to pull my hand from hers. I guess this is what friends do if that's what she thinks of us. Which she must, if she's paying for my dress.

"Desy?" I ask.

I'm slightly relieved when she takes back her hand. "Do you like it?"

"It's better than Inferno," I mumble.

"I'll take that as a yes."

I catch a glimpse of my reflection again. The warmth bubbling in my chest feels foreign. I smile, a real smile, and for the first time, I let myself enjoy it.

Portricia tells us it'll take her three days to have our dresses ready thanks to her super speed, which leaves me guessing that three days is fast.

"That's why you're the best, Trish," Aralia says, pulling out a little blue bag. She collects a huge handful of silver coins and puts them in Portricia's hands.

"Aralia." Portricia smacks Aralia's upper arm with the back of her hand. "This is too much!"

"Hide the extra," Aralia whispers with a wink and a smirk.

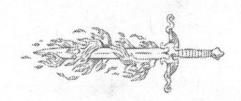

As per my routine, the next day I go to Leiholan before class, who I'm getting *really* fed up with. He's always drinking and rambling, and I swear he does it just to get on my nerves. But he teaches me to fight—the skill I need to save my mom—so I keep coming back.

Immediately, Leiholan starts rambling about how I need the kids to *think* I am important, even though I'm just septic scum. He doesn't say that exactly, but it's what he meant.

"Can we fight now?" I cut him off, my grip tightening around the hilt of my sword.

Leiholan grins lazily, his eyes bloodshot and far from sober. He points at me, his mouth opening in anticipation. Then it all fades. "No!" he shouts, grabbing his bottle from his desk and taking a sip. "Drunk. And getting more so."

"Leiholan?"

"Hm."

I lift my dual blade. "Draw your sword."

With his eyes on my hands, he lets out a half-drunken chuckle. "Sweetheart, with one swing, I'd knock that thing outta your hands."

I drop the weapon to my side, one end of the dual sword poking into the floor. It's a real pretty thing. The hilt between the two blades is silver—*real* silver—with blue stones engraved where the handle meets the blade. Completely pointless. It's made to injure someone, not put on a show. But if Damien's dagger could get a bottle of rena, I wonder what this could manage.

"Pick it up," he groans, and I do. His hands wrap around mine, guiding them into place. Immediately, I feel the difference, almost as if he added muscle to my arms. When he's finished, he pulls his sword from the sheath at his waist. "All right, sweetheart. Swing."

I do as he asks, swinging again and again, every screech of the clashing metal vibrating up my arms. But even drunk, Leiholan blocks my hits like he's swatting at a fly. With my blade struggling against his, he flips his down, fast and precise, causing my sword to drop from my hands.

"What are you? Scared of hurting me?" Leiholan scoffs—assessing me like I'm a book that's so easily read. "Come on now."

"Trust me." I pick up my sword. "The last thing I'm scared of is hurting *you*."

But is that true? It was only a few days ago that I started a fire—felt the same sick, electric rush I felt when I murdered two Folk. It was awful.

It was *power*.

Leiholan lazily presses his blade into my chest and keeps it there. "The weapon's not a weapon. It's an extension of you. Prove it."

I knock his blade aside with my own, then swing again. Yeah, maybe I'm scared of hurting *someone*, but I'm not scared of hurting *him*. A Nepenthe deserves it. I bring my sword back down on him, and I get another lovely speculation.

"You're predictable."

I don't have time for his babbling. I swing, and he knocks my sword almost out of my hand, but I flip it around in time, raising the other end of my dual blade. Again, and our swords are locked in battle, each taunting the other with the threat of losing.

Leiholan, much to my annoyance, continues, "You always step with your left foot before you swing to the right, which is your most preferred move." He knocks the sword from my hand, and I nearly scream in frustration as the metal clatters on the ground. "It makes you predictable."

*Not all of us can slip out of life with a bottle of alcohol and a habit of annoying his students.*

"And you pivot to your right before you aim for my torso. Or bend your left knee before you aim for my heart. *Every time*," I say between gritted teeth. "Predictable. But I still can't seem to beat you." I pick up my sword. "Predictability isn't the problem."

Leiholan just laughs. "Okay, sweetheart. Let's try again, and this time

*you* tell me the problem."

He must enjoy pushing my buttons.

I hate the Nepenthes.

Three fights and zero wins later, I try to leave, but Leiholan stops me, saying, "You have a better eye than I thought."

I sneer at him, my lips curling in disdain. "Guess you should scrap whatever else you thought. Or maybe not, seeing as I'm so *predictable*."

"I was *trying* to give you a compliment," Leiholan grumbles.

It's like fate has given me a gift—this time, I get to laugh at Leiholan's stupid comment. "Well, I didn't ask for one."

"My gods, Desdemona. If you could be a *nice* person for just" —he raises his thumb and middle finger, holding them close— "a second of your time, you'd get a lot further than you think!"

"That's rich," I say, my voice deep with humor.

"I already know where you're going with that, and I don't want to hear it." He shakes his head and crosses his arms. What? He's really just... giving up?

"How would you know anything?" I shout. "Right, right! I'm sorry I forgot—I'm predictable."

Leiholan just looks me in the eye, shaking his head slowly. "Because I know you, sweetheart, much to my distaste." His voice is laced with the venom that he holds in his teeth. "I may be drunk most of the time, but all I do is help you, and all you do is bite me."

I laugh bitterly. "Then why do you insist on helping me?" I start listing all of my less-than-pleasant qualities he's bestowed upon me on my fingers. "I'm insufferable, distasteful, unlikeable, predictable! Is there anything else you want to add?"

He sucks in his cheeks, and I can see the indentations of his fangs, reminding me of what he is, what he does. But his words sound the opposite of menacing when he speaks. "I've been where you are."

I think of my mom, trapped and probably tortured. Then I have to stop myself from thinking. I look him in the eye and say, "Doubtful."

I'm more than ready to leave—until I remember there's something I still need from him.

As he takes a long pull from his bottle of vesi, I wonder if he's right. I'm about to ask for his help—again. Did I not just bite him?

I know I did—but he bit me first.

"Thank you," I spit, the words tasting acidic on my tongue. Leiholan only nods, frowning. "And my apologies," I add quickly, getting it over with.

Leiholan laughs, a full, deep laugh. A real one. "You know, I wasn't holding my breath." He sits down on the floor, smiling at me like he's a kid and I've just given him something sweet. "What do ya want?"

I think of all the Nepenthes I've encountered, how they treated us Folk, trying to fight the strange guilt rising inside of me for someone as vile as him.

"I don't want anything—" I start.

Leiholan cuts me off. "Like I said, sweetheart, I know you."

Now I'm wondering if he really does. I mean, he saw right through me. The thought is anything but comforting.

"The Gerner," I say reluctantly. "I got a gold dress."

"Gold?" He laughs, clapping once. "Oh, sweetheart, you're going to be the belle of the ball." His words drip with sarcasm.

I ignore his laughter the way I wish I could ignore some of the other things he's said. "What do I do?"

He shrugs and takes another sip of vesi. "Use it to your advantage."

When he says nothing more, I ask the obvious question: "How?"

"By doing what I've been telling you to." He waves his hand in the air, saying, "Walk the walk. Show them what you're made of. Can you waltz?"

"I've never worn a dress before," I say, instead of the much more telling fact that I've never heard the word *waltz*.

"It's a dance," Leiholan explains, and I grow embarrassed at how easily he saw through me *again*. "Learn. And fast."

"I can't exactly tell anyone that I don't know how to dance," I whisper, but not harshly, the way I'd like to. I'm trying hard to be nice, see if it really gets me as far as he thinks it will.

"Say your parents sheltered you. Most balls in Utul are for debutantes, and the kids here know that." He smirks, raising an eyebrow. "Lucian knows that."

"I don't know what you're talking about," I say, making sure to maintain eye contact and *not* overheat when I think about who else has watched me watch him in class.

"Oh, please—"

I cut him off, my voice sharp. "And how do you know any of this? About the debutantes and Utul?"

Leiholan gets real quiet. He looks down and says, "I haven't been home in a while." And that's the only answer I get.

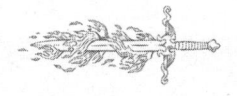

---

The next time I meet Lucian by the lake, I ask if we can dance instead of train—which is a change that I welcome because I don't like starting fires or being provoked into starting a fire.

"Why would we dance?" he asks, watching me with amusement in his eyes. It's something I've gotten used to, seeing as amusement seems to be his default emotion.

"I don't know how," I answer quickly. I'm good at lying, but I hate showing my cards. "My parents were strict."

The prince nods, like it all makes sense now. "That puts much into perspective."

I cross my arms over my chest, instinctively trying to hide myself. "What does that mean?"

"You're gauche." He smirks. "A terrible flirt, too."

I give him a quick—annoyed—flash of a smile back. "Just teach me how to waltz."

"Certainly, darling. But not here." He gestures to the nature around us.

Without arguing, I follow him back to the school and up dark, narrow steps. He grabs my hand, gently guiding me left and right, over and over, leading me effortlessly through the dim halls, until we enter a room I didn't know existed.

"What is this place?" I ask when the lights flicker on. The room is huge, with an entire wall of dusty books on shelves, fancy clothes on racks, and foreign silver and wood contraptions on counters.

"The floor was made for the Royals, back when every world had monarchies." He pushes a round table from the middle of the room and into a corner lined with bookshelves, then dusts the contraptions. "Now it's just my family and Kai's, and we don't come here often."

An entire floor, unused, while back home we have whole families living in a room this size.

Music fills the room, pulling me from my thoughts. It doesn't sound anything like the music I've heard in my life. It's slow, with various sounds and tones melding together. The music I know is upbeat, something they play in the factories to get the Folk's feet moving when they're tired or to lift spirits when they're down over the many things there are to be down about.

*Music must serve a very different purpose to the elites.*

Then Lucian *bows* on one knee, offering his hand to me. I worry I'm not doing a good job of hiding how utterly shocked I am. "My pleasure," he says, and I grab his hand.

He stands back, guiding one of my hands to the back of his neck. I don't mean to pull away as he reaches for my waist, but I do.

"We can switch positions for practice, but you'll be expected to dance the part of a lady during the Gerner," Lucian says, not at all unkindly.

I prefer his usual mocking edge. *Kind* is not a word I want to put to the prince, even for a second.

"It's fine."

I step forward, and his hand comes back to my waist. His grip is lighter now, hesitant, like he doesn't want to touch me—a far cry from before.

He explains how I'm supposed to move my feet, then says, "Just follow my lead," like I don't understand.

"Your explanation was lesson enough."

Lucian's hands skim down my hips, his grip barely there before he lets go entirely. "If you already know how, we don't have to dance."

I tighten my hold on the back of his neck, pulling him closer. "Just start."

"Unless this was all a ploy to get your hands on me." He leans in—close but still not touching—his lips hovering much too close to my ear and amusement flashing in his eyes. "If so, well played, Marquees. I've been waiting for you to make a move."

I laugh under my breath, drop my hands, and take a step back. "You have quite the ego."

"And you're bruising it right now, letting go of me like that."

"So *you're* the one who wants my hands on you?" I smile up at him.

Lucian smiles back. Different from his usual smirk. This is big, bright. The kind that highlights the dimples I didn't know he had. "I didn't think that had to be said aloud."

Is he *flirting* with me? It's by sheer force of will that my cheeks don't flush.

I grab his hand and put it on my waist. "Then you better milk it for all it's worth," I say, trying not to grit my teeth. Then I decide to just grit my teeth—better for Lucian to think I'm angry at him than myself. "Because this is the first and *last* time."

"You know," he says, lifting his hand from my waist to tuck a loose piece of hair behind my ear, "you're a temperamental little thing."

I hit his hand with the back of mine. "Am not."

"Oh, no." He lifts his hand with a smile. There's a red mark where I hit him. "Of course you aren't. My mistake."

"Is that a problem? Because I'm thinking of stepping on your toes next."

He *laughs*. I don't want to like the sound. "Anything but. I find it amusing."

I raise an eyebrow and ask, "You like when people step on your toes?"

"No, darling. I'd like to watch you *try*."

"Start dancing," I demand.

I watch our feet at first. He steps forward with his left foot, and I step back, just like he said. But when it's my turn to step forward, I aim right for his foot.

He steps back quickly with a laugh.

When his foot comes forward for *mine*, I pull my leg up. "Hey!"

Lucian smiles at me. "It's only fair."

"Okay, okay." I meet his gaze.

*Nothing about the worlds between us is fair.*

And I smile. "Truce?"

"Do you think I'd believe that for one second?" Lucian asks.

I pucker my lips, and in one fast movement, I smother his shoe under mine. "Nope," I let out the word with a giggle.

"Dirty work, darling."

"It's what I'm best at"—I smile—"*darling*."

"And there I was calling you gauche."

I step in, tugging a piece of his dark wavy hair out of his face, mimicking his earlier move. "A horrible mistake," I whisper mockingly. "I'm quite the flirt when I want to be."

Lucian grabs my hand where I had smacked his. "I knew I made you want to be a flirt, Marquees. Is it the hair? Or the eyes?"

He smirks, tracing lazy circles on my wrist. It shouldn't feel this good. I shudder at the sensation that ripples through me—the burning, the adrenaline, the churning in my stomach.

But I don't back away. Backing away would be a confession—to both myself and the prince.

"More like a sense of superiority," I mutter, and he grabs my waist, pulling me closer. My breath catches. I don't let it happen again when I say, "Someone has to put you in your place."

"If my place is here," Lucian says, his gaze drifting from my hand—still held in his—to my waist. "I'd say you should put me in my place more often."

I will not let his touch bother me. I do not care that his hands are on my body.

That his *eyes* are on my body.

I do not care.

"You still want to try to step on my toes, don't you?" I ask because I do care, and I need to back away before he notices.

Lucian's quiet for a moment, his fingers still drawing lazy circles on my wrist. Then, in a low murmur, he says, "How could I possibly think about anything else when my hands seem to be affecting you this much?"

This time, I can't stop the heat rising in my cheeks.

"Well, I happen to like beating you," I say, twisting out of his hold. "So give me your all, Prince."

He smirks, quickly rising to my challenge. "Oh, darling. I was planning on it."

His right foot rushes toward mine, and I twirl out of the way and around him, running to the other side of the room and surprising myself with a laugh. A *real* laugh. The kind that leaves me breathless.

He pursues, laughing right along with me. We stand, facing one another across the table he moved behind me. He makes mock movements toward me, and I pretend to step back, but neither of us stretches the distance between us.

The prince runs for me, and I jump on top of the dusty table. He waves his hand in the air and sneezes.

"You should get used to the dust, seeing as I'm gonna leave you in it," I tease.

He comes to the edge of the table. "How do you feel about flying?"

"What?"

The prince lifts me by my legs, then sets me back down and promptly steps on my toes.

"Not fair!" I laugh, grabbing his shoulders for balance as his hands wrap around my waist, steadying me.

He shrugs. "A page from your playbook."

"Quick study," I say.

"And there you were, talking about dust or something like that."

"Leave you in the dust," I correct, lifting my chin. "You've never heard anyone say that?"

He shakes his head. "No."

"Oh." I laugh, feeling a little silly now. "It's just like saying you'd surpass someone."

Suddenly, his hands feel very hot on my skin.

What is *wrong* with me?

This is the prince, someone who'd likely have me killed for a discretion like... kicking a rock. Or something. I just need to make sure he's on my side, because so far, he's the only one with the means to find my mom.

And I still think he knows more than he lets on.

"A dance?" I ask.

Lucian releases one side of my waist and grabs my hand. "I thought you'd never ask."

The dance is simple, really. The only thing that has the power to make me lose focus is the fact that his touch burns through my shirt.

I look up at him with a smug smile after three rounds of monotonous dancing.

"See?" I say, raising my eyebrows. "Easy."

In response, the prince spins me to the side and tilts me down so fast that I don't know what's happening until I feel his hand pressed to the small of my back, keeping me from falling to the floor, and I'm staring up into his midnight eyes. I never noticed before that there's a lighter shade of blue around his pupils, like the rarity of light in the night sky back home.

I never noticed the little divot in the middle of his bottom lip either.

He leans in closer and whispers, "Don't get cocky."

My heart beats so fast that I fear he can feel it. I just swallow and say, "I think cocky is your territory. It goes with your ego."

Then he pulls me up, drawing me a little closer to him. I do the same.

"The one you refuse to stroke?" Lucian says.

"There are other kinds of flattery." I dare to look him right in the eye. "If you can prove to me that you deserve them."

"Consider me at your mercy."

But I was wrong—there is another thing that can make me lose my focus.

The whispering.

# Chapter 12
## A Fool's Errand

# LUCIAN

Desdemona steps back, her gaze sweeping through the room as if she's expecting to find something new. It's a cruel contrast to the playful smile that once stole her face.

"What's wrong?" I ask, stepping forward.

"Nothing." She shakes out her hands, blowing on them as if to cool herself down. "It's just hot."

Her control needs refinement. I accepted her pleas to dance because I have to earn her trust. Her magic is still weak, barely a fraction of what it could be, but if she doesn't trust me, the entire mission is futile. When the time comes, I have to be able to persuade her to do as I wish.

*I think I'd like to do so without annihilating her.*

It's her ragged breath that draws me closer, and I pick up her hand, surprised to see a large scar on her left palm. The deep cut is long healed, undoubtedly acquired before she arrived. It's not at all the kind of wound one would get in Utul and further proof she's lying.

I don't trust her, not by a long shot. There is something more than her home that she's hiding. If it mattered to my cause, I'd investigate further, but all I need is her power.

I summon shadows from the corner of the room, coating my hands and tracing the lines of her burning palm. I cool her down as she heats me up, feeling her shudder beneath my touch.

My fingers glide up her arms, passing her wrist and moving over her hammering pulse. I smile as her breath catches—until I realize my heart is beating just as quickly, if not faster, than hers.

Desdemona looks up, locking her gaze with mine, her eyes wider than I've ever seen them.

*Her eyes.*

How have I never noticed her eyes?

They're the color of the warm rays of the sun, of leaves right before they fall from their trees, of the gold that we've deemed too precious to mine.

Her eyes are the color of free falling. Into the world, beneath its surface, through its core.

And the shape—not rounded and bulbous like they usually appear. No, they're wide and sharp, like a blade cut from sunlight. Her lashes frame them like a painter's strokes, making them seem deeper, more dangerous, as though she could see right through me if she chose to. I'm not sure why it's taken me so long to realize she's been using a glamour to appear more Folklike, though I must say I prefer her this way: sharp, steady.

Stunning.

A force that I can't look away from, even if I should.

Her entire face is an indiscernible map of her feelings. I should have spent more time committing her smile to memory, because suddenly the most treacherous thought I've ever known is that I will never see it again.

The song ends with a scratch, and Desdemona turns, walking toward the music player. Her back is to me now, but I swear I can still feel her eyes on me, pulling me in, dragging me closer with every step she takes away.

Then, without looking at me, she says, "Let's try again."

And I don't know if I want to hold on to what I'm finding in her, or try to let go.

Azaire has spent more time asleep than awake, recovering from the wounds he sustained during our break-in at the weapon facility. I'm in his and Yuki's room every day, weighed down by the guilt of what I did.

But no matter who was to blame, I'd still be by Azaire's side.

"Hey," I whisper, softly stepping into his room.

Yuki stops spinning in his chair and glances at me. "Hey."

Azaire stirs, his eyes slowly opening, and he looks between us with a weak, straining yawn.

Yuki raises his arms in mock protest, teasing, "See? I told him he was too loud, bro."

Azaire attempts a smile, but it's short-lived, a grimace crossing his face as he winces from the effort.

I glance at Yuki, my voice low. "Would you mind giving us a moment?"

He throws his hands up. "Yeah, sure, because I *love* being kicked out of my own room." But despite his complaint, he gets up, leaving the two of us alone.

When the door closes behind Yuki, I turn to Azaire, who's sprawled across the bed. "I am so sorry," I begin—the only person I would ever utter those words to.

"You don't have to say it every time I wake up," he replies, blinking slowly. "It was my decision."

"One you would not have made without my meddling."

"You know how I feel about your actions as of late," Azaire mumbles. "But a *weapon?* That's bigger than us. A little pain for future peace is worth it."

I look down, not wanting him to be able to read what must be clear. This isn't about peace. Not for me.

"Yeah," I say. "But I swear I won't let you get hurt again."

"It's not up to you." He grits his teeth, struggling to sit up.

"It's not everyone else's job to make sure I'm all right."

Azaire finally gives up, lying back down and pulling his dark-blue beanie over his eyes, shutting out the world. It's what he does when there's something weighing on him.

"What is it?" I ask.

"Wendy," he mumbles. "I think…" He sits up again, uncovering his eyes. "I don't know. I mean, the thing about her is that she feels everything, you know?"

"No, I don't. Perhaps start at the beginning?" I prompt.

"When I first woke up after fighting Freyr…" He gestures vaguely over his torso. "She said that 'whatever this is has to end here.' And that she 'doesn't know how to do this.'"

"Doesn't know how to feel?" I offer, considering how he began this confusing conversation.

"I think… She didn't take it well in class." Azaire clears his throat. "When she healed me, I mean."

I clench my jaw. I'd do anything Leiana and Labyrinth asked of me to keep Azaire safe, and it still isn't enough. They still gather people like him into a volunteer group, like animals, and force them to endure torture for the *betterment* of their academy's education.

"This was much worse than that," Azaire continues. "What I was saying before, about her feeling everything… She can't turn off her empathy like the rest of them. I think my being hurt scared her, but I want her to know that I'm okay *because* of her."

I see now. I've heard of the Eunoia who cannot turn off their powers of empathy. Those who are not Eunoia see it as a gift they take for granted, while those who are Eunoia view it as a curse they wouldn't wish upon their least favorite person.

Least favorite, because the Eunoia refuse to *hate*.

"I want to help get rid of this weapon," Azaire says with conviction. "Before it's used to cause more damage than we all can take."

"All right," I promise. "We'll destroy it. Together."

I don't know that it's a promise I'll be able to keep, yet I make it anyway. I can't look at my best friend, my brother, in this state and do nothing.

A light knock sounds at the door. I drag a hand across my face, suppressing the betrayal that brews there. A moment later, Lilac steps into the room. She offers me a solemn nod and sits on the bed beside Azaire.

"Here," she whispers, offering him a handful of herbs. "They'll help with the pain, accelerate the healing." Gently, she brushes lint off his beanie. "I can't believe they did this to you."

I cast Azaire a sharp glance—though he doesn't need a reminder. It was his idea to tell Lilac that his injuries were sustained in one of the volunteer groups, not at the facility.

That our parents' commands did this to him, and not *me*.

It's not a lie I like, though it doesn't have to be. The point is to keep Lilac as far out of danger as possible. The less she knows, the better.

"It's okay," Azaire responds. "I'm getting better already."

I gently place a hand on top of Lilac's, saying, "We should let Azaire rest."

Silently, she nods, rising to her feet. Together, we leave Azaire's room and step into the hallway. As we do, a group of girls walks past, offering a casual "Hi" to Lilac.

Lilac's cheeks flush, and she looks down as she mutters, "Hi."

I glance at her, confused. Lilac isn't shy—she's never had that luxury, given her position.

"You all right?" I ask.

"Sorry," Lilac whispers. "Since Calista it's just been… People don't really talk to me anymore."

"Do you want me to do something about it?"

"No." Her voice carries more strength than I expect. "The silence is nicer, actually. It feels like the only time in my life when I can exist without being noticed."

I know that's what Lilac wanted—something she'd never

have. A quiet life, full of love. As I watch her walk now, with her shoulders hunched and her head ducked down, I can't help but want to take every burden from her. If I could, I'd stay under Leiana's rule forever, if it only meant Lilac's freedom.

"My apologies," she mumbles softly. "We should be talking about Azaire. He's going to be all right, isn't he?"

"We don't—" I shake my head. "We can talk about *you*, Li. We can talk about anything."

Lilac glances at me, and I see the horror written across her face, as if talking about herself is the last thing she wants. She swallows hard. "It's all right. I don't have anything to add."

"Li—"

"My words would be treason anyhow."

Gently, I grasp her hand, pulling her aside. "Li," I murmur, "talk to me."

She meets my gaze, hollowing her cheeks. "Every day brings us closer to the betrothal," she says. "Soon we'll be bound to people we don't desire—and you'll be bound to the person *I* long for. Yet that's the cruelest part. That I *do* want her, after everything she's done. She broke my heart, took my friends, and somehow, I still love her."

There's conflict in her eyes that I cannot ease. She doesn't deserve this—she never has. Unlike me, she's always been kind, yet this is how the universe repays her. If only I could wield more than words to protect her.

"I'm sure Calista has her reasons—"

"I know that she does," Lilac whispers, her words heavy. "But at our core, we are different. She craves power, and I wouldn't be surprised if what she did to me was just another step toward that. Even if we had the chance to be together, it wouldn't work. Yet I can't release the daydream."

"What do you want to do?" I ask, knowing that I'd do anything I could for her.

"Get it over with. Put my head down, suck it up, and live the life I was born to."

I can see how much it costs her to say that—the strength it takes to smother her dreams for something more than this. It's resignation, not her choice.

"No, Li. If you could have anything—what would it be?"

Lilac frowns, shaking her head as if I've asked a silly question. "A gentler universe, Luc. If that weren't possible, then I'd want the same as you. To be as far from here as I can."

---

When I leave my morning training with Yuki, Wendy is waiting just outside the combat room, her posture tense, like she's been standing there for longer than necessary. I'd asked Azaire to talk to her for me, to convince her to dig up any information she could find about her mom, Isa, and the Arcanes. He convinced her, all right.

I knew I shouldn't have asked him, but I knew I needed answers more.

Wendy doesn't look at me as I approach. Her gaze locks onto the open armory, though I can't tell if the look in her eyes is shock or intrigue. It's probably her first time seeing weapons like these—Eunoia aren't allowed in Combat Training. The academy focuses on teaching them the art of healing, not destruction.

That's a job for the rest of us.

"What did you find?" I ask her, wiping sweat from my forehead.

"Not here." Wendy's eyes don't stray from the armory. "Are those all the weapons?"

"Not even close. Why do you ask?"

"No reason," she says, meeting my eyes. "Let's go."

I take a step, and Wendy follows, heading to the nearest exit —until she grabs my arm.

"We can't go past the barrier," she whispers.

*They're here.* The monsters have made it to Visnatus—there's no other reason she'd stop me. Still, they won't get past the barrier. It was cast a thousand years ago, back when the academy first opened. Nothing unwanted can pass through.

"What happened?" I ask, in case I've missed the mark. Though I know I haven't.

"A pernipe attacked me. I killed it." Wendy's tone is distant.

I should be scared, but truthfully, it makes me a little giddy. Too excited to not be considered maniacal. A monster near the academy means the puzzle is coming to me. So, too, will answers.

Not to mention, Wendy *killed* it—a Eunoia. It's not that I care, but the rest of her kind certainly will. Killing and Eunoia do not go hand in hand. Their power is life.

"All right." I nod. "I have another location."

I pivot and head to the dormitory wing to find Azaire. He's sitting on the edge of his bed, looking better than the day before but still pale. I sling an arm under his shoulders as he limps to his feet, helping him out of the suite.

Wendy waits in the hallway, nodding at Azaire as we approach, though she doesn't meet his eyes. The three of us make our way toward the staircase that leads to the Royal chambers.

At the base of the stairs, I glance at Wendy. "A little help?"

She hesitates, her eyes darting between the two of us. "Oh," she finally mutters. "Sure."

Sliding her arm around Azaire's waist, she helps steady him as we take the steps one at a time. When we reach the top, Azaire's face is flushed, whether from exertion or Wendy's proximity, I can't tell.

The room is still littered with remnants of Desdemona—the circular table tucked in the corner and her footprints faintly visible through the thick dust.

I pull the table back to the middle of the room, its legs creaking under the strain, its surface layered with years of grime.

Carefully, Wendy and I settle Azaire into a worn chair, then we both sit. Wendy runs a finger along the table's edge, disgusted, before reaching into her bag and pulling out a worn book. "I found this in my mom's study. It's glamoured."

A philosophy book: *The Mendacity of Good and Evil*.

"How do you know?" I ask.

"For one, this book is written by Shenlin, not Marto. Second, it doesn't feel like my ma or anything else in her study."

"Can I see it?" Azaire asks her softly.

"Yes," Wendy whispers, taking a deep breath as she hands him the book.

He flips through the pages, examining each one, and stops three-quarters of the way through the text. "They didn't get the book right."

"Whoever glamoured it was in a hurry," Wendy observes. "Whatever it is, it was valuable enough to not warrant destruction."

"Or it was indestructible," I offer.

"Why wouldn't they just take it?" she asks.

Azaire closes the book and hands it back to her. "Things are best hidden in plain sight."

"There's more," Wendy adds. "Whatever is truly under the book, I think it came from Folkara."

Azaire and I exchange a look, both of us thinking the same thing. It can't be a coincidence that the one man we find working on the weapon mentions Wendy's mother. Nor that glamour is Folk magic—no one but them can cast or strip one.

"May I see the book?" I ask Wendy.

When the book is in my hand, I try deftly to pull apart the components of the glamour. Glamour is a form of mental magic; the physical objects do not truly change, they only appear different to an untrained eye.

Perhaps it is because I am a Lyrian, or perhaps it's Labyrinth's unabating words about physical strength paling in comparison to mental strength, but I've always been adept at pulling apart a glamour to see the truth beneath. Not with this one, though. Try as I might, the glamour holds, said to be written by Marto when it was truly written by Shenlin.

I hand the book back to Wendy, and at last, a question is spoken.

"Why do you think it came from Folkara?" Azaire asks.

Wendy answers, "I found papers, all stamped with Folkara's crest and signed by King Easton and Queen Melody."

I exchange a glance with Azaire, both of us weighing our options. To disclose or conceal? The weapon is a dangerous operation, and her knowing about it could be considered treason.

Wendy gives us both a scrutinizing glare, her voice sharp as she says, "Tell me."

*Damn Eunoia*—she must have sensed our hesitation.

Azaire is the one to answer, "Folkara is making a weapon."

"You've seen it?" she asks, but it's more a statement than a question. She glances between us, her green eyes flickering to light with magic as she reads our emotions. "That's where you came from—when Azaire was half-dead?"

"Yes," I answer.

"You lied to me." She looks at me like I've committed the worst of betrayals.

"You would have known if I lied."

"At what point does omitting the truth become a lie?" Wendy says.

"When you're intentionally hiding something," Azaire answers.

"Yes," I admit to Wendy. "I lied."

"I told you not to be vague about my mother," she says, her voice rising despite her whisper. Then her gaze snaps to Azaire. "Did he tell you?"

Azaire stutters, "Tell me what?"

"I didn't tell him," I answer. It wasn't important, and I didn't think him bringing up her dead mother would aid agreement.

"Tell me what?" Azaire asks again.

Wendy stuffs the book back into her bag and glares at me as if I'm the culprit. "My mom's dead," she answers, her eyes flicking between Azaire and me. "Whoever gave you her name likely didn't even know that this was in her study. And if they did, they didn't think you'd find it." She finally settles her attention on Azaire. "They sent you on a fool's errand." Turning away from both of us, she adds, "I'm going to get the glamour stripped."

"Allow me," I say, "I'll take it to Calista."

Wendy pulls the bag closer to her. "I can do it."

# Chapter 13
## A Drink He Was Sharing

# DESDEMONA

Darkness covers the school as I sneak up the narrow steps.

When I get to the room, Lucian is leaning against the old table, wearing the most ornate suit I've ever seen: dark blue and beaded with silvers and moonstones that catch in the low light. It's the kind of thing that could save a family from starving *and* freezing in the colder seasons.

*A reminder of who he is.*

I clear my throat. "A little much for this, don't you think?" I gaze over the fabric, then gesture around the dusty room.

"You should see what I have for you," Lucian says with a smirk. Then I notice a long piece of cloth next to him—the same kind my dress came in—with a bottle of red wine and two glasses beside it.

*Wine.* That stuff is borderline mythical in the septic.

I step closer, eyeing the materials carefully as I ask, "What's this about?"

Lucian pushes away from the table and brings me the dress, covered in a black slip. "Dancing in a dress isn't the same as dancing in…" He eyes me up and down, his gaze lingering. The heat that floods my face is entirely irrational.

I snatch the dress from him and mutter, "How princely of you" under my breath.

He just chuckles.

There are multiple unused rooms on the floor—all reserved for Royals—so I walk to the next room over. I set the cloth down, surprised when I pull out a rich, emerald green dress. Shimmering gold thread outlines the bust, and gold fabric covers the sleeves. The slits running down the sides leave my torso exposed, except for delicate gold lace that crisscrosses over my skin.

Gold—something I didn't know of a month ago and can't escape now. It's quite heavy, too.

I have a hard time believing the prince picked this out, let alone brought it up here for me. But I guess he thinks I'm a lady of Utul.

I struggle with the laces of the corset in the back for far too long before I admit to myself that I need help. When I walk back into the room, the bodice clutched to my chest, Lucian is holding two glasses full of red wine.

This feels very romantic, and I wonder if it's a joke. Maybe Leiholan told Lucian I'd been watching him, and they set this whole thing up to get a good laugh.

But it still feels like a kind of *pinch me* situation, even though I'd never admit it. A prince, a fancy dress, and this mythical red wine that no one had ever been able to fathom having back home. It seems like the kind of dream I would've had as a child if I wasn't preoccupied with the notion of surviving.

"I can't tie the corset," I say, keeping my eyes fixed anywhere but on Lucian.

"I've only ever untied them." His voice is low, threaded with amusement—and something else. "But for you, I'll try."

He moves behind me, unhurried, like he's savoring every step. His fingers graze my back, and my breath catches before I can stop it. I hope he doesn't notice. But the goosebumps on my arm are probably a dead giveaway.

"There," he breathes, his lips brushing the shell of my ear.

I spin around quickly, despite his hands still being on me. But that was a mistake because now we're face to face—with his hands on my waist.

"You look…" He trails off, his eyes dragging over me like a confession he isn't ready to speak. Like I'm something he's trying not to touch and dying to all the same.

"Every bit the lady I was raised to be," I say quickly, breaking the moment and moving toward the wine glass he'd set down.

It's going to be a long night.

But the prince grabs my wrist before I can make it too far. When I turn into him, he doesn't let go.

"Breathtaking," he says. "You look breathtaking. Well enough to cover me in gooseflesh, as well." He pauses, gliding his fingers up my arm, coaxing *more* goosebumps from my skin. His gaze lingers, almost like he's trying to commit every inch of me to memory. "Well enough to make being in your presence excruciating."

No amount of self-control could stop my face from flushing.

"Wine break," I say, desperately needing to get some space. I don't know why either, considering I'm dancing with the epitome of these spoiled kids. The picture-perfect prince.

"A fine idea," he says, turning on his heel and picking up the glasses.

From the first sip, the wine slides down with ease, warmth budding inside of me like a sunrise. I try to act like this is something I've done many times.

But Lucian asks, "Is this your first time?" I give him a look, and he holds up his glass. "The wine?"

"Oh." I shake my head. "No."

He downs the rest of his glass in one sip. "It'll help with your nerves."

I take another sip, too. "I don't have nerves."

"No?" he teases, stepping closer.

He puts his hand on mine and guides my glass down, then brings his hand to my waist. He pulls me closer than he ever has before, leaning his head down so that his lips are brushing the top of my ear.

Beginning the waltz, he whispers, "Then what are you feeling right now?"

"Definitely not nervous," I whisper, but my voice is low and breathy and, worst of all, shaky.

The prince laughs a little against my hair. "Your voice betrays you."

I back away, grab my glass, and drink the rest of the wine in two gulps. The tingles in my stomach that were already there from his touch multiply.

Fast.

"Am I to believe that *wasn't* for your nerves?" he asks with a smile.

"Absolutely," I reply, raising a brow and pouring myself another glass.

The only other time I've ever gotten *really* drunk was with Damien, the day I left. I push the memory from my mind. I'm going to get back. It'll just take some time. And that's okay. I'm biding it well, learning to use my magic and fighting and drinking fancy alcohol.

I'm gonna go home a new woman.

With that, I have to wonder, what is the point of this? I can't tell anyone fundamental parts of me, and even if I could, I'm leaving anyway.

But I've lived my entire life keeping myself hidden. In a way, what I'm doing isn't much different than what I've always done.

I drink the next glass with three sips and spiral into another. *Maybe I should stop,* I think, but Lucian just matches me in all my glasses.

The next time we try to dance, I almost fall on my face.

Lucian catches me, and the stupid grin he gives me sets me off into a fit of laughter, which he joins me in.

But it's a sound I wish I hadn't heard. Rich and deep, like

nectar on my tongue, it bounces through the room, filling my ears and forcing me to wrack my brain. I haven't heard a laugh like this in a long time.

I would stop laughing to get a better listen, but I can't get over how silly he looked! His mouth was all lopsided, and his eyes were wide with emotion I've never seen from him before. Even the thought of it makes me laugh harder.

So now the two of us are just looking into one another's eyes and laughing like idiots, and I don't want it any other way. I love this! I feel like I can do anything. So I take his hand and lift it over my head, spinning in circles until the room spins with us.

When I'm done, I fall into him, laughing and laughing and laughing.

"I've never seen you like this," he whispers, and I'm sure I misheard him.

But I still stop everything while trying to figure out if he really spoke or not.

"What?" I ask. I can hear the smile in my voice, and it's so nice, so different from the way I'm used to living!

I really should just laugh more! This giddy feeling in my chest still hasn't dissipated, and I hope it never does.

"Your laugh," he says, his gaze never leaving my face, his eyes darkening as though holding back something he can no longer hide. "It's bewitching. I don't think I could ever get enough of it. I think I could get drunk off it."

Now he's looking at me in a way that scares me, and I feel suddenly sober.

I've never been called bewitching—my laugh or otherwise. And the way he continues to look at me tells me he meant it. He's staring as if there's something worthy of awe somewhere on my face. Maybe right now there is, with all of Aralia's glamour.

But while I look at him, I suddenly wish he was looking at *me*. So I skip away, my hands shaking with a nervousness I'd rather drink away. I grab my glass of wine and turn back, somehow managing to run right into Lucian. Red soaks his suit, and he laughs.

But I'm petrified. Shocked! Stunned! Mortified! I'm feeling a little goofy, too, because I've just ruined what must be the most expensive piece of clothing I've seen in my life, but he just looks at me.

His face is nothing but a picture of insouciance. It's infectious, the way he's looking and acting. His usually perfect hair is messed up, dark inky waves moving in every direction and into his eyes. I like the thought that *I* am the one who rumpled the perfect prince.

That *I* have the power and position to do such a thing.

I push him into one of the dusty chairs, a little too harshly, I think.

He looks at me, amusement filling his eyes. "What are we doing now?"

I grab the school's uniform coat I'd been wearing before I put on the ridiculously beautiful green-and-gold dress. Then I start unbuttoning his—*soft*—royal blue coat. Gods, what material is this? I want to wear it to sleep.

"Darling," Lucian drawls, watching me as I unbutton his coat. Then he shrugs out of it, leaving him in only a see-through, stained white shirt. And leaving my hands on a very *thin* shirt. "If you wanted to undress me, there are far easier ways than spilling wine."

I hit his chest with the back of my hand, a sloppy, drunken gesture that I hope distracts from the blood rushing to my cheeks. "I'm cleaning you."

*The outlines of his muscles are really quite easy to make out.*

"Ah. You didn't have to spill wine to do that either," he says with a lazy shrug.

"What?" I ask, laughing again.

He laughs, too, and my head falls on his shoulder from the

force of it. Have I said how much I love laughing?

"There are far more satisfying ways to get dirty, but if they all end with *you* cleaning me like *this*..." Lucian looks at my hands, both of them on him, neither of them cleaning. Not when half of me has fallen over on him laughing! Not that I care that much either. "Then I could get used to the wine."

"You talk like someone who's touch-deprived," I say.

"Well, I don't think I could ever get enough of you."

"You mean my..." I push my hands up his chest. "Glorious, glorious hands?"

Lucian smiles, and a laugh fills the room once again. "Oh, don't stop Marquees," he mutters mockingly.

But when I do stop, he grabs my wrists. And when I look at him, I find him staring at me.

"No," he says. "I meant it." I blink, and he answers, "Don't stop."

He couldn't possibly mean that, couldn't possibly care that much about my drunk hands on his abdomen.

The room is still spinning, but a little less—enough that I can see... "Hold still," I whisper, too quietly. My hand reaches out before I even think about it. "You have wine on your chin."

Lucian gently tightens his grip around my wrist, stopping me before my thumb can make contact. His gaze darkens and his lips part while he glances at mine.

"You have no idea what it does to me when you look at me like that," he murmurs. "I couldn't imagine what would happen if you touched me right now."

Then, using his free hand, he wipes his chin and lips. His eyes don't stray from mine for a second.

Warmth rushes to my face, and I shift awkwardly, trying to regain some control. I don't know what to say, and for a moment, I just want to hide.

But there's a small amount of relief to be found in the wine still smeared across his face.

"It's still there," I find myself whispering so quietly I doubt he heard me. "It looks like blood on your lips."

"And why are you looking at my lips?" he asks with *his* eyes on *my* lips.

"Because it messes them up," I say.

"Are you telling me you like my lips?" he teases, his voice low.

"No," I say, and damn me for smiling! "It messes up your whole face."

Lucian's smile turns smug. "Are you telling me you like my face?"

I shrug. "It's a nice face."

He leans back, looking up towards the ceiling. "I knew you thought so, Marquees."

I waste the last sip of my wine, splashing it on Lucian and the shirt I just briefly bothered cleaning. The room is spinning, but Lucian quickly sits up again, so I blame it on him when the wine lands on his face. He licks his lips and smiles. I can't help but laugh, mortified or mollified, I don't know.

"Now you *really* have wine on your chin."

"And my lips," he notes.

"Yes," I breathe.

"Would you like it back?" he asks, leaning in enough to make my pulse jump.

But I don't back away.

Messy hair, parted lips, drunken doings—I want it all. The power and the position to bring this out of him.

Does he?

I'm noticing all kinds of things I hadn't before. Like the way his nose actually slants a little to the left or that his right eyebrow is a little higher or that one eye has a speck more of the lighter blue that encapsulates his pupils.

All of it only makes him more endearing. Less the annoyingly perfect prince, more the man who takes time out of his day to teach me magic or dancing while he teases me.

Which, speaking of, I tease him right back, and he doesn't mind! I expected such a sheltered, spoiled person to have a bigger ego and thinner skin. But he's...

What am I even thinking? He's still the prince of Ilyria. He's still a part of the family who delights in the hardships of people like me.

*He's still the kind of person I loathe.*

I turn away, and he clears his throat. Wow. The room's really spinning.

"Perhaps we should retire for the night?" Lucian offers after a lapse of silence.

"No," I say before I can think. "I mean..." I blink and blink. And blink. What *do* I mean? I'm unsure as I say, "This was nice."

He smiles at me. "Nice? I'm not a pet, darling."

"Desdemona," I say.

"Lucian," he says absentmindedly.

"No, I mean my name is Desdemona."

He laughs. "I know your name."

"Right." I drop to the ground, tired of carrying the weight of this dress.

Lucian slips down and out of his chair, sitting across from me on the floor. "Do you know mine?"

"Of course I know your name," I say.

"You're welcome to use it."

I lean into him with an idea. "How about when you stop calling me 'darling,' I stop calling you 'prince'?"

He leans in, too, our noses an inch from brushing. A smile paints his face, and his eyebrows pull down when he casually says, "That's no fair deal."

"Yes, it is!" I say, almost gleefully.

"Isn't 'darling' *much* more endearing than 'prince'?"

"Do you mean to be endearing?"

"I do now, yes."

"So, you don't call *anyone else* 'darling'?" I tease.

"Only you," he whispers back.

"And why's that?"

"I suppose you inspire something within me," Lucian says with a sly smile.

I lean in without meaning to. "And no one else inspires such arrogance?"

"Oh, darling, I thought we'd covered that it isn't arrogance!" He taps my nose. "It's endearment."

"Did you just *flick* my nose?" I say with a loud and intoxicating laugh that takes over my whole chest.

"Why, yes, I did."

"Is that another thing I *inspire* in you?"

"Truly, it might be. Because I can't imagine another time I'd ever *flick* someone's nose." I can't help but laugh at his horrible impression of me. "But yes," he says a moment later, leaning in and singing, "only you inspire such *endearment*."

I don't know what to say. I inspire endearment in a prince? A perfect, pampered, pompous asshole. I *wish* I thought he was an asshole.

"Lucian," I faintly whisper, just to see how it feels on my tongue.

Just to hate it.

I like it.

"Hm," Lucian groans.

"What?" I ask, my eyes widening, suddenly alarmed.

"It almost sounds worthy of speaking on your lips."

"Your name?"

"I wish you'd have said it again."

"Lucian?" I whisper.

His head tips back, and he smiles. His dimples are showing—the ones I only see when his smile is *real*.

"Doesn't everyone call you by your name?" I ask.

Lucian looks back at me, the alcohol still staining his fancy attire.

*Attire he wore for me.*

He hesitates. Then, in a heady whisper, he says, "No one who matters to me."

I watch him for a long moment, willing my eyes not to waver. But maybe the alcohol is stronger than me. Maybe my feelings are, too.

"And do I?" I dare to ask. "Matter to you?"

Lucian fixes me with a gaze so intense it makes my breath catch. Heat rises to my face, and I drop my eyes before I can stop myself.

But he never answers my question.

I clear my throat and ask, "So what do the people that matter to you call you?"

He shrugs. "My sister calls me Lucy."

"Lucy?" I can't help but laugh. And laugh. "No, no, that's sweet. I'm sorry." I say with a nod, "I like it."

"It's grown on me, too." His messy hair falls into his eyes, and I long to ruffle it more. "Do you have siblings?"

My smile drops, but I don't mean it to. "Why?"

Lucian shrugs. "I don't…" His back falls against the chair behind him. "I suppose I'd like to know more about you."

That's not good. Not good at all. Very loud sirens begin to go off in my head, telling me to back up, retreat, stumble out of the room and into the surely spinning hallway. I have to get back to the suite before I make any more stupid decisions.

"No siblings," I say instead. My eyes shy down. His hands are in his pocket, moving something around. "What's in there?"

Lucian looks down and then pulls out something silver. It looks like a wolf, but it's back in his pocket quickly.

"A wolf?" I ask.

"A token," he corrects. "I spin it when I'm nervous."

I smile at that. I *like* that. "And I make you nervous?"

"Beautiful, entrancing, and deadly is a pretty nerve-racking combination."

I squint at him, laughing in a way that sounds like a scoff and hoping it distracts from my disbelief. "You think I'm *entrancing*?"

Lucian holds up his token again and grins. "I was talking about the wolf."

"Right," I say slowly as I study him.

Breathtaking, bewitching, and beautiful. Could the prince truly think that about me?

*Do I really think that about him?*

I extend my legs outward, trying to get comfortable, because for some reason, I don't think I'm going to be leaving. Lucian scoots back and extends his legs out in front of him, too, putting the bottoms of his shoes against mine.

"What are you—"

"Push." He smiles. "Whoever bends their knees first loses."

So here we are, two drunk idiots, pushing each other's feet all night, trying to get the other's knees to bend.

## Chapter 14
## There's What You Want and What You Get

# DESDEMONA

Aralia and I are putting on our fancy dresses when she asks, "Do you have an eye for anyone?"

"Nope," I say.

But I still feel the ghost of Lucian's hands lingering on my waist, the phantom of words whispering in my ear. The thought alone makes my stomach churn, and it's entirely irrational.

He's a *prince*. The epitome of what's wrong with the worlds. He's only ever going to perpetuate the system that lets people like me bleed and starve.

He's friends with a *Nepenthe*—knowing what they are and what they do.

*He is the problem.*

Letting myself forget that just because we danced was a mistake.

"Darn, you look too good not to," Aralia says, smiling as she holds up a dagger. The hilt—carved from orange memor stone—glistens in the light.

With a mocking bow, she presents it to me. "For you, milady."

I pick it up like it's a child. "It's beautiful," I whisper, staring in awe.

Aralia speaks fast when she says, "Yeah, I've had it for years, never used it. The real gold stuff is so expensive, the only people who could afford it are probably the gods, but I figured the orange would go well enough." She turns back to the drawer, rummaging through it. "I have a strap for it somewhere in here."

"It's beautiful," I say again. "But why are you giving it to me?"

Aralia looks at me over her shoulder with a smirk. "Every leg slit needs a dagger," she says, her voice deep and heady, clearly mocking the rest of the elites. "It's only the very *basics* of accessorizing." Her voice goes back to normal when she squeals, "Found it!"

I strap the dagger to my thigh and stare at my reflection, almost admiring myself. My cheeks are rounded, my jaw is soft, and so is my nose—all thanks to Aralia's glamour. I almost look pretty, and the dress is something else entirely. Gold and gleaming, nearly dangerous with the dagger equipped at my side.

Together, Aralia and I walk to the ballroom, which might just be the shiniest room I've ever stepped into. It's a world composed entirely of blue and silver, with chandeliers reflecting off the marble floors like stars in the sky.

And I am the only one in gold.

It doesn't take long for all eyes in the room to settle on me.

I'm used to this by now, being a Fire Folk and all. But tonight, their looks aren't all fearful. Or even pitying, for that matter. There's something else gleaming in this sea of eyes.

It's more than just students in this room. There are adults, too. Regal figures line the room, with sharp eyes and even sharper clothes. If I know anything about this school, I know they're also *ruling* adults.

"You didn't tell me the government would be here," I whisper to Aralia, feeling their scrutinizing eyes on me.

She gives me a quizzical look, her brows furrowed. "You didn't know?"

Right. I never told her I didn't know what the Gerner was. It kind of feels like I did.

"Visnatus educates the elite children of the universe," Aralia whispers. "In theory, everyone has a say in how it's run." She looks toward the adults. "Some more than others."

I think of Arson's Alley and the seamstress Portricia, of Aralia giving her the extra pence. "If every government is involved, why are we stealing from the poor?" I ask. "Can't they fund the school themselves?"

"Haven't you heard?" Aralia laughs, but it's a bitter sound. "Our universe is fucked up." She grabs my hand and pulls me. "Come. Let's get drinks before any of those Royal pain-in-the-asses make us dance."

"Vesi?" I ask, catching the attention of an older woman with bright blue eyes and dark hair.

"Duh," Aralia says, and I look away from the Lyrian—but I still feel her eyes on me.

We walk through the room of chattering students and adults alike. I've never had so many eyes on me. Suddenly, I'm extra grateful for the dagger strapped to my thigh... and maybe even the girl who gave it to me. I want to look like a worthy opponent, because among these glances, there must be someone sizing me up, ready to fight.

There always is.

Lucian's back is turned when we approach. He's with Yuki and the Nepenthe in the blue beanie—with warm olive skin, a long arched nose, and eyes that wander through the room. I glance in his direction, fixating on the second-to-top button of his suit, but I don't dare meet his gray gaze.

"Fill my flask?" Aralia asks, and if I didn't know to look, I would never see the sly passing of her flask to Lucian. It's filled and back in her hands before anyone even bats an eye. This must be a routine.

"Can't take your eyes off my body, Marquees?" Lucian asks, spinning the drink in his hand.

He knows why I'm avoiding his gaze.

All I can see now is the boy with the messed-up suit and hair, on account of me. The boy whose fingers brushed my cheeks and whose lips occupied my mind these past nights more than I'd like to admit.

*The boy I can never have, let alone want.*

"It's a nice body, what can I say?" I arm my voice with boredom, even though my heart is pumping blood at an obnoxiously fast rate.

Aralia spins me away before Lucian can say more, twirling my hand over our heads.

I laugh. It'll be good to look like I have friends.

"Save me a dance, Marquees?" Lucian calls.

Aralia stops, and I give her a look. Then I give Lucian one worse. "Don't bet on it."

Lucian smiles, a reminder of who he really is and what that night really was.

I knew from the beginning that it'd be best to keep my distance. But I pulled him in, and now if I don't push him out, I'm going to deal with the consequences.

Like being kicked out of the school and having *no* chance of finding my mom.

*Or getting killed.*

"Wasn't planning on it." Then he winks, and I'm turning around before I have the chance to think twice.

"What was that about?" Aralia says, but she's too giddy.

"Nothing."

I steal a glance over my shoulder, but Lucian is no longer looking. I don't even know why I'm looking back. It's ridiculous. I'll never belong here or with him, and I don't *want* to. Suddenly, I'm sure that the older Lyrian who won't take her eyes off me knows it, too.

Aralia picks up two glasses of pink tea on our way to the corner of the ballroom. Handing me one, she says, "Down it before the dancing starts."

"Are you gonna put the vesi in it?"

She grins a lopsided little smirk. "Already did," she says, like it's the easiest thing in the worlds.

With the Lyrian woman watching me, I'm not sure I should be drinking. But on the other hand, with the Lyrian woman watching me, I'm sure I *should* be drinking. I debate for a moment and drink half—just to be safe.

"You're not finishing?" Aralia asks before grabbing my glass and downing it herself. Then she's dragging me across the floor again, right to the center of the room.

I spot Leiholan in the back. Even in a gray suit and slicked-back hair, he looks like a drunk. I don't know how he got the position he holds at this school.

Aralia grabs my hand, pulling my attention back to her, and spins me, catching me completely off guard.

As we start dancing, I can't help but ask, "Where are the rest of your friends?"

She frowns. "They're not good friends."

I kind of hope she doesn't think I'm a good friend, because I'm sure that whoever *they* are would be much better for her than I am. But I dance with her while she makes pointed looks across the room—I guess at her parents.

"Do you want another drink?" Aralia shouts, the flask dangling in her hand. "The dances are going to start any minute."

"Who are we dancing with?" I ask.

"Anyone. Everyone."

I look at Lucian, then he looks at me, his gaze lingering. Immediately, I answer, "Yes."

I drink the vesi, the burn of it spreading through me, much different from the bubbly warmth of the wine. Minutes later, I'm holding the back of the neck of a man I've never met. He feels foreign beneath my palms, where I've gotten so used to holding Lucian. Dancing with him. I'd hoped I wouldn't miss it, but here I am, dancing with another and thinking of him.

Keeping up with the steps doesn't offer me any sense of

pride with Lucian on my mind. Noticing the older woman still watching me doesn't help, either.

And when Lucian's gaze flickers toward her, I wonder what kind of game he's playing.

Calista steps into the dance, cutting off my view of Lucian, and wraps her hands around my waist. I look at her, intending to ask what she's doing, but she avoids my gaze.

"I see you, you know," she whispers, her eyes fixed across the ballroom. "You've been watching him all night, and it's disgusting. He's *my* husband."

Finally, her head turns, and her eyes lock onto mine. They're furious, burning with intensity—and in that glare, all I see is my princess. The future queen of my world, Folkara. She's right, and I've forgotten how right she is. I have no claim to Lucian. I have no reason to be watching him, to be wanting him.

"Look, I'm not—"

"You're not trying to steal my king? Trying to take my throne?" Even though she's inches shorter, it feels like she's looking down at me. "I've seen your kind before. Impulsive little Folk who think they can waltz in and sweep the prince off his feet. Lucian isn't *that* gullible." She glares at me, taking me in from head to toe, as much as she can from her height. "He isn't even that desperate."

"That is *not* what this is—"

Calista cuts me off before I can finish. "Save yourself the dignity and leave him alone."

"There's nothing romantic happening between us. There's hardly a relationship between us!" I exclaim. "He's helping me with school."

Calista laughs. "Lucian? Helping you with *school?* Are you that daft?"

"Are *you?*" I ask, narrowing my eyes at her.

"Lucian is far from a sycophant," she says coolly. "He wants something from you. If you were smart, you'd be working to get something from him, as well. Perhaps I misunderstood your *relationship*."

She steps away from me, releasing my waist and offering a small curtsy—the signal that our dance is over. Begrudgingly, I bow before her, too.

Before moving on to her next partner, she steps in close, whispering in my ear, "Or perhaps you did."

Without another word, Calista glides away, prancing through the ballroom with the precision of someone who grew up in one.

A man steps in to take her place. It's Kai standing before me. I tense beneath his hands when I'm bombarded by the memory of dragging him to the woods and almost bashing Aralia's head in. I look away.

"Don't worry about Calista," he offers, misreading my discomfort. "She's quick to anger."

I shake my head. "It's not that."

"Not having a good time, then?" Kai asks.

I meet his brown gaze, reminding me, momentarily, of Damien. It lulls me into a false sense of trust. "Not particularly, no."

"It seems we have something in common," he says as we move slowly across the floor.

I don't know what to say, but I have to make a good impression. The prince is here, listening and talking to me. It's an ample opportunity. One prince is valuable to have in my corner; why not try for two?

"Really? I kind of figured balls would be your thing." I let out an exaggerated little laugh.

"And why's that?" He raises a brow, the gesture more playful than serious. Good.

"I don't know. You're a prince. Isn't this what you do?"

"Touché," he says.

We dance a few steps in silence before I ask, "So you don't

like being a prince?"

He shrugs a little, then smiles. "It has its perks."

"Like what?" I grin.

"No one can say anything when I do this." Then he's taking long strides, spinning me faster than anyone in the room. I'm a little dizzy, but when he laughs, I laugh, too. "I'd say it's well worth it."

"Oh, yeah," I say. "Me as well."

"I believe our time might be coming to an end." Kai presses his lips together in a mock frown.

"I think you may be correct." I smile. "Till we meet again?"

He lets out a second's worth of laughter. "Until we meet again."

My next three partners are far less entertaining than Kai. And while I watch Lucian dance with another girl, it's the most irrational part of me that imagines it's his strong, calloused, and familiar hands on my waist.

## Chapter 15
## Can't Save Them All

# LUCIAN

"Fleur," I say with a smile as she approaches. One hand falls to her waist, the other clasping hers as we begin to dance. "You look brilliant, as always."

"It's appreciated, Lucian," the Eunoia says with a smile and a small curtsy. "We missed you at the party."

"Ah, yes, I had other plans." I got drunk with Desdemona, who I'm watching watch me from across the room.

Yes, she dances with another, yet she is looking at Fleur and me as if it pains her. Which means I have a fraction of her feelings.

What scares me is that she has mine as well.

But fear is not enough of a reason to take my eyes off her. She's a vision no matter what she wears—she'd still be the most beautiful in this room draped in silver or blue. But clad in gold, she is more than captivating. She is truly and utterly devastating. Never have I glimpsed upon beauty so harrowing as hers.

Rarer than even the rarest ore that she dons the color of tonight.

She looks like a burning ember in the sea. An impossibility. A phenomenon one could spend their entire life trying to explain.

The dagger at her thigh is an interesting touch, a reminder that she is dangerous. Dazzling. That the results will be dreadful if I allow myself to continue with these daring thoughts.

So I force myself to look away. But I can never unsee her.

*Her image is seared into my brain like a brand.*

"Other plans? With whom?" Fleur asks with an edge to her voice.

"Desdemona."

Fleur laughs. "The Fire Folk? She can't even pass Elemental Magic."

Our shoes scuff against the floor as we move to the instrumental music. I exhale lightly. "And here I was, under the impression that she didn't want to kill the lot of us."

"You think she—" Fleur stops, pressing her lips together. "I don't want to talk about the Fire Folk any longer."

"That's more than all right," I say.

"I think we're going to have another party here in a few weeks, after all these fundraisers are over. You should come." She smiles.

"I believe I'm going to be busy that day as well." I have much more important things to focus on these days. We take our last step before it's time to switch partners, and I send her off while I say, "You will be missed."

My next partner approaches, and before I see Desdemona, I know that I am dancing with her by the heat of her body intertwined with mine. The way her skin hums beneath my touch.

The gold of her dress accentuates the bits of orange in her brown eyes, and up close, she is more than an ember.

She's a raging fire.

I find that I am entirely unable to take my eyes off of her as I ask, "How was Kai?"

Desdemona raises an eyebrow. "How was Fleur?"

"I wouldn't know," I say. "I was too busy imagining she was you."

For half a second, Desdemona looks almost shy. I wish she would allow me to glimpse her true faces. The ones she pulls back so quickly. The ones that betray her emotions.

She stiffens under my hold. "Well Kai was great. He's... fun."

I let out a short laugh. "Does he make your heart race?"

"What?"

"When I touch you," I say, my thumb settling over her pulse, "your heart rattles. Does *fun* do that for you as well?"

Desdemona looks and sounds unbothered as she says, "Not the way *infuriating* does."

But her pulse betrays her.

"Infuriating means you're burning for me, does it not?"

Her hand that I'm holding becomes very hot, as if even her body cannot deny what her mind longs to.

"If you wonder if it's reciprocated," I say under my breath, leaning in, "it's been my night's greatest challenge to keep my eyes on anything but you."

This time, I see it: my reward—the small amount of blush that softens Desdemona's cheeks.

"Oh, please," she huffs. "I'd burn you before I burned *for* you—"

She trips. I catch her before she reaches the ground, but not without smiling. Other than when drunk, Desdemona's more sure-footed than the kids with a lifetime's worth of training. This is almost a form of flattery.

"Are you sure about that?" I murmur. "Because I couldn't tell you the last time a girl tripped over herself because she couldn't get enough of me."

"Funny, because I could tell you the last time a boy did the same for me." She gives me a pointed look.

I shrug and say, much more casually than I feel, "But falling for you is such an easy thing to do."

*How I wish it wasn't.*

"What are you playing at here?"

"I can tell you what I'm playing for." I pull Desdemona a little closer. Not at all as close as I would like. Only enough for her to know I want her with me. "You."

Desdemona shakes her head and lets out a short, shallow

laugh. But her body tenses beneath my hands when I glance at Leiana. I tense too, even more so when I realize Desdemona's gaze is following mine.

"Who's the woman?" she asks. When I don't answer, her voice sharpens. "I know you know. I've been watching you look at her all night."

Resignation settles over me and I answer, "The queen."

Desdemona draws a breath, and I realize my fingers have curled tighter around hers—unwilling, *unable* to let go. As if releasing her would mean losing her to the pull of Leiana's gaze. That the wind will take her to a place I cannot reach.

"Why is your mother looking at me like that?" Desdemona whispers.

"I don't know." I'm not prepared to tell her that the queen has been asking about her since before I knew her.

"Am I safe here?" Her long, dark eyelashes flutter down over her sharp eyes. Her *real* eyes—hidden beneath the glamour I pull apart each time I'm granted the privilege to glimpse her. "Because I'll run. I'd be happy to leave, and if she's going to do something—"

"Where would you run to?" I ask.

Running could be her best option. I could find her, wherever she goes, pick up this rendezvous again, work with her and her power, make it to The Void when the time comes.

Prove to her that she's safe with me. Define these fickle feelings. Count the freckles on her face. Memorize the shape of her lips with mine.

*Gods.*

If I keep this going, it will not be me undoing her—it will be her undoing me. And that simply can't be, not with everything I have on the line.

But I can't imagine anyone I'd want to pull my strings more.

"I don't know." Desdemona pauses, her grip around my neck loosening. "I mean, when I find my mom, I'll go home. But I don't belong there without her."

"You don't belong in your home?" I ask.

Desdemona looks down at our feet. "No," she whispers.

"Why is that?" I want to pull her gaze back to mine.

"I don't know." She shrugs. "A lot has happened since I got here."

"You can talk to me," I say selfishly. "You know that, don't you?"

She finally meets my gaze. "Of course," she says softly. Her grip tightens around my neck. Her left hand.

A lie.

*Smart girl.*

I can't risk her running in the middle of the night and not telling me where. I can't risk her disappearing.

Because of the Arcanes. Nothing more.

Confessions of endearment and desires will be left in the past as what they are.

Mistakes.

"You are," I say. "Safe here."

I lie, too.

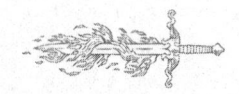

---

The next day, my private guards arrive at the academy to escort me to Ilyria. They lead me to the throne room, disappearing behind the heavy doors with an unspoken apology in their eyes.

Leiana and Labyrinth sit on their silver thrones, the blue carpets beneath them alight with the harsh white sun spilling in through the towering windows. Statues of the goddess Sulva stand on either side of their thrones, her crescent moon-shaped hair gleaming silver.

I always feel small before my parents, but never more so than here. Tiny in a grandiose room. Nothing compared to the power of the columns, wider than me. The statues of Sulva, heavier than me. The steps that lead to their thrones, taller than me.

The eyes of Leiana and Labyrinth, stronger than me.

"Darling, come," Leiana beckons, her fingers curling in a silent command. I prefer the word on my tongue, spoken for Desdemona.

It's less repugnant.

I approach their thrones, staring up at the rulers of our universe.

Labyrinth gives a curt nod, muttering, "Son."

I return the gesture, daring myself to ascend the steps. "Father."

Anytime I'm summoned here, dread curdles inside of me, knowing the outcome will be grim. Another task to carry out, regardless of what it means to me.

I am nothing more than their puppet.

"We won't waste time," Leiana says, her gaze sharpening as the light catches her moonstone earrings. "The girl in gold at the Gerner, when did she enroll?"

It's as I feared, as I knew—as Desdemona knew. Leiana could tell that Desdemona was the student she was looking for from one glance. Perhaps the gold dress was too telling.

*I wasn't the only one who couldn't look away.*

"I don't know," I lie, trying my best to sound indifferent.

"Hm," Leiana says at the same time as Labyrinth says, "Bring her in."

I twist my head to the entrance, scared of what Leiana has already done. Has my promise—my *lie*—to Desdemona already been broken?

Lilac is the one to walk in with wide eyes full of fear. She opens her mouth, and shadows wrap around the lower half of her face.

"Let her go!" I shout, emotion overcoming me. Besting me. But my sister meets my gaze, shaking her head, just barely.

"My apologies, Lilac," Leiana says. "I was afraid that Azaire wouldn't be *enticing* enough this time."

Fury trembles through me. My shadows wrap around my fingers like rings, up my arms like cuffs. I know I can't win against Leiana, not after the hundreds—perhaps even thousands—of people she's killed and drained the power from.

But I'll try, for Lilac.

Leiana weaponizes her shadows, faster and stronger, moving through the room—up the walls, across the windows, and over the ceiling, swallowing every hint of light. They linger around me, a silent threat, warning that the moment I strike, she will, too—twice as powerful.

Beneath the shadows, Lilac screams. It's a sad, muffled sound.

I can just make it out—one sentence repeated: *Leave him alone.*

I look to Labyrinth, pleading silently. *Stop this madness. She's your daughter.*

All hope shatters as he looks away.

It hits me all at once. I'll never be able to protect them all—Lilac, Azaire, and now Desdemona. Knowing me is a death sentence, or, at the very least, a sentence to torture.

"Let her go, please," I say to Leiana. I say to Lilac's *mother*.

Shadows pin my arms to my sides, trapping me. I look down to see darkness wrapping around my torso, and it isn't my own.

This time, it's Labyrinth who speaks, his voice booming through the room with the crack of his staff pounding against the floor. "The girl, when did she arrive in Visnatus?"

I look at Lilac. She is frozen still, petrified. Then Leiana looks at her, too. I know the look that washes over Lilac's face all too well. Her power—her life force—is being drained.

Leiana is killing her slowly, as she does me.

I never thought she would sink to such levels—abusing her own flesh and blood.

"Let her go, and I'll answer," I dare to say.

What could Leiana do with Desdemona's name? Surely something, if she wants it.

"That's not how our game works," Leiana drawls.

"Prove it to me," I spit, daring her with deadly words. "Go on, kill your future queen! Kill your *daughter*."

Leiana stares at me, her glowing eyes growing lighter as she sucks the power out of Lilac. I'm pinned in place, powerless. I hold my breath while I hold her gaze.

And I exhale when Leiana releases Lilac.

The darkness covering the room dissipates—some shadows return to their slanted positions on the floor, while most drift back to Leiana.

"Make sure Lilac stays conscious," Leiana instructs Labyrinth as she rises from her throne.

Then I am moving behind her, being carried by her shadows against my will. I've truly lost all autonomy over my body, and she's breaking the very little control I have left over my will.

She takes me to the dungeon, something she hasn't done since I was a child, back when she would force me to watch her kill the prisoners when I didn't follow instructions. It's why I'm so *compliant*.

If this is the worst she can do for my lies, then I'll be fine. I learned to put up a mental shield of steel years ago. I can handle this.

Leiana *pulls* me to the back of the dark dungeon. The deeper in we go, the more it reeks of iron and other bodily fluids.

It would be an understatement to say that I did not miss this wretched room.

She stops, dropping me suddenly to my knees but not releasing the shadows that hold me.

Then Leiana sinks her talons into my subconscious. As she tugs, it feels like claws raking through my brain, drawing blood, butchering my mind. Jagged nails against tender flesh. I pant, desperately holding back a scream.

"What's her name?" Leiana demands.

"What are you going to do with it?" I struggle to get the words out.

"That's none of your concern," she sings to me. "Not unless you've grown an attachment." Claws move through my mind like it's a file cabinet. "She's septic, Lucian. Whatever feelings you harbor are to be dropped, immediately."

How would Leiana know this?

I assumed Desdemona was middle class, from a family who worked in livestock or some other median-level job, though certainly not from Utul. It never crossed my mind that she could be septic.

Suddenly, I'm bombarded by foreign faces, unfamiliar places, memories that aren't mine. I'm in my body, but I'm barely in my mind. "What are you doing to me?" My voice is gravelly, a weak mess.

"A new little trick," Leiana says as though she wants a laugh to follow the words.

It feels as if my brain is being split down the middle, hacked at with a sword. I watch Leiana take the life force from a prisoner while I *feel* it. The prisoner collapses, dying, and I feel my body following. My entire *being* tearing to shreds, yet I'm perfectly intact.

"Her name, and this will be over."

Does she not know that I cannot even *fathom* speaking?

A scream rips itself from my throat, begging to be spared, exactly as the prisoner in front of me is doing.

Until I'm no longer in my body at all.

Then every feeling stops. I'm a husk on the floor. A shell of myself. The memories of the dead prisoner are gone, but the feeling of death is not.

I cannot move.

Leiana crouches in front of me, lifting my face while my chest hangs hopelessly against the floor. "You know what the Arcanes have taken from us—from *you*. But the girl might be what we need. Tell me her name."

I was right—Desdemona has the potential to reach The Void one day. She is, without a doubt, the key to my revenge.

Why would I give that to Leiana? Why would I surrender the one edge I have?

When I don't answer, Leiana releases my head, letting it crash against the hard ground.

She leaves me with one parting gift. "Your safety only goes as far as your usefulness."

My head splits repeatedly—like a hammer to rock. My cheek presses against the cold, pungent floor. I try to speak, but all that escapes is a low, desperate groan.

---

The moment I find my footing, I search for Lilac, dragging myself through Ilyria's corridors. I slam into walls and fall to my knees, but I won't stop until I know she is all right.

I kept Desdemona's name to myself. I'm not sure what good that will do her; Leiana can be persuasive, and she is surely persistent.

Perhaps Desdemona should leave. Maybe we both could.

I stop the delusions before they take root.

"Lilac!" I scream, staggering down the castle halls. "Lilac!" At least my voice echoes back. I am not entirely broken.

My private guard meets me, slipping her arm around me to keep me from collapsing. "Lilac went back to Visnatus," she whispers.

"Is she all right?"

"She's okay," my guard answers with a nod.

The relief would conquer me entirely if I could allow it. But I can't. There's another girl I need to get to.

"Would you open a portal for me?" I ask, and my guard looks at me with a silent question. *What did Leiana do?* I don't need to tell her that I can't share those details. She knows I'd never put that target on her back.

She opens the portal, and I drag myself through the halls of Visnatus. I reach Desdemona's suite, but it's Calista who answers the door.

"What do you want?" she asks, her gaze sweeping over me with disdain.

I push past her, my legs unsteady, barely able to stay upright as I stumble into the room. "I need Desdemona."

"Are you serious?" Calista's voice drips with disbelief. When I don't respond, she grabs my arm fiercely, yanking me back to face her and nearly breaking my crumbling form. "*I* am your wife," she hisses, her words barely breaking through the haze of my mind.

My vision wavers, and my knees threaten to give out. I meet Calista's gaze just as I collapse, her hand still anchored to my arm.

"You will be my wife in nothing but title, and we both know it."

Calista crouches before me, her fingers gripping the collar of my shirt as she pulls me close. Her words come out low and dangerous, each syllable a veiled threat. "You will not publicly belittle me, Lucian."

I grit my teeth against the pain and the exhaustion, thinking only of Desdemona. "Get out of my way, Calista."

She narrows her eyes at me. "And if I refuse?"

Slowly, I whisper, "Do you want to play that game with me?"

"You don't look like a very worthy opponent right now." Calista raises an eyebrow.

"Neither does Lilac."

The smug look vanishes from Calista's face in an instant. "Lilac?" she asks, her voice trembling with worry as she releases the collar of my shirt. I collapse, her sudden lack of support leaving me unsteady. "What happened to Lilac?"

"Tell me Desdemona is all right, and you'll have your answer."

Calista's lips form a frown, and she scowls. Turning her head to the back of the suite, she calls sharply, "Marquees!" When there isn't an immediate answer, she adds, her tone growing more impatient, "Fire Folk girl! Your *prince* needs you."

Moments later, Desdemona appears. The relief of seeing her unharmed is truly treacherous, a knife to the gut and a healing hand all at once.

"You're all right," I whisper, falling to my knees.

Leiana hasn't touched her. Yet.

"Are you?" Desdemona asks, her gaze soft where Calista's is cutting. Desdemona runs to me, sits next to me, and my head is in her hands in more ways than one.

Now that I know she's all right, there's nothing to keep me from reliving what I've just survived. Someone's death, and with it, the death of any hope I once had to be free of Leiana and Labyrinth. Forever their puppet, like it's written in the stars.

*Your safety only goes as far as your usefulness.*

Desdemona's gentle thumb brushes over my face, once, twice, until she pulls away. I look for her eyes, but she doesn't look for mine. "Can you take me to Lilac?" I manage to say.

"I will," Calista says instantly.

"I don't know where her suite is," Desdemona says.

Calista takes a step closer, reiterating herself. "I'll take you."

As she stands over us, Desdemona looks at her instead of me —both of them scowling.

"Will you come with me?" I ask Desdemona meekly.

Her gaze finally meets mine. It's farther from me than I've grown used to, as though something is coming between us. It could be any number of things—Calista, my secrets, Leiana— but I can't let it happen.

My feelings are one thing, but I can't let that cloud my judgment. She most certainly holds power against the Arcanes, and that, more than anything, is why I need to keep her close.

I sigh in relief when she whispers, "Sure."

"Let's go," Calista says, already on her feet.

Desdemona puts my arm around her shoulders and wraps her arm around my waist. I struggle to stand, leaning into her as we rise. We step into the hall and pass three suites before Calista knocks on Lilac's door.

Fleur opens the door, and the melody of Lilac's violin creeps out from her room.

"Oh, Zola," Fleur says, her eyes scanning over me. But her gaze lands on Desdemona for a moment. Then she calls, "Lilac?"

Lilac exits her room and looks at Calista with wide eyes. They hold one another's gaze for a moment, then Calista whispers, "Lucian needed you."

It's only then that Lilac looks at me.

"Oh, Sulva," she gasps, rushing to my side, and guiding me to her room. I glance over my shoulder at Desdemona, who is already leaving the suite.

Sitting at the edge of her bed, Lilac's voice trembles as she asks, "What did she do?"

"She killed me," I mumble, my voice distant. The shock of it all vibrates through me. The back of Lilac's hand presses to my forehead, then she pulls a blanket over me.

"She *killed* me," I say again. I felt it all, as if some sort of flip switched in my brain, and I was outside of my body. Only I wasn't looking down at myself—I was looking down at *him*. The prisoner she truly killed.

I saw it all, his childhood in the septic of Ilyria and all of the things that happened that led him to choose to steal from his station. He did it for his wife, his daughter, for the hope of a better life. I felt it all—his love, his desperation—then I felt his death. As if it were my own.

"I'm tired, Li," I whisper. The tears in my eyes feel like

stones.

"Sleep," she says softly, brushing hair out of my face.

"I can't."

It's the last thing I remember saying.

---

I wake up in a cold sweat, haunted by the dead prisoner and gasping for a breath that won't come.

"Shit, Lucian," Azaire whispers from the other side of the room.

*I'm in Lilac's room. I'm not in the septic of Ilyria.*

Groaning, I drag a shaky hand across my sweat-soaked face. I tell myself it was only a dream.

But it wasn't. It was his life. I will forever be inexorably tied to this man—as though his DNA is written in my soul. His blood is coursing through my veins.

"Do you want me to… soothe you?" Azaire asks. One word from him, a single hiss, and my inhibitions would be lowered. My anxieties soothed. Baneful bliss.

A power of the Nepenthes—the ability to soothe their prey.

"No," I rasp. Magic can't fix this madness. Nothing could decimate the dead man inside of me.

"Where's Lilac?" I ask, my voice barely a whisper.

"Getting dinner," he answers softly.

I lie back, mumbling something that barely resembles *okay*. I stare at the ceiling, and it quickly morphs into the man's life.

A looping image. Everlasting torture.

Hot tears slide down my cheeks, soaking the pillow as my chest constricts. As if I am dying all over again.

"What is it?" Azaire asks, his footsteps drawing closer.

"I died," I choke. "She put me *inside* a prisoner, and I felt it all when she killed him." I catch my breath, the words clawing their way out. "I can't—I can't keep living like this." I'm frozen to this bed, unable to move, just as I am unable to cut the strings that bind me to them.

To Leiana and Labyrinth.

*There is no way out.*

"You won't have to," Azaire says. He's too hopeful. "Soon you'll be king, and they won't have a say."

The hollow laugh that escapes me sounds like it belongs to someone else. "I appreciate your perspective."

"And I'll believe it enough for us both. No surrender?" he says, though his grip on my hand trembles.

The words feel distant and false as I mutter, "No surrender."

The door opens, and Lilac sets down a wooden tray of food before rushing to me. She hugs me as though she thought I wouldn't survive my slumber.

Gently cupping my cheeks, my sister examines my face with a tenderness I imagine only a mother could have. "Oh, Lucy." She hugs me again, her hands cradling the back of my head. "I was so worried."

"I'm all right," I lie, not wanting to worry her further.

Her hand is cool against my feverish skin, and her voice is more severe than I've ever heard as she asks, "What did they do to you?"

I meet Azaire's gaze and shake my head ever so slightly.

"Nothing," I answer.

Lilac removes her hands from my face, her nose twitching as she frowns. "You can't keep lying to me."

"I'm not—"

"I see it," she whispers, cutting me off. "I know the things you do to protect me—I *know* what they ask of you. I've watched you return from Ilyria, weaker every time." Lilac scoots closer, picking up my hand as she begs, "You can tell me. I can keep the secret."

But it's not that simple.

The last time I told my sister a secret, Leiana had a Folk wipe her memories, then made me kill the last living piece of my father. I've been trained from a young age in the art of obedience. The punishments for my failures were severe—even more severe than my sister, looking me in the eye and begging me to confide in her about the abuse I've suffered.

Keeping Leiana's secret as she's always trained me to—like a dog doing her dirty work—I mutter, "There's nothing to tell."

Lilac scoots back, clearly disbelieving. "I'm going to fix it."

"Lilac," I say, my voice trembling as I grab her wrist. "*Don't.*"

"I can't keep watching this happen—"

I cut her off, putting weight behind each word. "It will be over soon."

Her eyes widen, and the silence settles between us. Nearly imperceptibly, she shakes her head, staring at me as if I've become a stranger.

"All right," she mutters, pulling away as she rises to her feet. She grabs the tray she settled on her desk and hands me a ceramic bowl with cheesecake and a red berry reduction. "I got Elowen to make your favorite."

I smile, for her. Beneath it there is only fear—fear for what Leiana and Labyrinth will do if Lilac fights. The only hope is that they will treat her rebellion better than they would mine. She is their daughter, after all. Their bloodline and their flesh.

Though today Leiana proved that such ties no longer carry the weight I once placed upon them.

I hold the cake in my hand, saying, "A better remedy than any."

Lilac nods once before walking to her violin—but there's a sadness in her eyes. Worse than that, a determination.

She softly asks, "Would you like a song?" and I know the previous conversation has drawn to a close.

But she's yet to let it go.

If she were in my position, I wouldn't either.

"Always," I answer.

Azaire flops down beside me, the mattress sinking as we listen to Li's mini-concert.

## Chapter 16
### I'm A Killer Everywhere

# DESDEMONA

I stumble away from the dead body lying at my feet. A dead body I know—Bernice. I think I killed him, and now I'm just walking away, because what else can I do?

The trees around me catch fire. One by one, flames swallow the trees, each catching fire seconds apart. I run. Was that me? I didn't know I could set fires—*destroy*—yet. Mom always says my powers would manifest when I was older, but I'm not older. This is too soon.

The fire chases me, nearly licking my heels while my heart beats in every inch of my body. "Mom!" I'm calling, and my throat is growing raw. I'm running home.

I did kill Bernice. I must've burned him alive. And now, I'm going to kill a forest. He told me I was just as bad as the Nepenthes. Maybe he was right. Because in the end, I killed him, just like a Nepenthe would.

And now I'm burning everything in my path.

"Mom!" I scream, the words tearing from me, shredding my throat as they pass. "Mommy!"

A beat of silence. Then, I hear her respond: "Desdemona?"

Relief floods me—I'm safe.

"Mommy!" I slam into her, wrapping my arms around her hips.

She pulls me back, resting on her knees to meet my gaze, her hands shaking as they clutch my arm. She looks scared.

"You need to put it out," Mom demands, her voice shaking.

But I just look at her, frozen. The heat floods across my back, scorching me—the fire is right behind me.

"Put it out!" she screams, her nails digging into my shoulder as she spins me around, forcing me to face the fire. It's too close, threatening to consume everything in its path.

For some reason, I reach for it, and the flames wrap around my hand—first circling my fingers, like glowing rings, and then down my wrist like bracelets. I expect it to burn, and it does, but not in a way that's painful. It just… is. I stare at the fire in awe, but Mom's scream cuts through me, sharp with fear.

Then I jolt awake, heart racing, my scream joining hers.

But she's not with me anymore. I'm in Aralia's room, lying in bed. I was sleeping, and that was a dream.

I take a deep breath, my hand trembling as I raise it to my face, searching for burn marks. But my skin is perfectly fine, unscathed—and my hand feels unnervingly larger, twice the size it was when I reached for the fire.

Because I was a child in the dream. More importantly, the fire didn't burn me, and it didn't follow me outside of my mind.

*Obviously.*

*I'm safe,* I repeat in my head. I'm inside, there's no fire, and I'm safe. Sweat soaks through my clothes, and I'm lying in my own puddle, but I'm *safe*.

Only, I can't breathe. Something is caught in my throat. I choke on nothing—on the air, I guess.

"Des?" Aralia says, stirring in her bed across from me. "Des, are you all right?"

"Fine," I try to say while taking shallow breaths, but I can't manage to get the word out.

"What is it?" she asks, rising to sit next to me. Her hand rests gently on my arm as she mutters, "Gods, you're burning up." Then she moves her hands to my torso, right over my lungs, and uses her magic to fill my shriveling body with air.

"I'm fine," is all I can say. When I finally catch my breath, she gives me a look, and I know she wants answers. "Bad dream, it's fine. Go back to bed." Then I say, "I apologize for waking you."

"Don't worry," Aralia says with a small shake of her head, standing and returning to bed.

I lie for a while, unmoving.

When it sounds like she's fallen back to sleep, I grab my notebook, where I've started writing down the dreams.

I was six when I met Bernice. So why am I dreaming about killing him? Yeah, he was an asshole, but I never wanted him dead. I was six.

I start writing every detail—the screams, the way Bernice's corpse lay, and how the fire felt when it touched me. When it becomes too much, and I get hot in the room, I leave for a walk.

As I step outside, the waning moon shines on me, reminding me of Lucian. These past few days, he's occupied my mind for more time than I'd like to admit, and in turn, I've been ignoring him more than I'd like to admit.

It doesn't matter how I feel; what matters is who he is. He's going to be king, and if he ever finds out who I really am, he's gonna change his mind about me *inspiring endearment*.

Besides, he's just a means to an end, I tell myself. A way to find my mom. Someone willing to break Ilyrian law.

I walk to the lake, out of habit from meeting Lucian here every week to train, I guess. Sitting at the edge, I dip my feet in the cool water and feel marginally better. I rest my hands behind me and look up at the sky, counting the stars. I kind of relate to them. Everyone is looking, but no one is close enough to really see. At least, in the stars' case, they're not purposely keeping everyone at arm's length.

They're that way by coincidence, and I'm here by necessity.

Leaves ruffle beside me, and even though it's likely an animal, I'm on my feet in seconds. Then I spot a flash of red, a bit of shadow.

"Hello?" I call out.

Whispers answer. *Cause... act...* run.

I stumble back, tripping over a root and falling. Again, I spot something—a flickering wisp of red and black that vanishes before I can make it out. Like some kind of ghost.

But it feels like *more*, like my blood is boiling in its presence.

My magic surges inside of me, goosebumps rising along my neck. As I raise my hand, I feel my mom's—like she's right here, on the other side of an invisible wall.

And I hear one word. "Hide."

"Mom?" I call.

The ghost flees, and the world goes black.

The chill in the air takes over the boiling of my blood. Instantly, I know this is Lyrian magic—not whatever was here before.

"Lucian?" I call. No response.

*They don't feel like Lucian's shadows.*

Then those shadows are wrapping around me, constricting my throat, my mouth, and I can't breathe again. Strong hands grip my shoulders, and I know it's not Lucian.

Instinctively, I smash my head back, right into the Lyrian's nose. They groan, and their magic slips from around my mouth, but my vision is still compromised. I lash out, kicking and swinging blindly, desperately hoping to hit my attacker. My fist is caught, and my arm twists with a sickening *pop*. Pain forces me to gasp. I kick—once, twice—before they catch my ankle, and I crash onto my back.

Anxiously, I pull the dagger from my waistband. I haven't slept without it since Aralia gave it to me.

Stars begin to fill my vision from the lack of oxygen when pressure pulses in my shoulder. Instinctively, I reach for the pain and find the hilt of a blade that *burns*. Then I kick hard, hitting my attacker's knees before managing to stand.

I swing my dagger, slicing through the air, ignoring the dull ache in my shoulder. They grab my wrist, overpowering me and forcing my injured arm down, and I swear it hurts more than the blade in my shoulder.

My dagger falls from my hand, and there's no time to pick it up. But now I know where this Lyrian is.

I pull the knife out of my shoulder, and the second I do, it feels like layers of skin are being ripped from my palm. I sink the blade into their shoulder, getting the dagger out of my hand as quickly as possible. I'm surprised when I don't hear a yell or feel another punch.

And if I hit their shoulder, why are they gurgling? I aimed for their shoulder.

Right?

The shadows dissipate, leaving me standing in the clear night with a man at my feet and a knife lodged in his throat.

The hilt is red, and he is dead.

I fall to my knees, blood-curdling pain pulsing through my arm and shoulder as I bleed out. My shirt—Aralia's shirt—is entirely soaked, but her black jacket conceals it enough.

What am I going to do? There's no way I can carry him, not with my shoulder, and there's no way I can get someone to heal me, not without telling them what happened.

Not without admitting I'm a killer.

I'm a killer. A killer who's likely to bleed out if I don't *do* something.

I just have to get the Lyrian into the lake, then I can worry about bleeding out.

I walk to the man, but I can't take my eyes away from his. They're open wide, staring into the sky but not seeing. Bile rises in my throat, but I swallow it, forcing myself to stay sane.

*How am I going to pull him into the lake if I can't pull myself together?*

I grab the body by the ankles, but the strain on my shoulder sends a jolt of pain through me, nearly making me scream. But I don't drop the body. My muscles strain under the pressure, but I force myself to continue dragging the corpse.

Footsteps stop me, echoing from a distance. I hold my breath, trying not to make a sound. But as the footsteps grow louder, my stomach churns, panic rising in me.

There's only one option. I let go of the ankles and jump behind the nearest tree, hoping it will be enough to hide me. Then, my eyes catch the dagger Aralia gave me, sitting really close to the dead body. The orange stone of the hilt gleams in the shrinking moonlight, probably drawing attention.

Screwed, that's what I am. I'm screwed.

As Lucian's face comes into view, I realize just how screwed I might be. He glances around the area, his gaze—luckily—sweeping past the tree I'm hiding behind. But then he notices the dagger. Kneeling, he picks it up, fingers tracing its edges like it's something precious. There's no doubt he knows it's mine.

He knows entirely too much: my mom, my magic, and now the blood on my hands. It doesn't matter what he thinks about me, whether or not he calls me "darling" or why. I have to level the playing field somehow. But I know nothing, nothing I could use against him if it came down to it.

I carefully move out from behind the tree, grabbing the last weapon I have—the small knife I stole from the headmistress. Stepping before Lucian, I hold the blade to his throat. The pain shoots through my shoulder, sharper this time, even though I'm using the opposite arm. The intensity forces me to bite my tongue so hard I draw blood. I can't scream now; I have to appear strong.

"One word of this to anyone," I whisper, "and I'll slit your throat."

But doing this now, after what he's said, *what I've felt,* doesn't feel right.

It feels worse than not right. It feels entirely wrong.

I think about how I last saw him. He was lying on the floor,

217

drenched in sweat with eyes glossed over in a way that reminds me of the dead man at our feet. I was so gentle then, gentle in the way I never want to be, gentle in the way that makes me weak.

Lucian glances down at my blade and outstretched arm, but he doesn't seem scared.

"With a letter opener?" he murmurs with a laugh.

I force the shock of his reaction away. He was just lying there, *dying* on my floor, and now he's laughing at my blade.

I don't get him at all.

Scowling, I tighten my hold on the hilt of the blade—letter opener. Whatever. "I'll make it work."

Lucian smirks, shadows rising around him before darting toward me and pulling the blade from my hand. It hovers through the air a moment and lands right in Lucian's hand—ruining my plan before it's begun.

He holds up the dagger, taunting me. "I'll give back your toy when you're a little less murderous," Lucian mutters, giving a very pointed look at the dead man.

"He was going to kill me!" I emphasize quietly, each word taking more energy than I can afford to give.

"Okay," he says with a small shrug.

I step forward—nearly wincing from the movement. I stop short, saying, "You believe me, right?"

Lucian's face hardens. "Doesn't matter."

I shrug in my best attempt to act like I'm not scared beyond my wits' end. This time, the motion sends pain from my shoulder up to my neck.

"Well, I'll just burn you, then," I say, my voice growing weaker, smaller. "If you're thinking of saying anything." I clench my jaw and raise an eyebrow in defense, but stars begin to cloud my vision, and I'm not entirely sure I'm standing up.

Lucian chuckles. "You're more violent than I anticipated."

I'm going to say... *something*, but most of my energy is being spent trying to keep my head upright. The stars are filling my vision fast now, the world blurring. I'm going to pass out.

I *can't* pass out in front of him—not before taking care of the dead body. And the prince.

Lucian is already next to me when he asks, "What happened?"

My head tips to the side, and my legs lose their muscle. I'm falling. But something catches me. It's Lucian's arms around my waist, gently lowering me to the ground. I'd know this feeling anywhere.

My eyes roll back and forth and I try to hold onto the world, but the feeling of floating into unconsciousness is so much more appealing.

Lucian's hands move across my body, pulling my energy to his touch and keeping me awake. Every place his skin brushes feels like a jolt of adrenaline, power rushing through my veins toward him.

His hands move up my legs first, the coolness of his touch allowing me to relax for a moment, easing the constant burn in my skin. When his fingers reach my waist, a shiver runs through me, sending a shock straight to my brain. As he moves higher, his hands press against my shoulder and stop there. The fabric of my shirt tears, and the cold air stings my newly exposed skin.

Quickly, the chill turns to warmth, and all my body longs for is sleep.

"Stay with me," Lucian whispers, but he sounds so far away. Like either he's flying, or I am.

Then I scream as something cold and wet moves into my opened flesh. The shock of it passes, and my head sinks deeper into the grass, as if gravity itself is pulling me down.

"It's all right," he whispers. "You can scream."

But I don't want to scream, I want to *sleep*. I do. I fall further and further down into darkness...

"Marquees?"

I think I'm shaking.

"Marquees!" The name that isn't mine echoes. "Come on, Des—wake up!"

My face is shaking. It doesn't feel like mine.

*Cold* fills the wound, and my eyes open with a jerk. I reach slowly toward my shoulder. It's not just wet, it's *swelling*.

I squint up, noticing Lucian's bare torso. "Why are you shirtless?"

He holds up a wet cloth, a hint of sarcasm in his voice. "Because my shirt is covered in your blood."

I try to speak, but all that comes out is a croak.

"You don't have to talk," Lucian whispers. "But know I'm missing your witty remarks."

He smiles a little, and I can't help but think that it's for my benefit.

"Hey." It's only when I hear his voice that I realize my eyes are closing. "*Desdemona, stay with me.*" I look at him. "Yeah," he whispers. "Focus on me." His calloused hand touches my cheek.

"You said my name." My voice is scratchy.

"*Desdemona,*" he whispers back—like it's more than the name of a girl. Like it's the name of a god he's swearing to. "Desdemona, Desdemona, Desdemona." He twirls strands of my hair around his finger. "I don't know what I'd do if something happened to you and I hadn't said it aloud."

"You could say it over my grave."

"I'd prefer to whisper it in your ear." He smirks, the action sending my eyes to his lips. "Are you looking at my lips again?" he says joyfully. So carefree. Like it's a day in the sun. "Listen, I know you like them," he whispers. "Perhaps a little too much, if you ask me. But I do have other attributes."

I can't stop myself from laughing. The sound is a sorry one. "Ass," I mumble.

"It's all right," he says. "Soon you'll find better comebacks." He sounds so sarcastic, but the way his fingers rake through my hair feels anything but. "We can't all be witty *and* pretty."

"You sound like a bad poem," I croak.

"Well, if my words are too much for you, then go ahead and look at my lips again."

It's like his words are a spell because when he says look, I do. He smirks again.

*Ass.*

My hand reaches for the wound, but Lucian swats it away, mumbling, "Hold on." I watch as he fills the wound with shadows. "I have to do this bit by bit, so as not to freeze you," he whispers.

*He's keeping me from bleeding out.*

I don't want him saving my life. I don't want to owe him a thing. I don't want to talk about his lips and call him an ass.

I don't want to be reminded of the intimacy that I *can* feel for him.

But the magic doesn't seem to agree with my mind. As his shadows work to stop the bleeding, it feels like Lucian's touch is seeping into me, becoming a part of me. The cooling, the burning, the power, the adrenaline—each sensation lingers in me, odd and intense, almost as if his touch is being etched into my skin.

I try to sit up, but Lucian says, "You need rest."

"No," I croak as I sit up all the way, despite—or maybe even in spite of—the pain. "We have to…"

"We're not putting him in the lunar lake," Lucian says immediately.

"I never said—"

"You were going to," he says. "The body won't sink here. Sulva has a way with secrets. Everything comes to light eventually." Lucian gestures toward the woods. "If we take him to the coast, he'll be farther away when he does resurface."

"Okay," I say, my mouth dry. I rise slowly to my feet. "Let's go."

Lucian follows, his hands resting on my waist to stabilize me. "I can do it."

"Without me?" I ask. Why would he do that?

"Yes," he answers.

"No, I'm coming." I still feel dizzy and a little emotional, like I'm going to cry at any moment. "This is my problem. I'll take care of it."

"With a dislocated shoulder and a stab wound?" he questions.

"Yes!"

"Then grab his shoulders," Lucian says, and I can tell it's a challenge.

I walk carefully to the man on the ground, but when I try to lift him, the strain on my shoulder is too much. My vision blurs white, and I have no choice but to let go of the body. I fall beside it, sitting on the ground and staring at his limp limbs—never to be used again.

The *body*. That's all this man is now. What if he wasn't trying to kill me? What if he saw me clearly through the shadows and aimed for my shoulder on purpose?

I shake the thought away. *I aimed for his shoulder, too,* I remind myself. But that doesn't make it any better.

Without meaning to, I find myself looking at Lucian, speaking before I can stop myself. "I aimed for his shoulder. I swear. I–I couldn't see in the shadows, but I was aiming for his shoulder. I swear—"

Lucian sits beside me, just inches away from the body. "It's all right," he says softly—too softly. He never speaks this softly. His gaze is heavy as he stares at me. Intimate, even. Like he wants to make sure I understand him when he says, "I believe you."

Those three words are the emotional embodiment of putting shadows in my wound to stop the bleeding. I don't know why it matters that he believes me, but it does. It really does.

Lucian opens a portal and lifts the body with ease, moving as though he's done this a thousand times. The *body*. I've been here before, I've *killed* before, but this doesn't feel real. It never did.

When we reach the coast, I sit on the sand, knees drawn up to my chest. I watch Lucian drag the man to the sea, shaking uncontrollably, rocking back and forth, fighting a chill that isn't coming from the cold.

Then, out of the corner of my eye, I spot a knife strapped to the dead man's waistband, its hilt iridescent in the moonlight. *Moonstone.*

I get up, place a hand on Lucian's chest, and walk to the top of the body. I duck, finding the crest of Ilyria—tiny and covered by a scrap of fabric. Just what I was searching for.

"You told me I'd be safe here," I whisper without looking at Lucian. My eyes are locked on the Ilyrian crest. Someone from *his* kingdom sent this man to attack me. After the ball, after *his* queen was staring at me, he told me I was safe. He told me to stay.

"And now I've killed someone because I trusted you," I finish.

*Another someone.*

Lucian looks at me guiltily, and I realize he has both my weapons. Is this all a setup? Has his mother—the *queen*—told him to finish the job if the first soldier fails? It couldn't be. It could be. Lucian could've been lying to me this entire time. But to what end, for what purpose?

The soldier didn't try to kill me, either, I don't think.

"If it wasn't you, it would've been me," he says softly. I *hate* how soft his voice is. "That man wasn't making it out alive tonight. Not after what he did to you."

"That's not enough! I trusted you," I whisper, my voice breaking. "You said I'd be safe here."

But I'm a murderer in the septic, too. It's not like I had anywhere to actually go. I'm homeless, in my heart at least. I don't belong anywhere.

*I'm a killer everywhere.*

No matter where I go, I can never shed the bodies. The blood doesn't stop at the hands because I'm covered in it. I'm surprised no one sees it when I walk the halls of this school.

Now Lucian will, if he doesn't kill me right here and now. But he's had every opportunity to, and I'm the only killer here.

"I don't want to be this way," I whisper, my words thick with saliva and tears. "I don't want this," I say again.

But "say" is a sad excuse for what I really sound like. "Cry" is more like it. I don't want to cry. I wipe my tears and bite my tongue before he can see. I want Lucian to believe that I *would* slit his throat if he told someone. That if he comes close, I *will* burn him.

Crying about not wanting to be a killer isn't the way to do that.

Lucian drops next to me, the water soaking us both, and I can't bring myself to move. Maybe I could burn him if he tries anything. But I don't think that I actually think he will. I don't know. I wish I had the strength to push him away. Because if he's not here to kill me, he's here to comfort me, and I don't want to be coddled. I want to be *feared*. But I don't think I look very scary right now.

"You won't be the same," Lucian says in that soft tone again. "But you'll be all right."

And all it takes are those words for me to break entirely. I fall into myself, my head and shoulders collapse, and Lucian pulls me into his chest. It feels good to be held, and for a moment, I feel safe again. Like I'm five years old, and the war hasn't begun, and I'm sitting on my mom's lap with a cup of hot water while she tells me stories about her life before the septic.

For a moment, everything is okay in the world. Nothing bad has happened to me yet, and I'm not a killer. I breathe in the scent—pine and something sweet that chills my nostrils. It's comforting. Familiar and foreign. The fine line between childhood and what lies ahead for me. But I don't want to think about that quite yet. I just want to be held.

Lucian strokes the back of my head, brushing through my hair with his fingers, sending ripples of sensation down my spine. And when he whispers, "You'll be all right," I realize I'm still crying. I don't try to stop the tears this time—I just let them go.

*You'll be all right.*

---

Lucian takes me back to my suite, but instead of heading to my room, he knocks on Wendy's door. I've managed to do little more than nod since breaking down in his arms. I'm still breaking down. My shoulder's gone numb—or maybe I have. Every time I close my eyes, I see the dead Lyrian, sometimes the dead Folk in my dwelling.

Wendy opens the door and locks eyes with Lucian. The intensity between them makes me feel like I'm intruding on something. "What happened to you?" she whispers.

Lucian clears his throat, the steadiness in his voice faltering for the first time. "Desdemona needs your help."

Wendy's eyes widen, and she turns to me, her expression tightening with concern. "What happened to her?"

"Dislocated shoulder," he answers, and *she* winces, feeling the pain I've already gone numb to. It must be a Eunoia thing.

Lucian tilts his head toward the door, beckoning her, and without even glancing in his direction, Wendy says, "Okay."

She disappears into her room and returns with a tray stacked with glass jars. I follow as she steps toward the exit, but the pain makes me wince. Without a word, Lucian lifts me into his arms, and my head falls into the space between his neck and shoulder. His fingers gently thread through my hair as he walks silently through the school.

No one's held me this tenderly since my mom. It doesn't feel right—to feel safe. I know I should be on edge, put my guard up and prepare for the worst, but I'm too damn tired. Too comfortable in the arms of the last person I should be comfortable with.

We go up the stairs to the room where Lucian taught me to dance, and he lays me gently on a cot in the corner of the room.

Our eyes meet, and a jolt of electricity moves through me, my body forgetting that I'm half-dead, if not dying.

I quickly look away, and Wendy appears at my side.

"Can you?" she asks, gesturing to the wound.

Lucian waves a hand, and as the shadows pour out of my shoulder, a rush of heat floods into the injury. Blood starts to trickle down my shoulder, and I realize just how much the shadow had been numbing the pain. A wave of agony washes over me, returning me to the state of pain I'd been avoiding.

Without hesitation, Wendy applies a salve to the wound. When she's finished, she dips a gloved finger into another glass jar and holds it under my nose.

"Inhale," she orders.

I do, the scent pulling me toward unconsciousness. I can barely hold my eyes open until I decide there's no reason to anyway.

I'm greeted by the darkness.

That is until something tugs on my shoulder, and I wake up with a jolt. Wendy has her hand over my mouth before I can scream and keeps it there when she turns back to Lucian.

"Calista's working on it." Then she turns to me, tells me it's okay, and that I can close my eyes.

I follow her instructions, but this time, I don't fall into nothingness like before.

The silence stretches, and so does the room, drifting farther from me. I lose my grip on reality, slowly slipping into the cracks of the silence.

Then there's Wendy, but she seems to be off in the sky somewhere. I see her there, see her flying. "What's that about?"

she asks.

"What's what about?" Lucian's flying, too—up in the sky, light curling around his body.

"That feeling," she whispers. She's floating further down with every exhale.

"Is she out?" He's moving away from me. I can still see those midnight eyes of his and the little bits of light blue and the divot in his lip.

"Yes," Wendy answers. "Now, are you going to tell me what happened to you?" Silence stretches while they dance around one another in the clouds. "You don't feel the same."

Lucian's voice is barely a whisper when he finally says, "I'm not the same anymore." He's floating further and further away, but his words still echo through my mind. "But what matters now is Desdemona, then the book."

"She'll be fine," Wendy's voice softens as she floats over me, caressing my face.

"Yeah, she will," Lucian says as he leaves my view entirely.

## Chapter 17
### Innocence Don't Make You Feel That Way

## LUCIAN

Wendy's left for the night, and I sit at the table, watching Desdemona sleep on the couch, making sure she doesn't succumb to her wounds. Worry continues to gnaw at me—some kind of poison lingers in her body. Burns mar her stab wound and spread across her palm. I gave Wendy the red knife, but she found no trace of poison—nothing in Desdemona's bloodstream she could identify, and no way to cure it.

Before leaving, Wendy gave me a long list of warning signs to watch out for. I've stayed up all night, just in case something happens.

Occasionally, Desdemona stirs on the couch. Sometimes she cries out. I try to keep her dreams peaceful, guiding her subconscious away from the images that trap her.

But the nightmares always pull her back.

Leiana's fast. Within days of identifying Desdemona, she orchestrated both the taking of a life and the loss of one.

I close my eyes and see the unnamed prisoner.

Desdemona closes hers and sees her own version of that man.

A gift, I suppose, for us both.

When Desdemona cries out once more, I guide her into a dream of her mother, on a sunny day somewhere, lying in the grass.

It doesn't last.

Minutes later, Desdemona whimpers again. I've never had so many difficulties dictating dreams before.

I move next to the couch and try once more to bring her peace. This time, she screams.

When I enter her subconscious, she's... killing someone. The bodies are burning in front of her, but more than that, she's crying out, racked with guilt. She doesn't *want* to be harming them.

"Marquees?" I shake her gently, but she cries louder. "Marquees."

It feels like the lunar lake all over again—begging her to stay, to *live*, watching as she bleeds out before me and doing everything I can to stop it.

I barely know the girl, yet it feels like I know her intrinsically—like we're bound together by something stronger than this universe. There's no other reason for the terror tearing through me at the mere thought that she *could* have died.

She screams.

"Desdemona, wake up!"

Her eyes flash open, glowing orange, and land on me.

"Hey," I whisper. "You're all right."

Then the room grows unbearably warm. Sweat beads at my forehead, soaking through my shirt, and soon it feels like my entire body is on fire. My insides ignite, the burn scorching from the inside out.

Desdemona's gaze remains fixed on me, her glowing eyes unblinking, but her body is completely still.

"It's me," I choke out, reaching up to my burning throat, desperate for relief.

The heat spreads further, and I tug at my shirt, trying to free myself of some of it, but before I can do anything, I collapse. My body hits the floor, and I gasp for air as the heat claws at my lungs.

I reach into her subconscious, glimpsing the image she sees.

She's caught between a dream and waking, and in both, I am the enemy. Shadows coat my body in her dream, and each time one touches her, her power fades, sinking into dormancy.

"Des—" I try to speak, but my words are weak. "Wake up!"

"Aibek?" Her voice is a whisper, and in that instant, my organs stop burning. Actively, that is. Her power has ceased, but I am still very much overheated.

I clutch my torso, lying on the floor, disoriented, unsure of what just happened. I've never heard of a Fire Folk burning someone *internally*.

Desdemona crawls from the couch, clutching her shoulder in pain as she stumbles toward me. She reaches out, hands trembling, and gently cups my face like she's afraid I'll vanish if she doesn't. Her eyes search mine, holding a kind of vulnerability I've never seen in her before.

"Did I hurt you?" she asks, her voice fragile, breaking with the weight of the question.

I think of her dreams, the way the murder is haunting her. And in that instant, I know I can't be another wound she carries.

"No, darling," I manage to say, swallowing the pain. "I'm perfectly all right."

My heart beats vigorously, the heat lingering in my chest.

Desdemona nods and grabs the blanket Wendy brought her, wrapping it around her shoulders. She sits next to me, jaw chattering as she weakly says, "How did you know I'd be out there? By the lake?"

"I had a vision," I answer, steadying my breath. "I didn't know you'd be hurt."

"So you're one of those Lyrians?" she asks without meeting my eyes.

"I suppose, assuming I know what you mean by *those* kinds."

Desdemona is quiet for a while, still shivering, strangely. I wrap an arm around her, and she leans into me, her head resting on my shoulder—like we've done this a million times before. As if we've perfected this dance.

*As if she can be anything more to me than what she's become.*

"How powerful are your visions?" she whispers.

Few people know of the things I foresee. Every Lyrian has the propensity for them, but most Lyrians fall short with our magic: shadows, subconscious manipulation, all of it. It's said to be the most difficult magic to master.

Which also means that it's the most powerful, some say.

"They're never wrong," I answer. "Occasionally a detail is omitted, such as your injury."

"Oh… Okay."

She snuggles closer to me, silently telling me to hold her tighter. I listen. I even dare to stroke her hair, brushing my fingers through the short, soft strands. For the first time, I have the honor of holding her in the way I've longed to, yet I worry where we will go from here. In her dream, I was the enemy. In some part of her mind—subconscious or not—that is how she sees me.

Somehow, I understand. What else could I be to her, after all I've done?

"Can you tell me a story?" Desdemona whispers, her words breaking with the hoarse tone.

I hold her a little tighter, breathing her in, knowing that soon —sooner than I wish—I will lose this. "What kind?" I whisper into her hair.

"One of your own. What was it like growing up in a castle?"

I look at my hands, still covered in her blood. "Lonely," I admit, my free fingers absentmindedly spinning the silver wolf in my pocket. "Have you met Azaire?"

"I think so."

"When he moved in, it was less so." Desdemona's hair falls over her closed eyes, and I tuck it behind her ear.

All right, a story.

"When we were nine, we decided to sneak away for a night.

We walked far out into a neighboring village and found a pub. Barley's. There was some sort of ceremony, a wedding, I believe. Lots of Lyrians at the bar drinking and hollering.

"We sat with them, shouting and acting in ways we never could in the kingdom. The man next to us was a bit… drunk. He kept ordering shots and handing them to us. Naturally, we didn't know what it was, yet, also naturally, we drank them all. Azaire and I got so messed up that at the end of the night, when Barley found us, he gave us the key to an extra room and told us to sleep it off. After that, we went back as often as we could. Barley felt more like family than anyone in the kingdom ever did."

That was always Azaire's and my secret. No one knows about all the nights we've spent at Barley's, from nine to now.

"Hm," she mumbles.

Desdemona's eyes are closed, and her mouth slowly parts as sleep pulls her under. "Would you like to go to the couch?"

She groans softly, her eyes fluttering open. They have a sleepy look to them that tells me she's not fully here. "No," she whispers and pushes her head further up my shoulder.

There's something about Desdemona when she's unguarded. Her eyes soften, and her lips curve down. Her entire face becomes easier to see. To behold.

It irks and intrigues me that she is… *allowing* me to regard her in such vulnerable moments as this night has held. I don't want to do wrong by her.

I will *only* do wrong by her.

As I've thought of doing before—and swore I wouldn't—I count her freckles. I brush her cheek with my thumb; I graze her nose.

To touch her, to *have* her, would be a gift from the universe. But the gods have never been all that generous with me. They prefer my abuse to my award. My torture to my treasure.

I'm not sure what my penance is for, but it's always been

rather obvious that I am paying one.

Not being able to have her, not being able to allow her to have me, will be the greatest punishment yet.

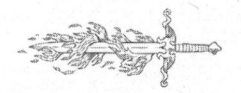

---

Wendy returns in the late morning, quickly pushing apart Desdemona's ripped and bloodied shirt to look at the wound. She frowns, examining the blistered and blackened skin, charred from some kind of poison. Green wisps of light flow from her fingers into Desdemona.

"You should get her to the couch," Wendy says, gently cleaning the wound without waking Desdemona. Then, she heads for the door.

I look at Desdemona's palm, burnt to a crisp. "Do you have any new theories on what the poison might be?"

"It's not natural," Wendy replies. She would know, the Eunoia of Visnatus Academy study all the plant life in the universe. "No fever, no signs in her blood—the only symptoms are around the stab wound."

Wendy reaches for the door. I'm about to ask what that means when she spins back, exasperated. "Look," she sighs, "all I can feel is her pain and your worry, and it's too much for me. I'll be back to check on her."

"Before you leave," I say, stopping her, "are you done with the knife?"

Wendy hesitates, glancing at Desdemona's sleeping form, then hands it to me with a shaky sigh. "There's nothing."

"Thanks," I murmur as Wendy slips out the door.

The knife is entirely red—the hilt, the blade, everything—and cold to the touch, nearly transparent. As I hold it, I sense how it feels alive, humming faintly, as if aware of Desdemona's presence. The power it radiates buzzes through me, familiar and electric—the same sensation I feel when I touch her.

Like it's a piece of Desdemona itself.

But I don't understand how that could be. The knife must be made of something other than metal or bronze—perhaps a stone of some kind. How it could be connected to Desdemona is beyond me.

Perhaps her burns are from a simple poison. Perhaps there is nothing more. But as I touch the hilt to Desdemona's forearm, her skin sizzles and burns, then she wakes with a jump.

I slide the knife into my pocket.

If it was poison, then the knife shouldn't still burn her. That means there's something else causing this reaction. I watch carefully as she sits up, breathless, eyes darting around the room.

"How long?" she asks.

"Only the night."

"Has class started?" Desdemona stands too quickly, swaying unsteadily. She leans against the wall for support, still blinking sleep from her eyes. Her free hand clutches her shoulder, and I move to her side in an instant, steadying her by the waist—pulling her close.

"Yes," I say, almost as if it's a question.

"Why didn't you go?" She looks up at me, her gaze searching.

"It's no big deal."

"No, it is!" she whispers, pulling out of my hold, her body trembling slightly as she steps away. Her words come in a rush, frantic with fear. "You said the body will resurface, and what if they find out the man died before we both skipped? And what if they go to Wendy and she tells them she healed me and they put it together and they find out *I killed him?*"

The *they* she's talking about are my parents. It makes sense for her to be this worried if Leiana was right about her being septic.

But I won't let them have her. I won't allow it.

I take off my jacket and put it on her shoulders. "Wear this when you go back to your suite." She looks down at her bloody, ripped shirt, then covers it with the jacket. "Take a shower and burn your clothes. If anything happens, I'll take care of it."

She looks up at me, her tone cold and harsh. "Why would you do that?"

I step into the space between us, my hand inching toward her cheek. When my touch reaches her, her breath catches.

I tuck her hair behind her ear. "That's why."

Desdemona doesn't move. Her voice is softer now—the cold edge has thawed. "Because you like playing with my hair?"

"No." I smile, dropping my hand and stepping back, scared at the truth of the next words and what they mean. "For the same reason your breath catches when I touch you."

Desdemona looks at me like she's scared I will look away. I believe I'm looking at her the same.

"Is that what you tell all the pretty girls?"

"Oh no," I say. "If that were the case, you wouldn't have made the list."

"Right." She looks down at her feet, clenching and unclenching her left hand almost imperceptibly.

"You're not pretty—"

"Yes, thank you, Aibek," she cuts me off, losing her balance.

She sinks against the wall, and I step toward her again, lifting her. When she won't meet my gaze I gently pick up her chin. I'm prepared for her to fight me, but there's not an ounce of pushback.

"You're haunting," I tell her. "It's been mere weeks that I've known you. And it's been weeks that you've been on my mind. Like a spell."

There it is, the second of something in her eyes that I long for. A softness, a sheepishness. A look that belongs to her face but not to her spirit.

"Maybe it is a spell," she says, the corners of her lips lifting. "Maybe I've been playing you the whole time, putting myself in the favor of a prince."

"You wouldn't have to play me to do that." I smile back at

her. "You've already won."

"Well then, Prince, that sounds an awful lot like being your downfall."

She finds her footing—just as mine falters.

"You could be any man's ruin," I whisper. "I might call it a privilege to be one of them."

I *died* for her. She *is* my downfall. Whatever becomes of me on account of her is bound to be baneful. I've known this; only now I am starting to think I'd let her make of me whatever she wishes.

Desdemona leans in, her fingers wrapping around my wrist and pushing it away, as if it's an act of defiance and not what I expected her to do from the beginning. "I'll add you to my hit list."

"So long as I'm your last."

Again, her eyebrows furrow, my wrist still in her hand. She watches me for a while, and I'm thoroughly pleased with the image of her stunned.

"You're well worth the wait."

Her eyebrows rise, her eyes harden, and she smiles. "That's what they all say." Then she stumbles toward the door, saying, "Thanks for the jacket," as if a jacket is far more than cloth.

## Chapter 18
## My Conscience Is Stained Red

# DESDEMONA

It's been a week since I killed last, a week since *Prince Lucian* saw me for what I don't want to be. Crying and murderous. Cowardly and manic. My lies are the only thing keeping me safe. In a way bigger than before.

Because the second he finds out who I am, killing one of his soldiers will not end well for me.

Since the dream, Bernice's voice hasn't left my head. He told me I'm just like the Nepenthes. I think he's right. I think I'm worse.

Wendy says my shoulder has been put back in place, but carrying my bag still hurts. She also says the wound will be healed soon. I've seen the Eunoia heal wounds worse than mine after Combat Training in minutes. So either she's weak, or my wound is strong.

I'm sure the burns around the stab are from my body trying to cauterize itself, but I don't know what's wrong with my hand. Wendy thinks those burns are poison, which is good. Mom told me to keep the cauterizations to myself. At least I haven't broken all her wishes.

I've been pretending that I am not injured and do not have a dislocated shoulder just to get through my days. I could make up a lie to tell, an explanation as to why I'm hurt, but if that body does resurface, Ilyria could easily figure out how long he's been dead. I don't want there to be any way of tracing this back to me. Wendy is already too much of a liability.

As Aralia and I are walking the academy halls, I pull the sleeve of my uniform further down my arm. Aralia turns to me, glancing at my burnt hand, but says nothing.

That's probably my favorite attribute of hers.

I hardly notice that Calista is coming toward us until her gaze snaps to Aralia and me. At her side, Fleur and Eleanora quickly go silent, and as they pass, Calista purposely shoves her shoulder into Aralia's.

Heat flares in my chest, and I turn to face Calista as she retreats. I don't know what I'm going to do, but Aralia grabs my arm before I can do it, tugging me back around.

"Eyes ahead of you, Inferno," she mutters, quickly taking her hand from my skin. I do as she asks and put my eyes ahead, but then I feel the heat flooding into my palms.

The odd anger that I feel from Aralia's mistreatment.

I brush my burning hands against my uniform skirt—and stop when smoke starts to rise.

"Why didn't you fight back?" I ask, genuinely shocked that she hadn't. It doesn't seem like Aralia.

"We used to be friends." Aralia shrugs slightly. "Then we weren't."

"That's all?"

"It's a long story," she answers, and I get her point: don't push me.

I offer her the same grace she gives me and don't say another word about it.

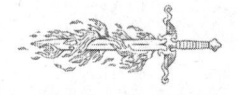

---

I go back to the coast. Every day, I check to make sure the dead Lyrian doesn't resurface. Some things don't add up. He had another blade on him but didn't stab me again, even when I aimed for his neck. He didn't fight back at all. I'm not sure he was trying to kill me, and that scares me more than anything.

*He wanted something else.*

And I don't know if I can even use that to exonerate my guilt. Because I know he attacked me. I know I was defending myself and that I didn't mean to kill him. But the worst part isn't that I feel guilty.

It's that I don't.

I've known all along that I should feel worse. That I should have felt *something*. But on the hardest day last week, instead of confronting that, I went looking for Lucian. When I got to his suite, Azaire told me to look in the art room. At the time, I didn't know Lucian was an artist—not until I stumbled in to find him in front of a canvas, paintbrush in hand.

I closed the door behind me, asking if Lucian thought we should have buried the man.

He looked at me for a long moment, his eyebrows falling as he took me in. It was like he saw the weight of it all. I didn't feel this bad after killing the Folk—not at first, anyway. I guess I didn't let myself. But in that art room, I felt the weight of both murders. And on top of that, there was the dream about Bernice. It felt like I'd killed three people that week, not just one.

For a second, Lucian just stood there. Then, without speaking, he crossed the room. His arms wrapped around me, his hands weaving up through my hair. I didn't have it in me not to grab onto him either. It felt good to be held but bad to be in the arms of the one person who knows too much.

When he finally finds out where I'm from, he won't go out of his way to protect me anymore.

"I'll take care of it," he'd said before, but he didn't realize that those words are a contingency; they don't mean anything to our future selves.

Whatever he feels about me is bound to change. So whatever I feel about him has to stay bound.

That day, when I was in his arms, I didn't know which was

worse—that the Lyrian's body *would* resurface or that I killed a man and didn't give him a proper burial. But the Lyrians don't bury their fallen like the Folk. They send them into the water. I had forgotten that, and before I remembered, I realized I was more scared of being caught, which just made me feel worse in the end.

I took a life, and all I care about is saving my own. It wasn't until today that I even thought about the man's family.

The memory fades as a wave crashes in front of me. I'm still here, looking into the sea like his body is going to float to the surface. I killed someone's best friend, or brother, or maybe father. And all I'm worried about is what's going to happen to me.

*My conscience is stained red.*

I think about writing—my notebook sits on the rock in front of me, waiting. But what's left to write when all that's left is death? A girl named Nova started showing up in my dreams—blonde hair and a laugh like a god's—and I've already written about her. She's the first person I've dreamt of who I didn't know.

I wonder when I'll kill her, too. That's what happens with the dreams, right? I just keep killing these people.

My thoughts spin in circles, all the way back to the blade on the man's hip. He aimed for my shoulder and didn't aim again. *He wasn't going to kill me.* That becomes more and more obvious with each day.

But it begs the question—was he going to do something worse?

I'm not surprised when the whispering brushes past my ear like the wind—inaudible hisses that make no sense. I've been hearing it since the day I killed the Folk in my dwelling, but it gets louder by the coast. I'm almost used to it, like the dreams. But this time, it's different. It's loud. It's debilitating. It infiltrates my mind, the only place where I can be honest. So, let me be honest: I *am* losing my mind.

Aren't I?

When the whispering fades to a steady hum, it leaves me hunched over myself, grasping for sanity. That was the worst attack by far, and if the dreams are any indication, it's only going to get worse. It will get worse, and I will get used to it.

My heart plummets when I catch movement from the corner of my eye. I snap my head around, toward the woods. If someone sees me here and the body resurfaces...

There's no one there.

But when I turn back toward the coast, something appears in the distance, concealed by the fog along the water. There's no mistaking the glowing eyes that watch me.

Someone's out there—someone who might know I'm a killer.

I stand up, ready to confront them, not entirely sure what I plan to do. But as I rise, they approach me, stepping out from the fog.

Not a person—a monster, its fur a light, luminous gray. The outline of its rib cage is visible, the fur so thin it's nearly translucent. Just beneath the jagged bone, a faint blue glow pulses with power. It stops before me, the thing standing on two feet and at least three times my size.

I reach for the dagger at my waist, but the beast makes no move to harm me, and I don't think I'd be able to take down one this big with something as measly as a six-inch bedazzled blade.

Besides, the beast is kind of... beautiful. Several furry antlers poke out around its head, and its eyes are the color of snow. Not that I've seen snow before, I just know it's white.

My grip tightens on the dagger, but I don't strike. I should be running. I should be afraid. Instead, I just stare.

The monster looks at me while I look at it. It looks pained, which doesn't make sense. Monsters don't feel emotions like people; they're lesser creatures that don't even have their own souls. And yet, its eyes look like any of our own.

*Causer... act... us...*

For a brief second, the whispering becomes coherent. But it doesn't stop me from palming my dagger.

The beast continues to look me in the eye as I hear, *Act... Never...*

"Is that you?" I ask, stepping toward the monster.

Its head tips down, as if conceding. I reach for it, but the craziest part is that the beast doesn't fight back when I rest my hand atop its furry nose.

"It is you, isn't it?" The monster makes a low grunting sound. "Tell me," I plead. "Tell me why I keep hearing you."

If this whole time the whispering has been the monsters... I don't know what that could mean. I just know that I need *more*.

"Please," I whisper, my hand still on the monster's nose. "Tell me—"

I cut off when I hear footsteps. They're quick, urgent; I barely have time to pull away before—

"Marquees! Run!"

The monster scurries away at the sound. I sit on the rock, letting go of my dagger and picking up my pen. Then I fall into my default mode.

A liar.

I look over my shoulder, forcing a smile for Lucian.

"Run from what?" I lie, shaking my head. Though, I'm not entirely sure why. All I know is that I can't let the boy who knows too much know more. Admitting that a monster might be trying to talk to me feels like admitting to *something*. Monsters don't approach Folk, and Folk don't hear whispering in their heads.

But he's also the only one who looks at me the way he's looking at me now—with wonder, like I'm some great work of art he's desperate to decipher, to trace every line and learn every color. I feel like a fraud when he looks at me like that, but I don't want him to look away.

"The moonaro," Lucian says with a sigh, but the monster is

gone.

"I didn't see anything." I tuck my notebook in my waistband.

He narrows his eyes at me but still nods. "Perhaps I'm mistaken."

Maybe he's the one I could tell the truth to, the one who would understand. I think I could tell him. It wouldn't take much work to say the words.

But it's not just words. It's the dreams, the septic, the whispering. It's not just the Lyrian I killed, either. It's the Folk.

It would be telling him, *Hey! I'm a liar and an even bigger murderer than you thought, and to top it off, I'm from the septic, too!*

So when Lucian says, "I need to tell you something," I have the horrific hope that it will be something I can use against him. Something to keep the boy who knows too much from divulging my secrets.

Lucian turns away, leaving the coast and heading into the woods, and I follow.

We stand beneath a canopy of trees, feet apart, as he assesses me. He's probably reconciling what he saw—the monster and me. I widen my eyes, clasp my hands in front of me, and stand as sweetly as possible. The image of innocence, I hope.

Lucian's voice is a whisper when he finally says, "The day we tracked your mom, monsters started attacking."

I think of Damien and how he thought a monster killed my mom, days *before* we tracked her.

"Are you sure you didn't see anything?" he asks again.

"Positive," I say, maintaining eye contact and forcing myself not to flinch.

"All right." Lucian looks past me. "We should get back inside the barrier."

Is following him an act of admission? I'm not sure, and I'm lost for words, so I do just that.

"What were you doing at the coast?" he asks as we walk through the woods, stepping on overgrown roots and crunching pebbles.

For some reason, despite everything, telling him that I was watching for a dead man to float to the surface doesn't seem like the right thing to say.

"Just studying. What were you doing?"

"Something similar," he answers. "The coast is peaceful." But the way he's looking at me is different than usual.

We walk back to the school in utter and unusual silence. I don't glance his way, out of fear my eyes will prove me guilty.

When we're within the walls, Lucian says, "I have a matter to attend to. I'll find you soon?"

"Yeah," I say gently with a smile. I hope it reaches my eyes. "See you soon."

## Chapter 19
## Birth Of A Vendetta

# LUCIAN

When Wendy steps into my suite and says, "We need to talk," I know that the glamour on her mother's book has been lifted, and my chest twists with excitement.

What was uncovered could unveil the connection between Desdemona's mother, Isa, and the Arcanes.

I head toward Azaire's room, but Wendy matches my movements, stopping me. "No," she says quickly. "It's not safe."

"What isn't safe?"

"You want to get Azaire," she whispers. "*He* won't be safe."

I sigh, trying to read the fear behind her eyes. "He's a big boy, Wendy. He can handle himself."

"I don't want him involved," Wendy pleads, clutching the strap of her bag tightly.

"Is this a romantic thing or a quarrel? I suppose they'd both stem from romance—"

"Neither." Wendy shakes her head, then opens her bag. She pulls out a folded paper, its edges delicate, and holds it up like it's an answer to my question.

I narrow my eyes at the paper in her hands. Could that be the book she found, stripped of its glamour and now reduced to a single piece of parchment? Glamours can hide anything from sight—though why go so far to hide a piece of paper?

The last time we were here, I'd had so much hope for what might lie beneath.

Now, I don't see how it could connect to the Arcanes or Isa. I don't see what purpose it could hold.

Is that why Wendy is here, or have I misread her arrival entirely?

We head to the Royal chambers and sit at the dusty table. Wendy places the paper down between us with a deliberate touch. Her fingers linger on the edges as she slides it toward me, as if she fears what the contents of the paper can do.

The moment my eyes settle on the parchment, I see this is more than I'd anticipated.

It's the weapon's blueprint, marked *Design No. 27*. At the bottom are the signatures of King Easton and Queen Melody of Folkara, alongside a blueprint destroy-by date from four years ago.

And yet, what can I do about this? I hardly have autonomy over my own choices in life. What am I to do about a weapon being made by another kingdom?

A dead end, surely, because Freyr gave me answers to the *wrong* question.

When Wendy pulls the blueprint toward her, ready to tear it, I have no qualms.

Until it doesn't rip.

"You were right." She sets it back on the table, her fingers trembling. "They glamoured the blueprint because they couldn't destroy it. My mother must have tampered with it, and the Royals retaliated."

"Retaliated?" I ask, wondering what kind of mess I've created for myself. "How?"

Pointing at the bottom of the page, Wendy says, "That date? Two days before a monster killed my mother. Monsters that hadn't attacked for centuries."

My eyes meet Wendy's glassy green ones, and I don't need to speak the question.

She feels it.

It's the weight of loss, of decisions made far above us costing everything below. I wouldn't wish it upon anyone. Yet, her confession clarifies her conflict. She understands what we're playing with—a weapon in the hands of a kingdom.

Everyone is fair game. No one is safe.

The Arcanian War was the last time a weapon was used. From the writings, it was said to demolish entire kingdoms, lay waste to villages. Weapons powered by the Arcanes' power were the reason the majority of life was wiped from the universe during the strife, a loss that the universe still hasn't recovered from, no matter what Leiana claims.

And now we're bringing them *back*.

"That's why you don't want Azaire involved?" I ask, already knowing the answer.

"I care about him, Lucian, more than I should." Her voice softens. "If something happens to him…"

"I meant what I said; Azaire can handle himself. As for caring about him, go for it. He's not only the strongest person I know, he's the most moral."

As I speak, I try to smother the unease curling in my gut. Wendy's better than me, wanting to leave him out of this, even as I know I need him involved. I've always needed Azaire. He keeps me grounded, keeps my head on straight.

It's never been a fair trade-off between me and him.

Wendy says nothing as I reach for the paper again. This weapon is grand, sure to be cataclysmic. But I can't bring myself to care about it the way I should. I have too many mysteries of my own: Isa and her connection to the Arcanes, Desdemona and her power, and now, the moonaro she swore she didn't see.

Not only had I seen her in my vision before I ran—thinking her life depended on it—but she insisted she saw nothing.

With her left hand scrunched into a fist.

This weapon is only going to distract me from what truly matters: reaching The Void and wiping the Arcanes from existence.

"I was there when my mom died," Wendy whispers, and I look up from the blueprint. "I'm the strongest in my family," she confides in me. "*Magically*. I should've saved her, but I didn't. No one ever said it, but I felt their blame. I still do."

I don't know what to say, and she senses this, filling the silence. "I'm telling you this because... if I let myself get close to Azaire and something happens to him... I already know how that feels." Wendy meets my gaze. "And I fear morality will become a weakness."

"But he has us," I whisper. "We'll protect him."

She offers a faint smile. "You're a fair friend."

"He's more than a friend. He's my family."

"Then you're fair family to have."

I shake my head. "He's better than I ever was—he'll take you, too, Wendy."

For a moment, Wendy says nothing. The smile she offered disappears, but this is more than a frown. She looks at me like I've said something truly awful. Then, she clears her throat, breaking our eye contact as she says, "There's something more. Isa, the woman who was taken... I remember her."

My interest piques, my focus sharpening. How could Wendy *remember* Desdemona's mother?

"You knew her?" I ask.

"Not well, but we used to visit her. I was trying to figure out why Ma would be involved in something like this." Wendy shakes her head, biting her bottom lip. "She kept journals. Over and over, my mom wrote the names Isa and Freyr and the word 'weapon.'"

*They were all involved.* That's why Freyr offered Willow Estridon's name in the welding facility, why he led us down this path. *They* built the weapon—*this* is why Isa faked her death. She was running from punishment.

Is that what Wendy's mother was doing before she was killed?

248

"You think they built the weapon?" I clarify before getting ahead of myself.

"Originally, yes. They thought they were doing something good. In her journals, Ma said the Arcanes returned and killed two little girls—Marbella and Annabetha."

*Cynthia's girls.* Her reason for wanting revenge, for our partnership.

"She wanted to make a weapon to stop them," Wendy finishes.

No wonder the Arcanes took Isa. She was trying to destroy them—trying to do what I *must*.

Perhaps I could use the weapon for its original purpose.

I pick up the blueprint with renewed ardor, running my fingers along the outline of the weapon. It's grand—a machine of mass destruction, perhaps powerful enough to obliterate The Void—but the only damning information I find is a note that reads: *Do not power on Folkara.*

Whatever it can do is awful enough to cause severe damage—possibly destroy entire planets.

"It's missing something," I mutter. "There isn't a power source."

"What do you mean?"

"Weapons like these don't function on their own," I say. "They need magic to fuel them."

Wendy's expression tightens. "Our magic?"

"Yes." My voice is grim as I scan the blueprint once more. "It would need a generator to amplify the power. That much magic would likely kill someone."

"My mom wouldn't do something like that," Wendy responds, her voice sharp.

The room falls silent, and I nod. The weight of the unspoken clings to the air between us: that I *would*.

Finally, I whisper, "You're probably right."

Though, that's the last thing I believe.

In front of me is the potential of a weapon, made to be used against the Arcanes. That means only one thing is certain: I have to know what it can do.

---

I lie on Azaire's bed, watching him stare at the tome on his desk, my thoughts drifting to the day Leiana discovered Desdemona. If only she didn't wear the gold, perhaps I would not have died.

Perhaps Desdemona would not have been driven to kill.

But I'm not ignorant. I know she was at the coast for the body. There's no way I couldn't know. I only wish I hadn't seen her with the moonaro—it complicates everything. Yet I'm also glad I did, because now I know for certain she's hiding something.

Though I fear I'll destroy the fragile trust we've built before I uncover the truth.

"How's Wendy?" I ask, breaking the silence as Azaire flips through his Universal Relations textbook.

"Still avoiding me," he sighs.

I push thoughts of the Gerner—and the gold that led to my partial demise—out of my mind. The party Fleur told me about is today. I came to Azaire with the single intention of dragging him with me.

"Then let's party," I say, needing the distraction now more than ever.

"I don't know…"

"Come on, when was the last time we had any fun?"

Azaire doesn't answer. In fact, he tugs on his beanie.

"Exactly!" I exclaim. "They're all going to be in the ballroom tonight."

Azaire turns slowly in the chair, locking eyes with me. "You've been keeping your distance from them lately," he observes.

"Yes."

"Why?"

"More important things," I answer.

"Well," he gestures to the textbook on the desk, "Universal Relations are more important."

I shrug. "Depends on priorities."

"Hmm." He nods. "What happened?"

"A few things." I gesture in the direction of the ballroom. "Could use a distraction."

"Luc," Azaire sighs.

"It's the weapon," I admit, feeling the pressure of every loose end I fear I will never tie.

I tell him about the latest discoveries—how both Desdemona and Wendy's mothers were involved in the weapon's initial conception. Then I tell him about the moonaro.

"A weapon *made* for the Arcanes?" Azaire repeats to me when I've finished, his voice wary.

"Yes."

He nods, leaning back in his chair as his shoulders slump. "Be careful, Luc." His gaze lingers on mine and worry lingers in his gaze.

I smile, mostly for him. "I will."

"And Desdemona? How are things with her?" he asks.

"If anything more happens with the monsters, I'll know who to question."

Azaire chuckles, shaking his head. "No, I mean... I saw you with her at the Gerner. I'm kind of surprised you haven't told me about her."

I stiffen—though I don't know why. Azaire is my best friend. It's no surprise that he noticed my infatuations.

Instead of confessing, I shake my head. "There's nothing to tell."

A lie. With her, there's an entire book to tell, one I both hope and fear will be written.

"Didn't look like nothing," Azaire says, raising his eyebrows.

*Leiana must have seen it as well.*

Desdemona and her gold dress and my eyes that betrayed me, unable to let go of the sight of her.

I don't allow myself to linger on the thought. Instead, I focus on Azaire's jab, grabbing a dirty shirt off the floor and hurling it at his face, a laugh escaping me despite the current circumstances.

"Oh, bro, this is Yuki's!" Azaire shouts, flinging it back at me. "You smell that!"

"Smells like roses," I say, holding the shirt at arm's length. "Nasty."

"So…" I grin. "Party?"

I have a desperate desire for a distraction.

There are more questions than I ever anticipated, a girl who's hiding something from me, and feelings I'm hiding from. A night of fun is due before the rest.

He looks at his book like he's going to miss it, then at me with a sly smile. "Party."

---

As I pull a bottle of vesi from under my coat, Azaire and I enter the ballroom. Stacks of furniture line the walls, and dim orange sconces barely light the room. It feels empty—bigger with only the small lot of us—as our footsteps echo off high, shadowed ceilings and marble floors.

"Lucian!" voices call at once, hands grabbing my shoulders and clapping my back—a reminder that I'm among people who consider me a friend.

"Yo, Zaire!" someone shouts, leaning into Azaire with a grin. "Where've you been?"

Azaire shrugs the guy off, replying, "Universal Relations."

"Who got the keys?" I ask.

Yuki steps forward with a smirk, brushing his shoulders off as though he's done something impressive. "Me, obviously," he says. "These duds aren't smart enough to steal from Cynthia."

"Better not let her catch you," a kid remarks, half-teasing. Someone else laughs, shoving Yuki's shoulder as we move toward the long table at the center of the room.

"She's not as vicious as you might think," I add.

"Never doubt their *special* relationship," Yuki teases.

"Let's *not* talk about the headmistress and me like that."

Yuki just laughs, tugging the bottle from my hand and taking a swig as we walk.

From the corner of my eye, I catch the flicker of white hair —Fleur, bathed in the dim light. "Lucian," she calls, sitting at the table we approach. I make my way over, taking a seat next to her and pouring myself a shot.

Before I have the chance to drink, Kai calls my name. "You up for a round of speed?" he asks, already lining up the shot glasses.

The room goes quiet, as if everybody is waiting for my answer. Suddenly, the ballroom feels too small for the both of us.

From across the table, Azaire catches my eye with a slight shake of his head. *Don't engage.*

I know Azaire is right, and despite my urge to win a fight, I shake my head as I announce, "Not tonight."

"Oh, come on!" Kai groans. "Everyone's dying to see the next King of Folkara down a few. Lucian! Lucian!" he chants, and the crowd joins him, fists pumping.

Fleur laughs, tugging on my arm. "What's changed?" she asks. "You used to be the life of the party."

She's right. Ever since Desdemona arrived, I've been... distracted. No—possessed. Preoccupied with *greater things*, I told myself. I've pulled away from everyone I know, searching for answers about the Arcanes. Searching for revenge.

But there's something else unraveling me.

It's not duty. Not even vengeance.

It's her.

That won't change after tonight, but perhaps, for the night, I can offer myself a moment of reprieve.

Fleur takes my hand, her fingers cold against my skin. She feels *nothing* like Desdemona. I nearly close my eyes, imagining Desdemona beside me instead, despite it all. A dangerous indulgence. A betrayal of the one thing I've sworn to forget. But I'm starving for the thought of her. I've grown drunk on the memory of her, even if I never truly had her.

Is it only now that I'm realizing how dearly I desire her, or have I known the whole time?

For she is the longing I must deny—the emotion I am forbidden to feel.

And yet I crave the unfinished things. The almosts. The not-quites. The ghost of her hand near mine. The space between our mouths.

Tormenting.

Tantalizing.

Unfinished.

My ridiculous, unrefined ramblings. My unrelenting thoughts.

I won't fall any further for her.

*It would be too easy of a descent.*

Perhaps that is the reason I force a smile as I say, "You know what? Pour the shots."

Kai smirks, doing just that before sliding the five glasses across the table to me. I take a deep breath, refraining from looking in Azaire's direction.

I don't need to see his disapproval.

Fleur counts Kai and me down. "Three, two, one."

I grab the first shot glass, downing it quickly. By my third, I feel the fire spreading in my chest. By my fifth, I can't stop myself from wishing the girl with white hair had fiery orange instead.

My shot glass clanks down against the table just before Kai's, and the room explodes in cheers. Fleur leans into me, half of her body falling out of the hickory chair. When she tugs on my arm, I allow her to guide it around her shoulders.

She feels like the personification of the past, the life I had once lived—one without hope. It makes me realize that, for the first time in a long time, I believe in something. And it's because of Desdemona—her power, her possibility. Her ability to reach The Void.

That is exactly why I have to keep her as a means to an end. I can't risk my feelings getting in the way of what must be done.

Fleur's white hair falls over my shoulder as Kai asks, "Again?"

"I welcome any invitation of friendly competition," I announce, raising an eyebrow at Kai as he glowers, clearly irritated by his loss. Our eyes stay locked on one another as the shots are poured.

I drink the next round in a blur, finishing my fifth by the time Kai has his fourth in hand. The cheers are subdued this time, the crowd growing tired of our game.

"You're only getting slower," I say, leaning back in the chair.

"Let's do it again, then," Kai slurs, making me realize I had as well.

"Oh, come on," Fleur says lightly.

Azaire stands, looking down at both of us as he says, "Yeah, guys, I think this is enough."

"Zaire's right," Yuki adds from the other end of the table.

Kai ignores them, turning to me and saying, "I'm ready for another. But if you're not…"

I hold Kai's gaze, resting my arm on the chair beside me. Perhaps it's the alcohol, but my patience for the prince is wearing thin. He's supposed to be my friend—my brother-in-law. Instead, he's acting like a little bitch.

I've already put him in his place. Must I do it again?

Smirking, I lean forward. "Pour the shots."

"Okay, okay, but what about the rest of us?" Yuki shouts, pushing to his feet at the head of the table. "You're gonna drink it all over whatever big-dick competition this is."

Kai lets out a bitter laugh, not even bothering to respond as he lifts a hand, signaling the reluctant bartender. The kid pours the drinks, and this time, Kai finishes a moment before I do. He throws his arms up, triumphant, shouting in excitement.

"Two to one," Yuki says with a shake of his head. "But I mean, three to zero would've been embarrassing." He doesn't say it with any malice—simply a dim-witted comment and a chuckle.

But Kai's eyes narrow as he stands, swaying slightly. "What was that, Yuki?"

I rise, prepared to defend my advisor, but the room tilts dangerously. Or my head is twisting. Or perhaps it is both. Faces blur around me as Kai slams Yuki into the table, rattling the glasses.

"Kai, calm down," I start, reaching for his shoulder as I try to convince him not to hit Yuki again.

He turns and punches me square in the jaw. The world spins, and I hit the floor hard, unsure if it was his force or my dizziness that knocked me to the ground.

Kai looms over me, his fist missing twice before he finally connects with my cheek. I feel… nothing. Either numb from the hits or the alcohol.

Then Kai disappears, yanked back by some invisible force—I quickly realize it's Azaire. I try to stand, to move toward Azaire, but Fleur rushes to my side, gently cupping my face and asking if I'm all right. Her touch is light, but it isn't Desdemona's. It isn't what I want.

"I'm fine," I say, pushing her hand away.

Her shoulders sag, the energy draining from her demeanor. For a moment, I feel sorry.

Azaire's groan snaps me back to focus. I'm on my feet as Azaire shoves Kai into the velvet blue drapes with unexpected force. Chaos erupts—glasses shatter, someone curses, and a kid hits the ground with a bloody nose.

"I always knew you were Lucian's bitch," Kai spits with a laugh, blood spraying as Azaire lands another punch.

I step forward, rushing to grab Azaire and drag him toward the exit, but Kai charges me before I can. His elbow crashes into my forehead, and for a moment, everything goes black—darkness rushing over my vision in a blur of pain.

"Just calm down," I hear Yuki call out. "It's not a big deal."

My sight returns in fragments, and through the spots of light, I spot Yuki pinning Kai to the ground across the room. Azaire stands beside me, steadying me.

I grip his arm for balance as I ask, "Are you all right?"

He looks at me, a black and blue mark blossoming on his jaw. "Yeah," he breathes.

Before I can say more, Fleur pulls me down to the floor. Her hands brush against my face as she whispers, "You're bleeding."

"I noticed," I mutter, my words slurred, and my eyelids flutter, closing against my will.

The hands on my face shift—no longer Fleur's pale, cold touch. This touch is different—hot, heavy, searing, pulling every ounce of my attention to the precise place where skin meets skin.

Where skin meets sin.

The touch is Desdemona's.

I force my eyes open, trying to shake away the daydream. It's Fleur's fingers that flutter over me now, the faint glow of green clouding my sight. It's precise, practiced, perfect. Her refinement is the exact opposite of Desdemona in every way.

Perhaps it was only Desdemona's oddities that drew me in—she exists outside the bounds of power plays and politics. She's reckless where others are rehearsed. Raw where others are polished. It's calming to attribute attraction to logic, to wrap desire in reason.

But I know better.

Gods, I've always known.

As my face begins to mend, worry pulls at the lines of Fleur's expression. I can't help but ask, my voice heavy with exhaustion, "Why do you care, Fleur?"

For a brief moment, she pauses, her eyes growing wide. She looks at me as if I've struck a nerve—likely using her empathic powers as a Eunoia to feel my interest in the question... and my disinterest in her.

Then, as if nothing happened, she resumes her healing, asking, "What kind of a question is that?"

"I mean it," I press. "I dated your best friend, I drink too much, I'm *engaged*. Why do you like me?"

"I don't..." She parts her lips as if to say more, but stops herself, shaking her head. "You're *the prince*," she finishes, as if it should've been obvious.

"I'm hardly a prince," I sigh. "You know it as well as anyone. I'm a pawn."

She ignores me, settling her hands on my wounds, but I catch her wrist, halting her.

The alcohol loosens my tongue, persuading me to say what's been simmering beneath the surface all night. "I want Desdemona, and I know you know that. But even that is something I will never give myself because, by nature of my position, it is something I can't have."

Fleur frowns, her eyes turning glassy as she looks into mine. Softly, she shakes her head. "What can't you have?"

Her words sober me, showing me my own shortcomings. We both know what I can't have, and I won't be forced to say it.

I clear my throat, dropping her wrist as I reply, "You're wasting your time healing me."

"Dude," Yuki groans, glancing at Kai, who's slumped on the far side of the spinning room. "You're bleeding all over the floor."

Kai spits another streak of crimson onto the floor, his voice dripping with sarcasm. "Surely not the first time in a place like this."

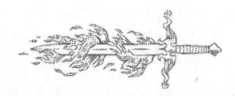

---

The next day, I awaken with a pounding headache and a goal.

There's a weapon, *built* to be used against the Arcanes.

There's a girl, who may be the key to reaching them.

My feelings, my hesitancy about the matter, have no meaning. I don't allow them to. *This* is what has to be done—not kissing a girl and counting her freckles or undertaking any other actions of madness.

Yet, despite my resolve, the walk to Cynthia's office feels impossibly heavy.

Crashing down on the sofa, I prepare to proclaim the whole truth. I gave myself a distraction last night, but all it did was pull the veil from my eyes.

I care for Desdemona—deeply, completely, and in a way that consumes me. A devotion that cannot be undone.

And in that realization, I understand my need for something more. Someone to hold me steady when I falter. Someone like Cynthia, who has the strength to do what must be done if a time comes where I cannot.

With a soft exhale, I whisper, "There's something I kept from you."

"Again?" Cynthia asks, her voice laced with amusement.

"Again."

The word leaves my lips, but it carries no humor. I don't share her amusement. No matter how I try to ignore it, there is a pang, a pleading feeling in my chest to *stop*.

I disregard it as I say, "When I tracked Isa to The Void, Desdemona nearly stepped through my projection. *That* is the true reason I've been training her."

I deliberately omit my feelings from the confession.

Cynthia's eyes flare as she leans over her desk. "Intriguing. Do you think she could make contact?"

"Unknown," I answer. "Perhaps."

I twist the silver wolf between my fingers, the cool metal a brief distraction. Then, I pull my hands from my pocket and stand, setting the red knife down on Cynthia's desk. She looks down at it, then up at me.

"And this is?" she asks, intertwining her fingers beneath her chin.

"Unknown. That's the problem." I sigh. "It scorched Desdemona's skin, but Wendy found no trace of poison."

Cynthia picks up the knife, balancing it between her fingers and holding it to the light. "Can I hold onto it?"

"You wouldn't want to. It was used to kill an Ilyrian soldier."

"Hm," she mumbles, wiping her fingerprints from the blade. Ilyria would be the last place to show leniency toward that kind of accusation. "Use it against another Fire Folk and see if they have the same reaction, then bring it back to me."

I grab the dagger, then take my seat. "It's not as if we have an overabundance of them running around here."

Cynthia shakes her head, as if my concern has no legitimacy. "You'll find one." She winks. "You have my undying faith."

I nod, annoyed, but another Fire Folk quickly consumes my mind—the one that led me to the weapon. Could Cynthia have orchestrated the whole thing? Sending me after Freyr, him mentioning Wendy's mother, and us finding the blueprint? I wouldn't put it past her. If she knows about the weapon and what it was originally built for, it only makes sense that she would send me to find it.

After all, a prince has the best chance of making it out of a facility like that.

And she retains every right to claim plausible deniability.

"You sent me after Freyr," I say. "Is it correct to assume you knew about the weapon?"

Cynthia smiles crookedly. She's always proud when I solve her puzzles—she believes it trains me to be a worthy partner.

Slowly, she answers, "Yes."

"And about Isa and Willow's involvement?"

Cynthia offers a delayed shrug. "I keep my tabs on such things."

"Have you seen the weapon?"

"I have not."

A dangerous, glorious idea creeps into my mind, not for the first time. "It's harrowing," I say, leaning toward her. "Originally built to be used against the Arcanes. I think we could use it."

Cynthia rolls out her wrist slowly, taking her time to say, "Careful, Lucian. Destruction rarely chooses its master."

"Perhaps this time, it has," I whisper. "If Desdemona can reach The Void, she could uncover what we need."

Cynthia's grin widens. "You're going to betray your untrustworthy beloved?"

My eyes meet hers, unwavering. "I'm going to make good on my promise of revenge."

## Chapter 20
### It's Strange How People Can Change

# DESDEMONA

In Elemental Magic, I channel power from Kai—who, for some reason, is sitting on the sidelines—to deflect my classmates' magical attacks.

One of the most annoying parts of my life is my power. The only reason I even try is because it will help save my mom, which would be the saddest part of my life.

"Miss Marquees!" Ms. Abrams's voice cuts through the room. "Focus on offense, not just defense."

The class watches with wide, fearful eyes. It's the only look I get from these kids. I pretend to be too focused on their stares to notice when Calista's eyes light yellow in my direction. A gust of wind hurls me into the marble wall, and once again, I wish pain wasn't always my plan B.

I'm just grateful my spine is intact while I hobble to Kai, cursing the intense pain in my shoulder.

"Hey," Kai says as I sit.

I'm surprised by the smile on his face. "Hey."

"*That* looked like it hurt." He reaches for my shoulder, the one I'm clutching—probably too conspicuously. "Here," he whispers, and small bolts of lightning flicker across his fingers. With a gentle touch, he sends a shock through my shoulder.

The sudden jolt—like a searing surge of electricity racing through my veins—makes my breath catch. I stiffen for a moment, the pain all-encompassing, before it quickly fades, leaving only a lingering twinge.

"It should help you heal," he murmurs. "Stimulate your nerves and muscles."

For a moment, his eyes remind me of Damien's: kind, amber, and utterly un-princely. Just a boy. Sometimes I just want to look at Kai, for that small taste of home.

"Thank you," I say.

He shrugs with the faintest of nods. "I feel I should apologize for Calista. She's been on edge."

"Is that part of the reason you're sitting out?" I ask with a little laugh.

"Actually, yeah." His tone is bitter when he mutters, "Calista and I have an *event* soon."

I eye him suspiciously, putting on more of a show than I want to amidst the clash of pains—my spine, my shoulder, and the lingering shock. "And only *you're* sitting out?"

"She fought to participate today." He leans into me subtly and whispers, "I think it was when she accidentally blew Ms. Abrams halfway across the room that she got her way."

"That would make sense." I reach for the back of my neck, scrunching my nose as I say, "It's no fun."

"Magic rarely is."

"Tell me about it." I think of the dreams, the fire, the metaphorical murders, and the ones I've actually committed. I want to shudder, but I don't let myself.

"It's the betrothal," Kai says abruptly, his tone bitter. "The reason I'm sitting out. They can't have me getting injured beforehand."

"Betrothal?" I ask and hope it's not a word I should know.

"An agreement to wed, bound by our magic," he says.

I don't know what to think about that. Yeah, it sucks to be forced to marry someone, but am I supposed to feel pity for someone who's about to inherit more money and power than I could ever dream of? There's no way.

But I play to my strengths, giving him the consolation he wants from me.

"All I can really think to say is that I'm sorry. No one deserves to go through that." I resist the urge to roll my eyes.

"I vaguely remember us having a conversation in this vein already," Kai says, his voice a little less dreary than before.

"You were pretty drunk at that party," I tell him. Another reminder of all the good magic does me. I nearly bashed Aralia's skull that night—and then I killed a Folk instead. "But I told you I was sorry, and I believe you told me that people normally say congratulations."

"Sounds about right." He presses his lips together. "That is what they say. Not one person has said 'my apologies' and here you are, offering the real thing."

"I think it warrants it." I nod with my words, putting on a convincing show.

"The only one."

---

As I leave the classroom, I spot Lucian waiting, and my heart plummets. The body's resurfaced; they've found it, and he's here to tell me to run, I just know it. I walk to him, concealing my panic.

"What is it?" I ask in an urgent whisper.

"We need to talk."

It's like someone took a knife to my stomach and cut until there was nothing left. I'm empty, but I could also puke.

I nod my head and say, "Okay." It's funny, my voice sounds so casual and lighthearted, but my heart is thumping in a way that could constitute death if it went just a beat faster.

Lucian walks, and I follow. I think of something to say to fill this silence, but I have nothing. All I can focus on is my worry.

We walk to the lake, a place we haven't been since I killed the man who attacked me. It only makes sense that he brings me here to tell me the inevitable—I have to run. I've been found guilty. I'm a convict.

But when we reach the lake, Lucian—abruptly—says, "I know where your mother is."

I shake my head a little and try to meet his gaze, but his eyes are everywhere but on mine. I want—*need*—him to look at me. What does he mean he knows where my mom is?

Did something happen?

My mind races to the worst—she was kidnapped by his parents, and now she's dead. She's dead.

She's *not* dead. I choke the thought before it grows.

"Is this some kind of a joke?" I find my voice, but vulnerability—*fear*—still laces through my tone.

"It wouldn't be a very funny one," Lucian replies, looking into the iridescent water.

"Okay." I press my lips together and keep my twisted tongue from twisting anymore. The body wasn't found, but Lucian found my mom. Is that right? "Where is she?"

Lucian still won't meet my eyes, even when he says, "The Void."

I can't stop the laugh from slipping out of my throat.

*Now* he looks at me. "This isn't funny."

The way he's looking at me isn't the way I'm used to—like I'm something *worth* seeing. Now he glares at me like *I've* done something wrong here, when he's the one playing some kind of sick joke on me, using my mom as the butt.

"It kind of is. You're saying that my mom is in a world where the bad boys and girls go when they don't follow rules." The Void and the Arcanes that live there are a *story*, taught to children so that they behave—or else they'll be stolen in the middle of the night, the memory of their existence taken with them.

It's bullshit.

"It's not a world; it's a universe," he corrects me, and I can't hide my shock at the adamant tone in his voice. "The first time we tracked her, you almost stepped into my projection."

Suddenly, I'm looking at him differently, too. He really believes my mom is in The Void. Which, even if it were real, still doesn't make sense. I wouldn't remember my mom. No one would.

That's the first rule in every story about the Arcanes.

But worse than his delusion—there's a sliver of truth in his words. He thought he *knew* where she was, and he still promised me he didn't.

"You've been lying to me? You knew where she was this whole time, and you've been lying to me?" I ask, ignoring the fact that I've been lying to him too.

My lies are justifiable; he'd have me sent back to the septic if he knew who I was, leaving me with no chance of finding my mom. At worst, he would have me killed for killing the Lyrian.

Lucian won't meet my eyes when he says, "Yes."

Everything is cracking, crashing, crumbling into a million pieces.

"What do you mean I almost stepped into your projection?" I ask, hope flaring in my chest for a single, brief moment. If there's a chance of finding her, I'll take it. But this is a boy who's been lying to me this whole time—a boy *I've* been lying to. There's no trust lost between us, and I don't know what to do with that. "Do you mean I could be there right now?" I finish.

"Your mind, possibly. Your body, probably not."

That flicker of hope in my chest explodes. There's a chance that I could see my mom, that I could speak to her—that she might tell me where she really is and how to find her.

"Then we're doing this again, right now. I'm going to find my mom right now!" I nearly jump into the water on the spot, ready to track her just as we had before.

I begin tearing off my shirt, so I have something dry to get into when this is over.

Then I stop, trying not to eye Lucian as I tug the shirt back over my torso.

He took me to the lake. *This is what he wants.*

For me to jump into that water and locate my mom.

But why? What does he want with her? What does he want with *me?*

When his mom was looking at me with murder in her eyes, he was the one who told me I'd be safe. When I killed a man with the crest of Ilyria, he was the one who came to my rescue.

He's the reason I'm still here when I could be far away—in a place where I would've never killed that man.

*The boy who knows too much is certainly taking claim to the weapon he's wielded with such information.*

"All right," he says, and I step back, reaching for the dagger tucked in my waistband.

"I mean, I can't believe you've lied to me this entire time!" I continue to inch away from him, just far enough to give me a head start before I run back to the school. If I could just get to Aralia, or even Leiholan, I'd have someone to hide behind.

Another step back.

"You know I trusted you, right?" I shout. "I've already trusted you, and now I find out you're lying!"

Another step back.

"Marquees?" he says.

"What?"

The prince looks at me like I'm his prey. "I know what you're doing."

I stop. "What am I doing?"

"There are two ways this is going to end. You'll run, and I'll catch you, or you'll get in the water and do this without the needless games you're so fond of."

It's all been a lie. Every glance we shared, every touch that *did* make me catch my breath, every word from his mouth that I believed. Every time he looked at me like I was something more than what I am.

A lie.

How can I really be surprised? His family, Kai's family, both of them are the reason I've lost *my family*.

My hand grips the dagger's hilt when the prince murmurs, "Please don't make this bloodier than it has to be." He sounds actually pained, like he's the one seeing what I really am instead of the other way around.

I run, one foot in front of the other until his hands are on my body again, and I'm doing anything but catching my breath. I'm screaming.

"Get off me!"

His fingers dig into my shoulder, no longer gentle. No longer soft as he pulls me back in, like he's afraid I'll slip away forever if he lets go.

"Please, Desdemona," he says, and I curse myself because I've waited so long to hear my name roll off his tongue.

But I never imagined it like this.

"Help!" I rasp.

"Let me explain," he's saying, but I'm screaming.

"Someone help me—"

"Your mother tried to kill the Arcanes!" he whispers into my ear, and I grow quickly silent, waiting for him to finish. "She made a weapon, and when Folkara's Royals found out, she faked her death."

I go still against him. Conflicted because too much of my attention is on the way his hands feel around my waist. How his chest feels against my back—every drop of my energy rushing to the surface just to get a glimpse of his skin on mine—instead of the very realistic explanation he's just given me.

I gulp, loudly. "Why are you telling me now?" I ask, all while getting ready to smash my head back and hopefully break his nose.

"Because things have gotten more difficult."

"You've been using me this whole time then?" I whisper, turning so I can make out his eyes. Not that they'll tell me anything. Apparently, he's just as good a liar as I am.

His voice drops to a low murmur as he answers, "Yes."

It's ridiculous, really, the way I feel very palpable pain in my chest.

Defeat drips from my heart and into my bloodstream. My body falters, momentarily collapsing into Lucian. I close my eyes and force myself back together again. This is okay—it's more than okay, it's good. I found my mom. I have a reason to untangle from the prince.

I force myself out of Lucian's grasp and turn to him, masking every bit of emotion I'm feeling. Either he's doing the same, or he's really feeling nothing.

"And I'm not going to like die or something if I do this?" I'm shocked and relieved at the steadiness of my voice. I continue, "I don't think I'll be able to swim with my shoulder."

"I won't let you die," he swears to me, nearly sounding like the person I thought he was. It's almost like an oath—no doubt trying to fool me into thinking he cares about my life. *Again.*

But there's one thing that outweighs whatever game he's playing.

"And I'll get to see my mom?" I ask.

"If all goes right, you'll get to talk to her," he says. "If you're able to, I need you to ask what the weapon was made to do."

*So, that's what this is all about.*

"Anything else?" I ask sarcastically.

"The original power source," the prince offers, and I roll my eyes. "If you find this out, we're one step closer to taking out the creatures that have her."

Right, the not-so-mythical Arcanes.

"Fine," I say and walk toward the lake.

But Lucian grabs my uninjured shoulder, turning me back to face him. For a moment there's more than nothing in his eyes, then that semblance of something disappears.

"Keep your wits about you," he says like Lucian. In the tone I'm used to.

But I won't be played again.

Without looking back, I dive into the water. I don't take my clothes off either, dry clothes be damned. I've already put too much skin into this game.

I watch Lucian from below the surface, and when he opens his arms like he did the first day, I close my eyes and picture my mom. Moments later, the images become a portrait of her sitting in a dark, dirty cell, just as before.

It's difficult to move here—to breathe—like I'm wading through contaminated waters. Shadows flicker at the edges of my vision, shifting and twisting into unusual shapes. I hear whispers, but they're barely audible. They brush my ears, but never fully penetrate my hearing.

"Mom?" I call, stepping closer.

She looks up, her eyes searching but never landing on me. Her face is covered in dirt, bruises, and cuts. The sight of her battered makes me nauseous. Even as I run closer, she still doesn't see me.

"Mom, I'm here."

"Desdemona?" she whispers. "You can't be here."

I'm sitting in front of her, reaching for her hands. I fail to grasp them, but I can feel her touch. The grounding warmth.

"I'm so sorry," I mutter. "I haven't done enough. I should've gotten to you sooner."

Her voice is stern. "No. I told you, you wait for me to find you."

"Are you in The Void?" I have to know.

Instead of answering, she looks at her hand—the one I'm holding.

"Can you feel me?" I ask, hoping she can.

"Yes," she answers. "Yes to both."

"The Arcanes are real?" my voice cracks.

"You can't come for me," she says.

"Is this what we were running from?"

My entire childhood flashes before my eyes—every time we ran, leaving our lives behind just to do it all over again.

I cough quickly, then say, "I was supposed to ask you about a weapon you made."

She looks up fast. It's almost like she could be looking at me. But then her gaze wavers, still searching. Still seeking me.

I frown, and she doesn't see.

Her voice trembles, barely above a whisper. "Who's asking?"

"The prince of Ilyria."

"What does he know?" she asks, her tone urgent.

"I'm not actually sure," I answer, coughing again.

Mom looks away, her eyebrows furrowing, lips tightening.

"Mom? What does the weapon do?"

She blinks, as if in pain. "If we had powered it properly, we predicted it could shred the fabric of any universe we used it against," she says, looking up. So close to my eyes. "But it wasn't powered, and it never will be."

I cough again, struggling for breath. "That's why we always ran?"

"Yes." Her head jerks up, searching for something behind me. "Desdemona, go back. *Now.*"

I clutch her hand tighter, only to realize I can't feel it anymore. "I miss you," I whisper. Our time is running out. "I miss you so much."

"And I miss you," she says. "But you can't come looking for me."

"Mom—"

"Promise me!"

My hand slips through hers, and water gurgles up my throat, spilling from my mouth and over my chin.

"Mom?" I try to call, but the words are muffled, and it seems she can no longer hear me. "Aibek!" I call for Lucian.

But liquid floods my lungs, and I choke, begging for air that isn't there. Darkness captures the corners of my vision.

"Aibek?" I try to scream again, but it sounds like I'm talking underwater.

Because I *am* underwater.

# Chapter 21
## The Things That Break Are Never Fixed

# LUCIAN

*A weapon that can destroy a universe.* Sickening, and exactly what I need to finally bring an end to the Arcanes.

In the projection, Desdemona sits beside her mother, clutching her hand through gleaming bronze-gold bars. Gold is a rarity in our universe, yet in The Void, it's used as a tool of imprisonment. It speaks volumes about the values these wretched creatures hold dear.

Then the image shatters, and I am left alone, gazing out at the lunar lake.

Perhaps Desdemona severed the projection herself. She's no longer tethered to me; I don't feel her presence.

I dive into the water.

The last time I swam down this lake after her, my focus was on her mother, not her well-being. Now, it's the latter that occupies my every thought.

*Every* inch of her pulls me in, and I'm drowning in the feeling of something I know I'm not supposed to want. I never stood a chance.

So why did I let her do this when I knew it was dangerous? Why did I let Azaire? Is my revenge truly worth their lives?

Desdemona wasn't ready. And still, I pushed her—just like I pushed Azaire into the weapon's facility.

When I can't find her body, a sharp instinct rips through me. I swim deeper, faster, harder, driven by a need I can't name. I have to find her. I swore I wouldn't let her die.

It's not the fear of failing to reach The Void that panics me—it's the fear of losing her.

And yet, I went into this knowing I would. In one way or another, I know how this ends. I've *always* known how this ends—with her slipping through my fingers.

*Keep swimming,* I command myself. *Faster.*

My heart pounds. Panic rises with every beat. I push harder, my lungs burning as I scan the depths, my eyes straining to catch a glimpse of her.

Finally, I find her, drifting further down the lake. The sunlight barely reaches this far below, but I fight my way toward her. Small bubbles float from her nose—the only sign of life.

I wrap my arm around her waist, pulling her closer, my chest tightening with relief and terror in equal measure. I swim toward the surface, but every stroke feels like it could be my last. The weight of this moment, of what she truly means to me, is too much to bear.

With a final effort, I haul Desdemona out of the water, collapsing onto the grass with her in my arms. I hold her, frantic, desperate for any sign that she's still with me. My hands fly to her chest—no breath. No pulse, either.

*Losing my wits in this moment will do her no good.*

As gently as I can manage, I tilt her chin back, bringing my lips to hers. I breathe into her lungs, willing life back into her, then press my hands against her chest, each compression precise—at first. But as the seconds stretch and she remains unresponsive, my movements grow wild—desperate.

She remains motionless beneath my hands.

"Come back to me," I whisper, my voice a foreign sound—hoarse and raw with anguish. But words alone will not bring her back.

I press harder, faster, each movement fueled by rising panic. My control fractures with every agonizing second of silence.

Then a shudder rips through her. Desdemona convulses violently, her chest heaving as water spills from her lips, cascading down her chin before foaming at the edges.

Yet her eyes remain closed. Unmoving.

I cradle her face, my thumb brushing away the foam clinging to her lips. "Marquees?" I call for her, though doubt creeps in. That was never truly her name, was it? Dalin was never her father.

Realizations tighten in my chest, but I push them aside. Now is not the time.

I try to steady myself, to remain calm, but my composure unravels into a scream: *"Desdemona?"*

No reaction.

I close my eyes, forcing myself to reach for her subconscious. I do not find it. Have I killed her? Lost her in between time and space the way people get lost between portals?

Have I not only killed her, but damned her to oblivion?

I thought I could handle this, yet I find my heart beating faster, my arms shaking, my body growing cold and rigid. My magic withers under the strain. I'm panicking. She's dying, and I'm panicking.

What little use that will do for her.

If her subconscious is no longer within her physical form, then it has been severed—left behind in the last place it existed: The Void. It's either there, waiting to be reclaimed, or lost beyond reach. Beyond even my own.

With a final, frantic attempt, I grasp her wrist, searching for a pulse. It thrums weakly beneath her skin. But her body radiates heat, enough to set kindling ablaze with a single touch. She's still out there, somewhere.

She has to be.

Losing her isn't just emotion.

It's consequence. Catastrophe.

She's the only one who can reach The Void. The only one

who can help me kill the Arcanes. The one thing standing between survival and collapse. Between vengeance and failure.

Losing her wouldn't just mean losing a person; it would mean losing my last chance.

My only chance.

I close my eyes once more, seeing nothing but her. The wide angles of her face, the thirty-three freckles that dot her nose and cheeks—her true self, concealed beneath the glamour she wears. It frightens me how easily I can conjure a mental image of the girl. Even in my mind, she is beautiful in a way that is perplexing.

*Beautiful in a way that is haunting.*

I delve deeper, summoning every last vestige of my power. I draw upon all that I am, hollowing myself out in the process—willing to burn if it means finding her.

Fear grips my heart. Panic squeezes my lungs. Darkness presses in around me, a vast emptiness ready to consume. But I think only of her—of the girl I can't seem to outrun, no matter how hard I try.

I think of everything she is—brilliant, stubborn, unbreakable. She's survived the septic. She's survived the academy. She will survive this.

Then, at last, Desdemona appears—her form unstable, flickering in and out of solidity, as if she is turning to water, caught between worlds.

And I feel myself drowning in that very uncertainty. Drowning in the thought that maybe I won't be able to pull her back. Maybe this time, I've lost her—like I always knew I would.

She sits across from her mother, still clutching her hand.

I don't know how to step through the way she has, how to tether myself to my projection as she's done. I attempt to call her name, and she doesn't so much as glance away from her mother.

She wasn't strong enough yet.

I have only one option left. I reach, once more, for her subconscious. This time, I find it. There's an odd resistance, as if she doesn't want to let me in—or perhaps there are wards placed to keep me out—yet I step through with unsettling ease. The strain on my mind is subtle, like a firm pressure, pulling me deeper into her. It's not a feeling I've experienced before.

Then *everything* disappears from view. I'm in an entirely dark void of nothingness—Desdemona's subconscious. While the realm of the mind is purely immaterial, I feel the effort physically as I walk, the darkness like a universe of its own. I feel the solidity of my form, the skin on my bones, which shouldn't be. Not in the mind.

A maze begins to materialize around me. It's a forest, much uglier than the academy woods, meaning it must be the septic. Leiana was right. I ponder—not for the first time—how Leiana knew Desdemona was septic yet did not know her name.

But I have a much more daunting task to focus on. The forest is on fire. This is how Desdemona's subconscious has chosen to protect itself. That means she knows how difficult it is to make it through. I, myself, do not. I'm used to snow and ice, the wind and the bitter cold of my world—Ilyria. Not the heat of fire.

Though my body isn't truly here, sweat gathers beneath my shirt. Here I cannot wield shadows, because this is a realm of thought and space. Immaterial by nature. I can't be hurt—but I can be trapped.

I sprint down the only path that has not yet been set ablaze.

From here, I climb the nearest tree, searching for a path through the maze. But the forest goes on forever—ash-choked and endless in every direction. There are no mountains, no bodies of water, nothing new except a patch of barren land—of nothingness—in the middle. It's my only option.

The fire closes in on the tree, and I have no choice but to jump, cursing when I land wrong. Running on my newly sprained ankle is certainly a nuisance, and amidst the pain, there's little comfort in knowing my real body remains perfectly preserved on Visnatus.

I turn left, then quickly right, only for my path to be blocked by fire. The flames lick at my shoulders as I double back to where I started.

Then I trip, collapsing to the ground, the leaves scalding my skin as I stumble.

I get to my feet to see that I tripped over a *body*.

I run, twisting left, right, then left again. I find a building, though "building" is a generous way to describe it. It's more of a dilapidated hut.

And it certainly wasn't there when I looked down from the tree.

Perhaps Desdemona is trying to help me reach her. I open the door. The structure appears better on the inside than out. There's one bed and a few tools in the corner—a pot, some weapons, and animal skins. The building reminds me of the hunting huts in Ilyria's septic, where hunters would stay while on their expeditions.

A small girl with fiery orange hair stands beside a woman—a younger and less haggard-looking Isa. As I look between them, I realize it isn't a hut.

This is their home.

"What happened to my eyes, Mommy?" Desdemona's little voice is as small as she is.

Isa visibly recoils. "What, sweetie?"

"My eyes." Desdemona taps the bone below her eye twice.

Isa opens her mouth as if to speak, but a heavy sigh escapes instead. "Shit," she mumbles and grabs the pendant at her chest. It's a large stone, its surface a muddy shade of orange.

"Wait," Desdemona beckons. "Every time you do that, something funny happens."

Isa clutches the stone tighter. "Do what, sweetie?"

Desdemona taps her chest twice, where the pendant lies on

Isa's.

"Gods dammit!" Isa shouts and tugs at her hair. This time, it's Desdemona who recoils. Isa takes the necklace off and stares at the stone, shaking her head. "Fucking Willow."

"Mommy?"

*Willow.*

Isa puts the pendant in Desdemona's tiny hand and says, "Close your eyes and just... *feel.*"

She wants her daughter's magic—there's no other reason for such a request. Could it be for the same purpose I have in mind? To defeat the Arcanes?

Little Desdemona's hands clasp the stone, and they begin to glow. I watch as the child's face grows more intense. Her eyes close tightly shut, and her hands go from glowing orange to on fire.

Whatever this necklace does, Desdemona is powering it.

Then the little girl looks at me, and in a voice more akin to the one Desdemona carries now, she screams, "Get out of my head!"

I stagger out of the hut, nearly collapsing. The woods return to view, and only one path isn't engulfed in flames. I take it. My shirt catches fire as I run, the flames searing through to my skin. It hurts as if my body is truly being injured. As I turn, I rip the shirt off, hissing as the wind hits my burns.

Finally, I receive a brief vision.

If I keep going straight, there will be a fork to my right that leads to the patch of nothing. This is what I do, pressing forward to my destination.

The forest vanishes as I step into the darkness.

*Everything* vanishes. This is absolute nothingness; dark, empty, lonely, except for Desdemona. She sits in the middle. Her hair burns like fire—the only beacon of light. Her legs are tucked up against her chest, and her forehead rests on her knees.

For as much as I'd like to try, I'd never be able to capture this picture with a brush.

Everything here feels like her. The very air sets fire to my skin, sparking every nerve and sending shivers down my arms and spine, as if raising the hairs on parts of my body I never knew existed. As if she's coaxing the very power within me with her own.

I could never depict this essence that I'm finally able to define as *her*.

I long to sink into it—to drink her in like breath itself, like she is my lifeline and I, a man starved for the will to live.

As if worshiping a deity at her altar, I sink to my knees before her. "Desdemona?" I whisper, the name slipping from my lips like a prayer.

She looks up at me, chest rising and falling in quick, shallow breaths. Her hair is no longer merely hair—it rises around her like smoke stirred by flame, as if the very air bends to her will.

And her eyes… gods, her eyes.

They are not the brown I've come to memorize in silence, not the ones I've stolen glances at in moments too fleeting to count.

They burn with fire. With fury. With something divine and devastating.

"Can you see me?" I ask, all while I contemplate which is worse—my lies or hers. Has she lied to me even with her eyes? Every time she looked at me and I knew she felt what I felt, was that, too, a deception?

At last, Desdemona nods, and I say, "I can get you out of this, all you have to do is allow me."

She shakes her head. "I don't think I want to leave."

"I see," I whisper, lowering myself beside her, as if sitting closer might somehow pull her back to me.

She watches me as I sit, and I can't stop staring at her—not in reverence, not in awe. It's fixation—feral, feverish—fueled by fear and the kind of longing that festers, a hunger I can't name without choking on it. It's everything I've never said, everything I don't know how to say—twisting beneath my ribs like a curse.

*She is the flame, and I am the moth.*

"Why don't you want to leave?" I ask in the silence.

"I have nothing in here," she says. "And nothing out there. Only one of those options sounds somewhat peaceful."

"You have me," I murmur—not as comfort, but as confession.

"Do I?" Desdemona asks the darkness beyond her.

I don't answer.

She presses her lips tight, nodding slowly. "Didn't think so."

We're both taken into the silence. I don't know where her mind is, but mine is on her. What happens when Leiana tries, again, to get to her? When I discover how to use this weapon, originally made by her mother? Or when I know what she was doing with the moonaro? Why she's able to semi-step into a projection of The Void?

This would never work. A king-to-be and a girl from the septic. She *burned* me. She must have been lying about knowing the extent of her powers all along, especially if she's been powering her mother's necklace since she was a girl. Yet today, when she could've used those powers against me, she went for a knife and ran. When the Ilyrian soldier was trying to take her, she stabbed him.

Then she cried in my arms, begging to be believed. Had horrifying dreams the entire night.

I don't want to think about all the ways she might be *good*. I'd prefer to focus on her lies, put her back in her original place as a means to an end. But her lies don't seem all that tantalizing anymore. *I* do. *I* betrayed her.

Revenge truly is stronger than matters of the heart. Or perhaps it is a matter of the heart.

"Come back with me." I reach my hand to hers. "Please?"

She finally looks at me, but she doesn't accept my hand. "So you're pleading now?"

Yes, I am, and I am not ready to see the depths to which I will take said pleading for her.

Desdemona's eyes are wide, on fire with what I can only read to be anger. "You've lied to me about my mom this whole time." Her head shakes so subtly, I wouldn't have noticed if I weren't watching her so acutely. "Did you see? They're torturing her, and there's no way for me to *actually* get there."

She's right, and the torture is an oddity. Why not just kill Isa? The Arcanes have never been known to play with their victims. They're deliverers of death, nothing more.

It makes no sense.

"What if I could find a way to bring us there?" I whisper, questioning whether I am pushing this too far.

I can't reveal my plans to her—and yet, she has her own reasons for wanting to reach The Void. She *is* my way there. She is the means to my end. Perhaps this was always how it was meant to be.

Perhaps I never should have deceived her in the first place.

Desdemona's eyes light up, though they couldn't possibly burn brighter. "To The Void?" The corners of her lips lift ever so slightly.

This is what we will become to one another: partners in crime—if she'll still have me. If her rage burns anywhere close to mine, she will.

A smile splays across my lips.

"Yes."

I look at her. Or she looks at me. Her eyes are wide. Her eyes are fire.

"You can get to The Void?" she asks eagerly.

"Working on it," I say with one nod of my head. "If you stay here," I shrug, "you'll never get there."

Her nose twitches at me, and she raises an eyebrow. "Dirty work, Prince."

I smirk. "It's what I'm best at."

"Lucian?" Desdemona scoffs, and despite her tone, despite everything, I decide I never want her to *stop* saying my name. Then she shakes her head. "Just get us out."

The light of the sun is blinding when I pull Desdemona and myself through to the land of the living. I'm surprised when I glance at her, and she opens her eyes. I hadn't been sure she would come with me.

Tears are caught in her eyelashes and brushing over her flushed cheeks. In her subconscious she looked like a god. But here, she looks like Desdemona—the girl whose face I've committed to memory, with no wonder of it lost.

She wipes her eyes before glancing at me, a frown overcasting her features. Without a word, she rises and walks away.

"Wait," I find myself calling for her.

Desdemona looks back in my direction. "How could you not tell me she was in The Void?"

There is no use in lying now, so I say, "Because I needed to make sure you were powerful enough first."

She steps closer, both her fists clenched tight. "And am I?" She seems to be trying to ask it tauntingly, but it comes across morose. "Am I *powerful* enough for you?"

"No," I tell her, a hint of sadness in my voice. "No, I need you to be able to get through."

"So do I, Prince," she whispers, turning her back on me. "So do I."

As I step, a sharp pain in my ankle makes me falter—the same one I'd twisted when I leapt from the tree. I stop, watching as Desdemona disappears from view. I couldn't have brought this injury back from her mind. It's not possible.

My body wasn't *there*.

Once Desdemona is out of sight, I lift my shirt. Right at my side is a long patch of burnt skin, pink and blistering.

## Chapter 22
### Somebody Might Die, But Everybody Gets Hurt

# LUCIAN

I did it. I've alienated Desdemona entirely. Now, the only question that remains is whether it was worth it.

But I know what the weapon can do, and I'm one step closer to using it for myself. When it comes time to go to The Void, I'm certain Desdemona will help me, driven by her desperation to save her mother.

It wasn't the wrong thing to do, yet I can find countless reasons why it wasn't the *right* thing.

One of those reasons, and one I try not to think of, is the disdain in Desdemona's eyes.

"It's as we thought," I tell Cynthia. "Desdemona's consciousness can make it through my projection, but not her body. If she tries again, she'd likely die." As I finish, *all* I can think of is the disdain in Desdemona's eyes.

I can't stop thinking about her, but not for the reasons I should. It's not the questions that surround her that occupy me —it's only her.

It's the way she lifts her head as if she's said something argumentative, when, in truth, it's exactly what I expected. Or how she raises her left eyebrow when I say something flirtatious, always responding in kind and outdoing even my own wit.

It's her smile—her *laugh*—when she isn't holding onto the myriad of masks she wears. It's the sparkle in her eyes that I catch only for a fleeting moment before she conceals her true feelings again.

It's the adrenaline, the power, the excruciatingly exquisite nature of her *being*.

In a perversely comfortable way, sitting in her subconscious felt more natural than being in my own. Like a home I was made and molded for. Like a fate my life is too fickle to grasp.

Images of her flash in my mind again, as if she's a ghost whose dying pact was to never let me go.

I spin the little silver wolf in my pocket, my fingers trembling with the weight of decision. I *have* to let go. The promise of revenge is all I have. All I can ever have.

"Don't look so glum," Cynthia muses.

I sigh and deflect, changing the subject. "Isa, Willow, and Freyr crafted the weapon to destroy The Void and all the Arcanes within it. To my understanding, they weren't able to make it work."

"Perhaps you should meet Freyr again," Cynthia says.

"Azaire almost didn't get out last time," I remind her. "Freyr set us up."

"He set you up… yet you found more than you hoped for." She offers me a lopsided little smile.

"You don't think Freyr was lying?"

"What good would it do to protect the people who imprisoned him?"

How typical of Cynthia to respond to my question with one of her own.

It's yet another idea she's planted: those Fire Folk, or at the very least Freyr, are working in that facility as punishment for past crimes against Folkara.

Going to Freyr again would be dangerous. I certainly couldn't involve Azaire again. If the rulers of Folkara find me there, I'm not sure I'd leave with my head intact. Heir to their throne or not, I'm still a Lyrian—still, for all intents and purposes, loyal to the Ilyrian throne.

Folkara breaking the weapons accord could end in war.

Before I can dwell further, a prophetic vision flickers at the edges of my mind—a disorienting blur of green, brown, and red. It pulls me with an urgency I can't ignore. I'm on my feet in an instant.

This isn't some trivial premonition, like the next move of an opponent. No, this is the kind of vision that once drove Leiana to force me to paint as a child, demanding to see what my mind's eye revealed.

The weight of the vision is pressing, urging me forward as I leave Cynthia's office without another word.

---

My head drops, and I try once more to grasp the vision. It's right there—it's *been* right there—and yet I've been standing in front of the empty canvas all night. My eyes hang heavy, and when I allow myself the sweet relief of closing them, I see Desdemona. Her hair alight with fire, her eyes burning red where they should be brown.

This is pointless, because no matter how I try, she's the only thing I see. With that, I leave behind the art room and whatever the future may hold. Today, it can wait. The first and most important thing is the consumption of the vesi that sits under my bed. I tear off the cap, seeking solace in its bitter burn for my last day of phony freedom.

Azaire knocks softly, his voice interrupting my thoughts: "Your face looks better."

"You should've seen the other guy," I remark.

"You looked worse."

"Thanks."

I take another slow, deliberate sip.

"Do you think drinking before this is a good idea?" Azaire probes.

Lowering the bottle from my lips, I take a deep breath and say, "The subtle poisoning is the only silver lining today."

*If it could be called that.*

"And are you ready? For today?"

I begin to respond, but a vision rips me from the room, thrusting me into a blood-soaked future. It's the same vision I've struggled to fully see. I can *feel* that. Then a girl appears, her face obscured, lying in the woods beneath the sun.

The rays of sunlight dim as the trees fade away, and suddenly, I'm back in front of Azaire, breathless, the vision fading fast.

"As ready as I'll ever be," I mutter as I pull the white, shining shirt and sapphire blue vest from my closet.

But before I can put it on, blood begins to seep from my hands, soaking the pristine garment. I turn to the mirror, seeing a shirt I've not yet worn, already coated in crimson.

This isn't real—it's the vision. Worse still, it feels pressing, personal. The more emotionally demanding a vision is, the harder it becomes to channel.

I look away from the mirror and button my bloody shirt, watching as the blood vanishes with each movement.

"Luc?" Azaire murmurs. "What happened?" He is always understanding. Too understanding. When I don't answer, he asks, "Do you want me to come with you?"

Yes, I do want him to come, but I can't subject him to this—the threats and stares from the Folk.

"No," I answer, "I can handle it."

I fasten the dark-blue cloak around my neck, its interior embroidered with the figure of the goddess Sulva in delicate silver threads. Even I can commend the craftsmanship it took to create this cloak by hand—though, when I do, the blood returns. And with it, the vision of the girl in the woods. Her face remains obscured, yet the deep slash across her stomach is unmistakable, the wound running deep enough to expose her ribcage.

Immediately, I run toward the woods. The cloak tightens,

suffocating with each step, but I don't loosen it. I can't imagine the fuss if I were to arrive at the betrothals without the garment of my kingdom.

When I reach the river, I clench my eyes shut, begging Sulva for another glimpse of the vision. Once again, I see the girl—somewhere beyond the protective barrier of the academy.

Could it be Desdemona? Is that why I kept seeing her while trying to see the vision?

My heart plummets as I make out a hint of dark hair on the nearly lifeless girl. It can't be... It just can't.

I open my eyes, rushing toward the barrier. If it is her, it makes sense why the vision was so hard to grasp. The closer you are to something, the more difficult it is to see it for what it truly is.

But it can't be her.

A scream shatters the silence.

I run toward it, praying I'm wrong. As I approach, I see Aralia, her hands trembling as she cradles a girl in her lap. I don't want to recognize the dark hair and the torn skin around her nails.

*Lilac.*

I drop to my knees, pulling my sister into my arms. Her lifeless weight drapes over me, and without a second thought, I race back to the academy, her blood soaking through my clothes.

Never did I think Lilac would meet her death at the hands of a *monster*. No, all my anxieties, all my fears always pictured Leiana as the culprit.

When Lilac was nine years old, Leiana first made a threat against her, all because of me. I made a vow to Sulva that I would do everything in my power to protect her. One I've failed to keep.

To protect someone at all costs is a sacrifice, and it has not come cheap thus far.

What was Lilac doing in the woods? She was supposed to be

getting ready. How long had she been there bleeding out? If only I could've seen that accursed vision sooner.

Healers rush Lilac's limp body into a room, rubbing balms into her gashes and ground herbs under her nose. They prick her finger and let three drops of blood fall on a round crystal plate.

There are only a handful of healers in the academy at any given time, here for the injuries we acquire in Combat Training. But they're Eunoia, and their magic is honed to save people. I repeat that to myself as three healers stand over Lilac, green energy wisping from their fingers into my sister.

*They have to save her—they're trained for this.*

I sit beside Lilac, my gaze never leaving her, until I can't afford to stay any longer. I make a feeble attempt to scrub the blood from my clothes before I portal to Folkara.

The moment I step into Folkara's kingdom, I'm met with the sharp tone of Piphany, Leiana's advisor. "You're late."

I'd like to tell her that a forced betrothal doesn't warrant my punctuality, but instead, I meet her gaze and say, "My inadequacy."

Piphany's eyes flicker over me, her breath hitching as she stumbles over Lilac's blood, stark against my clothes. She runs a hand through her white hair, trying to regain her composure. "*What*," she breathes, "is on your attire?"

"Blood," I say with no effort to suppress my scowl.

Piphany inhales sharply, as though swallowing a scream.

*She and I both.*

"We will have to get a seamstress to fit you a new suit."

"There will be no need," I reply, turning on my heel before she can argue. Unfortunately, she follows.

"Excuse me?" Piphany asks in a tone unfit for addressing Royalty. Then again, she is Leiana's pet.

"I will not be changing," I say firmly.

Piphany laughs—a loud and deranged sort of noise. The color drains from her already pale face, her ice-blue eyes lighting with an unspoken power, as though she might try to wield it against me—though she knows she can't.

"Where is Lilac?" she asks, her voice tight with desperation.

She's clearly on her last string.

"Lilac will not be attending," I say, staring ahead as we walk to the throne room.

"And why is that?" Her voice squeaks.

I stare at Piphany, content in my silence.

We make it to the back staircase of the throne room, and she all but pushes me as she insists, "Get in there."

I walk down the stairs, stepping past Kai to stand next to Calista. She links her arm through mine, staring ahead at the steps we prepare to ascend, crafted of unfinished wood, with dark vines and violet flowers twisting around the banister.

"Where is Lilac?" Calista whispers.

"Lilac isn't coming—"

"Welcome," King Easton's voice booms through the room above and the one we stand in below. "We are gathered here today to watch and honor the union between the future King and Queen of Folkara and Ilyria as they make their vows of promise."

That's our cue. Calista and I make our way up the sprawling staircase, each step feeling like a march toward doom. At the top, we stand before a room of nobility.

Gasps echo as we step onto the aisle, all eyes on the blood staining my shirt. I keep my gaze ahead of me.

As expected, Leiana and Labyrinth are nowhere to be seen. This should be no surprise. They control our lives but never bother to witness the disasters they demand. I pray for a miracle—like a monster breaking past the kingdom's defenses, putting a finish to this farce.

Reaching the thrones, I turn to Calista and take her hands in mine. Once we do this, there is no stopping our future marriage. We will share our power, share our essence, and on the day we ascend to the throne, if we refuse to marry, our very souls will beg for what we deny. Beg for the release of the binding we begin today.

Beg for the release of the pain we are sure to endure if we try to fight for our freedom.

From this day forward, an invisible noose ties Calista and I together, asphyxiating us both.

Yet here I am, putting on a show the way Leiana has always trained me, announcing, "I, Lucian Aibek, hereby solemnly vow to take Calista Contarini as my wife and future Queen of Folkara on the day of our shared coronation. I will love her as I love myself; I will protect her as I protect myself; and our powers shall be bound in unity, in the name of the lunar goddess, Sulva."

We are here to placate those in this room, easing their minds by showing that the alliance between Ilyria and Folkara is in good hands.

It's a charade. A game of politics.

And we are the pawns.

Calista clears her throat before reciting, "I, Calista Contarini, hereby solemnly vow to take Lucian Aibek as my husband and future King of Folkara. I will love him as I love myself; protect him as I protect myself; and our powers shall be bound in unity, in the name of the goddess of balance, Zola."

There are small echoes of approval from the crown. But when Kai arises from the staircase alone, the room gasps in horror once more.

"Lilac isn't with us," Kai announces. The audience reacts with even more horror than when I stepped out covered in blood.

"Very well, we shall begin the feast." King Easton's voice is strained, but he smiles and gestures to the tables.

I make my way to the Lyrian table and sit beside Lilac's empty seat. The table is full of my kind, but none meet my eyes as they feast on traditional Folk foods—seeded breads, jams made from every fruit the Folks' world has to offer, steaks from their cattle, and even some of the organs, all to be washed down with an array of wines. I don't touch a thing.

I am too consumed by Lilac's absence to consume their foods.

Halfway through the *ceremony*, Calista and Queen Melody both leave the room, one after the other, and I find myself believing there may be a silver lining after all. Perhaps Melody discovered Calista's snooping. Following them could lead to answers.

"If you'll excuse me," I announce to the table, setting my cloth down before exiting the throne room.

In the halls, I follow behind until Calista and Melody enter the portal room. I sneak in once they are out of sight. From a distance, I watch as Calista steps into the infirmary of Visnatus.

*If she is doing anything that pertains to Lilac, I will be there.*

I race to the nearest reflective surface, opening a portal of my own and stepping back through to the academy.

The infirmary is far different from Folkara's kingdom. It smells of blood and flowers—two scents that don't belong together. From the corner of my eyes, I spot Calista walking into room twelve—Lilac's room. I follow after her, peering through a narrow crack in the nearly closed door. Calista stands over Lilac's bed, pinching her nose and clasping a hand tightly around her mouth. Silent tears fall from her eyes, silver makeup staining her skin.

"Oh, Lilac," she whispers and picks up my sister's limp hand. "You have to know I'm sorry. I'll always be sorry."

I step inside, misinterpreting Calista's words as a threat. Then she pries open Lilac's eyes, and her own glow yellow, casting a faint light across the room.

She's going through Lilac's memories.

There's no reason she should be able to—Lilac has the same wards as I do—unless my sister offered the princess of Folkara access to her mind before. I suppose she must have, back when they trusted each other.

I fear Lilac might still trust her.

Calista holds my sister's hand for far longer than I expect. Her hands shake, and her jaw trembles as she finally lets go, turning to see me watching from the door.

"Why are you here?" I ask.

Calista's eyes flicker between me and Lilac's body, unable to settle on either.

"What are you up to, Calista?" I press, taking a step closer, narrowing the space between us.

Her breath quickens, heavy and uneven, her chest rising and falling sharply. "My mother told me to find out what happened," she stammers, her voice trembling. "I didn't know it was Lilac, I swear."

How is it possible that Melody already knows what's happened?

"Why does your mother want to know anything?" I ask, narrowing my eyes.

Calista shakes her head. "She wanted to know who was nearby when Lilac was attacked."

Against my will, I think of Desdemona. The vision of her and the moonaro, her hand nuzzled on its nose, both of them comfortable in one another's presence. Then, I watched the beast run from her when I approached, while she lied to me, over and over. I saw *her* in my visions when I was supposed to see Lilac. It's not enough to convince me Desdemona has anything to do with this. Nothing would be enough. She couldn't possibly.

*Could she?*

"What did you see?" I ask, and Calista shakes her head once more. "What did you *see*, Calista?"

She bites the inside of her cheek, and her rounded face squishes together. With a deep breath, Calista reluctantly answers, "She ran when she saw the monster, but she tripped." Her lower lip quivers, but she forces it still. "When it was close, Lilac grabbed the creature and then… I don't know how to explain it. It just felt gross. Lilac almost fainted, and when she let go, the monster slashed her stomach."

Calista wipes a tear from under her eye before it can fall, her composure wavering for only a moment. The quiver is gone from her voice—as if by sheer will—as she says, "She watched herself bleed out before losing consciousness."

All I can picture is Lilac, alone in the woods, bleeding out and believing she was going to die. I think about the power she must've realized she had at that moment, how it must've made her feel.

I should've known. I should've put it together.

It makes sense. Stealing life force is a rare power—no wonder it's hereditary.

Her mother has been stealing mine my entire life.

I steady myself enough to ask, "What did this to her?"

Calista's lips quiver, and she turns away from me, cupping her mouth again and plugging her nose. Her body trembles with silent sobs before she turns to me, her whisper barely audible as she says, "A moonaro."

# Part 2:
# The unraveling

## Chapter 23
## An Arsonist's Lullaby

# DESDEMONA

I throw another rock into the river, then I scream into the trees. Birds chirp back at me, filling the space with their cacophony, and I decide my next rock will peg one of them.

It's one failed attempt after another, every single day.

This isn't the way to open a portal to The Void. This isn't the way to reach my mom. I'm stupid for coming out here every day, thinking something will change. If no one's made it to The Void before, me and a portal in the river aren't going to do it. Maybe that's just the way things go—people like me never get what they want.

But people like Lucian *do*. It doesn't matter that he lied. It *can't* matter. Not if I want to get to my mom.

I wouldn't be in this position if I hadn't left her—if I hadn't let her push me through the portal to this school. I should have fought harder. I should have *stayed*.

The next rock I hurl strikes a bird mid-flight, straight to the skull. And another. And another. Each one falls to the ground without a thought from me, as if the weight of the worlds is lifted every time a bird dies.

One rock distracts, and the next kills.

It's like a meditation. The one thing I'm good at. The one time I get what I want.

When killing birds grows boring, I wait for the whispering, which I've been doing every day. That, like opening a portal to

The Void, has only ended in failure. But I swear the whispers were trying to say something when the moonaro approached. I swear I heard *words*.

What if it's the answer to saving my mom? The answer to *everything*.

But the silence presses too hard, so I grab the dead birds and bring them to Elowen. I have to say I've missed the hunt.

Reaching the kitchen, I hold up the birds by their legs, offering them to Elowen.

"Where'd you get those?" she asks, crossing her arms over her chest with a knowing smile. Of course she knows I'm not some rich kid—no rich kid would do this.

"Anger and accuracy. A little bit of annoyance, too." I return the smile.

Elowen lays a wooden plank on the counter in front of me, instructing, "Put 'em here. I'll whip something up."

I set the birds down and take my usual seat across from her.

"How ya doing?" she asks.

Now, that is a weighted question. I've spent days at the river, trying and failing to open a portal and screaming at birds. Aralia hasn't left her bed the whole time, I guess because Lucian's sister was attacked. I have a feeling that Lilac is one of those old friends she doesn't like to talk about.

I take Aralia's silence as grief, but she won't divulge anything to me. I thought I'd earned her trust more than that, but I think she's smarter for keeping it to herself.

At least I know I made the right decision when I lied to Lucian about the moonaro and the whispering, or the wind, or whatever it is. I won't let anyone clump me up into a mess that involves the princess. I've already gotten too tangled with the prince.

Avoid and deflect is plan A. Lie and gaslight is plan B. I'm trying not to think of plan C.

As for Elowen's question, I'd tell her I was fair if I didn't already admit to being angry and annoyed.

"Angry and annoyed," I mutter, bringing my elbows to the counter.

"Here," Elowen says, leaning down until I can't see her. She pops back up, sliding a dish over to me. "Have a pie."

I smile a little, fiddling with my fingers over the newly presented pie. "I'm all better now."

---

Long after the sun has set and the stars have taken over, I stand in front of the mirror in my room, coating the stab wound on my shoulder with glamour. Even as it burns, I *keep* putting it on.

Every time I see the thing, I think of the dead Lyrian.

I coat my hand too, since there's no way to explain why my palm is so badly burnt. The skin is charred, the color of ash. But it doesn't hurt anymore. More often than not, it's numb.

And I'm probably going to need more glamour soon.

When the wound disappears from view, I slide the dual sword into the sheath strapped to my back. Not that I want to train, or learn to swing a sword to wound my opponent, or do *anything* but find out how to get to the not-so-mythical universe we call The Void. But I don't know how to talk to Lucian anymore. He's my only lead, and after everything with my mom—and his sister—it doesn't feel like I can ask him for anything. I'm just waiting for him to come to me.

"I'll be back soon," I call to Aralia, but she stays silent.

The school is quiet tonight. As I walk the empty halls, I close my eyes, pretending it's early morning, just before sunrise, and that I'm hunting with Damien. Mom's in the dwelling, getting ready to head to the factory, while I wait for a possum to fall so I can throw a dagger into its throat.

The weight of the sword on my back is nothing like the small dagger in my hand. The indoor air replaces the morning breeze.

And I'm all alone. Pretending I have company only reminds me of how little I have here.

Leiholan is waiting in the combat room. I don't greet him, and he doesn't greet me. I only unsheathe my sword, and he raises his. I'm not in the mood for banter or blame, or for much of anything, actually. Every swing of mine is filled with anger.

After I lose yet again, he shouts, "Good!" He points his sword at me, flicking it up and down in assessment, as if I'm finally worth something. "You're improving."

"Yeah, I tend to be at peak performance when I'm pissed."

We go back and forth again, before he inevitably pins his blade to my throat. I've grown used to the steel on my skin.

I've grown used to the sting of defeat.

The next time, two quick swings and a nick across my collarbone are all it takes to make the sword fall from my hands.

I tug my shirt higher to hide the wound before it cauterizes, then pick up my sword again. The same thing happens once, twice, three more times.

It isn't until we've finished that Leiholan says, "I think I like you better this way."

"Pissed?" I sneer.

"Quiet." He smiles.

When he isn't paying attention, I swing at his sword with all my strength, finally knocking it from his hand.

---

After hours of training with Leiholan, I return to the suite, lying in bed and pulling the covers over my head—just as Aralia has been doing. I do nothing but try to breathe, keeping my eyes open. Every time I close them, I see my mom covered in bruises, blood, and dirt.

I do this all night.

The next morning drags by, no different from the last. Aralia won't get out of bed, and I'm starting to realize how much drearier this place feels when my roommate is acting dreary. I dress quickly, trying to go through the motions like nothing's changed.

But *everything* has changed. I know where my mom is, but no matter how hard I try, I can't open a portal. So instead of heading to the river, I go to the library. I search for any book that might tell me something—*anything*—without triggering alarm words like "Arcanes" or "The Void." The Arcanian War is the first thing I look up, even though that's risky, too.

For as much text as there is on the subject, there's not much information. A thousand years ago the Arcanian War destroyed the universe. But one world emerged nearly unscathed: Ilyria. The Lyrians come up again and again. They survived the war, then saved the universe, opening Visnatus Academy to mold the universe's future leaders in *their* image. There's not a thing in these texts about the Arcanes or The Void—what it is, how it was created, why the Arcanes were sent there, or *how* to get there.

Defeat has never tasted so bitter—like the dirt and blood that covers my mom.

Just as I begin to close the last book, a scratching sound—like nails on a chalkboard—rises from the pages. I flip through the book, searching for the noise, and stop when I see words being etched into the paper in ink the color of blood.

*The Void awaits you, Desdemona.*

I snap the book shut, holding it in my trembling hands for a moment. The Void awaits me. *Me.* Excitement pulls at my muscles—urging me to *do* something.

Quickly, I slide my pile of books into their shelves as the librarian approaches. She offers to help, but I decline, worried about what she'll think if she sees all the text regarding the Arcanes.

The old woman snatches a book anyway—the one with the eerie message. I stiffen as she examines the cover, hoping that she won't open it.

With a hoarse, grouchy voice, she demands, "Why are you looking for the Arcanes, girl?"

"I'm not," I lie, my heart racing. Not because I'm scared of the message—I actually like it. I don't care what it means or why; I'm *going* to get to The Void. My only concern is the librarian seeing it and thinking I'm connected to such an ominous evil.

"It's no school project," the woman grumbles, her eyes magnified through her thick glasses. "We don't teach about the Arcanian War anymore."

She opens the book, and I hold my breath. Licking her finger, she turns the pages dreadfully slow. I watch, heart pounding, as the paper flicks beneath her fingertips, each turn closer to the scarlet script.

But she makes it through the entire book, and there's not a single remnant of red.

I nod, shoving the rest of my books back and trying to slip away, but her gnarled, wrinkled hand clamps down on my wrist. I try to pull away, but I can't, not without hurting her. She's surprisingly strong.

Her gaze meets mine, her voice like a threat as she warns, "Some things are best left forgotten."

"I understand."

She doesn't respond. Her gaze stays fixed on mine for a moment before finally releasing me, and I run. I leave the school, weaving through trees and rocks, heading back to the river. When I reach the water, I drop to my knees, staring at my reflection.

The Void awaits *me*. The place where my mom sits bruised and battered wants *me*. So why, for all my aggravation, can I not open a damn portal there?

I try again, reaching out to my reflection, setting my hand on the water. I try to imagine that place, those gold bars that held my mom, the strange shadowy figures that seemed to lurk—but

I don't feel any power. All I feel is wet.

I've portaled from Folkara to Visnatus. I traveled between *worlds*. Can a universe be that different? Why can't I do it *now*, when they *want* me?

I try again, and I fail again, when the necklace Mom gave me begins to pulse against my chest, thumping like a heartbeat. I reach for it; I *remember* it. The chain had snapped the last time I'd opened such a powerful portal. The necklace fell to the floor of my old dwelling in the septic, and power flooded me.

I killed a man with a simple scream.

Mom always disdained my magic. But it was for the same reason I did—she didn't want me to die. Right?

Cautiously, I reach for the necklace, tied around my neck with one of Aralia's corset strings.

I untie it.

Slowly, I set the pendant beside me, my fingers lingering for just a moment. But the instant it slips from my hands, I'm yanked out of the woods, and the world around me blurs into greenery I've known for years.

I'm in the septic.

There are no villages in sight. Mom and I sit deep in the woods, settled in front of an unlit fire pit dug in the ground.

"You can do it," Mom says softly. She holds a stick with her catch skewered on it and leans it against a tree trunk. Then, she picks up my hand and rests it over the kindling. "All you have to do is feel."

"I'm scared," I croak, looking back through the trees.

"Good," she whispers, tugging my hand. I turn my head back to face her. "That's emotion. That's power. Use it."

I nod and close my eyes, blood rushing through my body, heart beating loudly in my ears as I feel the heat prickle beneath my fingers like needles.

When I open my eyes, I'm sitting in front of the river again. Back on Visnatus—not Folkara. Not in the septic, but at the school.

I lie on the ground, my hands burning up, the needles still pricking my fingers.

But this might be what I need.

I sit up quickly, frantically placing my hand to the water, trying to summon every ounce of power at my disposal. Once more I close my eyes, imagining The Void, my mom.

Am I really going to make it this time? Is that what the note in the book was telling me—that I can finally find my mom?

I feel it. *Really* feel it—the power rushing in my hands, in my chest where the necklace once was. I swear the water is swirling beneath me—the portal is opening. It isn't turning to darkness, like it always does. Instead, the water turns red, and through the crimson, I see the bars of Mom's cage.

I've done it.

I open my eyes, ready to step through the portal, but when I look, nothing has happened.

Nothing has happened at all.

---

With a heavy heart, I drag myself to Elemental Magic. I've choked down more than my fair share of tears today. It isn't because I'm sad, not exactly. It's because I'm so close to my mom, and I'm still failing.

I'm failing her.

I try to get to the back of class, to go through the day ignored, but Ms. Abrams pulls me aside, saying, "I wanted to give you a heads-up that you will not be passing."

I catch the hint of a grin tugging at her lips. She enjoys this, and I'm not cut out for it. I wasn't made to be poised and proper and powerful. I'm the opposite of it all—I'm manipulative, I'm vulgar, I'm… powerless.

And I won't apologize for it. I'm strong where they're stubborn. Clever where they're clueless. Cunning where they're cautious. It's why I'm alive, and it's the way to get my mom—which is all I have to do before I can get out of here.

I just have to get out of here.

I just have to get something.

"Okay," I say. "Is that all?"

"Yes, you may be excused."

I want to punch her, to set her hair on fire. Instead, I force a smile and walk back to the table where the Air and Light Folk are working on their defense. I get to be briefly suffocated, or electrocuted, or whatever else they want to do to me that I can't do to them.

"Don't worry," Kai says, but I don't see him. It's a trick the *Air* Folk can do—amplify and isolate sound—but Kai is a Light Folk. His power is electricity. "I won't let her ruin your future in the kingdom."

*My future in the kingdom.* I don't let my face fall, but I can't stop my stomach from churning.

"Thank you," I whisper, but I don't think I mean it.

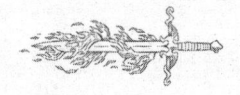

---

When class is over and I'm thoroughly beaten up by my fellow Folk, I find myself running into Kai.

"Walk with me," he says in a hushed tone and doesn't stop.

I match his stride, and for a fleeting moment, I'm back beside Damien, walking together like we did every morning.

"I'm going to tell my father about Ms. Abrams," Kai says, glancing over at me with a sideways smile. "Discrimination against the Fire Folk isn't permissible."

I think I understand what he's saying; he wants to get Ms. Abrams fired. *For me.* If he knew I was from the septic, he wouldn't do that. I don't even think there's any kind of rule against discrimination back home.

"Why would you?" I ask.

*She's just a mean teacher. And I'm just a Fire Folk.*

"Life has been more than poor for me as of late. You're kind of the only person who has taken my feelings into consideration. I owe you."

The prince of Folkara *owes* me? I could use that, but to what length? I'm glad the bullshit I've been spewing has led him to believe I take his feelings into consideration.

At least I'm doing something right.

"Oh, no, you don't owe me anything," I say with a short—fake—laugh. "I was just doing what any good Folk would do."

"Then you're the only good one here," Kai says quietly. I think he's actually saddened by the sentiment—and somehow, that makes me a little sad, too.

"Can I ask you a question?" I ask. It's a slow descent into what I want to know.

"Shoot."

"Was it you who amplified your voice when you spoke to me in class?" What can I say? I'm curious about what else we don't know at home.

"Yes," he answers.

"You used air magic?" I ask, just for the clarification.

Kai lets out a short chuckle and says, "Yes, why?"

*So it is possible.*

"I didn't know you were so powerful," I say softly. Then, "Can you show me?"

Kai looks around the hall quickly, then grabs my hand and takes a sharp turn. Looking over my shoulder, he says, "It has to be our secret."

If I could use magic other than fire, I'd be better off. I wouldn't have to risk killing myself to protect myself. I *need* this. So, I smile and say, "Of course."

He smiles a little, his eyes perusing me up and down. There's something in the way he looks at me, like he's impressed—

maybe even intrigued. After a moment of staring, he says, "Then follow me."

He turns toward the exit, walking through the garden, and into the woods—but not beyond the barrier.

The trees close in around us as we walk deeper, the decaying leaves crinkling beneath my feet. Back home, they wouldn't fall until... well, now, actually. We're past three hundred days of the Collianth Cycle. The year is almost over, and I've been here for months, doing... what?

Kai steps into a pile of fallen leaves and holds his hands out. His brown eyes begin to glow with power, but they don't turn purple, the color that's associated with light magic. They turn yellow.

Air magic.

The wind howls, and the leaves beneath him sweep up into the current, swirling around him. A Light Folk using air magic. I can't believe my own eyes. Then the leaves fall abruptly, settling around him, and Kai looks like he's catching his breath.

"Are you okay?" I ask, stepping forward, then curse myself for not saying *all right* like Lieholan always insists I should—especially in front of a prince.

"Yes." After a minute of heavy breathing, Kai says, "Channeling a component you don't inherently possess takes more energy. I wanted you to know what to expect."

"Oh," I say. "Thanks."

Kai sits on the ground, then gestures for me to do the same. When I don't join him, he says, "Please."

I sit.

"All you have to do is open yourself to a new element, the same way you had to open yourself to the one you *have*," he says. "Close your eyes."

Begrudgingly, I do.

"Air, light, water," Kai says. Then he pauses before adding, "*Fire*... I have everything inside of me." He repeats it again, like a mantra, and I do the same.

The wind picks up, brushing through my hair and against my ears.

"Reach for it," he whispers.

Power rises in my stomach, bubbling up into my chest. It courses through my blood, taking me over entirely. I am nothing but the adrenaline in my veins. The rush of my heart.

"And release it," Kai says, and I do.

It leaves me feeling pleasantly dizzy. My mind hums with a sort of silence I've never experienced before. My whole body vibrates with it.

It's the peace of sleeping without the horrors of my dreams, and I could sit in it forever.

But someone's calling my name. I try to block them out, and they only get louder.

Kai is in front of me when I open my eyes. Fire roars behind him as he screams, but I still can't fully hear him. He pulls me to my feet, and we run.

Kai's cursing, and I don't know what to do. When the sun shines on my face, I can suddenly feel the heat that's surrounding him and me. It's from the fire chasing behind us.

I didn't tap into a new element; I unleashed my own. The Flame.

"What are we going to do?" I yell, losing my breath and trying to catch it.

We're getting closer to the school, but the fire follows close behind. Back home, *this* is how we die—and I'm about to kill countless others.

"I'll get the headmistress," Kai says. "She can stop this."

There's only one person that I *know* can fix this.

"No," I shout, "get Lucian."

"*Lucian?*" Kai echoes. "The headmistress is much more powerful than him." The way he speaks doesn't leave much room for debate.

"Then get her. I'll run toward the lake."

I don't wait for a response before I turn from him and run for the water. I know the fire is following me—the Flame always chases its igniter. Once the fire starts, it has one goal: survival. It will go on until it can't anymore, and I hope the lake's lunar power is enough to let me see the end of this.

I do my best to ignore the fire catching in my lungs, not daring to look back until I'm almost at the lake.

Maybe I'll survive this—be one of the lucky ones.

When I turn again, Kai and the headmistress are there, but the fire still rages.

"Get Lucian!" I scream, desperation choking my voice. But even that feels hopeless. I mean, Kai said it himself—Headmistress Constance is stronger than Lucian. Lucian has subdued the Flame before, but never anything this big. Maybe it's just impossible to stop me now.

To save my life.

I'm not one to plead, but I find myself doing just that as I dive into the lake, begging Zola to let me live.

## Chapter 24
## Hole Hearted

# DESDEMONA

Can fire kill me underwater? That's the question, and it's followed by the thought that maybe a higher class of education would be more useful than I thought.

The fire starts to spread across the surface of the water. My ears pop and burn as I swim deeper, but I don't stop. When I finally look up, there's no light. I endure another searing moment before I swim toward the surface.

No fire.

But Lucian is the first thing I see, and an unexpected pang hits my chest when I take him in. The bags under his eyes are black, and so are his irises. His hair is a mess, and his scruffy jaw is the only part of his disheveled look that suits him.

Our eyes meet for just a second before he looks away and toward Kai. Headmistress Constance stands before them, her expression the opposite of the two boys. Where they scorn, she admires, offering me a hand and pulling me from the water.

"Very fair, dear," she says.

"What?" I ask. My core is shaking, and I can't hide it.

"Few in your place would have survived." She removes her coat and wraps it around me. "In the end, it's astuteness that keeps us breathing."

Her voice echoes Lucian's earlier words: *Keep your wits about you.*

The headmistress leans into me and whispers, "Especially for a girl with your upbringing."

Right.

I turn, searching for Lucian. Did he save me? He must have. But before I can do anything about it, he walks back to the school—not even turning to glance at me.

"Come, dear," the headmistress says, wrapping a hand around my waist to help me walk.

By the time we reach the school halls, Lucian's gone.

"I can take her to her suite," Kai offers Headmistress Constance.

I wonder if she's thinking what I'm thinking—a girl from the septic has managed to not just secure one, but two princes' help. I wonder if she's in awe or disgusted.

"Thank you, Kai," the headmistress replies, removing her hand from my waist, but leaving her coat on my shoulders. Under her breath, she whispers, "Good luck, dear."

She leaves without another word.

Kai clears his throat, shifting uncomfortably as he meets my gaze. "I don't know how to adequately apologize."

"Apologize?" I echo.

But he doesn't respond. Instead, he takes the headmistress's place, guiding me through the halls in silence. I think I could walk fine on my own, but I let him, not wanting to tell off a prince.

By the time we reach my suite, Kai pauses in the middle of the living room, his face twisted with guilt. "I almost got you killed," he whispers.

I shake my head, falling on the couch in the middle of the suite, surprised by my exhaustion.

"It was my magic, not yours." I force a smile, trying to ease the tension, but it doesn't work out in my favor.

Kai walks toward me, saying, "Magic you wouldn't have used if I hadn't—"

I quickly say, "It was a survival lesson. Maybe I should thank you."

Really, I just want him to leave so I can lie down and stop thinking about the potential I have in killing myself.

He's clearly not convinced by my thanks when he says, "I apologize, Desdemona."

The formality of his words isn't one I like. I mimic it as I say, "I accept your apology, Prince Kai." I pause. "*If* you'll answer another question."

"Anything." He nods.

I lower my voice, rising to my feet and stepping closer. "What do you know about The Void?"

His eyes go wide. Shit. At least I didn't mention the Arcanes.

"What do you know?" Kai asks.

"Nothing, really." *That's the problem.*

"Is anyone here?" He looks over my shoulder.

"There shouldn't be, no."

He scans the room, then says, "Supposedly, there were these creatures that fought during the Arcanian War. After the ruin, they left the universe." His soft brown gaze meets mine. "It's a presumption, and I wouldn't advise you to bring it up again."

Shit. "I won't," I promise.

He nods, lips pressed tight.

"I'll see you tomorrow?" I ask, trying to get him out quicker.

Kai takes a step back, nodding. "Yes." Then, he disappears through the door.

Shit. Shit!

*Where* is Lucian? How can he screw me over and then disappear when he becomes useful?

I wait until Kai is long gone, then I go to Lucian's suite, where I refrain from barging in and instead knock at the door.

Azaire has a lovely greeting. "He's not—"

"I need to talk to him," I say, pushing past Azaire. Their suite is like ours, with dark blue decorations instead of beige, but I've never been in Lucian's room before. "Which door is his?" I demand.

"Look—"

"Aibek?" I call, opening doors one by one and being greeted by the empty rooms.

"Desdemona." Azaire puts his hand on the next doorknob before I can. Must be Lucian's. "Stop."

I face him. "Shouldn't you be in class?"

"Shouldn't you?" His tone is soft as he shrugs.

"Do you know?"

I mean, he's the boy who *made the kingdom less lonely*. He and Lucian are close, that much is obvious.

"Has he told you the truth?" I demand.

Azaire shakes his head, but he says, "Yes."

I can't help but laugh. "Brilliant." I pull my hands through my wet hair. "Just brilliant." I pound on the door. "Aibek!"

After a moment, Lucian comes out with a bottle in his hand, smiling.

"We need to talk," I say, but this sight makes me feel like I've lost the upper hand.

"Do we?" he asks, his voice tinged with humor.

I step closer to him, into his room. "Yes."

He stretches out his arms, knocking my shoulder with the glass bottle and chuckling. I step fully inside and close the door on Azaire.

His room is different than I expected. Paintings line the walls, but my gaze settles on one in particular. It's a man with the same features as Lucian—right down to the uneven eyebrows and crooked nose.

His gaze follows mine to the painting, and when I look back at him, all the humor has left his face.

It takes too long to find the courage to say, "I need your help."

"You *need* me?" Lucian takes a slow sip, glancing away from the painting. "How endearing."

"It's not supposed to be endearing." I whisper, "You know I can't find my mom without you."

"I see." He nods as he takes another sip. "In all the time I spent waiting for you, this partnership has grown stale."

He drops the bottle, fakes a frown, and turns away from me, walking to the door. No doubt to open it and kick me out.

I catch his wrist, my voice cracking as I say, "*Please.*"

He looks down at me. "Another thing I was waiting for. Should've made a bucket list."

"You wanted me to plead?"

"No," he shrugs. "But *I* almost did." Lucian laughs, running a hand down his face. "I almost *begged* you for something so simple as your time."

"You don't have to beg me, I'm here voluntarily!"

"Yes, well," he says shallowly. "I wouldn't anymore."

I let go of his wrist and take a step back, my heel knocking into an empty alcohol bottle. "What's going on with you?"

"What's going on with me?" He laughs.

"Yes! What is going on with you?" I shout.

"My sister's in a coma!" His voice cracks. "And you"—he points at my chest but keeps his distance—"how long have you been lying to me?"

Oh, shit.

"What?" I say, trying to laugh a little, to make it seem like what he's just said is the most outrageous thing I've heard. "I've never lied to you."

"On the day we first tracked your mother?" he offers.

"Besides that day, never!"

"Okay," Lucian slurs. "Then tell me the truth and I'll believe you. Tell me who you are, and I'll stand beside you."

He steps closer, and a part of me believes it's the alcohol in his veins that makes the desperation in his eyes so clear. But when he reaches for my hands, then pulls back—as if reconsidering—I realize something *has* shifted between us. Something deep.

"Give me a reason to believe you," he says, his voice heavy with defeat. "And I will."

It would be easy, wouldn't it? The words aren't the hard part.

*I'm Desdemona Althenia. I've been running my entire life. I've never once told someone who I am.*

*I'm from the septic. I've murdered three. A few more in my dreams.*

*When the moonaro came close, this whispering that's been in my head since I first killed became louder than it ever has.*

*And then I lied, because I'm a liar, too.*

*I don't know how to show myself.*

*I don't know how to handle being seen because there's this part of me that swears to the gods that, once I am, I'll lose everything again. Because that's how my life goes.*

*I've never once gotten to keep something.*

The words aren't the hard part. It's what's behind them—what they mean. I can't let him see me… because then it's all over. He'll hate me—just like everyone else.

Being alive means being unknown, and despite my feelings against it, the prince is the single most important person to keep at arm's length. So I look him in the eye and say, "I'm exactly who you think I am."

Lucian scoffs, stepping back and furthering the distance between us. "You know," he sighs, "your left hand clenches when you lie."

I freeze when he calls me out, my hand instinctively moving to clutch my left palm. My mind races to hide it, but it's already too late. The tremor in my hand betrays me, and I feel like he's seen something much deeper than I ever intended him to. His eyes seem to peel back layers of me, like skinning an animal.

And like a child, my only rebuttal is, "Does not."

"Does."

I step away. "And how exactly did you figure this out, Aibek?"

His entire face stiffens. "Because I happened to enjoy looking at you."

"Happen*ed?*" I echo.

"Happened," he confirms.

"So this?" I point between us. "This is over?"

The prince takes one last sip from his bottle before answering, "Long over."

So that's it. I've lost him in every way that matters.

I reach for the door and slam it behind me.

There's no one on my side anymore. There's no way to The Void. It's all I can think as I walk back to the suite and step into Aralia's room, spotting the lump in her bed. Then I remember it's just my sulky roommate. Joining her in the sulking, I lie down and pull the covers over my head. It gets stuffy fast, and I throw them off.

Lucian could tell anyone about my mother, about the Arcanes, about everything I've worked so hard to keep hidden. He could unravel my world with a few words—and why wouldn't he? I should have been more careful.

I should have made sure he saw less.

The panic hangs over me, too heavy, too close, threatening to tear it all apart. It's too much because it's *true*. This could happen at any moment.

And then, I do something stupid.

"Aralia?" I ask.

She pokes her head out from beneath the blanket. Her black hair is a mess, like a raven's nest, and her lips are twisted into a scowl.

"Are you okay?"

Aralia turns away and mutters, "No."

I wince when I ask, "Do you want to talk?" But I wince even more at the sudden emotion that fills me—the overwhelming hope that she'll say yes. "I miss you," I add, hoping it sounds convincing. "And I almost died today."

Aralia fidgets under the covers, then looks at me. She stares, for a long, long time. Then, finally, she says, "I can't stop thinking about what will happen if Lilac doesn't make it."

I knew her behavior had something to do with the princess's attack.

"I didn't know you were close," I say.

"We were best friends." She fidgets more before adding, "When Calista and I got back from Acansa, a lot changed. Before that, it was always the three of us."

*Acansa*, an elite all-Folk school Aralia told me about.

"The three of you?" I ask.

"Calista, Lilac, and I."

I'm shocked, but I don't know why. Her parents are the king and queen's head advisors. She grew up in the kingdom, with Calista.

She's practically Royalty adjacent.

I'm surrounded by people who'd hate me if they knew the truth.

"Calista was the first to cut us off. It was just Lilac and me for most of the year, until I did exactly what Calista had done to us." Tears build in Aralia's eyes. "What Calista did still hurts me, and Lilac went through that twice." After a pause, she says, "And I miss her."

Oh. It isn't grief—it's guilt.

"I'll check on her for you," I offer, thinking of my mom, how the image of her, bloody and bruised, fills my mind every time I close my eyes. "So you don't have to see her like that."

"Thank you," Aralia whispers, swiping at a tear. "How'd you almost die today?"

"Oh." I roll onto my back. "The Flame."

"Oh," she says, her voice cracking.

"Yeah," I sigh. "Oh." When the ceiling gets boring and my thoughts get repetitive, I say, "You know, you're the only one here who's taken an interest in being my friend. Everyone else looks at me with either fear or pity."

*I'm more likely to self-combust than graduate. That truth terrifies me.*

"My dad was a Fire Folk," she says quietly.

*Was.* I look away from the ceiling to find Aralia looking at the window between our beds and all the pictures on the sill. They're *his* pictures on the sill, I realize.

"I don't think you should be ignored because you have a power that's difficult to maintain," she adds.

I don't mean it as I say, "I appreciate it." But I do.

"It's not a big deal. You're kind of my best friend at this point."

"Best friend?" *That could be useful.* "Yeah, you too." I shift topics before my white lie slips. "How well do you know Kai?"

"I grew up with him," Aralia says. "Why?"

"I think he likes me," I say instead of explaining today's ordeal.

"Careful with the Royals," Aralia says with a small hint of the sarcasm she once exuded. "I only have a fraction of their fucked-up-ness, and I can tell you, it's a lot."

"Noted."

"Plus, his real name is Malakai," she says, and I can certainly hear her smile.

I smile, too.

---

I start checking on Lilac every day and giving Aralia updates. It quickly becomes my new routine. The princess looks better with each visit. Color returns to her face, and the bandages around her torso become less and less restrictive, no longer needed to cover as much of her wound.

Today, when the healer changes Lilac's bandages, she takes me into account.

"I see you here a lot," says the woman with green eyes and white scrubs. "Are you a friend?"

"We have a mutual friend," I answer. "I check on Lilac for her."

The Eunoia smiles, her lips widening slightly. "That's sweet."

I take the opportunity to ask, "Do you know what happened to her?"

"Based on the traces of magic we found in the wound, we know the monster that attacked her is from Ilyria."

I fight to keep my composure. A monster from Ilyria attacked the princess, and I know for certain a moonaro was here.

*The princess's brother knows, too.*

"Thank you," I say, mumbling a goodbye to the unconscious girl before leaving the infirmary.

Screwed. I'm screwed. Lucian must know that the creature that attacked Lilac *didn't* attack me. I have to watch my back. Could he pin this on me?

*Would* he?

I can't think of any reason why he wouldn't. He hates me now, maybe even did the whole time. He only ever kept me around because of my mom, and I made the foolish mistake of thinking a prince could see anything more than the *scum* in me.

I continue going to class, checking on Lilac, looking for Lucian. He's never here. The paranoia over what he might do has put me in a frenzy. I'm not sleeping well, not that I ever was, but certainly worse than before. I keep one eye open, waiting for another Ilyrian soldier to attack me in the night and drag me off to the dungeon.

Eventually, Leiholan announces that we're doing hand-to-hand combat. Lately, our chats and "training" have gone nowhere. Basically, he gets annoyed with me quicker than usual, and I tell him to shove his vesi up his ass. It's frustrating, but it's the most human interaction I've had these past weeks, apart from Aralia.

At least I don't have to constantly put on a show for Leiholan.

"You get three daggers. You drop 'em, you lose 'em," Leiholan slurs. "Desdemona, you're with Yuki."

Hearing my name nearly knocks the wind out of me.

*This is my first challenge.*

Yuki meets me on the mat, and I'm anything but hopeful. What if Lucian asked for this and Leiholan is setting me up?

This anxiety only worsens when Leiholan *keeps* pairing me with Yuki. Every day I fight—and lose—while watching the door for Lucian.

That unwavering fear finally comes true when Lucian shows up, looking every bit the prince. The last time I saw him, his hair was a mess, his words were slurred, and his eyes were tired.

Today, he's perfectly groomed.

When I'm called to fight again, it's not Yuki that meets me on the mat. It's Lucian.

What if he doesn't wait for a soldier to drag me away to the dungeon? What if he kills me right here?

If I know one thing, it's that Lucian has a plan at play here, which means I have to have one too: stay alive at all costs.

I swing first, aiming for his face. He blocks. I go for his side —blocked again. Lucian's fist comes at me, but I knock it away and strike twice more. He blocks both—until I land a kick to his stomach.

Lucian moves fast, trapping my bicep and landing two punches to my side. I knee him in the gut, then aim for his throat. He spits blood, stalking closer. I throw another punch, but he ducks, and I fall flat on my face. The impact of his blow to my shins sends waves of pain through my body.

His foot comes for my nose. I roll out of the way and scramble to my feet, the room spinning around me.

He throws a punch at my face, but I block it with my forearm, pain spiraling up into my shoulder. Another punch lands in my gut, and I drop to the floor again.

I kick at his shins, but he doesn't flinch.

Before I stand, I grab my dagger, getting to my feet and preparing to throw it. But Lucian punches my wrist, and the blade clatters to the ground. I draw another dagger and swipe upward, from his torso to his neck—but all I manage is a nick on his shirt.

I go in to stab him, but he catches my wrist, spinning me so my back presses against him. I stand on the tips of my toes and smash my head back into his with a *crack*. My vision fills with specks of light, but I wrench myself free.

His nose gushes blood, now more crooked than usual.

I kick him once, twice, but he blocks the third and pulls my leg out from under me. I fall onto my back, the wind knocked out of me. Then Lucian straddles my waist, pinning my arms above my head, and presses a knife to my throat. His dark hair brushes my eyes as he leans in.

I'm dead.

"Tell me what you did to Lilac," Lucian hisses.

"Nothing," I choke, the blade pressing harder into my neck.

"I'll put it this way—tell me, or I'll tell *them*."

"Tell them *what?*" I snarl, digging my nails into his wrist and drawing blood. Trying, with everything I have in me, to get away from him.

To survive.

Then, suddenly, he relents, standing in triumph.

*He didn't kill me.* I'm amazed, and I'm worried. What's next?

"Everyone," Lucian's voice echoes through the room with sheer power.

I force myself to stand, ignoring the pain rippling through every inch of my body, the blinding stars crowding my vision.

"Desdemona has been lying to you all for some time now."

The class lowers their weapons, every eye locked on the prince, waiting for what he'll say next.

I'm waiting, too.

He stares down at me, and I meet his gaze. His voice is loud and clear as he says, "She's from the septic."

*No.* How could he know? I want to take his head and hold it under the lake until he stops breathing. I want to take this dagger and put it through his throat. I want to… I want to…

Everyone is looking. Everyone knows.

I want to run from this room full of spoiled brats staring at me like *I'm* crazy. But I can't move. Can't breathe. I can't do anything. Frozen—I'm frozen. They all know. Everyone in this room knows who I am now—and soon, everyone outside will, too. They know, they know, they know. They have my weakness when I want theirs.

A hand grips my arm, pulling me down the hall. My body falls to the floor like I'm no more than a rag doll. Cold water splashes on my face once. Twice.

"Stop it," I mumble to no one in particular.

"You're burning up, sweetheart."

It's Leiholan and his sweetly impersonal voice. He dragged me from the class. He helped me.

I try to focus, but everything blurs. I can't believe they all know who I am. I can't believe the prince knew this whole time. I picture their faces—*Lucian's* face—staring down at me while he tells the world I'm from the septic. It takes the air from my lungs. The composure from my being.

What else does he know?

"You can calm down," Leiholan says softly, and I listen to him, suddenly unsure as to why I was getting so worked up in the first place.

Then I realize what he did.

"Don't use that shit on me," I huff, throwing a weak punch at him. He catches it with ease. Damn Nepenthes and their ability to soothe their prey. At least he won't use it just to kill me.

I think.

"It was that or let you burn down the building," he says casually and sits next to me, patting my knee like I'm a child.

I turn to face him. "Why did you help me?"

"Been in your shoes." He tries to smile, but it falls severely flat. Then he whispers, "You're not doing a very good job at being likable."

"Yeah, well, no one was gonna like me anyways," I grumble.

"Especially not now." He chuckles.

"You're not helping."

"I'm sorry, I forgot that was part of my job description—*Help Desdemona*."

I glare at him, dropping my head in my hands. "What am I gonna do?"

"About your utter lack of charm or the students knowing you're a septic bum?" he asks with a smile.

"The latter," I say. "They're gonna hate me."

Leiholan leans closer, whispering, "They already do."

My palm connects with his shoulder, and I push him back. "Then they're gonna hate me more."

"Good," he says, giving a small shrug.

"Good?" I stare at him while I'm slumped against the wall, half lifeless.

"You're not good at being liked. We'll make you formidable." The idea excites me a little more than I think it would excite a normal Folk. "Still, you'll need to be careful. No one is going to care if you die. The law isn't here for you, the staff won't be here for you, and the kids are gonna be out to get you. Got it?" His voice is intense, growing in emotion with every word. Like he… cares.

"Hence making me formidable?" I say like a question, but we both know it's not.

"Exactly," Leiholan replies with a small smile—different from the others in terms of sincerity—that I'm sure is only for my benefit. I probably look like a mess.

"Could you do me a favor?" I ask with a smirk, and the simple gesture makes me feel marginally better.

"Depends."

If formidable is what I'm gonna be, then there is something I'm going to need.

"Can you get me some throwing knives?"

# Chapter 25
## Let The Hero Die

# LUCIAN

Since Lilac's attack, I haven't slept more than two hours a night. From the moment I wake to the moment I black out, vesi drips down my throat just like the IV drips into Lilac's veins.

Now, standing before a murmuring class—shocked to learn that a student at their high-and-mighty academy is from the septic—I nearly pass out from exertion. Or alcohol.

The moment slips sideways. Present collapses into memory, dragging me back to the first few days after Lilac's attack. I'd confined myself to my room then—a self-imposed prison in the likeness of her coma. Most of it is a haze of silence and vesi, though one day burns through the fog, clearer than the rest. Perhaps because of what Azaire said. Perhaps because of the fire.

"Lucian," Azaire had urged, "you've got to talk to me."

"I can't," I said. "I can't think about anything other than Lilac and her sliced-open stomach."

My thoughts spiraled, a constant loop I couldn't break. Desdemona and the moonaro haunted my mind, their presence too vivid to ignore. I couldn't shake the thought that I'd invited the culprit—and allowed her to stay.

All I could hold onto was the faint hope that I was wrong.

"Because you're hiding from the world," Azaire responded. He didn't look at me; he looked at the bottle on my bedside.

"I'm putting together a plan," I muttered.

"With alcohol?"

"Copious amounts."

Azaire exhaled sharply. "More revenge?"

I was unsure if it was a good or bad thing as I answered, "You know me irrevocably."

"Do you ever think that maybe you could live your life without... hurting more people?"

I sat up straighter for the first time since I'd planted myself in bed. "The Arcanes are not people. They're monsters. They *ruined* my life; they took *everything* from me."

Azaire's voice was too soft, his heart too kind, so ready to understand, to forgive, when he said, "What will ruining *them* do?"

"It will make up for what I've lost!"

"But it will never bring it back," he whispered. "You have to start learning to live with what you have now, to find peace with the past."

"Azaire, I know you had it rough. But it's not the same."

"No?" he questioned. "I may not be forced to do things in the same way you are, but I am, nonetheless. There can still be contentment."

"Peace and contentment can wait until the universe and I are even."

Azaire fell silent, the only sound the soft crack of his knuckles. After a long moment, he said, "We should get out of here, maybe head to Barley's."

I shook my head. "I don't think I can ever go back to the septic." The dead prisoner from Ilyria's septic had faded a bit, but he will always be present.

*Carved in my soul with the sharpest of blades.*

Azaire gave a faint smile. "Or something?"

"Yeah," I said, grabbing the vesi. "I'll let you know—"

I was cut off by the screaming of my name. I didn't know at

the time what kind of revelations this would bring. I didn't know how deeply ill I could become for the girl who'd put my mind in a mania.

I didn't know how sickly it would be to navigate such a fine line between love and hate.

"Lucian!" Kai screamed again.

I took another swig, preparing myself for whatever mess Kai was going to lay at my feet. A fight I could take. In fact, I wanted a fight.

I cracked my knuckles, summoned my shadows, and prepared for battle.

Kai barged into the room. Shadows surrounded him and he let out a steady string of curses.

"It's Desdemona," Kai breathed, and instantly, I hated myself for faltering. For releasing my shadows and *listening*. "There's a fire—Headmistress Constance can't put it out."

I stood immediately, suddenly forgetting every single thing I swore to remember. I followed Kai, heart pounding, running to the garden and toward the lunar lake.

The trees bordering the garden glowed orange, set ablaze. The air was thick with smoke.

My shadows snuffed out bits of the fire as I walked to the lake, easily extinguishing the remaining flames.

*Cynthia couldn't handle this?*

A chill ran through me. An untrained Folk set a fire that one of the most powerful Lyrians couldn't put out?

I looked for Desdemona, ready to see her face and declare it guilty. Not only had she given Cynthia difficulty, but she'd survived the Flame. That's something even the most powerful of her kind rarely manage.

But she was nowhere to be seen.

Until suddenly, there was nothing *but* her.

I felt true fear at that moment. Not the kind I should have. Not in the way I wished to.

Because I knew that one day, my eyes would land on her, and I would never be able to move them again. I would be trapped—incapacitated—like death to its coffin. Frozen in her warmth.

I've never known hunger, but for the first time, I felt it. Not the kind that gnaws at the stomach, desperate to be filled. No—this was something else entirely. Something insatiable. Something that refused to be named, because naming it would mean admitting I could never rid myself of it. This wasn't a hunger that could be put into order—because there was no order to my heart, no rhythm to its thrum—only the frantic beating of a bird's wings, encaged.

And if I weren't so eager for her heart—held in my hand to rupture or revere; I've not yet decided—perhaps I wouldn't have run. Perhaps I wouldn't have rescued her. A girl who is as treacherous as she is tempting, as terrifying as she is irresistible. A girl whose very existence made everything else seem insignificant. A girl who could burn the entire universe down, and I'd still run back in, as if it were a blazing house and I'd left my most prized possession behind.

That's why I ran. Rescuing her was dangerous enough. I could not risk revering her.

*That* would be my ruin.

After that, the days blurred into blackouts—Azaire pushing me to talk while I pushed him away.

That spiral only broke this morning, when Leiana and Labyrinth summoned me to the kingdom—pulling me back into a world I've spent weeks trying to avoid, and the obligations I've never been allowed to refuse.

Leiana kissed my cheeks. Labyrinth clasped my shoulders. I already knew what would happen—the same thing that always happens. They'd demand something I'd have no choice but to obey, no matter how much I despised it. They'd force me to do something that makes it harder to look myself in the eye.

*At least I'll be ready for it,* I had thought.

After an exhausting display of niceties, Leiana dropped the ball. A thousand-pound ball, that was about to drag me under the current.

"Lilac is healed," she said. "Her physical injuries, that is."

"What does that mean?" I blurted, too eager, too *emotional* for Leiana's liking.

"It means that there's something else keeping her from waking," Labyrinth said. He had the decency to act discomforted.

Fool me once, shame on you. Fool me twice, well, Desdemona already had. But fool me three times, I would make sure that was an impossibility.

I stood by Desdemona, lie after lie. I took a man's death as my own, for her. I've scarred my very soul for eternity. Every time I close my eyes, I'm watching a man's world, then I'm feeling him die. Always and forever, for her. *Because* of her.

I watched her in a vision, touching the moonaro, looking at the thing like it was *human*, days before a moonaro attacked my sister.

If something was keeping Lilac asleep beyond her wounds, it had to be Desdemona.

"We need you to bring Lilac to us," Leiana said. "We can't let the… *others*," she spat the word like a slur, "talk."

*Others*, as in those less than her—which means everyone. She is the queen of the strongest world in the universe. A world that honors a woman's intuition before a man's instinct. There is no one above her.

I did what she asked, because there is never another option. I brought Lilac to Ilyria, and that was when Leiana instructed me to hand her over to Piphany. She wasn't even going to take her daughter to the infirmary; she was having her advisor do it.

I looked at Piphany, the personification of snow itself: pale skin, ice eyes, white hair. I imagined that if I gave her my sister, Lilac would freeze on impact.

"No," I said, holding tight onto Lilac. "I'll take her." I looked at Piphany. "You'll follow me."

Piphany scoffed.

"Darling, there is no need for theatrics." Leiana laid her hand on my back and pushed me. "We'll go together."

I knew we were trapped, right then and there. I tried to breathe, tried to keep my anger from overtaking me. If I tried to run, what would happen to Azaire? When Leiana caught up, what would happen to Lilac?

I forced down my fear—there was no other choice—and walked beside Leiana and Piphany. But, when they stopped, I kept moving forward.

"Here, darling," Leiana said, halting me.

I turned around. They stood in front of a dingy room, empty except for a single bed. A room of isolation.

"That's not the infirmary," I said, as I noticed a faint shimmer flickering across the threshold—a Light Folk's barrier. Once Lilac went in there, she wasn't coming out, not without being electrocuted at least half to death.

Not until Leiana decided she was ready to let her out.

"You're locking her away?" I demanded.

I already knew.

"For her own good, darling," Leiana said, her voice chillingly devoid of emotion. "We need to make sure she is betrothed as soon as she wakes up, without trouble. She's never been as"—her cold hand settled on my cheek—"compliant as you."

I must have shown signs of defiance, because Leiana looked down at Lilac and began draining her life force. Her cheeks hollowed, her skin paled, and her lips turned gray.

I knew I'd be willing to die if it would save Lilac. But dying that day would've doomed her. Doomed Azaire. It would've negated everything I've done—the reason I've complied.

I looked at my sister, unconscious, defenseless, and on the verge of dying. I made a choice that, like so many others, I fear I'll never be able to clear from my conscience. I handed Lilac to

Piphany, then I lived with the disgust and my deepest fear—that I will only ever be allowed to survive under their hands.

I turned away like a coward, unable to face the consequences of his choices.

But as I dropped Lilac's hand, I no longer stood in Ilyria. The world around me blurred, leaving me standing in the sand—on the coast of Visnatus Academy. It was the same vision that had brought me running to save Desdemona from the moonaro, but this time there was more.

The monster towered over Desdemona, yet she reached for it without a hint of fear on her face. The moonaro lowered its head for her, almost reverently, allowing her hand to rest gently on its nose.

She tilted her head, just slightly, and the creature mirrored her. Small noises began to pass between them.

*Barrier... Broken... Master.*

Desdemona's mouth moved, but I could not hear the words. All I knew is that she spoke to this creature. *Commanded* this creature.

*Master*, it said.

But I didn't know what to do with that. And clearly, I still don't. The matter should probably be handled with care, though I didn't feel very careful today, not after what Leiana did to Lilac.

And now, here I am again—back in the classroom, back in this body. The whispers about Desdemona haven't stopped.

I open Leiholan's cabinet and pull out a bottle of vesi.

Then I drink.

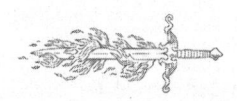

---

I keep my gaze trained on the steel-reinforced cave in Folkara, waiting for the welders to emerge. I've been watching them for days, searching for the most opportune time to strike.

Once a day, four welders come out and four go in, and it's

always the same eight men working.

I expected no less—eight workers is already a risky gamble when crafting something as treasonous as a weapon. I haven't been here since Azaire was nearly killed, but I imagine that the security has only improved since then.

With every passing second, my pulse quickens, adrenaline surging in my veins. I have to be quick. One misstep, and I'll be discovered; Queen Melody and King Easton will find out I was here, and they'll likely kill me. They can't risk what I know.

But all I need is Freyr.

As soon as the steel door lifts open, I bolt forward, knowing what's at stake. I slide under the door and jump to my feet, only to be met by two Fire Folk, gripping iron poles.

There's no time for idle chat before they attack. The searing iron swings inches from my cheek. My shadows swirl around me as I unsheathe my sword, cloaking it in darkness to combat the heat.

The iron snaps on impact, and I lift the armed man onto his toes, shadows coiling tightly around his neck. He dangles in the air, his thin limbs trying to claw at my restraints.

"Now, boys, we can go about this civilly." I flash a sharp smile. "Can't we?"

The other Folk are looking down from the main room—the *only* room—where the weapon is displayed in the center. The space is small and nearly circular, carved into the mountain's core, the walls rugged with raw stone.

I glance quickly at the weapon.

Then I take a smoldering fist to the jaw.

The stench of my burning flesh fills the air.

I duck beneath his next swing and drive my fist into his gut, doubling him over. The man I'm choking with shadows struggles to speak. When the burly one strikes again, I string him up beside the other, choking the air from both their lungs.

The last Fire Folk and Freyr advance, their hands glowing

orange, ready to strike. I weigh my options: strike first and kill, or try to talk my way out.

I choose the latter—but only to keep Freyr alive.

"I could kill your men with a twist of my fingers," I warn. My voice is steady, but the shadows around me twitch—waiting for a command. "I'm only here to collect Freyr."

Freyr scans the room warily as the thin man I'm strangling gasps, struggling to speak. He drops to the ground when I release him, choking out, "He's the prince of Ilyria." He holds onto his neck while he pants like a dog.

"Yes," I draw the word out. "It is I. If you'll allow me to see the weapon and collect Freyr, I'll be but a moment."

"I'm sorry, Your Majesty, but we're under strict instruction not to let anyone pass," the Folk next to Freyr says.

"Let's put it this way." I clap my hands and dare a smile. "You spare the man and some of your time, and I will spare your heads when I am crowned king."

"Or we could take yours," Freyr says, stepping forward. "Here and now." His eyes glow orange, and I become keenly aware of the tension in my bones coming from holding the burly man *without* killing him.

I take in Freyr's stature, certainly twice my size. Perhaps nearly thrice. "If you want a rematch," I say. "I won't be so inclined to keep it to physical combat." I tighten my hold on the burly man, and he makes a deeply unpleasant sound.

This is it—the moment I test how far I am willing to go for answers. If any of them are to swing right now, I don't believe I will be leaving without spilling blood. Though I can't spill Freyr's.

"Choose wisely," I warn. "*Friend.*"

Freyr swings his smoldering fist at my already burnt face. The other two men advance on me, one of them equipped with another burning rod that comes for my side. I move out of the way in time, but I do take a punch to my other side.

I twist the burly man's neck—the snap easing the tension in my shoulders—before slashing another Fire Folk across the chest, blood spilling from his wound.

Amid the struggle, I force my way into Freyr's subconscious.

But Freyr fights back. It's as if there's a door blocking me from his mind, and every time I push, it slams shut. If this were his first—or even fifth—time, he wouldn't have the faintest idea I was invading his subconscious. *Failing* to invade, because he resists my every attempt.

Freyr's fist cracks my nose, still healing from the fight with Desdemona. I punch him twice before binding his wrists with shadows, rooting myself to the other Folk's mind. The last one standing.

His mind gives way easily.

*"Open the door,"* I command.

The man whose mind I'm controlling walks to what must be a control panel near the cave's entrance.

Freyr slams his foot into my stomach, sending me crashing against the steel door.

"What are you doing?" Freyr yells, running to the control panel.

"Opening the door," the Folk replies, absentminded.

"Have you lost your bloody mind?"

I let those two work it out and run to the weapon. The body is rounded, constructed of dark metals that ripple like water. From beneath, a light pulses, heating the air around it until the world blurs.

It's twice the size it was when Azaire was here. The blueprint Wendy found from four years ago was *Design No. 27*. If they've made this much progress since then, what design number are they on?

What in the worlds is it made to do now?

I slide beneath the weapon, looking for anything that could tell me what the power source is. There's nothing but a mass of molten gold, feet away from scorching my face. It dances against the dark metal, melting together, though never fully mixing. Yet I can feel the potential—almost as if it's *waiting* for something.

But there's nowhere for it to go.

I summon shadows, smothering the burning metal as best I can as I search.

There are no levers, no buttons, no controls. No indications of how it works—what commands it, let alone powers it.

It's just a hunk of magical metal with no answer. No end in sight.

No beginning, either.

No way to turn it on, and worse yet, no way to turn it off.

I run back to Freyr, who's still struggling against the man I control. Grabbing Freyr's restrained arms, I pull him with me. He headbutts me in my already broken nose. My eyes tear until my vision is taken from me.

"Open the damn door!" I shout.

"If he does, the Royals will be alerted!" Freyr yells at me. "We only have clearance to open it once a day."

I command the man to *open the door*, knowing time is running out, before wrapping Freyr entirely in shadows and saying, "Luckily for your comrades, they'll only think it's you who ran."

The steel door opens, and I drag Freyr out, pulling him beside me with every tiring step as he fights.

At the river's edge, I catch my reflection—the burns along my jaw—and I don't look away. I press my palm to the water and open a portal to the dungeon Cynthia gave me the key to.

The moment we step through, I shove him into a cell.

"The weapon," I say. "What's the power source?"

Freyr spits on the ground.

"The power source." I clench my jaw. Freyr does nothing but stare at me blankly. "Not to worry, I have other questions. Such as… Isa Althenia!" His eyes widen, but he says nothing. "What's your relation to her?" I crouch down to meet his gaze. "Ever, I don't know"—I shrug—"conceived a child?"

Freyr spits again. "What do you want from me?"

"Answers."

"Well, I'm not talkin'."

"And I'm not above torturing you."

He sweeps his eyes over me, stopping at my bloody, broken nose. "Been through worse than you."

*Leiana?* Is that how he blocked me from his subconscious?

"You say that now." I rise to my feet, and my shadows rise with me.

They circle him, forcing his mouth open and entering his body. The shadows curl inside him, ready to freeze him from the inside out if I lose control.

"Scream when you're ready to talk." When he begins to dry heave, I add, "Or at least try."

## Chapter 26
### Infamy's A Dish Served Cold

## DESDEMONA

I stand across the counter from Elowen, eating meat I've never had—and would never have admitted to before yesterday—when suddenly, I can't move. My torso is cinched tight, bound from ribs to throat. I try to step back, but it's like my muscles have turned to stone.

The harder I pull, the tighter I'm restrained. My mind begins to scream for control.

But nothing comes of it.

Panic sets in—each flinch drawing the bonds tighter.

Elowen looks at me—then past me—and her green eyes flare with light.

Sensation returns in sharp bursts, like static skimming down my limbs. When I can move again, I twist around to find two Folk behind me—one with a knife, the other with electricity crackling between their fingertips. Both are pinned to the walls by writhing vines.

One of them electrocuted me, and the other was going to *stab* me.

"Get. Out. Of. My. Kitchen," Elowen orders.

The vines snap back, releasing the kids from their grasp. Then, they bolt.

Elowen's jaw tightens. Her face is flushed, pulse beating visibly in her throat. But when her gaze returns to me, it softens.

"How long have you known?" I ask.

Elowen smiles at me, but it's the kind of sad smile I fear is coupled with pity. "No one from Utul is as hungry as you are." She reaches over the table and pats my hand.

I go through the day with eyes on the back of my head. I've never been so abruptly popular. Suddenly, everyone wants to fight me. A sore difference from when everyone avoided me.

Now they want to see if they can kill the *septic scum*.

Well, I have seven throwing blades, and I'm not afraid to bury them in someone's skull if they so much as *think* of killing me.

But even with this new popularity, the one person whose avoidance is the most annoying is doing just that—since she's my roommate. At least I doubt Aralia would try to kill me in my sleep.

After a thrilling hour of studying the gods—and if I don't count the angry stares, no more attacks—I meet Aralia outside of her first-period class, like every day.

She meets my gaze with a frown.

"Hey."

"Hey," Aralia says slowly. "I have to go see Mr. Bayley, so I'll see you in class?"

"Yeah, sure," I reply, but I know she would've asked me to join her yesterday.

In Combat Training, we stand around the three mats, waiting for Leiholan to call out our partners. Without warning, Eleanora walks toward me, proclaiming that she can "take me."

"Anyone could," one of the boys says—Jermoine. "She's septic." His smirk deepens as his eyebrows flick upward, a strand of his long brown hair falling loose and brushing against his cheek.

"I wouldn't piss her off," Leiholan says with a nod.

I do what we practiced: turn, unsheathe a dagger, and let it fly —right into the eye of my target across the wide room.

Eleanora rolls her eyes, but Jermoine narrows his and says, "Nice show. But what's Leiholan got in your corner? Any reason he's protecting you?"

I step forward, drawing another dagger and spinning it between my fingers. "He's no more than a pain in my ass. But you're gonna be a sack of burnt flesh if you take another step closer." This time, *I* smirk.

Not that I could do that. They just have to think I can. Lucky for Leiholan's plan, I'm a great liar.

"You're not allowed to use magic in this class," someone says from behind me.

I smile and even force a little laugh for the show. "Watch me."

I don't take my eyes off Jermoine. He's twice my size, could easily take me on the mat, and I have no business threatening him. But his shoulders drop ever so slightly, and I take it as a victory.

"Partner up!" Leiholan says. "We'll resume challenges tomorrow."

Yuki walks to me, and I try not to give him any of the attitude I've been feeling. He's been nothing but cordial to me, and I doubt he knew what Lucian was going to do. We fight like usual, and one out of the seven rounds I land on top, with my blade to his throat.

I've never been prouder.

I don't like expecting attacks, but the next day in Elemental Magic, I'm prepared. In this class, there are no restrictions against using our magic.

I'm not the least bit surprised when a blast of wind throws me across the room. My back slams into the—luckily padded—wall, and when I step forward, pain stabs my leg, pricking like a thousand needles.

*A Light Folk barrier.*

I'm cornered in the room.

I spot the boy stalking toward me—Jermoine—and I'm not sure if he's the Air Folk who slammed me against the wall or the Light Folk who traps me now.

Unsheathing a blade, I say, "Take it down right now, or this goes in an artery."

"I'd like to see you try." Jermoine bares his teeth. Obviously he didn't heed the warning I displayed in Combat Training yesterday.

I balance the blade's weight in my hand, then hurl it right into his shoulder. He jerks back, but it hits its mark.

"Bitch!" Jermoine's hand reaches for the hilt. I can't believe *these* are the kids they're training to be the universe's leaders.

I grab another blade and growl, "Take. It. Down." Then I tilt my head, just to look like a menace. "Or the next one's going in your skull."

Jermoine's face goes red as he takes another step, but he stops when I lift my blade. He signals to the boy behind him—Breck—and when I try to step forward again, I make it through.

Jermoine runs. Presumably to find a healer.

I spot Aralia watching from the other end of the room, but when I look at her, she looks away. The same thing happens with Kai.

Ms. Abrams steps in front of me. Ms. Abrams, who *wasn't* replaced like Kai offered. "You stabbed a student."

"He attacked me."

"This is Elemental Magic. Attacks are welcome. You should've countered with *elemental* magic." She enunciates, as if I'm hard of hearing.

"Would you like me to burn a student to death? Or maybe the school?" I narrow my eyes on her. "Besides, I'm already failing, right? What more are you going to do?"

"You could've done something with your education here. It's a... *pity* you chose to throw it away. Although, what more could we expect from you septic Folk?"

My jaw pops from my clench-unclench routine. "How about I burn *you* and show you just what to expect." She's taken aback, but I fill the silence. "That's what I thought."

"Threatening a teacher. You know what—"

"What?" I lean in closer. "You're gonna fail me? I'd rather be in the septic than in your face."

Ms. Abrams shakes her head, taking in an uneven breath. "Even when we give you people opportunities, you can never overcome your nature."

"Guess not." I step away from her and look at the class. "Anyone else wanna try me? I have six good blades left and a bit of anger to feed off of." I turn around the class. "No?" I shake my head. "That's what I thought."

I sit down, hiding my shaking hands under the table.

When class is over, I do something stupid—I catch up with Kai. If anyone can help me now, it's a prince. I don't know what those boys were going to do to me in class, but I do know those girls from the kitchen were going to kill me.

"Hey!" I say with a smile and a buoyant tone, walking beside him in the hall.

"What?" he asks, picking up his pace.

"How are you?"

"What do you want from me?" He gives me a scornful look, no more than a second-long glance. Like I'm not even worth looking at.

"I—I don't know. I just wanna talk."

"Well, I don't." He keeps walking.

I reach for his arm, turning him to me. "Please?"

"You lied to my face, Desdemona!"

*His* face—*his*, as if I lied only to him, as if lying wasn't a matter of my survival.

"News flash, Kai! I lied to everyone! I had to."

"No, you didn't." Kai turns away.

"What?" I follow after him "If you knew I was from the septic, would I still be a *good Folk* to you?" I shout, shaking my head. "Do you really think I'd believe that? Even if it were the truth?"

"I don't know." He looks at me for a split second before

averting his gaze. "But I also don't care."

Of course. I knew they'd hate me for who I am—*what* I am. This still feels absurd. Am I that different from them?

I guess I am. I mean, that's what I've been telling myself from day one. I'm *not* pampered and polished, but they're certainly not *good*. Not in the way they think they are.

They may be poised, but they're not pleasant.

The first thing I do back in my room is rifle through Aralia's drawers until I find her stash. Then I smoke a joint, and I swear if anyone tries to break into my suite to kill me, I might actually burn this place to the ground.

When my head is a little fuzzy, I do the only rational thing I can think of. I throw my new knives at shit. I challenge myself with any little mark on the wall I can find, hitting almost all of them.

Seventeen holes in the wall later, I collapse to my bed. I want the dagger I buried in Jermoine's shoulder back.

The door creaks open, and I'm on my feet, wielding a knife behind the entrance in a second. But it's just Aralia. She grabs a book from under her bed.

"Hey," I whisper.

Aralia frowns. "I have to get back to class."

She brushes past me, toward the door. "Are you serious?" I ask as she reaches for the knob. She twists it, and I put my hand on top of hers. "Aralia!"

She takes a deep breath, tipping her head back so she's looking at the ceiling instead of me. "What?"

"Can we talk?" I wait for her to say something, anything. When she doesn't, indignation prickles my body like the Folk's electrical attacks. "I was almost *killed* today, and all you did was watch!"

She finally turns to me, both her hands lifted into fists at her ribs. "It's not personal—"

"He was going to kill me!" I'm pretty sure the entire wing can hear me now.

"No, he wasn't." Aralia shakes her head. Like *she* has any reason to feel exasperated by this conversation.

"Are you kidding me?" She drops her gaze, and I have to clench my fists to keep from strangling her. "You know that was the second time someone tried to attack me today? Call me paranoid, but they were both going for the kill. The boy will be fine. A healer will fix his pretty little shoulder, and he'll go about his day. But if they killed me, I'd just be dead. And no one here would give me a second thought."

My hands start shaking, and I shove them into my pockets, only to realize my throat is tight with the threat of tears.

"It's not personal, Desdemona. It's survival. I'm the advisor's daughter. I can't be seen with someone from the septic."

"So if my life was in danger, you'd just watch?" I say, looking at the door.

That's the reality of the situation. I'm septic scum—and I'll be treated as such. Even from someone who declared me her best friend.

I shove the door open, and without a word, Aralia walks out, ducking her head and holding the book she came to grab.

I slam the door behind her.

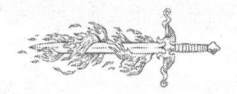

---

Aralia doesn't return by the end of the day. I tell myself I don't care. I go to the kitchen to get dinner—beef with roasted red berries. Elowen asks how I'm doing, and I tell her I'm fine. Because I am. I still have a plan. I know where my mom is, and I'm going to find out how to get there. Then I'm going to get her and get home.

In the dimly lit halls, on my way back to the suite, I have the strange feeling that someone is watching me. I glance over my shoulder, hearing footsteps—but I don't see anyone. The second floor is empty, too. I leave the dining hall, pass through the class wing, and turn toward the suites.

As I round the corner, someone steps in front of me, a long sword dangling in their hand. There's no way my little knife could fight that. Then I make out the face.

Jermoine.

*You've got to be kidding me.*

I turn around and, lookie here, there's Breck. What a joke.

"Are you guys serious?" I say. It's been a long day. "What, you're gonna stab me?"

"That's exactly what we're going to do." Jermoine steps closer.

Before I can say anything more, Breck's sword comes straight for my chest. I duck, tumbling out of its way, and get back to my feet. The second I grip the cold steel of my dagger, Jermoine's sword nicks my wrist, drawing blood.

Jermoine makes a sound like a "tsk" and says, "You won't be doing that again."

Then a thousand needles prick every inch of my skin, all at once. The hair on my arms stands on end, and my body shakes uncontrollably. I can't stop it—until I collapse, stunned. They're really going to kill me, aren't they? These two assholes are going to best me.

What a joke. What a dumb way to die.

Breck steps over me, and it's by sheer force of will that I push my attention to his pant leg.

Light, light, *light*.

Heat rushes through my body, up my stomach, down my arms, into my fingers.

Then he's on fire, and I let out a small gasp of relief while he screams, frantically slapping at the Flame. Pushing harder, I'm able to wiggle my fingers. Then, my wrist. The sensation of *feeling* my body moves up my arms and down my torso.

Just in time for Jermoine to bring his sword down toward my

abdomen. I twist, barely avoiding the full blow, but the blade still slices through the side of my stomach. A sharp, searing pain shoots through me, and I gasp, my vision blurring as the world tilts. White floods my sight, and the coppery scent of blood fills the air as my shirt soaks through with crimson. The floor beneath me feels unnervingly slick, as if I could just slide away in my own blood.

I can barely see as Jermoine's blade goes for my heart this time. I fold my legs in, pushing with all my strength and sliding up the polished floor. Then I get to my wobbly feet.

The right side of my body is uncomfortably sticky with hot blood. But it's nothing compared to the heat coursing through me; whether from the fire across the room or my body's attempt to cauterize the gash in my side, I don't know. Only the wound is too deep, and the whole cauterizing thing doesn't seem to be working. I'm bleeding out fast.

"Why don't you put down the sword and fight me like a gentleman?" My voice is rough, and when Jermoine smiles, I know he heard the strain. The weakness.

I unsheathe a dagger, ignoring the blistering pain creeping up my body and the sweat that's threatening to pour into my eyes. When Jermoine takes a step, I throw the blade, aimed for his throat, but he's out of the way right before it lands.

"Fool me once, am I right?" He laughs—then swings.

I duck. Drawing another dagger, I plunge it deep in his thigh. The blade sinks like he's made of butter. Without hesitation, I punch his knee—but the pain in my fist is nothing compared to my side, the movement tearing my wound wider.

I bite my tongue, forcing myself to rise as Jermoine falls to his knees. Dizziness overwhelms me. I fall again.

Jermoine doesn't.

He stands, looming over me as I remain on my knees, weak and vulnerable.

He doesn't say anything—no parting words, no sympathy, no

*humanity*—as his sword comes down for my head. I'm about to die. Shit. I'm about to die.

Inches from my neck, I catch the sword with both hands. Before I can bite my tongue again, I scream. Maybe it's more of a shriek.

Then the heat goes to my head like a drug.

I meet Jermoine's gaze, biting back a heady laugh. His mouth opens his shock.

And he screams—his pain curdling in my ears.

Silver coats my hands, dripping down his sword and covering his forearms. The blade slips from my grasp, and Jermoine collapses, a ragged cry escaping him. Blood and thick silver liquid paint my palms, and the air fills with the stench of scorched metal and searing flesh. I stare at him, the boy writhing on the floor, and then at his sword.

I blink. The blade—it's gone. There's no edge. No tip. Nothing where my hands just were. Just a molten stub, dripping silver down his forearms.

Because I *melted* it.

On the other side of the room, Breck is still on fire. But he doesn't move. He doesn't even make a sound.

Only Jermoine screams.

I get up and run. The pain from ripping open the wound my body is trying to cauterize shatters any rational thought with every step. I killed them—I must have.

Palming a knife and sliding it up my sleeve, I go to the last person who can fix this. I knock on the door to Lucian's suite. Yuki answers, and I walk right past him.

"He's not here," Azaire says, stepping into the main room of their suite.

Yuki glances at the blood seeping from my side. "What happened to you?"

I have to play it down. If I just give my body time to rest, it will cauterize itself. I think. "It's not my blood," I say.

"I think it's still bleeding."

*Thank you, Yuki.*

"It's nothing. Where's Lucian?" I ask Azaire. My voice is strained, cracking. I'm not doing a very good job at my only job.

*Lying.*

But Azaire's answer is, "I'm sorry for what Lucian did."

"What did Lucian do?" I keep my face still, not moving a muscle.

"Told everyone you were from the septic."

I don't wince. "What are you, his babysitter?"

"Sometimes, yeah." Azaire shoves his hands in his pockets. "They try to teach us here to hate anyone from a septic, forgetting Nepthara is the same kind of thing."

I cringe, tasting actual bile at the thought of being grouped in with the Nepenthes' world.

"Right," I say slowly.

Did I just step into some sort of alternate dimension? *He's* the first person to try to console me—not that I need it. But *him*, a Nepenthe? I guess only the Folk have been treating me differently.

Trying to *kill* me.

I'm still not sure I trust whatever this is.

"It's why we're not allowed to contact our homeworlds for the first two years. They don't wanna foster any sympathy here," Yuki says, leaning back and resting his hands behind his head with a smile. I've watched him almost every day in Combat Training, and I don't think I've ever heard him speak until tonight.

"Thanks," I say, looking between the two of them and trying not to hold onto my side. I had no idea they weren't allowed to contact their families… and as *children*. As far as I know, most of the students here started before they turned ten. "But do you happen to know where Lucian is?"

"I don't," Azaire says. Yuki just shrugs.

"Okay." I nod. "Thanks." Without giving myself time to think, I turn and walk out.

I leave the boys' wing and turn toward my suite, but I don't want to go back there. I want to *do* something. Besides, I'm pretty sure there's a kid burning on that side of the school.

In a turn of events that must be sheer luck, Lucian walks toward me.

"Aibek!" I shout as he approaches.

But with every step he takes, the clearer the details become.

He's covered in blood.

Well, so am I, but I don't think it's his.

He gives me a look that can only be described as wicked, and I don't let myself miss the days when he looked at me like I was... *more*.

I take a step toward him, the dagger still cold in my hand. "You need to tell everyone, right now, that you lied about me being from the septic." My voice lowers with each word. I don't know what I'll do if he disagrees—my anger is already red hot, close to boiling.

"That won't change a thing." He shrugs. His entire jaw is badly burnt, and his nose still looks broken. I'm glad I broke it. I want to break him.

"Why not?" I press.

"Because no one will believe it."

"Then lie. Say it was a social experiment. Or something."

"No."

In one quick movement, I shove him, the marble wall pressing against his back. Then, I raise my dagger to his neck. "Tell them it was a lie, or I will slit your throat." My eyes go wide with what I hope is malice—or something else that will break his cold exterior.

"Oh, how I've missed your daggers." He sounds *amused*, and it infuriates me. How could he mock me *now*?

I hold the knife tighter, pressing it to his neck and wondering if I could kill again. The prince, no less, which would put me in a very tricky position. I'd have to run and hide for the rest of my life and maybe never find my mom. I already have enough problems on my hands. Then I think about the very real possibility that I may have just killed two Folk *again*.

*This is what it takes.*

On top of all this riveting contemplation, the dagger scorches my hand. But I can't let go—I won't. The fire inside me moves, catching in my bones and blood, and it's not a feeling I like. It feels like power.

*Like murder.*

I kick Lucian's knees and watch him stumble to the floor. My hand shakes as I hold onto the dagger for dear life. As I tip it to his neck, I can feel his heart beating beneath mine.

I hope he's afraid.

"Do it, or die, Aibek."

"It would be a pity to die by *blade*," he mocks, and I swear I could do it.

I *should* do it.

"I'll do it!" I scream.

He leans into the blade, daring me to push it deeper.

"Burn me," the prince whispers. Then he laughs. "You *can* do it, can't you? It would be a shame to have spent all that time training to have you come out useless."

His hand rises to my cheek, and I'm not sure if I'm about to lean into his touch or really go through with the whole slitting-his-throat thing.

But neither of those things happen when he grabs my wrist —his hand impossibly cold against my skin—and twists in an unnaturally painful way. The dagger falls from my hand, and I bite down so hard I feel it in my temples.

Then *I'm* shoved against the wall, both my wrists being held over my head. I look up to meet his eyes, then down when I can't bear to see the malicious gaze. It sets something off inside me—I mourn all the things that could have been if I'd manipulated him better.

But I didn't, and he hates me.

That hate makes it impossible to meet his eyes. Instead, I stare at his neck—at the fresh burn mark in the shape of my blade.

Something cold wraps around my legs, winding around my skin like rope—shadows. They're his, holding me still. My body isn't mine anymore—my hands are trapped in his, my legs are trapped in shadow. At first, I struggle, trying to free myself. But slowly, his fighting excites me. He wouldn't do this if he weren't scared—if he didn't think I could best him.

*Kill* him.

Then I meet his eyes, a rogue smile taking over my lips.

He's afraid of me.

But it doesn't matter that his hands are on me in *threat*. There is still an all-too-palpable sensation to his touch. This time it isn't longing—no. It doesn't matter that my power, my *fire*, rushes to his touch. It's fueled by loathing, ready to burn him if I need it to, and he knows that.

He *fears* it.

Lucian leans in so close that our noses touch. His eyes scan my face, and I miss the days when my heart would hammer out of something other than the panic it's pumping through my blood right now.

"Has anyone ever told you how cute you are when you're angry?" Lucian whispers, a taunt wrapped in the remnants of something more—something we both used to feel.

I know I'm not cute. Cute doesn't kill two boys. Cute doesn't fantasize about killing *him*.

"You'd almost be terrifying if it weren't for your broken magic. *Unless...* that was an act? In which case"—he smiles—"I'd be happily burned by you."

I scowl.

"No?" the prince says, still smiling. "All right. Tell me how to wake Lilac, and I'll do as you wish."

I grind my teeth. "I don't know what happened to Lilac."

"Then I'll leave you with one last farewell," Lucian whispers in my ear. "When I unravel, you're coming with me."

He steps away, but he doesn't release his shadows. He puts more in place, coating my wrists like shackles.

The prince wants to keep me in place—to keep me from following him and using my dagger. To keep me from *burning* him, despite his earlier words.

But just as he steps back, an alarm shrieks through the hall.

Taking advantage of his distraction, I lunge forward, aiming my head at his throat, hoping to bruise his windpipe—something to remember me by.

Instead, shadows yank me back, hard, and my head cracks against the wall.

He looks down at me, his gaze violating—like he knows something he shouldn't.

"Was it you?"

"Was *what* me?" I seethe.

"The fire alarm."

*I'm burning down the school, aren't I?*

Lucian releases my wrists, picks up my dagger, and presses it into my hand. The hilt is the shape of my closed palm.

"I'll only clean up your messes for so long," he mutters.

I swear his eyes flare when they hover over the wound at my side. He freezes, taking me in—the blood soaking through my clothes, the sweat pouring from my skin.

I enjoy the look of him shocked.

His voice is deep, a rumble, when he says, "Who did this to you?"

My voice is breathy, a whisper, when I answer, "It's not my blood."

I'm counting on the wound not being around for long—and

the prince is the last person I want to know that.

When one of his hands reaches toward my side, I catch his wrist. He pauses, his fingers lingering just a fraction too long against my skin, as if he's feeling the pulse of power beneath my touch. Then, his gaze meets mine.

It's heavy, unyielding, and worst of all desperate, making it hard for me to choke out, "It's *not*. My. Blood."

His gaze narrows as he leans into me. "And I'm not ignorant. Who did this to you?"

His voice is deep and urgent, as if he's unraveling inside. His wrist is in my hand, and he makes no effort to revoke my grip. His eyes are on mine, and there is no choice for me to take mine off of his.

He is everything wrong with the worlds. He's everything wrong in *mine*.

It's with that in mind that I find the strength to say, "*You* did."

Something in his expression falters, fractures, then falls. My grip on his wrist softens, though I'm not sure if it is my doing or his.

Then he walks away, melting into the shadows that line the hall. Becoming them.

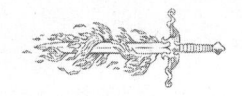

In the spirit of not going back to my suite, I go to the combat room to throw more knives at shit. But when I walk in, there's a passed-out Leiholan in the corner. Alcohol seems like a better way to drown my sorrows than throwing knives, so I grab the bottle from his limp hand.

Leiholan wakes with a start. He pulls a knife from his boot, bringing it to my throat.

I have to admit, being on the other end of this isn't fun.

"It's just me," I mutter.

Leiholan opens his eyes, then squints them toward the bottle.

"Whatchu got vesi for?"

"It's yours." I take a long sip.

He swipes the bottle back and drops his knife in one movement. "Then get your own."

Leaning against the wall, I drop my head in my hands. A second later, the bottle taps my shoulder. I grab it from him, offer a smile, and take a long chug, then I hand it back. We go on like this for a while, passing the bottle back and forth in utter silence until the room spins.

I probably wouldn't have come here if I knew that Leiholan would be my company, but—for the first time ever—he doesn't seem terrible.

"What's your problem?" He burps.

"I seem to be a harbinger of chaos today." The words feel numb on my tongue as I stare at the target—the cluster of knife wounds I've made, kind of like the ones being carved into my own life.

"What about you?"

He looks over his shoulder at me, the movement reminding me of a snake.

I shrug, adding, "You don't drink this much for no reason."

"No." He shakes his head. "We're not having this conversation."

"I wanna know." A bitter laugh escapes me at the realization. "You're kind of the only person I have left in my life."

"Kind of?" he retorts.

"You *are* the only person I have left." A Nepenthe—who's actually not that bad.

He smiles, and his fangs make me reconsider that last drunken sentiment.

The almost empty bottle comes back to me, and I take another long sip. I don't know how he drinks so much of this stuff. It doesn't burn, but everything is…

"Thank you." My words sound groggy, but I don't know if

they came out that way or if it's just my brain that's groggy.

Leiholan chuckles. "Didn't know those words were in your vocabulary."

I sluggishly shove my shoulder into his bicep before draining the bottle. My hands, still covered in metal and blood, look bigger through the glass. I'm thankful Leiholan didn't push for an answer because I don't know how I would've told him that I think I killed two boys tonight.

Five. That's how many people are in Damien's family. I've killed the equivalent of Damien's family.

With how far away I am, it's almost like I could've killed them.

Unexpected tears slide down my cheeks before I can stop them. Three tears turn to ten, and those ten turn to sobs that rack my body so thoroughly I can barely breathe between them.

"Come here, kiddo." Leiholan's arm wraps around me, and I lean into him, sinking into his solidity.

I think this is the first time I've ever wanted to fall apart in someone's arms.

## Chapter 27
## Lines We Don't Cross

# LUCIAN

The screams are piercing.

One is on the floor, burning, burnt, dead.

The one who still breathes is the one who's screaming. I quench the flames that turned Breck into a corpse and rush to Jermoine. He writhes on the floor, his cries drenched in agony. I try to calm him, but he's too far gone.

His arms are covered in silver, and a sword with only half its blade lies a few feet from him.

*Clearly Desdemona can take care of herself.*

I pull Jermoine into my arms and sprint to the infirmary, his weight dragging my every step. The second a healer takes him, I walk away, leaving behind the guilt that won't wash away with the bloodstains—the responsibility I can't shake.

I'm responsible for what they must've done to Desdemona. She killed them because I told the school she was septic. She was attacked because of *my* actions.

As I enter the suite, Azaire asks, "Whose blood?"

I already know he won't condone my actions, but I don't lie. Not to Azaire.

"Freyr's." The blood crusts under my nails, the metallic stench clinging to my skin. A scent that reminds me of my childhood in the dungeon.

I never thought Azaire and I could be tense, but at this moment, the weight of his stare feels like a stranger's judgment.

"What did you do?"

"He's in the dungeon," I answer, walking to my room and stripping the blood-soaked coat.

"Luc…" Azaire sighs. "What are you doing?" I stare at him, and he sits at my desk. "I know you want answers, but"—he looks me up and down—"you're covered in blood. You ruined a girl's life, and whether or not she deserves it remains to be seen. But now you've kidnapped someone?"

"I'm doing what no one else has the guts to do."

"For answers?" Azaire frowns. "For revenge? You know you'll always be my brother, but you take things too far."

"For the weapon! For us, for our plans!" I exclaim.

"Luc," he whispers, "you wouldn't be drenched in blood if you only wanted to destroy the weapon."

I'm quiet for a moment, looking into his eyes until I can no longer bear being seen. "I need to—"

"Will it make you happy?" He cuts me off. "Seriously." He pauses. "Will getting answers and revenge make you happy?"

Azaire is always the best part of me. But…

"It's not about happiness."

"Then refocus. You, more than anyone, deserve a good life, but you're going to forge your own grave if you keep this up." He stares at the burns on my cheek. "What you did to him—whatever it was that produced that much blood—that doesn't leave you."

My throat tightens, and I force down a mouthful of heavy saliva. "This is bigger than me and happiness."

It's about survival. About making sure the Arcanes can't hurt me, or anyone else, anymore.

"It doesn't have to be." Then he says those words. The words I've always feared. "In our choices lie our fate. And I know you've had a lot of those taken from you. So, it's the ones you do get to decide for yourself that matter most." His eyes are full of sympathy, sympathy I don't deserve after cutting a man open again and again. "Don't let them take more of you."

"Desdemona could be a monster," I say, avoiding the rest. "She has to be why Lilac won't wake up. She could be in league with the Arcanes!"

She all but reached The Void. That's no coincidence. I was a fool to think it could be.

*I was a fool for her.*

Never have I been so blindsided by a pretty face. Because she was *more* than a pretty face.

She was a lie.

The worst kind. *The kind you want to believe.*

"She might be, yeah. But if you find out she's not, how are you going to feel about what you did to her?" A line of worry creases between Azaire's eyebrows. He looks away, farther than the room, whether to the past or future, it's hard to say. "When that was me, I thought I was worthless. I lost my parents, was thrown into this new world where everyone hated me, and I took it personally."

He was my suitemate at six and didn't say a word to me until I let him win a duel in Combat Training. He told me he knew what I did. I asked if he wanted a rematch. He reached for his beanie and zipped his lips.

"Does that sound familiar?" Azaire asks. "Desdemona lost her mom, she was thrown into this world, and everyone hates her now—because of *your* choice. The Arcanes could be around her family for a bigger reason, or it could just be about the weapon. Everything else could easily be a misunderstanding."

"I'm not willing to bet on that," I say.

"A month ago, you fought against Leiana to protect her."

*I don't need reminding.*

"Do you think that's why you're so quick to want revenge?" Azaire asks.

"When did you become my therapist?" I try to laugh, but I fail.

"I don't know. Desdemona called me your babysitter earlier."

My attention sharpens. "You talked to her?"

"I told her I was sorry."

*Sorry.* We don't use that word. It's considered informal, too personal.

"If by some miracle we find this isn't her fault, I'll issue her my apologies as well."

Azaire faintly nods, his gaze holding mine as he says, "Good is relative. You decide where the line between it and evil stands, but there *is* a line. And I know you, Luc; you're undoubtedly good. Just find your line again."

I nod, and Azaire exhales, his shoulders dropping with the release of the tension.

Then, he says, "You know Wendy and I can handle the weapon."

I stiffen. I can't let that happen—not if I want to destroy The Void. I can't risk the weapon being destroyed before I get my hands on it.

"No," I say. "I'll handle it. It's my mess to clean up." Then hesitantly, I say, "Forgive me. How's Wendy?"

Azaire smiles, the kind of smile that he hasn't had on my account in far too long. What if he's right?

"Really good." His cheeks flush crimson as he pulls a leather cord from under his shirt. Just above his chest, a small rose dangles, its petals preserved. "She gave me this amulet for protection," Azaire says, his fingers brushing the rose. "Then she kissed me, and it's been"—he laughs to himself—"really good. I think I love her."

The happy words are a hit to my heart. How have I missed this? My best friend, my *brother*, in love.

"That's great." I smile, for him. "You deserve it. More than anyone."

Azaire shrugs, still smiling. "I think the same of you." But my smile falls, and eventually, so does his. "Can I ask you something?"

I don't answer. Not because he *can't*, but because I know he will, and it will be a question I don't like. He wouldn't ask otherwise.

"Are you still planning on destroying the weapon?"

I inhale before answering, but it's enough for Azaire. He nods.

"Zaire." My voice is rough. "It consumes me. I always knew it would come down to this—I'd get my fighting chance, and I'd have to do something you wouldn't like. Perhaps it's selfish—I know it is—but I want you to do this with me."

Azaire shakes his head and tugs his beanie. "What are you going to do with it?"

I take a deep breath. I've played this conversation out in my mind countless times, yet now that it's real, the urge to retreat—to keep my true intentions hidden—grips me. But I don't lie to Azaire.

"I'm going to power it and use it against the Arcanes."

Azaire is quiet for a moment, his gaze flickering with agitation—betrayal. Then, his voice tightens. "That's the exact opposite of what Wendy wants—of what *I* want!"

I look him in the eye, silently praying for his understanding. His is the only approval I need. "I'm so close now, Zaire. You've always been my voice of reason. For better or for worse, I fear that I'll lose that without you."

"But what happens when you get it, Luc?" His voice is heavy, tired. I open my mouth, but he continues, "What if this elusive revenge costs you something you're not willing to lose?" Again, I try to speak, but he presses on. "What if it's just one thing after another until you've wasted your entire life? When will it end?"

The words dry in my throat, choking me. For as many times as I tried to speak before, I am stumped. "I'll swim the sea when we get to it," I mutter.

"If you can tell me right now," he says, "I'll do it. I'll be your voice of reason; I'll choose *you*. Your revenge and your vendettas, I'll make them mine." His dark eyebrows fall down his face, an undisguisable look of anguish in his eyes.

This is my brother, and he'd follow me into war, even though he knows the cost of spilling blood.

Yet I don't know that I'd follow him into peace.

"When does this end, Luc?"

I fall silent, lost in thought. I want to say something profound—something that matters. But the words do not come. Instead, thought itself slips away, leaving only certainty.

I know what I must do.

Give Azaire a reason to quit before we begin.

Finally, I say, "I don't know what comes after."

I've been thinking of this beloved revenge for seven years. It's grown in my mind to become all-encompassing. It's the thing I would fall asleep to on the worst of nights in the kingdom and the academy alike.

It was my saving grace amidst the abuse.

I can't imagine what comes after.

I don't know if there's peace for me.

And Azaire *shouldn't* follow me into this. He deserves more.

"What do you want?" Azaire asks me. "When you close your eyes, what do you see?"

"The Arcane," I answer. I *feel* it. Hot and fluid. I *see* it. Still and lifeless. It's all I've ever wanted. "Dead."

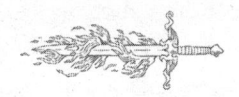

---

I drag Yuki with me back to the dungeon. The chances are slim, but if there's any hope of Yuki being able to read Freyr's mind, I have to take it.

I have one goal—getting an answer—and one plan if he doesn't oblige.

Torture.

I haven't told Yuki what happens down here, but as we descend through the trapdoor and climb down the ladder, he groans. "What is that smell, dude?"

"Decomposition."

Yuki gives me a grave look, but I continue down the ladder.

I'm unsure whether the dungeon ever served the academy's purposes. The world of Visnatus was once a free land—a sanctuary for magic-wielders of all kinds—before the academy was built. Those who chose to live on this world in the early days constructed the dungeon when the Arcanian War was ramping up—whether as a refuge or a prison, history does not say.

Though I don't need a tome to know it's never been cleaned.

Freyr isn't responsible for all the rot—just the current stench of sweat and iron.

We settle on solid ground, my boots crunching against the stray rocks on the unpaved floor as we approach the prisoner.

When Yuki sets his eyes on him, he quickly turns away, gagging. "Dude, what the fuck?" He sighs, shaking his head.

Freyr looks up at me from the corner of his cage. Most of his fingers hang at unnatural angles. One eye is swollen shut and dark with bruising, while the other is barely open. I lift a hand, pulling the last of my shadows from his convulsing body, something I was too exhausted to do last night.

"Are you ready to talk?" I ask.

Freyr gives me the kind of look that tells me he's closer to killing than confessing. I think about what Azaire said—of what I already know. *What I do to Freyr won't leave me.*

It's why I brought Yuki. A foolish hope. Perhaps Freyr's mind won't be protected, and I won't have to torture him.

I doubt it.

Whatever I do after this is necessary.

Yuki keeps his back to Freyr, one hand braced against the grimy cobblestone wall to steady himself.

"He isn't that bad," I say.

Yuki meets my eyes. "Remember when your bone snapped through the skin in Combat Training?"

Instinctually, my hand moves to my forearm, and I flex.

"I *still* have nightmares about that," Yuki finishes.

I glance back at Freyr. It's only blood, broken fingers, and black eyes. Nothing compared to the torture in Leiana's dungeon—severed limbs, missing eyes, among other things I force myself not to recall.

Yuki's hesitancy reminds me that there's still gentleness in this universe.

I haven't told Yuki about the weapon, and I don't plan to unless it's necessary. "Just search his mind for Desdemona," I tell him.

My advisor gives me a pained look. "But I have to look him in the eye."

I clasp a hand on his shoulder and whisper, "The smell is worse."

Yuki groans as he straightens his posture, turning to face the prisoner. Freyr clenches his jaw, but a moment later, his Folk brown irises glow purple—the color of the Draes, a clear sign that Yuki is using his power.

The two stay silent for a while, their stares growing more intense. Yuki groans at times, and Freyr's eyes flicker, as if caught in a battle of wills. Then, finally, Yuki snaps out of it. Their irises return to their usual colors, and my advisor falls back, groaning.

He takes a few solid breaths, then answers, "He cares for her. But there's no way I'm getting anything else out of him."

If that's all Yuki can get, there's no reason to tell him about the weapon. I'm not sure hearing that Freyr *cares about a weapon* will help my cause.

"Thanks Yuki," I mutter. "I'll meet you in class."

"You want me to…" He gestures toward the trapdoor.

I nod. "Yeah."

He steps back. "When I get nightmares—you're the one who has to come cuddle me. Got it?"

I smile at my advisor. His easy humor in the face of a prisoner being tortured is a lightness I think we both needed. "Just say the word, and I'll be there."

Yuki chuckles, heading toward the ladder. I wait for the trapdoor to close behind him before drawing the little red knife. I've held it on my person for ages—ever since the night it scorched through Desdemona's skin with a simple touch. No matter how long I hold it, I can never get past the power pulsating within the material. I doubt it was a poison that burned Desdemona; it was something greater. Today, I'll discover if it has anything to do with her power.

Cynthia told me to find a Fire Folk to use the blade on—and now, I have.

I run the screeching blade along the bars, placing my attention back on the prisoner. Freyr sits defiantly, like a rabid dog—at any moment, he might strike, if my shadows weren't holding him back.

"This is your last chance to speak of your own accord," I mutter.

Freyr just smiles. "I'm not speaking. Period."

Holding the knife up, I spin it between my fingers. "I will cut you open, stitch you up, and do it all over again."

Freyr's voice is a ragged whisper when he says, "I meant what I said."

"And what was that?"

"Been through worse."

"I'm going to Folkara today. I need the name of the project."

Freyr's swollen eyes meet mine, but his body remains slouched, as if he can't move it at all.

"What am I looking for?" I rephrase to put it into simpler terms for him. When he doesn't answer, I lower my sword toward his neck. "Are you protecting someone? Is that what this is about?"

"I'm dead either way." Freyr's crumbling body sags with every word spoken. "And I don't talk to people like you."

"People like me?" I prod.

"Entitled fucks." He spits on the dirt-streaked floor, the wet sound echoing through the dungeon.

I step back—though only slightly. "I'd rather not get blood on my shoes, since, as you said, I'm an entitled fuck. Though, in the end, I'll get new shoes, and you'll be dead. I suppose the point of this pontification is to ask: Is your pride worth spending your last days in agony? Or do you want to answer my very simple questions?"

Freyr rasps, a sound that could pass as a laugh, but is more akin to a death rattle. "I didn't mean you'd be the one to kill me." He barely gets the words out. "Something far worse is waiting for that honor."

I'd ask him to elaborate, but I know he won't. I decide to go with the simpler option and follow through on my promises of agony as I cut him open.

The red knife slices his skin with sickening ease, and I'm not surprised when it doesn't burn him.

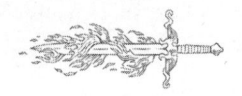

---

I force myself to class, to uphold appearances, naturally. I'm in Psychology, where we rehearse the same age-old questions and tactics of control. Today Hogan is talking about the subconscious and how we can influence it without the powers of my kind—the Lyrians.

I answer Hogan's repetitive question. "The easiest way to manipulate someone is to do so without notice. That's why the books boast about short sentences and pretty pictures. They'll read the same thing tens, hundreds of times a day, and the message will begin to embed."

"*Actually,*" Desdemona cuts in, "contrary to the popular opinion in these books"—I turn to face her seat, where she holds the book like it's poisonous—"we're *not* animals, and we're not much dumber than the lot of you."

Across from Desdemona, Fleur rolls her eyes, muttering, "Oh, come on."

"No, no." Hogan lifts a finger. "What better way to learn than from them?"

"Whatever." Fleur turns away.

"Yeah," I say, goading Desdemona. "*Come on.* I'd love to hear the kind of insight you have."

Desdemona leans forward, sneering at me. "Well, for one, *'the key to peace is compliance'*? That's one of your favorite statements, for all those who don't know." She looks around the classroom. "It's total bullshit. No one reads that and thinks slaving their lives away is doing them any good. It's meant to make us feel self-important, but it doesn't."

No, compliance is not peace. It's torture.

Against my better judgment, the words slip out, "Yet it works."

"Your *words* don't work—your actions do," she says. "Forcing people to work by threatening physical punishment if they *don't* is what gets results. But my point is that we're not idiots."

"No, you're not—"

Desdemona interrupts. "Your fancy book says to make us tired and feed us ideas. Which obviously means that you know we wouldn't believe your propaganda if we could have a minute to think."

I open my mouth to retort, but her words take the opportunity away from me.

"You want the people to work more? Give them more to survive on. Starvation, dehydration, and a lack of sleep are only going to give you less production. But you're all so focused on the mental aspects of everything." Desdemona leans back in her seat, crossing her arms defiantly. "Physicality is just as important."

I repeat Labyrinth's phrase, "Wit wins wars," though it feels more like regurgitating.

"Partially, yeah," she says. "You need someone to plan where to aim, but what would you do if your soldiers couldn't swing?"

Someone whistles behind me, and Fleur turns furiously.

It's Andy, hesitantly nodding. "She has a point."

"I do have a point, because I'm not dumb, and you all know where I'm from." Her eyes shoot daggers at me. "Including you, *Aibek*. So should I mention that night? With the wine, and the dress, and... what was it? Oh, right!" She smiles, and I know it's mock enjoyment. "You trying to kiss me." She enunciates each word slowly as she says, "A *prince* wanting dirty, septic *scum*. Now what do your books make of that?"

As she finishes, her eyes hold mine—and for a moment, I'm not sure I could look away even if I wanted to. She isn't twisting the truth for leverage. She hasn't been lying at all. This is unfiltered, brutal honesty. Because, as I stare at her, all I can see is that night. Choosing the green dress because I knew it would suit her hair. Bringing the wine because I wanted a moment that was real—something shared, not performed. Watching her lips, wishing to kiss her against all my better judgment.

It feels like lifetimes have passed since then. But for some inexplicable reason, I want to go back. To that moment. To her. For however long, for whatever time she'll give me.

The murmurs around the room grow louder, shaking me from my thoughts and replacing them with vindication. The past has passed. Now, I would sooner be damned before I allowed her to maintain the higher ground. I'd like to tip over this newfound pedestal she's sitting on.

"Tell me," I taunt, "does your fire require mental or physical strength?"

Desdemona's smug smile falters, and for a fleeting moment,

fear flickers in her eyes. It's the same look she had the night she nearly burned me alive in her sleep. I'd lied to protect her, then.

I won't do that again.

"What?" she whispers.

Eleanora speaks before I can. "He's asking if it took mental or physical power when you killed Breck."

Desdemona takes a sharp breath, her face going blank, then it turns angry. "Neither," she barks, looking around the class with a sneer. "Seeing as it was so damned easy."

"Okay!" Hogan says with a clap and a falsely cheery tone. His eyes remain pinned on Desdemona. "It seems we've gotten far off track. Let's—"

"You don't belong here!" Eleanora shouts, cutting him off. She twists furiously in her chair toward Desdemona. "You're crass, uneducated, violent *scum*."

Desdemona's face remains blank, unyielding, as she turns to Hogan. He stands with his arms crossed and a slight look of disapproval on his face.

"Really?" Desdemona says, sounding resigned.

Hogan, however, does not acknowledge her challenge, and she falls silent for the remainder of class. Yet, he hasn't let it go.

As the lesson ends, he calls for her to stay behind. I linger by the door as the other students file out, uncertain why I hesitate—but I do.

From where I stand, I cannot see them, but I hear Hogan's measured voice: "I think you know why I asked you to stay?"

"I can't speak to the prince that way?" Desdemona answers, and it is clear from her tone that she does not care for the topic.

"We welcome debate, but—"

"But *what?* I can't make a solid point because, well, I'm *septic*," she says, all too sarcastically. "Right? Well, get this. I'm a little tired of kissing everyone's asses around here. I know where I stand. You made it *abundantly* clear. So if you want to send me back, take it up with the headmistress. But I'm *done*."

Then Desdemona storms out, stopping in the hallway when she sees me.

Scoffing, she says, "If I didn't know any better, I'd think you were obsessed with me, *Aibek*."

But she doesn't walk away.

"I don't think you should speak to a prince in that way," I mock. "Perhaps titles are in order."

I step away, smiling to myself when she follows.

"Yeah? Well, my *apologies*. Which one should I use? Prince? Or pathetic?"

I shrug. "You could have called me yours."

Desdemona extends her arm against my chest, halting my movement. She walks around me, her finger trailing over the fabric of my shirt and coat. Even with the layers between us, I feel the heat of her touch. Beneath her finger, even beneath my coat, my skin prickles. Pins and needles of power fluster, waiting to be used. Waiting for her. I imagine she loathes and loves this sensation as much as I do.

"I'd like to call you dead," she whispers, now standing in front of me, her gaze steady.

"All right." I grab her wrist, press her hand to my throat, and say, "Kiss or kill me then. Your choice."

Her breath hitches as her eyes narrow at me, but she says nothing. I imagine this is the face of hatred, and if it is, I feel the same. Distrust her even more.

But keep your enemies close, right?

After a moment, Desdemona yanks her hand back. Love and loathe, indeed.

"I'd like to smack that smirk off your face," she finally says.

"Is that what your insults have been delegated to? How very puerile." My smirk deepens, enjoying the flicker of frustration that crosses her gaze. I press on, searching for more of a reaction. "And anyway, you love my face."

Her hand reaches for my forehead, tousling loose tendrils of hair. Then her eyes fall to mine. "Your nose is crooked, and one of your eyebrows is higher than the other," Desdemona says in the most monotone voice I can fathom. "One night, I thought that said something more about your character than it truly does. But you are *exactly* who I thought you'd be."

"And who is that?" I whisper, my voice dropping.

"The spoiled, pompous prince, who gets everything he wants and doesn't care about the lives he ruins in the process."

Mimicking her, I touch her hair, wrapping an orange strand around my finger. Her breath still catches, much to my amusement. "You have thirty-three freckles on your cheeks and specks of gold in your eyes. But I never thought your appearance had anything to do with your character." I drop my hand and meet her eyes. "You're the modest, humble girl from the septic." I shrug. "Who happens to murder people as a pastime."

Desdemona recoils as though I've struck her.

"Breck is dead," she says, somewhere between a statement and a question. But I don't miss the hollow, broken tone in her voice. "You told Eleanora."

"I didn't have to. Half the hall is charred and reeks of burnt flesh," I point out.

She looks away, her shaky exhale barely masking the tremor in her fingers. When she turns back, her eyes are vacant shells. If I were to open the doors, I don't know if I'd find anything beyond their threshold.

Not for me, at least.

"This blood on my hands is only half mine," Desdemona says. "Remember that."

## Chapter 28
### Nothing's More Dangerous Than A Scorned Lover

# LUCIAN

With all other options regarding the weapon either exhausted or nonexistent, I search for Calista, who is nothing short of dispirited to see me. She pulls me into her room, her voice trembling as she asks, "Is Lilac harmed?"

Yes, she is, if for no reason other than Leiana holding her captive. But I answer, "She's breathing."

Calista narrows her eyes at me. "Then why are you here?"

"Is the room soundproof?"

"Of course it is," she snaps.

I nod, relieved—but I don't drop my defenses. There is always someone stronger, someone listening. "Where did you find the map that had the weapons facility marked?"

All the concern on Calista's face melts into anger. She crosses her arms and glares at me. "You're still chasing dead ends?"

I expected this response—and I didn't come ill-prepared.

"It's in your best interest for Ilyrian law to punish Folkara *before* you're queen," I say. "Wouldn't you agree?"

She shifts her weight back and forth, shaking her head. There's a hint of disbelief in her tone as she bites out, "Lilac would never do that to me."

"Nothing's more dangerous than a scorned lover," I say flatly, hiding the truth. Lilac would never harm her, but desperate times can always blur the lines of loyalty. I'd say the four of us taking the thrones would be desperate times indeed.

"I'm going to destroy the weapon," I finish. "Not your family."

"Remember when you said this could get us out of our marriages?" Calista scowls. "Look at you now. I'd almost think you're some kind of sicko who's excited."

"It's never exciting to have your choices taken from you."

*If only this ended and began with a forced marriage.*

"Work with me, Calista. The only thing this weapon could do is revive our strife."

Not that my motivations are entirely noble. They're driven by self-interest, by a thirst for revenge. I only want the weapon to be used properly, in the way it was intended—against the Arcanes.

"It never died," she says gravely—and she's right. The last war ended only ten years ago, but the strife between worlds has only grown since then.

I understand her fears.

"I know the marriage is hardest for you," I reply. "Giving you a king of your own world." A world that holds the king at a higher value than the queen, the men more valuable than the women. The opposite of Ilyria.

For a moment, her eyes grow distant.

I step closer, finishing, "I was raised a Lyrian. I will not strip your autonomy the way our parents have with ours."

She meets my gaze, her eyes brimming with unshed tears. "I believe you," she whispers. "But circumstances change—and I see the way you look at Desdemona."

The mention of her name shakes something inside of me. But she's no longer an issue. There's no longer a *way* I look at Desdemona that does not involve hatred.

"At any moment"—Calista shakes her head—"you could rip me from my throne to be with her. The one you truly desire. And that will never be an option for me."

I step closer to her, closing the space between us. "I would never do that to you, not out of any sense of decency, but because I'd never do that to Lilac. She loves you, and in turn, I care for that bond."

Calista releases a bitter, humorless laugh. "*Loved* me," she mutters. "There is no possibility she still feels that way about me."

"You underestimate my sister's capacity for emotion," I reply quietly.

"As you underestimate the cruelty of my parents." She hastily wipes a tear away before it can fall, her expression hardening as the emotion fades from her face. Her voice is distant as she continues, "There's a tunnel system you can access, three stories below my kingdom's south wing. At the far end of the castle, down another floor, there's a vault. It's where we keep everything of priority. Our technology." She shrugs. "Secrets."

I'm grateful she's shared this with me—though, I knew she would. Calista may seem bitter on the outside, but there's a reason Lilac loves her. Besides, keeping secrets from Ilyria is a perilous game, and by involving me, she makes me just as complicit.

"Thank you." I give her a small bow of my head.

Calista removes the pins keeping her dirty blonde hair intricately woven around her head. "But there are wards, as I'm sure you would expect. One can only enter alongside Contarini blood." She pulls a jacket over her academy uniform and shifts her hair to cover half her face. "We go now, or not at all."

"Now it is."

Calista presses her hand to a mirror, the air shimmering as a portal opens before us. We step through together, into Folkara's kingdom.

"Keep your head down," she whispers. "We only have two hallways to get through to reach the entrance. Don't ruin your plotting by being seen."

Doing as she says, I lower my head. The halls of Folkara

stand in stark contrast to Ilyria's. Here, the kingdom is bathed in a muted yellow hue, with most of the structure crafted from oak wood. Sunlight pours through the windows, a sharp difference to Ilyria, where the skies are almost always cloaked in clouds.

As we traverse the halls, an overwhelming number of soldiers and warriors pass us by. Their faces are hard, their steps deliberate, as if they are preparing for something more severe than I realized.

Perhaps the strife has done more than revive by now.

Perhaps it's thriving.

Calista stops at a dead end, and I almost summon shadows, believing she's brought me here for harm. Before that happens, she taps a spot on the stone wall, revealing a hidden entryway. We enter the dark stairwell, the air damp and thick with mildew, and the door closes behind us.

There's little light as we descend the steps, entering a hallway paved with sandstone. We look over our shoulders with every few steps, until we come along a large, circular steel door.

It lifts for Calista, and she grabs my hand, pulling me through.

The room is bigger than I would've expected from the outside. Shaped like an L, the right side is long, with shelves sagging under the weight of ancient tomes and maps.

Including one of Ilyria.

*Secrets, all right.*

The left side is quaint, with a chipped wooden table and purple cushions on the chairs. Behind it is a shelf with crystal glasses, liquor, stones, and herbs.

Calista moves farther into the room, down the narrow path cluttered with books. I follow, picking up the first tome that catches my eye. It's only a history book, but what catches my attention is that it's dated seventy-eight AA. That's seventy-eight years after the Arcanian War and the subsequent burning of the Irisan Archives—the library that once held nearly all of the universe's knowledge.

Opening the book, I find that it was written by Ilyrian scholars—highly educated Lyrians who piece together the history lost in the flames. As I flip through the pages, one name keeps appearing: Mial. There's no explanation for its significance—only that the name was scattered across the universe. By page two hundred, I learn that Mial is why people believe entering The Void erases a person's existence, leaving them forgotten by the universe.

It was the only explanation the scholars could devise.

"Lucian!" Calista whispers. Setting the book down, I make my way to the back of the room. "This is where I found the map. And remember, this is your problem," she adds, casting me a sidelong glance. "Not mine."

"This is soon to be everyone's problem."

I've never seen this iteration of the map of Folkara. There are increased welding and mining villages. Soldier camps—where they take and train Nepenthes—are littered everywhere, in every continent and mountain peak. Azaire would have been sent to one of these camps if it weren't for his snakes. A power like his is rare, something that was best kept in the hands of the elite, in case of another revolution.

The Nepenthes have long resisted the Folk's oppression. The Neptharian War was the first time the Nepenthes got close to victory. It tipped the scales of power and showed the people they *could* win.

But Folkara wants to make sure that can never happen.

The maps show Folkara's decades-long preparation for war. Against the Nepenthes or Lyrians, it's hard to say. Perhaps both.

"How many meetings do you sit in on?" I ask Calista.

"I'm a *princess*. No more than a glorified trophy here." The bitterness in her voice is cutting.

"None?" I surmise.

"None," she says bitterly.

*She has no idea what this map means.* I knew Folkara viewed the women differently than Ilyria, but I hadn't realized they silenced even their princess.

"When you first discovered the weapon, what else did you find?" I ask.

"I only saw it on the map."

"No plan?"

"All you asked for was a location." I can tell she's still bitter about the circumstances by her tone.

"Look for anything regarding the weapon," I instruct.

Within moments, I'm scurrying through the maps, papers, and books. Dust hangs in the air, mingling with the scent of old ink on withering parchment, making it difficult to breathe.

Calista clears her throat, and I look up to see her arms crossed over her chest.

Relenting, I say, "Please."

She rolls her eyes. "So much for not taking my autonomy," she mutters, walking over to the shelf of books at the other end of the room.

Most of the books aren't titled, seeming to be nothing more than handwritten journals and accounts of earlier wars. Still, I skim through them all—book after book—until my eyelids grow heavy and my shoulders ache.

But I can't leave here with nothing. There's too much at stake. My desperation mixes with my desire as I force myself to continue my search.

*The Hidden Powers* is one of the few titled books I come across. As such, I do more than skim, finding that Lyrian powerists—those who specialize in technological advancements—had been working to multiply the Soul Stones over the years.

This goes against every belief held by Zola.

The six stones—one for each divinely crafted world—were placed by Zola herself to manage the magic.

They were tampering with the goddess's balance.

The Soul Ruby is repeated—a Soul Stone they've worked to maximize. They broke pieces off the original, expanding them while slowly eroding its core, until only weakened fragments remained.

More harrowing, the Soul Ruby was the key component in The Void's creation.

What if that's what Isa meant when she told Desdemona the weapon would never be powered? They sought to use the Soul Ruby to destroy the very universe it had forged, but its power had been worn away beyond use.

Suddenly, footsteps echo down the hall, and my pulse races as they draw nearer. I shove the tome back onto the shelf and stand as nonchalantly as I can manage as a woman appears at the entrance. Her eyes widen when she sees us. The crest of Folkara is on her shirt, but there's no distinct marker of her rank.

My shadows coil around her ankles before she can run.

"Bad timing," Calista says, surprisingly calm, walking to the entrance and kneeling in front of the fallen woman. I follow.

"P-princess Calista," the woman stutters, "what are you doing here?"

"What are *you* doing here?" Calista asks while looking down at the woman. She sounds much more uncanny than I've ever heard her before. The woman opens her mouth, and Calista whispers, "Honest answers only."

The woman only stutters.

Calista shakes her head, her voice taking on an almost seductive quality. "I'll have to take your memories, but if you answer correctly, I won't have to take your life."

The words fall from the woman's mouth in such a rush they're hard to make out. "I was only sent to pick up a tome."

"Hm," Calista muses. "Which tome?"

The woman looks at me and shakes her head. It's almost answer enough: something pertaining to Ilyria.

Calista places her fingers on the woman's temples. The

woman stares blankly as Calista's irises glow yellow, her magic seeping into the woman's mind like a haze. Minutes later, Calista turns to me. "Pull back your shadows."

I do as she asks, ready to subdue the woman again at a moment's notice. But Calista pushes the woman in the direction she came, and she doesn't turn as she walks away.

The first thing I say is, "You kill your staff?"

"Gods, no," Calista says, disgusted. "I only learned how to get my way around here. She won't remember anything except not being able to find the tome." She gives me a wide grin. "And I found something you won't like."

My voice is stiff. "What?"

"Come along." She walks to the table and leans over one of the chairs. "Does this look familiar to you?" Between her pointer finger and thumb, there is a moonstone earring, embedded in silver. Calista laughs, her smile sharp. "Your perfect family isn't so perfect after all."

They're Leiana's earrings. Ilyria could know everything I've discovered and more. Do Leiana and Labyrinth know of the power supplies they have on Folkara? The soldier training camps? The extra mining and welding villages?

*The weapon?*

Has every fight in the meetings been staged?

"You've always known we were never perfect," I mutter.

I reach for the earring, and Calista flicks her hand back. "Perhaps I want the worlds to know, too."

"You'd do that to Lilac?"

Calista answers with a frown.

My idea of stopping—*ending*—the Arcanes has gotten so muddled beneath the layers I keep pulling back. I always seem to end up feeling hopeless.

Lilac won't wake up, Desdemona has something to do with it, I have a man in a dungeon who won't talk, and like Azaire said, what I do to him will never leave me. His blood will always haunt me. There's a weapon being made, and my desire to use it against the Arcanes doesn't seem to be what the two strongest worlds want when that's *all* they should want.

I have a laundry list of questions that need answers, and I've only managed to obtain a headache.

I only wanted the power source.

Frantically, I begin grabbing book after book from the shelves, piling them in my arms until the weight is too heavy.

"*Lucian*," Calista whispers, clutching her stomach. I turn to face her. Her skin is always pale, but right now, she looks like a corpse. Dark purplish-green circles sag beneath her eyes, and a gray pallor coats her sharply defined smile lines. "We need to get out before someone else comes."

Her bloodshot eyes meet mine. Altering the woman's memories has burnt her out.

"I can't leave with nothing," I say quickly, my hands shaking as I sift through page after worthless page.

"We won't leave at all if we don't—" she stops.

I turn. Exhaustion weighs her down, and I realize she's right. If we don't leave now, she might not be able to leave at all.

I drop the books and hurry to her, slipping an arm around her torso. As hard as it is to give up, I say, "Let's go."

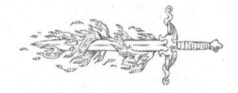

---

Back at the academy, Calista and I both go our separate ways—I to Lilac's room, while she disappears into who knows where.

I grab my sister's violin—hoping it might soothe her if she wakes—and open a portal to Ilyria. Perhaps seeing her in stable condition will grant me some measure of peace. More than that, I hope she will awaken.

I intend to be there when she does.

As I step through the portal to Ilyria, the cool air cuts through my clothing. This level of the kingdom is quieter than the bustling public floors—home to workers, nobles, and the royal council—yet people still pass through. They pay me no mind.

I stand beyond the shimmering boundary of Lilac's room, staring through the enchanted barrier. Lilac lies still, her breath shallow, her face pale. My fingers tighten around the violin's neck.

I do not step inside.

Because I am a coward.

*I put her there, and I can't bring myself to enter.*

Even as foam gathers at the corners of her mouth.

"Lilac?" I whisper, knowing it's futile.

Her eyes do not open. She does not respond. Instead, her body jerks violently, and my heart skips a beat as her back arches off the cot. My hand trembles as it rests against the electrical barrier, its shock shooting through my body. But nothing compares to the strangled, wet sound of Lilac gasping for air against the foam.

I sprint through the halls, my heart beating far too fast, searching for a Light Folk to break the barrier. My sister is seizing, and I run.

I feel like something worse than a coward.

Nobles, soldiers, and workers stare as I rush past. All of them have blue eyes—only Lyrians, who can offer no help. Not one Folk who can free her.

Despair presses down on me. What kind of moonaro attack results in a seizure? Moonaros carry no poison. I don't understand why Lilac won't wake. Leiana said her physical wounds had been healed—that something else is keeping her asleep.

Suddenly, I stumble, shadows wrapping around me as I fall. Then, Leiana looms above me, the darkness fading away. "Why are you here, darling?"

"Lilac," I gasp, scrambling to my feet. "She's seizing; she needs help."

Leiana waves a hand, dismissing me. "She's fine."

Desperation claws its way out of my throat, making me shout, "She's foaming at the mouth!"

Leiana steps forward, grabbing my chin and peering into my eyes for a moment too long. Her dismissive tone shifts into concern as she says, "You're right. There is something wrong with her. We don't know what." She lets go of my chin harshly. "You're still keeping an eye on the septic girl, yes?"

"Yes…" I answer. "Why?"

"I instructed you to bring her to me in the beginning, but I fear I underestimated her crimes and the lengths it would take to prove them. If you have the opportunity to strike, Lucian," she says severely. "Don't miss."

Before, Leiana wanted Desdemona in her possession, and I believed it was her power she desired. Now, she wants her dead. I hadn't realized how deeply I wanted to be wrong about Desdemona until this moment. Because it seems I've been right—there's something off about her presence.

"What crimes?" I ask. "Why would you need to prove them?"

*Proving crimes has never been within her worries.*

"Because the target on her back is interchangeable. Be careful with her. For now, get to class. Appearances are important, darling."

Leiana walks past me, moving in the opposite direction of Lilac. I don't know why I expected anything different. I have long understood how little I mean to her—yet, somehow, I believed Lilac meant more.

I return to Lilac's prison. No one comes, and I don't go in. She convulses on the cot for far too long before falling still. Even after, I linger at the threshold, watching her chest rise and fall, making sure she still breathes. Then, I sit in the hallway, scanning every person who walks by.

I should be in there with Lilac. But I can't bring myself to. I'm afraid.

It's been years since Leiana locked me in the dungeons, but the thought of being under her thumb again—trapped at her whim—terrifies me more than any phobia. And yet, I'm allowing it to happen to Lilac.

When a Folk finally passes, I rise.

With quick movements, I grab the man, pulling him toward the room. I place him before the barrier, my voice trembling as I demand, "Take down the barrier."

The man looks between me and the threshold, hesitating. "Prince Lucian, I—"

I grab the collar of his vest, throwing him against the wall. Lilac is trapped. He is the only Folk I've seen in these halls. He *has* to help.

"Please," I whisper. "It's my sister. She's—" I break off. I don't know what she is. I don't know what's wrong. "I need to help her."

The Folk draws a deep breath, his brown irises flickering to yellow. His tone is cold, emotionless—just an explanation—as he states, "I'm an Air Folk, sire. I don't have the precision needed to take down another's barrier."

With a strangled sigh, I release his collar, not deigning to speak another word as he scurries away.

I rest just beyond Lilac's room until the sun sets, unable to help—powerless to Leiana. The helplessness weighs on me, until I search for the only escape I can think of, fleeing to the wine cellar.

It's full of every wine imaginable. I grab two bottles and sit on the floor.

After finishing half a bottle, inspiration finally strikes. There's one place I haven't searched that may be ripe with answers. I portal back to Visnatus, and when I get there, I head straight to Desdemona's room—a place I haven't entered since Lilac moved out.

There are two beds now, as opposed to the single room Lilac

had. One bed is cluttered with books and clothes, the other is perfectly neat. I suppose that is Desdemona's. She likely doesn't have many belongings.

I open the drawer next to the bed laced in green. There's only a small glass jar, a journal, and a pen.

I go for the journal.

*Again. I killed again. In my dreams, in my waking hours, it's always the same. The guilt carries past the barriers of sleep. The two Folk back home and the Lyrian make three, but the dreams make a number that I don't care to count.*

Again.

I keep reading, page after page of torturous dreams: starting fires, killing people, burning them from the inside out.

Like she did to me.

Then I read what I had glimpsed in her subconscious after she entered The Void. The little girl and her mom—Desdemona and Isa—in a small hut. They talked about Isa's necklace, then about Wendy's mother, Willow. Afterward, Isa shoved the necklace into her daughter's hands and instructed her to power it.

"What are you doing?"

I put the notebook down and turn to face Desdemona, who's standing at the door and wielding a blade. She steps forward, ready to press it to my throat and make empty promises of death, no doubt.

But she's a killer. Those empty promises could soon be fulfilled.

She's my sister's assailant.

I bind her wrists with shadows, pulling them back and forcing the knife to the floor. Then they crawl up her neck, tightening.

Answers and revenge, getting to The Void, the weapon—whatever it is that initially started this rendezvous isn't nearly as important as taking her out.

*She's dangerous.*

"Aibek." Her head jerks back under the pressure of my power. "Aibek, stop," she croaks.

How I'd love to kill her for what she did to Lilac. For the havoc she's wreaked on my life.

For what she did to *me*.

"One last chance to answer," I say, Desdemona's face flushing more by the second. "What were you doing with the moonaro?"

More than the moonaro, it was the Arcanes who stole her mother—every reason for her to obey if they called upon her. I can't ignore that she reached The Void and spoke to Isa. If she could reach her, then she could reach the Arcanes as well.

These creatures killed my parents. If they've uncovered my plans, they have every reason to come for me next.

A feeling lingers—a sense that the monsters and the Arcanes are bound by the same thread, woven into the same web. A web that Desdemona has become a part of—whether by choice or by force.

Her jaw clenches—the only part of her that can still move. I loosen my shadows, allowing her to speak. "You'll have to kill me," she breathes, "because I didn't do *shit*, and I don't have an answer—"

I tighten the shadows once more, and as her mouth opens, only a squeak escapes. I step closer, pick up her knife, and hold it to *her* neck this time. But before I can do a thing, her knee slams into my groin. My shadows falter for a moment, giving her enough time to grab my shoulders and knee me again, harder.

I collapse, and she claws at her neck, unable to grasp the darkness that holds her.

"I'll burn you alive," Desdemona chokes as she gets on top of me and punches. Her hits are weak, and she eventually falls, gasping. "Lucian!" She writhes next to me. "*Please*."

We lie on our backs, her legs kicking the floor. The only color on her face is red. I don't dare look at her, because I know I'm killing her. But at the last moment, I begin to release my shadows, until a faint orange hue fills the air. Her glowing eyes lock onto mine.

I forget where I am, the fight I'm in, and all I can see is her.

Her thirty-three freckles. The flecks of gold in her eyes. Her tanned skin and lips that I've tried to make twist into a smile more times than I can count.

I see her strength—every attempt that's been made on her life by people more powerful than she's ever been. By elites and leaders and even my own soldiers. And suddenly I know, unequivocally, that she is going to survive *me*.

I see her mind as both a tunnel and the light at the end of it. She's a falling angel. A faithless god. She's everything right in the wrong way. Contradictory yet so utterly captivating. *Controlling*, because even now, even as I know her sins, I want to absolve them. Even as I try to kill her, *I long to kiss her*.

Her beauty is one thing, incomparable to all else. But it's her spirit that I'm drawn to, like a moth to a flame, a finger to a thorn, a shipwreck to the sea.

Hope to a lost cause.

Sweat moistens my forehead, and I become keenly aware of the heat pooling in my palms. It rises up my arms, into my chest, and down my body, settling into every organ—squeezing them, *shriveling* them.

*We're going to kill one another.*

Despite it all, I don't have the strength to do that.

It might be a weakness, perhaps a wonder, but I withdraw my power. I restrict my shadows. Desdemona breathes. As I look at the ceiling, kicking the floor with a red face, I decide it's all right —death by her hand.

Then the burning stops. The only noise for a long moment is our ragged breathing. Until, still out of breath, Desdemona says, "Why'd you stop? Scared I'd best you?"

"No," I breathe, lying across from her on the floor and staring at her cold face, sharp with anger, full of fire. "Not scared. Expecting."

She turns to me, sweat beading on her forehead, her hair sticking to her face and wisping into her mouth. I almost reach to pull it back.

"You don't get to do that!" Desdemona roars. "No more flirting. No remarks! Fight me so I can kill you." Her voice trembles, and her irises begin to pulse with orange light.

"What are you?" I whisper, my groin still throbbing, my body still overheated.

The burning knife, the burning *me*, Cynthia not being able to put out her fire.

"You're not a Folk, are you?"

She draws a breath, her eyes returning to brown. "What are you talking about?"

I look at her neck, where I'd cut her in Combat Training. Then, I recall the wound on her left palm and the injury to her side, inflicted by Jermoine and Breck. There isn't a flicker of that pain now, but the dislocated shoulder from the Lyrian soldier had bothered her for weeks.

Slowly, I ask, "Your wounds cauterize themselves, don't they?" I despise the curiosity I feel when cunning should be in its place. "What are you?"

Desdemona stands, breaking my gaze. "How about you tell me when you figure it out, seeing as you know so much."

I stand, too, and when she turns to walk away, I grab her hand—the one burned when she killed the Ilyrian soldier. The skin is flawless, not a mark or even a scar. It looks perfect.

The glass jar in her drawer must be a glamour, and she's using it to conceal more than just her facial features.

Desdemona pulls her hand back. "You said that when you unravel, you'll be taking me with you. But what you didn't think about, Prince, is that I'm going to be your undoing. So threaten me again," she says slowly, a dagger gleaming in her hand.

She presses it into my chest, and I burn as the blade pierces my skin. One line over my heart, then another. Blood—*burning* blood—pours down my chest.

It's a pain unlike any other. A pain only she could inflict.

"And I will do *so much worse* than sink this blade into your heart."

---

I study my chest in the mirror of my suite, staring at the "X" Desdemona has graciously left carved there. It's not bleeding. It's not even an open wound. It's *scabbed*, pink and orange around the edges.

Cauterized.

She burned me as she carved, like a brand. A physical mark to represent how she's marred my soul.

As I brush my fingers along the scar, my eyes shut, refusing to open. Utter darkness surrounds me, silent and still, until a scream pierces the facade.

In front of me, hundreds of people fall to their knees, magic swirling around them as their red eyes glow in the darkness. It's horrifying, but I recognize this magic. I know this feeling.

It's the Arcanes. I watched this power kill my father.

Then I fall to my knees, crying with the lot of them, if only from the memory. I'm helpless to it—the burning, boiling, blood-ridden sensation all around me. All within me.

When the magic ceases, finally relenting, the bodies look worse than corpses. They're burned down to the bone. Their skin is charred and flaking, like embers from a dying fire.

One stands from the pile of corpses, like a man coming back to life. As if death is only a holiday. He sheds his burnt skin like a snake, each scale shifting into the form of my deceased father. Slowly, he stalks toward me, each step dragging the weight of the past.

This doesn't feel like a prophetic vision, because it doesn't feel like the *future*.

It feels like a warning. A reckoning. It feels Arcane. Not just magic—but something planted.

Something they want me to see.

My father's hand reaches for me, a breath away from my face. Perhaps if I thought this was real, I'd lean in. Perhaps I'd reach for him, desperate to grasp him the way the living grasp for ghosts.

But his voice is an unrecognizable rasp as he says, "Bring me the child."

I gasp, nearly screaming, as my eyes fly open.

I'm standing before my mirror, my chest convulsing with panicked breaths. My feet are on solid ground. My body is in my room.

It wasn't real—and that was never in question—yet I feel as though that red magic is suffocating me now. It clings to my lungs, as if I inhaled it like smoke. I cough, my breath initially steady, until I force myself to choke, to expel whatever I've breathed in. But nothing emerges except my own mucus—no tangible trace of the vision I witnessed. It might as well have been a dream.

There's one thing I can do—the only thing I ever do when a vision is forced upon me.

I grab charcoal and paper, sketching image after image. The burning bodies, my deceased father, and then I scrawl the words: *Bring me the child.*

I can't even think of the last time I've seen a child—not since I've been one myself, surely. This academy, my life and its politics, are no place for a kid. There's no reason I would have a vision regarding one.

*I'm not sure it was a vision at all.*

I try not to let it sidetrack me; I tell myself that the future can wait. But I feel the future curling in my gut, turning to acid. I continue to sketch: burning bodies, skeletal remains, my father.

Bodies, remains, father—like a madman.

By the end, scattered sheets of paper surround me, yet I've made no progress, only trapped myself in a suffocating loop.

I stand, the crinkle of paper beneath my feet a war drum, urging me out of my room. The vision clings to me like soaked clothes, weighing down every step, but I head for the dungeon—the path I'd intended before the vision struck me.

Freyr sits in the dimly lit corner, mostly mended by whichever poor healer Cynthia sent. I sit just out of his reach.

"Have you tried burning these yet?" I tap on the bars, knowing that would've been the first thing he'd try. They're made from an alloy with a melting point higher than the Flame.

Freyr only looks at me, his eyes visible for the first time in days.

"Isa Althenia had a child after faking her death," I say, though I know he's aware of this. "I need to know if you're her father."

Freyr jerks his head up. "Desdemona?"

He even sits like her. He is the father—she *is* a Fire Folk.

"Yes," I answer.

"She's here?" There's a hint of panic in his voice.

I nearly smile. I finally have him in my grasp. "An answer for an answer."

Freyr grunts. "Fine."

"Are you Desdemona's father?"

"I don't know," he says. A lie, I assume. "Is she here?"

"Yes," I answer.

The words tumble from his mouth in panicked cohesion. "What happened to Isa?"

"It's my turn," I say, watching as Freyr clenches his healed jaw. "When did you start building the weapon for Folkara?"

"Eighteen years ago," he bites out. "What happened to Isa?"

"The Arcanes took her. She's in The Void."

His face pales, and his shoulders sag as the weight of my words settles on him.

I study him carefully before continuing, "Do you know what the weapon's power source is?"

"By the gods." He lets out a harsh laugh, dragging his hand through his unkempt beard. "You think us Fire Folk would ever be granted that kind of clearance?"

"It's not your turn for a question."

"It used to be *us*—Isa, Willow, and me. Then Willow and Isa cut me out when our agreements... slacked. Now Folkara has changed the design so many times throughout the years, I've lost track." Then he asks, "How long has Isa been in The Void?"

"Three months, give or take. Why do they keep changing the design?"

Freyr shrugs. "I don't know. It's not doing what they want it to do?" He studies me for a moment, through his freshly healed eyes. "Look, all I know is every time we rebuild it, they take it. Most times they give it back, but the materials aren't reusable. Has Desdemona been using her magic?"

"Yes," I say. I want to ask why that's important, but I'll save it for my next question. There's something even more pressing. "What is the weapon being made for now?"

"Honestly? No idea. They change it too often. My best guess is something they can use against the lesser planets."

As in, every planet except Ilyria. Which would mean one thing—Leiana and Labyrinth *are* involved.

Freyr leans against the wall, resting his elbows on the tops of his knees. "Unfortunately for you, I've run out of questions."

# Chapter 29
## High Hopes and Huge Falls

# DESDEMONA

Breck is dead. I burned him alive. I knew it, but I didn't want to. The acrid scent of charred flesh clings to me, like it's woven into my skin, my clothes. Like it followed me into the headmistress's office and settled in the walls. But if I didn't kill him, he would've killed me. That's the only thing I'm certain of.

I lift my gaze to Headmistress Constance and ask, "What about the other boy?"

"Jermoine lost his forearms, but he lives," she says, like it should be comforting.

But all I see is the metal, melting when I grasped it, pooling down his arms while he screamed. It must've burned his skin right off his bones.

I assumed Lucian told her it was me, but she said no other Fire Folk in Visnatus could have caused the damage I did.

I still think he told her.

"What's my punishment?" I spit, masking the fear of what she might do to me.

But instead of the harsh response I expect, I'm met with something far worse.

"I don't punish the Folk for reaching their potential," she says with a shrug. As if murder and mutilation are my potential.

*It is, isn't it?*

The only thing of value I've ever done is kill.

"Okay." I grip the chair arms, pulling myself up. "Am I free to go?"

"No," the headmistress says, nodding toward the chair and motioning for me to sit back down. I follow her silent instructions. "I believe you're looking for something?"

I meet her eyes, keeping my face blank. There's no way she has proof that I'm searching for forbidden texts. The only suspicious thing I searched for was the Arcanian War. Not illegal.

"I'm not looking for anything," I lie.

My mom, a way to The Void, a way home. I don't show any of my longing, I swallow it, stuff it down so far that there's no possible way she could sense it.

Everything I want sits untouched in the deepest pits of my stomach.

The headmistress leans back in her cushy chair, fingers intertwining as though she's already decided my fate. "I'll aid you," she says, "for a favor."

I prepare to get defensive—to double down on denying that I'm looking for anything. But curiosity gets the best of me. Worse than that... hope.

"Aid me in what?" I ask, trying to pick apart what she knows, what she's offering.

"Finding your mother. What else?"

My heart stops as she smiles. She *smiles*. I have to take a breath of air, get my heart pumping blood again, and find out what she wants before I blindly accept.

"My mother is dead."

"Desdemona, dear?" Headmistress Constance leans closer. "Don't treat me as if I am puerile."

My eyes burn—with tears or power, I can't tell right now. "Did Lucian tell you?"

"That's not important."

The headmistress stands and walks to the back corner of the room—to her bookshelf. No way. There's no way she's about to give me what I need. I can't let my hopes get too high—but I already feel it. She sits back down and opens a book, an old one.

No way.

"Did you know the Arcanes weren't born?" she asks. "Most people hold a common belief that they were Ayan's descendants. And perhaps they once were."

*Most* people? I briefly wonder how old she is. No one talks about the solar god—Ayan—anymore, and *most people* believe the Arcanes to be myth.

"But what the Arcanes became used to be seen as a punishment." She pushes the book across the table toward me. "Take a good look, dear. It's one of the last surviving tomes from the Irisan Archives."

Nothing is written in the common language. Not even with the same letters. But in the middle of the page, there's an image of three creatures falling into each other. The first is tall, with wings the size of its body and a heart the size of its chest. The second lost its wings, and its heart is half the size. The last has no heart, its wings reduced to bones, hunching its back.

Instinctively, I run my fingers along the edges of the page.

"You've heard the story?" she asks. "That the Arcanes were the catalysts for the Arcanian War? They were too powerful, too dangerous—nearly unkillable. As a result, the leaders devised a solution—they banished the Arcanes to a universe called The Void. A universe supposedly devoid of magic."

I tear my eyes from the unreadable words and strange pictures, struggling to digest her words. "That's not the story we're told back home," I mutter. "Arcanes are like ghosts."

I try not to hesitate, but when she frowns and narrows her eyes, she becomes a different person. Her face becomes gaunt, her skin ashen. She must be ancient; Lyrians don't begin to age until after their second century of life.

"They take bad children and workers." I shrug. "And everyone forgets you ever existed."

*But I remember my—*

"But you remember your mother?" The headmistress raises her eyebrows, bringing some life back to her face.

My instinct is to deny, but I swallow my pride. "I do."

"You see, the reason that became the common legend is that, after the Arcanes' defeat, mentions of someone named Mial were found throughout the universe." She clasps her hands under her chin. "But no one remembered him. Not even those who wrote his name."

I need to get up. I need to move. I stay entirely still under her scrutiny. The hope I felt before? It's dwindling.

"That's very interesting." My voice comes out flat, too controlled, and I worry it sounds fake.

"My apologies. We've gotten off track."

Headmistress Constance settles her hand on top of mine, and I try not to visibly shiver. While her hand is cold like Lucian's, it's not the least bit comforting. It doesn't soothe my constantly burning skin. It just feels like dead weight.

"The Void," she begins, "a universe created to be devoid of magic. But a universe *can't* be devoid of magic."

She's right, it goes against everything I've ever known. Magic *is* the fabric of a universe. So what does this mean for my mom? Assuming these aren't the ramblings of a lunatic.

"That's your answer," the headmistress murmurs.

"I didn't ask a question," I respond.

"Of course you did. You want to get to The Void. Everything you've learned claims it's magicless. Though it's only a universe with a different language." The headmistress leans over, opens a drawer, and pulls out something small, juggling it between her fingers. "Find yourself an Arcane, learn their way, make it to The Void. But beware—if you return, nothing will be as it was."

I can't laugh. I can't even scoff. Is she really this delusional?

"They're already here," she says, answering another question I never asked.

I make out what's in her hand now: a white and blue box.

"They've been back for centuries, waiting."

"Waiting for what?" I mutter.

"To finish what they started." The headmistress leans closer, her voice barely above a whisper. "A thousand years ago, they waged a war with one objective: to wipe out every species not descended from the gods."

"But that's *everyone*," I say, shaking my head.

The Arcanes have my mother—and they haven't killed her. If the goal of the Arcanian War was annihilation, how could I have never heard it?

Except... I have. Not in words, but in silences. In what history never said. In every account of the war, one thing rang true: the Lyrians came out unscathed. The most powerful creatures in the universe—descendants of Sulva, some claim, the lunar goddess herself—untouched by the devastation.

I stand as the headmistress strikes a match, hissing against the box as it sparks. She tosses the flame toward me, the fire leaping onto a pile of books, too fast to not be doused in something flammable.

"Put it out," she whispers.

My knuckles are white as I grip the armchair. My heart beats just as fast—if not faster—than when I danced with Lucian.

I look over my shoulder at the headmistress. "Are you insane?"

"Perhaps." She shrugs. "Put it out."

The fire comes closer, close enough for me to *feel* this woman's insanity. But suddenly, it feels like I have no choice. If I don't try, this fire will burn me alive, sealing the death I've envisioned my entire life as fate.

So I stare into the eyes of destiny, begging it to be rewritten.

It happens slowly at first: the heat that flickers around my fingers, the scream I let out before I realize it doesn't burn. The fire feels as natural as my own blood.

Maybe she's right. Maybe I can stop the fire. I've always known I was different, that there was something slightly off. So this time I don't beg destiny—I demand it.

The fire flickers out with ease, and when I look up, the headmistress's face is twisted into something eerie, almost inhuman.

I stand, my chair screeching against the floor as I turn to the door. My hands hover just over the knob when she says, "You could be the most powerful of them all." My fingers freeze. "Imagine that: a girl from the septic outranking the elites."

When I turn, she throws the box of matches at me. I catch them.

"And you think *matches* are gonna get me there?"

"No, dear." The headmistress smiles. "I will."

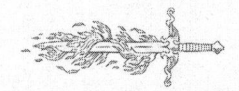

---

I go to the last person I can turn to—Leiholan. What does it mean that the person I trust most is a Nepenthe? He has the same eyes and powers as the keepers but not the same nature; no keeper would hug me while I cried, drunk and guilty over a murder I committed.

Four deaths, not five. By that count, it's as if one person in Damien's family still breathes, only without their arms.

As I head to the combat room, a hand grips my shoulder. In a heartbeat, I twist, my blade pressing into Lucian's chest. He smirks, placing his hands on the hilt of the dagger and over mine. His touch feels different, the same hands with a different intention.

I force myself not to shudder when I think about his shadows choking the life from me.

*Or branding him.*

I don't know what came over me, but I don't regret it. He'll remember it forever—a reminder that I'm far worse than a worthy adversary.

"What do you want?" I lower the blade to get my skin away from his.

Lucian smiles at that, as if he can sense my tension. "I may have found your father," he replies, his tone stiff, like he's commenting on the weather.

"I'm not in the mood for jokes." I turn away from him. To the worlds, my dad is Dalin Marquees; to me, my dad is unknown; and to both of us, he's dead.

"Freyr Alpine is waiting for you in the basement."

"I don't even know who that is," I spit without looking at him.

Lucian spins me around, and for a moment, I consider punching him. With my knife.

"He was engaged to your mother before she… you know." He lazily drags a knife over his neck, nearly touching the skin.

*My* knife. I rip it from his hands.

"You really think I'm going to go to the basement with *you?*"

"I think you've always wanted to go to the basement with me."

"I think I liked you better when you weren't a complete sociopath, *Prince.*"

He smiles. "And I think I liked you better with your hands on me, *Marquees*. Or should I say Alpine?"

I turn away. "Screw you!"

"I'd have considered it if you'd said please," the prince sings.

I don't have a second to think better of myself before I unsheathe a dagger and throw it, just south of his ear. He lifts two fingers to the graze and pulls them away, red.

"Sadistic," he notes.

"Only for you," I drawl, mocking him.

Then I go to the combat room, searching for Leiholan. It feels like the universe has flipped itself inside out.

"You know I only have so many hours of free time in my days, and you're starting to take way more than your share." That's how he greets me.

"How well do you know the headmistress?" I ask while staring at the bullseye across the room.

"Not well."

"Then why were you with her and Hogan when I first showed up?" *I thought they were all close.*

"Coincidental." He shrugs.

"No, no way. Don't lie to me, Leiholan. You are literally the last person in this universe I trust right now." *Please, don't lie to me.*

"I'm truly *touched* that you trust me, sweetheart, but I'm telling you the truth." He leans back and rests his hands behind his head. "Ever wonder why *I'm* the only person you have left?"

"Because you're the only one who didn't leave." I shake my head. Pointless, this is pointless.

Leiholan chuckles. "Or, for your consideration, because I'm the only one you didn't lie to."

I raise a finger at him. "That's not why I'm alone." *I lied to you, too.*

He pouts and looks around the room. "Oh, it's not? Please, tell me why you're alone. I'd love to hear what story you've cooked up."

"Hm, well, I don't know. Maybe because you're all a bunch of pompous assholes!"

Leiholan leans forward again. "Do you ever stop and think," —he shrugs, raising his hands and gesturing toward me—"that maybe *you're* the problem."

"What is wrong with you?" I shout. "Everyone here wants me dead, and you think *I'm* the problem?"

"My mistake." Leiholan smiles like he finds this humorous. "I think you *have* a lot of problems, and only one of them is who you are."

"Gee, thanks."

"You'll figure it out." He pats my shoulder before he drinks, and I don't stop him.

There's something else on my mind. I wait for the alcohol to bring his faculties down before I ask, "That first day, why didn't you believe me when I told you my real name?"

He curses under his breath and rubs his hand against the scruff of his jaw, but doesn't turn to face me.

"Leiholan?"

"Yeah?" He doesn't look at me, but my eyes are burning into the back of his head. "I knew someone with your surname once. *Althenia*," he says slowly, savoring the syllables. Almost like he misses the name. I do, too. "I thought you were talking about her."

"And she couldn't have a kid?"

"She's dead. Then again, so is your mom, but I knew Anise during the war."

During the Neptharian War, when I was six. "She was a Folk?" I ask. Althenia is a Folk name, not Nepenthe.

"Yep," he says, taking another sip. "My wife, too."

"Did you fight?" I ask. "In the war?"

"I did." Another sip. "And before you get snippy, Anise survived it."

I try to keep my voice kind. We're talking about his dead wife. But he *fought*. No matter how different he is from the keepers— he killed my kind. He ambushed our world. He could've been the very same Nepenthe who killed my neighbors, my friends.

So no, my voice is far from kind when I ask, "What killed her, then?"

"Your Royals." He laughs bitterly, pointing his bottle at me and spilling the silver liquid on my feet. "Oh yeah, you should've seen what they did to us in the aftermath." He tips the bottle back again. "But they'd never show you."

"They kept bringing *you* guys back to the septic, to kill us, even after the war. They kept you all employed—"

"Who do you think trained us to kill like that? All our facilities and schools are run by the Folk. Trust me, it's no accident that we're your *keepers*," he spits. Before I can tell him off, he adds, "I'm not having this conversation with you."

"You never want to have any conversation other than the ones where you're telling me what to do!" I shout, walking to the back of the room and swinging open the armory, grabbing another sword.

I used to hate the dual blade, but now I can't imagine fighting with anything else.

"On day one, you told me if I won in a duel, you'd *grovel* for my cause," I remind him. "New rules: I win, and you tell me your version of the *truth*." I raise the dual sword just like he taught me.

"My version!" Leiholan shouts. His face is red, and a vein protrudes from his forehead. "You Folk are so conceited. The saddest part is this:

*you'd* be the first of the kids here to understand. What they do to you in the septic is exactly what they do to us on Nepthara." He takes the sword that's strapped to his back, and I raise mine, ready to fight. But he throws his blade, clattering at my feet. "I'm not going to fight you, sweetheart. One of these days, when you're ready to listen, maybe I'll talk. For now, get the fuck out."

I hurl my sword down next to his, then I get the fuck out.

What is *wrong* with me? Is Leiholan right? Am *I* the problem? He just told me his wife is dead, and I—no, *he* turned it into a fight, not me. He started going on about how bad the *Folk* are when the Nepenthes have always been the killers.

I start searching for the basement of the school—where Lucian seems to think my father is. It scares me that he could be right, that there could be a man still living in this world who's half of me. With nowhere else to go, I keep searching. I open every door I've never considered before, but they're only classrooms and closets. I try to ask students where the basement might be, but most hurry past, avoiding my gaze.

The rest of them run.

Until one Folk, who barely reaches my shoulder, tells me, "There is no basement."

*You've got to be kidding me.*

Lucian could've been lying, and yet, if he was, what's his goal? If he wants to kill me, he could do it anywhere, at any time. No one would stop him; they'd be closer to cheering him on.

After an hour of opening doors and seeing things I probably shouldn't, I head outside into the rain. It drums against the dense leaves and grass in a steady rhythm. As I walk further, the cold drops seep through my clothes, adding weight to every slippery step.

There are a few doors along the side of the building, wooden and withered, and the few that open are rooms full of webs and no stairs. I walk along the building for a while longer.

And step on a trapdoor. It's rusted to the ground, but as far as I can tell, it's not locked by magic. I do the sane thing: find a big rock and smash it until my hand and head hurt and the lock snaps in half.

Gray, dirty stairs meet my eyes, then my feet as I descend.

It smells like bodily fluids and rain, and it's not a basement. There are tons of *cells*. Why would a school need cells? At least they're empty.

But the last one isn't.

## Chapter 30
### Facing What I Turned Away From

# DESDEMONA

A man crouches in the corner of his cage. A small window high in the stone wall lets in dim sunlight, just enough for me to see his auburn hair. He glances at me and exhales shakily, muttering, "For fuck's sake," under his breath.

"Freyr?" My voice betrays the emotions I'm trying—and failing—to hide.

Freyr's voice is harsh when he asks, "What's your name?"

"Desdemona." I sound unsure of myself, like maybe my name isn't Desdemona.

I can't just ask if he's my dad, can I?

Light floods the room as the trapdoor creaks open. Against my will, heat rises through me—*power*. My hands tingle with barely tamed flame.

But it's just Lucian.

It's *Lucian*. He feels safe in this scenario and like the most dangerous person in every other.

The reality of the situation is this: we're anything but safe together, and he's one wrong move away from becoming my next human torch.

*What am I thinking?*

I shove my hands into my pockets, and it does nothing to ease the burn.

Lucian points at me, smiling as the door slams shut. "You

found him."

"You didn't give me much to work with," I spit.

"The plan was for you to come with me." He walks closer to me.

"Plans change," I say, but the words are heavier than I intended.

"That would be the first time you told me the truth."

"What are you doing to him?" My voice shakes with fear I don't deserve to have. It was only a few days ago that I killed a boy and took another one's arms.

The heat in my pocket begins to feel very real. And very dangerous. But if he tries to kill me again, it will become my saving grace.

Lucian's gaze shifts to the cell, cold and assessing, just like his mother's, as he asks, "Would you answer *her* questions, Freyr?" Then he looks at me, and I feel the chill of his shadows as one brushes my cheek, too close to my neck. I swat at it, but my hand passes through.

"She shouldn't be here," Freyr snaps at Lucian.

"Well, news flash," I say, waving my hands at him, "I am here. So talk."

"Why shouldn't she be?" Lucian demands.

"There's a reason Isa raised you in the septic," Freyr says, finally looking at me.

Again, Lucian speaks before I can. "Other than to escape punishment?"

I crouch, lowering myself to Freyr's eye level. "Why did she take us to the septic?" My throat burns with the embarrassing threat of tears, and my eyes sting with the deadly threat of fire.

I'm far more concerned about the first.

But Freyr's eyes tear from mine as he stares at Lucian with disdain. It's the kind of disdain I've only seen when Folk look at the keeper who caught them with extra rations—which always ends in a whipping.

"I won't talk with him here," Freyr says.

Looking up at Lucian, I'm scared that I'm one "no" away from pleading. My eyes do the begging that my vocal cords refuse.

Lucian looks down, and for one second, I glimpse the boy I knew. But it's gone before I get the chance to drown in the dark blue seas that swarm in his eyes. Then he's gone, too. Light fills the space for a moment before the trapdoor comes crashing down again.

I'm still staring into the distance when Freyr says, "Show me the memor."

I turn back to him, seeing him with new eyes. He knows about the necklace. He knows that *I* have it—something that was always my mom's. There's a spark of hope, a glimmer of trust, however fragile.

I pull the necklace from beneath my shirt and hold it up for him to see. Freyr shakes his head, his frown deepening as he stares in silence. It's in that silence that I understand the truth.

He is who Mom was before me, and I am who she became after him.

"She didn't run to escape punishment," he tells me, his gaze sliding away from the necklace. I tuck it back beneath my shirt. "Isa ran so she could raise you." He struggles against the shadows wrapped around his wrists and legs, but they don't budge.

"I'm sorry about this," I say, moving closer to the bars—a show of faith.

"I'm glad it's not his mom."

"Yeah," I mutter, thinking of the queen's berating gaze at the ball and the man that attacked me after. "So, why did my mom run to the septic to raise me?"

Freyr nods slowly, as if weighing the question before answering, "The Althenias used to be highly regarded in the court of Folkara. They fell from grace when your mother and I were caught making the weapon."

It takes years to build and seconds to destroy. That was my entire life, building with broken blocks. Gaining a life and losing it. A fate that I'm not even close to breaking.

"Isa didn't trust what the court would do with you," he finishes.

"Are you—" Damn this burning in my throat and the tears threatening to spill. I force them back. "Are you my dad?"

Freyr shakes his head, muttering, "You don't want me as a father."

That's his answer. Every question I have slips away like sand through my fingers. Barely managing, I get the next question past my frown: "What will the Arcanes do with her?"

I catch the shadow of his furrowed brow. "If she's still alive, I don't know. She was a good woman, Desdemona."

"She *is* alive," I croak. "I'll get to her."

"Don't." He shakes his head. "It's not worth it."

"How can you say that?" I scoot back, his words burning like betrayal in my chest.

"I know more about them than you do."

Despite what he said, this suddenly feels very much like I'm talking to a dad. *My* dad.

"Then tell me," I say.

"If the prince is listening—"

"He's not."

"Look, all I can say is that when I was young, there were stories about the return of the... *creatures*. The Rising, they called it, before the stories were banned," Freyr tells me. "They want vengeance against us, for casting them away. Me and your mother, we were fools. We thought we could stop them. It's a mistake we'll pay for for the rest of our lives."

Lucian wasn't lying. My mom made a weapon, she tried to stop the Arcanes, and now both of us are paying for it. But I need more. I need something that can help me save her.

"I already know they're coming back," I snap, unable to help myself. "They've been here! I don't need a fancy title for what's *already happening.*" I drop my head in my hands, composing myself. "Tell me how to fight them. How can I win?"

"You can't," Freyr's words are sharp. "Getting out alive is winning."

"Theoretically, how do they die?" I ask, my voice tight with the threat of a plea.

"You steal their life force, but no mortal can contain it."

"We're *all* mortal." I can't hide the strain from my voice. That heat is quickly turning to anger.

"Does Cynthia still work at the academy?" Freyr asks.

I'm confused for a moment—I've only heard that name once before. Then I realize where: Cynthia Constance.

"The headmistress?"

"Headmistress?" He laughs. "That's good for her." I think I hear sarcasm in his voice.

"Is that all?" I ask, trying to arm my voice with disinterest, but sorrow seeps through. "Any words of wisdom or parting sentiments?"

"I'm not your father," he whispers, meeting my gaze. "That's for your sake."

Doubting that he'll see it, I nod once as I stand, turning away. The tears that have been building slide down my cheeks, and I wipe them away before I open the trapdoor.

And lucky for me, Lucian is waiting just outside. I close the door before I look at him, scowling.

"What do you want?" I sniffle, hyper-aware of my eyes that are probably rimmed with red. I tip my head toward the sky, hoping the rain will wash away any evidence of my tears.

"I want the truth," he replies.

"You know everything," I say, my voice quieter than I intended.

He nods once, stepping closer to me. The rain coats his hair, dark, loose curls falling into his eyes. It's only now that I notice the stench of vesi.

"What do you want?" My words come out strained.

Lucian looks at me like I'm both his deity and the bane of his existence as he whispers, "Your very existence has torn mine to shreds. I want to know what you've done to me."

*Good.* He told me I was haunting. I hope I'm haunting him still. I hope these thoughts of me take him to his grave.

I like that I'm a nuisance to him. I want to be worse.

*I want to be his ruin.*

"I wish you had never come here," he says with a hint of finality.

I can't help but laugh. It's bitter in my throat. "Do you think I *don't*? All I've thought about *every day* since I got here is getting back home!"

Lucian smiles the kind of smile that makes me want to slap it off. It's the kind of smile that doesn't belong on a boy who seconds ago told me I'm tearing his existence to shreds.

But, despite that, he leans closer to me, sending chills down my spine when he whispers in my ear, "Because I'm fairly certain your mind was on… *other* things while we were dancing."

I shiver and hope that he'll blame it on the rain and my soaking wet clothes—not his voice.

"It was." I slam my forearm into his chest, and he hits the wall with a satisfying groan. Rain drips into my eyes, and I lean into him, looking up. "I was thinking about all the ways I could make you want me." I raise an eyebrow. "And how to weaponize your longing."

*I wish that were the truth. I wish I'd thought so far ahead.*

This time when Lucian smiles, I memorize the hint of pain in it.

"I don't believe that," the prince whispers.

I wish he'd fight me back, just to give me a reason to take this further.

"Just remember that you've already played your best move

against me." I eye him up and down purposefully. "And you have no clue what mine will be."

"I can always see what you're going to do next, Marquees. And it isn't nearly as pretty as you are."

"You're bluffing," I say, narrowing my eyes.

If he's a Seer—a type of Lyrian who can invoke visions at will—what has he already seen of me?

Lucian smirks. "Perhaps I wanted an excuse to call you pretty."

"What is wrong with you?" I drop my arm from his chest and take a step back. "I *hate* you." He wouldn't think I was *pretty* without Aralia's glamour. "You tried to kill me!"

"And you almost killed me," he says with a shrug.

"And I *will*. You know I will."

Lucian grabs my wrist, pulling me back to him. I inhale sharply. Then I shake my head, mostly at myself. I've held knives to his throat, but I could never do anything of real consequence. And I'm not gonna do anything now either.

*When did I become so weak?*

"I urge you to say it again," the prince whispers. I can feel my pulse thumping against his thumb like my heart is in my wrist. "Without clenching your left hand."

The one he's holding.

"Please," I say, even though I'm a bit scared that he is right— that I am lying and do have a tell. "The only reason my hand is clenched is because I'm fighting the urge to punch you."

Then his fingers lace through mine, pulling my fist apart before returning to grip my wrist.

"Say it," he murmurs, leaning in close. Too close. "Say you hate me."

I gulp. I don't clench my fist. And I say, "I hate you."

Lucian smiles. Like he wanted to hear it. Then he spins me around and presses *me* into the wall, the wet ivy slippery beneath me.

"Have you ever kissed someone you hated?" he asks.

I'm stunned, annoyingly—obnoxiously—frozen beneath his electrifying touch.

"I'd imagine it's not so different from love. The spike of adrenaline." His hand inches up, his fingers grazing over mine. "The pounding of your heart."

It's the ghost of a touch, enough to get me going but not to keep me satiated.

"The *electricity*. In fact…" His fingers intertwine with mine briefly before pulling away. Then he picks up my chin like he really would kiss me. "I'd even bet it to be *more* lustful."

"Well, you'll have to find someone else who hates you," I push the words past the lump in my throat.

"Because you don't?" His tone is so clearly teasing. Mocking.

I grab his wrist from under my chin, twisting it enough to at least sprain. His sharp intake of breath, masking the pain, makes me smile.

I lean into him, tightening my grip. "Because I'd kill you before I'd kiss you."

"Oh," Lucian says while smiling. Like I played right into his hand. "But you can't see the future."

---

I avoid the headmistress, convincing myself it's because I don't believe Freyr and not because my power terrifies me.

It's funny—I thought I was alone before all this. But this week, with Leiholan no longer being a reliable person I can turn to, I'm realizing it's been a long time since I've truly been alone. Even though I've been lying to everyone—and still am—that's how things have always been. Even Damien, Elliae, my own mom.

I'm just a damned liar.

I don't know which word fits me better now: damned or liar.

I guess I'm both.

My room reeks of joints and vesi, and Aralia's gone again. She is more often than not now. I don't miss her, not by a long shot.

I miss anyone. Everyone. No one. What I never had.

The dreams still happen every night, and when I wake up in hot sweats, sometimes Aralia stirs, but she never asks if I'm okay. At least last night she said *something*.

She turned toward me, our eyes meeting in the dark and said, "You talk in your sleep sometimes."

I was still breathless, but not like the night I killed the man with the crest of Ilyria…

"Oh," I muttered.

"I wanna say I'm…" She trailed off. "Sleep better."

I hate her.

The dreams are all repeats. Recurrences. Same old shit. I've carried out nearly everything that occurs in them now—set a forest on fire, taken a life. I guess I've become exactly who I was scared I'd be in those dreams. At least I get to hug my mom in them. I guess, in a way, it's worth it.

The Folk in Elemental Magic stop attacking me. Now they run away instead. Formidable—and I did it without Leiholan's help. Because he never told me to kill someone and take another someone's arms. That was all me.

Maybe he's right about the Folk, because I'm turning out to be worse than they are.

I wipe my eyes, even though I'm trying to wipe my mind. I did what I had to do to survive. Someone weaker would be dead now. I'm lucky. I'm smart. I'm strong.

I'm *burning*.

I shake out my hands and blow on my fingers, hoping for a moment of relief. Elemental Magic would be the one place where my power is permitted, but I have a feeling that permission only goes so far.

Ms. Abrams instructs us to pair up and test our progress with our elements. I glance at Aralia, but she quickly averts her gaze.

Right. Alone. It makes sense, with this reputation of mine.

In my next class—Psychology—I search for Lucian, just like every day. When I find him, I turn away, and when he's not looking, I watch his back.

Fantasizing about the day I'll get to stab *him* there.

I prefer it this way. Gentleness is weakness; tender hands and touching words are treacherous. They tear down strategically placed walls. They tarnish armor that was crafted for a reason. And in the end, it's not gentleness that sends a blade through your opponent's heart.

It's rage.

Rage is strength. Rage has kept me breathing.

All I feel for that man is rage—exactly as it should be. One day, perhaps when I care less about my own life, I'll cast aside the consequences and give him the payback he deserves.

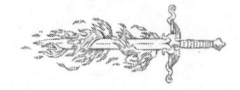

---

A week later, I haven't said a word to anyone—and no one's said anything to me either. I think if I tried to speak, my throat would snap from the strain.

In the halls Aralia and I used to walk together, Fleur, Eleanora, and Calista close in on her again. The princess shoves her shoulder into Aralia's. A book slips from her bag, a picture sliding out.

Aralia reaches for it, but Eleanora steps on it first. Then suddenly, I'm standing in front of her, glaring at the others, my eyes burning so intensely they sting.

"Move your foot, or I'll burn you alive," I threaten through clenched teeth.

Eleanora quickly steps back, falling in line with Fleur and Calista.

"Do you want to wait and see if I'll do it?" I scream, the fire nearly reaching my fingertips.

"Calm down, Inferno," Aralia says, setting her hand on my shoulder.

Air rushes into my lungs, forcing me to take a deep, unsteady breath.

I hardly notice when the three of them run away.

Shrugging Aralia off, I mutter, "You didn't deserve my help."

She reaches for my hand. "Des—"

"Don't," I cut her off.

I shouldn't have gotten involved. But I glance at the photo next to my foot, and I recognize the man from our windowsill. It's Aralia's dad, the Fire Folk—the reason she spoke to me in the first place.

Life would be so much easier if she'd just stayed away.

Can't I go to Leiholan now? Or at least find the courage to face the headmistress? I can't decide which is scarier, so instead, I walk, staring at my feet.

"I'm sorry, Des," Aralia's voice echoes through the hall. "I've been sorry this whole time." Her tone softens, quieter now, like she wants the words to be just for me.

I can feel the weight of eyes on me, so I keep my head down and try to slip away.

Suddenly, I'm stopped by a body, and something *forces* me to look up.

It's Wendy. She reaches for my wrist, her eyes glazed over, fading to a washed-out shade of green. Then, from her mouth, comes the most eerie, toneless voice I've ever heard.

"Time fractures with the stone.

The one who leaves returns alone.

When the cracks in the universe divide,

love will be your demise."

Wendy's eyes clear, and her hands jerk away. She trembles uncontrollably, swallowing hard before she runs, disappearing from sight.

Aralia is by my side immediately, asking if I'm all right, but I step away from her.

"Here," Aralia hands me a piece of paper. Whatever Wendy just said to me is written down. "It's a prophecy," she explains.

I shove the paper in my pocket and look at Aralia. "Apologizing in front of twenty people"—who are all staring at us—"doesn't make us friends."

"Yeah," Aralia says. "But you still wear my clothes. And use my blusher. I don't know how many Folk share their clothes with people they don't consider friends."

"Then I'll stop wearing your clothes," I spit.

I speed down the hall when she whines, "Des."

"Save it!" My voice echoes around me, while the so-called prophecy reverberates inside me, heavy with meaning. It was about my mom. It has to be.

It must mean she's closer to home—which means I'm closer to saving her. And that means I need more. I need power.

Temptation pulls me toward Headmistress Constance.

*Nothing left to lose.*

The moment I step in the room, the headmistress smiles down at a pile of paper on her desk. "Fair to see you again, dear."

"You know why I'm here," I say, stepping further inside.

But before I can react, a sharp pain erupts as a letter opener drives deep into my bicep. Every nerve in my body lights up with heat, the burn spreading quickly. I grab the hilt, ready to rip it from my flesh.

"What is *wrong* with—"

I stop.

"Go on." The headmistress gestures to the letter opener, still lodged in my arm and gripped in my hand, and smiles. "Heal."

The heat is dizzying as I scramble for another convincing lie. Oh, whatever.

"I don't heal," I spit, pulling her bloody, bedazzled letter opener from my arm with a stifled whimper. It clatters against her desk. Blue looks good with blood. "My body burns the wound shut, but trust me, it hurts like a bitch for a long time after."

"Fascinating," she whispers, her voice slow, like my body burning itself is some kind of twisted art.

"Got any more blades you wanna poke me with?"

"If that's an invitation…" The headmistress wipes my blood on a small, red handkerchief. "But no." She raises the letter opener, the hilt facing me. "I want you to melt it."

She knew about Jermoine, how I took his arms. What will happen to me if I do it again?

What will happen if I *can* do it again, whenever I please, to whomever I wish?

Power—but more importantly, power that won't kill me— sounds pretty damn good. Power is murder; power is power. I don't know which I believe, but I know I want it.

That's why I came to her.

"Fine."

Hastily, I grab the letter opener from her and close my palm around the blade, just like the last time. I think of the adrenaline, fighting for my life and being so close to losing it that my only instinct was to *grab* a sword coming for my head. My heart races just thinking of how close I came to death.

That heat overwhelms me, singing my nostrils and burning my vision. I grip the blade tighter, pulling blood, and when the heat rushes to my palm to cauterize the wound, the metal crunches like a leaf just before it melts.

A laugh rumbles up from deep inside, forcing its way out. Gods, does this feel good. Every cell in my body is *electrified,* and not from pain—from *power*.

I meet the headmistress's icy blue eyes, where she smiles before her mouth does.

# Chapter 31
## Soul Sucker (For You Only)

# LUCIAN

"You don't start with your strongest unit," Yuki says. "Not right away."

The teacher's stone-cold face shifts slightly, his gaze meeting mine as he asks, "Why wouldn't you send your strongest soldiers?"

In War Strategy class, we're participating in a mock battle. Currently, we're defending the Great Sea, the largest and most powerful body of water in the universe, located just below my kingdom. As with all of these mock wars, we are fighting the Nepenthes—whose population is barely a fraction of Ilyria's.

"To move yourself from defense to offense," I answer. "You use your weakest soldiers as collateral, tiring the enemy before sending in your best for the kill."

That stone-cold face smiles. I know what he's thinking—I've heard it many times before: *You'll make a fine king*. "Fine" meaning ruthless.

He pushes forward gray pieces on the battle board—gray representing our lieutenants, the soldiers who have seen the least battle. The collateral.

"If it's the Nepenthes you face, you can wear them down quickly by forcing them to overuse their abilities," the teacher says, repeating what we all know—Nepenthes tire faster than any of us when they rely too heavily on their heightened senses.

As he speaks, my personal guard steps into the room.

I expect him to come to me, but he stops in front of Kai, waiting by the door as Folkara's prince stands. I do the same, following behind him. Kai looks at me, only to scowl, and doesn't say a thing.

"You're not called to Ilyria, Prince Lucian," my guard says, using my title in front of the other prince.

"Not a bother," I reply.

Lilac must be awake. It's the only reason Kai would be summoned to my kingdom. Their betrothal is imminent.

I have to be there for her, so I say, "I'll be joining."

The three of us walk to the nearest portal room in silence. My guard presses his hand to a mirror, and we step through. The bite of the air on Ilyria makes Kai shiver. My guard and I are more than used to the bitter cold.

My guard leaves us at the door where I last saw Lilac. The look in his eyes is an apology.

"Lucian." Lilac's voice quivers, her body pinned to the bed. She struggles to move but barely shifts against whatever holds her down. She says my name once more, her voice more a whimper than a word.

I step through the threshold, my heart nearly stopping as I pass the electrical barrier and reach my sister's side. Indigo energy hums around her, restraining her with the same force that keeps her trapped in the room. Her head is fixed to the ceiling, but her eyes dart frantically.

Her voice cracks as she whispers, "I can't move."

I turn to Kai, desperation in my voice as I shout, "Get her out of this!"

He's a Light Folk—he can control the energy field binding Lilac.

Kai's eyes widen, the concern I knew he felt evident on his face. His irises glow indigo, and I realize that he's trying to free his future wife from the hold of our parents.

Until they appear behind him.

Kai stiffens, the color draining from his eyes, taking my hope with it.

"Take down the barrier, son," King Easton says, almost sounding like Labyrinth.

Kai doesn't so much as glance at his father. Instead, he gives me a look full of shame and sorrow as he lifts his hand. The tension tightens his face as the indigo light pulls into his trembling hand. Breathless, Kai doubles over, bracing his hands on his knees.

The kings and queens step inside the cramped room.

"No," Lilac cries out. "No!" Her voice is barely strong enough to shout. "Let me out!" She tries to thrash against the restraints, glaring at Leiana. "Mother! Mother, please!" Tears stream from her eyes. "I love someone, Mom," she whimpers. "*Please.*"

Leiana's face remains expressionless.

"Father!" Lilac begs. "Father, do something!"

"Son," the king of Folkara says.

Kai's face twists with turmoil. We both know who Lilac loves. When Kai looks at me, I know he's thinking of Calista.

But he steps forward, a foot from me, and takes one of Lilac's hands. His arm trembles, struggling against the magic binding my sister. Anyone other than a Light Folk would be electrocuted, but Kai withstands the currents.

"Kai, please!" Lilac begs.

"I told you she'd be a pain," Queen Melody mumbles.

Her words snap something inside of me. Slowly, I turn to her, my vision blurring with fury. "Excuse me?"

"Your sister should follow in your stead," Melody says.

She clasps her hands together, but my shadows surge to life around me. Then they coil around her and King Easton, darkness tightening at their throats until their strangled breaths echo through the small room. Leiana's lips curl into a cold smile—like she finds this entertaining.

"Lucian!" Lilac cries.

I press their necks tighter, the pressure of power pulsing within me. With every squeeze, I lose another breath of air, strangling my sanity.

Then I'm shoved into the wall, Kai standing in front of me as his hand grips the collar of my shirt. My shadows rise, but so do his currents. Lightning wraps around my chest, squeezing the air from my lungs, while my shadows tighten around his.

My heart pounds faster than ever. His fingers curl, twisting as if turning a rusted faucet. Sparks of electricity fill my chest until I can hardly feel it anymore.

He's going to give me a heart attack.

"Lucy!" Lilac shouts. "Someone, do something!"

I pull my shadows around Kai, choking him, stealing the air from his lungs. He coughs, his face turning bright red, but he doesn't let go. It's as if his hand is wrapped around my heart, squeezing tight, and I'm about to explode.

With the last of my strength, I grip his shirt and slam him against the wall, again and again, waiting for him to lose consciousness—to let me go. Blood splatters across the marble when his head hits it for the last time.

"Enough!" Labyrinth roars.

Both Kai and I release our magic, leaving me with the blissful emptiness of nothing. My entire body hums, as though this absence of magic is an enlightenment.

It's hard work to keep myself standing.

Laughter erupts from our parents, and I am left looking at the cold, bloodstained floor.

"Are you two done with your power-measuring contest?" Queen Melody says, as though the whole thing was amusing to her.

Why is she not mad that I bested her moments ago?

Neither of us responds—I'm not sure that I can—and she says, "Wonderful. Kai, seal the betrothal. And, Lucian?" She narrows her eyes at me, whispering, "Remember what we've given you."

As if I ever wanted their throne.

Lilac looks at the ceiling, her gaze held there against her will. Kai glares at his parents, mirroring the way I regard mine. He barely manages to step forward, take my sister's hand, and recite his vows.

---

The servants take Lilac to her room on Ilyria and bring her food, tea, and new clothes. She lies on her bed, the silence broken only by the growl of her stomach.

Our rooms in the kingdom no longer reflect who we are—or perhaps they never truly did. These are the finest rooms in the castle, with beds large enough to fit ten people, blankets crafted from the richest fabrics, and pure silver accents on every piece of furniture, art, and duvet.

Her room is adorned in pastel blue and cream, mirroring the dress she was meant to wear to our betrothal in Folkara.

When the servants clear away, she turns to me. "How could you act like that?"

"Which part?" I ask carefully.

Lilac sits up, folding her arms over her chest. Seeing her move, seeing her *breathe*, is enough to paralyze me with relief. "Attacking the only other two people who can make your life a nightmare!"

"I didn't attack Calista," I reply, forcing a smile.

"Calista wouldn't do anything akin to her parents."

Calista isn't a queen yet, nor am I a king. Who knows what we will become by then? If it's anything like what we discuss in War Strategy, it won't be good. Though, perhaps not as bad as the current rulers. That's the impractical hope I hold.

"You're right," I appease her. "She wouldn't."

Tears roll down Lilac's cheeks, left untouched as they fall. "I hate that she's half of me."

I settle on the edge of her bed, reaching for my sister's hand. "You'll never be like Leiana," I say firmly.

She *has* to know this. Yet, her bottom lip still wobbles.

"It's her power that runs through me." She shakes her head, avoiding my gaze. "I'm a *soul sucker*."

That's what some people call this power of Leiana's—and now Lilac's—soul sucking. It's the ability to steal a person's life force, draining the very essence that powers their magic and sustains their life. If anyone other than the current or future queens of Ilyria wielded such a deadly power, they'd likely be killed on the spot.

But I have to believe that Lilac won't use it as Leiana does. I have to believe in her heart.

"You'll never use it the way she does," I reassure her. When Lilac's glassy, red-rimmed eyes narrow in my direction, I squeeze her hand tighter. "It saved your life this time. Perhaps it will do so again."

She likely escaped the moonaro because it lacked the power to fight her—power she had taken for herself.

"I knew the moment it took hold," Lilac whispers, her head falling against the headboard with a dull thud. "My visions had already shown me the inevitable... They were pulling me out there. When I grabbed the moonaro, all I wanted was more. It felt vile, like sludge in my veins, but I still craved its power. When I tried to pull away, it lashed out—and honestly, I can't blame it." She wipes her eyes with the back of her hands. "I'm not sure I can blame Mother anymore."

Can't blame Mother? I shift in my seat. Can't blame Mother for the years of torment she's inflicted upon me?

But Lilac doesn't know the extent of what Leiana's done to me. I've protected her from that, at the very least. She only knows I had to watch Leiana take the prisoner's life force—not endure it.

"No, Lucy," She reaches for the wrist of my retreating form, but her eyes don't meet mine. "That's not what I meant."

"I'm glad you're awake, Li."

"That's not what I meant," she says again, grabbing my hand and holding it tightly.

"It's all right," I say. "I understand."

Lilac nods, though her frown remains heavy.

"There's another question I've been meaning to ask you," I continue. "Do you remember Desdemona?"

Her eyebrows draw together, a crease forming across her forehead. "Calista's roommate?"

"Is that *all* you remember?"

Lilac hesitates before faintly shaking her head. "Yeah. Why?"

"Just curious. Did anyone explain why it took you so long to wake up?"

"Yes," Lilac exhales, "Mother said something similar happened to her when she first discovered her power. They said I took more life force than what was sustainable for my body."

If that's true, that would mean the moonaro attacked because of what Lilac did to it, not another party's intervention.

*Not Desdemona.*

I push the thoughts aside and whisper, "Okay."

# Chapter 32
## No Future, No Past

# DESDEMONA

*The one who leaves returns alone.*

I've been trying to figure out the prophecy. I think it means my mom will come back with or without my intervention, but I don't know. As for *time shattering* and the *universe dividing,* I'm entirely stumped.

There's also *love being my demise* and all that. It must be about my mom. My love for her will take me to dark ends to get her back. Right?

I knock on Wendy's door, but when there's no answer, Calista suggests I check Azaire's room. Though I wonder if this is another trap from Lucian, there's no sensical way it could be, so I go.

I knock on another door, and a few minutes later, Wendy walks out, her hair messy and the top button of her uniform pants undone.

"Follow me," she instructs.

We walk to a corner of the garden. A fountain sits in the center, and the woods start just behind it, meaning we're within the barrier. The fountain must represent Zola, holding a scale in one hand—with the sun on one plate and the moon on the other—and tree roots coiled around her other arm. What more do I need to decipher the goddess of balance?

Wendy pulls off her gloves, saying, "I felt something when I channeled the prophecy. I can share it with you."

Of course she understood. I mean, what else do we have to talk about?

I grab her outstretched hands.

Then I have to let go. *I have to let go, but I can't.* It's like her hands are glue. I can feel my brain slowing, my hands going limp.

Agony splits through me, like there's a zipper down my body and someone's undone it and is *pulling me out*. The next part is agonizing loneliness, worse than I've ever known. It's debilitating. It's everyone I love and could have loved, dead. I'm stuck in a blank, empty room, and the only chair is their bodies stacked one on top of the other.

I rip my hands from Wendy's grip the second I'm able to, taking a deep breath to steady myself against the physical pain that still lingers.

When I can, I shout, "What the fuck was that?"

"Your prophecy," she answers, her eyes darting toward my chest. "It's what I felt when I channeled it."

"And you can just pull up that feeling whenever you want? *Give* it to someone else?"

"Pretty much." Wendy frowns.

I had no idea the Eunoia could share their emotions.

I frown too, asking, "You *feel* it?"

"I just did," she says plainly.

"I'm sorry," I croak.

Wendy shrugs it off, like it's inconsequential. But her eyes are hollow in the same way that feeling that prophecy must have made me look. "I'm surprised you weren't found out sooner," she whispers. "No one here says sorry."

Another bit of bullshit about this place. Basic human decency is beneath them. They aren't training future leaders here; they're making callous kids, then offering them crowns. It's no wonder our universe is so fucked up.

"Well, I am," I say, my voice steady.

I mean it. If she had to feel that pain on account of me, the least I can be is sorry.

"It's fine." Her voice doesn't sound fine. Her eyes cloud with emotion, and she avoids my gaze, as if saying more would be too much. "I've felt worse."

Worse? It wasn't just losing everything I ever wanted; it was pure agony. Is that what this prophecy means? Am I doomed to something even crueler than what I've already endured, over and over again? Leaving every village with my mom was painful, but this? This was something else entirely. This was death incarnate.

"What could be worse than that?" I ask, the words falling from my lips, each syllable more fractured than the last.

But Wendy looks me dead in the eye as she says, "The real thing." Her voice is sharp, yet steeped in sadness. Then her eyes drop, again, to my chest. "Time fractures with the stone—it's the catalyst for the prophecy." She lifts a finger, pointing at me. "It could be the one you wear."

Instinctively, I reach for it. I thought I'd kept it hidden. It feels like the pendant is heating up, trying to burn my skin as punishment for being so careless. I guess it's just my guilt over my mom manifesting. She told me to keep it hidden.

I have no idea how Wendy saw it.

"What kind of stone is it?" she asks, her gaze sharpening.

"It was my mom's," I answer.

"Why do you wear it under your shirt?"

*And why does this feel like an interrogation?*

"To keep it safe." My grasp on the stone tightens. "It's all I have left of her."

"Is it the Memorium?" she asks.

What an absolutely ridiculous question. She actually thinks *I* have a Soul Stone, one of the most powerful artifacts in the universe?

"You do know I'm from the septic, right?"

"Answer the question," Wendy says, her green eyes glowing.

422

I think it's a threat. She's trying to see if I'm lying.

*As if I'm scared of such a docile creature.*

My power courses through me, heat flooding my bones. I laugh at the ridiculous idea that *she* could best me and say, "It's not the Memorium." My tone goes so bitter that I have to spit the words out, "We don't get to keep the precious stones; we only mine them."

"The Memorium is a Soul Stone," Wendy replies, like I'm dense.

"All the more reason I can't get my grubby hands on it." I can't stop myself from sneering at her. "Thanks for showing me the rest of the prophecy." I don't feel very thankful as I walk away. It just felt like death.

But I stop when the wind kicks up, coming from the direction of the woods. As I turn to face the trees, not a single gust touches my skin. Only the whispering reaches me—growing stronger with each step I take toward the woods.

*"Help us,"* I think it says.

"What is it?" Wendy asks.

My eyes stay locked on the trees as I mutter, "You should go."

"What's out there?" she demands.

"Nothing."

"It's certainly something. I can *feel* you," she says, just as a dark-gray cloud of smoke with four, long arms hovers toward us.

*"Help me."*

So it has been the monsters—this whispering that's haunted me for months, that's only now becoming coherent.

Its tentacle-like arms stretch toward me while the wind pleads. I reach for them, too. I have to hear what it has to say to me.

The monster locks eyes with me, and I return the stare, just like I did with the moonaro. My hand settles at the center of its body, which towers at least a head above me. I hadn't expected the roughness of its scales.

Out of nowhere, roots erupt from the ground, followed by branches that coil tightly around the monster's hovering form. The creature writhes, struggling against the tree's tight grip.

*Wendy.*

She just saw everything—maybe felt it, too.

"Thanks," I say, playing it cool, just as Wendy says, "We need to drain its blood."

Every monster has a specific way it must be killed. Fail, and the magic will bring it back to life. I'm glad one of us knows what we're fighting, but neither of us has a weapon. And, more importantly, I need to get rid of Wendy.

"Go to Leiholan," I tell her.

We need a weapon. But I'm not sure I want to kill it.

When the creature shatters its bonds and breaks free, it hovers toward Wendy, moving wildly through the air.

"Go!" I scream.

Wendy looks at me like I have two heads, but in the end, she nods and runs for the school. I grab hold of the creature. It doesn't resist. Its head swivels toward me, ready to listen, I think.

"Help you what?" I whisper.

The creature seems to soften, almost relieved, as if it's been waiting for me to ask. *"Causer of our pain, you are,"* it hisses in my mind.

"Me? Why me?"

The creature shakes its head slowly, its dark eyes blinking in what almost seems like sorrow. *"Never could we act for us."*

"Then why did you pass the barrier? *How* did you?"

*"No more."*

"The barrier is broken?" I ask, trying to get a clear answer and straying further from it.

*"For you, pain awaits. Free us and accept. Your fire draws you closer to the home."*

"That's it?" I say a little louder than necessary. "That's what you've been trying to say to me? That makes *no sense.*"

*"Not me,"* it says. *"Our master."*

I grip the creature harder, pulling it closer to me as I step forward. "Who is your master?" I beg.

The creature only shakes his head.

"Is this a prophecy or something?" I ask. I can't do another one of those.

*"Not future,"* it says. *"Now."*

Then, right in front of me, a tree rips itself from the ground, its roots writhing like living things as it wraps its branches around the creature, subduing it.

I stumble back, crashing into Leiholan. He shoves me aside and unsheathes a sword I've never seen before. The blade isn't silver—and not by design—it's rusted away, unsharpened and forgotten.

Leiholan steps forward, moving toward the tree.

Something cracks—a deeply unsettling sound, like bones snapping.

Leiholan lifts his sword.

Another sharp snap.

Then a *snake* breaks through the trunk of the tree. Two of the monster's four arms slither out from the gap, twisting toward us with inhuman speed.

One tentacle lashes right for me, and in a moment, Leiholan is in front of me. It wraps around his calf with bone-crushing force, and he screams. Then he collapses.

I look to Wendy, waiting for her to do something, to save him. But her hands drop to her stomach, and she crashes to her knees, gasping like there's no air in her lungs.

Then the tree snaps in half with a crack that sounds so… alive.

Leiholan drags across the ground, Wendy is still sprawled out, and all I've got are my throwing knives.

I quickly unsheath one, gripping it by its tip and closing one eye. It's just a possum, I tell myself. A possum that Damien barely electrocuted and happens to move faster than I can.

I release the blade, somehow severing the arm that drags Leiholan. But the snake—the monster's tongue, I realize—takes its place. The snake bites so deep into Leiholan's leg that I'm not sure he's going to get to keep it—if he gets to keep his life at all.

He's yanked violently along the ground, his body passing over rocks with a sickening scrape. The remaining three arms of the monster uncoil, wrapping around Leiholan as he disappears into the tendrils tightening around him.

*With the sword we need to kill it.*

I run, throwing knife after knife. Then the snake lunges for my head. I fling a knife straight into its eye, but its tongue coils around my neck. I thrash and claw at the dry, rough thing, but it's no use.

And suddenly, I don't seem to care at all! This is funny. I'm being choked to death; I know *that,* but I'm entirely at peace with it. The suffocating stillness in my lungs feels strangely comfortable. Death is the only promise, and I'm just happy that something is being promised at all.

Stars dance across my vision as everything fades. There's nothing I can do, and I'm okay with it.

I'm happy I finally get to rest.

Darkness takes over, and I revel in it, the quiet consuming me entirely.

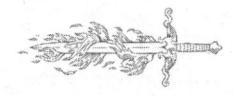

---

When my vision clears, a tree branch clings to me, the world tilting as it moves toward me, then away. Everything spins, making me dizzy, but I catch a glimpse of two severed tentacles beside Wendy, her hands glowing green with power. I take a deep breath, my gaze shifting toward the monster. I'd forgotten about the fight.

I was at peace with death. If it weren't for Wendy, I would have died without any resistance. I don't understand why. I don't know why I didn't fight.

From the ground, two trees grow, reaching toward the monster. They pull at the last of its limbs—one final arm.

Leiholan tumbles out, unconscious. His leg is severed just above the knee, the bottom half hanging by a thread while blood pours from him at too rapid a pace.

He's going to die, and I don't want him to.

Wendy grabs the sword from Leiholan's limp body, her fingers tightening around the hilt as she raises it high above her head. She plunges the blade into the center of the creature.

With a sharp, jerking twist, she drags the sword downward, carving through the monster's flesh. Blood sprays out from the wound, coating Wendy—her arms, her chest, and face. She gives the sword one last push. The tip of the blade emerges from the other side, dripping with blood and guts.

The monster shudders, its black and blue intestines spilling to the ground as it collapses. Wendy stumbles back, her knees buckling as she falls. She clutches her stomach, gasping for breath, her face twisted in pain.

I run to Leiholan, dropping to my knees beside him and shaking him roughly. "Come on, Leiholan," I mutter, but I already know—he won't walk again. His leg is... I could tear it apart with a flick of my finger.

His pulse is faint, barely there. I press harder against his skin, begging for life to return to him.

"You have to heal him!" I shout, turning to Wendy.

Her breaths are shallow, and suddenly I'm not sure she can do anything.

"Leiholan?" I slap his cheek. "Open your eyes!" Slap, slap, slap. "Now!"

*He can't leave me. Not yet.*

Blood gushes from his leg like a waterfall, pooling beneath me into an overflowing river.

I turn to Wendy and hold out my hand. "Channel me," I say. "Use my power."

Her eyes meet mine, the green of her irises duller than before. But she nods, her movements sluggish as she stands, walking slowly to sit beside me. Slowly, she pulls off one glove and takes my hand.

From the moment my skin touches hers, it feels like life itself is draining from me. My heartbeat falters, slowing to match the faint, dying rhythm of Leiholan's. A pit forms in my stomach, nausea rising with a force I can't control. When I finally puke, Wendy lets go of my hand, and it all dissipates.

I had no idea channeling power felt like that.

Wendy gives me an odd look, sizing me up. It reminds me of the way I looked at her earlier: shocked by her true power. Then she grabs one of Leiholan's arms and pulls him halfway upright, gesturing to me to grab his other side.

Together, we carry his limp body to the school, his barely attached leg dragging behind us. Blood splashes against my ankles as I step through the crimson puddles. With every rock his foot hits, I worry his leg will fall right off.

We drag him into a room filled with plants and herbs lining the wooden walls—the school's infirmary. Three Eunoia rush around us, pulling him into a room and onto a bed, but no more come.

He's going to need more of them.

Wendy nods to me once, her face still covered in blood, then leaves. I follow into the room where Leiholan lies.

One of the Eunoia says to me, "We can't mend his leg."

I recognize her. She told me Lilac was attacked by a monster from Ilyria.

"But he'll live?" I ask.

The woman sprinkles powder over his leg. *I don't know how*

*that could help.*

"Possibly."

Her hands glow green, and the bleeding from Leiholan's leg begins to slow, the Eunoias' magic working its way through his damaged body. But the three healers quickly stop working, heading for the door. The bleeding hasn't even stopped.

"You're done?" I call, my voice sharp as I stop the woman in her tracks.

"The next group will come in soon," she replies, her tone matter-of-fact and her eyes distant—emotionless.

I glance between Leiholan and the door the Eunoia tries to escape from.

"But he's still bleeding."

She offers a solemn shake of her head. "We can't risk burnout."

"What about his life?" My voice rises despite my best efforts to keep it steady.

"It's up to Zola now," she says to me like I'm a child. "He's lost a lot of blood."

"Then give him more blood!" I thrust my arm toward her. "Give him *my* blood."

"The Folk can't give to Nepenthes." She stares, her expression frozen in shock, as if my offer is absurd.

"Please," I whisper, "just keep him breathing."

She frowns, and for the first time, emotion floods her gaze. I wonder what they teach the Eunoia—how they prepare them for the grief of losing so many. How they teach them to shut it all out.

The Eunoia are natural empaths. If they didn't protect themselves, they'd feel it all—and I think the healer before me is doing just that.

She turns, quietly locking the door. "There are rules about what we're allowed to do to heal the Nepenthes."

"Okay," I answer, but she locked the door, so I know there's more.

She exhales a trembling breath. "You're a Fire Folk, aren't you?" the healer finally whispers, and I nod. "If you cauterize his wound, that's his best chance of survival."

Me. *I'm* Leiholan's best chance.

I stare at my hands like they are... what they are.

The enemy and now the savior.

"I—" My voice cracks. "I can't."

"It will take at least three rounds for us to stop the bleeding, and I don't believe he has the time."

My breaths grow shallow and uneven, coming too fast and returning too slow. "He'll die if I don't?" I ask, even though I understand her.

"Possibly."

"Can you look away?"

The healer nods sympathetically before turning her back. I unsheathe one of my throwing knives, the blade gleaming faintly, and draw another shaky breath. All the ways this could go wrong flash before my eyes. I could end up killing him, like everyone else.

I should just leave this to the healers. They know what they're doing. I sheathe my knife again, my fingers lingering on the cold steel, and I'm about to tell the healer I can't do it when I notice Leiholan's shallow breathing. A knot tightens in my chest. I can't help but think of the last time I saw him. I was about to *fight* him. And for what? I can barely recall.

What I can recall is the headmistress handing me another, bigger, dagger.

"Without wounding yourself this time," she had said, and I grabbed it by the blade. "Magic is a tool. You don't learn to build a kingdom before you can quarry your marble." Her eyes met mine as my blood spilled on her carpet. "You can withstand the blood, but can you control the heat?" she whispered. "Focus on the metal in your hands. Your energy will go where your attention flows."

All I thought about was the metal. And the blood.

Now, I stand before Leiholan, unsheathing my knife again and cutting open both my palms. The blade presses so deep that I have to bite my tongue to keep from gasping. *There has to be a better way of doing this,* I think as I press my bleeding hands to Leiholan's severed leg.

Fire fills my entire body until my eyes are just prickly balls of ember and sweat drips down my forehead like I'm nothing but a blazing bundle.

My hands are so hot I can't tell if it hurts or if it's just invigorating.

The heat intensifies, and I fear I might burn Leiholan alive instead of saving his life like I'm supposed to. When I'm sure that I'm going to hurt him, I pull my hands away.

The stump of his leg is a blistered, bloodied mess—swollen and charred. It's gruesome, but better than the gore before.

"I'm done," I say, my voice shaking as dried blood flakes off my hands.

The healer turns around, examining my work. She leans in, inspecting the stump closely. "You did well."

With that, she leaves the room.

Another team of three arrives a few minutes later. They exchange confused glances, then turn to me and resume their healing.

I hope they take his pain.

The woman from before comes back with a knife and a pair of scissors. I look away while she cuts the rest of his leg off.

"We called for more healers after the princess was attacked," she says, her gaze focused on Leiholan.

But I see her words for what they are: a distraction. I guess it's supposed to be kind.

"I heard there've been a few attacks lately," I say.

"There have been. My sister works on the council in

Eunaris."

The Eunoia's homeworld. I've heard a bit about their council and government. It's strange—nothing like the monarchy of Folkara. It's a group of two hundred men and women, a few from every village, who come together to make decisions for their world's greatest good.

"They're trying to figure out why the monsters are attacking again," she says.

"It's been months, and they still don't know?" I ask.

"Nature is slow."

*Great answer, thanks.*

---

It's the middle of the night by the time Leiholan wakes. There's been an announcement declaring that the entire academy is in lockdown and we have to stay in our rooms, but nothing was said about the monster attack.

I don't understand why they're keeping it a secret. The people need to know.

"Oh, gods," he groans, twisting his neck back and forth. "Where's my vesi?" Then he glances down, and his eyes widen. He sounds less groggy when he says, "Where's my leg?"

"Maybe in a cooler somewhere," I say.

His eyes narrow at me. "Desdemona," Disappointment laces his voice like venom.

I try not to frown, but it's even harder to keep the sorrow from my voice. "Yep. Desdemona."

"Thought you were someone else," he mutters and closes his eyes again.

"Well, I'm not." My throat burns. "But I did just save your life, so maybe I could get something more than that?"

Leiholan lifts his chin high, frowning, but not unhappily. He's only assessing me. I've seen this face many times. "Bullshit."

"Yeah," I say hastily. "I did." I don't like him one bit. But I care about him more than I disdain him. "Doesn't mean I like you."

"I find you uniquely unpleasant, too, sweetheart." He raises a soft finger with his words. "Where's my vesi?"

"Are you not concerned by your missing leg?"

"Alcohol first, missing limb second," he mutters with a yawn as his finger falls to the bed.

A few seconds later, he snores.

## Chapter 33
### Remember The Pact of Our Youth

# LUCIAN

There's a bottle of vesi in my hand when Azaire walks into my room.

We haven't spoken deeper than surface level since I tortured Freyr—who is still in the dungeon beneath the academy.

It would be a shame if a monster got to him before I did.

Azaire slips in quietly, slumping against the wall. "Can I have some?" he mutters, his words soft.

I hand him the bottle, and he takes a long, deep swig—longer than I've ever seen him drink. He gulps it down, then he belches, a sound that shocks him more than me.

Azaire wipes his mouth as he hands the bottle back. "I think Wendy broke up with me."

The words hang heavy between us, and I shift, unsure if anything I say can smooth them over.

"Why would you think that?"

Azaire shifts, tugging at his shirt as if he can't quite sit still. "She came asking about the rose amulet she gave me," he mutters, as if that alone should explain everything.

"I don't follow."

He exhales sharply, and his voice drops lower. "The lockdowns are because of the monsters. She fought the one that got past the barrier."

"I still don't follow."

He rubs his eyes, twisting Wendy's preserved rose between his restless fingers. "It was the way she spoke. The amulet is some sort of protection token, and... I don't know. She wasn't telling me something. There were gaps in her story." He pauses, looking up at me with tired, bloodshot eyes. "She still hasn't told me she loves me."

I open my mouth, but hesitation knots my words. What could I say? That you don't need words to show love? It feels cliché at best, hollow at worst.

Azaire shakes his head with a heavy sigh before continuing, "It's not that I don't think she loves me. I just don't think she believes in me the way I believe in her."

I take another drink, the room tilting slightly. Then the bottle slips back into Azaire's hands.

"Look, I'm the last person you want relationship advice from," I mutter. "But perhaps you should talk to her."

"I talk to her all the time, Luc." He leans forward. "I *know* her. Something's different, and I'm not sure if it has to do with me." After taking another sip, he says, "I think she thinks I'm weak."

"Show her your snakes again," I suggest, though I've never seen them myself. In fact, Wendy is the only person alive who has.

Azaire tugs at his beanie, frowning. "Normally I feel free with her. It's okay that it feels different now. Things change—and no matter what happens, I'll still love her. I know that. Even when I feel like this."

"How do you feel?"

His eyes wander around the dim room. This is the expression he wears when he doesn't want to admit something.

He exhales sharply, running a hand down his face. For a moment, I think he won't answer. Then, quieter, "Incapable." The word lingers on his tongue before his face twists, as it tastes bitter. "But–but I don't blame her for that."

"Zaire, you are the most capable person I know," I say when he's finished. "If Wendy thinks you're weak, that only means she has more to learn of you." Anyone who has endured what Azaire has and turned it into something that makes them stronger can't be called weak.

"I don't know what she's thinking right now. Maybe that's part of the problem. She always knows what I'm feeling and…" He drinks, then laughs to himself. "She'd gladly give up that power, and I'm wishing I had it, just for her."

I lean toward him, plucking the bottle from his hands. Alcohol never sits well with Azaire; it amplifies his doubt.

He turns the rose between his fingers again, slower this time, like he's afraid of crushing it.

"I want to go back to yesterday," Azaire mumbles. "Everything changed today."

Yes, it did, but in a way that's far different for me than for him.

Gently, I ask, "You said she fought another monster?"

"A kapha," he replies. "She washed the blood off in our bathroom."

Wendy's becoming quite the fighter—first a pernipe, now a kapha. No one would expect that from a Eunoia. Then again, no one would expect a Nepenthe to be so soft-natured either, yet here Azaire is, sitting across from me.

With a sigh, I sit beside him. "Monster or not, killing's never easy," I say. He knows it. We both do. "Wendy's empathic power means she feels everything. It's different for her. What she said that made you feel incapable? Perhaps it was her way of saying she doesn't want you to have to kill."

Azaire stares at me for a long while, his eyes searching mine. Then, he asks, "Can I have more vesi?" He takes another drink, letting out a hollow laugh. "You sound more like me than you."

"I should hope so," I shrug. "I could stand to be a little more like you."

But the thought slips away with the room, my vision blurring as it morphs into the academy hallways. A vision. Azaire stands beside me, but this version of him wields a sword. We fight in a blur of steel and instinct. In the end, I stand over the fatta scorpion's corpse, its heart in my hand, its blood on my sword. Another fatta stands frozen, turned to stone.

I know what this means. The monsters will breach the last of the academy's protective shields, and Azaire and I are going to kill two of them.

This could be my only chance to uncover why they are here. To find out what happened to Lilac and how Desdemona is involved with the monsters.

The vision fades, and my room reassembles itself, like pieces of a puzzle being returned to their rightful place. Azaire watches me closely.

"What was it?" he asks, knowing when I slip in and out of my visions.

"There's something we have to do tonight."

I lay out a collection of swords on my bed and ask Azaire, "Which do you want?"

"I don't know about this," he mutters, even as he hones a sword. "It's a *fatta scorpion*. Those things are, like, borderline mythical."

"Exactly!" I exclaim. "That's why we do it together, like always." I pour honing oil on my sharpening stone and gesture to Azaire. "At least let me sharpen that old thing for you." I already know he'll take the short sword—and it suits him. That's the weapon he held in the vision.

He pauses before saying, "You know the consequences."

The fatta scorpion isn't only deadly—it has soul-ceasing venom within its stingers. Known as filumaniram, the venom's name roughly translates to "shredder of souls." Not that it's a concern.

"Consequences be damned," I mutter. "I've seen how this plays out. We win, game over."

Azaire rests the sword on his knees. "That's not exactly your best strategy."

"Happens to be my favorite." I smile, meeting his gaze. "No surrender."

"Why are you so set on this, Luc? Just because you have a vision doesn't mean you have to follow through." He sighs. "You can let the future be what it is without trying to tamper with it. I kind of worry about your choices lately."

By "lately," he means since I found out about the engagements. I may be acting recklessly, but I'm not blind to it. I see the path I'm going down. When your life isn't your own, you'll do anything to hang on to that last bit of control you have.

At least I will.

"It's about taking some agency," I say. "Let the consequences be damned because there won't *be* any. We'll kill it, then you and Wendy can talk about your shared experience."

Azaire lowers his head, pressing his lips together, his gaze fixed on the floor. Slowly, he says, "She doesn't want me involved. That's what made me feel weak. She doesn't think I can do what she did yesterday."

"Then show her you can." I sharpen my blade, then pause. It wouldn't be right to pull Azaire into this fight under false pretenses. I don't simply want to kill a monster; I seek to do what he warned me against.

I wish to alter the course of the future.

I think about telling Azaire it's my battle, that he doesn't need to join. But he *does*. The vision showed that one fatta was killed by his snakes. If he's not there, I don't know what will happen.

"I'm going to get inside the fatta's subconscious," I tell him. "Find out why the monsters have come."

"I see," Azaire responds flatly, yet he doesn't object. He witnessed what the monsters did to Lilac, and now the turmoil they've stirred in Wendy. He, too, must want to understand their objective.

"I didn't tell you before," I begin, my voice low, "but I had a vision of Desdemona. She *talked* to the moonaro."

*That's* why I have to fight the fatta scorpion. It might know more—something I've missed—and I have every promise we'll walk away from it unscathed.

Azaire stiffens, his expression shifting as he understands the gravity of my words. "Luc, that's..." He shakes his head. "That's huge. Why didn't you tell me?"

I look past him, afraid of what I'll see if I don't. "A part of me wished to handle it alone. A larger part hoped I was wrong. This fatta is the only way to know for certain."

This is my one chance to find out—for once and for all—what Desdemona is truly here for. Why every rule about the Arcanes seems to bend around her. And what, if anything, can be done about it.

Handing Azaire the short sword, I say, "No surrender, right?"

At first, the short sword looks awkward in his hands, but he fixes his grip and becomes every bit the fighter I saw in my vision. In a way, though, it looks wrong. He's not a fighter.

"No surrender," Azaire says, shaking my doubt.

---

With blades drawn, Azaire and I move cautiously through the academy's silent, shadowed halls. Every lamp has been turned off, making the crescent moon and glowing trees the only offering of light.

"I don't think anything's here," Azaire says cautiously, pausing at the west wing.

"I can feel it."

A heat pulses through me in stark contrast to Desdemona's

warmth. While she feels like the sun's gentle rays, this burns like the smoldering of a soul.

As the heat intensifies, I know we're drawing nearer.

When we round the final corner, a creature stands ahead, far uglier than any depiction we studied in class.

I resist the urge to shut my eyes, overwhelmed by the sting of its power. Its enormous form looms above us, a long, soul-ceasing stinger hanging just a foot above its body, while six limbs click and scrape against the stone floor as it draws closer. Its shell is a dark, murky red, the color deepening at the bottom of its limbs.

Azaire turns to me, and I nod, prepared to fight. Shadows wrap around the fatta's stinger, and with a shrill cry, it rises onto its back four legs. I swing at its claw, the clash ringing like I've hit full metal armor. The fatta's heat pours down my blade, and I fight to hold onto the burning sword while I cover it in shadows.

But I'm not fast enough.

The beast's strike burns as it hurls me across the room. I slam into a marble bust, then crash to the floor, my head smacking against the cold stone. The world blurs around me as Azaire charges toward the fatta, leaping onto its back. From the floor, I work to restrain the venomous stinger, then the claws, and the fatta struggles under the chill of my power.

Azaire strikes with his sword. A sickening crunch—like brittle bones snapping—echoes through the hallway. The fatta jerks up in response, throwing Azaire off its body and slamming him to the floor.

Every ounce of my sanity screams at me to trap the venomous stinger. Yet, as the creature rises and stalks toward Azaire, it forces its way past my shadows.

I struggle to my feet, deliberately scraping my longsword across the floor, drawing the monster's attention. The fatta turns away from Azaire, and I swing again as a distraction.

The stinger raises, aimed directly at me.

I lunge into its mind, and the sensation is like swallowing a searing ember. The deeper I delve, the more the burn fades, replaced by a growing ache.

*Come on.*

The pain presses against me. It's a deep hunger, a dark desire. A dream of freedom. The beast is just as trapped as I am.

Then the stinger shoots toward me, poised to stab, to steal my soul.

It's a split second from impaling me—

"*Stop,*" I command when I've finally anchored myself into the monster's mind. "*Be still.*"

The fatta freezes.

"*Can you speak to me?*" I look into its black, beady eyes as it tries to move but fails. "*Answer me!*" I demand.

"*Yes.*" The voice in my head is delicate, far more fragile than I expected. "*I speak.*"

"*Why are you here?*"

"*I feel you in my mind, Sulva's child,*" the fatta whispers. "*You know these actions are not of my desire.*"

"*Whose desires are they?*" I press, struggling to maintain my control. My physical body strains as my mind desperately holds onto the fatta's. "*Is it Desdemona?*"

"*It is not the child. It is the master. The barrier is breaking; the borders are crumbling. That is the desire.*"

"*What borders?*" My voice trembles, even through the mental link.

"*Universal.*"

"*You're breaking universal borders?*"

"*Not us,*" it sings.

"*Who?*" I beg, my hold on the monster faltering.

"*You know.*"

I'm about to ask for clarification when the connection snaps, my control withering away. The fatta's legs move; its claws shake, and the stinger bounces.

*"Hold still,"* I demand, though I have no power over the beast anymore.

The fatta's claw swings at me.

"Zaire!" I shout, raising my sword just in time to block the blow. Its stinger lunges toward me, aimed straight at my chest. Just as it's about to pierce, it halts mid-air.

I step back, the stinger grazing my skin—barely brushing death.

"Zaire, beanie off!" I shout, my voice strained as I raise my hand, summoning the shadows to form a shield around us.

*"You do me a favor, Lucian Aibek. Fighting you was against my duties."* The fatta's vibrant red fades as its body stiffens into stone.

I wish it wasn't dead. I want to know more. It isn't Desdemona that controls them, but it's certainly someone.

Luckily, there will be a second fatta.

Azaire lets out a small groan, and I turn to him, ready to come up with our next plan and tell him what I've heard.

Only, he isn't.

A small stinger, half the size of the fatta's we'd just defeated, sinks itself into Azaire's stomach. He's looking down at the stinger, then he's looking into my eyes, tears falling as his mouth opens wide in shock.

The snakes on his head hang limp. Dead.

"Azaire!"

I run to him, slicing through the stinger. A guttural cry roars from the fatta behind me. Azaire falls to the floor, and the sound echoes through the hallway.

*What have I done?*

My shadows push the smaller fatta into place as I drive my sword into its heart, grinding it against the filthy creature's shell. Then I shove my hand into the beast's chest and rip out its heart, twice the size of my bloodied hand.

This is it—the vision I saw.

It didn't feel this painful.

Dropping the heart, I run to Azaire. *I run to my brother.*

I scoop his bloodied body into my arms and continue running. "You're not going to die," I promise him.

Azaire coughs, blood spewing from his mouth. "Don't lie to me." His voice is already weak.

"It's not a lie," I proclaim.

But it is, isn't it? We're too far from the infirmary to make it before he bleeds out. The stinger pierced straight through his body; I can feel it poking my torso as I run.

"Please," he coughs, "stop."

"What?" I keep running.

"Just let it be peaceful," he whispers, the blood in his mouth forcing out a sickening gurgling sound with the words.

"What?" Tears sting my eyes, but I blink them away as I run.

"Look at me, Luc."

His voice is so weak that there's no way I can't do what he's asking of me. I stop against my will and look into his glassy—soon to be lifeless—eyes.

*No.* He'll make it. He has to make it.

There isn't a world where he won't make it. There isn't a time—there isn't a universe where he dies, where he doesn't exist.

I won't allow it.

I force shadows into every inch of his bleeding wound. It stanches some of the bleeding but not a worthy percentage.

*Even magic can't fix fatality.*

Mortality.

The stinger is too far into his body.

*No.*

"I'm ready to surrender." Azaire grabs my arm, but his grip is loose. Lifeless. "I surrender," he whispers again, weakly nodding his head.

"No," I shout. "*No!* You're not dying because of me!"

"I love you, brother," he whispers, his eyes shuddering closed while he strains to keep them open. His hand slips down my arm, trying to clasp onto me but failing to hold on. I pick up his limp hand for him. "It's not"—Azaire chokes—"your fault." His eyes open for one, single second. "I'll never blame you."

I run again for the infirmary. They can do something. The Eunoia are *made* to heal. They can mend him.

Blood oozes from his mouth. "It doesn't hurt, Luc," Azaire whispers. I can barely hear him. "Peace." His eyes are closed, and his red mouth is open. His heart is beating. It won't be for long, will it?

*I surrender.* Those words permeate my brain. *Peace.* I suppose I can give him peace.

I lay him down on the floor and pull the stinger from his body, praying that the venom hasn't spread enough to cause permanent damage to his soul. I hold his hand, hoping I can offer my brother some semblance of his final wish in his final breaths.

## Chapter 34
## Death Does You Well

# DESDEMONA

I've finally given in to Leiholan's *incessant* whining about vesi. Besides, the cold sweats, vomiting, and night terrors aren't pretty. I'm sure every healer in the infirmary agrees with me.

The man just lost his leg, and all I have to offer are the three bottles of alcohol I grabbed from the combat room.

When I step into the halls, brown hair streaked with blonde catches my eye, shining in the faint moonlight spilling through the windows. No one's supposed to be out, but I haven't seen my room since the lockdown, so who am I to judge?

The curls shift, revealing a familiar face. "Desdemona?" the girl calls.

It's Eleanora. Why would Eleanora be talking to me?

"Yeah?"

"It's you?" She takes a step closer, and two more people step out of the shadows.

"Why?" I ask wearily.

*Do I really have to do this again?*

At least I have my knives.

"You're hard to find!" she exclaims, laughing. "Why ever are you so hard to find?"

"You know the school is in lockdown, right?" I take a step back.

When there's no response, the phantom of fear creeps over me, and I turn the other way. I can just take the long way back to the infirmary.

But a hand spins me around, and I'm face-to-face with Eleanora. My fingers reach for the sheath at my side.

"Come with us, and we won't do any more damage." Her voice deepens, turning toneless. Eleanora's mouth smiles, but the rest of her remains rigid.

In one swift motion, I pull out a knife and shove it into Eleanora's shoulder. The vesi bottles shatter at my feet, and I'm careful not to slip as I shove her and run. But my feet go numb. It's not the tickling kind that can be shaken off but the kind that makes me wonder if I'll ever walk again.

I begin to fall.

Eleanora steps in front of me, and the others rush up from behind, four hands gripping me to keep me upright. She pulls the knife from her shoulder, blood spraying across my neck. Her wound closes almost instantly.

The tip of my dagger draws a line from under my eye to my jaw, drawing blood. I can't suppress the sharp, "Ah!" that escapes my lips.

"Do you prefer pain?" Eleanora's soft voice is back. "From here, it seems like it. Everywhere you go, you institute it."

I grab Eleanora's wrist, the one clutching my blade, and twist as hard as I can. The dagger falls to the floor. Then I bite my free hand until the metallic taste of blood finds my tongue, and the wound begins to cauterize. Pain surges through me as fire courses through my hand, and I shove it in her face.

This time, *she* screams, and it's music to my ears. The stench of burning flesh floods my senses, but I don't move.

Then my hand goes numb, just like my feet, and I worry I'll need three amputations by the end of this fight.

*My penance for taking Jermoine's arms.*

Eleanora's body is shaking while a shadow writhes just beneath her skin, like it's trying to force its way *out* of her.

"Bacstair, Eaman!" she screams. "Exit!" The two kids behind

me collapse, and I topple onto their bodies.

I don't feel them breathing.

Eleanora falls next to me and manages to fix me with a glare. This close to her, I notice that her eyes aren't brown anymore—they're red. The same red as the men who took my mom, and the man I killed in my dwelling.

"Power, dear child, is not your saving grace," she whispers.

Reality hits me with stunning ease. "You're one of the Arcane," I murmur.

Eleanora smiles, but it feels like someone else is staring through her eyes. Her face is nothing but boils and seared flesh.

Because she's possessed—they all were.

"What do you know of my power?" I ask.

"What your mother never told you," the Arcane hisses.

"I'll go with you." I hold out my hand, but she doesn't take it, so I grab Eleanora's instead. "*Take me.* I'll go."

"Can't you see it's too late for me?" Eleanora's hand pulls away from mine. "I happen to be the most benevolent of us. In death, I will tell you. When you come to The Void, as we know you shall, you will be forgotten by all… but not by your mother. Now, end me for my mercy."

"End you?"

"*Kill* me. I no longer wish to reside in this wretched body."

I blink, drawing in a deep, shaking breath.

"Do not worry about the Folk," Eleanora's strained voice says. "It is rare to survive possession."

I freeze. I'm being asked to murder. I don't know how.

I don't *want* to know how.

It's not Eleanora's voice that roars, *"Do it!"*

I don't know if it's fear or power that drives me to think of her burning the way the man in my dwelling did—the orange and gray shadow that escaped him in death—and to decide to do the same to her. White-hot fire surges through my body, and I can feel my limbs again as I watch what has to be some small part of the real Eleanora's eyes go wide with the realization that she's going to die with the Arcane.

A dark orange shadow spills from her body, solidifying as it rolls over me. I struggle free from its dead weight and look down at the massacre.

*My* massacre.

Eleanora's face might be badly burnt and unrecognizable. There might have been an *Arcane* within her body. But in the end, I killed her. I wonder if I'm responsible for the deaths of the two students I was just lying on top of. I check for pulses, desperate for any sign of life.

Nothing.

Four bodies in front of me.

Eight in total. I've killed enough people to fill two families. What about *their* families? I imagine their parents crying over a letter, insincerely written by the headmistress, letting them know that their child is dead. Is this what Breck's parents felt? His siblings and friends?

Who *am* I? I told myself I would never do what I did in my dreams, but every day I come closer to that person. I best her in barbarity.

Is this what it means to value my survival above theirs?

Is this what it means to be human?

And yet, with all this guilt, I'm also wondering if this could look like a monster attack because I worry about cleaning these bodies and getting back to Leiholan.

*This* could've been Leiholan yesterday. What if I cared about these people? Because there *are* people who care about them, and I'm responsible for their pain. If I could, would I bear it for them?

I don't think I would. The pain I carry is too much, yet here I am, delivering it to others a thousand times over.

One by one, I drag each body into the woods. I give each of their faces one last good look, committing them to memory, vowing to carry them. Because that's the price I pay for every death, isn't it? Killing is a promise that I will hold them for the rest of my life—because what else could it be?

Luckily, I'm not far from the training room, so I grab Leiholan three more bottles of vesi, using one to douse the dead. I take a deep breath, struggling as I force myself to kneel before the bodies I've gathered.

*It's okay. I'm not afraid anymore.*

That's a lie, but I repeat it anyway as I summon the fire and guide it to the massacre.

The heat burns my face, but I sit a foot from it, forcing myself to smell the acrid smoke that comes from their burning flesh. It's what I have to do—it's what killing entails.

Punishment.

## Chapter 35
## The Only Thing I Know Is That I Know Nothing

# LUCIAN

A single word echoes in the hollow silence: "No."

"No, no, no."

Wendy lowers herself beside me. She touches Azaire's snakes as if they're alive, his face like he's breathing, his mouth like it's smiling.

But he's not. And he never will be.

"How long?" she whispers.

"It's too late." If the stinger has deposited its venom—and it surely has—there's no way it hasn't spread.

I cradle Azaire's dead body and *soul* in my lap.

He's gone.

"I won't accept that," Wendy says as she picks up half his lifeless body. I do the same, unsure if our desperation will make a difference.

*I killed him.*

This is all my doing.

Wendy leads the way into the woods, and I follow in silence.

This is all my fault.

The foul stench of burning flesh fills the outside air, and for a fleeting moment, I wonder if this is all but a dream. I'd like it to be. None of it feels real. Each step feels heavy, lifeless—like Azaire himself.

Weighted with guilt.

Azaire, my brother, dead. I can't fathom why I once thought

such a thing could never happen. Why I had immortalized him in my mind. Because it's happening now. He's gone.

Deep in the woods, we lay Azaire's body on a bed of grass and mushrooms. I look at him, yet past him, into nothing.

I did this.

Wendy kisses his forehead as she weeps. Her whispers feel distant, as though they are being spoken in another life.

"I love you, Azaire," she murmurs.

They're the very words Azaire longed for—the words we had only just spoken of. Love. He has it now.

Shouldn't he be smiling?

Then, Wendy speaks our parting words—the ones we offer only to the dead. The moment they leave her lips, I know they aren't real. They can't be.

I was never meant to say these words. Not to him.

"May we meet again."

She rises, walking to me like a ghost—a figment of my imagination—and places a weak hand on my shoulder. I can never let her know that this is my fault.

I kneel beside Azaire's body, gently placing his beanie on his chest. I try to speak, but nothing comes out. Suddenly, my knees buckle, and I collapse, clutching Azaire's lifeless body.

My tears fall on his cooling skin. "I'm so sorry, brother."

*If only I'd listened.*

"I'm so irrevocably sorry," I sob.

I can't get up, even as Azaire's body rapidly loses heat. His blood isn't pumping; his heart isn't beating. I'll never hear his voice again.

He's gone.

It can't be real. He was just here. A moment ago, we spoke. "Zaire?" I can't stop myself. "Azaire, talk to me," I plead, shaking his limp body.

He can't be dead. He can't be gone. This isn't real.

If I beg hard enough, won't he come back? He always has

before.

Wendy hugs me. I feel her sobs as she must feel mine. "Come," she whispers in my ear, pulling me to my feet.

The blood of Azaire coats us both.

But it coats me in an entirely different way.

I killed him.

Wendy keeps me upright as we walk a few feet from Azaire. Letting me go, she holds her arms out, trembling as if weighed down by the air.

The world quakes beneath us.

Perhaps it is a dream.

The grass grows around Azaire's body, covering him entirely. From the green, the trunk of a tree sprouts, growing into the sky and sprouting gray flowers.

Is that really it, then?

A person doesn't leave like this, doesn't cease like this. He's still out there somewhere—he has to be.

But that's not how it works.

I pull Wendy close. She gasps before turning to me, hugging me back as we cry.

That's how we spend the entire night, crying in the silence and watching the sprouts of Azaire's tree sway in the wind.

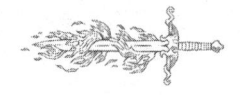

---

There is no funeral for Azaire. No mourning. There are no looks of pity, no whispering.

No one knows Azaire is gone.

I'm not sure I believe he's gone, either.

Wendy stays near in the days following his death. She doesn't say anything. Sometimes she's in the suite; other times, she's in Azaire's room. Sometimes we sit by his tree.

When I can, I venture alone into the woods, fighting what I find.

Today, vacancy is the only thing I feel—even as the kapha's snake of a tongue bites deeper into the flesh of my arm. Its blank, dark face stares at me, though I can't make out its eyes.

I've already killed two of its kin. Comrades. Other pieces of its soul, for all I care.

I'll kill this one next.

I'm not a monster. They tried to kill me first. I don't seek bloodshed—it seeks me. Even if I ventured into the woods, shouting for the creatures to come, cutting myself to lure them with the scent of my blood.

It's not like I have any control anyway. *My choices become my fate?* My ass.

If I had control over my choices—if I could say *no* to Leiana and Labyrinth—do I have the choice of my will?

My visions force my hand as much as the fear of Leiana and Labyrinth do.

The kapha's venom is getting to my head. Either there are three more of them, or I'm losing my grip on reality. I don't care which.

I slash my short sword through the snake—the monster's tongue—its teeth still sunk in my arm. It recoils with a shriek.

When the kapha flees, I shout, causing the birds to fall silent.

"What about vengeance?" The beast stops as if it understands me. "I killed your friends." I drop the short sword, holding out my arms. "Come on, get me back."

It *scurries* away. What is wrong with this universe? I pull another blade from my sheath and hurl it into the kapha's back.

As the kapha falls, so do I. The world spins so wildly, I might as well be upside down. I tip my head back into the grass, staring into the carousel sky.

*You got me again, universe.*

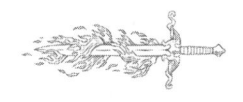

Something kicks my shoulder, and I twist away from the shoe.

"Are you an idiot?"

My eyes snap open, meeting Desdemona's with an intensity I didn't expect. Shoulder-length hair frames the world around me, sunlight streaming through her locks, casting everything in a warm orange glow.

Everything feels beautiful here.

She steps back, slipping from my sight, her presence pulling away like a fading dream. But then, her hand is in mine, pulling me to my feet, her arm winding around me like a delicate, dangerous tether I can't escape. I'm half walking, half being dragged —but I don't care. I'd follow her anywhere.

"Do you have a death wish?" Desdemona snaps. "You can't be out here right now."

"Perhaps," I reply, feeling the venom cloud my thoughts. The world shimmers with a glassy sheen, as if my eyes are covered in tears. Perhaps they are. "What happened to staying away?"

"I *thought* you had better survival instincts than this." Even with my blood soaking her, she sounds more annoyed than concerned.

"If bleeding out grants me your attention, perhaps I'll try it more."

Desdemona stops and pulls her arm away from my torso. I nearly fall to my face. "Are you kidding me?"

My feet grow wobbly, and I reach for her. When she steps back, I collapse to my knees.

Looking down at me, she says, "You *ruined* my life. You have my full attention because I should be burying a knife in your back, not carrying you to the infirmary."

*To be stabbed in the back by such pretty hands would be a privilege.*
Surely I am delusional.

"Why are you?" I ask, looking into her eyes. In the light, they look more red than brown.

"I heard about Azaire," she whispers.

I look away, red eyes be damned. "Save your condolences."

She kneels before me, gently lifts my chin, and draws my face toward hers. "I'm sorry. No *condolences*. Just the things you can't say."

Shaking my head, I say, "I don't want any of it."

"It's your fault," she mutters. "You do know that, don't you?"

I recoil from her touch, which suddenly feels colder than it ever has before.

"*You* dragged him into this," she accuses, "because *you* needed revenge. He had no skin in this game."

"How do you know this?"

"Wendy told me," Desdemona whispers.

"Wendy?"

"Oh, yeah. She blames you, too. You didn't stab him, but you put him in front of the blade." She runs her finger along a knife that wasn't there a moment ago, drawing blood.

A shiver runs through me, something I've never felt around Desdemona. If anything, I'm *hot* in her presence. Yet this is more akin to Ilyria's weather.

She pushes me down into the grass. I hit the ground, my back sinking into the dirt and worms, the maggots and bones. Desdemona hoists herself on top of me, and her blade hovers over my chest.

"Wake up or die," are the last words she whispers before my eyes force their way open.

A fingernail, attached to a hand so brutally burnt I'm not even sure it's human anymore, slices down my chest. A line of blood trails all the way down my stomach, and my back burns, as though I'm being held over an open fire, roasting alive.

"We want you, creator," the beast whispers.

The pressure vanishes, leaving me staring at the sky. The sun has retreated, yielding to the stars. Time has slipped away from me, and I don't know how long I've been lying here.

I jerk my body up, only to collapse again, coughing violently and vomiting until there's nothing left but foam. The venom must be working its way through my body. The two monsters I killed lie lifeless on the ground, yet in the surrounding stillness, there is no sign of Desdemona.

When I'm able, I pull myself up, stumbling through the desolate halls and to the infirmary. There have been no monster sightings within the academy walls since Azaire, but we remain in lockdown.

In the infirmary, my regular healer glances at me, pinching her lips in that familiar way she does when I've annoyed her. "Room thirteen." She points to an open door down the hall, and two Eunoia come to assist me.

Both healers pinch the skin around the bite—spread across most of my forearm. Blood rushes out, but my skin seals itself back together as the magic flows from their fingertips.

"Marquees?" I croak as a girl with orange hair passes by.

My voice is raw, tired from the tears and catching in my throat. But when she stops, I know it's Desdemona. I need to talk to her, find the truth once and for all.

*Or perhaps I just need to talk to her.*

There's a bottle of vesi beneath her arm, and it's as good an excuse as any.

"Can I have some?" I ask, my voice quieter now.

Desdemona tugs the cap off with slow deliberation. She lifts the bottle to her lips and takes a long chug, her eyes locked on me the entire time. Then, without breaking her stare, she flicks the cap at my face, hitting my forehead.

"No," she answers before walking away.

I've dragged myself so deep into the unknown that I don't know up from down anymore. It's as if I've lost this game between us as I call, "Please?"

Desdemona steps back into view, frowning. She hesitates, her eyes flicking to my wounded arm as she mutters, "What happened to you?" Her face remains blank, but I can see her fingers tightening around the bottle, betraying the tension in her.

"Kapha bite."

"They're really making their rounds," she sighs, shifting her weight.

There's a stretch of silence between us. She looks at the bite on my arm; I look at her.

"What are you doing in the infirmary?" I ask.

She mirrors my words: "Kapha bite."

I glance over the length of her, using her answer as a worthy excuse to admire what I should be admonishing. "You look fine."

"Yeah." She turns slightly, as if preparing to walk away, but something flickers in her eyes. The emotions ripple through her, too fast to pin down. "You too."

"Des," I murmur, the name barely more than breath, a plea hidden beneath the word.

A prayer.

Not a girl's name on my tongue, but a god's.

Desdemona steps closer. I'm sure she didn't mean to.

"I've never stopped thinking about you," I whisper, nearly against my will. The words slip out—beyond my control.

She laughs roughly, as if she can't believe my audacity. I can't either. I don't know why I'm reaching out to her like this. I don't know what I'm trying to grasp.

It must be the venom.

"Neither have I," she mutters. The bottle moves between her hands as she approaches, her voice lowering. "I've been trying to choose the best spot to level my blade."

"Anywhere. Level it anywhere." I look into her eyes, searching for something I know I won't find. "Anything. Do anything to me."

Her gaze flickers from left to right, like she's searching for the same.

"I'll always miss you," I tell her. "It feels like a part of me left when you did."

Desdemona pulls away, stepping back too quickly. "I didn't leave. I don't leave people. *You* do. You *did.*"

"I've been wrong about everything—"

"And I told you you were wrong."

The nausea—pushed aside by Eunoia magic, until now— creeps to the surface, the kapha venom swirling within me. I collapse forward, retching until my stomach empties, choking on the words I'm not strong enough to say. The foam hits the floor, the sickly taste burning my throat.

"Aibek?" Desdemona kneels in front of me, pulling hair out of my face. Her voice is sharp, but her fingers are gentle, making me smile against the pain. "We need a healer over here!"

She wipes the foam from my mouth with such care. It must be a dream. Even if it is, I want to stay in it forever. I'd give up reality to be in her arms again. Even if this is some cruel hallucination, it's the kindest thing the universe has offered me.

I've never felt hands this gentle, this kind. I've never felt more undeserving of help. She's right—what she said in another dream—*I ruined her life.* And here she is, showing me kindness, showing me something I never thought of before.

Mercy.

She's too good for me.

I hate that she is better than I'll ever be—beyond my reach, beyond my best intentions.

*I hate that I am the reason I will never have her.*

I choke again, this time on the taste of blood.

"Desdemona," I gasp, grabbing her wrist and bloodying it.

She doesn't even seem to care. Her eyes meet mine, big and wide and forgiving. "What?" she asks. "What do you need?"

"This. *You.*"

She looks stunned, the breath catching in her throat. A single moment of stillness before she tears herself from my grasp.

"Are you kidding?" she mutters.

"Not in the slightest," I reply, my gaze never leaving hers.

She shakes her head, leaning further away, as if desperate to put space between us.

"I *hate* you, Aibek," Desdemona snaps, shoving my face away and getting to her feet. "And I will always hate you. I'm sorry I let my human decency get in the way of that—because decency is something you will never have."

I don't deserve her mercy, her affection, not even her kindness. Yet, somewhere deep inside of me, I crave it more than I'll ever let myself admit. I close my eyes for a moment, bracing myself. Her hatred, her disgust—it's more than I could've hoped for. Because it means she still feels something. Even if that something is contempt.

"Good," I murmur, and I mean it. "That's all I deserve from you."

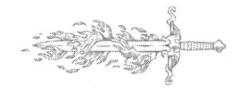

---

The healers keep me overnight, extracting the venom from my blood, and when I wake again, I feel better, though I'm disoriented. They run a few tests, ensuring the venom has left my system, then they allow me to leave.

I walk straight to Azaire's room. There's much I have to tell him—all the new pieces of information scatter through my brain. Desdemona wasn't controlling the monsters, it seems.

When I open the door, the silence settles. His room is empty. It hits me all over again.

*It will always be empty.*

I leave the suite, making my way to his tree, the only piece of him left. A fucking tree.

I walk through the woods, but I'm not sure why—what I'm expecting to find, if anything. All I know is that I went to his room, and he wasn't there.

All I know is that I know nothing.

Wendy sits in the shade of the leaves. I settle across from her, staring at the trunk, both wishing it is and isn't him. I wish he weren't a tree, yet I hope his soul lingers somewhere within.

Whichever the truth may be, it's my fault.

"Why do you feel guilty?" Wendy whispers, her voice low. It's the first time she's spoken since his death.

"Because I am." *I pushed him to fight.*

Wendy turns to me. "Because of Desdemona?"

Hearing her name stumps me. I should have seen it coming, should already be used to the way she lingers in my mind. Yet hearing her name aloud—hearing Wendy say it—shakes something within me. A fear, one that whispers I won't be able to do what needs to be done.

What does Wendy know? Has she pieced something together that I can't even admit to myself?

Would it even matter if she had?

"Desdemona?" I repeat, every vowel both familiar and foreign on my tongue. It's a name I've thought of often, nearly reverently, but rarely spoken.

"Oh." Wendy's eyebrows rise as she quickly turns away, her gaze settling back on Azaire's tree. "It's not."

"Why do you bring her up?"

"I—" She shrugs, cutting herself off. Every movement she makes is stiff, her hands trembling at her sides, as if she's carrying a weight she can't release. She takes a deep breath before continuing, her voice uneven, "I thought that you thought she was involved. After your theatrics."

*I did.*

"Do you?" I ask. "Think she is involved?"

The same question runs through my mind, lost to the tide— would it even matter if she did?

Wendy runs her hands through the grass, hesitating. "Yes," she says at last, meeting my gaze. "She's a smart liar."

She is. I've seen it in action—how has Wendy?

"How so?" I ask, pressing her further.

"Never once have I been able to catch her."

"Perhaps she was telling the truth."

"No." Wendy shakes her head. "She just knows how to get around a question."

"As you know how to get around a subject," I observe. "What aren't you telling me?"

Wendy looks up to the sky, emotion clouding her gaze. "There was a prophecy," she says, her soft voice trembling, as if the words themselves burn through her tongue. "It felt like… the *end*. I tried to kill her before it could commence. I didn't try well enough."

Every muscle in my body tenses. My heart races, but the rest of me remains frozen in place. A prophecy tied to Desdemona. She could be connected to *all* of it, exactly as I thought, yet be entirely unaware.

"Go on," I mutter.

Wendy continues, her words flowing more easily now, like she's losing herself in the events, the cadence of it all. "Then there was the kapha. I could feel it trying to communicate with her." Her gaze locks onto mine. "If we can stop the prophecy at its source, we have a moral obligation to. And if she's involved with—"

She falters, Azaire's death too painful to say aloud. Merely thinking of it is agony.

"A prophecy isn't a good enough reason," I say.

I don't believe that Desdemona had anything to do with Azaire. I *can't* believe it.

"*The end of everything*—that's what we're facing. That's what the prophecy was!"

"Tell me. What was it?"

Wendy shudders, taking a breath as if to steel herself against the words.

"Time fractures with the stone.

The one who leaves returns alone.
When the cracks in the universe divide,
love will be your demise."

I shake my head. "That's too vague—"

"You didn't *feel* it!" she shouts. Tears fill her eyes and muffle her words. "You haven't been out here for days thinking about what you could've done differently! Like, if I'd just been able to kill Desdemona, maybe the monsters wouldn't have attacked. The kapha came for her, Lucian, I swear it!"

But isn't this the complete opposite of what Azaire begged of me?

*Just because you have a vision doesn't mean you have to act on it.*

I can let the future be the future.

"This isn't what Azaire would want," I say, tears dangerously close to taking my voice. "He wouldn't want his death to lead to more death. Peace, Wendy. You know he always wanted peace."

"I can't do it!" she cries. "There is no peace without him. I feel everything! *Always!*" Wendy turns to the tree, resting a hand on the trunk. "But I can't feel him. He's not here. His soul is gone. *He's* gone. And it's like—it's like I can't even grieve when she's still around." Her eyes go cold in an instant. "I have to avenge him."

*It's me,* I should be saying. *I am the one who has to die to avenge him. I am the one who forced Azaire to fight.*

*I am the one who killed him.*

"She'd take you in seconds," I say. "You don't know the extent of her power."

Pressure clamps down on my arms as branches wrap around them. My body lifts from the ground, each limb being pulled in opposite directions, as if Wendy is silently showing me the extent of her own.

"Wendy," I warn, struggling against the branches. "Don't take this path—"

She cuts me off. "Do you care for her?"

Her head tilts in silent command, and the branches tighten, pulling me further apart. I feel my skin stretch over muscle, straining to hold together.

There are no shadows in the woods to command, no way to free myself—not until the sun shifts a mere inch through the sky. Not until shadows are cast.

"I think she's hiding something," I gasp, choking against the pain.

"No," Wendy breathes, her irises sizzling green as she glares at me. "Beyond that. What do you feel for her?"

The truth spills out of me like I am a broken faucet, her power somehow severing through my wards. "I *want* her to be hiding something because I don't want to face the fact that I've never been more attracted to a person in my life."

I, myself, was not entirely sure what the truth was. I think I could've gone this lifetime without knowing that.

I think Wendy could have, too.

"I've lost everything!" she screams. "Twice!" The branches continue to pull, stretching me as if I'm made of rubber and not flesh and bone. "And you're worried about your attraction to a killer?"

The truth tears from me, like skin ripped from its bone. "It's more than attraction."

Wendy freezes, and for a blissful second, the branches still. Then she speaks, as if the words are only now dawning on her. Her voice is a whisper, a gust of wind, magic seeping into every syllable. "The prophecy isn't only hers."

I'm silent, waiting for an elaboration and refraining from pushing Wendy down another rabbit hole.

Her eyes dull to a pale green. "Love won't just be *her* demise, Lucian. It will be all of ours."

As her gaze settles back on me, a dangerous glint sharpens in her eyes.

Then, the branches snap back into motion, their pace doubling.

I gasp, choking for air, fearing that, with even the smallest movement, my body will be torn in two. "Are you trying to kill me?"

Wendy's eyes widen, darting between me and the branches. Her breathing picks up, but the branches slow down. She shakes her head, opening her mouth but unable to speak, until, finally, she screams.

"I don't know!" Wendy falls to her knees, clutching her stomach as if she could stop the sobs that tear through her. "But one of you has to die."

When her body begins to tremble, the world does too.

I'm tossed violently between the branches, praying the tree will snap and finally grant me freedom—then the ground cracks open below me. It's nothing but a pit of darkness, a crack in the world. I am held above my death by nothing more than the branches clutching my arms.

Branches that continue to pull me apart.

With each tug, my vision blurs, my consciousness flickering—perhaps my mind is shielding itself from the inevitable torture of being torn in half. The pressure intensifies, the pain unbearable, and I long for my mind to finally give out—until suddenly, it stops.

I fall.

My hands shoot out instinctively, catching the nearest branch just in time to stop my descent. As I hang above the pit in the world, my weakened hands slipping, Wendy looks out into the woods, distracted. I seize the opportunity to climb—each movement burns my limbs, but I force myself higher. Then I jump, barely managing to land on solid ground, mere inches from the gaping rift.

I take a deep breath, glancing at the darkness in the world. There's no ending in sight. If someone were to fall down, I fear they'd be falling forever.

Then, I catch sight of what Wendy was staring at in the woods. A moonaro, only steps away from her. I have no weapons, but soon I will have shadows. I can help hold the moonaro off long enough for us to survive.

Yet it looks at *me* the way it did at Desdemona.

Then the beast runs away from us both.

Wendy turns to me, her voice breaking. "You're a part of it?"

"Why?" I ask breathlessly. "What did you feel?"

"It wanted to *save* you."

Against my will, I think of the night I got Azaire killed—of what the fatta scorpion whispered in my mind moments before its death.

*You do me a favor, Lucian Aibek. Fighting you was against my duties.*

Wendy looks at me with disgust. Then, she looks at the rift, not with shock or surprise, but with malice. I step away from it, the darkness gaping beneath me, and lift my hands, searching for shadows.

I need something to defend myself.

Another damned branch flies straight for my chest with enough force to punch my heart out, and I drop to the floor.

"Wendy!" I gasp.

The trunk of a tree pushes itself from the ground, prepared to impale me. I roll out of the way, breathless. Then, a sliver of shadow shifts into view. I call to it, halting a branch mid-air as it lunges for my head. With another shadow, I bind her hands and throat, choking her.

She glares at me, though not with fear—nor a plea for mercy. No, it's different, and I feel it. Her anger and desperation. The grief.

The darkness isn't just in her.

It's in me.

Because right now, I could do it. I could kill her.

For just a heartbeat, the thought tempts me.

But killing her would mean killing a piece of Azaire. I would kill a part of myself.

"Do it," Wendy chokes. "Finish it. Because I love him—and he would hate what I've become."

I know the feeling. I know it all too well. But there's more than that.

Azaire was good, and the pieces of him that live in me are the best parts of who I am. I can't forsake him any more than I can stop myself from hearing the echoes of what he would say.

*If there is love in grief, then there has to be love after.*

"I don't want to hurt you," I barely manage to say as I drop the shadows from her throat. "But touch Desdemona, and I will kill you."

---

Cynthia invites me to her office. I haven't spoken to her since Azaire died. Priorities, I suppose. The grief that drove me to kill the Arcanes has been replaced with a fresh wound.

The ghost of my former self occupies the seat as I sink into it.

"My condolences." Cynthia pours me a glass of vesi, and as she hands it to me says, "The prices we pay."

I turn the glass in my hand, waiting for more. Azaire *died*, and all she can offer are *condolences*?

He won't even have a coffin.

He died because of me, my grievances—grievances he took on as his own. He died because he loved me, because he was my brother, and I was too wrapped up in vengeance.

Was he right?

*I've paid the price with something I could never afford to lose.*

"Is this what revenge becomes?" I question. "Death upon death?"

Cynthia is slow to answer, her gaze heavy as she glances at me. She has the decency to frown as she whispers, "That is the very definition, my dear."

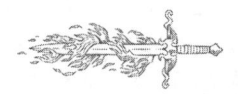

---

Yuki's waiting in my room when I get back. A pile of clothes taller than him sits on my bed. His shoulders and mouth sag, and his head hangs lower—physical manifestations of the pain I've caused everyone.

He must miss Azaire, as well.

"These are from your parents," Yuki says, gesturing to the clothes. "For the Collianth."

The words slam into my temples, pulsing through my mind. Azaire is dead, yet Leiana presses on. I'm still expected to be the prince, to go to the ball, to ascend the throne. It's not surprising, not in the slightest. It's just tiring.

I don't blame Yuki. He's simply my advisor. This is his role in the universe. But I can't handle another moment of this—not right now.

I rub my temples. "Get out."

There's a crater in the middle of the woods that Wendy can't close. A moonaro that wanted to save me. A prophecy that Wendy swears will be the end of everything. A girl who has been on my mind every day for months—from fantasizing about kissing her to killing her.

And a brother who, no matter what I do now, will always be dead.

"What? Luc—"

"Get. Out." Shadows flare at my command, and Yuki quickly rises.

Once he's relieved me of his presence, I sit beside the insanity of what must be twenty different suits.

*For the Collianth.*

# Chapter 36
## Pot Meets Kettle

# DESDEMONA

Leiholan continues to gain momentary consciousness, chug his vesi, and slip back into sleep. But this time when his eyes open, there's something different. They're not foggy. There's clarity in them—a hint of lucidity that wasn't there before.

I throw myself on top of him, hugging him as tight as I can and trying not to cry into his shoulder.

Is this our routine now? Will I run to him every time I drown in guilt, each time I sink deeper into the truth of what I am—a murderer?

"Am I missing something?" he mumbles groggily into my shoulder.

"Just your leg," I whisper.

I'm pleasantly surprised when he laughs a little and hugs me back. "It was due in time. Most soldiers don't make it out with all their limbs."

I stiffen, and I know he can tell because his hands flatten on my back. I push myself up. This isn't how I wanted this conversation to go.

"You've killed Folk?"

Leiholan groans. "You know the answer, Desdemona." He scratches his overgrown beard. "I don't want to talk about this—"

"I'll listen," I tell him, locking my eyes on his. "I'll hear you."

He scoffs, and I say, "Maybe I was wrong, because you're the person I care about most in this school."

I think of Portricia, Aralia's seamstress, with her split tongue and kind nature, gingerly wrapping my body in golds and blues. That's not what a merciless killer does.

Besides, I've killed Folk, too. It feels like I've killed every kind of creature under our sun. Maybe *I'm* the merciless killer of this duo. Because Leiholan jumped in front of the monster to save me, someone he doesn't even like.

And I don't know if I'd do the same for anyone.

"So I'm listening," I finish.

"I'm touched, sweetheart. Truly. But can we do this later?" He gestures to his leg, groaning in pain. "It's been a long few days."

"Oh, right," I mumble, and heat flushes my cheeks. Of course he needs to rest. I shouldn't have pounced on him the moment he woke up.

I slump back in the chair, sitting in the corner of the room and closing my eyes. Not that I've gotten much sleep these past few days.

Or months.

Leiholan sighs, and my eyes snap open, knowing that sound means something. He lies on his cot, not meeting my eyes as he whispers, "No one good ever thinks they can win a war."

I sit up a little taller, leaning in like it will help me hear him better. He grunts in pain as he sits up.

"And I thought we would." His eyes meet mine, and for the first time, I don't think I'm angry about the color of them. "I put winning over compassion. Cost me everything."

His words land heavily, almost like they're tailored just for me.

If no one good thinks they can win a war, then no one good wins the war. Isn't this what he said last time? Blamed the Folk?

"What happened to Anise?" I ask. It may not seem relevant

469

to him, but to me, it seems like everything I'll need to know about him.

"The Royals killed her," he says.

"That's what you said last time."

"That's because it's the answer. You didn't want to hear it."

"But you were saying it was all of us—"

"No, I wasn't," he interrupts.

"You said we did terrible things to you after the war, but so did you—"

"This isn't a matter of me and you, Desdemona." Leiholan's voice is sterner than I've ever heard it. "We don't have a say here. A girl from the septic and a Nepenthe never held any weight. Why do you hold such loyalty to the people who kept bringing the keepers to your land?"

I glare at him. Loyalty? To the Royals? The very people who are to blame for every misfortune I've endured?

"I don't," I snap.

"You believe in them more than the keepers, but the keepers wouldn't be there without the Royals."

"But that's not—" I shake my head, cutting myself off. "The keepers treated us like we were below them."

"Who granted them that power?"

I watch him in silence, his eyes boring into me and his words echoing through my brain.

"The Royals," I finally say. Admitting it hurts me, a little. Because the last time we almost had this conversation, we were talking about his dead wife, and I fought against what I'm admitting now. "What did they do to her?" It's hard to get the words out.

Leiholan glances away, tears forming in his eyes but never falling. When he speaks, his words are full of emotion, even though I can tell he's only relaying a story.

"When the Folk won, Folkara gave us two choices—bind our loyalty to them with magic, or die. Clearly, I swore my allegiance.

They gave me my position here, said it was because I was the most skilled soldier. But I was the only Major who didn't choose death. My parents, my brother, and Anise... they were executed as punishment for my involvement."

The room moves in slow motion. Every single movement I make feels delayed, slowed down by a force beyond me. That last conversation we had comes back to me.

In my head, I'm picking up that sword again, raising it toward him, and telling him to fight me. Only, this time, I know what I'm doing is wrong.

I'm at an utter loss for words, and Leiholan continues. "It's like I said, who do you think taught the keepers?"

I open and close my mouth a few times before I can form the words. "Why would you keep me around when I always..."

"I saw the same qualities that led me to fight in the war within you." He doesn't sound sad, just resigned.

"What?" I say too harshly. "This was just some save-the-septic-girl operation?"

"Did I save you?" he asks, his tone muted. Resigned. Almost sterile. His eyes drop to his missing leg, and he mutters, "Not physically."

I shake my head. "I didn't need saving."

"You mentioned it, sweetheart. Not me." He shrugs.

It's quiet for a long time. Leiholan doesn't look at me, but I don't stop looking at him. How could I have gotten him so wrong? He's not a bloodthirsty and menacing Nepenthe. He's a man, trying to make it through with a bottle of vesi and a sword that was forced into his hands.

"I don't know if I'll ever like you," I say without looking him in the eye. "But I love you."

"Yeah?" Leiholan mutters. "I feel the same about you." He looks at the wall directly behind me, and I do the same to him.

"Why do you stay?" I ask when the silence grows palpable.

"Vesi," he grumbles. "Nothing to gain."

"Aren't you angry?" I nearly shout.

"If I am anything, it's angry. Just not the way you're thinking." Leiholan looks at the pillow beside my chair. "You should get back, sleep in your own bed."

I don't move.

When he speaks again, there's a softness in his voice that I've never heard before. "We'll talk soon, I promise. Get some rest." He closes his eyes, and I close mine while I struggle to get comfortable. "In your own room," he mumbles.

I don't get up, not until the sun shines through the window. Leiholan's been up a few times; I know because his bottle of vesi has been drained.

Heading back to my suite, I wonder if we're still in lockdown, and when I open the door to my room, Aralia perks up.

A wine-red dress is draped across her lap, and a green one lies beside her. "I got you a dress," she says.

I throw the school bag on the dresser. I haven't opened it since before Leiholan lost his leg. Funny—it was only a few days ago, but it feels like a lifetime. The anger I feel toward Aralia is still there, just buried beneath everything else.

"Thanks," I mutter—unconvincing even to myself—and fall onto my bed.

We didn't have beds like this back home, and after spending three nights in a chair, I remember what it felt like those first nights here. Like a patch of thick, cushy grass.

"Des—"

"Stop calling me that," I snap.

I guess I knew Aralia would hate me if she found out, considering everything they have printed in their textbooks about the septic. *Printed by the Royals*. Despite realizing Leiholan has been right all along, there's this part of me screaming that he's wrong.

"You have to know—"

"How sorry you are?" I cut her off, my tone mocking. "Got

it." Aralia opens her mouth, and I sit up with more force than Leiholan's sword, speaking before she can. "You don't deserve my forgiveness. And I don't want your dresses or your pence."

"I know I don't deserve it," Aralia says, every muscle in her face sagging with regret. "I–I should've done something when you were attacked. I know that now. I'm not looking for pity or– or anything, but... I wasn't lying when I called you my best friend."

My *best friend?* Says the girl who watched me nearly die and then told me it wasn't *personal.*

"Well, I was," I say coolly, even as anger knots in every fiber of my being.

Her eyes squeeze shut so tightly that her face crinkles. "I have to tell you—"

"No," I say and turn on the bed, lying on my side and facing the wall.

Aralia speaks anyway. "I knew you weren't one of us. For a little while, I was trying to figure out who you really were, and the more time we spent together—" She cuts herself off, and I seethe in silence.

*Was everything fake?* Lucian wanted me to get closer to the Arcanes, and Aralia wanted me to see if I was septic.

I curl up, knees tucked tight against my chest.

"I cared about you fast," she begins again. "Then you didn't flinch in Arson's Alley, and I saw the scars on your back one day when you were changing—"

I turn to face her, my voice sharp. "Do you think this is helping?"

"No." Aralia shakes her head. "I want to be honest, that's all."

"You want me to see where you're coming from." My eyes narrow on her. "Is that it?"

"I'm telling you that I grew up with a specific view of the septic. Knowing you showed me how wrong that was."

I laugh bitterly. All those layers peeling back, all this anger burning hot. "I'm so glad you could have that cozy little lesson. I'll make sure to tell all my neighbors back home that the girl with the *kingdom mommy* learned that the septic Folk aren't disgusting. I'm sure they'll be thrilled. Better yet, maybe it will fill their stomachs!"

"Desdemona—"

"Screw you. You know, I hope someone traps you in the corner of a room and comes at you with a sword while I watch and do nothing." Her frown grows further. "We're not just not friends," I say, and even though I don't mean the next words, fury pushes me forward. "I hate you."

I watch her neck work while she swallows, and I hope to the gods that it hurts.

"I got the green one for you." Aralia looks at the dress next to her. "Portricia and I thought it would suit you."

For the first time, I wonder what the dress is for.

# Chapter 37
## You Can Never Go Home Again

# LUCIAN

It shouldn't come as a surprise when I'm called to Ilyria. The moment I step across the threshold of the throne room, a dagger of shadows shoots toward my throat. With a twist of my wrist, the shadows dissipate like smoke, though my senses remain on high alert.

"In times like these, wit is our greatest weapon," Labyrinth says. "Good on you for seeing it."

I nod, the collar of my formal attire cutting into my neck. I don't bother responding. I simply wait for my command.

"Two things." Leiana steps forward. "Lilac will be returning to the academy."

"And the monsters?" My voice tightens, matching the clench of my jaw.

"The situation has been taken care of," she waves me off.

"You didn't send soldiers," I say. Is this why they are allowing the Collianth Ball to proceed? Because they believe the threat has passed?

"Fighting was not required in this case," she answers.

"How was the situation taken care of?"

"Don't trouble yourself with matters beyond your reach," Leiana replies.

A hand made of shadows caresses my cheeks and almost freezes my face in the process. I stand still beneath it, waiting to hear the reason I've been summoned.

The longer I remain unresponsive, the more impatient Leiana becomes. Her shadows withdraw, but the chill they leave behind lingers. Then, her voice deceptively sweet, she asks, "How is your darling Desdemona doing?"

My body instantly stiffens. *I never disclosed her name.*

"Superb," I reply, praying that my worry doesn't show.

I still don't know what to believe about Desdemona. I wasn't sure before the moonaro supposedly protected me, and I'm less sure now.

My confusion does not mean she has been absolved.

*But my feelings might.*

With each passing day, I grow more certain that she was there —sitting beside me, her touch gentle as she wiped away the blood and vomit, her hand steady through the worst of the poison.

No matter how it ended—no matter the truth of her parting words—she stayed by my side, even after I wronged her. In my delirium, I knew she was too good for me. I hated myself for not being worthy of her.

I fear I still do.

I'm her villain, her enemy, and she has become the object of my every desire.

Leiana assesses me, and for once, I return the favor. I watch her with a careful eye, rather than a waiting one. I'm not sure there's a thing she could do to hurt me anymore.

I've already punished myself.

Slowly, I ask, "How did you know that Desdemona was from the septic?"

She exhales, a tired sigh that feels too practiced. "Tongues travel faster than thought."

"And the second thing?"

Leiana perks up, though there's a stiffness to her movements—a sign, perhaps, that she senses I won't be so easily controlled anymore.

But her unease melts away the moment she speaks. "Ah yes, darling. You will be speaking to an audience about the monster attacks. You shall see Lilac after. Piphany will prepare you."

Leiana shoos me out of the room, and I find her advisor, Piphany, waiting for me when I exit. She walks fast ahead of me.

When I sit in front of the vanity mirror, Piphany looks at my reflection from behind me, glancing at the dark circles beneath my eyes.

"Not sleeping?" she asks in a high-pitched, emotionless voice.

"Let's do this without chatter, shall we?"

Piphany gives a smile that never reaches her eyes.

I've spoken to a live audience before—Lyrians and Folk, their pens and papers poised, driven by their idle thirst for gossip. I am no stranger to the pampering as she sweeps damp brushes beneath my eyes.

A few minutes later, more Lyrians swarm into the room, measuring me or applying makeup.

"We all offer you our sincerest apologies," Piphany says, plucking at my eyebrows again and nodding without sympathy.

"How does it feel?" I ask slowly.

"Hm?" she mumbles, her focus taken by my eyebrows, but I don't miss the slight pause of her hand.

"To be the head advisor to the queen of Ilyria, yet still be responsible for plucking my eyebrows?" Her fingers falter just enough for me to feel it, and I meet her eyes through the mirror. "Pity."

Piphany scoffs softly, and it quickly turns into a short, bitter chuckle. "Did Queen Leiana give you your briefing on what it is you are to do?"

For a moment, the only sound is the rustle of fabric as the attendants work around us.

"No," I answer.

She pushes my eyes closed and brushes powder on my eyelids. "You'll be pandering to the wealthy and influential people of our kingdom. Those who *matter*."

*And Azaire wasn't one of them.* She doesn't have to say it, not when it's lined between her words and filling the gaps in her teeth.

"Yes, Piphany. I'm well aware of what my title entails."

"Pity," she whispers my word back to me slowly, the room falling silent.

But I embrace the silence for what it becomes—temporary bliss. The moments before disaster strikes. For I am not naive enough to think that there wasn't a reason Leiana told me I'd see Lilac *after* this meeting. It was a threat.

*Do as I say or Lilac will suffer the consequences.*

When the crew clears out, I'm dressed in another extravagant suit—bright white and iridescent, like Ilyria's Soul Stone, the Stone of Light. A display of power and rebirth.

As I glare at my reflection, I try not to ponder the question: what dark deed am I forced to do now?

Walking to my sentencing, I slide the short sword Azaire last held down the sheath at my back. Then I pass his room, the one he uses when he visits Ilyria with me.

*Used.*

Without a second thought, I step inside.

The room is a blank slate, his belongings gone. Every trace of Azaire's existence in Ilyria has been wiped clean, as if his blood could ever be wiped from my eyes.

The world will never look the same again.

The view from his room is more familiar than my own—it was once a hiding spot. I spent more time here than anywhere in the kingdom, but never without him. Now, I'm the one left standing in the hollow silence, once full of laughter, despair, and childhood. A space that was once full of Azaire.

It isn't fair. The universe needed more of him—and less of me.

Yet, it received the very opposite.

The snow falls thunderously outside, landing in the Great Sea that borders the kingdom. I sit on the barren bed, watching it blanket the glaciers in white.

Is Azaire's soul truly gone, obliterated by the venom of the fatta scorpion? Or is he part of the universe now, scattered among the stars, his atoms drifting through the cosmos? Perhaps he's even forming the snow that falls from the sky.

For as much as I'd like to believe that to be true, he's probably just gone, his body tangled in the roots of a tree, his essence never to be felt again.

---

I drag myself to the courtyard before the audience arrives. A translucent tarp stretches across the skyline, blocking the snowfall for the neighboring planets—those who can't handle the burning cold.

The courtyard is enclosed by glass walls, three facing into the kingdom and one overlooking the Great Sea. Only Leiana, Labyrinth, Piphany, and the guards are present in the space. Piphany sets up the raecrium—a device that projects images through its partners, something only the wealthy and noble acquire. The people I will be speaking to today.

The people who *matter*.

"You look dashing," Leiana says as I approach.

Labyrinth stands tall, his silver staff gleaming in his hand. "You have an hour to prepare, son. You're the face of our conquest—carry yourself accordingly."

When he's finished speaking, Leiana hands me a scroll. I skim through the material before asking any further questions.

The *conquering* of the monsters. My defeating a single fatta has been ramped up to my defeating them all. Are the monsters truly gone, or is this all a facade so they can still have their ball?

My eyes snag a quarter of the way through the paper. Azaire's name, emblazoned in blasphemy.

They want me to say that Azaire forced me to fight.

Because a prince can only be a prince, not a soldier. Entering battle is bad press—no one wants their king on the front lines, not unless they want their king dead. A king is a show of strength, and who is stronger than those who control an army? Certainly not someone who fights in the army. Not to the Lyrians, who honor subconscious manipulation and wit far more than brute power.

The entire page is anti-Nepenthe rhetoric. *For how is a creature so thirsty for blood any different than the monsters who attack in their leisure?*

This is what I'm supposed to say. This is why I'm not allowed to see Lilac until after I've completed their *mission*.

"How much of this is public?" I ask, the words bitter on my tongue, searching for a way to undo this and still see Lilac.

"Everything," Labyrinth says, clutching his staff. "The people only need to see their savior now."

"The monster attacks on the other worlds have ceased?"

"After you killed the fatta, they all seem to have retreated." Labyrinth's expression is as impassive as ever.

They don't know I've spent time in the academy woods, still fighting off these creatures. The monsters have most certainly not retreated—though, they didn't try to kill me either.

"Fair to hear," I say. "I'll stay in the halls until we begin."

They both nod, and I depart, a myriad of contradictions clouding my judgment. I killed him, and now I am expected to slander his name. And yet, what choice do I have? What choice have I ever had?

I read through the scroll—the *script*—three times, memorizing every lie until they are easy on my tongue, all while hoping that it will twist. I have to do this for Lilac's safety and no longer for Azaire's. Because *I killed him.*

Sometimes my visions show me how someone will swing from the front, yet I fail to see the knife in my back. My own thoughts evaded me when I said *let the consequences be damned*. I never meant it—I didn't think there would *be* consequences. I certainly would've never said it if I knew it was Azaire who would face them.

He should've been the one to live, not me.

*One day I will show the worlds what he is.* I made that promise. Yet here I am, about to not only go back on it, but shatter it entirely.

If choices create our fate, at what point does compliance define me?

The crowd shuffles in, and I watch them from afar. The faint glow of the raecrium signals it's active. It's not only the hundred people in this room who are going to hear this. There are thousands across the worldly borders listening in.

Leiana and Labyrinth take the front of the room together, but my attention drifts to the audience. My heart pounds, threatening to rise from my throat.

This is the moment I lose all honor; every *good* piece of Azaire that I carry with me will be gone with his soul when I say what I have to.

I take my place, staring into the raecrium at the back of the room, past the people with their notebooks and recording devices. It's pure propaganda. I don't need psychology lessons to see that. I'm promoting the hostility against the Nepenthes—the exact mindset that's been used as a weapon.

"As we all know, monsters have risen, attacking the people and destroying our homes," I begin, as the words on the scroll instruct. "Some have made it so far as to break past the protective barrier of Visnatus, killing Azaire Wenejad."

A sigh ripples through the crowd, though not one of despair.

I continue, "Your queen and king wanted me to come forward and say a few words about the situation—and my heroics. The moment that I knew there was no choice but to stop the fatta before it stopped me." There's a conviction in my voice that I do not feel an ounce of. "Azaire took the path I hoped he wouldn't. As we all do, I wanted him to rise above…" I pause, forcing myself to go on. "His nature."

I pause, draw a slow breath, and feel my hammering, traitorous heart. I look into the audience instead of the faint light behind them.

*Don't let them take more of you than they already have.*

How can I kill my brother and let his words die with him, unanswered?

"Azaire wasn't just the finest Nepenthe I knew; he was the finest person. Probably with a stronger moral compass than anyone in this room." I meet the eyes of several recoiling faces. "It was *my* idea to fight the fatta, *my* idea that got him killed. And in the end, do you want to know what he asked of me?" A shiver runs down my spine. "He asked me to give him *peace*.

"A Nepenthe, a creature you've deemed aggressive and murderous, was dragged into battle by *me* and killed at *my* hands." When the people scoff and stand around me, my eyes grow cold. I let my shadows rise, a clear warning, and I say, "For those of you thinking of leaving or disrupting this broadcast, you're going to want to sit down. This next piece of information will be a story worth your life."

They all sit, and for once I value my name, my status. I'm doing something worthy with it.

"For the last eighteen years, the rulers of Ilyria and Folkara have been secretly collaborating on a weapon designed to annihilate the *lesser* planets," I announce. "Boycott the kingdoms, take their powers." I search for Leiana and Labyrinth in the crowd, meeting their gazes. "They were never going to do anything worthy with it."

The entire room buzzes, but no one stands up to do a thing. I escape the courtyard and race the kingdom halls, looking for Lilac. I need to reach her before they can act against us.

Room after room and floor after floor come up empty, until I find one of my personal guards. "She's underground, in the dungeons," she tells me.

"No," is the only sound I can manage to make.

Then I run down to the place where I was forced to spend much of my youth. Could they have done to Lilac what they did to me? Force her to watch and feel the dead? Or are they making her bring about the death?

In every cell lies a corpse, and in the back of the dungeon, Lilac sits shackled to the floor. When she looks up at me, her eyes glow bright blue with over-exertion.

Leiana had her kill every prisoner, I realize. Lilac stole the life force from them all.

I run to her, shoving shadows into the keyholes of the shackles. They don't unlock—that would be far too easy. I grip the chain, pulling on it with all my strength. When it doesn't give, I coat my hands in shadows, using the extra power to snap it in two.

The shackles still cling to her wrists, but she's no longer tethered to the ground.

With a desperate cry, Lilac collapses into my arms, her body trembling like a candle flickering in the wind. Her voice barely escapes her lips as she whispers, "I didn't want to."

I hug her tightly, wrapping her in the safety I promised. "It's all right, you're safe now," I breathe. "You'll never have to be here again."

Lilac pulls away, her gaze flicking over my shoulder. I follow her line of sight to the lifeless bodies of the prisoners. Cell after cell, body after body.

Corpse after corpse.

"They made me," she whispers, her voice cracking with tears.

I grab her shoulders and force her gaze back to mine. "Then you're stronger now," I promise. It feels as though Azaire is whispering in my ear when I add, "Don't let them take more of

483

you than they already have."

Does she know he's gone?

"We have to run," I say, my voice tight with urgency as I glance to the side, my eyes locking onto the contraption.

*The weapon.*

What is Ilyria planning?

"Do you know why this is here?" I whisper, my gaze fixed on the cold metal, a dread sinking into my chest as Lilac stumbles, nearly collapsing beside me.

I shift my focus back to her, catching her before she falls.

"They wanted me to channel the prisoner's life force and power it," she answers.

For some reason, I'm stunned. I knew they wanted to power it—I didn't know they would use their own daughter to do it. All at once, I feel what I should have felt for the weapon this entire time.

Revulsion.

"Did you?" I ask, my voice weak.

Lilac shakes her head. "It didn't work."

The relief her words bring is all the proof I need. Everything I thought I wanted unravels, slipping through me like rain from a cloud. I am emptied. If the hope of destroying the Arcanes grants Leiana and Labyrinth the means to further their dominion over the universe, then I cannot continue.

Azaire's words lash past like a storm. My compliance—my inability to see beyond vengeance—could bring about catastrophe.

*It already has.*

I've already torn my world apart with bloody claws. I've surrendered everything, and gained nothing in return.

Suddenly, the answer is clear—clearer than it has ever been.

The shadows rise around me, spiraling like a tornado.

"What are you doing?" Lilac asks weakly.

"What I always should have."

The shadows gather speed, crashing into the weapon and seeping into its crevices as I work to tear it apart.

The first crack rings out like thunder. The next like the groan of a collapsing world.

Yet the metal does not yield as I expected. The shadows seep in, only to emerge moments later—transformed. They're no longer black, but deep blue, iridescent where the light touches them.

Worst of all, I can no longer control them.

Lilac grabs my arm, pulling me back as the echo of racing footsteps fill the room.

"We have to go," she urges.

I shake my head—the weapon is still intact. I haven't done enough. My body stiffens, the weight of my shadows settling on my chest as I fight harder to tear the weapon apart.

The footsteps draw nearer. The creaking of the metal becomes a roar.

"Lucy!" Lilac cries.

I have to keep going; I have to finish this, have to atone for all my failures this far.

But then it strikes me—this same line of thinking got Azaire killed.

I look away from the weapon, swallowing my regret. It's the sight of my sister—whole and alive—that pulls me back. No matter what Leiana has done, no matter what Lilac was made to endure because of her, she's still here.

I reach for her. The moment she takes my hand, we run.

We make it barely a floor higher before six guards block our path, their figures crowding the underground stairwell.

Lilac trembles.

"Your Majesty," a guard says. "Queen Leiana asks for you."

He speaks calmly, yet each of the guards has their weapons drawn. Either way, we're surrounded by shadows. We're all fair game.

I lean closer to Lilac, whispering, "Close your eyes."

When she does, I summon shadows, weaving them into tendrils that snake around the guard's torso, crushing the breath from him and wrenching the weapon from his grasp. At the same time, one of the others retaliates, sending dark wisps to twist around my throat.

But I'm stronger—and I make that known. I rip his shadows from my throat, forcing them to wrap around my chest like armor. Then I grab Azaire's short sword, releasing the other guard's limp body. The rest approach with caution.

I let go of Lilac's hand and step in front, placing myself between her and the danger.

"I've never been above death," I announce with a smile. "Choose wisely."

One guard swings. I duck, extending my blade to slice his stomach. Rising to my feet, I block the next blow—a life-threatening swing. His sword clatters to the floor with a metallic clang, and I kick him in the stomach. There's a sickening crack when his head collides with the cold stone wall, and blood stains the floor as he falls.

I block a swing to my left, then another to my right, but darkness yanks my head back, exposing my throat. I know they won't kill me—not unless the order came from Leiana—but the blade still comes, perfectly placed to take off my head.

Steel glints inches from my skin. I reach for the remaining shadows—but there's nothing left to grasp. I brace for the pain, my last thought Lilac's safety—until the guards are suddenly flung against the wall, most of them collapsing into unconsciousness.

I turn to Lilac, my shadows no longer shielding her, and see her eyebrows furrowed sternly. Her hands rise, fingers twisting in unnatural shapes, shadows coiling around her arms as though she were a master.

But there's a darkness in her gaze as she stares at the bodies—then at me, frowning.

It's the first time I've seen such power from my sister.

One of the guards, sliced open and groaning, clutches his stomach and reaches toward us. Perhaps if someone finds them soon enough, he'll survive.

"Are they dead?" she asks, her hands beginning to tremble.

I step toward Lilac, reaching for her shadow-veined hands. "You saved my life," I say, unsure of the guards' fates.

Lilac's eyes are distant as she takes a deep breath, nodding. "We should run," she mutters.

"I agree."

We move quickly, running up flight after flight without resistance until we reach the ground floor.

The daylight blinds me.

I can't imagine how it must feel for Lilac—how long she's been in the dungeon, without sunlight, without hope.

I glance around, searching for the quickest escape without running into another legion of guards—then Leiana and Labyrinth step into view.

Dozens of guards stand at their side. That's good—that means they think we're strong enough to beat them now.

Shadows from all corners of the room rush to Lilac, wrapping around her limbs like branches. Before she can make a move, Leiana flicks her wrist, and Lilac snaps upright. She gasps as her head jerks back, shadows spiraling out of her mouth—her life force.

I hurl my short sword at Leiana's chest like an axe. I know it's an impossible task, but I pray it finds her heart.

The sword halts midair, then clatters to the floor in a wisp of darkness. Before it settles, I call it back—my power guiding the blade into my hand as I step closer to Leiana.

The guards raise their swords, drawing nearer in turn. One presses a blade to my chest.

But I already have mine leveled at Leiana's throat.

Glancing at the guards, I say, "Kill me, and your queen dies."

The sword pierces my skin, ripping into my heart—right above the X Desdemona carved into me. I do something dangerous, pressing my sword into Leiana's throat, nearly drawing blood.

She gasps.

I'm guessing it's been a long time since she was this vulnerable.

Just as the blade sinks deeper, tearing into muscle and nearing the bone that guards my heart, darkness spills from the guards' eyes and mouths. It swirls through the air, rushing toward me with force.

But it never touches me.

The shadows cover Lilac instead, seeping into her eyes, spiraling up her nose and mouth—even her ears.

"Lilac!" I scream.

Then every single guard drops to the floor, lifeless. My sister stands taller, darkness dripping from her hands like blood, an influx of power at her fingertips.

She took the guards' life force. She killed, though she never wanted to, to save *me*.

Lilac moves in front of me and steps around the fallen men as she says, "No one kills my brother."

Leiana raises an eyebrow, her bare hand reaching for my blade. She grasps it, moving it away from her throat as blood spills down her arms.

"My daughter," she says with pride, stepping toward Lilac.

Instantly, a chill runs through me. I fear what comes next—that she's going to tell Lilac what I was never allowed to, just to get under her skin.

To take her from my side.

Slowly, Leiana shakes her head. "He was never your brother," she says.

I glance at Lilac, willing her to understand. She stares at

Leiana, her shoulders slumping.

Leiana's gaze snaps back to me, a deep frown etching her lips. "He's barely even your cousin with the way his parents treated us," she spits.

Lilac turns to me, her eyes wide as she whispers, "What is she talking about?"

"That's it then?" I say, stepping in front of my *sister*, shielding her from Leiana. "She can't know until you allow it? Or is this all for theatrics?"

*And she plans to use the Folk to wipe Lilac's memory again.*

Labyrinth's eyes dart nervously to Leiana, silently saying what I'm thinking: *Don't.*

"Will you defend the boy who's deceived you your entire life?" Leiana taunts Lilac, who looks at me like she's contemplating the truth of this claim.

"It's true," I mutter, looking at Lilac and no one else.

My whole life, I've dreamt of this moment, the day that Lilac could know. But seeing the betrayal in her eyes—after every time I tried to tell her, every time Leiana reduced my choice to nothing—makes this moment feel like failure.

"My parents are dead."

Lilac releases a trembling breath. "That's not possible."

"I know."

"Leiana!" Labyrinth warns.

"The truth always comes out," Leiana says, ripping Lilac's attention from me. "So what will it be, Lilac? Your *brother*, or your true bloodline?"

At that, Lilac snaps.

"I have the power of every dead guard and prisoner—so you're going to answer *my* questions!" she yells louder than I've ever heard from her. "Lucy?" she says, her voice softening as she turns back to face me.

"You're my sister by heart, cousin by blood."

Lilac looks at Leiana again, and the only choice I have is to believe in hers.

"You think I'll side with you because you're *my mother?* When have you ever treated me like your daughter!" she screams, her face scrunching up into the same configuration it always does when she cries. "I choose Lucy. Every. Time." Her hand shoots back to me, and all I can feel is relief when I grab it.

*What will she think of me when I tell her Azaire's gone?*

Together, we turn—foolish, perhaps, to believe we'd be permitted to leave. Labyrinth's voice halts us, bellowing across the room.

"Tell me what you know about the weapon," he demands with a hint of... is that *fear* in his voice?

I meet his gaze, unflinching.

"It's important, son," he says, as he always has. As though he ever had any right to that word.

I turn from him once more—a deliberate act of shunning—and Lilac follows.

"It's not what you think!" he shouts, desperation in his voice. "You were the only one whose power could be used against the Arcanes at the time. You were only a contingency. I loved my brother. And I hold love for you, as well."

*Contingency? Power?* What is he talking about? If my power could be used against those things, I'd be in The Void by now. They'd be *dead* by now.

"Yet you did nothing of worthiness when he was killed," I say without turning.

Labyrinth didn't just fail to act; he banned the speaking of the creatures that killed my father. He hid the truth of the Arcanes from the universe—hid the very dangers we're facing. If I *did* have power against them, then he's the reason I was never able to use it.

I was six when my father was murdered. Six when I discovered by whom. And six when speaking of the Arcanes was declared forbidden.

"Lilac may not be my sister by blood," I mutter. "Yet I'd never betray her the way you betrayed my father."

"You're projecting your current mind onto your future self," Labyrinth says softly. "It's hard to know who you will be before it becomes you."

"Trust me." For the first time, I look him in the eye. "You've made me exactly what I am."

"Let's go," Lilac says, tugging on my hand and pulling me away from our parents.

As we leave, Leiana calls, "I'll see you at your weddings, darlings!"

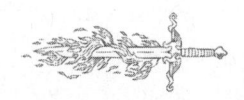

---

I expect Lilac to berate me, to demand an answer—but she only sits across from me on her bed in Visnatus, staring.

Unsure of where to go from here, I begin explaining. "I was six when—"

"I don't want to know," she cuts me off. "Too much has changed."

"I'll always be your brother," I whisper, meaning every word. I won't lose her because of what Leiana made me do.

Lilac's tone is dry as she says, "There's no need to say silly things when we both know them to be true."

That's where we leave it. Lilac says nothing more, and I sit with Azaire's name on the tip of my tongue, unable to spit it out. Eventually, I excuse myself without telling her the fate of our friend and venture out to the abandoned dungeon. I'm somewhat surprised to see Freyr still alive, though he's surely starved. I drop a bag of pence at my feet and toss him bread and water.

There are puddles in his cell from the rain. I imagine he drank from them when I forgot to feed him after what happened to Azaire.

Freyr devours what little sustenance I offer, and I unlock his cage. He struggles to his feet, collapsing against the wall three times before finally reaching me.

"You're letting me go?" he asks groggily.

"You're a free man," I whisper. Freyr shakes his head, denying my sentiment. "The bag is yours. Twenty thousand pence, enough to start a life far from the septic."

"My life's been over for a long time now." Freyr picks up the bag and notes, "You seem remorseful."

"Yes, well…"

"You want to make up for it? Help Desdemona. If she's here, danger is coming, and she's not ready for it."

"Please," I whisper. At first, I want to ask what he knows—want to dig deeper and deeper for answers until I lose myself entirely. The words that leave my mouth go against my every instinct. "How do I help her?"

"Don't let the Arcanes get to her."

# Chapter 38
## Three's A Ball, and One's A Killer

# DESDEMONA

A ball! Do none of these people have common sense? Leiholan lost a leg, and I've even heard rumors of a boy dying, yet we're supposed to dress up and celebrate the Collianth—a holiday only the rich love. The one day a year the lunar goddess and solar god cross paths.

*Of course* we have to celebrate Sulva and Ayan. No matter what happens. No matter what we lose.

Aralia sits by the window in our room, smoking her third joint of the day, and I'm ready to call a truce just for a drag. The dress she got me is phenomenal, but not phenomenal enough to earn forgiveness. Neither is a joint, so I stick to my side of the room as I get dressed.

The gown looks even better once I put it on. Olive green and floor-length, the top half is covered in flowers embroidered in dark green and gold, with tiny black beads catching the light. Small vine-like patches stretch down and billow with the material at my waist.

I strap on four sheaths, two on each thigh.

"You look great," Aralia says from across the room. Her dress is the color of the wine I drank with Lucian, who is yet *another* person I'd like to avoid.

I allow myself one good look at her before turning away. "Thanks."

Remembering what Aralia said about my scars, I apply more

glamour to my exposed back.

Then, with reluctance, I turn to her and ask, "Can I?" while nodding toward the joint.

"Oh, yeah." Aralia smiles a little as she hands it to me.

I refrain from telling her to grow a spine.

As I blow smoke out the window, she says, "I heard that the boy the fatta killed was Azaire."

I freeze, choking on the smoke. *The boy who made the kingdom less lonely.* Lucian's best friend. I shouldn't care. But I do.

For some reason, Aralia continues. "That's what my mom said. Apparently, there was some drama with Lucian and a meeting—"

"I want to hear about Lucian even less than I want to talk to you." I shiver at my instant remorse. What is wrong with me? Both of these people would've left me to die.

Screw them.

"Then no more for you," Aralia says, almost humorously, plucking the joint from my hand.

I kind of missed that edge to her voice, and have to force my smile back down.

Am I being too harsh with her?

"Thank you for the dress," I say shyly, testing the waters. "Truly."

"Is that a smile?" There's a faint, playful tone to her voice.

Against my will, I smile more. But screw her, no. I force it down.

Aralia takes a long drag, taps the joint into the ashtray, then says, "Oh, right. We're doing the sulky thing." She passes the joint to me and frowns. "I can sulk too."

I glare at her, hoping my eye holds a dangerous glint, while I smoke her joint.

"I love you, Des," she says morosely, like a child whining that they want their toy back. "You mean a lot to me, and I'm not giving up until you forgive me." She plucks the joint from my hand, again. "But I might just stop sharing my drugs with you until you do."

"I could just lie," I say. "Say we're fine and steal your joints."

"That'd force you right back into my proximity until it was true." Aralia smirks. "I made you smile twice already. That has to count for something."

"You know what I don't get?" I ask, and Aralia raises her eyebrows, the joint still between her lips. "Why you still kiss my ass after I told you I hate you."

She blows smoke from her mouth. "Because I don't believe you." Before I can respond, she adds, "Be my date."

"Huh?"

"You hate me, and showing up to the ball with the *likes of you* would do negative numbers for my reputation."

Right. For her, punishment means ruining her reputation.

This time, I pull the joint away from her, but I don't answer. Instead, I ask, "Are you sure it's Azaire who's dead?"

The spark in Aralia's eyes fades. "Yeah."

I inhale the smoke deeper than ever before.

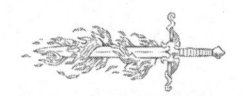

---

Reluctantly or not—I can't tell—I enter the ballroom with Aralia on my arm. I feel eyes on us, and Aralia gives me a sly smirk, as if to say, *I told
you so*. Oh, whatever. This is nothing compared to what she's done to me.

Besides, in this dress I almost defy reputation. It can't be *that* bad for her.

Green vines drape elegantly over the gleaming glass-and-silver chandeliers. The tables where government officials sat during the Gerner are nowhere in sight. Good, I'm glad they won't be here again. That turned rather sour for me.

The night drags until Aralia begins gathering her drinks, and this time, I don't bother refusing.

I scan the crowd for Lucian, thinking of the last ball, unable to stop myself from wanting to talk to him.

There's something deeply wrong with me. Aralia all but told me she would've let the Folk kill me, and Lucian is the reason they wanted to. Yet here I am, still thinking about both of them.

More eyes turn our way—mostly at Aralia. They're looks of contempt or disdain, and I wonder if she really is going to pay a price for this. She links her arm through mine, just like we used to when walking to class together.

Worried she'll say something stupid, I whisper, "I don't want any more attention on us."

"Noted."

Then, after a few beats, I ask, "I'm not going to have to dance again, am I?"

"You might. The dancers are picked at random to offer a balanced selection to Sulva and Ayan."

Right. Because it's not just the new year—it's also the supposed day the gods collided and created our universe. I'm about to mock how ridiculous this all is when someone shouts, "Arcane!"

I glance around the room, searching for the Arcanes—looking for a way to my mom—when suddenly, I'm not in a room at all. I'm standing in the withered woods of one of my old homes.

*This is the village I lived in when I was six, a place I never thought I'd see again.*

"Well, Mom and I have to leave a lot," I say to Bernice while we walk to school. "So I don't think we should be friends."

*I'm so short it feels like I'm standing on my knees.*

"What do you mean you have to leave?" Bernice asks me.

"I never get to stay," I tell him. I don't say that I've never had friends. "It's not happy."

"Oh," he says softly. "I'm sorry." Then, "Why do you leave?"

I stop to think.

*Don't tell him. Knowledge is a weapon.*

I feel like I should share. "Because we have to."

"Why do you have to?"

I kick a pebble. "I don't know."

*My feet are so tiny… This has to be a dream, but it feels different. I've never been able to think as* myself *in them. Something about this feels sharper—like I'm not remembering it, but reliving it.*

Bernice grips my hand. "This time you don't have to."

"Why?" I ask, giggling.

"Because we're friends now!"

*Friends? We were never friends—he always hated me.*

"Okay."

"You should meet Nova," he tells me. "She's funny like you."

"Okay."

I meet Nova at school. She's pretty. Her hair is long and blonde, and her eyes are big and round. Her laugh is pretty, too.

*Nova, from the dreams.*

"I'm Desdemona," I tell her.

"I like your name," she says. "It's so pretty."

That's the first time anyone has called any part of me pretty. My smile stretches across my whole face. "Thank you."

The three of us begin spending every day after school together, since we live nearby. I tell them about my mom and all the places we've lived, the three villages before this one.

*No, there have been eight. My mind feels split down the middle—I'm both six and eighteen and there's no common ground between the two versions of me.*

They think it's cool that I've seen so much of the world.

One afternoon, the three of us venture into the woods. "Show us your fire, Des!" Nova shouts.

"I don't think that's a good idea," Bernice says.

"Don't do that." Nova smacks his arm. "I've never seen a Fire Folk before. I think it would be cool."

But Bernice goes red in the face and shoves Nova. "There's a reason you haven't seen them," he mutters.

"Come on, Des, *please*."

I look between them and back up into a tree.

"It would be so cool. Wouldn't it, Bernice?"

"I guess," he shrugs.

*I think I know how this ends. I think I've had this dream before.*

I lift my hand and *feel*, just like Mom taught me. The flicker of heat starts in my stomach and moves through me like wind in my hair. When it enters my chest, I know it's working.

Fire flickers in my palm, spreading across my fingers. I wiggle them, and when Nova looks at my hand with awe, I smile.

She likes it. Mom never does.

"That's so cool!" Nova says.

"Thanks."

When I go home, Mom is looking at me like I've done something wrong. I don't know how I recognize this look, but I do.

"You used your power today?"

*She knows I have power?*

"Yeah." I scratch my arm.

"You know you can't use it unless I'm nearby!"

"I'm sorry."

*My voice sounds so small. I want to say more, but I physically can't.*

Mom rubs her eyes, her knuckles pressing hard against her skin. "Gods, Desdemona, do you never listen? No. Magic. Do you understand me?"

I gulp. "Yes."

"You can't do this again."

"Okay."

"Supper's on the table."

I eat and try to savor the small amount of water in my dry mouth. Then I lie on the bed, and when Mom lies next to me in her spot, she holds my hand and rubs the top of it.

"It's important to watch people." Her hand moves to my chin, rubbing my jaw. "You're old enough now to know that there will come a time when everybody needs to fight, and your most powerful weapon is knowing your enemy. Do you understand?"

I nod.

"Good." She lets go of me and turns away.

When Nova says she wants to see my fire again, I tell her no. Three days later, she asks again, and I tell her no.

I think of what Mom said. I don't know what she meant. I don't know what an enemy is.

*No, I know exactly what an enemy is.*

When Bernice and I are alone, I tell him, "My mom doesn't want me using magic anymore."

He's quiet for a minute.

"I think she's right," he says.

"Why?" I ask, frowning.

"The Flame isn't safe." He kicks at a tree trunk over and over. "You could hurt people."

"I don't want to hurt people." I kick the tree, too.

"Then don't use your magic."

But months pass, and when Nova asks again, my hand lights on fire, and she looks at it like it's a moon. Bernice steps back, arms crossed tightly over his chest.

"Wow," Nova says, stepping closer.

Her long, blonde hair brushes against my hand, and in an instant, her entire head bursts into flames. "Desdemona!" she cries. "Stop it!"

I think I step back—or maybe I don't. It's hard to tell.

"Bernice!" Nova shrieks. "Bernice, get my mom! *Get my mom!*" she cries.

Then she's just screaming as the fire swallows her face, racing down her clothes and consuming her entire body. "Someone, help!" are the last words she shrieks.

I glance at Bernice, who's frozen in place, too. His eyes are fixed on Nova's burning body, wide and horrified. I swear I know this look.

I swear, it's always been aimed at me—people are scared wherever I go.

"I told you it wasn't a good idea!" he finally shouts.

"I—I…" I shudder, taking in a shaky breath.

Bernice walks past me, heading toward Nova.

She's stopped screaming.

"You're a monster!" he shouts.

"I—"

"This is what the Nepenthes would do!"

"I didn't mean to—"

"You're no better than them." He jabs an angry finger at me. "I wish you left when you said you would!"

"I'm sorry—"

"You're a killer! A monster! And I hate you! I'll hate you forever!"

"Berny, I—"

"I hate you! I hate you! I hate you!" he shrieks.

"Stop it," I cry.

"You're a monster. You knew you could hurt people! You said you didn't want to! You knew your mom was right, and you did it anyway!"

"Bernice—"

"She knew you were a monster! That's why she told you not to use your magic! She knows what you are!"

"Stop it!" I cry. The rage closes around my heart and pierces every bit of sympathy I have, bleeding me dry.

The Flame stirs within me, and I tell it to burn him.

For half a second, Bernice's pupils are on fire, then he falls to his knees. The shock knocks me backward, but I don't move. Instinct tells me to shout for my mom, but when I try, the words stick in my throat. *I try to look away from Bernice*, but I watch as his body falls forward, while mine burns.

Killing him. *I'm killing him.* I'm both aware of it and entirely confused about what's happening. The trees around me catch fire, *like in the dreams,* and I run, *like in the dreams.*

This time, when I call for my mom, the words finally break free. I run into her arms, *like in the dreams,* and she tells me to put the fire out, *like in the dreams.*

"What happened?" she says, holding onto my arms.

"Bernice," I cry. "I think he's dead, Mommy."

Mom grabs my hand firmly, saying, "Show me where."

We walk together in heavy silence while I cry, stopping beside Bernice and Nova's very dead bodies. Mom's hand goes stiff in mine, and my fear pumps adrenaline into my blood.

She reaches down and puts her fingers on his pulse. *I don't remember this part of the dream.* She looks at me as if I were a stranger—an evil, volatile, malevolent stranger.

"Is he dead?" I squeak.

I can't say anything more. The words won't physically leave my mouth, no matter how hard I try to force them out.

Mom shakes her head, her brows furrowing and her lips twisting in disgust—a look I could never forget. She hates me. I know this irrevocably. This is the face of hatred.

*This is the look I think I've always feared.*

"Is he dead?" I ask again.

She looks away from me like she can't stand the sight. "Go home, Desdemona," her voice is sharp. "Don't mention this to anyone and just go home."

"Mommy—"

"Go. Home. Now."

My lower lip trembles uncontrollably as I walk back to the dwelling, collapsing into bed to cry.

When Mom finally returns, she marches toward me and seizes my cheeks. "Knowledge is a weapon when you know how to wield it. Do you understand?"

I nod.

"Stronger than any Flame."

I nod.

"Do you understand?"

I nod.

Mom presses her necklace into my hand, and just like when we practice my magic, she tells me to feel.

When I catch sight of my reflection, my irises are red. The color of fresh blood.

*Oh my gods.*

Mom takes the necklace back, and my head feels fuzzy. All I can remember about today was Bernice screaming at me that I'm a monster after I told him everything about myself.

And something else. Something that has to do with Mom...

*Oh my* gods.

Mom says again, "Knowledge is your weapon of choice. Do you understand?"

Knowledge is a powerful weapon. Bernice knew it. He knew me. He wielded it against me.

*She's been taking my memories.*

"I understand."

I close my eyes, and when I open them again...

I'm in the ballroom.

I'm still here? It feels like months have passed. It feels like I should be shorter.

It feels like I'm six.

Aralia stands before me, her arms outstretched as three students crash against an invisible barrier.

"I could use a little help here!" she shouts.

I can't seem to move my body. I can't do anything.

I'm petrified, aren't I? That look in my mom's eyes—the disgust—will never give me the peace of purging itself. I will remember that face for the rest of my life.

Students charge all around me, screaming and shouting.

"Arcane!" they cry out, again and again.

But beyond the noise, one feeling stands out above all—the

absence of weight around my neck.

I clutch my chest, muttering, "My necklace," before dropping to my hands and knees. I try to crawl across the floor, but I'm stopped—there's a shield of air surrounding Aralia and me.

"Drop the shield!" A familiar voice shouts. *Lucian*. "I'll take her to safety."

"My necklace," it's all I can say. "I need my necklace!"

"Behind you," Aralia yells.

Someone charges for me with a sword in hand, and I'm only just getting to my feet when Lucian steps in front of me.

A severed hand falls to the floor. A scream rings through my eardrums.

I can hardly see through the panic.

Lucian crouches, grips my waist, and throws me over his shoulder.

I claw desperately at his back. "Aibek, I need my necklace!"

"And I need you *alive!*"

"Why?" I ask, barely loud enough for him to hear me.

Lucian glances over his shoulder, but he doesn't even offer me the decency of a response. My fingers grow numb from clawing at his heavy coat, and I finally let my body go limp against him. What could he possibly do to hurt me when I can apparently burn anyone to death?

In the darkness of my mind, I see Mom shake her head, striding quickly to the entrance of an old dwelling. Her hands swing around the neck of a man. *He looks like Freyr*. I notice her chest trembling with quick, uneven breaths.

"I've missed you," Freyr whispers into her hair.

She holds his face in her hands. "And I've missed you."

"How is she?" Freyr steps toward me, and I recoil. *Even though I tell my body not to*. He looks over his shoulder at Mom. "You wiped me from memory?"

"I can't give her any more instability. She's destructive enough as it is." Her voice sounds nothing like the one I know—it's cold and distant, like she's angry with him.

Or me.

"Isa—"

"I know, I know, nurture trumps nature." Mom sits next to Freyr. "It's easier said than done." The way she looks at me... It's like she despises me. "She's already taken lives."

"Isa," Freyr says sternly, turning to her and holding onto her shoulders. "You can't keep saying these things in front of her, then wiping her memory clean. The emotional scars will never fade."

"I know, I know—"

"If you can't love her, find a way to give her love. She's a sentient weapon. Handle her with care."

"Gods," Mom drops her head into her hands, "what were we thinking?"

"Regret won't save us now, my love." Freyr's hand shifts to her cheek, and they stay looking at one another. It's so... tender. "Is someone helping you? If there is, I understand."

"There's never been anyone but you." Freyr tilts his head, and Mom clarifies, "There never will be."

"Okay." He looks away.

Mom freezes. "Why? Is there someone *helping* you?"

"Never. I spend my entire life in that facility." A beat later, he says, "Have you spoken to Willow?"

"I've seen her a few times. But she's not doing well. As much as I try, she won't tell me what they're making her do."

Freyr nods in response.

"Do you have any more questions about the past?" Mom asks. "Because right now, I want to be here with you."

"Just one last thing... I know you don't want her." Freyr looks at me, and only now do I realize I can't hear myself when I try to speak. My mom's a Light Folk, and sound is Air's territory.

*She's been hiding the truth from me my entire life. She was one of the privileged once, too. Is that all she sees in me—the septic? The life she was*

504

*forced to give up?*

"But by nature, you are good," he continues. "She can be, too."

"Is that everything?" Mom asks.

"Yes." Freyr drops his head.

She picks it up and kisses him.

## Chapter 39
## Losing Track of What I'm Fighting For

# DESDEMONA

I don't recognize where I've woken up, and when I see a figure at the foot of the bed, I jump to my feet. My knife rises to his throat as his knife presses into my chest, but our eyes lock, unwavering.

*Do it, or I will.*

I push the blade deeper into his neck.

"Gods, Marquees," Lucian breathes, glancing at my blade like it's nothing more than a feather.

"Relent," I say through clenched teeth. I'll kill him, I will. He deserves it. I can *do* it this time.

"Everyone outside this room wants you dead," he says. "I'm doing you a damned favor."

"I'd like to see them try."

"No. You don't."

I angle my knife beneath his chin, pressing until he's forced to look up. Good. I don't want to see his eyes.

"Yes, I do."

I'll kill them first. I'll kill them all. Everyone who wishes to take away from me what is mine—the *only* thing that belongs to me. My life.

Lucian mirrors the pressure, his blade cutting into my chest. "Do you want this to end in a bloodbath?"

"I don't know." I press the knife deeper, drawing blood from beneath his chin and muttering sarcastically, "I did think we were kind of like Amun and Eira."

The first two humans—one immortal and one Lucent. They both died in the end.

With his gaze forcefully on the ceiling, Lucian remarks, "Would you say you've seen my charming attributes yet?"

"I've seen more of you than I ever wanted to," I bite.

"Drop the blade, Marquees."

"Why don't you say it louder and bring the *bloodbath* to me?"

In a move too fast for me to follow, Lucian drops his knife and both his hands grip mine. Then he pulls my blade down, pressing it to his throat and forcing me to look him in the eye.

Why not just take it?

"Would my throat be where you choose to level your blade? Or would you prefer my heart?" He leans in, nearly drawing his own blood. His breath is a whisper against my skin, his lips dangerously close to mine. "Go on, tell me all the ways you've imagined killing me."

I didn't think he'd remember that day in the infirmary, not after puking blood or his eyes rolling to the back of his head.

I lower my voice to match his. "I'd prefer your back."

"Think you'll falter if you're too busy staring into my eyes?" he taunts, his tone like a song.

I slam him into the wall, making his breath hitch. "On second thought, your throat will do just fine."

His grin widens, a dangerous thing, but there's a flicker of something else in his eyes—something softer, maybe more knowing. "Don't get me wrong, I love when you hold your dagger to me—"

"Why would you love that?" I spit the words out, a bitter laugh on my lips.

"—but we need a plan," Lucian finishes, studying me like I'm here for his delight and not his death. Like I'm both a puzzle and a prize. After a pause, he says, "Your whole demeanor changes. Most of the time you look dreadfully passive, but this? There is no word to describe it. I think I see the person you truly are. It's incomparable."

"And who am I?" I challenge, the words burning in my chest. "*Truly*."

"A survivor." His voice drops, almost a whisper now. "Something fiercer than what meets the eye. Someone who'd kill a prince. I must say I like her much better than what you pretend to be. Though, if I were you, I wouldn't kill me just yet. You should wait until I get you out of here alive." His lips curve in a slow, knowing grin. "Then you can have my back or my throat, though I'm more inclined to think you'll choose my lips."

I don't know why I'm surprised he's paid so much attention to me—seen through all my masks, all my false fronts and concealment. But I wish he hadn't. It just means he's gotten too close, and now he knows something else he can use against me.

"Still cocky, I see."

"Well, yes," he drawls, his voice dripping with arrogance. "I see the way you look at me. But I think you've forgotten the way I look at you."

I don't know why I do it, but I press the dagger harder against his neck. "You want to keep me alive?" I ask. "Then why bring me somewhere you have to get me *out* of?"

"It was the safest place at the time."

"Why bring me *anywhere*?"

Lucian glances down at the knife I have to his throat. "Because I'm a glutton for punishment?"

"Hm, funny," I mutter.

Then I notice the empty space against my chest. The dagger falls from my hand—foolishly. I'm unarmed now. Am I defenseless, too? I can't bear the weight of the question against the weightlessness of my neck.

"My necklace," I breathe. "Where's my necklace?" I back away from Lucian, searching for something reflective.

*My eyes*. They really are red. I touch the bone beneath them and stare, hoping if I look long enough, they'll turn back to brown.

They don't.

Something inside me splits. A seam, maybe. Something that had been stitched closed without my permission.

Nova. Bernice. They were real. They were my friends, and I killed them.

I killed them *all*.

Every dream I had wasn't a dream at all. They were memories—real ones. Memories I never really forgot, but just wasn't allowed to remember. Because my mother stole them. Hid them from me.

I don't want to think about how she truly feels toward me. I don't want to think about Nova and Bernice. I want to believe that Bernice is nothing more than a *living* asshole.

"Why are you protecting me?" I ask, louder than I should, given that we're hiding. But Lucian knows what I am. He knows I'm a killer, and now he's seen my red eyes.

*He knows what my mom knows.*

"Why do you think, Marquees?" he whispers, his tone laced with defeat.

"You should have killed me," I say, but I don't mean it. I don't want to die. I never did.

Lucian's face falls, stunned.

"I *have* seen your charming attributes, Aibek. But the bad in you far outweighs the good," I snap.

"Desdemona... I—"

"I'm going back to sleep." I walk to the bed and throw the cover over my head. "You can try to save my life in the morning." I close my eyes, but I have no intention of sleeping.

The dreams were real—and I've become exactly the monster I feared I was within them. I swore to never become that, but how many people have I killed in these last few months?

My mom knows me, better than anyone. And she never

wanted me. Did she ever even love me? Was it all just an act, what Freyr said? *If you can't love her, find a way to give her love.*

I see her eyes, looking at me and full of malice.

But *she* took those memories from me. They were accidents, I swear it. If she hadn't made me forget, then I could've learned. I could be in control.

This is *her* fault. I see it now. I learned to fear being known because of her. I learned to fear my magic because of her. I killed countless people because of *her*.

And I think I'm going to do it all again because it's the only way I know how to survive now.

But if Bernice was right, if I am a monster, then my mother made me one.

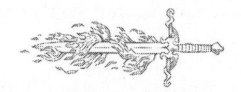

---

I realized I loved Bernice and Nova moments before they died, and I didn't remember them until yesterday.

I didn't remember *them*, but I could never forget the feeling. The wave that crashed over me when Nova begged me to stop. The knife that carved into me when Bernice spoke those words.

*You're a monster.*

I believed them instantly.

I didn't know what love was, but I felt it turning sour when Bernice screamed. I could taste it growing rancid when he fell.

I could smell it rotting in his burning flesh.

I learned what love was in death, and I didn't remember it until yesterday.

---

I must have slept, because when I open my eyes, the sun is up, and Lucian is gone. *I'm trying to get you out of here alive.* Yeah, whatever. At least I still have my knives. I'll get out alone, and I'll kill anyone who stands in my way.

I don't need anyone. Not even Lucian.

Surprisingly, the door is only locked from the inside. I slip out, a blade clasped between my fingers. I keep my head down, concealing my eyes as kingdom members pass through the hall.

Guards are everywhere. Soldiers, too. I wonder if Lucian was right—are all these people here to kill *me?* I have to assume they are. There's no benefit of the doubt in such severe cases as my life.

Doors line the left wall, windows to my right—no favors there, since light is exactly what I need to avoid. I can't afford to be recognized, and I have no idea how to get out, which means I'll be fiddling until I find the exit.

We must be several stories above ground—the sea through the glass wall seems too far away. I focus on the stairwell ahead. I have to make it there. I pick up my pace, determined to reach the steps.

But a guard locks eyes with me. Panic surges through me, but maybe he didn't notice. I duck my head lower—he doesn't.

It's too late.

The guard approaches, closing the gap between us with each step.

Without thinking, my hand moves, and the knife flies through the air—finding its mark.

The guard's breath catches as he raises a hand to his throat, blood spilling into his palm. His eyes widen in shock as he gurgles, then collapses.

The room freezes in stunned silence.

Every eye shifts to his falling form, then to me. Nobles in soft blue, guards armed with swords, soldiers with bows and blades—all staring at me.

I bolt, running for the guard and yanking the knife from his throat—knowing more murder lies ahead of me. But that's what I'm good for, isn't it? I can't think of anything else I've accomplished. I've killed animals for food and people for survival.

Even with all this power, I couldn't find my mom. I could only kill.

*And she never saw me as anything more than that, either.*

So when my wrists are wrenched behind my back so hard my spine cracks, I don't hold back one bit. My hands might be restricted, but my power never will be.

I can't even count how many I've killed, not after all those memories came flooding back. And I didn't even have to touch *one* of those Folk.

Guards close in from the front, and I'm sure more are at my back. Shadows wrap around me, chilling my core—but I don't mind the cold.

It soothes the fire tearing through my veins.

Fire that I now use as a weapon to kill.

One guard falls, and if I had to bet, I'd say his eyes are on fire like Bernice's. I remember this feeling before I understood what it meant—a muscle pulling from somewhere deeper than I can fathom.

Three more go down.

No one will kill me now. I'm a weapon, a murderer, a monster, and that won't change the moment I *need* to be. Every organ inside me burns as I focus on another guard. I choke back the urge to gag at the familiar stench of burning flesh.

It smells like burning hair and sweat that's sickeningly sweet.

Then, scalding steel presses against my throat, bringing blinding pain. There's nothing but blaring agony, drowning out every thought. I thrash at the shadows binding my hands, pulling until my wrists are raw, desperate to escape the pain before I crumple beneath it. But they won't budge.

*Stop, please—stop.* I try to speak, but all that comes out is a wheeze. My chest convulses as the heat spreads, devouring me from the inside.

I try to beg for relief that doesn't come.

"How does that feel?" They're behind me. Burning me.

Whatever this is, it pierces my skin, burning my blood. Every beat of my heart is agony, molten nails shearing it to shreds. I'd welcome death if it meant this torment would finally end.

"Queen Leiana wants her alive," a voice commands.

It feels like the skin is being torn from my neck, layer by layer. Ripping, ripping, *ripping*. Slowly, sweetly, like they enjoy the view of my flesh.

The steel presses harder, and it's no longer just my skin and blood. It's my *bones*, carved apart like brittle bark.

Darkness creeps into my vision as the burning fades to nothing.

Then the world does, too.

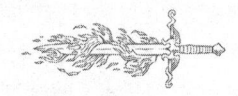

---

I wake to find shackles around my wrists. Immediately, I pull against them, trying to rip myself free, but they don't move. I'm frozen in place, and something feels wrong—different.

I don't feel hot. For once, I just feel... warm.

*My power*—they took my power. I thrash harder against the steel holding me, screaming like a maniac. Without my magic, I'm dead for sure. This is where it ends.

The world is a blur, but I see a woman in front of me. "Hey!" I scream, my voice hoarse. "Fucking look at me!"

I can barely make her out as she turns to face me. She drops to a knee, eyes fixed on my neck.

Her voice is unnervingly calm as she says, "He burned you good, didn't he?" She traces the wound on my neck—at least, I think she does—but I feel nothing. "Fascinating what a resilient thing you are," she murmurs, almost to herself.

I blink hard, trying to focus as the world slowly sharpens. The woman from the Gerner leans in, inspecting my neck. It's Queen Leiana—Lucian's mom.

"Do you know what you are, darling?" she asks, and I strain against the shackles. "The things you're capable of achieving?" She grips my chin like she owns it. "Unfortunately, I can't have you."

Her blue eyes gleam, fading to an unnatural pale white that casts a sickly light across the room.

"Where's Lucian?" The words spill out before I can stop them.

I didn't even realize he was on my mind.

The queen frowns. "You two have truly gotten under one another's skin. Is Lucian all you care to ask about? Come on, think *deeper*."

My mind feels blank, as if being beckoned by something beyond me. "What are you going to do to me?"

"Hm." Her smile widens, as if my fear pleases her. "I'm going to let you go, and you will run." The queen's hand clamps around my cheeks with such force that my jaw aches. Speaking slowly, she says, "You will never stop. At any sign of trouble, you will run again. And you will do so because the one chasing you is far more powerful than even I, if you can imagine such a thing."

My words are muffled, because she has me fish-lipped with her death grip around my cheeks. "You want me to run?" I want to whack her hand away from my face. I clench my jaw against the pain. "Why not just kill me?"

"Don't bother with riddles that have no answer. If I killed you, you'd just come back."

Between her and the headmistress, I'm tired of people talking in circles. What does that even *mean*?

The queen's grip finally relents, releasing me. She reaches for something—a key. Salvation is the only word that comes to mind. "If they find you, death would be a mercy. Do you understand?"

"Run. Got it."

*Been doing it my whole life anyway.*

514

"What concealed your power before?" she asks, twirling the key between her fingers. "Can you retrieve it?"

*The necklace,* I realize. Which means my eyes are red, and the dreams are real.

What does that mean for me?

"A memor," I answer, my voice hollow. "But it's gone."

"A memor?" Queen Leiana's eyes widen, a sharp breath escaping her. "Where is it?"

I would reach for my chest if my hands weren't restrained.

"Stolen," I say, fighting the urge to sneer and keeping my face blank instead.

"Stolen in Visnatus? At the academy?" she probes.

"Yeah."

The queen stares past me, lost in thought, until she suddenly jerks awake again. Looking me in the eyes, she says, "I'll cover you, but it won't last. Nor will it hide your eyes. You can escape the kingdom unnoticed, perhaps into our septic. I wouldn't advise you to stay on Ilyria."

I nod numbly. Is she really going to let me go? On the pretense that I *run?* It just seems too good to be true. Good things usually are. But I'm a sentimental idiot, and I ask, "What about my mom?"

"Oh, Sulva," the queen mutters. "She is gone. Dead. Do you understand?"

"No, she's not. I saw her."

Definitely a sentimental idiot.

"Hear me well and hear me once, child." She leans in close. Maybe I could smash her skull in. "You never will again."

I pull against the shackles. I don't care what Mom said. I don't care about the way she looked at me. I don't believe it. I can't believe it.

But all I say is, "Okay."

If I can just get out of these shackles, I'll get my power back, and I can figure out my next move.

I'll go back home—back to Damien. Yes. For the first time in months, this hope feels real, finally possible. Maybe Mom is still out there, but would she even want me to find her?

"I'll run," I tell her, "like you said."

The impassive sneer on Queen Leiana's face melts into something almost human—relief. For a moment, I question the truth of her words—that something terrible is hunting me. Something terrible enough that she fears it, too.

"This will hurt." The queen raises her hands, shadows twisting from the room and spiraling into me.

I gasp as the darkness floods me, seeping into every crevice. I become so thoroughly frozen that the aching grows dull. I'm not even sure my heart still beats.

I don't even think the blood moves in my veins.

With a forceful sweep of her arms, the queen draws the darkness back, leaving me empty. But I feel its ghost. I drop, choking on air, condensation clouding each breath.

"You're not far from the exit," she says. "When you leave this chamber, turn left. In three hundred paces, you will find the portcullis, and it will be open. Cross the moat and head south, beyond the Great Sea." The key slides into my shackles, and with a gratifying *click,* my hands are released.

"Got it." I nod and run, eager to get far away from the queen. I turn left, trusting her—if only because of the genuine fear I think she felt.

These halls are different from the ones before. No marble or glass—just dark stone.

I hear the portcullis open before I see it. I'm only feet away when a squad of seven guards marches down the hall, walking in formation, heading straight for me. I'm so close—but I can't make it without risking them seeing me. I press myself against the wall, hiding between two columns.

The guards move slowly, their pace unhurried. I shrink against the wall, holding my breath to stay silent. As they pass, I remain hidden in the shadows.

Then I spot him—Lucian, trapped among the guards. He looks almost dead, his breath shallow, but his eyes still find mine, locking onto me with unsettling intensity. His gaze flicks to the open portcullis, then back to me.

He nods. When I don't move, his lips part. He mouths something, but the words are lost in the distance.

The last words he'll ever say to me are ones I'll never hear—because this is it. Our final moment. I'll never see him again.

As I turn to run for the open door, I hesitate. What will happen to him if I leave?

I try once more to plant my feet—to stay—but my legs move of their own volition, carrying me to freedom.

With every step, I cling tighter to the memory of Lucian telling everyone I'm from the septic—just to make leaving easier. It does. If only slightly.

The blinding light strikes me as I step outside. A thick blanket of snow crunches beneath my feet, coating the bridge and making it difficult to walk.

The difficulty only increases as I leave the bridge, my legs sinking through the snow, nearly to my knees. But I push through, each step harder than the last.

I head south, like the queen instructed, putting space between the castle and the sea that surrounds it, when I hear the portcullis begin to close.

I continue forward, not looking back—even as I think of Lucian being hauled away by the guards. I push the image away. At least, I try.

But then, the memory shifts. A flicker of sound I hadn't registered in the moment. One word. A breath caught between silence and surrender.

*Go.*

That was Lucian's last word for me.

My body turns, even as my mind screams *no*.

He told everyone at school I was from the septic. He made me fear for my life more than once.

But even in his defeat, he told me to *go*. In our last moment, he could have begged me to save him.

Instead, he saved me. He saved me in the ballroom. He saved me when I killed the Lyrian soldier, too.

He never looked at me like I was a monster.

*The way my own mother did.*

Before I even know I've made a decision, I'm sprinting toward the kingdom's entrance, lifting my gown through the snow. It soaks through my shoes, numbing my toes.

The portcullis lowers slowly, but from this distance, it feels like it's falling fast. I force my legs to move faster.

But I'm afraid I won't make it.

Lucian was right. His touch did make my breath catch, and it *still* does, despite everything that's grown between us. Beneath all the hatred and the anger, there's still respect. There's still trust.

He wouldn't save me if there weren't—and I wouldn't be trying to save him.

He and Leiholan are the only two people I haven't severely censored myself around. They're the only ones who wouldn't run if they saw me for what I truly am.

Maybe not all of me. Not the nightmares turned memories.

And maybe Lucian will stop wanting to *kiss me*—and I would, too, if I were him—but the overwhelming feeling of wanting him, the one I've been running from, is finally catching up to me.

I miss the smile he would give me when his voice was full of amusement. I miss dancing in dusty rooms and stepping on his toes and laughing in a way I haven't dared to in years.

I miss the way he'd tuck my hair behind my ear and the strange sense of safety I felt when he looked at me like I was worthy of being seen.

I just miss him, whether there's hatred between us or not.

When my feet finally hit the steady ground of the bridge, I let out a sigh of relief. The portcullis is nearly closed, the spikes inches from locking. There's no choice now. I throw my body beneath them, making it just in time to *not* be cut in two.

Once I'm inside of the kingdom, I run in the direction they took Lucian, hoping their slow pace will make up for my slow heart. When I come across a staircase far grander than it ought to be, I take my chances. I scan every hall I pass, searching for any sign of him.

After three flights of stairs, I finally spot the guards' square in the distance.

I clutch my knife against my wrist, hidden. As they turn the distant corner, I quicken my pace. The door slams shut just as I round the bend.

I run for it.

The door is locked—but I remember the headmistress's lessons.

I grip the knob, summoning heat from deep within me. It surges through my fingertips like molten veins, pushing into the mechanisms of the lock. The metal groans, then softens, warping to the shape of my palm. I push harder, and I'm practically breathing fire by the time the knob melts and the door yields, opening with a silent push.

Inside, chaos unfolds. A vial is forced into Lucian's mouth, but his elbow strikes the guard's face, sending blood spraying from his nose. The guard fumbles, and the vial slips from his grip, shattering and spilling blue liquid across the floor.

Another guard grabs Lucian by the throat, choking him. But they won't kill the prince, will they?

I don't wait to find out. I send a dagger flying into the guard's back—but that leaves me with only three knives.

The guard falls against the wall, and Lucian gasps for air. No one spares a glance in my direction.

I step further into the room, watching Lucian's movements.

He drives his knee into a guard's face, but another slashes his arm, drawing blood and forcing him into a corner. Swords clang against the wall as he crashes into them.

That's when I take in my surroundings—an armory. The walls are lined with blades, axes, and bows, and in the center stands a metal contraption. It glimmers in the dim light, its surface reflecting what seems like a million colors, not just the cold gleam of metal. The air around it ripples, half infused with the vibrancy of heat, the other half shimmering like waves of water. It seems to distort reality itself.

*It's the weapon my mom created,* I realize.

I step closer to the weapon when something cold wraps around my throat. I gasp, reaching for the source. They're shadows—but they feel far different than Lucian's ever did.

They're weaker.

I scan the room, hunting for the person controlling them—then throw a knife into his chest. The pressure releases from my throat as he crumples to the floor.

Too easy. Two left.

Another guard sneaks behind Lucian while he's busy asphyxiating another. My second-to-last knife hits its mark—his throat. The guard drops.

And Lucian's eyes finally meet mine. The smile that flicks across his face is irreplaceable. He runs toward me, and the way he grabs me makes my head spin.

I think he's about to kiss me when he lifts my chin, but he only raises my head higher, examining the burns on my neck. I wonder what it looks like now. Concern flashes through his eyes, but nothing more. I guess he didn't have the same realization I had at the sight of him.

"Who did this to you?" he breathes.

"A guard," I answer. "I didn't see who."

Lucian's jaw tightens, and without warning, he sweeps me off my feet, pinning me into the wall with his body shielding mine.

An arrow whistles past, missing his head by a hair.

We stay here for a moment, but it feels much longer. For the first time in ages, his skin brushes against mine, and I feel every inch of it. I take a deep, shaky breath, and he smirks—just like he used to.

But a battle rages around us, and it's as good an excuse as any to avert my gaze.

"Duck," I mutter, and when Lucian does, I throw a knife at the archer. My last one.

Lucian grips my hand. "Run."

He pulls me through the hall in a zigzag as arrows whistle past. One grazes my shoulder, sending me off balance, but Lucian catches me. There's a bite of heat as the wound cauterizes.

"Do you trust me?" Lucian calls as we burst into a room, slamming the door behind us and heading for the balcony.

"Do *you* trust *me*?" I retort.

He answers without hesitation. "Yes."

*Bullshit.*

Footsteps thunder behind us, and I have no choice but to follow Lucian as we climb to the top of the balcony's white marble railing. The wind lashes my face. I should be afraid. This fall could kill us both—but the soldiers chasing us definitely will.

I look to Lucian, but he doesn't flinch. He's looking at me like I'm something he'd follow into the sea or the sky. I don't know if he's brave or broken. Maybe both.

But I follow him anyway, forcing myself not to look down, because there's no other option.

I squeeze my eyes shut.

And I fall.

# Part 3: The Falling

## Chapter 40
### In Your Choices Lie Your Fate

# LUCIAN

We crash through the surface of the sea, the world vanishing beneath the water. For a moment, there's nothing but the pressure of the cold. We hold our breath, not in triumph, but in desperation.

This safety is relative. The soldiers will reach us soon.

We'll have to survive until we can find a reflective surface to open a portal through.

Desdemona's muffled gasps bubble up from the water as she struggles to swim, her dress tangling around her legs and pulling her down with each frantic stroke of her arms. I catch her gaze, and panic flickers in her eyes as she taps her thigh urgently.

I release her hand, and the moment we're no longer connected, the freezing water stings my skin and burns my eyes. Despite the numbing sensation spreading through my fingers and toes and quickly claiming my arms and legs, I swim beneath her.

My head comes to rest at her knees. My hands barely brush her waist, as though I might shatter something sacred if I hold her too firmly. As if I know that I do not deserve to touch her.

She isn't simply above me in this moment—she is above me in them all. I glance upward, and she looks down, her gaze meeting mine with a silent trust I'm certain I don't deserve. And in that moment, all I can do is accept it, knowing that I am both unworthy and utterly consumed by her.

If the only thing I can ever be in her life is the guy who rips her dress to free her, then that's what I'll be. And maybe that's enough. Though, gods know how I wish there were more ways to tear her dress.

With a quick motion, I rip the seam, the fabric relenting in my hands as it releases her from its hold.

I offer her my hand, bracing myself to swim to the surface. Shock surges through me as she takes it. She still accepts me—in some way, however small, despite everything.

We swim, desperate for air, but the surface shatters again. Soldiers plunge into the sea, their swords still strapped to their waists and backs. The weapons will slow them down, offering us a fleeting advantage—if we can escape fast enough.

But if they catch us, I fear what they will do with those blades. No one brings swords into the water unless they intend to use them.

I tighten my grip on Desdemona's hand, pulling her forward. Together we push through the water with all the strength left in us.

But a sudden force yanks me back. A soldier seizes my hands from behind, ripping me away from Desdemona. Another clamps down on my legs.

My mouth opens, attempting to scream her name. The water swallows the cry before it's born.

A guard restrains Desdemona, her face pale and her eyes wide with the same fear I feel—they came armed. Leiana must have decided that whatever use I once had isn't worth keeping me alive.

All the while, my lungs burn with the need for air. My heart pounds until the pressure is unbearable.

I fear Desdemona will run out of air before I do.

As if we didn't have enough problems, something worse approaches. From the sea's deep darkness, a massive creature emerges—its glowing orb swaying from its head, casting fractured light through the water.

The soldiers drag me back, and Desdemona is pulled in the same way. I thrash against them, but my limbs are heavy, my strength slipping away with every second we're underwater.

Then, something shifts. The current changes, as if the sea is recoiling.

The light draws closer, illuminating the dread building within me.

The creature comes into full view—a monster the size of the fatta scorpion. Instead of claws, this creature has fins, slicing through the water. Instead of a stinger, rows of razor-sharp teeth glint in the shadows it casts.

It won't be Leiana or her soldiers that take me down—it will be this monster.

It charges toward me, jaws unhinging, ready to snap my head off. The soldiers release me, lifting their swords underwater as if they stand a chance.

I twist toward Desdemona and grab the guard holding her. He reacts too late. With a sharp crack, I snap his wrist—the sound swallowed by the sea. She slams her foot into his gut, wrenching herself free.

Knowing she's safe, I close my eyes, bracing for impact.

In the darkness behind my eyelids, a wave of red floods my vision. For a brief moment, I believe it to be my own blood. Then, a fleeting thought—could it simply be my imagination, a trick of the mind borne from the deprivation of air?

When nothing follows, I force myself to open my eyes slowly, taking in my surroundings with careful precision.

The water is stained crimson, and half a body floats by, severed clean. The other guards float through the water with gashes on their chests and necks; some are simply bodies without heads. I barely catch sight of the monster as it retreats into the depths of the sea.

Wendy's words strike me once more—the moonaro wanted to protect me. This monster must have done the same.

Desdemona's eyes widen at the gore around us, though she quickly shakes off her shock. She swims toward the severed torso, the crimson waters parting for her. Grimacing, she yanks the sword from the mangled body's back. When she looks at me, a smile curves across her lips, even amidst the horror.

She is every myth I was never meant to believe.

Every deity I was doomed to fall before.

Then she raises the sword—a shining, *reflective* blade.

*I've met my match, indeed.*

I swim toward her, pressing my fingers to the cold blade. The steel shimmers beneath my touch as I focus, and the portal begins to open—an image of wintry woods stretching across the reflective metal. The portal widens, growing until it's large enough to swim through.

Desdemona presses her hand into mine, and together we swim forward, gasping for air as we emerge miles away in a vast, snowy expanse.

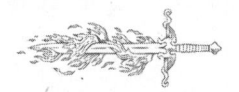

---

Soaked and nearly freezing, we stand in a world cloaked in white—typical of Ilyria. The trees surrounding us are mostly pine, though I've never seen them without a coating of snow.

Desdemona shivers, and I shrug off my coat. It's too thin to offer much warmth, but it's all I have to give. She eyes it like a weapon, then nods faintly. I drape it over her shoulders. As soon as I let go, she pulls the coat on, its hem falling past her knees, and hugs it tightly around herself.

The cold gnaws through my thin, wet shirt as Desdemona asks, "Do we have a plan?"

"Yes," I answer. "First, we find somewhere warm to rest."

"And after?"

"We find food."

I don't mention that I'll have to return to Visnatus for Lilac

—not yet. It's not safe for her to join me. Not that it's safe for me to go when *I'm* the power source of my parents' weapon. I'm their key to destruction. That's the reason the guards brought me to that room and tried to force that liquid down my throat. Why Labyrinth told me I was a contingency. I'm sure of it.

I should have ensured the weapon was destroyed before I fled with Lilac. No, I should have destroyed it when Azaire wanted to.

Desdemona's teeth chatter as she asks, "How exactly are we going to find somewhere warm in all this snow?"

"I know a place."

She stops, and despite the danger, I stop, too. Which we really shouldn't, not with the kingdom's soldiers likely trailing us.

"My eyes," she whispers.

This is the first time I've truly seen her without a blade to my body or a haze of adrenaline keeping me upright. This is the real her, eyes and all. Is it depraved of me to think she's the most beautiful person I've ever seen? When she's the very creature responsible for my parents' deaths.

If that's the case, there's this unabating knocking in my head, repeating that while she came into my life as a puzzle, she's now a piece of me. Because there are very few things I can control— in fact, I can count them all on one hand.

And my feelings for Desdemona Marquees are not one of those things.

Arcane or not, evil or good, it doesn't matter. She could burn the universe down, burn me inside out, and I'm sure this feeling would not falter.

I want to sink to my knees before her and pray for her forgiveness. I want her to serve me my retribution.

I want her to look at me the way I've been trying not to look at her.

"It will be dark," I say, choking on my words. My confessions. *Coward.* "Keep your head down and stay hidden."

It'll be dark enough. It has to be.

"Keep my head down?" Desdemona whispers with disbelief. "Wish I'd thought of that sooner."

I scoff a laugh. "Yes, as do I. Would've saved us the trouble."

For a brief moment, her face looks soft, unguarded. She quickly pulls herself together, though the daggers in her eyes don't have their usual intensity.

"Where are we?" she asks, her hand drifting absentmindedly to her chest.

"We're in Ilyria's septic," I say quietly.

The snow crunches underfoot as the trees loom around us, their bare branches weighed down by ice.

Desdemona lights up, her eyes widening. "Then why don't we go to Folkara?" she whispers, her breath visible in the cold air.

"Let's focus on immediate needs for now. We'll figure out the rest tomorrow."

She stiffens, eyebrows falling in confusion. Her gaze flicks between me and the cold surroundings, as if weighing my offer. After a beat, she asks, "We?"

I can't tell if the word is spoken in anticipation or animosity.

"I can't very well leave you to navigate a world you don't know."

Her eyes sweep down my body, then back to meet my gaze, as if seeing me for the first time. "Just until I find my way home."

"Until you're home." I nod.

To my surprise, she frowns. "Right. Let's keep moving."

She barely takes three steps before she stumbles into a tree well. I grab her waist just in time, pulling her free.

Desdemona turns toward me, stopping suddenly. Her eyes scan my face, searching for something, flicking up and down. I watch her intently, waiting for her to say something, anything.

After a moment, she pulls away, the warmth of her body flooding out of mine, a loss that leaves me colder than I expected.

"Thanks," she whispers.

Her gaze remains ahead of her, and mine stays on her. My mind shifts to all the things I'd like to say. All the things I feel for her.

We walk in silence. When I spot another tree well, I tell her.

She steps back. "Thanks again."

We keep moving, as do my thoughts.

I could just say it: *My apologies.* But it wouldn't be enough. Sulva knows it wouldn't be enough.

"What's your favorite food?" I ask when I can no longer bear my milling mind.

"What?" Desdemona gives me an incredulous look.

"Your favorite food," I say again, trying to sound casual.

Her eyebrows furrow, and she looks at me like I've lost my mind. Maybe I have—at least, when it comes to her.

After a moment, she speaks, her voice slow and contemplative. "Anything I get to eat."

"Favorite color?"

She says, in the same way, "Anything I get to see."

"Very interesting."

"*Endlessly.*"

"If you could see any color and eat any food, which would you choose?"

Desdemona glances over her shoulder, a smile tugging at her lips. It's a face I haven't seen in far too long and one I want to remember for the rest of my life.

But that's far from fair, and I'm far from deserving of it. Not when I know what's hidden beneath it, the things I can't fix, the things I've already broken. Still, I let myself want it.

"I have one answer for your two questions," she mutters, trudging through the snow and giving me a sidelong glance. "An orange."

"Why an orange?" I ask.

"Because they're made to share. My mom always said that." Her smile fades, and before I can ask more, she says, "What about you? Your favorites?"

"Cheesecake with red berries. No favorite color."

"I wouldn't have taken you as a sweet tooth."

"No?" I raise an eyebrow, surprised. "And what about you?"

"Savory all the way. We didn't get many sweet things back home."

"What *do* you get back home?" I ask.

There's nothing in her tone to tell me what she's feeling when she answers, "You know what a possum is?"

She lived on possums—scruffy, nearly inedible little animals. I always thought I knew her strength, always believed she could endure even the worst atrocities. Yet, somehow, I'm left questioning if I ever truly grasped the depth of her resilience.

With a nod, I answer, "I do."

"Hunted those," Desdemona says as she looks up at the trees.

"Oh," I say slowly, in an effort to tease. "You're a hunter. That makes sense."

"Why's that, Prince?"

That word—my title—reminds me of the world between us. Even if, somehow, I *was* worthy of someone like her, there's still that insurmountable wall standing between us. And it's not just the name I carry. It's everything else that I can't undo, can't change. It's all the things I've done to her and the things I can never be for her, no matter how much I wish I could.

I look at her while she looks at the snow ahead. "You're strong," I whisper. "Stubborn. And you have astonishing aim."

Desdemona stops, turning to me and lifting a finger to the ear she nicked before, when we were far from where we are now. At first, she seems solemn, then she smiles and says, "You better start wearing armor. I might aim for your heart next."

The crimson of her eyes gleams like the blood that stains coffins.

"Had you not already?" I ask.

Desdemona lifts her chin, but her gaze stays fixed on mine. I swear, for but one second, she blushes, the kind of reaction that makes my chest tighten. Maybe it's just wishful thinking, or maybe it's the way her eyes linger just a moment too long.

Stepping closer, she says with a quiet certainty, "You'll know when I do."

I don't know whether to be relieved or terrified by that answer.

The setting sun peeks through the snow-covered trees, turning the whole white world purple. As much as I love her staring at me and—truthfully—me staring at her, I softly say, "Look up."

Desdemona does, turning away from me and staring into the sky. "Wow," she breathes. "This is something."

"Yes," I answer, my eyes lingering on her as she watches the sky. For a moment, I forget everything exists but her. "It is."

If it's wrong to long for the same creature that killed my parents, then I will be wrong.

I will await my damnation.

But even in damnation, I would never grow used to the perplexity of her beauty.

The perplexity of *her*.

We continue trudging through the snow after sundown. The closer we get to Barley's, the more townhomes begin to emerge. Their chimneys release tendrils of smoke into the cold air, while a blanket of snow covers their roofs.

Desdemona glances up, her brows furrowing in disbelief. "This is what you call septic?" she asks, her tone edged with incredulity.

"Yes," I answer, my own tone carrying a hint of confusion. "Why?"

"We don't have anything this nice back home."

I glance at her, but my expression must be far less inviting than I intended because she gives me one quick look before her eyes return to the path ahead.

"I mean, it's nothing compared to Visnatus," she says, "but when I think septic I don't think… infrastructure."

It dawns on me that I have no idea what she has truly endured—of what has forged the girl standing before me now.

I want to know her thoroughly.

The red and orange lights from Barley's pub cast a warm glow over Desdemona's face as she mutters, "What are you waiting for?"

I haven't set foot in this place in what feels like an eternity, though it's only been a few years. Barley has always been a second family to Azaire and me. A second home.

The thought that I'm here without him feels impossible.

I stall for a moment, but when Desdemona steps forward, I follow.

"Keep your head down," I murmur.

"I know," she mutters dismissively, as though my words are barely worth responding to.

"I'm Andrew, and you're Catarina."

"Got it," she sighs.

I push the door open, the once-familiar bells barely audible over the noise of the drinking crowd. The air shifts, thick and warm with the stale scent of the pub. I glance at Desdemona—whose head is down. Perhaps it wasn't worth responding to.

"No shit!" Barley shouts from behind his bar, a grin in his voice. "It's been ages!"

He approaches and pulls me into a tight hug, a hearty slap landing on my back. I return the gesture.

"You're freezing, bud," he continues, tossing off his coat and wrapping it around me like a blanket.

"Long time, huh?" I ask, trying to match the cadence of his voice.

It's been so long since I've played the role of a commoner.

Once, it came to me as if second nature, but now, it feels like more of a struggle. Somewhere along the way, I lost the small cracks in the universe where I could be something other than a prince.

Something better.

"Much too long. Come," he mutters with a casual wave of his arm. "Sit by the fire."

We walk through Barley's pub, and he leads us to a circular table positioned in front of a fireplace. Desdemona extends her hands toward the warmth, her gaze fixed on the flames. Around us, the murmur of conversation rises—glasses clinking, the raucous laughter of drunk Lyrians filling the air.

Barley sits beside me. "Where's Elijah been?" he asks.

*Azaire.*

My heart lurches, the weight of his absence settling like lead in my chest. I hold onto the hope that my few redeeming actions might make him proud, though I do my best to push away thoughts of what he would think of the guards I've killed.

"He's caught up with the family business," I answer.

In the imaginary worlds we once created as children, his family was still alive. I glance at Desdemona, as if seeking some quiet understanding, and she meets my gaze, her chin lowered.

*She knows.* It's etched in every line of her face.

"That's too bad," Barley says as he gestures toward the bar. "The two of you look like you need a shot."

A waitress approaches, setting a glass in front of each of us. Desdemona and I knock them back as if the day hasn't been filled with anguish.

"Thank you, sir," I say, exhaling deeply. "This is Catarina."

Desdemona glances up for a quick moment. "Hi," she whispers, offering a faint smile.

"Good to meetcha, Catarina. Sure Andrew told you, but I'm Barley." He reaches across the table to shake her hand, offering a smile. Then his gaze shifts back to me. "So, what's the story with these get-ups?"

Desdemona's bloodied and torn green dress lies beneath my embellished coat—its fabric, too, stained with the remnants of a day we can never undo.

I lean in closer to Barley, lowering my voice. "It's been a rough day. By any chance is that room—"

"You two in trouble?" he asks.

"—still free?" I finish.

"No trouble, sir," Desdemona answers before I comprehend the question.

"None at all," I second. "Just far from home and a bit too tired to make it back."

"If there is trouble, you can tell me." Barley reaches into the pockets of his apron, pulling out the key and sliding it across the table to me. "The room's always yours, bud. The missus is upstairs; she'll find you both something warm and comfortable." He flashes a crooked-toothed smile. "Free of charge for my favorite young friend."

"I much appreciate the title upgrade," I say with a grin, and Barley chuckles.

"Yeah, go get some sleep," Barley mutters. "We'll catch up in the morning."

I meet his gaze and offer, with the utmost sincerity, "Thank you."

Pocketing the key, I guide Desdemona toward the concealed stairwell, leading her up the steps and down the hall to the spare room.

It's exactly as I remember it. Every inch of this room is an assault on my memories—reminders of the truths shared with Azaire on the days we escaped from our lives.

I sit on the bed, facing the wooden wall, my back to the window.

I surrender.

How I wish I could follow that path. Is it an option for me?

*Consequences be damned* is what I said, and it was never what I meant. There were never supposed to *be* consequences. There wasn't supposed to be a world without him.

He's not next to me, but he is in this room with me. He's leaning against the wall, under the window, telling me more about what lies under his beanie. He's under the bedspread shivering, while I tend to the fireplace, stroking the flames as I tell him the truth about my parents.

He's understanding me as I confide in him about all the things Leiana has done to me since my father's death.

We're in this room, together, alone, on every one of my real birthdays that I was never allowed to celebrate.

He's everywhere, and he's nowhere, and for the life of me, I can't understand it. It's not like my parents—I hardly remember them. Perhaps I couldn't comprehend this grief then, either. Because he was here all but a moment ago.

So, where did he go?

How can he be gone?

If there's a soul, and fatta venom kills that, I don't understand where that leaves him. In the snow?

In this room?

I won't believe him to simply be gone.

"Aibek?" Desdemona's voice is soft, the polar opposite of how I've ever heard my last name fall from her lips.

I stand. "I'm going to get us something more comfortable."

## Chapter 41
### When Bones Turn To Ash

# DESDEMONA

Snow is every bit as beautiful as my mom described. I've been watching it fall for what feels like an eternity. But Lucian must be joking—telling me *this* is the septic. There's no way. They have glass windows and real beds with sheets and all, just like Visnatus.

I'd rather think about the possibility of this being a joke than the probability of my mom. Everything I've fought for means nothing because she wouldn't fight for me. I don't even know who I am—*what* I am—to her.

A girl who killed children and chased her from her home? A girl who chased her from her lover?

I pull my knees closer to my chest.

The room is mostly empty—just a bed in the middle, a cluttered table to the side, a fireplace set in the wall, and a single light overhead.

When counting snowflakes becomes entirely too boring, I dig through the firewood and find kindling beneath the pile. I stack the wood and put the twigs in the middle, but I don't use my magic, I just stare at my handiwork.

Lucian walks in, his vest gone and his white shirt untucked, carrying a pile of clothes and a face full of sorrow. I sit against the bed on the floor, and he takes his seat beside me.

"I suppose," he whispers, "we're in this together."

A dry laugh escapes from my throat. "How about we're in it

together until we find individual safety?" When Lucian doesn't respond, I turn to look at him, but he doesn't turn to me. "You wouldn't want me as a partner." I look back at the window. "I'm not really a good person."

"I see you clearly, Marquees." He speaks like it's the truth.

"Not if you think I'm good," I whisper, like I'm scared to say it at all.

"Never said I did. Remember all the times you've held a blade to my throat?"

"Remember when you told the entire school I was from the septic?" I snap.

"Yes." He sounds almost remorseful. I can see he's looking at me, but I don't face him. He slowly whispers, "I'm truly sorry about that."

His words prickle at me. I never wanted—or expected—an apology. I wanted him to *fix* it. But that seems well beyond us now.

"Yeah, well, I have a lot to be sorry about, too," I mutter, my mind drifting to all the kids I killed. Even the X I carved in his chest—the rage that drove me to insanity. I had to release it, and I did. I scarred him.

"No, you don't," he says. I turn to face him as he adds, "Not to me."

"Right."

"No," Lucian says again, moving in front of me and picking up both my hands. He holds them like they're Soul Stones. Like they're stars. Like they will both grant the universe light and burn it to the ground. "Never apologize to me. There's nothing you can do or have done that requires my forgiveness."

Lucian's eyes don't leave mine, even as his cheeks turn red. I've never seen Lucian flush a day in my life.

I don't know what to think. There *are* things I've done that require forgiveness. And if my own mother couldn't offer it to me, no one can.

He doesn't know what he's saying. That much is clear. Or at least, he doesn't know *who* he's saying these things to.

Multiple, long exhalations later, I ask, "So you trust me, then? Or was that just an act to get me to jump off the balcony?"

Lucian is unwavering when he tells me, "I trust you."

He shouldn't. I don't know why he does. I don't know why he's thinking or saying any of this.

I also don't know why I say what I say next. Maybe I'm testing him to see how far his proclamation of trust will go. Maybe I want to arm myself with knowledge for the day that he turns on me again.

Or maybe I just want to know.

"Then tell me something about you no one knows."

Lucian's expression shifts from smug to faltering. His grip around my hand loosens, if only slightly, and he stares blankly at me. He blinks at least ten times in rapid succession before he says, "I killed a wolf when I was ten."

I can't help but laugh. "Is that what a prince thinks a secret is? I've probably killed a thousand animals."

"No." He shakes his head. "He wasn't an animal to me. He was my best friend, the last present my father gifted to me before he died."

Suddenly, I freeze. Every shard of humor I've clung to shatters. I ask, my voice tight, "Why'd you kill him, then?"

*Wait, isn't his father the king?*

"It was my punishment. Leiana was draining both mine and Bao's life forces, and she told me that if I didn't kill him, she'd kill us both." He looks away. "If I died then, Azaire would've, too. I did what I had to do. But that doesn't make it any easier, does it?"

A better person would give their apologies. But I am not a better person.

"No," I say, thinking of my readiness to crack Aralia's skull and my wavering remorse for the Folk I killed and all the misdeeds I've committed from then to now. I did what I had to survive, too.

But I'm not sure how much that matters anymore.

"It doesn't make it any easier." I have nothing more to say—even though I should—except, "A punishment for what?"

Lucian fiddles with the sculpture in his pocket for a while before answering. "When I was one, the Arcanes killed my mother. When I was six, they killed my father. Leiana and Labyrinth took me in, not as their nephew, but as their son. I had to lie about my birthday because it was only three months after Lilac's. One year, on my eighth birthday, I gathered the courage to tell Li that small truth."

I watch him, his gaze vacant as he stares at the snow outside. How deeply I've misjudged him. I want to say something, I want to be able to convey my sorrow.

"I—I'm sorry," I manage to choke out.

"For laughing?" he finishes for me. But no, I think it's more than that. "Don't be," Lucian says. "I can only imagine how silly it must sound."

"What?" I whisper.

"Having an extra mouth to feed," he answers.

"I wasn't thinking about it like that," I tell him.

"It would be justifiable."

"Why are you telling me this?"

Lucian meets my gaze, and with a single nod, he says, "I chose to trust you. Should the next question be whether you truly trust me?"

I pause. He shouldn't trust me. If it came down to his life or mine, I'd choose mine in an instant.

I will always choose myself.

"No," I whisper, my voice low. "It shouldn't."

"Noted," Lucian says to the silence.

And that's where we sit for far too long—my knees tucked to my chest and his long legs stretched out. His posture is better than I could ever hope to have.

Another person would've given him the answer he wanted. A better person would've told him the truth—that I'm not trustworthy. But a better person would also be trustworthy. Faulty logic, I guess.

"I put my survival over compassion," I say, telling myself it's to fill the silence, but I think it's because I want to answer his unspoken question: something about me I've never told. "But I think that's what it means to be human, isn't it? Just an instinct to survive?"

Lucian's eyebrows crease like he's deep in thought, and he says, "Being human means you get to find where the line between good and evil is. Then it's your job to stay on the right side of it."

"Right." I look out the window. "I don't even know what it means to be a good person, then. Let alone where the line is. That's what I've never told anyone."

But deep down, I think I know where I stand. My mom did, too. I really can't blame her for not wanting me. She basically said my nature is evil. And I don't have the courage to disagree.

"You trust me then, Marquees?" Lucian finally looks at me.

"I don't know," I mumble. "It's not over until the bones turn to ash."

"What?"

I smile, only a little. It's nice to know something a prince doesn't—no matter how morbid it is.

"It's something we say back home," I explain. "It means don't presume the outcome before the event is over. It's really just about the death count from a fire."

Lucian looks at me like what I've just said is insane and not the truth of my life. "That's... vile," he mutters.

"The septic usually is," I say. "What you have here is a joke by comparison."

My words come out almost cheerfully, but Lucian's expression darkens. His gaze sharpens, and I find myself staring right back.

"What was it like?" he asks. "Growing up there?"

"Probably not much different from growing up in a castle," I answer without thinking. "Let's talk about this later?"

Why don't I just tell him? I want to tell him. I want to be heard.

*By him.*

I want to make him feel awful for what he did to me.

More than that, I want to prove the universe wrong. Knowledge might be a weapon, but maybe it's not a weakness. But Mom didn't look at me with hatred because she didn't understand me. And Bernice didn't call me a monster because he wasn't sure.

Are the worst parts of myself who I really am? Or is that all there is?

Did the universe make me this way, or was I born backward?

If the universe is to blame, can it be undone? Can I revert back to some sort of purity? Or am I too far gone?

I don't want to be too far gone. But I know that if it came down to killing all those people again or losing my life, I wouldn't change a thing.

But maybe one person can hear my reasoning and understand. Hear what the world has done to me and not think I'm a monster.

*Not see me the way I'm starting to see myself.*

"It was hard," I say. "And I mean, obviously I didn't know it. As a kid, it felt normal. But, um, before the Gerner when I saw you in the Royal's room, or whatever, with your fancy suit and the wine, I thought… this is what I would have dreamt of as a kid if I wasn't dreaming of more food to ease the constant pit in my stomach or… being able to live in one place long enough to make a friend." *Or killing people*, I don't say. "It didn't hit me how much it sucked until I got older and realized there are people out there *not* fighting every day just to make it to bed. So yeah, it sucked."

I want to feel awkward or awful for sharing all that, but the only thing I'm wondering is: Does it exonerate me?

"It wasn't all bad," I say. "Sometimes there was music and dancing. Stories and poems. I think most of you posh people would be surprised by how strong we are."

I'm looking at him, waiting for a response and trying to gauge his feelings from eyes alone.

But Lucian walks away from me. *Not* exonerated, then. And he was just here saying I could never do something that he needed to forgive… or whatever that declaration was.

I should've known better. I used to. He's a *prince*.

*Oh, how he must see me now.*

A *click* and a rich symphony of sound pull my attention to him.

Lucian stands, leaning against the lone table in the room, his gaze fixed on me—with something like hope in his eyes. "Do you still hate me?" he murmurs.

Confusion sweeps through me, but it's this looming feeling of inadequacy that makes me answer, "Debatable."

Lucian steps closer, saying, "Perhaps I could change your mind." Then he bows in front of me, like I'm the Royalty of this duo, and his hand reaches up in invitation. "A dance?"

I stare at his hand, unsure.

"To rewrite the dreams," he whispers.

A smile pulls at his lips, and suddenly I see this situation for what it is: the *prince,* on his knee for *me.*

"At least hate me the way you used to." His voice is rough, almost a plea. "When you cared enough to use my longing as your weapon."

"Who says I still don't?" I whisper, accepting his hand.

Lucian pulls me in, our chests pressing together. He leans close, his breath warm against my ear as he whispers, "It used to be far easier to make you nervous. But I like it this way as well." His gaze seems to break through my barriers. "There's not a single part of you I wouldn't crave."

My blood pumps faster when I feel his heart thumping.

He's... *nervous.*

I like that I told him. I like that he knows about my screwed-up life and still looks at me with some kind of wonder. I like that he's seen me kill and still craves me.

I like that I can be awful, and he still asks for more.

"Well, my favorite is the part that hates you," I say with a smile.

"So long as she still touches me. But for you, darling, I'm not above begging."

*He hasn't called me darling in months.*

I lean back, wondering if Lucian can see the emotion written on my face, even as I try to hide it. Because the way he's staring at me is too intense—too intimate—that it has me looking at his hand until he says, "No one deserves the life you've had. Least of all you."

*I don't know if I'm anything more than the bad.*

I let out a soft laugh, changing the subject. "And here I was, thinking I'd never inspire endearment out of you again, *darling!*"

"Oh." Lucian chuckles, too, but it's short-lived. "Every time I look at you, I think about doing things I shouldn't."

I blush. Which is ridiculous. He could be talking about killing me for all I know.

"Then tell me," I say, desperate for something a little less serious. "In what ways do I *inspire* you? Other than terms of endearment and flicking noses?"

I mean it teasingly, but Lucian sways us through the room, lifting my arm over my head and spinning me. Then he pulls me into him, my back pressing against his chest. If I turned my head just an inch, my nose would touch his chin.

"I fall to pieces," he whispers.

"I told you I'd be your undoing," I say, but my voice is anything but steady.

"I never doubted it." His voice is so low, I'm not sure I didn't imagine it.

Spinning again, I turn to face him, and he pulls me in, whispering like it's a secret, and we're really in a ballroom. "If you meant what you said about not being a good person, I don't know where that leaves me. Beneath you, perhaps. But I think that's where I've been this entire time. Because I swear, the moment I first laid eyes on you, a part of me knew this was where my life ended and began. Falling for you."

I want to believe it. I want to look into his eyes and *know* he means it. Instead, I mutter, "You're good at this."

"Charming you?" Lucian whispers sarcastically.

"Spewing romantic shit and seeing if it sticks."

Then the world flips as he dips me back. But I think I trust him enough to know he won't let me fall.

His eyes crash on mine like a storm.

"Tell me I'm not crazy, Desdemona." He's not, but I might be because my name on his tongue is driving me into a frenzy. "Tell me you feel what I feel. Tell me your heart is on fire every time your eyes are on me. Tell me that through every harrowing hour of hating me, you couldn't forget what it felt like to hold me."

"Aibek—"

"Because I couldn't."

I try to swallow this lump in my throat.

"If you still hate me," he continues, "you'll have to hate me enough for the both of us. Because despite all my efforts, I could never *not* want you."

I open my mouth, but nothing comes out. We stay like this for a moment, dangling in the silence, waiting for something more. But it never comes.

Lucian pulls me to my feet, letting his hands fall from my

body. It's the most irrational part of my brain that demands me to tell him to *put them back*. "Perhaps I should have kept that to myself, but—"

I cut him off. "No—"

"—but if I do one thing—"

"Lucian, I—"

"—I will bleed until we're even."

I grab the collar of his fancy, untucked shirt and pull his lips to mine.

Heat rushes to my skin, to my face, my lips, and I feel so *alive*. My hands slide from the collar of his shirt to his neck, inching further back until my fingers slip into his hair.

I pull away, only hoping that my eyes will speak the words my tongue fails to.

*I feel it, too.*

The intensity of his gaze tells me he understands as he reaches up around me and pulls the pin from my braid. Hair cascades around me.

His calloused hand holds my cheek, his thumb grazing over my jaw, then my lips. He looks at me how I look at the sea—lost to its magnificence, wishing I could steal some for myself.

Then he kisses me.

His hands come to their place on my waist as he pulls me closer, impossibly close, like this space between us can be remedied on a level deeper than physicality. The hands that move down my body set a path of blazing hot fire everywhere they go, awakening every inch of me that they touch.

I'm trying to catch my breath in the milliseconds between the merging of our lips when his hand presses into the small of my back. I arch against him as his lips move to my neck. I'm unable to suppress every moan that escapes me when he finds what must be a delicious spot on my neck because he won't *stop* kissing it. And I would do anything to make sure he never does.

My back hits the wall with a thud, and with his lips on my

neck and one hand on my back, I pull his face to mine and crash my lips into his. Taking every kiss like it's the last human feeling I'll ever experience. Taking every touch like they absolve my lack of morality. His tongue slips past mine, deeper into my mouth, and mine does the same.

I kiss down his chin and stop on the apple of his neck. The sound of his groaning is more than gratifying, and my hands track down his torso, finding their way underneath the edge of his shirt and touching him the way I think I've longed to for months now.

Touching him like he's *mine*.

The music stops, and the chatter from downstairs resumes, but it feels miles away. Especially when Lucian's hands grip my thighs, pulling me up his body. My legs wrap around his waist like that's where they belong.

He carries me to the bed, dropping me down and kissing me, kissing me, *kissing* me from my lips to my cheek to my ear and down my neck to my collarbone until I crave for these lips to touch every inch of my body.

I sit up as he kisses me, my clumsy hands fumbling with the corset's ties until he reaches behind me. In one swift motion, he undoes the corset, letting it fall from my body.

I push up and climb on top of him, tugging off his shirt and pulling his chest to me so we can be as close as possible. Skin on skin on skin. My fingers graze his cheeks, jaw, lips.

*He's so impossibly beautiful.*

How am *I* kissing this boy? Skin to skin with a *prince*.

My hands graze over his back—over the scars that feel so much like burns.

There's a knock on the door, but neither of us is in the right mind to answer it, and his lips come to mine.

Another knock.

Then the door crashes to the floor.

# Chapter 42
## Doing What You Have To Isn't Easy

# DESDEMONA

Lucian pulls my corset back up, reaching for the laces. When his fingers skim my spine, I hate that I shiver, despite everything else he's already seen.

It's the only time that it happens. His hands know restraint, even now, after all this.

I almost wish he didn't.

But we don't have time for this. For softness. For touch.

For all the things I've always longed for and never got. Not until him—the same man who nearly killed me.

Figures.

For just a second, I let his touch consume me.

Then, I murmur, "We have no time!"

Lucian leans into me, his breath brushing the shell of my ear. I wish we had a moment. I wish we could linger, just long enough to believe this meant something.

But we can't.

"The window," he whispers.

Clutching my bodice, I force myself to my feet, running across the room. I grip the window, my fingers turning white as I pry it open.

A sharp breeze slashes across my face just as soldiers burst into the room.

My fingers scrape the empty leather at my thighs.

*I'm out of throwing knives.*

It really isn't over until bones turn to ash.

I climb out the window, scaling the side of the building. My fingers grip the icy, slippery stone as I fight the urge to look down.

The cold wind claws at my skin—as if this escape isn't already hard enough with my dress half on and half in my hands.

The narrow footholds are slick with snow, forcing me to test each step before taking it. When one shifts beneath me, my heart stops. I scramble, fingers digging into stone until I regain my balance.

Lucian climbs out after me, his movements swift despite the burden in his hands—a coat, no doubt meant for me. But the added weight will only slow him down.

I'm ready to shout for him to ditch it, but he yells, "Go!"

I hurry, jumping the last few feet to the ground and landing hard, but the thick snow cushions my fall. Lucian lands beside me, grabs my hand, and pulls me forward, but my corset slips from my grasp.

When I trip, I rip the dress over my head, clutching it under my arm as we run. I cling to the heat of adrenaline, ignoring the bite of the snow against my bare shoulders.

But my footing falters, and I stumble again, collapsing to my knees. Before I can gather myself, Lucian is there, trying to pull me to my feet.

My gaze locks on the soldiers, steps away from us. I could run, try to get away. But even if I stood now, I doubt we'd make it.

Fire builds in my lungs, burning with every breath, and consuming my every thought. It writhes under my skin, begging for release. Then it surges from me, igniting in the snow and rushing straight for them.

The heat warps the world, and the Flame burns my eyes—but it's a rush like no other. It may be sinister to laugh, but I can't help it as their faces twist in horror, realizing they won't be taking *my* life. Not today.

Not tomorrow.

Flames rise like a wall. The soldiers' shadows curl around it, trying to choke the fire with fear. But it's useless.

My power is inescapable.

I try not to look at Lucian, scared that he'll long for the version of me that might've stopped. But when I meet his gaze, there's no horror or retreat. There's acceptance.

There's desire.

The laughter rumbles through me, making every flicker of fire burn brighter. Never in my life has killing felt like this— catharsis. But for the first time, I'm not the victim. I'm not begging for sanity.

I'm spilling the blood, and I'm not sorry.

It's a line I'm crossing, and with every small step, I worry I will never be able to go back.

That should be horrifying.

I'm not horrified.

The fire winds around my spine like a lover's finger, whispering that I'm more than what they made me. That I could burn my name into the stars, and no one would ever forget it.

I tilt my head back, listening to every promise of power, every whisper wound with want. *Give yourself to me,* the Flame says.

*Yes*, I promise.

White-hot fire flows in place of my blood, and I rise to my feet. Some of the soldiers run from the fire. The others burn beneath my power, screaming.

My body moves before my mind can catch up, the remnants of heat keeping me going. I run beside Lucian, the chilling snow no longer cold at all, but burning hot beneath my feet.

A part of me knows I'll never be the same again. But another part, the part that always feared my power would be the death of me, is glad to leave the old me behind.

I let her burn with the rest of the bodies.

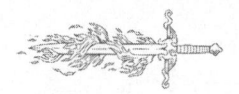

---

Lucian and I reach the spot where we portaled in from, the remnants of my fire still glowing in the distance. As I step back into my dress, my hands are unsteady, my pulse still thrumming from the fight. Flame still flickers across my fingers and knuckles—as if this power in me isn't ready to be put out.

Without a word, Lucian steps behind me, gathering the corset in his hands. His fingers move swiftly, but there's a tenderness to them—careful, reverent. Like he's lacing something far more delicate than fabric. Before I can say anything, he tugs gently on my hair, the motion so startlingly familiar it sends a shiver straight through me.

"Are you... braiding my hair?" I ask, but I'd know this feeling anywhere. My mom used to do the same.

"Why?" Lucian murmurs. "Does that surprise you?"

I nod, but I don't know if it's a yes or just a reflex.

He exhales softly, finishing the braid and pulling it over my shoulder. His fingers graze my collarbone as he lets go. "It's not very good," he says quietly, "but seeing as I ruined your last one, I figured I owed you."

When he steps around to face me, I tilt my head, studying him. "Is that why you tied my corset, too?"

He shrugs, his smile crooked, boyish, like we've got all the time in the worlds. "I did untie it."

Heat crawls up my neck. I doubt Lucian can see the flush in the dark, but even after having his lips on my body, I still don't want to risk him noticing.

"To Folkara?" I ask, clearing my throat.

Lucian's smile fades. "No. I have to go back to Visnatus. Lilac's still there."

So, this is where we part.

"Then I have to tell you something," I say, the words heavy on my tongue.

I didn't want to tell anyone, didn't want them to be able to chalk it up to me murdering four people without reason. But someone other than me needs to know.

"Arcanes attacked me the night the Leiholan lost his leg. They got past the barrier. They got into the school."

Lucian steps back, shock flashing in his eyes. His face shifts —calculating.

"What is it?" I whisper.

"That's why the monsters were attacking," he says under his breath, as if he doesn't want it to be true. "They were breaking the barrier for the Arcanes."

But that doesn't make sense. I shake my head. "If the Arcanes were only trying to get into the school, why would they have the monsters attack on other worlds?"

"If they're looking for someone, they can't risk that person escaping."

The words linger—more specifically, one word. *Someone.*

That someone is me, and I think we both know it.

The Arcanes already did get through the barriers, and they came looking for me. I *killed* them.

All the pieces click into place with ease.

"You think they're going to attack the school?" I ask.

"Entirely," Lucian says. There isn't even a hint of doubt in his tone.

"But why would they?" I just want to go home. And they want me—if the thing that Eleanora became was right, if my eyes are any indication. "What's the point? What good would it do them?"

*"Good?"* Lucian's expression darkens, his voice sharp. "These things aren't *good*. Their actions don't have to benefit them if they destroy us. That's all they want. They're harbingers of chaos."

Funny, that's how I described myself to Leiholan after I murdered a boy.

I step back, and the action doesn't go unnoticed by him. His gaze flickers—calculating, unreadable—before he taps his temple. "Whatever you choose," he says, voice softer now, "I'm with you here."

Instantly, I understand that unreadable expression.

Looking at the ground, I say, "You know."

"You're going home," Lucian observes, without a trace of pushback in his tone—something I'd expect from anyone else.

"Yes."

"We do what we have to do, even when it's hard." He reaches into his pocket, pulling out something silver and small—the token I'd asked about the night we drank and danced. He picks up my hand, and the gesture pulls my gaze to his. The chill of the object in my palm cuts through the fire still burning in my veins.

"I'll find you when this is over," Lucian whispers, his breath uneven. "I swear it."

I nod, trying to find something to say and coming up utterly dry.

"Until then, keep your wits about you, Marquees."

He lifts my hand, pressing his lips to my skin. Then he turns, opening a portal without another word.

And just like that, he's gone—leaving me alone with the silver wolf in my hand.

I open my own portal home, stepping through it into the Welding Village. Each breath clings to my throat. I'd forgotten how thick the air is here—heavy with soot that settles in my lungs. But I don't care.

My legs move on their own, carrying me to Damien's house as if my body remembers the path better than my mind does. I'm home. I got my life back. These last four months can be forgotten, and I can just be me again.

The me without Lucian, Leiholan, and even Aralia.

Suddenly, I'm not entirely sure what that looks like.

But when I see Damien, it all goes away. He opens the door to his dwelling, stepping out onto the dirt. His eyes meet mine, going wide—like he's seeing a ghost. Then he moves, fast, throwing an arm around my waist and lifting me off the ground, spinning us in circles.

I laugh. Really laugh.

It bursts through me like a second breath—lighter and freer than anything I've felt in months.

*I got back what I lost.*

Damien laughs, too, setting me down. My feet hit the ground, and he just stares, like he still can't quite believe I'm here.

"My gods, Des," he breathes, "I thought you were dead."

All I can say is, "I'm back."

His gaze roams up my body, falling on my smiling face. His eyes lock on mine, and just like that, the warmth drains from them. He's never looked at me like this.

My knees go weak, and I nearly reach for him to steady myself.

But for some reason, I don't.

I did it. I made it home—what I've been trying to do for months. I fought so hard for this.

I thought this was the part where everything would finally be okay.

"What? What is it?" I ask in a rush, confused at first.

He must be shocked to see me after so long. He thought I was dead—he must be adjusting to me being alive. He just needs a second, but with every one that passes, fear fills his gaze.

Then realization strikes me.

He's not seeing *me*. He's seeing what I look like now. The red eyes.

Air escapes my lungs and becomes twice as difficult to take back in.

Damien stumbles back, and I step forward, following him.

He falls but still tries to crawl backward. "Mom!" he shouts. "The Arcanes are back!"

"No," I try to explain. "I'm not—"

He shakes his head, hand straining for the door knob.

"I'm not an Arcane, I swear!" Panic laces my blood, my words tripping as they spill from my lips. "What do you mean they're back?"

Damien doesn't even try to answer.

His sister, Elliae, appears in the doorway. Her eyes widen as she drops to her knees, clawing desperately at Damien's shirt as she tries to pull him inside.

"Please, let me explain!" I shout as Elliae cries, pulling Damien beyond the barrier of the door.

They slam it closed in my face. They can't seriously believe this would keep out an Arcane. That this would keep *me* out.

I knock on the door again. "Please, Damien. Just talk to me. Elliae! I'm not an Arcane, I swear." Knocking turns to pounding and pounding turns to pleading. "Do you know how hard I've fought to see you guys again? Please, just talk to me!"

*This was everything I wanted.*

My legs fold under me. I sink to the ground, forehead pressing to the door like it might hear me if I'm close enough. Tears cloud my eyes, and snot clogs my nose.

"Please," I whine. "You're all I have left! My mom's probably dead, and she never even cared about me. You guys are all I have. *Please*. Don't leave me alone."

Please, please, please.

## Chapter 43
### I Know What I Didn't Before

# LUCIAN

This room of mine reflects a person I've lost, someone I'm not sure I want to hold onto.

I look back at the mirror I stepped out of, the hopeful part of me thinking she's followed.

The better part of me knowing she's gone.

Adrenaline keeps my exhaustion at bay, but I can feel a fight coming—I'm certain of it. There's one thing I have to do before it arrives.

As I leave my suite, the stillness of the academy is unsettling—it's hard to tell if it's under lockdown or if the silence is just a byproduct of the late hour. I approach Lilac's suite and knock, the sound echoing through the desolate halls. Fleur cracks the door open just an inch, her eyes barely visible through the narrow gap.

"What are you doing here?" she whispers.

"I need to see Lilac."

"No, we were all told you weren't coming back." The corners of her lips lift. "But I'm glad you're here."

"Told by who?"

"King Labyrinth announced it."

A chill runs through me at the thought of what would have happened if Leiana and Labyrinth succeeded in using me to power their weapon—if they had been able to force that liquid down my throat.

Would I be catatonic? Trapped in a nightmare from which I could never escape, while my body became nothing more than a vessel for their will, slaughtering those they deemed worthy of death?

Fleur's tone falters as my silence stretches. "Have you seen Eleanora lately?"

I have a hard time pushing past the horrors of my thoughts. This weapon—one I once desired to wield myself—was meant to draw its power from me.

*You were the only one whose power could be used against the Arcanes at the time,* Labyrinth had said. *You were only a contingency.*

If I were nothing more than a contingency—why are they using me now?

With a concentrated effort, I cast aside the thought, trying to recall the last time I saw Eleanora. It's been ages.

"No," I answer. "I haven't."

Fleur looks down, nodding solemnly. "Okay."

She opens the door, and I enter the suite, heading straight for Lilac's room. As soon as I step inside, she pulls me into a hug.

"Is it true?" Lilac asks. "He's dead?"

She's heard—and I wasn't the one who told her. I allowed another to bear the burden, because I couldn't.

"Yes," I whisper, still struggling to say it. "He's gone."

Lilac shudders. "He's gone." The words seem to settle in.

These are the consequences—my sister looking at me with tears in her eyes as she realizes exactly what I can't fathom: he's gone. Our brother is gone.

"They said it was a fatta," she whispers, looking down.

I nod, the word difficult to speak. "Yes."

"So that means he's…"

"Wendy brought him to the woods and anchored his spirit to a tree," I explain, though I'm not certain that's what happened. I fear Azaire was already beyond saving by the time we arrived, yet another truth I cannot bring myself to tell her.

"Have they started evacuating the other students?" I ask.

Lilac's head snaps up. "Evacuate? Why?"

"The Arcanes are coming." I lower my voice. "I can take you to Ilyria before they arrive—"

"No way. I'm not going back there."

"All right," I breathe, exhausted. "We'll find you a safe place to hide." Could the Royal floor be safe? I'm not sure anywhere in any world is safe from the Arcanes.

Lilac shakes her head firmly. "I'm not hiding this time." Her shadows close the door behind us, and she smiles. "I've become a worthy adversary."

"If anything happens to you, Li—"

"It won't." With a long exhalation, she follows her last sentiment with, "I don't know how many Leiana made me kill. But I have their power now. This time, I'll protect you."

Other people care about my life, too. With Azaire, I think when I disregarded the consequences, I'd been thinking about them in terms of *my* life. At that moment, it felt inconsequential.

*It wouldn't have felt inconsequential to Azaire.*

Consequences be damned, as it turns out, was an entirely ignorant thing to say.

I should've never dragged him into that battle, vision or otherwise.

"Azaire died," I murmur, the words feeling anything but real, "because I dragged him into that fight. I'm not ready to lose you, too."

"*I'm* ready." Lilac extends her hand, her shadows picking up a sword from the corner of her room and pulling it into her grasp. "I'm probably even stronger than you now. Consider my fighting a favor."

She grins, and I can only pray this doesn't end like it did with Azaire, because I can't stop her. Try as I might.

"Where did all this snark come from?" I ask, raising a brow.

"Years with you, brother. Calista ,too."

"In that case—" I jump into Lilac's bed, untucking her sheets.

"Hey!" she yells with a laugh.

It isn't until I'm lying down and ready for sleep that I notice what's missing.

"Where's your violin?"

Lilac doesn't answer.

"Li?"

"In the closet," she mutters hastily.

"Why?"

"I don't know, I got tired of seeing it."

Her violin, her prized possession. Tired of seeing it?

I sit up straight. "How are you holding up?"

"Fine." Lilac doesn't meet my eyes.

Perhaps it was a mistake to hide the abuse from her all this time. She deserves to know what our parents are truly capable of, that she isn't alone in this.

"I spent much of our childhood in that dungeon," I tell her; I *finally* tell her. "I watched as Leiana drained the life force from hundreds… before she did the same to me. I don't know how much of my life force she's taken, but I know it was more than I should have been able to survive. Whatever you endured, I may never fully comprehend, but I will make every effort to understand."

When Lilac finally looks at me, her eyes glisten with unshed tears. She opens her mouth to speak, but only a sob escapes.

I hold out my arms. "Come here."

Lilac collapses onto her bed, crying into my shoulder. "It was awful, Lucy," she chokes between sobs. "Person after person. I can still feel them—like I got more than their life force. I took their souls, too."

"We'll figure it out," I whisper, keeping my voice steady for her.

"There's no escaping," Lilac says. "I see that now."

"No." I pull her back and look into her eyes. Her gaze is distant, vacant, as if she's ready to give up. "We'll get out from under their thumbs," I promise her.

Her bottom lip quivers, and she shakes her head. "I'm becoming her, Lucy. I can feel it already."

"You will *never* be her."

"I have her power. I get it. Even with the disgust, there's a longing for more."

"You have her power, but you have *your* heart. You have what she never did." I smooth out the hair at the top of her head. "If I know one thing, Lilac, it's that you are better than her in every way."

"I don't know."

"Whatever good is in Leiana lives in you. I swear it."

"Okay." She nods, wiping the tears from under her eyes. "You should get some sleep."

"I'm more than all right to stay up."

"You need your strength. I'll wake you at the first sign of trouble."

---

I wake, and the taste of Desdemona lingers in my mouth. I savor it as if she's here. Though, I'm not sure where I am.

"Lucian," a voice calls, shaking my shoulders once more.

I take in my surroundings, the pastel room and my sister standing before me.

"Where did you sleep?" I ask.

Lilac's cheeks flush as she looks down. "There's trouble." I sit up instantly, and she continues, "Calista found a necklace—she believes it's the Memorium. Out of nowhere, it levitated and disappeared beneath the door."

Calista found the Memorium—the Soul Stone of Folkara, lost for hundreds of years.

I fasten my sword, knowing it's useless against an Arcane—

and dreading the destruction they could unleash with a Soul Stone in their unkempt hands.

"All right." I move toward the door. "Stay here."

"Where are you going?" Lilac asks.

"I'm getting Yuki and more weapons."

Lilac tosses a sword over her shoulder and declares, "I'm coming."

I shake my head, every instinct urging me to leave her behind, yet something warns me that it isn't my decision to make.

"Straight to my suite," I tell her.

Lilac makes a face, then, with a mocking tone, says, "Okay, Dad."

"If things go wrong, focus on the fight in front of you."

"Okay!"

"Please," I whisper. "Be careful."

Lilac's expression sobers, and she nods. "I promise."

I let out a sigh and turn toward the door.

The moment I step into the hallway, something feels off. I glance down at my feet, half-expecting to see bodies littered across the marble floors. Instead, they're as pristine as ever. I look at Lilac, but her expression doesn't falter.

She doesn't feel this.

We move through the silent halls, our hands hovering just above the hilts of our swords. Approaching the boys' wing, I notice the first sign of life—someone walking toward us.

Lilac grabs my wrist, stopping me. "Is that... Wendy?"

I watch the silhouette, which increasingly resembles Wendy with each step. As she draws nearer, I notice red in her eyes—red that, before Desdemona, I'd only seen once before.

When an Arcane killed my father.

"Lilac, run."

Instead, Lilac draws her sword. I raise mine.

"Oh, my boy, I have no desire to fight you," Wendy's voice lilts, both familiar and foreign; the voice belongs to Wendy, though the inflections and tone do not. "I know how skilled you are, and I'd prefer not to kill you."

I try to push the familiarity away, but it lingers in my body. Lilac swings.

"Don't," I say, too late.

Azaire loved her. *We have to try to save her.*

Before Lilac's blade lands, Wendy raises an arm, freezing her mid-strike. My sister stands, awkwardly poised—one foot lifted on its toes, the sword suspended in the air.

I step in front of Lilac, shielding her body with my own.

"Neither of you, for that matter," Wendy says.

"I can't move," Lilac says, panic lacing her tone.

"Let her go," I demand.

The Arcane inside Wendy grips my chin, forcing my face down until we are eye to eye. It's not Wendy's gaze I am met with. Instead, I lock eyes with something far older. Here, there is life, death, experience. The familiarity in that stare strikes me with an unsettling force, a presence I wish I never knew.

The Arcane nods, as if reading my mind, and an approving smile curls across its lips. "You know," *it* says.

I rip myself from the creature's hand, the blood in my cheeks thrumming as though its touch were engraved into my skin.

"Yes," I spit. "I know."

Wendy steps back, her voice carrying the weight of a challenge. "But not the whole story, I presume."

I shake my head, hoping to silence the Arcane before it speaks. I don't need Lilac to hear about my past. When I tried to tell her, she didn't want to know, and I want to protect her from it—the darkness that has haunted me since my parents' murders. That's mine to bear.

Meeting the Arcane's cold stare, I steady my voice and demand, "Let her go."

The creature's gaze flickers over my sister. "She seems... defiant."

"She won't attack again," I promise.

The Arcane sneers, and the scar running down Wendy's chin protrudes. "If I must."

With the wave of a hand, Lilac is released. Her sword falls forward, her body carrying through with the swing.

"So who am I, really?" Wendy smiles.

But the curve of her lips is wicked.

"Luc—"

"It's all right, Li," I say gently. This isn't her fight. It's mine. And I can't draw her into it the way I did Azaire. Facing the Arcane, I answer, "You killed my parents."

The creature lets out a deep, guttural laugh—one that echoes through my body and sends shivers down my spine. The cacophonous noise ceases as the Arcane says, "Well, yes. I must admit, I'm almost ashamed you don't know the full story. I expected my offspring would be more astute."

Lilac steps forward, determination in her eyes, but I raise my arm, halting her.

"I'm no Arcane," I retort—yet even as I say it, doubt knots my tongue. These creatures are darkness incarnate: born from hatred and driven by a hunger for destruction.

Exactly as I am—driven by vengeance.

Where does their darkness end, and where do I begin?

"Come now. I know you feel it, boy." I do—yet I can't possibly allow myself to. The Arcane steps around me and hisses, "It's in your bones."

I step away from it. "What do you want?"

"A reunion." Wendy's hands are as hot as Desdemona's when the Arcane brushes a piece of hair from my forehead—though Wendy's touch only burns. "To bond... with my son."

The words fill me with revulsion.

"I am *not* your son."

Wendy steps back. "There's much hidden, my boy. Starting with Silas and Ramona. Give me your favor, and I'll enlighten you of your true history."

"Don't," Lilac says strictly.

"Do," Wendy says softly.

"What do you know of Silas and Ramona?" I ask, my voice betraying a waver I can't control. Father and Mother. Shadows swirl beneath my feet as Lilac prepares to attack, but I block her power.

From the corner of my eye, I see her glare at me.

"Everything where it pertains to you," the Arcane answers. "Your favor?"

This is it, something I've thought of all my life. This is where I get to learn why the Arcanes did what they did to me.

"Your name?" I answer.

"Lucian!" Lilac shrieks.

"Icarthus," Wendy says.

I recite, voice steady, "You have my favor, Icarthus."

My defenses diminish, and I turn, grabbing Lilac's shadow-ridden wrists before she strikes.

"If you kill *it,* you kill Wendy," I say.

Lilac jerks her wrists from my grip. "What are you doing—giving your favor?" she shouts.

"It knows my parents, Li. But you should go."

"I'm not leaving you this time." She picks up her sword again. "You're my brother by choice now."

"I didn't just *know* your parents," Wendy's voice cuts between Lilac and me. "I *chose* them—the two most powerful Lyrians." Lilac grabs my arm, pulling me back as Wendy's tone deepens. "In the body of your father, I used the Soul Ruby to impregnate your mother, creating *you,* with the power we require." It leans closer, whispering, "That's why you bear the scars."

"That's absurd!" Lilac shouts.

Icarthus ignores her. "I am ready for my favor now."

I stare into those red eyes. Red eyes I've seen before—the creature who killed Father. Yet this story is a work of fiction. It can't possibly be true. The *Arcanes*—the creatures I seek to destroy—forged me?

It isn't right.

"What was the first gift my father gave me?" I demand.

"I gifted you a silver carved wolf," it replies with chilling certainty.

I freeze, the air catching in my throat, and my voice cracking as I ask, "What was hidden about Silas and Ramona?"

"They were the true king and queen of Ilyria." It speaks slowly as its voice dips into a deep whisper, "You didn't ask me the clearest question." It tries to mock my tone and fails, *"What is the power you require of me?* A fine question, son, as it pertains to my favor. Bring me Desdemona."

The word forms in my chest, but it doesn't make it past my throat.

*No.*

I will not.

"The two of you were never supposed to *fall* for one another. You were made to *destroy* one another. Lucian Aibek, I command you, in return for my favor, to bring me—"

Shadows surge forward, slamming into Wendy with force and sending her staggering backward. A puff of orange-gray smoke bursts from the top of her head, dissipating in the air like a fading flame. Then Wendy crashes into the marble wall, her body still as it slumps toward the floor. The Arcane is seemingly gone.

But it won't stop the command.

Already, every inch of my being is pulling me to find Desdemona—even more than I've already longed to.

For this isn't longing—it's compulsion. I *have* to find her and then I *have* to give her up. I can't do it. Yet I know I will. The prickling in my bones has already begun, and it will turn to pain, and the pain will turn to debilitation.

My legs twitch with instinct. My throat tightens. The pull is everywhere—under my ribs, behind my eyes.

And as I fight this need that courses through me, I finally realize, *I wanted Desdemona to be responsible for Lilac.*

Because just as I am doing now, I have to fight this feeling in my chest. I have to deny this longing in my being.

I have to face the fact that I fear my heart is opening, and I'm not prepared to let another one in. To have another person to fear for, another person to protect, another person to lose.

*Another person to love.*

Because love, for me, has been nothing but pain and punishment. Torment and tactics. It's having the life sucked out of me. It's having to kill to protect. It's having to die to save. But now, having to truly doom her against every part of my shattering will, I can't deny the way I feel.

It's like… I've laughed for so long that I have to force myself to stop. To breathe. And my whole body is humming with a feeling that dares to be so fleeting. I want to hold onto it. Wrap my hands around it and carry it with me for the rest of my life, whether it's hours or days. Minutes or years.

But I can't. I can only welcome the fleeting moment.

That's what she is to me.

The fleeting moment.

The breath after the battle.

She is the peace when I've finished laughing.

I see her smile, and it lifts years of pain from my shoulders. I remember the wine glass trembling in her hand—how she tried to hide it, how I noticed her nerves. The way her lips always curve in defiance, like she's daring me to look away.

I never could.

She made following her feel like the only option.

And I would follow her anywhere.

I would do anything to hear her laugh again. To catch the real her, slipping through in the quiet moments, like a secret only I was meant to see.

And I wish she were responsible for everything bad that's

ever happened in this world and the next.

"She's dead," Lilac whispers. I only now notice that she is across the room with Wendy's body, gently closing her eyes.

I crouch beside Wendy. Another part of Azaire—gone. Will he fade from me, too, little by little? The best parts of me have always come from *him*. His words in my mind. His beliefs in my bones.

Will that fade with time? Has it already?

I fear I don't have enough of Azaire in me to carry him forward. What if I never did?

"I have to go to Folkara," I say, barely aware I've spoken aloud.

Lilac looks at me, bewildered.

"No," I mutter, as if it will undo what's already begun. "Don't let me go, Li." I shake my head, wishing it could shake this madness from me.

"I won't," she promises, voice tight. Her eyes flick down to Wendy's still form. "What do we do with her?"

I pull my jacket off and drape it over Wendy's body, saying, "We'll return for her once this is over. But until then, we fight."

And as the dawn breaks, so, too, does my will.

# Chapter 44
## Please Have Mercy on the Wicked

## DESDEMONA

I have nothing. I have Lucian.

I always had nothing. I never had Lucian.

Did he ever truly know me? Did Damien? Did *anyone*?

I thought I knew what it was to have nothing. But I think I was wrong. Because realizing that no one, in any world, knows who I am makes me question if I even do.

If knowledge is power, letting people know me means handing them the weapon. But if I'm left in just as much pain as if I'd given someone the knife, what does that mean?

No one stabbed me in the back, but I stabbed myself at least in the foot.

I'm alone by my own doing. I pushed everyone away because of my mom's words. The words of a woman who never loved me. Was it deliberate sabotage? Or is she just as screwed up as I've become?

My forehead is still pressed to the door. My knuckles ache from knocking, but I don't move. "Damien," I cry again, knowing he won't answer.

Wind brushes through my hair. For a second, it feels like comfort—like the past is reaching for me. But it slips away, cold and impersonal. It doesn't remember my name. Doesn't remember me.

The soot in the air presses against me, trying to shove me out.

This entire village is forgetting me, moment by moment, shunning me the same way Damien has.

I thought I belonged here, but even the elements disagree.

Does this prove my mom right? That I am a monster—something worthy of being feared?

"Girl!" someone shouts. "What are you doing out here past curfew?"

*Curfew?* I turn to the voice—a keeper. I meet those gray eyes, and I can't help but think of Leiholan's words. With that Nepenthe in mind, it's hard to hate this one.

"Family fight," I mumble, rising to my feet. "I was just leaving."

*Am I really giving up this easily?*

The keeper pulls a metal rod from his belt. "What's your name?"

"Catarina," I answer.

He steps closer before stopping in his tracks. I hold his gaze as his eyes widen, his breath hitching before he backs away.

"I'm not going to hurt you," I call, following after him. "Just... What have the Arcanes been doing here?"

He turns sharply, and I take the last step between us, closing my hand around his wrist before he can escape.

"Don't," I rasp, my fingers tightening to keep him in place. "Run."

He lets out a strangled cry, and I quickly let go. A red mark, the size of my hand, spreads across his wrist as the faint scent of scorched fabric fills the air. I must have burned him.

"Please. What's happening?" I ask.

The keeper practically wheezes as he says, "They've been rummaging the area. Looking for a Desdemona."

Is this why they've kept my mother alive—to find me?

"How long?"

Groaning again, he says, "A few months, maybe. They only stopped recently."

"Thank you," I push the words out. Then I point toward Damien's dwelling. "The woman who lives here can help with the burn." I don't wait for a response before turning to run.

The Arcanes are looking for *me,* undoubtedly. Can I stop them? I don't know, probably not. But I think of Leiholan lying hopelessly in the infirmary without his leg and Aralia smoking a joint unknowingly when some red-eyed Folk comes into the room looking for *me.*

And Lucian going back, *knowing* what he faces and choosing to face it anyway.

I could stay here. Hide from it all. *Run,* the way I always have. The way Queen Leiana told me to.

But there's nothing for me here anymore. Everything I want sits across the universe. So when I make it to the mirror, I make the same decision I made months ago.

To open a portal back to Visnatus.

As my hands settle against the surface, I catch my reflection—the red eyes that drove Damien away.

The eyes that change everything people thought about me. Eyes that change what I am.

I meet my own gaze, just long enough to wonder if Damien was right to be afraid.

Then I plunge through the portal.

My boots skid against the school's marble floors as I break into a run. I head first for Lucian's suite but stop short at the sight of a figure on the floor, draped beneath his jacket.

Kneeling, I pull it back; Wendy's face stares up at me.

Her lips are parted, like she'd speak if there was air in her lungs. Her eyes, glassy and fixed on the ceiling, don't recognize me because they can no longer see. My hands hover over her gaze, unable to conceptualize that she's gone.

That bodies just stop working like this.

*What number is she?*

She isn't breathing, but there's no wound, no sign of what

stole the beat from her heart.

I lean down, trying to breathe life back into her. I press on her chest—once, twice, three times. Warmth pulses beneath my skin, curling through my fingertips, and I shove it down. Now is not the time for fire.

But the more I fight it, the more I realize this warmth is different. It doesn't flicker—it pulses. It doesn't burn—it hums. It's beneath my skin, but not in my bones the way the Flame is.

I don't *know* what this is, so I stop fighting it. I give my all to save Wendy's life. I feel every bubble in my blood, every prayer in my pulse.

Maybe I'm a better person than I thought. Months ago, I came back to this place to save my mom. Today, I came back to save everyone else.

I'm giving something I don't understand to a person who's already judged me. Saving a life instead of taking one.

That's the opposite of selfish, right?

I continue to press Wendy's chest. It takes seventeen times before she sits up, gulping for the air that she's lost. Her fingers clutch at her throat, her breath ragged, as something wet trickles down the side of my neck. A slow, sticky warmth. My stomach twists as I swipe at it, and when I pull my fingers away, they're smeared with black.

Not red. Not human.

Something isn't right.

"What... what happened?" Wendy asks weakly, her voice barely a rasp.

It's a question I don't know how to answer. Instead, I grab Lucian's jacket and wipe away the liquid coming from my ear.

"Something isn't right," Wendy mutters.

She stares at me for a long time, like she's trying to read me. Then, shockingly, she grabs my wrist, looking at the black that stains my fingers.

"What did you do?" she asks, her voice low. "What *are* you?"

Her words freeze me. I don't know what I did.

But I know what I am. Don't I?

Ripping my wrist from her grasp, I spit, "I saved your life."

Wendy looks away, trembling, her mouth open in shock. I take a moment to look at my hands, studying the darkness that coats them. I try not to look for too long—to think about what this means.

"I'm gonna find Lucian," I say. "You can come, or you can mope. Your choice."

I stand, not waiting to see what she chooses. I've spent too long begging for people to understand me. Now I need to find the last person who tried.

To my surprise, Wendy rises—but it's probably for Lucian, not me. She follows, limping, and I put my arm around her torso, half-carrying her.

"Thank you," Wendy mumbles, quieter this time. Like she means it.

I nod, but I don't look at her. I can't. I don't want sympathy slowing me down.

When we make it to Lucian's suite, I don't knock; I just push the door open and call his name. It's Kai who appears.

"Where's Lucian?" I demand.

Kai's eyebrows scrunch as he leans slightly closer—getting a good look at my eyes, no doubt.

"You're one of them," Kai says. I'm getting really tired of people's fear, as if that would save them.

"Great, so you chose the unhelpful option. Thanks." I slam the door behind me when I leave.

"Calista can find him," Wendy rasps, putting what must be more than half her weight in my hands.

"Calista?"

"They're betrothed. They share a little of the other's power."

Right. Lucian is quite literally bound to another, and there I was kissing him and thinking he could be mine.

"That's good," I whisper.

"She should be in our suite."

I nod. "That's good."

We walk in silence, and—to avoid everything else—I make a mental list of the weapons I'll gather. I could grab my dual sword, but it'd be easier to carry a few throwing knives.

My avoidance doesn't last very long. Every single person who's seen my eyes has run the other way—except for Wendy, who is quite literally clutching onto my arm right now.

I finally break the silence. "So why didn't my eyes scare you?"

Compared to the boy who's known me for years, this reaction from a girl who doesn't know me at all is unsettling.

Wendy takes a while to say, "Calista and I stole your necklace. We thought we could get ahead of the prophecy."

*Time fractures with the stone.*

My memories—a lifetime's worth of memories—came rushing at me, bombarding my mind with images of existences I never knew. From my childhood to the age of fourteen, before we moved to the Welding Village. Before Damien.

They stole my necklace, a *stone*, and suddenly I wasn't eighteen anymore. I was six, seven, ten, twelve...

"Really?" I try to keep the anger from my voice, and I fail. "'Cause it seems like you just made it happen. And I don't see what this has to do with my eyes."

"Your memories were inside it," she says softly, like a confession.

I'm ready to throw her on the ground and leave her there. What a gross invasion of my privacy. I'm scared of the things she saw me do.

"I saw your mom, Isa. I grew up seeing that face. She was my mom's best friend, so..."

"Got it," I say. I don't want to talk anymore about Isa than I have to.

Wendy stays silent for the rest of the walk to our suite. When we get there, Wendy knocks on Calista's door, and I go into my room.

"Des!" Aralia sits up and walks toward me. "You're all right."

"Fine." I grab my dual sword from the wall. "Got any more little knives?"

"A few," Aralia mumbles with a shrug.

"I could use them." I strap the sheath to my back and slide the sword in.

"You're going to fight?" Her eyebrows furrow.

I think about giving her a quippy response, but I decide time is of the essence and settle for, "I need the knives."

Aralia rummages through the desk between our beds while I pull myself out of the dress, opting for something more suitable for battle.

*Battle.* What am I thinking? As if I could even fight a classmate, let alone some ominous magical evil thing. I'm in over my head.

Well... maybe not. I'm quite the killer.

"Here." She hands me three silver daggers. I guess they'll have to do. Then she does exactly what I did: puts on clothes more suitable for battle.

"What are you—"

"I'm not leaving you hanging this time. We're fighting the Arcanes? Perfect—maybe we can win. We have one on our side."

"Who?" I ask.

Aralia turns to me, rolling up her shirt sleeves. *"You."*

I smile like she's told a joke, but she doesn't. *"Me?"* I ask in disbelief. "I'm a Fire Folk."

"Tell that to your eyes," she says, walking past me and leaving me momentarily stunned. "Are we going or what?"

"I'm *not* an Arcane!" I call after her. "They tried to kill me—they made my feet stop moving, and I couldn't do a thing about it."

As the words leave my lips, I realize they aren't entirely true.

The Arcanes never tried to kill me. They tried to *obtain* me.

"Maybe we're wrong," Aralia says, her voice gentle—like I'm a wounded animal. "It's just your eyes. We could be wrong."

"Wait." I grab her arm, stopping her. "So, you couldn't accept that I'm from the septic, but you can accept that I'm an *Arcane?*"

"It's like I said," Aralia whispers, "I had an idea of what Folk from the septic were, and I realized that was wrong. That didn't change because your title did."

And my title is Arcane. That can't be true; it isn't right. I would know if I was one of them. I can't even do what they can —they literally *stopped* my feet from moving. I'm not that, but of course people think I am.

They've always enjoyed assuming the worst.

Including my mom, who spent my whole life hiding my eyes and stealing my memories.

"Aralia?"

"What?"

"That's insane," I spit.

"All right," she says with a small smile and an annoyingly lavish voice.

I missed it.

Calista and Wendy are already in the common area when we exit our room.

"He's still in the academy," Calista says to me, but not without glaring. Whatever.

"Then let's go," I say.

Calista doesn't wait for further words. She navigates us through the hallways, searching for Lucian and carrying Wendy at her side. We round a corner, stopping when we see Lilac. She's leaning against the stone wall, but her eyes flick to us as we approach.

"Lilac?" Calista whispers in a rush, walking to her and gingerly touching the sword she holds. Her fingers brush Lilac's hand. "You're fighting?"

But Lilac's eyes are on mine as she whispers, "No." Then she looks at Calista, shaking her head. "Yes, I'm fighting. Get Desdemona out of here. Now."

"No—" I step forward, cutting myself off when Lucian walks out, his eyes immediately landing on mine.

Before he seems to fully register it's me, he steps toward me in a single, long stride, his hands coming up to cradle my face like I'm a falsity. His thumbs trace the lines of my jaw and cheeks, his gaze never leaving mine. But there's something else there—something different. Slowly, his grip tightens. His fingers press harder against my jaw, digging into my cheeks.

"My darling Desdemona," he murmurs, and I had expected more... I don't know, *elation* from him. But his voice is filled with regret. "You're *ruining* me."

A chill prickles up my spine. Then shadows surge around me, grabbing my hands and yanking them behind my back so violently that my entire body arches in response.

"Lucian!" Lilac shouts.

Lucian's eyes close, and his face contorts with a painful effort. The shadows slip from my wrists, and his voice cracks when he whispers, "Run."

## Chapter 45
## An Ode To You

# DESDEMONA

"Run, *now!*" Lilac shouts when I hesitate.

My legs don't move at first. Not because I'm brave—because I'm frozen. But when shadows snap toward me again, something primal inside me takes over.

So I run, and no one follows. I turn around, and they're all fighting to hold Lucian back, even Kai. My entire body shakes with confusion so strong that it errs on the side of fear.

I've always had nothing; I never had Lucian.

Even while I run, I'm a mess of emotions and nothing more. I have no idea what I'm supposed to do anymore. My mom doesn't care for me, Damien and his family are scared of me, and who knows what's going through Lucian's mind.

I keep running like it will save me, but all I've ever done besides kill is run, and it seems to have gotten me absolutely nowhere.

I turn into the ballroom. The ground is stained with blood, but I find a clean enough corner and tuck my knees into my chest and my head to my knees. I try not to hyperventilate, but that's exactly what I do.

You can't go home again, and you can't go to school either, I guess. There's no place for me, and maybe there never was. And what, I'm an *Arcane* now? I think of Lucian calling them harbingers of chaos, and I think that's all I am, too.

But what does that mean? I go and live in The Void with

these creatures and my mom who hates me? No, thanks! I have so few options, and I hate them all.

Actually, I think I have no options.

The scariest question of them all arises: would I be better off if I'd just been honest? If I hadn't hidden who I was like a disease? If I'd told Damien about the dreams and the cut, would he have been scared of me then, or would he have understood me now?

If I'd told my mom, could she have protected me? Clearly, she already knew everything. Could she have stopped this?

Could she have stopped me?

And Lucian… He probably learned that I killed more than just one person, that I killed *eight* in the time we knew each other, and now he sees me as a monster because that's what I might be. Telling him that I had a sad childhood doesn't make up for that. Obviously. I was stupid for thinking it could. He's probably sure he's doing the right thing by taking me out, and all the others telling me to run just don't know what he knows.

Footsteps echo from the entrance, and I curl into myself a little more, as if I could disappear.

"You can't hide from me, darling," Lucian's voice echoes. It doesn't sound menacing, even though I think it's a threat. "I feel you everywhere I go."

*I'm all out of options.*

So I stand, looking him in the eye. For too long, it's just me and him across the ballroom from one another. Staring like it can save us. Aching like it could absolve us.

But when he moves, I clutch onto my dagger, aiming for his heart.

I try to let go of the blade. It's perfectly aimed for the most important organ. He'd be on the floor in seconds, dead in minutes.

But I can't. Not to him. And those words I thought not long ago pierce through my mind like a ceaseless song.

*When did I become so weak?*

"They want me to bring you to them," Lucian croaks. "I'm trying to fight it."

*The Arcanes.*

I have no other option, do I?

"You're trying to fight it?" I whisper like I don't believe it.

Why would he? I'm probably no better than them. I don't even know how much blood coats my soul.

I'm scared to see the hideous thing.

"Okay." I step closer and closer until I'm in his arm's reach. "It's okay."

If I can't kill him, then I have no other option.

"No." He steps back, and it looks like it pains him.

"I mean, it was always going to end this way, wasn't it?" I try to smile. "Septic scum and future king. Lyrian and Arcane. Like Amun and Eira," I croak as the words fall from my lips.

"I won't do it," Lucian pushes the words out, but the shadows that spread from him to me say otherwise. His jaw clenches so tightly that I want to ease the tension. "But you need to run. You need to *fight me!* Because I *will* strike, and I won't miss."

I stand, staring, trying to collect my thoughts in a meaningful way. Trying to think of something to say other than, *You're doing the right thing, stopping me. You're doing what everyone else should have done.*

In the silence between the words I think and the words I want to say he breathes one that helps me collect my own.

"Run."

I step closer to him, the darkness swirling beside me with every step. "I'm done running." I pick up his cheek and force his gaze to mine. "I've been running my entire life," I whisper. "It was never worth it."

His face sinks deeper into my palm, and his hand holds my wrist. At first, it's tender, but I can feel his fight to keep his grip from tightening.

"I'll go," I say. "Just let me go."

"I *can't*."

"You can."

Lucian raises his head. Veins pop in his forehead, coated in a sheen of sweat. He's trying to inch away from my touch and give into it all the same.

"Desdemona, you don't understand—"

"That no one will remember me?" I whisper, and at first, Lucian looks shocked. Then only pain remains. "I understand. But there's too much misery because of me. Too much pain."

"That's not true—"

Maybe the truth is easier than another lie.

Suddenly I have no more to spew. No more weapons to wield.

"I've killed eight people since I got here," I confess. "Even more as a child, but I can't remember them all. Whatever this is, I deserve it. And you—" I pause, the weight of us settling in. If there ever was an us. "You don't have to *bleed* until we're even. It was never going to be a fair fight with me in the game."

Lucian points at his chest, but the gesture is weak. "And *I* lied to you. *I* got close to you to use your power for myself. *I* kidnapped and tortured your father!" His voice cracks, and I watch the tears well in his eyes. The shadows around the room start to swirl again. "I... I killed my best friend. Whatever you did to think you deserve this, I've done worse. And I won't doom you, too." He strains, his breath shaky. "I can't."

Lucian reaches for me, but his hand trembles. Like he wants to touch me but his body—whatever spell has him—won't let him.

I pick up his hand, and the second I do, the shadows wrap around my legs. *Good.*

"Then we've both done terrible things," I mutter. My lip quivers and it's beyond my control. "But I'm yet to pay for mine."

The cold wraps around my throat, tightening until I can't breathe. My vision blurs with the onslaught of tears, and I don't fight it as the world blurs. Good—this is good. He's doing what he has to do. Lucian's hand trembles in mine as he screams out my name. But as the light of the room goes out, so does his voice.

Until the sound of a slow, mocking clap fills my ears, echoing through the room like a cruel taunt.

The shadows loosen—but barely—and my breath slowly returns. When I open my eyes, I'm staring at Lucian.

"You should have run," he whispers.

"Good, son," someone says.

My eyes land on the most horrifying sight I've ever seen: a charred figure, its skin scorched to an ashen gray, blisters bubbling grotesquely across its body. They're almost like the burns on my hand and forearm—the ones left by the red knife, now visible since the glamour's worn off.

"Lucian," I wheeze, clawing at the immaterial shadows.

I couldn't use my weapons against him, but I'll use them against *that*.

This is what people think I am?

But I glance at my palm, unable to stop myself. It's nearly identical to the creature. The truth of everyone's fear of me becomes impossible to shake.

I won't believe it.

"Let," I breathe, "me go."

The moment the shadows relent, I fall to my knees, where I stay to catch my breath. Lucian turns to the creature. There's only one measly guy. We can take him.

But Lucian doesn't raise his weapon.

"Lucian," the Arcane says.

Lucian's hands clench tighter, the veins in his arms sticking out like overgrown tree roots. "No," he chokes out. His face is red as blood.

"You'll have to forgive my son." The Arcane turns toward me, closing the distance between us. It kneels before me, extending a long, burnt finger toward my face. I catch its wrist before it can touch me. Our eyes meet—*red, like mine*—and I hold its gaze with all the intensity I can muster. I hope I look dangerous. I hope I look terrifying.

I hope it doesn't see how afraid I am.

I hope Lucian does.

But the thing smiles. "He's going to be so happy to finally meet you."

"Meet me?" I whisper. "Why? Who?"

The Arcane doesn't answer as it jerks its wrist from my hold and turns to Lucian. "Lucian Aibek, I relieve you of your favor."

Lucian's fists unclench, and the trembling in his body finally stills. With a single, powerful motion, shadows rise from every corner at his command, wrapping around the Arcane. They consume the creature entirely, as if it was never there to begin with.

I glance at Lucian, a smile tugging at my lips—he smiles back, and for a fleeting moment, everything feels still. It's over. I push to my feet. We did it.

But as I take a step toward him, a rasping noise fills the air, followed by a sickening grinding sound.

"You are her ruin," it says.

We both turn toward the noise—to the Arcane, tearing the shadows away with deliberate slowness. Black tendrils writhe and hiss as they dissipate into the air, and the Arcane's blistered body emerges—unscathed.

"Not mine," the creature finishes.

Then, suddenly, Aralia and the others burst through the door, their footsteps frantic. They barely hesitate as they surge into the room—but I don't move. My mind is still tangled in those words, trying to comprehend.

*You are her ruin.*

All of them draw weapons, prepared to fight. But the Arcane

doesn't do so much as glance at them. It meets my eyes, and its gaze doesn't move.

"You will choose your friends' lives over your own?" The Arcane smiles, its teeth yellowed and decayed. I can smell the stench of rot from a few steps away. "When you are what we've been waiting for."

I unsheathe a knife and throw it at its throat. The Arcane barely reacts, pulling it out as if I've done no significant damage at all. The blood wipes clean off the blade, swirling through the air and back *into* the wound. Then, with a sizzle, the wound closes.

Kind of like mine.

The Arcane glares at me. While the rest of its form lacks humanity, there's so much in its eyes—so much that I notice when disappointment crosses them.

"Very well," it says.

The sound of shattering glass echoes through the room as two more grotesque creatures crawl through the broken window. They advance toward us, and Yuki wields his sword.

"Oh, that's insulting, dude!" he shouts. "Only three to eight? Where's the rest of you?"

Three against eight could be an easy fight, if my knife trick had worked.

The first Arcane turns to him, its eyes glowing to life. Tension spreads through me—like I'm feeling its magic—but Yuki is the one who falls to the floor, clutching at his chest. He tries to breathe, but strange gurgling noises are all that comes.

I drop down, trying to help without knowing what to do. Placing my hands over his, I can feel the frantic thrum of his heart through the armor.

But when the same thing happens to Aralia, I run in front of her before I can stop myself. I don't know why—it's the last thing I ever thought I'd do. Then the Arcane's magic turns on me. Immediately, my vision dims as the screams of pain pass my lips. My heart races, quickening with each passing second, until I'm certain it can't *possibly* beat any faster.

I fight to stay upright—I give it everything I have—but my knees buckle beneath me. I crash to the floor, the weight of my body multiplying tenfold. I can hardly move, as though my blood has been turned to stone.

As sweat beads at my forehead, as I claw against the floor, I understand what's happening—I'm dying. They have my heart in a vice grip.

Lucian calls my name, just as an unfamiliar voice says, "Oh, ease up on her."

Each word drops in volume as it's spoken, like the voice is pulling away. But as the screams of pain around me—including my own—grow fainter, I realize it's my ears that are betraying me.

A second bitter voice says, "She killed Ciella."

Then all sound ceases to exist, and I writhe on the ground in sheer agony. The world around me begins to move slowly. Darkness creeps into the edges of my vision. With every ounce of my strength, I try to crawl, to move any part of my body. I can barely lift my chest. Then I can do nothing at all.

Lucian runs toward me, swinging his sword wildly. He severs a burnt hand. But nothing will stop this pain. It's in my chest. It's going to kill me.

*"Desdemona!"* Lucian shouts. It's the only sound that cuts through the pain before he falls to the floor.

I try to extend my hand, to reach for him. I think my body moves, but I can't see it. I'm not sure it's doing what I ask of it.

It feels like nothing.

Suddenly, the rapid beating of my heart stills. The twitch of my fingers ceases. The darkness at the edge of my vision takes me entirely.

It's funny how you sometimes hear of deathbed woes. I never thought I'd have any. I thought all my decisions were certain, all my logic sound.

But if I could go back and do things differently, I would. I think I'd be forthright—in all my fears. I think I'd be softer—in all my strength. It's a shame it took me so long to get here, to decide I'm finally ready to tear back every mask and burn every burden. Because it seems I'm out of time.

Because now… there's nothing.

A flicker of light.

A fire so hot I swear it's *melting me*.

A layer of soot, a gasp of air, and Lucian across the room, looking at me while he clutches his chest in shock.

Moments before, he was running for me, trying to save me.

"No," I gasp, trying to sit up, but pounds of *ash* hold me down.

*They're doing to him exactly what they did to me.*

And I expected my heart to stop beating.

He's taking this pain for me. Instinct tells me to look at him as the enemy—the monster that ruined my life.

But I can't see that right now, not after everything. I see someone who shattered my world. I see someone who picked up the pieces. I see someone I can never have.

I see a person I want to protect.

"Stop!"

Yuki and Kai lie unconscious, barely breathing. An Arcane holds a knife to Aralia's chest, and she hardly stirs. Calista and Lilac are frozen in place, their eyes the only movement. Wendy lies on the floor with a blade lodged in her thigh, but there's no blood.

Most importantly, all of them are breathing.

"We didn't kill them," the Arcane who called Lucian "son" says. "*For you*. We have no qualms with murder, though, if it will encourage you."

I can barely hear the words as I claw my way through the ash, desperately trying to reach Lucian. I breathe his name, watching as he sweats like he's being burned, clutching his chest as if his heart might explode.

When I reach him, I stop, pressing my hands against his chest, trying to stop this madness. If I'm an Arcane, then I should be able to stop their power.

Shouldn't I?

Nothing I do works.

"Stop it!" I shout in desperation, finally understanding the Arcane's last words. The leverage that I hold.

They nearly killed me. They *did* kill me, for all I know. In that moment between life and death, in my stillness, they could have taken me. But they're still trying to *encourage* me to go with them.

It only stands to reason that they can't make me go against my will—otherwise, they would've taken me in the school hallways or my old dwelling. They had plenty of chances to just take me, but they want something more. They want to persuade me.

Taking a deep breath, I say, "I'll go with you. But only if you let me say goodbye."

"No—" Lucian chokes.

"Let him go, Aisling," the Arcane says.

I don't know why it shocks me that they have names.

Lucian's grip on his shirt—over his heart—loosens. His chest rises and falls heavily as he catches his breath, and I drop beside him.

"Don't go," he pleads. His trembling hand reaches for my cheek, and he whispers, like a vow of love, "I can't forget you."

Right. Because if I ever feared losing my life before, that was child's play. What I'm about to do is worse than death.

I glance around the room, at how easily these three Arcanes have taken down the eight of us. I don't even have an inkling of hope that we'd stand a chance if we had a do-over.

"It'll be okay." I hold tightly onto his hand. "You'll go on."

And I'll give up my life to save him, Aralia, Wendy, Yuki, Kai, and Lilac. Even Calista.

Suddenly, what I used to call nothing doesn't feel like nothing. What I have here feels like everything.

Lucian, Leiholan, Aralia—they know me better than anyone. They care more than I ever thought someone could.

And I'm about to give it all up.

"May we meet again?" I whisper.

Lucian shakes his head, hard, his lips trembling while a tear rolls down his already sweat-dampened face. "No. I'm not doing this again."

Was Mom wrong? Was *I*? Is being truly *known* a weakness?

Or could it be a strength?

Because there is no world in which he would fight for me if he didn't know me.

And I thought getting to know him would reveal his weakness, but instead, it's made losing him feel unbearable.

We fight for one another because we care. And there's no real caring without knowing. I guess I see that now.

I know what I didn't before.

"May we meet again," I whisper, leaning down and kissing his shaking forehead.

Lucian shakes his head beneath my touch.

"*No*," he chokes, his voice breaking apart. He grips my wrist like it's the only thing anchoring him to the moment. "If I do anything, I *will* find you. I will hunt to the ends of this universe and the next to remember you again."

I want to be worthy of this devotion. But leaving, the way I'm doing now, feels like the most worthy thing I've ever done.

"Maybe you should write that down," I say, tears breaking through my walls, wetting my cheeks and making it hard to speak. "So you don't forget." I hold onto his hand, gently placing it over his chest and sliding the little wolf back into his palm.

I could've had it. I could've put my trust in someone other than myself. I could've had everything, before I even knew I wanted it.

I could have opened my heart.

But Lucian puts his hand on top of mine and slides the wolf right back. He whispers, so quietly it's almost inaudible, "Keep it close."

There's something in his eyes, something written on his

sweaty, tired face, that convinces me to take it. I nod once and stand, walking toward the Arcanes. I can't tell them apart, but when one says, "Are you ready?" I know it's the one who called Lucian "son."

This is what I wanted from the beginning—to go to The Void and find my mom. But after everything I've seen, after all she's done to me, she might be the last person in the universe I want to be with.

I thought I had nothing—now I'm about to learn exactly what that is.

Still, I whisper, "Yes."

With my left hand balled into a fist.

# Chapter 46
## An Ode To Nothing

# LUCIAN

I stay there, shaking on the cold, hard ground as the people around me slowly regain movement. Wendy sits up, pulls the blade from her thigh, and stares at the clean metal in disbelief.

The wound should've left blood. But the steel glints like it never touched her.

More than that—she's alive. When Icarthus left her body, he'd taken her pulse with him. Yet here she is, moving and breathing.

It makes no sense.

Aralia, Yuki, and Kai barely manage to get to their feet. Lilac, Wendy, and Calista glance around the room, pausing where the Arcanes once stood.

There's nothing left of them—no blood, no magic, no ash. They beat us down, then left. For what? To prove they could?

None of it adds up.

I push myself upright, each movement heavy with exhaustion. My limbs drag, as if they don't belong to me. Like I've come back into a body I only half-remember how to wear.

As I step forward, every gaze in the room shifts to me. Their expressions are awed, and I'm unsure what I did to deserve it.

"You did it," Lilac says, a slow smile breaking across her face. "You stopped the Arcanes."

I regard my sister in silence, waiting for her to say more—because I don't remember any of it.

All I feel is the absence of my little silver wolf... and something else I can't quite name. A feeling that lingers in my chest, like a stone I could almost reach. A sensation I could almost *see* —if only it would show itself.

The longer I dwell, awaiting an answer I never receive, the more my chest begins to burn. I reach for my heart, only to find it cool to the touch. Though I can't find it within me to let go.

There's something more here—something deeper.

A pressure, more than pain.

I unbutton my shirt, my fingers tripping over the fabric as my desperation grows. I tear the cloth away, revealing an X, branded over my heart. It's already scarred, an old wound that feels like it should be remembered. Far too clean to have been left by accident.

The Arcanes must have done this—their magic must have made it seem weathered—though I can't recall when or how. I trace it with two fingers and flinch. The longer I touch it, the deeper the X seems to etch past my skin and bone—into my heart.

Is it a curse? A signature? A sentence marked on my body while I was left unaware?

I half expect someone to remember what happened. To recognize the mark. To see what is missing.

Looking to my sister, I silently plead for an explanation.

Lilac says nothing more.

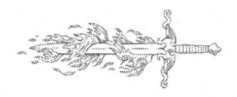

---

That evening, I sit hesitantly in my room, staring at the scar. I touch it again and again—chasing the sensation. A rush to my brain, a lack of oxygen, a sharp high.

There's something exhilarating, and each time I reach for it, it slips away.

A knock echoes through my room, and I scramble to cover

the X. It's not that I want to hide it—I want to hide my fear of it. My fixation.

The longing to understand.

"Come in," I call when my shirt is adequately on.

It's Wendy who opens the door, standing tentatively at the threshold. I stare at her, as though she's an impossibility.

The Arcane who called himself my father killed her, and here she stands. Her features are muddled—shadows beneath her eyes, a gray tint to her dark skin, and most odd, a loss of depth in her green eyes.

Yet, she's here.

"Are you busy?" she asks, her voice weak and cracking around the edges.

I shake my head, unsure. It feels like there are a million things to do—though I can't pinpoint one.

"No," I answer.

Wendy enters the room, closing the door and leaning against it. Looking at the ceiling, she takes a deep, trembling breath.

Weakly, she says, "I feel I'm morally obligated to tell you that I remember."

My gaze fixes on the wall just behind her. Remember what? I'm fairly sure there is something I've forgotten. Yet each time I reach for it, it scatters like sand in the wind—until even the act of remembering fades into nothing.

Then understanding settles over me—Wendy remembers the conversation I had with Icarthus while he controlled her body.

She knows the truth of my parents.

That they are dead, and I was never Royal by blood.

"I'm beginning to forget why I ever cared to keep Leiana and Labyrinth's secret," I mutter.

Wendy pushes herself away from the door, straining with the effort. Her gaze drifts past me, lost in thought, as she sits beside me. "I'll help you find the truth about your parents if you help me."

She speaks as if all is forgiven between us. Though, I suppose it is. I don't wish to hold a grudge over any piece of Azaire.

"What truth are you looking for?" I ask.

"Two things," she says nervously, releasing a shaking sigh. "First... my magic is gone."

My eyes snap to meet hers, and she frowns at me, her bottom lip wobbling.

With a subtle shrug, she says, "I don't *feel* anything... even when I try. Your emotions are as much a mystery to me as anyone else."

Her eyes grow distant, tears beginning to stain her cheeks. The longer I look, I begin to see what's changed in them. They've lost their vibrance. Instead of a deep green, her irises are closer to gray.

Closer to Azaire's.

"And the second thing..." she says, her voice hoarse and choppy. "When the Arcane stabbed me, I didn't feel anything then either. No pain."

Her tears drip down her cheeks, falling on my bed.

Wendy clears her throat. "Do you remember what happened after the Arcane... *left* me?"

Shaking my head, I whisper, "You died."

I had hardly processed it when it happened. Lilac had thrown Wendy's body across the room, and once Icarthus released control of her, she had no pulse. But she sits before me, breathing.

"That doesn't make any sense," Wendy mutters.

"Nothing about today makes sense." One moment I was dying, and the next the Arcanes were gone.

I'm not sure if it's anger or dissonance that I feel. I waited my whole life to face the Arcanes, and in the moment I finally did, I faltered.

And even if I had killed them, I'm not sure it would've mattered. It wouldn't have granted me freedom—I've never had that. It was vengeance. And now even that feels impossible to claim.

I lost Azaire because of it.

Perhaps I'm disappointed. Perhaps I expected it to end this way. I'm full of feeling, none of which I can decipher.

Nothing makes sense anymore.

After a long pause of silence, Wendy takes a shaking breath and says, "The only person I want to talk to is gone."

My heart hitches as I look up at her. The tears she shed offer a hand to me. I try to hold mine back, but they prove their strength as they break through.

"I know," I whisper.

I would do anything to talk to Azaire.

Yet beneath that, there's something else. A silent ache. A gory grief.

"You do," she says.

There's an odd comfort in that. We carry the same ghost. We keep him alive by carrying the pieces he left in us.

This does not make the loss feel any more real, however.

---

The monsters are gone, supposedly, and classes begin again. I try to attend like the dutiful prince I am, though every breath feels false in the old facade.

I've cracked the shell. I can't shove my body back in.

On occasion, I venture to Azaire's room. I knock at his door, waiting for him to answer—thinking of how long it's been since we talked. It's odd because normally I see him every day.

There are so many things I have to catch him up on.

Each time, Yuki opens the door with a frown.

And each time, the loss hits me all over again.

Today, I look past Yuki, staring at Azaire's side of the room. The desk where he usually sits is empty. His bed is made.

He is gone.

It is silence that is truly suffocating. Not the fight, not the physical pain—but the aftermath. The reckoning. The moment when you realize what it all cost.

I wonder if I'm dead, too. If I died that day with him, and was left in the world as some form of purgatory.

Some depth of damnation.

"My inadequacy," I mumble, turning away from the room—before I reach for something that isn't there to hold.

"It's all right, man," Yuki says.

I shake my head. Nothing is all right.

In the days that follow, I begin to search for something. In Azaire's room—which I frequently forget is now empty of him—by the lunar lake, in the dusty Royal chambers upstairs.

I don't know what I'm hoping to find. A sign, maybe. An answer. Something to take me back.

I never, however, find what I'm looking for. It feels as if it's right around every corner I turn, yet the only thing that follows me are the cheers and applause. To the masses, I've been granted the title of a savior—though only against the monsters. No one but our small group knows about the Arcanes.

And they, too, think I led us to victory.

One evening, on my endless pursuit for something more, I find myself walking through the girls' dormitory wing. It feels as if I'm being carried here. There is a light beneath my feet, a fire at my heels, chasing me.

At first, I assume I'm looking for Lilac, but I find myself stopping before Wendy and Calista's suite.

I consider walking away—I have nothing to do here. As I try to turn myself around, instinct stops me.

There's something here I have to see.

I knock on the door, and Aralia answers.

"Oh," she says. "Hi."

I look past her, into the suite, searching.

Aralia moves, placing herself in front of my gaze. "Is there something you need?"

"Yes," I say absentmindedly, stepping around her. The air is warmer inside. A silent stillness. The sensation crawls inward, toward the mark over my heart.

My head turns of its own volition, as if my body is trying to teach me a lesson I never learned. My gaze stops, looking through an open door into a bedroom.

The sheer curtains billow in the breeze from the open window. Dust clings to the desk between the two beds, and I step closer before I realize why.

"What are you doing?" Aralia asks, her voice low.

"Is this your room?"

"Yes."

"I thought there were only three girls in this suite," I mutter.

"There are," she whispers, hesitation in her tired tone.

I step back, confused why I even began this line of questioning. I'm about to mutter my apologies when I notice something odd.

The second bed is made—one that should be empty if there's only three suitemates. It feels... deliberate, a message I haven't yet learned how to read.

"Why is the bed made?" I ask.

Aralia glances over my shoulder, at the neatly made green covers. "I didn't notice," she mutters, her gaze lingering inside the room.

A dull sheen crosses her eyes, as if she's looking through something rather than at it. She lingers in that momentary trance before her focus sharpens, eyebrows rising in silent question. Her gaze snaps back to me, wide-eyed, as if piecing together what just happened.

Then, she adds, "I don't even like green."

"That's rather odd," I murmur, more intrigued by her reaction than the bed.

But for some reason, the back of my neck prickles, like I've just missed something important.

"Yeah," Aralia says thoughtfully. "It is. You know, there was something else kind of odd."

I give her a look that says, *go on*.

She hesitates. "I found a notebook under the bed... with a name I've never heard before."

# AUTHOR'S NOTE

If you've made it here, first: thank you. Thank you for reading this strange, twisted, vulnerable story—for following these characters through their pain, power, and impossible choices. Whether you screamed, cried, or quietly unraveled somewhere along the way, I'm honored you let this book into your world.

Before anything else, if this story meant something to you, the absolute best thing you can do right now is leave a review on Goodreads, Amazon, or wherever you picked up your copy. Your words make a real difference. Ratings help this story reach new readers, signal to bookstores and publishers that it matters, and tells the algorithm gods, *"Hey. Pay attention to this one."*

This is how books like this survive. This is how they spread.

So if you have thirty seconds—or a single sentence to spare—I'd be wildly grateful.

Des was born from the feeling of never being seen clearly—and fearing what will happen when you are. Lucian came from the weight of expectation—and what happens when you begin to crumble beneath what you think people want.

This story isn't about grand victories—it's about what it means to find softness in a world that demands you be steel. About how terrifying, and necessary, vulnerability can be. If any part of this story made you feel less alone—then it was worth writing.

With all my heart,
Caroline

# ACKNOWLEDGMENTS

The first person above all others to whom I want to give my utmost gratitude is my dad. This book wouldn't have come to be without him, for many, many reasons. When I began writing *A Liar's Twisted Tongue* I had no intention of ever sharing this work with the world. But the second I told him I was writing a book, he was nothing but supportive. He believed in me before I began to believe in myself. From the beginning, he told me he had a feeling it was going to be great. And he is *not* the kind of person who has feelings things are going to be great. Sorry, Dad, but you're a bit of a pessimist. Or, as he would say, a "realist." But it was that belief from a guy like him that made me think I could do this.

To my brother, Dominic (don't mind me checking off the familial obligations). No, I'm kidding. He was the first person I told about this project. I plotted key parts of the book while we were watching *The Wolf of Wall Street* one night and when we finished, he sat with me in the kitchen for two hours while I all but acted out the entire story. I had no intention of telling him every detail. I told him every detail. In the end, he told me that one of these days, he was going to think about this story, want to finish it, realize I was the one writing it, and bug me about it.

He did, in fact, bug me about it. A lot. For a whole year.

He read the very first draft, and it's come a long way since then.

My brother, Anthony, for all his support. Thank you for the phone calls and ramblings that you sat through. Having the support of both my brothers was incredible as a younger sister. It's those childhood dynamics that shaped Lucian and Lilac's connection. Same with Calista and Kai in the many, many deleted scenes.

To Rae Ramey, my brilliant developmental editor. Thank you for holding space for this story's evolution and offering me so much expansion within the book. Your vision helped me dig deeper and trust the complexity of the world.

To Gabriel Hargrave, for your deeply personal and insightful copy edits. I cherished every note you left in the margins—specially the ones where you screamed at me about the peril I put the characters through. Your attention made this story sharper, and your reactions made the process unforgettable.

My friend Talia and my cousin Tommy, who each got about a million videos of me talking about this book and working through plot holes. Thank you for putting up with that.

Stefanie Saw at Seventhstar Art, for the beautiful cover! It would not be what it is without her and her creative input. I could not overstate my gratitude to her.

Joe, the man who made the map, from Caffee Cartography. He was so attentive and is a wizard with his pen. If you don't believe me, go look at the map again! It was everything and more that I had envisioned in my mind. Both of these two brought this world to life.

Thank you to Jan, for the lovely illustrations you see inside the book.

To my first copy editor, Mallory Bingham. In the world of self-publishing, finding a reputable and honest editor can be tough work, and she made it easy.

Lastly, and of course, thanks to you, dear reader. The fact that you had enough faith in this story to not only pick up but read it through to the end is world-shattering to me. No dramatics. I am endlessly grateful that you're here today. I am endlessly grateful to you. Thank you.